THE RED
GLACIER

THE RED GLACIER

Book Four of
The Guardian Cycle

JULIA GRAY

www.orbitbooks.co.uk

An *Orbit* Book

First published in Great Britain by Orbit 2002

Copyright © Julia Gray 2002

A CIP catalogue record for this book
is available from the British Library.

ISBN 1 84149 123 3

Typeset in Erhardt by M Rules
Printed and bound in Great Britain by
Mackays of Chatham plc, Chatham, Kent

Orbit
An imprint of
Time Warner Books UK
Brettenham House
Lancaster Place
London WC2E 7EN

Talkin' 'bout my generation . . .

This book is dedicated, with much love, to
Ross and Lyn, Gail and Miles.

Thanks for being friends as well as family.

PROLOGUE

'And do you know what the sword was called?'

'Slayer?' Yarek replied, getting it wrong deliberately so that it wouldn't spoil his grandfather's story.

'No.' Takkara smiled at the boy's innocent expression. 'It was called the Peacemaker. Strange name for a sword, eh?'

Yarek nodded.

'It was called that,' the old man explained, 'because it made the warrior who wielded it invincible. His foes would fall before him, making the ice run red with their blood, and only when they were all defeated would there be peace.'

'So why don't our generals use it?' Yarek asked.

'It's not as simple as that. The Peacemaker was lost long ago, many centuries before even I was born.'

'How could anyone lose anything so important?'

'That's a good question,' Takkara replied. 'The only answer I can give you is that the gods are sometimes capricious – even cruel.'

'Who forged the sword?'

'No one knows for certain, but it must have been a very great wizard.'

'Then why can't one of *our* wizards make another one?'

'Because the magic was lost too.'

The boy nodded, looking thoughtful.

'No one knows where the blade is now,' Takkara went on, 'although most people assume it's buried deep within the ice that never melts, guarded by the Lonely Peaks. And that's not all.' The old man's voice fell to a conspiratorial whisper. 'The sword only becomes visible when the Red Moon is full and all the other moons are new – and that's a very rare combination. You'll be lucky to see it once in your lifetime.'

'Have *you* ever seen it?' Yarek asked.

'No, but my father did, when he was not much older than you are now. He told me that all the mountains, all the snow fields, all the glaciers turned red, as if the gods themselves were weeping blood.'

'Did he look for the sword?'

'Of course! But he was too young to go very far, and much stronger men had to turn back that night. Many men died and even more lost fingers or toes to the bitter cold, but no one even caught a glimpse of the sword. Some say that only a hero who can walk on through the winter dark will ever be able to find the Peacemaker.'

'But that's impossible!' Yarek objected.

'Who knows what a true hero can do?'

The boy still looked doubtful, but decided not to argue. He knew that he'd been lucky to have his grandfather to himself for so long. Takkara was the best inspirator in the whole of the Black Quarter, and his services were much in demand. This late in the season the generals called for him less often, but there was usually one last campaign being planned, one last daring raid on the White or the Gold, and it was rare for Takkara to be able to return to his village home for more than a few hours at a time. It was rarer still for him to be persuaded into retelling one of the old stories. When he was not working he liked to take a rest from such things – but he found it almost impossible to refuse his grandson.

Yarek could see that the old man was tired now, and wondered how he could keep him talking. If he did not, the boy knew that one of the women would soon come and drag him back to their world, to the tedium of lessons, of cooking and sewing, of building fires and weaving cloth. Yarek preferred the world of adventure and battle, and ever since his father had been killed, his grandfather represented his only direct link to that world.

'Can I fetch you a drink, jokull?' he asked, using the term that denoted respect for an elder. Literally, it meant 'ice-wisdom', implying that the person had a great deal of experience and was known for the proven worth of his advice.

Takkara nodded his assent and watched as the boy scurried away. Sometimes, as with most children, his motives were transparent, but there were other times when it was clear that Yarek's mind worked on several different levels. Watching him now, as he dipped the ladle into the mitral cauldron and filled a metal cup, Takkara could not help wondering about his grandson's future. Yarek had always been good-natured, but recently there had been something disturbing about the intelligence hidden behind that deceptively cherubic face. Someone so young should not question things as much as he did. Takkara was about to say something to this effect when Yarek beat him to it – and in doing so, deepened the old man's disquiet.

'But it's not really true, is it?' he asked, as he handed over the cup. 'I mean, the sword is just a myth, isn't it?'

'Myths can be real. They have to begin somewhere. And there are some things we just have to accept on faith.'

'Why?'

'Because that is what it means to be a soldier,' the inspirator replied awkwardly. 'And you'll be a soldier soon, like your father.'

That silenced the boy for a while, and Takkara felt a wave of sadness envelop them both. He reminded himself that his son had died in glory, that he now strode across the Great Plain, but the pride he felt in Borgar's sacrifice did not wholly counteract the ache of his absence. Nor did it quell the old man's anger.

'What if I become a wizard instead?' Yarek asked eventually.

Takkara laughed, glad that the boy had returned their conversation to the future rather than dwelling on the past – even if his question was ridiculous.

'You mean a neomancer. That would be good too. You could—'

'No. A wizard,' Yarek stated with solemn persistence.

'That's impossible!' the old man snapped, angry now. 'And you know it.'

The boy retreated into silence again, realizing that he'd gone too far this time. A short while later, Takkara's curiosity overcame his misgivings.

'Do you think you have talent?' he asked tentatively. 'Enough to gain a sizarship?'

'I hope so,' his grandson replied, though he sounded less confident now.

'Life under the pyramids is not easy,' Takkara told him. 'And any glory you may earn will be at second-hand. You may never see the results of your work. Are you sure that's what you want?'

Yarek didn't answer and Takkara took a sip of his mitra, which was growing cool now. As always, the infusion of herbs tasted bitter, but he was used to that. Their scent filled the house almost constantly – which was only right and proper. He watched his grandson over the rim of the cup, wishing he could tell what the boy was thinking.

'You're a bright lad,' he said, when the silence had

dragged on long enough. 'I'm sure you can do anything you set your mind to. But be careful you don't anger the gods.'

'I'll be careful, jokull,' Yarek promised earnestly.

'Besides, you don't have to decide yet. And you'll soon have the chance to sleep on it.' Takkara smiled, and the boy grinned back, but – as so often now – there was something hidden behind his large, pale blue eyes.

The reference to the long winter sleep had indeed set Yarek thinking. When he'd been an infant, he'd accepted the hibernation as natural, just another part of the life that was organized for him by others. By the time he was a few years old, it had frightened him, and his mother had been ashamed of his crying. He had grown out of that and had returned to unquestioning acceptance once more – though with a little more understanding this time. And now, as the days grew shorter, Yarek was actually looking forward to it. When the spring came, unlike most of the others, he would remember his dark dreams. And it was in those dreams that he learnt so much, *saw* so much.

That was his great secret, the reason he knew he was destined to be a wizard – no matter what anybody said. Unwittingly, his grandfather had confirmed his faith. 'You can do anything you set your mind to.' Rules were meant to be broken. Yarek had decided that long ago. And if the greatest wizard the four Quarters had ever seen could not break some rules, then who could?

PART ONE

MYVATAN

CHAPTER ONE

Far off the starboard bow, the sea was burning.

'I bet you've never seen anything like that before,' Kahl remarked. 'However far you've travelled.'

Terrel stared at the fire, wondering how such a thing could be possible. As he watched, another burst of flame erupted, sending a shower of glittering red sparks into the air and burnishing the surrounding waves as though they were made of bronze. Above them, a pall of black smoke and grey steam trailed away on the wind.

'There'll be an island there come the autumn,' Kahl added knowledgeably.

'An island?'

'The fire comes from the heart of Nydus,' the sailor explained. 'And as it rises up from the seabed, it brings rock with it. Those sparks you saw just now, some of them were boulders bigger than your head, and they're all made of stone so hot it turns to liquid and glows like a blacksmith's furnace.'

Terrel turned to look at his companion, trying to judge whether he was being serious or not. Kahl was one of the few crewmen who had been willing to talk to him and Terrel had tried to establish some degree of friendship with him. He had told the sailor a little of his own travels, and hoped for information in return. He was heading towards another alien land, and seeing the ocean burst into flame had emphasized just how little he knew about this region of Nydus.

'But when it hits the water and cools, the rock becomes solid again,' Kahl went on, apparently quite in earnest. 'And it gradually builds up until there's a new island for us to sail around.'

'I'm glad you said sail *around*,' Terrel commented. 'I wouldn't want to get too close to anything like that.'

Even from a distance it was an awe-inspiring sight. From close to, it would have been terrifying.

'Nor me,' the seaman said. 'The captain wouldn't like it much either, and he's kept us in clear water until now. Of course, one of them could break out right in front of our bows. There wouldn't be much we could do about that.'

Terrel found this idea extremely alarming, but saw that Kahl was grinning now.

'Don't worry,' the sailor said, relenting. 'We've done this run a few times now and no one's suffered so much as a singed beard.'

'Let's hope it stays that way,' Terrel replied, feeling the uneven stubble that now covered his own chin.

'Mind you, it's not just the new islands that make navigation tricky,' Kahl added. 'The fires under the water make their own currents too. Sometimes it's difficult to tell what's going on, especially now the tides aren't reliable any more.'

Terrel was already aware of that anomaly – and the reason for it. For several years now the Dark Moon had been behaving erratically – in defiance of all the precise astronomical laws laid down by the seers of his homeland – and recently, it seemed that the changes in its speed and size had begun to affect the orbits of the other three moons. This meant that predicting the rise and fall of tides had become increasingly complex.

'Of course,' Kahl went on, 'once the fire-islands are in

place, they can actually help us, give us reference points when we're out of sight of land – provided you can recognize them from one month to the next.'

'You mean they keep changing?' Terrel guessed.

'Sometimes. See those islands there?' He pointed further ahead, to where three black mounds rose from the sea. 'They weren't even there two years ago, and each time we come past they've got bigger. They still smoke sometimes too, so we steer well clear.'

Terrel squinted into the distance, studying the irregular cone-shaped rocks, and tried to imagine them growing out of the ocean.

'These are dangerous waters,' he commented.

Kahl shrugged.

'Any sea can be dangerous. This one more than most, maybe.'

'Then why do you cross it?'

'The usual reasons. Gold and adventure.' He grinned. 'But mostly the gold.'

'They have gold on Myvatan?'

'Loads of it. We wouldn't bother trading with them otherwise. They've got precious little else we're interested in. I'm more interested in why *you* want to go there.'

Terrel had several reasons, but none that would mean much to a practical man like Kahl.

'I don't know, really. I've been travelling so long, it seemed like one of the few places I hadn't been to yet.' This contained at least an element of truth. 'And I've heard it's different from anywhere else.'

'That's one way of putting it,' the seaman remarked. 'But there must be some purpose to your travelling.'

'Not really.'

Although Kahl was clearly not convinced, he chose not to press the point.

'Well, a person with your talents is going to find a welcome in most places,' he observed.

Terrel's healing abilities were something he accepted now, though he never took them for granted. He had paid for his passage on the *Skua* by helping the ship's first officer make a speedy and complete recovery from a nasty fever. In return, Ostan, the captain, had been only too willing to take him aboard – one extra passenger cost him very little – and, since then, most of the crew had benefited in some way from Terrel's skill.

'So have you decided which side you'll work for?' Kahl asked.

'Side?' Terrel queried.

'In the war.'

The healer had heard several rumours about Myvatan, including one claiming that the island had been in the throes of civil war for many years. However, few people had been either able or willing to talk about the place at all, so he'd remained in ignorance for the most part. His decision to go there had been made in a rush. Sailings were rare, especially this early in the year, and Ostan's offer had been dependent on his being able to leave immediately.

'Neither,' Terrel answered eventually.

Kahl laughed.

'You'd better make up your mind one way or the other before we dock,' he advised. 'Say the wrong thing in the wrong quarter and you're dead.'

Terrel looked at him in dismay.

'I've no interest in the war,' he said.

'Then what are you going to Myvatan for?' the sailor asked. 'Apart from gold, the war is all they have.'

Now I know *cats are mad*, a familiar voice complained. *This one hates water as much as I do, but it's chosen to live on a ship!*

Alyssa! Terrel exclaimed, sliding out of his hammock to kneel in front of her.

He had been aware of the cat's presence earlier in the voyage. The crew called it Dranga, which meant rat-trap, and it usually prowled the lower decks in search of prey. The animal's face was heavily scarred, one of its ears was torn and its left foreleg was slightly lame, but its ginger coat was glossy, testament to its success as a hunter. Until now it had paid Terrel little attention, and he'd been surprised when it had stalked up to his sleeping place that evening. But not even in his wildest imaginings had he thought that Alyssa's spirit might have taken over the cat's body. Not only did she dislike the devious nature of feline minds – of all the other animals she had tried, horses were the only creatures she found as difficult – but, as her opening remark had implied, she disliked large bodies of water even more. In the past, the mere fact that Terrel had crossed an ocean had prevented her from joining him for some time, even after he was back on dry land. And when he was actually *on* water, there had been no chance of proper contact. And yet here she was, inhabiting a cat, in the middle of a vast and dangerous sea.

I didn't expect to see you so soon. Even though Terrel's delight at her arrival was as great as ever, he was perturbed by the fact that she had forced herself to overcome her fears. What was so important that she could not afford to wait a few days?

I was never meant— Alyssa began, then broke off as the ship shuddered under the impact of an unusually large wave. The cat staggered, its mismatched ears twitching, and its fur stood on end. Hissing, it dug its claws into the deck – and Terrel saw the 'ring' looped around one of its forepaws. The ring was made of twine interwoven with one of his own hairs, and although at first Alyssa had worn it as a joke, it had soon become the precious link that helped her to find him wherever he was. Seeing it always made him think of Havenmoon, his home for the first fourteen years of his life – the asylum where Alyssa's comatose body still lay.

You're quite safe, he reassured her, sensing her unreasoning terror.

Why aren't you back in the palace? she asked. *That would be safe, not this. I won't be able to stand this for long.*

Was there something you wanted to tell me? he asked quickly.

The cat hissed again as the *Skua* rose with the swell.

This time I'm not even going to try to sing, Alyssa declared, looking around wildly.

The irrelevance of this remark made it clear to Terrel that she was more than usually deranged, and he wondered whether he'd get any sense from her at all.

You don't have to, he said. *Just give me your message and you can go.* Much as he wanted her company, he couldn't bear to see her suffering.

What message? She sounded bewildered.

I thought—

Oh, that! she interrupted. *All the windows are closed.*

What?

Muzeni says ... She paused, apparently trying to remember something elusive. *Muzeni says* ... *the crystal's broken, isn't it? Smashed.*

What does that mean? he asked, desperate now.

Be careful where you choose to follow, she stated tonelessly, as if she were reciting the words from memory. *Don't fight the wrong war. And don't trust your instincts.*

More confused than ever now, Terrel was about to speak again, but Alyssa overrode him.

I'm sick, she announced. *And if you think I'm coming up on deck, you're crazy.*

Sick? Terrel queried, his heart sinking. *Let me help you.*

I have no need of your healing, she replied, sounding a little calmer at last. *Just your love.*

You have that always, he told her.

But there are others in your path who are in terrible pain, Alyssa added. *Look ahead. Even the sky is at war.*

And then she was gone. Terrel caught a last glimpse of the ring as it faded away – and then the cat was just a cat again. Dranga wandered off, with a puzzled 'miaow'. Terrel remained where he was, too stunned to do anything. Whatever message Alyssa had intended to bring had been garbled by her terror. Her utterances were often obscure, but under normal circumstances Terrel could usually interpret the meaning beneath the words. This time he was completely at a loss.

The one instruction that had a potentially relevant interpretation was the last. *Look ahead.* Coupled with Alyssa's apparently pointless refusal to even consider going up on deck, it did at least give Terrel something to do.

Leaving the long cabin he shared with several of the crew – all of whom had been quite unaware of the silent conversation – he climbed up the steep wooden steps to the foredeck. As soon as he emerged, he knew instantly that the windswept night was lit by more than normal moonlight, but he was not prepared for the sight that greeted him.

Ahead of the ship, the sky was filled with a shimmering arch of greenish-white luminescence, stretching from horizon to horizon. Along its upper rim, even brighter beads of light moved at incredible speeds, leaving behind them glittering silver trails that trembled like the strings of a star-born lute. As Terrel watched, spellbound, the archway expanded and transformed itself into a swaying curtain of unearthly light. Streaks of green and blue tinged the white as the delicate fabric moved slowly on an unseen wind. Finally, as the rest of the astonishing display began to fade, the entire spectacle was suffused with an eerie crimson glow. As the other colours splintered into separate swathes and shards, the red mist remained constant, until it too vanished back whence it had come.

'Not a bad show tonight, eh?'

Kahl's voice made Terrel jump. The sailor's soft boots had made no sound as he'd come up behind him.

'Do you see this often?' Terrel whispered.

'Often enough. But there aren't many nights it's as bright as that.'

'It was beautiful.'

'I suppose so.' Kahl did not sound unduly impressed. 'Though they say that the winter lights are ill-omened when they turn the colour of blood.'

That gave Terrel pause for thought as he stared into the now empty darkness.

Even the sky is at war.

CHAPTER TWO

Terrel's dream that night made the fire he'd seen rise from the ocean seem like a candle flame. Above him the sky was obscured by a threatening dome of thick cloud, which extended to the horizon in every direction. It blotted out the sunlight so that the scene below was illuminated only by its own infernal glow. There were huge lines of fire snaking across both land and sea, dividing them into distinct areas, which were themselves in turmoil. In places the ocean boiled, spitting forth great gouts of steam and flame. Elsewhere the waves were discoloured, with swathes of red or brown running through the grey waters. On land the conflagration was, if anything, even worse. Molten rock spilled from open wounds in the ground and flowed like rivers of fire, consuming everything in its path. Other eruptions hurled debris into the sky with an incandescent fury, their smoke and ash adding to the all-encompassing gloom. It was as if the entire planet was in the grip of a vast convulsion.

Gradually the fires dimmed, and without the sun to warm it the world became a frigid wasteland. Seas froze over, and snow and ice blanketed the darkened land. But the forces that were destroying Nydus were not done yet. There was movement, slow but massive, as whole continents drifted into each other, creating another type of upheaval. Mountains rose and were smashed, complete oceans were thrown aside, only to inundate other regions and form new seas. And in the midst of the tumult one island floated free, finding its own escape route from the chaos.

At first Terrel thought it must be Vadanis, but its contours were unfamiliar. It was too big and too cold to be his homeland. By the time he'd realized that it must in fact be Myvatan, the dream had taken him closer, so that he could see individual landmarks within its bleak terrain. Much of what he saw was bewildering. Steam rose from pools of muddy water, even though they were surrounded by snow; crevasses in the great sheets of ice glowed bright blue, although the sky above was still an unremitting grey; and the interior plains were daubed with great splashes of colour – yellow, ochre, green and mauve – as if they'd been attacked by an insane artist.

And at the last, just before he woke up, Terrel saw the first indication that this daunting world might once have been inhabited. Atop one of the coastal cliffs, a huge boulder had been carved into the shape of what looked like an enormous fish. Although it resembled nothing Terrel had ever seen before, its fins and tail were undoubtedly meant to be part of a marine creature. He had seen another, much smaller and simpler, representation of the beast once before. And seeing it now gave him a surge of hope. This at least was a sign he *did* understand.

'Are you sure?' Terrel asked excitedly. 'Like a giant fish?'

'Yes. It's a whale,' Ostan repeated patiently. 'I've seen it many times. Why?'

'That's where I want to go ashore.'

The captain of the *Skua* looked at Terrel as if he were mad.

'That's impossible.'

'Please. It's very important.'

'It's just a sculpture,' Ostan said. 'I mean, it's impressive all right, but you'd get just as good a view of it from the sea. Better, in fact.'

'That's not the point.'

'Then what is? Why is this so important to you?' Ostan was aware that several of his crew were standing nearby, listening to the conversation with interest. Passengers were usually tolerated on board, rather than welcomed, but Terrel had been more acceptable than most – for obvious reasons. However, that would change quite rapidly if the foreigner became more trouble than he was worth. Ridiculous requests like this would not help his cause.

'There's a path I'm bound to follow,' Terrel replied, looking uncomfortable now. 'I swore an oath, and this is part of it.'

Ostan didn't know what to make of that.

'You're not making any sense,' he said. 'There's no path near there.'

'That's not what I meant,' the healer said, but Ostan ignored him.

'In fact, that part of the coastline is treacherous,' the captain went on. 'There are shoals and rocks just below the tide line and the currents are dangerous, especially when the tides are turning. I probably wouldn't be able to put you ashore there even if I wanted to. And if I did, you'd have to scale the cliffs to reach the whale. You don't look like much of a rock-climber to me. Then—'

'That's *my* problem,' Terrel cut in. 'Won't you at least try?'

'No. You obviously don't understand—'

'You wouldn't have to put me ashore yourselves. Just get me close enough so I can swim for it.'

Ostan's expression changed from one of puzzlement to

outright incredulity, and Terrel saw that some of the sailors were grinning now.

'I can swim well enough,' he claimed, but then began to doubt his own words. He was much stronger than when he had escaped from Havenmoon, and he'd been able to swim even then, in spite of the fact that his right leg was twisted and his right arm was withered so that the hand was little more than a rigid claw. The heavy clothes he now wore as protection against the cold disguised his deformities a little, but he would never be genuinely athletic. What was more, although he'd swum in various lakes and rivers, he had never been in the open sea – especially one as rough as this – and if the coastline was as rugged as Ostan claimed, he was just as likely to be dashed upon the rocks as he was to drown. And there was another factor he had not even considered.

'I'm sure you can,' Ostan conceded, 'but in these waters no one would survive such an attempt. You'd soon be paralyzed by the cold, and dead after a very short time. It would be suicide.'

'There must be some way,' Terrel pleaded.

'We could probably get the skiff close enough to the shore, if we time it right,' the captain admitted, 'but it's not going to happen. It's too risky.'

'But I'm willing to take that risk.'

'I meant for my crewmen,' Ostan stated flatly. 'Someone would have to row you ashore and bring the boat back. Give me one good reason why I should jeopardize any of my men.'

Terrel was silent, racking his brains for a way to convince the captain without sounding like a complete lunatic.

'Besides,' the seaman added. 'Supposing we did get you on to the rocks somehow and you *were* able to climb the cliffs. You'd still probably get yourself killed inside an hour.'

'Why?'

Ostan stared at him, obviously wondering whether the strange young man could possibly be as naive as he appeared.

'You really don't know anything about Myvatan, do you?' he said eventually.

'I know there's a war there, but—'

'So you know you'd be walking into a forbidden zone?'

At this Terrel's face lit up with renewed excitement, which he knew would make Ostan doubt his sanity even more.

'That's where I have to go!' he exclaimed.

'Are you *crazy*? Both sides would kill you in an instant if they found you there.'

'Why?'

'Because you're an outsider and it's a *forbidden* zone,' Ostan replied with heavy emphasis, then paused. 'Unless . . .'

'Unless what?' Terrel asked hopefully.

'Unless you've been lying to us all along.'

'What do you mean?' The healer felt genuinely uneasy now. Which of his half-truths was Ostan referring to?

'Which quarter do you follow?' the captain demanded.

'I don't know what you mean.'

'Which moon, then?'

Terrel shook his head in bewilderment.

'Forget it!' Ostan snapped. 'I'm not taking you to Whale Ness. You're coming with us to Port Akranes – and that's final.'

Terrel's bitter disappointment could not be dispelled even by the enchanting sight of a school of dolphins swimming alongside the *Skua*, effortlessly matching her pace and occasionally leaping from the water as though they were playing. He wished Alyssa would return – and bring the ghosts with her – so that they could discuss the situation properly, but he knew he was on his own, at least until he made landfall. And by then it might be too late.

'Don't take it too hard,' Kahl advised.

Terrel was sitting, huddled in several layers of clothing, near the bows of the ship. He had been deep in thought and the sailor's approach had taken him by surprise.

'Do you make a habit of sneaking up on people?' he asked, glancing around.

'I could've been wearing hobnail boots and singing at the top of my voice and you still wouldn't have heard me coming.'

'Probably,' Terrel conceded. 'What shouldn't I take too hard?'

'The skipper's decision,' Kahl replied. 'Ostan did some pretty reckless things himself when he was your age, but he's older now and more responsible. Or so he'd like everyone to believe. I reckon you could get him to change his mind.'

'Really?'

'Aye. But you'll have to come up with a better argument than before.'

And that, Terrel thought, is the problem. He'd been trying to think of a way to convince Ostan, but hadn't got very far.

'Why don't you talk to Kjolur?' the sailor suggested. 'He might be able to help you. Myvatan's his homeland and he knows more about the place than any of us.'

Terrel knew who Kjolur was, but had assumed he was just another member of the crew. Now that he thought about it, he couldn't recall ever seeing him at work on board or in the rigging.

'He keeps himself to himself,' Kahl went on, 'but he's not a bad sort.'

'You've met him before, then?'

'He's sailed with us several times. He's a merchant of some sort. Quite secretive about his trade, but he pays well to add his cargo to ours, so we've no quarrel with that.'

'I'll talk to him,' Terrel decided. 'Thanks.'

'Just so you know,' Kahl said, 'he's been asking a few questions about you, on the quiet, like.'

'What did you tell him?'

'What *could* we tell him? We don't exactly know much ourselves, other than you've a way to take the ache from a man's bones.' Kahl paused, perhaps hoping that his companion would volunteer some more information about himself, but Terrel had no intention of doing that. He was too busy wondering whether Kjolur's interest in him stemmed from idle curiosity or something more.

Terrel found the islander sitting inside a coil of thick rope, near the stern of the vessel. It looked like an uncomfortable seat, but Kjolur seemed quite relaxed. As he drew closer, the healer was astonished to discover that the merchant was reading a book – which immediately marked him out as unusual. In all his travels, most of the people Terrel had met could neither read nor write. Indeed, some of them – like the Toma in the desert land of Misrah – had no written language at all. And everywhere he'd been, books were considered rare and valuable objects, with many people regarding them as mysterious and even magical artefacts.

'What are you reading?'

Kjolur looked up sharply, but did not seem particularly surprised to see who it was. The islander had a thin, pinched face, with pale green eyes.

'It's a collection of old legends. My great-grandfather made a point of writing them all down. I'm not sure why.

But they help to pass the time on a voyage like this. Do you read?'

'I do,' Terrel replied, 'but probably not in your language.' They were speaking in what the sailors called 'the northern tongue', which was common to many lands bordering the cold ocean and which, according to Kahl, was widely spoken on Myvatan. That had come as a relief to Terrel, because it simplified the process of communication. Psinoma enabled him to learn new languages quickly, but he still felt guilty about the necessity of prying into other people's minds. However, he had rarely had any need to become familiar with the written word.

'Then you've travelled far,' Kjolur concluded.

'I have, but I don't come across books very often. May I take a look?'

'Of course.' The islander passed the slim volume over and Terrel flicked through a few pages of the precise calligraphy. This was enough to tell him that it was quite indecipherable.

'It's beautiful,' he said, handing it back, and remembering a time at the haven when he'd had access to a whole library of books. For the first years of his life, those books had been the source of everything he'd known about the outside world. The reality – especially after he'd left Vadanis – had proved rather different.

'The tale I've just been reading says that Myvatan once floated free in the ocean, like a gigantic ship. Can you believe that?'

'Perhaps,' Terrel replied, amazed at the apparent link to his dream – and to his own homeland.

'My people apparently ruled all of Nydus from their mobile fortress,' Kjolur went on, 'but then one of our enemies put a curse on the island and froze it in place, isolated from all the other countries. That must have been some sorcery.' He was grinning to show he regarded the story as no more than an imaginative myth, but Terrel wasn't ready to dismiss it so lightly.

'I come from an empire that's made up entirely of floating islands,' he said.

'Really?' It was the merchant's turn to be amazed.

'The main one is called Vadanis.'

Kjolur's expression made it clear that he had never heard of it, something that did not surprise Terrel at all. His homeland no longer seemed real, even to him.

CHAPTER THREE

By his own reckoning, Terrel was now twenty-one years old, and he was a very different person to the terrified boy who had been cast adrift from Vadanis. It was incredible to think that his exile had already lasted more than seven years, and that there was no immediate end in sight. During all that time he had been almost constantly on the move, and he'd experienced more than he could ever have imagined when he was growing up in the confines of the remote madhouse. His bargain with the elementals, the strange creatures who had no substance or shape and yet who wielded immense power, had become the core of his existence – and it drove him onward still. However, he had begun to feel that the circle was closing at last, that he had passed the furthest point in his long journey. He had come to believe that each step along the unknown road now took him *closer* to home.

That feeling had been reinforced by his most recent meeting with his ghostly allies. Their latest theory was that his trip to Myvatan might be the end of the road, the point at which he could finally fulfil his bargain, and thus set himself free to return to Vadanis – and to Alyssa. The hope that this might be true had given Terrel the strength to carry on, after a long period in which he had not seemed to be achieving anything.

Three and a half years – an eternity in his young life –

had passed since he'd left the deserts of Misrah, and since his last encounter with one of the elementals. When he'd crossed the northern borders of that territory he had been full of expectation, sure that he would soon find out what his next task would be. But although he'd hoped that this would begin with his 'going to the other side of the mountains' – the first part of his journey – he had subsequently been presented with an almost limitless succession of choices, and had been given little or no guidance. He'd been left to trust his own instincts – instincts he had begun to doubt more and more as time passed – to decide where he should go next at each stage. It was only recently that his goal had become clear, which was why he was now aboard the *Skua*. Yet in his heart it was not Myvatan but another island, on the other side of the world, that he longed for. Although Terrel was indeed a different person from the boy he'd once been, he still sometimes felt like a homesick child.

'You *are* a long way from home,' Kjolur commented, bringing Terrel back to the present with a rush. 'What brings you to this part of the world?'

Once again Terrel wondered how to answer this most obvious of questions. If he replied truthfully – that he came in search of a shadow-born entity that possessed intelligence and strength but no physical body – he would be dismissed as mad and would lose any prospect of being helped by a potential ally. After some consideration, he chose to move one step closer to the truth than he had done with Ostan.

'The seers of my homeland prophesied that I would make this journey. I swore an oath to follow their guidance, wherever it led.' He paused, trying to assess Kjolur's response, but the islander's expression was unreadable.

'Seeing into the future,' Kjolur said, nodding slowly. 'That's a useful talent.'

Terrel couldn't tell whether the other man was being genuine or facetious – and wasn't sure whether he agreed with what the islander had said. Prophecy had been his travelling companion for seven years, but it had brought as many pitfalls as triumphs.

'It is sometimes,' he said cautiously, 'but augury isn't an exact science.' That was one of the seers' favourite axioms.

'I find that rather reassuring,' the merchant said. 'I wouldn't like to think that everything was preordained.'

'Me neither,' Terrel agreed, remembering one particular vision in which he had seen the moment of his own death.

'And yet you're sailing to Myvatan because of this prophecy?'

'Sometimes you can't argue with destiny,' Terrel replied, knowing it was a feeble response. He was aware that his companion was studying him intently, and guessed that Kjolur was a shrewd character. It was obvious that the islander was not only weighing up his words but also the expressions on his face. Was it possible that those pale eyes could somehow see beneath the surface of their conversation? Could it even be that Kjolur was skilled in the use of psinoma, and thus able to read Terrel's thoughts without him knowing it? This was an unnerving idea, but the healer was able to convince himself that it couldn't be true, that he would know if his mind was being probed.

'Those are old wounds?' Kjolur asked, indicating Terrel's misshapen limbs. 'Were they received in battle?'

The abrupt change of subject took Terrel by surprise.

'No,' he replied. 'I was born this way.'

In fact the injuries *had* been caused by a battle of sorts – but not the kind Kjolur meant. Terrel had been in his mother's womb when he'd been crippled by his twin brother. Their enmity still caused occasional conflict between them, even though they were many hundreds of miles apart. Jax was the Emperor's son, the acknowledged heir to the Floating Islands. Terrel had been discarded at birth.

'Old wounds indeed,' Kjolur said. 'That was bad fortune.'

Terrel shrugged; his misfortunes had played a part in making him who he was.

'Too late for our healing pools to be of use,' the islander added, still watching Terrel closely.

'Healing pools?'

'You've not heard of them? Each quarter has them, but their efficacy is limited. And most are restricted, kept for military use. A soldier's injuries can be repaired if they're treated quickly enough, so that he can return to the war. But after a certain time . . .' He spread his hands in a gesture of futility.

Terrel belatedly caught the implication of his words.

'You think that's why I'm going to Myvatan? In the hope of healing these?' He tapped his right hand on his leg.

'The thought had crossed my mind,' Kjolur admitted. 'I've seen it before, with those who've had no luck elsewhere. There are legends told about the pools – there's one in this book, in fact – of miraculous cures, and when all other hope is gone that's the sort of thing people cling to. It's generally women who make the voyage, though.'

'Why women?' Terrel asked curiously.

'Because a supposedly barren wife once gave birth to twins little more than nine median months after bathing. A tale like that soon turns to myth if enough people want to believe it. But only the truly desperate come now. They know they have very little chance of even getting close to the waters. The army guards them jealously.'

'Well, that's not why I'm here,' Terrel said. 'I didn't even know about the pools, and I'm not sure I'd want to be cured even if it were possible. I'd like to see them in action, though.'

'Your line of work,' Kjolur said, nodding. 'You might be lucky. I may even be able to help.'

'That would be wonderful. Thank you.'

'I'm not promising anything, mind. A merchant only has influence with the generals when he's got something they want.'

'And do you?'

'Ah, now that would be telling,' Kjolur replied with a smile. 'You have to allow me a few trade secrets.'

'I'm sorry. Curiosity is one of my vices.'

'What are the others?' the islander asked, still looking amused.

'Now you have to allow *me* some secrets,' Terrel said, grinning back.

'Tell me, as you've never been to Myvatan before, how do you know about Savik's Whale?'

Coming so soon after their good-natured exchange, the question sounded abrupt, and it caught Terrel off-guard. He began to suspect that this was exactly what Kjolur had intended.

'I didn't know it was called that,' he said, stalling for time so that he could collect his thoughts.

'Savik is the god of stone and earth,' the islander explained. 'Who else could have carved a life-size whale from a granite cliff? You haven't answered my question, though.'

'I saw it in a dream.' Terrel's honesty was instinctive. There had been times in the past when he'd had to disguise his real motives – as much to avoid ridicule as for any other more sinister reason – and he had come to recognize that deception or dissembling were sometimes necessary. On this occasion, however, he saw no reason to lie. And he had learnt from experience that telling the truth whenever possible caused fewer complications later on.

'Are you a seer yourself, then?'

'No, not really. But dreams are sometimes meant to show us things.'

'I wouldn't argue with that,' Kjolur said, surprising Terrel again. 'Still, what makes you so sure you want to go ashore there?'

This question was not as easy to answer. The truth was that once Terrel and the ghosts had determined that there might be another of the elementals on Myvatan, Shahan and Muzeni had returned to their study of the Tindaya Code and discovered a passage referring to 'a land ice-carved and sea-girt'. The same section of the ancient inscriptions also described an ocean voyage that would end by alighting 'where the rockbound giant of the sea guards the gateway to a forbidden realm'. When Terrel had seen the sculpture in his dream, and confirmed its existence in the real world, he'd been in no doubt that this was his intended destination. Explaining all that to Kjolur would be much too complicated, though. He needed something simpler.

'I have a task to do here,' he said. 'And that's the starting point.'

'What is your task?'

'I don't know yet.'

'Then perhaps you need to dream some more.'

Terrel wasn't sure whether Kjolur was being serious or sarcastic. Not knowing how to respond, he glanced up and saw the Amber Moon, two thirds full and waxing. Against the azure of the midday sky it looked like a coin of pale gold.

'Which moon do you follow?'

Once again the conversation's sudden turn disconcerted Terrel, and he sensed that the question was important. Ostan had asked the same thing but hadn't waited for an answer. Kjolur, he knew, would be more patient.

'All of them,' he replied eventually.

'All of—!' the islander exclaimed, apparently caught off-guard for the first time. Then he was silent again.

'Did I say something wrong?' Terrel asked.

'I don't think you understood my question. We all fall under the influence of a particular moon. It decides our allegiances, our place, our whole lives. There must be one – just one – for you. Which is it?'

Terrel was aware that he was on dangerous ground now. More might depend on his answer than he realized. Yet he obviously had to say something. He followed his nature once more, thinking it better to suffer the consequences of the truth rather than a lie.

'The Dark Moon, I suppose.' It had always been the one he felt a strong connection to.

'Black, then,' Kjolur said. 'That makes sense.' He seemed relieved. 'We should be natural allies, at least.' He unbuttoned and lifted an epaulet on the shoulder of his coat. Underneath was a small circular patch of red cloth.

'So the red and black are allies?' Terrel queried. 'In the war?'

Kjolur looked startled.

'Surely you know that much,' he said.

Terrel shook his head.

'Tell me.'

Over the next half an hour, Terrel learnt more about Myvatan than he had in all his previous conversations put together. And almost all of it was unpleasant.

'Akranes is in the Red Quarter, of course,' the islander

concluded. 'I wouldn't be on board if we weren't heading
for one of our ports. You'll find a welcome there if you
can't persuade Ostan to take you to Whale Ness.'

'Which quarter is that in?' Terrel asked.

'Theoretically it's in the Black, which would be good for
you, but ownership of the headland is disputed, which is
why it's a forbidden zone. You still want to risk landing
there?'

After what he'd been told, Terrel's doubts were growing. But then he remembered the words from the Tindaya
Code and knew he had no choice.

'Yes,' he said. 'If Ostan will give me a chance.'

Kjolur looked thoughtful.

'Do you think you could persuade him for me?' Terrel
ventured.

'I don't think my word counts for much with the captain,' the merchant said apologetically.

'More than mine, at a guess,' Terrel muttered.

'I wish you well, though,' Kjolur added. 'Every man
must follow his own path, no matter where it leads.'

Increasing cloud cover and a lack of strong moonlight made
that night darker than usual, but Terrel was fascinated to
see patches of almost luminous colour – white with traces of
pale green – floating upon the waves around the ship. He
eventually realized that they were chunks of ice, and the discovery made him shiver in spite of his warm clothing.

As he went below decks to try to get some sleep, he
wondered whether Kjolur might really prove to be an ally
in his quest. The merchant was difficult to read. Terrel
still didn't know whether the islander had believed his own
answers, nor did he know whether everything he had been
told was true. Had Kjolur's version of events been the
whole story?

Terrel continued brooding once he was settled in his gently swaying hammock. Just before he fell asleep, it occurred to him that although he had been told quite a lot about Myvatan, and had in turn revealed a good deal about himself, he had learnt almost nothing about the merchant — or his trade. Had they both been hiding things from each other?

CHAPTER FOUR

Terrel was woken by Kahl the next morning.

'The skipper wants to see you.'

'What about?' Terrel mumbled.

'He didn't tell me. You'd better go and find out.'

'Do you still want to go to Whale Ness?'

'Yes.'

'Then we'll go. I think you're mad, but it's your life.'

'Thank you.'

Ostan waved aside any gratitude.

'What made you change your mind?' Terrel asked.

'The sad look in those eyes of yours,' the captain replied. He'd spoken with a straight face, but several of the crew were smiling, and Terrel knew he wouldn't get a straight answer.

Although Ostan's reference to Terrel's eyes had been a joke, the healer was used to people making remarks about them. His eyes were indeed remarkable. The irises were almost colourless, like pale diamonds – which gave the impression that they were almost crystalline – with only occasional rainbow flashes deep within. Strangers often found them intimidating at first, but as Terrel pointed out, they were just eyes.

If necessary, he could disguise them – and other aspects

of his appearance – through the use of the glamour, the trick of making people see what they wanted to see. But he only ever used this now as a last resort. As Alyssa was fond of telling him, there was a price to pay for such magic, and in this instance it came at the cost of making himself vulnerable to his twin's malign influence.

The weather worsened during the day, and Ostan kept his crew busy with almost continuous adjustments to their course and the set of the sails. When a ship was out of sight of land, navigation could be difficult, and Terrel knew that the seamen used a variety of observations to help them. Ostan and his second-in-command studied the angle of the waves, cloud patterns, the position of the sun during the day and the stars and moons at night. They even noted the colour of the seawater around them, and the types of seaweed within it. However, that afternoon Terrel watched as they prepared to take a completely different set of measurements. He didn't like to interfere but he was intrigued, so he sought out Kahl.

'What are they doing?'

'We're coming into shallower water now,' the sailor told him. 'The rope they're preparing is knotted every four paces, so that when a weight is tied to the end and we lower it over the side, we can tell exactly how deep the water is. That'll give the captain a better idea of where we've got to. Sometimes they spread tallow on the base of the weight. That way, when it touches the sea bed, some bits get embedded, and when we draw it up again, Ostan can tell more about where we are, depending on whether it's sand or pebbles or mud.'

'Ingenious,' Terrel said, impressed.

'It's called fishing for treasure,' Kahl added. 'To my knowledge no one's ever come up with any gold, but sometimes – especially if you're lost – information can be just as valuable.'

From his own experiences, Terrel knew that to be true.

'I hear we're going to Whale Ness after all,' Kahl said, as they watched the rope being carefully lowered over the side of the ship.

'Yes. Do you know why Ostan changed his mind?'

'That's not for me to say. But I *can* tell you he spent some time talking with Kjolur last night.'

'Kjolur told me his word wouldn't carry much weight.'

'No,' Kahl agreed. 'But his gold might.'

That evening, Terrel found himself becoming increasingly restless. Kahl had had no proof of his theory. The idea that money might have changed hands was pure supposition, and neither Terrel nor the sailor had been able to come up with a reason why Kjolur should have thought such an arrangement worthwhile. Nevertheless, there had to be some reason for Ostan's abrupt change of heart. But if Kjolur *had* intervened, what was his motive? Simply to help an ally of one day's standing? That didn't seem likely, but Terrel couldn't think of any sensible alternatives. And – assuming the islander *was* responsible – then why was he seemingly intent on acting anonymously? He'd made no attempt to talk to Terrel that day, and had spent most of his time below decks.

Terrel wasn't sure whether to confront Kjolur or simply accept his good fortune. Eventually, however, his curiosity overcame his reticence and he tracked the merchant down to his tiny private cabin. When he knocked and announced himself, a few moments passed before the door was unlocked – and from the various noises within, Terrel got the impression that the islander was tidying some things away before letting his visitor in. However, when Kjolur eventually opened the door, he was smiling and his welcome seemed genuine.

'Come in, come in. It's a bit cramped, I'm afraid. Would you like a glass of meletar?'

Terrel looked at the clear, honey-coloured liquid and shook his head.

'No, thanks. I don't have a good head for drink.' That was a simplification of the truth. His very real aversion to alcohol stemmed from more complicated reasons.

'Shame. This is good stuff.' Kjolur took an appreciative sip from his own glass. 'What brings you to my lair?' He settled himself and waved Terrel to take a seat at the other end of the narrow bunk.

'I was wondering whether you had anything to do with the captain changing his mind about Whale Ness.'

'Would it be so surprising if I did?'

'We've only just met. Why would you want to help me?'

'Don't you believe in first impressions?'

'Sometimes.'

'So do I. Call it intuition, if you like. My powers of persuasion are obviously greater than I thought.'

'So you didn't pay Ostan, then?'

Kjolur did not respond immediately. His smile faded slowly, and Terrel felt as if he were being impaled by the calm gaze of those uncanny green eyes.

'I'm a businessman, Terrel,' the merchant said at last. 'Why would I do that?'

'I've no idea.'

'There's no profit in it for me, is there?'

'No, but—'

'Tell me, have you revealed everything about what you're going to do on Myvatan?'

'I don't know everything myself.'

'Fair enough. But have you told me all you *do* know?'

Terrel's hesitation betrayed him. He wasn't sure where the conversation was leading, but Kjolur had succeeded in putting him at a disadvantage.

'It's all right,' the islander said. 'You don't have to answer, and I've no intention of prying. Every man is entitled to keep his own counsel when he wants to.'

'Including you,' Terrel said, finally seeing the point the other man was making.

'Including me,' the merchant said, nodding.

They sat in silence for a while. Kjolur seemed perfectly at ease but Terrel was nervous, not quite knowing what to say or where to look. He took note of the few things he could see in the cabin, but knew it would be both pointless and rude to enquire about the ledgers or the small casket that sat in one corner.

'Well,' he said eventually, clearing his throat. 'You have my thanks. I'm in your debt.'

'Few foreigners come to my homeland,' Kjolur responded. 'Most of my people prefer it that way. Even Ostan and his crew won't venture more than a few paces from the docks. For myself, I wish it were otherwise. Perhaps you're the first of many visitors.'

From what he'd heard, Terrel felt it unlikely that Myvatan would attract many outsiders, but he chose not to say so. Instead he tried to bring the talk around to the merchant himself.

'Do other Myvatanians travel as you do?'

'Very few. We're an insular breed in more than one sense. And for much of the year our climate is not conducive to travel.'

'Is it true that the sun never rises in midwinter?' Terrel asked. It was one of the tales told about the island that he'd found hard to believe.

'It's true,' Kjolur confirmed. 'Just as it's true that for two months at midsummer the sun never sets.'

'Really?' Terrel breathed, his astonishment plain.

'You get used to it,' the islander said, smiling again. 'Of course, we sleep through the darkest months anyway.'

'You actually *hibernate*?' Terrel was even more astonished now.

'For about two median months each winter,' Kjolur confirmed. 'If you'd made this trip much earlier in the year, you'd have found us all asleep.'

This idea took a bit of getting used to. Although Terrel had come across long-term sleepers of a quite different kind, the prospect of an entire community deliberately falling asleep every year was bizarre.

'It's really a very practical arrangement,' the islander went on. 'We save on supplies at the bleakest time of the year, and conserve our own energy for when the light returns.'

Terrel nodded, even though he still felt that – practical or not – it was one of the strangest things he'd ever heard.

'Do you do the same thing on your travels?' he asked.

'No. When there's light and warmth, I've no need to. My body adjusts. I might feel weary, sometimes, but that's probably just old age creeping up on me.' He grinned.

As far as Terrel could judge, Kjolur was probably about thirty. Old enough, but hardly ancient. He grinned back.

'There's a story in here,' the merchant said, picking up his book, 'about Savik's Whale. I reread it last night after our talk.'

'Will you read it to me?' Terrel asked eagerly.

'Not the whole thing. Our poets tend to be a little . . . overelaborate, shall we say? But the gist of the tale is that it's more than just a sculpture. It's a beacon, a marker for the gods. They take notice of anything that happens there.'

'That's a daunting thought.'

'It is rather, but I shouldn't let it worry you,' Kjolur advised. 'As far as I know, the gods haven't put in too many appearances lately. What's more interesting is the fact that there's supposed to be a funnel that leads all the way up from a cave at sea-level to the top of the whale, where it emerges at the creature's blowhole.'

'Its what?'

'Blowhole. Whales aren't like other fish. In fact, some people say they aren't really fish at all. Sounds crazy, doesn't it? It's because whales have to come up to the surface every so often. They breathe the same air we do, unlike true fishes. The blowhole is on top of their heads, and that's how they breathe. Blowing water out and taking air in. But that's all beside the point. The stone whale mimics the real creatures in a most ingenious way. If there's a storm, and the wind is in the southwest, the waves force water up the funnel until it bursts out at the top in a spout.'

'That must be quite a sight,' Terrel commented.

'I'm sure it is,' Kjolur agreed. 'And according to the legend, anyone who stands beside the hole when it appears – especially if they're splashed by the seawater – is granted a vision of the future. Sound familiar at all?'

'It's certainly an odd method of prophecy,' Terrel said, 'but then it's a strange process by its very nature.' He was intrigued, and wondered whether he might be able to climb the sculpture. Then something else occurred to him. 'I'd rather there wasn't a storm when we get there, though. If Ostan's to be believed, going ashore's going to be hard enough as it is.'

The next morning, Terrel was beckoned over to the starboard rail by one of the sailors, who pointed to something in the water some distance away. A smooth black hump rose above the waves, then sank again. It was replaced by a fluid shape that looked rather like a double-sided black sail. This rose, streaming foam, flipped over with slow grace, then slid back into the sea.

'What was that?' Terrel asked, though he thought he already knew.

'A black whale. That was its tail there at the end, when it dived.'

Terrel stared in awe, but saw nothing more. He had glimpsed only the top of the creature's arched back and its tail, but that was enough for him to tell that it was enormous. Which meant that the life-sized sculpture would be just as big.

Two days later, a shout from the lookout in the bows alerted both Terrel and the crew to the fact that their voyage was almost over. The healer gazed at the purple smudge on the horizon and knew that it was his first view of Myvatan.

CHAPTER FIVE

When Terrel eventually set foot upon the rocks of Myvatan, his first impression was not of the bitter wind that threatened to overbalance him, or of the black water that swirled around his perch. It was not of the daunting cliffs that towered above him, or of the seabirds that shrieked and whirled overhead. It was not even the sheer relief of finally having had the courage to leap from the skiff, timing his jump with the swell, and managing to gain a foothold on solid ground. The feeling that swept over him and through him, filling every particle of his being with a chill dread, was an almost overwhelming sense of madness.

This was not the harmless and occasionally benevolent lunacy of someone like Alyssa. This was violent, furious, unreasoning and yet malicious. Evil. What was even more disconcerting, it seemed to be coming from the island itself. It was as if the whole place was insane.

The initial onslaught was so savage that Terrel instinctively clutched at his head, then staggered and almost fell back into the sea. He recovered just in time, tried desperately to shield his mind, and went on. As he clambered over the barnacle-encrusted rocks, taking himself further from one peril at least, he heard yells of encouragement from Kahl and the other oarsmen who had brought him ashore. He couldn't pick out their words, but knew they

were glad both that he had survived the first stage of his
journey and that their part in his escapade was over. They
were pulling away again now, returning to the *Skua*.

Catching his breath once he was no longer in any
immediate danger of being sucked back into the icy water,
Terrel watched the skiff's retreat. Doubts assailed him.
He'd been so sure that coming ashore at Whale Ness was
the right thing to do, and yet now his decision seemed
incredibly rash. Even without the all-pervading sense of
madness, this was a bleak and forbidding place, where any
number of dangers might await him. Even if he succeeded in climbing up to the island proper, there was
nothing to suggest he'd be able to survive long enough to
achieve his purpose there – whatever that was. He could
die of cold or starvation. Even a minor injury could prove
fatal.

That's all irrelevant, he told himself. You're here now.
There's no going back, so you just have to make the best
of it.

Readjusting his pack, which contained his few belongings and the food he'd been given, Terrel got to his feet
and moved further inland. His first intention was to get
well out of reach of the waves, even if the wind freshened,
and then to try to find some shelter. It was already growing dark and he had no intention of attempting to scale the
cliffs that night. He concentrated on each footstep, on
making sure his boots did not slip, and tried to focus on
his immediate practical problems. But no matter how hard
he tried, he couldn't dismiss the atmosphere of insanity
from his mind. As a healer he felt it as a sickness, an
unnatural state, but treating such a disease was clearly
beyond him. The best he could hope for was to ignore it –
and to ignore the implications for his own mission. This
was easier said than done.

'Don't you believe in first impressions?' Kjolur had asked.

Terrel was beginning to wish he didn't.

It had been late afternoon by the time the *Skua* had dropped anchor off Whale Ness, but Ostan hadn't given his passenger the choice of waiting until morning. The captain's words had been succinct. 'It's now or never, Terrel. Make up your mind.' One of the reasons for his haste had been the fear of encountering local naval vessels. Sea raids apparently played a major part in the war, and Ostan hadn't been willing to linger near a forbidden zone and risk being discovered by military forces. And he and all his crew had also been anxious to reach Akranes and complete their trading so they could sail for home as quickly as possible. The detour had already cost them several hours, and any further delay was out of the question.

The little Terrel had seen of Myvatan had not been encouraging. He'd already known it was very different from Vadanis. For a start, it was much bigger and – of course – it was not moving. But from the sea it had not really seemed like land at all. So much of it was covered in snow and ice, some of it apparently permanent, that it looked more like a piece of ocean that had frozen over, like a giant iceberg. Even from a distance it was clear that the mountains of the interior were huge. They were mostly shrouded in mist or cloud, but when the sunlight finally broke through, their peaks shone like pure white beacons.

As the *Skua* sailed closer, the rugged nature of the coastline had become apparent. Where the slopes were too steep to be covered with snow, much of the rock was black or dark grey, but even that sparkled, as if it were studded with crystals. Finally, Terrel had caught a glimpse of the fabled sculpture. Although he'd known it would be impressive, the real thing had taken his breath away. The manner in which its sinuous lines mimicked life, almost as though it were swimming in the air above the cliff, was remarkable. This was no crude shaping of a convenient piece of rock; this was a true work of art, as beautiful as it was astonishing. And the fact that it could achieve this effect on such a huge scale was truly awe-inspiring. The stone whale was colossal. To conceive of such a structure, let alone actually shape it, did indeed seem to be the province of gods rather than men.

As the *Skua* had drawn round into the lee of the headland, Terrel had gazed up in wonder. For a moment he'd thought that perhaps a real creature had been frozen in stone many ages earlier, just as the dragon-lizard and her eggs had been preserved in the desert of Misrah. But he'd soon dismissed the idea. Savik's Whale was a deliberate creation, not an accident of history.

He had been given no more time to stare and speculate, as preparations had quickly been made for his departure. At least the weather had been kind, with the sea as calm as it was ever likely to be. Terrel's blithe assumption that a landing would have been possible whatever the conditions had seemed very foolish then. If it had turned rough, he would have had no chance at all. As it was, he'd already begun to doubt his own decision, purely because of the nature of the terrain he would be entering.

'I hope you know what you're doing,' Ostan had said in parting.

'Be careful,' Kjolur had advised. 'The Gold Moon is full tonight.'

Terrel had not known why this was relevant – and at that moment, as he climbed down the rope ladder to the waiting skiff, the position of the moons had been the least of his worries. The rest of the crew had been silent or, like

Kahl, had simply wished him good luck. By then, Terrel had known he was going to need it.

He spent the night huddled in a small, salt-smelling cave, which he fervently hoped was above the highest tide line. The darkness proved to be almost complete, with just a little moonlight filtering through a canopy of cloud. Terrel found that when he could see nothing, the relentless, ever-changing noise of the wind and sea seemed even louder and more threatening. He kept imagining that the waves were coming closer and would soon flood his meagre shelter, plucking him from his refuge like a clam being pulled from its shell. He was cold and afraid, and although he knew he ought to get some sleep to prepare himself for the exertions of the next day, both his body and his mind remained restless.

Part of the reason for his long journey towards Myvatan had been the advice given to him by the ghosts about their latest discoveries in the Tindaya Code. But that was not the whole story. Many years ago, in what seemed now like another lifetime, he'd had a dream which at the time had seemed nonsensical, but which in retrospect had granted him brief glimpses of places he would one day visit. The fog-bound valley, with its dwelling that floated on the surface of a lake, and the shimmering desert populated by camels and women with tattooed faces, had been so far outside his experience of the world that he'd thought them ludicrous visions. And yet both had proved to be fragments of his own future. That same dream had also featured a frozen sea of blue-shadowed ice.

And in addition, for the first time in all his wanderings along the unknown road, Terrel had felt the influence of another, new force shaping his destiny. Although he couldn't explain it, he knew that it stemmed from the

Ancients. Having now met three elementals and struck a bargain with them, twice renewed, Terrel was sure that there was a permanent connection between him and the strange creatures. He had been responsible – at least in part – for reassuring each of them that it was not alone, that it had 'brothers' elsewhere on Nydus. He had subsequently come to believe that they were not separate entities at all, that they were somehow part of the same being, sharing memories, abilities and fears, even though they were separated by enormous distances. As a result, it seemed entirely possible that the three might have concluded that there was at least a fourth elemental, and possibly more, somewhere on the planet. If that were the case, they might well be trying to help Terrel to find the rest of their 'family'. Such guidance as they had given him had begun as he left Misrah and, although it had certainly not been continuous or even straightforward, he felt that they had been with him – in some sense – ever since.

Although these thoughts should have been comforting, now that he'd reached the ice-covered island nothing was clear any more. Insanity had invaded Myvatan's air and rock, and Terrel couldn't help wondering if there was some connection between this and the presence of an Ancient – assuming that one of the creatures was really here. This possibility, together with Alyssa's last instructions – which had been unusually obscure even for her – did little to reassure him. *Don't fight the wrong war* was presumably a warning not to get involved in the island's internal conflict. On the other hand, *Be careful where you choose to follow* could mean anything. Surely being careful was just common sense? But the phrase that caused him the most concern, and which kept returning to his thoughts now, was *And don't trust your instincts*. That made no sense at all. He had relied upon his instincts in all his travels. If he couldn't trust *them*, then what was left?

Until Alyssa returned, this was a question he couldn't answer.

Terrel's last thought before finally falling asleep was about something Kjolur had said. In the Floating Islands, the Amber – or Gold – Moon was said to be the harbinger of dreams, and this belief had been reflected in the various lands Terrel had visited since his exile. And as with any of the moons, the Amber was at its most potent when it was full.

The crystal city rose from the waves of a dark sea that was dotted with luminous pieces of floating ice. He had seen the city before, although he could never go there, but this time its fractured beauty was gone. It was an ugly, crumpled mass of glass splinters and piercing light. It had never been real; he knew that. But it was *important*. Seeing it in ruins made him tremble. He wanted to scream, to warn her, but he had no voice here. He watched in dismay as the city began to break into jagged shards and sink below the icy water.

A different sea claimed him then, the pulsing crimson ocean he thought he'd left behind for ever. The blind realm of red terror was from a time before he'd been born – a world ruled by Jax and his malevolent energy, where Terrel's only defence had been to make himself small, invisible.

When Terrel woke, drained and shivering, something else Alyssa had said was running through his mind. *The crystal's broken, isn't it? Smashed.*

She knew.

Although the message had apparently been from

Muzeni, it hadn't sounded like something the old seer
would say – even taking into account the fact that he'd
been a heretic when he was alive. On this occasion, Alyssa
had been speaking for herself.

She *knew*.

Terrel understood the dream a little better now.
Although earlier visions had been incomprehensible, he
had learnt that the crystal city represented the shield
around Alyssa – and presumably the other sleepers – a
shield that both imprisoned and protected her. And
because the fate of the sleepers was inextricably linked to
the Ancients, it followed that the vision must somehow
come from them. In a sense it *represented* them. But if that
were the case, the elemental here on Myvatan was not only
very ill, it was also hopelessly unbalanced and possibly
beyond help. It was not an encouraging thought.

It's just a dream, he told himself as he forced stiff, cold
muscles into reluctant action. He had used this argument
before. He hadn't believed it then and he didn't believe it
now.

Morning spread a chill light over the empty grey-green
sea. The *Skua* was long gone, and Terrel was on his own.
He had no way back. He could either stay where he was,
and die, or he could climb.

As he settled the straps of his pack over his shoulder,
and retied the laces of the specially adapted boot that
fitted his crooked right foot, Terrel realized that the madness he had sensed the night before was still there. But
now he found he was able to treat it as a constant part of
the background. Unnatural though it was, it was like the
noise of the sea. After a while you still heard it, but you
ceased to listen. In the same way, he was still aware of the
insanity, but it no longer threatened to disorientate or dis-
able him. At least now, unpleasant though it was, he had

a possible explanation for the sickness that had permeated the very fabric of the island.

As he left the cave, he looked hopefully up at the wheeling gulls and other birds that inhabited the cliffs and coastline. He longed for one of them to be Alyssa, but no matter how welcome her aid would be just then, there was no sign of her. And there wasn't likely to be until he got further from the ocean. He was on his own.

Terrel was relieved to find that the cliff face was not entirely vertical, as it had appeared from out to sea, and that it was possible to scramble up parts of the lower section in relative safety. It was rough going, and he had to be careful where he planted his feet, but he made steady progress. Higher up, the slopes became steeper and keeping his balance was more difficult, but at least the surface of the rock was drier here and less slippery now he was some way from the water's edge. Eventually, however, it became a matter of real climbing, rather than scrambling, and on several occasions Terrel scouted a possible route only to be faced by an impossibly sheer cliff or an overhang. Each time this happened he was forced to backtrack, and as his frustration – and fear – increased, he was reminded of when he'd climbed Makranash. The arid heat of the desert had made his partial ascent of the mountain a very different proposition, but he had succeeded there and was determined to do so now. The other difference was that in Misrah he'd had friends, both on the mountain and at its foot, who might have been able to rescue him had he suffered a mishap. Here any such failure would almost certainly result in his death.

Eventually, as his desperation mounted, Terrel discovered a narrow vertical crevasse. He was able to wedge himself into it, bracing himself on either side, and edge upwards like a sweep climbing a chimney. His lop-sided physique made some movements impossible, and several of the necessary contortions were very painful, but at least he was moving upwards again. The fingers of his good hand were already raw from cold and the rough stone, but at least the exertions of his latest attempt warmed the rest of his body.

The crevasse had many twists and turns, and there were several awkward moments when Terrel had to negotiate various jagged protuberances or a particularly narrow section. However, apart from one occasion when he made the mistake of looking down – and then had to rest for a while until his limbs stopped shaking – he made constant advances. By midday he was high above the ocean and, knowing that a fall now would be fatal, he was moving with great caution. He had no way of telling how far he was from the cliff top, but he fervently hoped that the chimney continued all the way there. If he reached a dead end now, he wasn't sure he'd have either the physical or mental strength to make the long descent, let alone try again elsewhere. He kept looking up, longing to see his goal, but it remained tantalizingly out of reach.

Far above him, the clouds had dispersed and the sky was a pale but clear blue, and Terrel was glad of that. The sun's rays held little warmth but it was better than nothing, and any rain, sleet or snow would have made his task even more of an ordeal. As it was, he was apparently trapped in a nightmare where every new hand- or foothold seemed to make no difference to his overall progress.

On two occasions, something startled him to such a degree that he almost lost his grip. The first was when a loud clap of thunder burst in the air above him. The shock almost dislodged him, and in its aftermath, as the blood pounded in his ears, Terrel dreaded the arrival of the storm that was surely on its way. However, what sky he could see remained clear, and he'd just begun to think that the thunderclouds must have moved away again when two large, white birds flapped past him as they emerged from their eyrie. They were squawking furiously at his invasion of their territory, and the noise and flurry of their wings set Terrel's heart racing once more. Ducking away from their assault, he almost slipped again, clinging on only by his fingertips. He didn't have enough breath left to shout at the birds, and could only hope they'd leave him alone once he was past their nest.

And then it seemed that his worst fears had been realized. The crevasse appeared to end in a blank, horizontal roof, which would be quite impossible to pass. Even so, Terrel was not willing to give up yet, and went on. A few moments later he was intensely relieved to find that the crevasse did not end, but veered sideways in a sort of open-sided tunnel that was big enough for him to be able to crawl along it quite easily. What was more, to his great joy he could see level ground, with a covering of threadbare grass, at the end of the traverse. By the time he reached that, he knew he'd achieved the first of his goals. He was at the top.

As he stood there, taking in deep lungfuls of the cold, clear air, Terrel wondered for the first time what he was supposed to do now. The Tindaya Code had led him to this spot, but it had given no indication as to what was supposed to happen next.

Looking round, he saw that Savik's Whale was only a few hundred paces away and, without thinking, he set off towards the great sculpture. However, before he'd gone very far, movement from a little further inland caught his eye, just as the faint sounds of clashing steel and raised voices drifted to him on the wind.

Terrel stared in horror, knowing that he'd overcome one danger only to find himself embroiled in another. What he had stumbled into was not a forbidden zone but a war zone.

CHAPTER SIX

The terrain over which the battle was being fought was uneven, but Terrel was on relatively flat ground, with no vegetation to speak of, so there was nowhere for him to hide. His first instinct was to throw himself flat, in the hope that he could avoid being seen by the combatants, but as soon as he'd done this he realized that the battle was moving in his direction. He still felt horribly exposed, and knew that he'd have to find a better hiding place if he was to have any hope of remaining undetected. Going inland was out of the question – that would simply take him closer to the fighting – and behind him was the cliff edge. His only alternative was to go along the coastline one way or the other. In either case that would mean crossing a stretch of bare earth and rock, covered only by sparse patches of grass and a few pockets of snow. To the east the land rose slowly, but there was nothing large enough to conceal him there. The only possibility of cover to the west was Savik's Whale, but going in that direction would take him further out on to the tapering headland, making it more likely that he'd be trapped there as the battle went on. However, this was clearly his only chance, and so he took it. Heedful of Alyssa's warning, he wanted nothing to do with the islanders' war, so he scuttled along the cliff top, keeping as low as he could and hoping he would not be seen. The awkward movement sent needles of pain shooting through his twisted leg, but he limped on.

With every step he expected to hear the shout that meant he'd been spotted, but it did not come. In fact, the noise of battle seemed to have receded a little, masked now by a rising wind that was blowing from the other side of the headland.

When Terrel finally reached the whale, and staggered under its massive upraised tail fins, he crouched down in the shadows where the belly of the creature joined the granite below. As he caught his breath, he saw that the sea was now flecked with white and a rolling swell was building up. He heard – and felt – waves crashing into the base of the cliffs on the windward side of the headland, and shuddered to think what might have happened if he'd tried to come ashore in such conditions.

Renewed shouting brought his attention back to the soldiers. For the first time, Terrel was able to see how the battle was being fought. It was difficult to tell how many men were involved, but both sides seemed to be operating with groups of archers to the rear, who provided some protection for the advancing patrols of foot soldiers. These troops were continuously manoeuvring for position, making use of what cover the terrain provided, sheltering behind outcrops of rock and drifts of snow, or in the deeper gullies and hollows. Most of the fighting came in short but bloody skirmishes between these patrols, before one side or the other retreated, allowing their archers to fire on the enemy forces left behind.

Even from a distance, Terrel could tell that the conflict was in deadly earnest. He had seen some terrible things during his travels, but little to match the savagery of this encounter. The field was already littered with the bodies of the dead and dying, and it was clear that neither side was showing any mercy. No prisoners were being taken; the wounded were butchered where they lay.

The appalling carnage was already making Terrel feel sick, but what happened next left him not only horrified but also astonished. Out of nowhere a swirling dark cloud appeared, low over the battlefield and growing in size by the moment. By rights it should never have been able to form in such conditions, and even if it had, the strong wind now racing across the headland should have either dispersed the sudden mist or blown it away completely. But neither of these things happened. The cloud moved back and forth over the combatants, writhing as though caught in a vortex of several opposing gusts of wind, but never moving very far one way or another. What was more, within its churning shadows a strange light began to flicker, and the air all around it began to hum and crackle. As Terrel felt the hairs on the back of his neck stand on end, he realized what must be coming next. Flashes of lightning burst from the cloud, each accompanied by a deafening concussion. The strikes were obviously directed at a group of soldiers, and Terrel watched in horror as the men were smashed to the ground in blackened heaps or thrown into the air by the impact. He could hardly believe that such a primeval force could have been used for a deliberate attack, but that was the only possible conclusion.

Almost immediately, a second salvo of lightning leapt from the cloud, but this time it never reached its intended target. Instead of hitting the ground, the lightning fragmented, apparently deflected by some sort of invisible shield surrounding the forces under attack. This took the form of a pyramid that shimmered briefly with each bolt of fire, then vanished again.

Terrel had no idea what was going on. The use of such weapons – and the defences used against them – was quite beyond his understanding, though he couldn't help thinking of the much bigger magical dome that the sharaken had built over the palace in Talazoria, and of the murderous chaos that had reigned within. What he was watching now was also clearly the province of sorcerers, which made the nature of the battle even more horrifying.

After some time the cloud began to break up, and finally it drifted away on the wind, its unnatural potency clearly exhausted, but the fighting was far from over. The various advances and retreats continued, interspersed with bouts of violence, the bowmen still firing volleys of arrows. There was no indication as to how long the battle was likely to rage, but there seemed no possibility of escape for Terrel. The fighting now stretched across the entire width of the headland, effectively cutting him off from the rest of the island. To make matters worse, one patrol was coming closer to the whale, apparently trying to outflank their opponents, and Terrel knew he had to find somewhere else to hide.

Stooping to walk beneath the smooth curve of the sculpture, he made his way under a fin the size of a small roof and moved towards the whale's head — which was positioned so that it looked out over the point of the promontory and was therefore as far from the battle as possible. Terrel hoped that by positioning himself there he would not be seen, but as he crouched under the gigantic jaw and looked around, he thought of a better idea.

The whale's mouth formed a small cave that had been visible even from the *Skua*, and if he could get inside, there would be little chance of anyone spotting him. Moving out to take a look, Terrel saw that the opening was easily big enough for him to climb in. The only obstacle was the rows of widely-spaced, inward-facing teeth, both above and below the entrance. He decided that as long as he was careful, they should present no real problem. In fact, the lower set provided him with excellent handholds when he pulled himself up. After that it was just a matter of edging inside into the semi-darkness and then keeping very still.

He was just congratulating himself on having found the perfect refuge when a harsh grating sound – which reverberated through the hollow stone – made him unsure once more. It was a few moments before he realized what was happening – and then he couldn't believe it. The grinding noise was coming from the sculpture itself, as the lower jaw moved slowly upwards. At first Terrel was too stunned to react, and then it was too late. The two lines of stone teeth had clamped together, barring his way out. The giant mouth had closed. Savik's Whale had swallowed him.

Panic gripped Terrel by the throat and squeezed the breath from him. He crawled back to the enmeshed teeth and, bracing his back against the roof, tried with all his might to push them apart. Nothing happened. Then he tried hitting one of the teeth to see if he could break his way out, but all he did was hurt his hand. He sat back, telling himself to be calm. There was no rational explanation for what had happened, but as the whale's jaw had closed of its own volition, there was a chance that it would simply open again and release him. In the meantime, he had to be ready to escape.

Still afraid, but able to think a little more clearly now, Terrel took stock of his situation. There was nothing in his pack that could help him. He had the curved dagger given to him by the Toma, but it wouldn't be any use against such immovable stone. He wondered whether he should stay close to the teeth or try to explore the rest of the cavernous mouth. Looking around, he saw something white in

one of the deeper recesses, and realized that the back of
the cave was not entirely dark. There was obviously a
source of light there, which meant that there might be
another way out.

Crawling awkwardly on his hands and knees, Terrel
made his way towards the patch of light. As he passed the
white object he stopped to examine it – then wished he
hadn't. His eyes were growing accustomed to the dim
light now, and as soon as his probing fingers turned it
over, it was all too obvious what it was. The empty eye
sockets of a human skull stared back at him above grinning
rows of exposed teeth. Other bones lay scattered beyond it.
Terrel was obviously not the first person to have walked
into this trap. If the gods of Myvatan really were responsible for the giant sculpture, it seemed that they had a
particularly unpleasant sense of humour.

Terrel could hear the sounds of battle again now, echoing faintly in the chamber, and he knew that the fighting
must be coming even closer. For a moment he considered
calling out, hoping to attract the soldiers' attention.
Whatever they might decide to do with him, it could
hardly be worse than the fate of the one-time owner of the
skull. However, he knew that the chances of anyone hearing him amid the tumult of warfare were very slim, and
decided that he'd still prefer to try to find his own way
out. He went on.

The light was coming from a narrow tunnel at the back
of the whale's mouth. The tunnel was circular and barely
wide enough for Terrel's shoulders. The sides looked
rougher than the ridged floor of the mouth, but unless it
became an even tighter squeeze, that wouldn't be a problem. He told himself he should at least explore, and find
out where the light was coming from. He could always
return if the tunnel led nowhere. Taking off his pack, he

wondered whether to take it with him or leave it behind, and quickly decided on the former. If he did discover a way out, he wouldn't want to have to come back for his belongings. He pushed the bag into the tunnel. Unfortunately, this had the effect of blocking off most of the light, but Terrel couldn't think how else to keep it with him.

As he crawled into the hole, shoving the pack ahead of him, he was immediately aware of the sharp points of rock digging into his belly, arms and legs. The skin of his good hand was caught painfully as he pulled himself forward, but once his feet were inside the tunnel his boots were able to get a good purchase and he moved forward more rapidly – albeit at the cost of a few more scratches.

He had not gone far when his pack came up against an obstruction, and pushing only seemed to wedge it tighter. Whatever was ahead was not shifting. Terrel tried to squash the pack to one side and peer around it, but he couldn't see anything. So he reached round with his good arm to see if he could find whatever was barring his progress and dislodge it. His fingers encountered something slim and hard, lying across the width of the tunnel, and he had no need to see it to know what it was. He'd found part of another skeleton. It was one of the larger bones that was now wedged tightly, blocking the whale's throat.

With no way through, Terrel reluctantly decided that he'd have to go back. He began to wriggle around, and immediately cried out in pain. The stone points that had been mere nuisances earlier now stabbed at him like sharp knives, snagging his clothes and sticking into his flesh. Almost immediately he saw what had happened and cursed himself for not having recognized the peril earlier. The whale's throat was lined with backward-facing 'teeth', which allowed him to go in but not back out again. So now he really *was* trapped, unable to move in either direction.

Fear, coupled with the sheer stupidity of having got himself into such a situation, made Terrel want to weep. After all he'd been through, the idea of his life ending in this horrible, farcical manner was too much to bear. He thought of Alyssa, and wondered if she'd ever be able to find him here — alive or dead. He heard once more her words about being careful where he chose to follow, and wished he'd heeded her advice. Following the man whose skeleton lay ahead had not been a wise move. He had let her down. He had let them *all* down.

'No!'

He had been breathing in convulsive gasps, and was startled by the sudden roar that burst from his lips. It had come from a surge of burning anger, a rage against fate, and it fuelled a new and furious determination. He would *not* surrender meekly. If he couldn't go back, then he *would* go on. And no flimsy skeleton was going to stop him!

Squirming even closer, so that his face was pressed up against his pack, Terrel used his crooked arm to hold this out of the way as best he could while he reached forward with his other hand. Locating the bone, he felt along its length to find the central point, where he hoped it would be at its thinnest, then aligned the heel of his palm, drew his arm back and slammed it into the obstacle as hard as he could. The impact jarred his shoulder and sent spikes of agony through his neck and chest, but it had no effect on the bone. After a few deep breaths Terrel tried again, with a similar lack of success, but he was in no mood to give up now. He repeated his assault.

On the seventh blow, when his arm and shoulder were hurting so much he had almost ceased to notice the torment in the rest of his body, there was a loud, sharp crack and the bone snapped in two. Breathing heavily, almost weeping from the effort it had cost him, Terrel shoved his pack forward again and found, to his immense relief, that it now moved easily. As he crawled on he passed other bones, but none of them impeded his progress.

After a while the tunnel began to slope upwards and the light became stronger, which gave him a little hope. The passage was soon almost vertical and was joined from below by another, much smaller tunnel. This was smooth-sided, and Terrel could hear the rumbling of the sea far beneath him. However, by then he wasn't concerned with this curiosity. He had just glimpsed the sky through a gap above him, and he hurried on up to the open air.

Although he had to be careful still, the stone teeth actually made it easier for him to climb now, and he stuck his head out of the hole, finding – as he'd expected – that he had emerged at the top of the sculpture. Looking down over the smoothly curving sides of the whale, he saw to his dismay that fighting was going on all around him now. The soldiers had abandoned any pretence of strategy and had settled for a pitched battle on the relatively open ground of the promontory. In just a few moments Terrel saw several men cut down, and there seemed to be no end in sight. Both sides appeared intent on fighting to the last man. He had no wish to become embroiled in such violence, and decided to stay where he was until the slaughter ended or moved elsewhere. Preoccupied as they were, it was not likely that the warriors would notice his head poking from the top of the sculpture.

The wind had risen considerably since he'd been inside the whale and was now blowing at almost gale force. Out to sea, a huge swell was building up, and although Terrel couldn't see them, he could hear some of the waves crashing into the base of the southwest-facing cliffs. The next thing he heard was not so easy to explain. It was a loud, mournful whistling, that rose and fell in an echoing, melancholy song of the sea. He had never heard anything like it before, but it seemed to be all around him and he knew, with a sudden intuition that he did not question, that this was the whale's song.

The extraordinary noise had clearly been heard by some of the soldiers too. There was a brief lull in the fighting and many of them glanced at the whale, their faces betraying a mixture of surprise and fear. Terrel ducked down, trying not to impale himself on too many of the stone teeth, then found that he was now under threat from another source. A huge thump from below, louder than any that had gone before, had not completely died away. The vibration was augmented by a rushing, gurgling sound that grew louder by the moment – and Terrel realized what was going to happen just before the source of the noise reached him. He was standing in the whale's blow-hole – and it was about to blow.

Directly below him, water exploded from the smaller tunnel with incredible force. Expanding to fill the larger space, it lost some of its momentum, but was still strong enough to lift Terrel up bodily and propel him towards the open air. Flailing and spluttering, he found himself momentarily weightless as spurts of seawater, foam and spray flew past him into the sky. The next thing he knew he had been deposited, almost gently, on the whale's back, next to the still-gushing fountain. He had landed on his feet, upright, his boots resting on solid rock. It was almost as though the water had set him aside so that it could get on with its proper business of shooting towards the stars, and had decided that his entrance would be more dramatic if he was not just sent sprawling to the ground. He was soaked through, and the water was so cold that it seemed to burn his already bruised and scratched skin, but otherwise he was miraculously unharmed.

The rush of water next to him subsided as the pressure from below relented, and what was left drained back to the sea and into the whale's mouth, dribbling out between its clenched teeth. Terrel stood where he was, too shocked to think, only gradually becoming aware that the only sound he could hear now was the soughing of the wind. Even that seemed strangely hushed.

The warriors were still there, but the fighting had come to a complete stop. All the men seemed to be frozen where they were, some with their swords still raised for a blow that had been halted in mid-strike. Terrel found that vaguely worrying. But what was more worrying still was that every one of the soldiers was now staring at *him*.

CHAPTER SEVEN

The silence seemed to last for ever, and then was broken by a banshee wail that was recognizably human in origin but which also sounded like a deranged echo of the whale's song. The effect this had was remarkable. Soldiers on one side of the conflict took up the cry – which had presumably come from one of their own number – and at the same time they began scrambling to get away from the battlefield. A few dissenting voices – their officers, perhaps – tried to stop them from running away, but to no avail. The retreat became a disorderly stampede, carrying even the objectors along with it.

Meanwhile, those who were left – who were clearly not at all interested in pursuing their fleeing enemies – stood where they were, still staring in amazement at Terrel. He found it hard to believe that his appearance – even popping up out of the whale like a child's jack-in-the-box – could have brought such a dramatic end to the fighting, but he couldn't think of any other explanation.

He could see that the remaining soldiers, who were now drawing close to the sculpture as if pulled by some mysterious force, wore gold flashes on the shoulders of their uniforms. Now that he thought about it, those who had run away had worn similarly placed black patches. Their allegiance to their quarter – and their moon – was evidently signified by the colour of these badges, but unlike

Kjolar's hidden epaulet, theirs were worn in the open. In the confusion of battle, such markings must be a convenient way of distinguishing between friend and foe.

Exposed as he was, there was nowhere for Terrel to hide, and he felt desperately vulnerable. But the soldiers showed no sign of aggressive intent. Rather than enmity, their regard seemed to be tinged with awe, even reverence, and he realized that – for the time being at least – he had no need to hide. One of the soldiers laughed nervously, and for some reason it made him think of Jax. He heard his brother's mocking laugh, and then his voice sounded inside Terrel's head. *Now this looks like fun!* Then he was gone, and forgotten.

An impulse Terrel could not explain made him glance to his right and look out over the sea. He spotted several black shapes amid the surging waves and sensed, rather than heard, their mournful song. As if in response – or perhaps as a repeated summons – the stone whale called again. The ethereal whistling flowed over the headland, then faded into the noise of the wind.

This time Terrel knew what the strange music presaged and, as another loud thump shook the cliffs below, he stepped carefully to one side, distancing himself from the blowhole. Without a human presence blocking its path, the seawater shot into the sky in a single stream which was eventually bent and split apart by the gale, sending spray in a wide arc over the headland and beyond the cliffs on the far side. For a moment, a shaft of sunlight created a small rainbow within the fountain before that too was blown away on the wind.

As the last droplets pattered down, Terrel returned his attention to the soldiers. One of them, a bloodied sword still hanging limply from his hand, gazed back.

'What do you want us to do?'

Terrel had not known what sort of greeting to expect —
if any — but he could not have anticipated this. Moreover,
he had no idea how to answer. As he stood there, shivering, with icicles forming in his hair and at the bottom of
his sleeves, he recalled the legend which said that anyone
splashed by water from Savik's Whale would be granted a
vision of the future. As far as the soldiers were concerned,
he had not only been doused but had actually emerged in
the midst of the eruption. He still didn't understand why
this should make him an object of awe, but a more calcu-
lating part of his mind decided that he should try to take
advantage of the situation. They clearly thought he was
someone — or something — that he wasn't, and this presented him with both an opportunity and a problem. He
could try to exercise his supposed power, and perhaps be
obeyed at first, but sooner or later they would find out the
truth. So what *was* he supposed to do?

'Is he reading the far-crystals?' another soldier asked,
misinterpreting Terrel's distracted air.

'He has eyes like ice,' another breathed — and suddenly
there was a rush of questions.

'Is he really the child of the whales?'

'Who else *could* it be?'

'Is this the time of change, then?'

'Why doesn't he speak?'

'Quiet!' The voice of the swordsman who had spoken
first easily overrode all the others. With instant obedience
the rest fell silent, their military training overcoming their
curiosity.

'I command this company,' their leader told Terrel.
'Tell me what you need us to do.'

Paradoxically, the earnest expression on the warrior's
face made Terrel want to laugh. He was so cold and confused that logical thought was almost beyond him, but he

quickly realized that he should pretend to have seen a vision of the future – a future that included his own safety and comfort. The soldiers would presumably do their best to see that this came true. If and when his deception was discovered, he would deal with the consequences then. However, lying had never come easily to Terrel, and he hesitated before forcing himself to speak.

'I saw ...' The words came out as an almost inaudible croak, and he found he did not have the strength to go on. His tongue seemed frozen and his lips were numb.

'What did you see?' the commander asked eagerly.

But Terrel did not get the chance to even try to answer. As the soldier finished speaking, an arrow slammed into the side of his neck, sending him sprawling to the ground.

Terrel stared in horror, knowing that the man was dead, but his comrades reacted with more presence of mind. Shouted orders filled the air, and suddenly there was movement everywhere as the Gold forces prepared to resume battle. However, they were now at a considerable disadvantage, bunched together on open ground with their enemy having both the element of surprise and a greater readiness for the fight. The black-fletched arrows took a terrible toll, and those who were left were outnumbered and demoralized. The battle became a massacre.

Terrel was forced to watch all this from his elevated position. He crouched down, trying to protect himself from the freezing wind – and to make himself as small a target as possible in case one of the archers decided to take a shot at him. Other than that he was helpless, unable to influence either the course of the remorseless carnage or his own fate. Now that it was obvious that the renewed conflict could only end one way, he wondered whether the earlier retreat might have been a ploy, enabling the Black forces to turn the tables on their opponents. At the time their fear had seemed genuine, and that had either been exceptionally good acting, or their leaders had subsequently persuaded them to overcome their doubts and return to the action. Terrel was inclined to believe the second option, but in the end it did not affect his own plight. Before long, it was clear that he would be at the mercy of men who were capable of inflicting a truly merciless defeat upon their enemies.

'I could easily get one of my archers to shoot you down,' the commander of the victorious Black company pointed out. 'You're an easy target up there.'

The battle was over, and Terrel was now being watched by an entirely different group of soldiers. Some of them were obviously nervous, but there was none of the reverence he had seen in the faces of the Gold troop. In fact, several men seemed to regard him with unmistakable hatred. Still recovering from the revulsion he'd felt at the recent slaughter, Terrel was nonetheless bemused by the diversity of the reactions to his presence. Clearly, the legends surrounding Savik's Whale could be interpreted in more than one way.

'You'll freeze to death soon anyway,' the soldier added. 'You're soaked through. It's your choice.'

He had begun by insisting that Terrel could not stay where he was and had then demanded his surrender, which seemed a little superfluous. What could one unarmed man do against such a force? Terrel, who so far hadn't spoken, soon realized that there was more to it than that. His appearance had initially caused them to flee, and it seemed that some of the men still harboured suspicions about him.

'How am I supposed to get down?' Terrel asked, through chattering teeth. The question had been in the back of his mind for some time. Returning through the tunnel would be impossible, but simply leaping from the top of the sculpture would almost certainly result in his being badly injured or even killed. The frozen ground would not be a forgiving landing place.

'How did you get up there in the first place?'

Terrel explained, and although he sensed that at least some of his audience did not believe a word he was saying, their commander seemed a little more open-minded.

'Well, at least that makes more sense than the rubbish about you coming up out of the sea,' he remarked contemptuously.

Was that what the other soldiers had believed? Terrel wondered. It seemed barely credible, but their awed reaction had indeed been puzzling. If they had truly thought that he was some kind of supernatural creature from the ocean, it would at least explain their attitude. However, he had the feeling that his arrival had had a more specific meaning for the Gold troops. But he would never know what this was. The bodies of those soldiers now lay still, growing cold on the windswept ness.

'I guess you'll just have to jump and take your chances,' the commander said.

'It's too far down,' Terrel objected. The sides of the sculpture were smooth, affording no holds, and sooner or later he would slip and fall.

'Move back a bit, and see if you can slide down to one of the fins,' the commander suggested.

'Captain?' one of the others ventured. 'It'd be better if he went down to the lowest part of the tail. Before it turns up again. We could help him from there.'

'Aye, with a prod of steel if necessary,' one of his colleagues added, waving a metal-tipped spear.

'So, Terrel, where do your allegiances lie?'

The healer had made it down unharmed, and had told the captain his name.

'I have none,' he replied. 'I'm not from Myvatan.'

'Then why are you here?'

'I . . . I'm just a traveller.' He was aware that the mood among the listening soldiers was becoming even uglier, but he didn't know why.

'That's not good enough. Which quarter do you belong to?'

'The Black,' Terrel claimed.

'Good guess,' the captain sneered. 'You do realize you're in a forbidden zone?'

Terrel nodded.

'So if you're one of us, you'll know the password for this phase.'

The newcomer's bewildered expression was all the answer the warrior needed.

'Thought not,' he said.

'I'm not a soldier,' Terrel began. 'I don't—'

'I can see that,' the captain cut in, flicking at the plain shoulders of the healer's jerkin. 'You've no markings.' Turning aside and addressing one of his men, he asked, 'Find anything there?'

One of the soldiers had been rummaging through Terrel's pack.

'Not much,' he replied. 'There's this.' He held up the nomad's dagger. 'Not a lot of use unless you're planning to kill someone by stealth. The rest is just food, clothes. Nice belt.'

'Any markers on it?'

'None that I recognize.' The soldier paused uncertainly. 'The only other thing is this. The gods know what it is.' He held up a small object – the only thing that had accompanied Terrel on all his travels.

'It's a clay pipe,' the healer volunteered. It had belonged to Muzeni when he'd lived in the observatory at

Havenmoon. Terrel had taken it from the heretic's long-dead hand himself.

'Does it have power?' the captain asked.

Terrel wondered again about lying, about whether to claim that it was the magical artefact his interrogator clearly suspected, but he couldn't see the point. Any such claim could be easily disproved.

'No,' he said. 'It's just a pipe.' He couldn't understand why such a commonplace article should create such unease.

'What's that?'

'You put tobacco or herbs in the bowl,' he explained, once he'd realized the question was serious, 'light it, and breathe in the smoke through the stem.'

Many of the soldiers clearly thought this was hilarious, but their captain was not amused.

'You think to mock me?' he demanded. 'What is its real purpose?'

'I've told you,' Terrel said, frustrated by the fact that telling the truth only seemed to be getting him into more trouble.

'Put it away,' the commander snapped, and the soldier replaced Terrel's belongings and closed the pack.

'What now?' the healer asked.

'Are you one of Reykholar's people?'

'No. I've never heard of him.'

At this there were more smiles from the soldiers around him.

'But you still refuse to tell me where your loyalties lie?'

'I *told* you—' Terrel began, but another warrior interrupted him.

'He's a spy, Captain.'

'A brilliant deduction, Pjorsa,' the captain remarked sarcastically. 'Of course he's a spy. Do you think I'm stupid?'

'No, sir.'

'What I'm wondering is who he's spying for and why. But there's no doubt he *is* a spy.'

Terrel saw others nodding in agreement.

'So shall I kill him now?' Pjorsa asked. 'Or should we torture him first?'

CHAPTER EIGHT

'Oh, I think we'll hear a little more of what he's got to say before we kill him,' the captain decided. 'But I'm not going to hang around here till my fingers drop off. Let's get back to camp. Narvat, your detail set the lookouts. Stykkis, make sure the wounded get the help they need. Pjorsa, organize the collection of tags. The rest of you, move!' As his men hurried to obey, their commander turned back to Terrel. 'You stay in front of me, where I can see you. And don't try anything funny.' His hand rested purposefully on the pommel of his sword, making it plain what would happen if the prisoner *did* try anything.

Terrel nodded meekly. After the recent exchange he was grateful just to be alive, and in his current state his best chance of remaining that way seemed to be to stay with the soldiers. Without their help he was likely to die from the cold before too long. And anyway, he couldn't think of anything funny *to* try.

He was given a dry cloak to wrap himself in and, at the captain's prompting, he began walking. The entire company went on their way, leaving the bodies of both friends and enemies where they lay. Terrel was simply glad to be on the move. Although their pace was determined by that of the wounded soldiers, it was still fast enough to test his depleted reserves of energy. But at least the exercise warmed his limbs enough for him to be able to concentrate on other things.

His fate evidently hung in the balance, but any delay could only work to his advantage. He still had the chance to learn a little more about his captors, to plead his case, and hopefully to prove that he wasn't a spy. He already knew that these men were capable of killing in cold blood, so he'd have to tread very carefully, but surely it should-n't be beyond his skill to persuade them that he would be worth more to them alive. His main chance would come when they reached their camp and the injured needed treatment. He could offer his healing abilities then. In the meantime, he had to come up with a story that would be convincing enough to ensure his safety. In particular, he had to decide whether or not to mention Kjolur. As a merchant loyal to the Red Quarter, he was theoretically an ally of the Black soldiers, and the fact that he'd been at least partly responsible for Terrel's arrival at Whale Ness might count in the healer's favour.

This reminder of Kjolur set off a whole new train of thought. Terrel knew that he and the merchant had both been hiding things from each other when they'd talked aboard the *Skua*. Assuming that Kjolur *was* the one who had made Terrel's landing at Whale Ness possible, why had he wanted Terrel to go there? Had he had an ulterior motive? And if so, what could it have been? Could he possibly have guessed what was going to happen, or what was likely to happen? He'd been away from the island for so long that this seemed a remote possibility. Surely no one could have foreseen the extraordinary events that had just taken place at Savik's Whale – nor the fact that two groups of soldiers would have been there to witness them. Even so, Terrel found it difficult to believe that everything that day had happened purely by chance.

*

The soldiers' camp was not what Terrel had expected. It lay within a low-walled fortress which appeared to have been built out of blocks of ice and compacted snow. This bizarre structure would presumably melt in the warmer summer months, but for now it was solid enough, and provided both an excellent means of defence and — even more important — shelter from the ever-present wind. Inside the enclosure there were a large number of tents and, much to Terrel's delight, several glowing fires. Left under guard beside one of these, his clothes dried out at last and he felt himself begin to thaw. The intense tingling in his hands and feet was agonizing, but it was preferable to the awful numbness that would have meant he'd suffered permanent damage. For the moment, this was all he could think about — but when the captain returned with several of his lieutenants, Terrel recognized that he was still in considerable danger.

'Feeling better?'

'Yes.'

'Good. Some of my men think we should have cut your throat and left you out on the headland. Failing that, they'd like to kill you now. Can you give me any reason why I should stop them?'

'I'm not a spy,' Terrel replied. 'I've no interest in your war. I'm just a traveller. And a healer. If you let me, I can help your wounded.'

'You're not touching any of my men,' the captain retorted sharply, revealing the depths of his own mistrust.

'But I could lessen their pain, help them to recover more quickly.'

'Pain is a warrior's reward. They'll bear it until we get them to the pools.'

'Won't some of them die before then?'

'Probably,' the commander admitted, without sounding overly concerned.

'Then let me help *them*,' Terrel pleaded. 'I may be able to save their lives.'

'Are you a magian, then?'

'No.' He didn't know what the term meant.

'Then how do you heal?'

'It's just a talent I was born with. I know how to deal with pain.' He indicated his twisted limbs.

'You said you're from the Black Quarter. If you're a foreigner, what made you say that?'

'He was just trying—' Narvat began, but the captain waved him into silence.

'The Dark Moon has controlled my fate since the day I was born,' Terrel replied.

'Where were you born?'

'On an island called Vadanis, that floats in the Movaghassi Ocean.'

It was clear that his answer meant nothing to the soldiers.

'It floats?' the commander asked sceptically.

'All the islands of the empire do. They travel in a complex pattern, determined by the passage of the moons.'

'He's crazier than a cut snake,' Pjorsa remarked.

'You realize we have ways of making sure you answer our questions truthfully?' the captain asked.

'Why should I lie?' Terrel argued. 'Why would I make up something like that? What good would it do me?'

The soldier nodded, conceding the point.

'What's that marker on your hand?'

Taken aback by the sudden switch in the questioning, Terrel glanced at the tattoo on the back of his left hand. It depicted four concentric circles, representing the four moons, and it had been put there to identify him as one of the inmates of Havenmoon.

'I was a slave once,' he said, repeating a story he had used before. 'This was my owner's brand.'

His audience was clearly not convinced.

'If it's a marker, we can negate its power by cutting off his hand and burning it,' Stykkis said.

The captain seemed to consider this suggestion for a few moments, then shook his head.

'No. I don't think he's any danger to us that way.'

Terrel's relief was short-lived.

'Does anyone else have any questions before we decide what to do with him?' the commander asked.

'What made you go to Whale Ness?' Narvat asked. 'There are easier ways to come ashore.'

'Many of my travels have been foretold in an ancient prophecy,' Terrel replied, hoping he was doing the right thing. 'The stone whale was part of that.'

'You're an important person, then,' Pjorsa commented dryly, 'if prophecies are being written about you.'

Terrel couldn't think of a suitable response.

'You don't look so important to me,' the warrior added. 'Even Savik's Whale decided to spit you out.'

That brought a few smiles to the gathering.

'He did do us a favour, though,' Stykkis pointed out, 'distracting the Gold scum.'

'We'd have beaten them anyway, no matter what he did,' the captain claimed.

Then why did your men run away when I first appeared? Terrel thought. What did they think I was going to do? He said nothing, but wondered whether he could still play on that initial fear. The soldiers had obviously been able to overcome their original panic – they were even able to joke about Terrel's sudden arrival now – but could he somehow reinstate it? *Why* had they been afraid of him? Apart from his healing, the only reliable magic he could call upon was the glamour, and he would only use that as a last resort, if it looked as though they really were going to torture or kill him. But there were limits to what he could do with the glamour – changing the colour of his eyes was unlikely to impress these men – and if he used it and didn't make much of an impression, his pointless sorcery would only reinforce their suspicions. Such magic could just as easily condemn him as save him.

'Anything else?' the captain asked.

'I met one of your allies on the ship that brought me here,' Terrel volunteered. 'He helped me get to Whale Ness.'

'What's his name?'

'Kjolur. He's a merchant from the Red Quarter.'

'Never heard of him.' The soldier's disdain for a mere tradesman was clear.

The ensuing silence went on until Terrel could stand it no longer.

'If you're not going to kill me,' he said forcefully, 'can I have something to eat?'

His bravado brought some approving smiles and even a little laughter from the soldiers.

'Bring him some food,' the commander told one of the guards, 'but keep a watch on him. I don't know what to make of this one.' He paused, considering. 'We'll take him back to Saudark. The generals can decide what to do with him.'

After three days' march through an unremittingly dreary landscape, the soldiers and their prisoner reached the stone-built city of Saudark. It nestled in a wide valley, beneath the great bulk of a mountain whose lower slopes were bare rock but whose summit was a bright mass of ice and snow, rising above the layer of mist that lay over the city itself. The weather during their journey had been foul, with constant strong winds bringing showers of snow, sleet and hail, but as soon as they entered the valley the temperature rose appreciably. Terrel discovered the reason for this as they made their way to the fortress that was their final destination. One section of the town was cordoned off from the rest, with guards stationed at every entrance. Only military personnel were allowed inside and, as their own wounded were admitted, Terrel realized that this must be the site of the healing pools – and the water within them was obviously so hot that it made the climate of the entire city more pleasant. The cloud that hung over Saudark was not mist but a blanket of steam.

The rest of the party went on to the generals' castle and there, after certain formalities, the captain, his lieutenants and Terrel were all admitted to the central keep. They were eventually shown into a large bare room where they met with an adjutant called Myrdal.

The commander's first duty was to present the tags that had been collected from the battlefield. These enabled the dead to be identified so that their families could be informed.

'You lost some good men,' Myrdal said solemnly, looking at the slivers of metal, each one punched with a unique design.

'We did. But the Gold lost more. We wiped out an entire company.' There was grim satisfaction in the captain's voice. 'There was no one left to take *their* tags home.'

'The generals will be pleased. Give a full report to the recorder in the morning.'

'Yes, sir.'

Myrdal was several years younger than the commander, but his rank – and his influence with the generals – meant that he commanded respect.

'You've earnt some time to rest, Captain. Make the most of it. You'll be getting new orders soon enough.'

'There's something else, sir.'

The adjutant glanced at Terrel, who was standing between Pjorsa and Stykkis, his wrists bound together.

'I'd like the generals to see the prisoner,' the captain said.

'Are you sure it's worth it?'

'I think so. The circumstances—'

'I'll see what I can do,' Myrdal cut in. He was obviously a busy man. 'You can wait in the anteroom, but I'm warning you, you could be there a long time. They've just begun a conference to plan the new campaign.'

'That's fine.'

'Treat anything you overhear in the strictest confidence, Captain.'

'Of course.'

'What about the prisoner?' Myrdal enquired.

'It won't matter what he hears. He won't be going anywhere once we've finished with him.'

So saying, the captain turned and signalled for his lieutenants to follow him. Having no choice in the matter, Terrel went with them.

CHAPTER NINE

'What was that?'

'We've captured a spy, General,' the captain repeated.

'We execute spies, Captain. Why are you bothering us with this?'

'He's a little unusual, sir. I thought you might want to interrogate him first.'

'You thought?' General Pingeyri turned back to the group of senior officers who were sitting round a large table cluttered with maps, sea charts, goblets and plates of food. 'A captain *thinking*,' he declared. 'A dangerous precedent, eh, gentlemen?' His colleagues laughed obediently.

'He claims to be foreign, sir,' the soldier persisted, ignoring this good-natured mockery.

'Well, he would, wouldn't he? Look, Captain . . . Raufar, isn't it?'

'Yes, sir.'

'Myrdal tells me you did a splendid job on your last sortie. I'm sure there'll be an official commendation when all the reports are in, but right now we don't have the time to interrogate prisoners. If you really think it's important, let him wait. When we're finished here – ' Pingeyri waved a hand at the gathering around the table ' – we'll take a look at him.'

'Yes, sir.'

Raufar glanced at Myrdal, who gave a resigned shrug as

if to indicate that he'd done his best. The captain returned to the anteroom, where Terrel sat on a bench, still bound and still being watched by the three lieutenants. After a whispered conversation, Pjorsa and Narvat left, but Raufar and Stykkis sat down, looking as though they were prepared for a long vigil. Pingeyri's booming voice carried to them easily as the general returned to his staff conference.

The door to the main chamber remained open, and both guards and prisoner were able to see into the room.

'Well, gentlemen. The season's just getting into full swing. What shall we do to start the year off nicely? Colonel Davik, I understand you've got a suggestion.'

'Yes, General. It occurs to me that a raid on Hvannadal would be the ideal way of demonstrating our resolve to strike at the very heart and soul of the White Quarter this season.'

There was a moment's silence while the others considered this proposal. Then everyone started speaking at once, their voices betraying a mixture of enthusiasm and concern – which made it impossible for Terrel to make out what anyone was saying. The general quickly called the meeting to order.

'I think it's a capital idea,' he declared. 'Set the tone for the whole campaign. So, what's our strategy here? Davik, this is your brainchild. What would be your plan of attack?'

'We can't do this by the book, General,' the colonel replied. 'We have to take some chances, balance the need for surprise against generally accepted methods.'

'Daring against common sense, eh?'

'Exactly. We need a mixture of the two. The White will be expecting us both to play to our strengths and to try to prey on their weaknesses. Ordinarily those would be sound tactics, but if we're too obvious their foreknowledge will wipe out our dominance.'

'Most battles are won and lost before they're fought,' one of the others commented.

'Planning is vital,' Davik agreed. 'Which is why it's essential that we confound the enemy's expectations, while at the same time avoiding any situation that puts us at too great a disadvantage.'

'And how do you propose to do this?' Pingeyri asked.

'Let's examine their expectations one by one. Firstly, they may not even have considered the possibility of an attack on Hvannadal. The springs are a considerable way inside enemy territory, and they've long been regarded as sacred, even by some from our own quarter. That sort of belief is outdated, of course, but preconceptions can often get in the way of clear thinking. In any case, it's possible their outer defences might be lax. Any such complacency would play into our hands.'

'But surely we can't rely upon it?' another officer queried.

'That's correct, Brigadier. Such speculation is by its very nature dangerous. My point is, the White will certainly be far better prepared to defend other sites precisely *because* Hvannadal is such an unlikely target. By going there we may gain the advantage of surprise, but at worst we'll be doing something they couldn't have expected or planned for. Of course, we need to prepare a response for when they recognize our intention.'

'If necessary we could mislead them by creating a diversion,' Pingeyri suggested. 'Pretend we're heading somewhere else before we tip our hand.'

'An excellent idea, General,' Davik said, pretending that he hadn't already thought of this himself. 'But sooner or later we will, as you put it, have to tip our hand, and that brings us to their next expectation. They'll assume we intend to march our main force over the Sorendur Pass.

That's the most direct route, and by far the easiest. It's also accepted practice to keep an invading army together, sacrificing speed and stealth for strength in numbers. It's a method that's served us well in many campaigns, but now might be the time to change our strategy. I'd like to divide our men into smaller units which can move fast and strike quickly along any of the minor passes either side of Sorendur. That way each captain will be able to advance or withdraw on his own initiative, and keep the enemy guessing, before we eventually consolidate our forces on the far side of the mountains. It may even be possible to attack the fortifications in Sorendur from both sides.'

'I like the sound of that,' the general rumbled.

'However,' Davik went on, 'the White know that the pass is the best route, and they know that we know it, so they may be wise to such tactics. If they realize we're intending to use all the other high valleys, we could be faced with a stalemate. That's why I'd like to send the bulk of our force by sea, into Hofnar Fjord.'

This announcement caused quite a stir, and in the ante-room Raufar and Stykkis glanced at each other, their eyebrows raised in silent comment. Terrel couldn't tell whether their expressions were meant to convey disapproval or merely surprise.

'That won't be easy,' the brigadier said.

'In part, that's the point,' Davik responded. 'We'd have to go in at night. If the boats were spotted too soon, they'd become sitting ducks and any landing would be impossible.'

'It'll be damn near impossible anyway,' the brigadier stated. 'Hofnar's all cliffs!'

'There are sufficient inlets and low-lying areas near the inner end for our purposes,' the colonel replied.

'But that would be right next to the glacier.'

'I know, but if we can get there before they're able to set up defences, we can do it – and once the army's ashore, the route to Hvannadal is relatively short and very difficult to block.'

'We'll have them in a classic pincer movement,' the general said, nodding his approval. 'What about timing?'

'Well, using the same reasoning, they'd expect us to wait until the lunar alignment favoured us before we launched any major offensive. That's when their defences would be at their most alert. On the other hand, if we go when the moons favour *them*, we'll have the element of surprise again. But we'll have to be careful, because their neomancers will be comparatively powerful. My suggestion is that we pick a date that's neither one thing nor the other, so we can give Tofana and the rest a chance to instruct their people in exactly what will be needed, but at the same time retain at least some element of surprise.'

The other officers considered this for a while, and Terrel had the impression that they were waiting to see how the general reacted before speaking themselves. The healer's brain was already buzzing with questions. Why were the springs at Hvannadal so important? What they were contemplating seemed a huge operation for such an objective. And why were the springs considered sacred? Who or what was a neomancer? But getting answers to any of these questions was impossible. Raufar and his lieutenants had been eavesdropping too, but they remained silent, and Terrel knew that any inquisitiveness on his part would not be appreciated.

The situation he found himself in seemed unreal. He had to keep reminding himself that he could soon be arguing for his life. The very fact that he was being allowed to overhear the deliberations of the council of war was in itself ominous. Unless he could convince them that he was on their side – and having already disavowed any interest in the war, that was going to be difficult – they were hardly likely to let him go free now that he knew so much.

'When is the next counterbalance in our favour?' Pingeyri asked eventually. 'Myrdal, where are the latest tables?'

'Here, General,' the adjutant replied promptly, passing over a parchment covered with various symbols and columns of numbers.

'Damn lunarists can't seem to get anything right any more,' Pingeyri grumbled, running a thick finger down one of the columns. 'Always changing their minds. Is this the one?'

Myrdal leant over and glanced at where the general's finger had stopped.

'Yes, sir,' he said. 'Twenty-seven days from now.'

'Black Moon full. White new. On the same night.'

'And the others?' the brigadier asked.

'Red half full but waning. Gold exactly the same.' Pingeyri grunted in surprise at his own discovery.

'That would be the perfect alignment for us,' Davik said. 'Which is why I think we *shouldn't* go then.'

'Because they'll be expecting us?'

'Precisely.'

'So do we go before or after?' another officer asked.

'Both have their attractions,' the colonel replied. 'If we go earlier we might catch them unawares, and if the campaign lasts for any time, the fact that such a day is coming up will certainly work in our favour. For morale if nothing else.'

'It would certainly prey on my mind if it was the other way round,' the brigadier remarked.

'On the other hand,' Davik went on, 'if we wait until

after, they may relax after having been so vigilant. Mentally, they'd be dealing with an anticlimax once the time of greatest danger seemed to have passed. We'd catch them off guard.'

'Before sounds better to me,' the general declared. 'Apart from anything else, it would mean we'd be able to see some action sooner rather than later. That's always a good thing, especially so early in the season.' He paused, looking around the table. 'So, gentlemen, what's the verdict on the colonel's proposal?'

'Hvannadal's bound to be heavily defended,' the brigadier said. 'Whichever way we approach it.'

'True,' the general conceded.

'And any damage we could do to the springs would be limited. We can block or poison them for a time, but there's no way we can achieve a permanent occupation, so they'll be able to restore them eventually. It'd be a temporary victory at best.'

'True.'

'If they get wind of our plans, or see us coming in Hofnar,' one of the others put in, 'getting ashore will be the least of our problems. Just getting anyone out alive will be hard enough. It would be easy for them to collapse part of the glacier and swamp the fleet.'

'True.'

'No one's ever done anything like this, so we'd be in unknown territory – in more ways than one.'

'True.'

'And it would be imprudent for all of us to be there in person,' the brigadier added.

'True.'

'In fact,' the brigadier summed up, 'the whole thing is absurdly risky.'

'True.'

There was a pause.

'So when do we leave?' the general asked.

Terrel had been astonished to see the officers smiling as they listed the various perils they'd be facing. They had sounded positively gleeful. It was almost as if they regarded the war as some sort of game, and their apparently light-hearted attitude contrasted starkly with the reality Terrel had seen on the battlefield at Whale Ness. The action there had been anything but light-hearted. He glanced at Raufar and Stykkis to see whether their reaction was the same as his, and found that they were smiling too.

Is this whole island and everyone on it mad? Terrel wondered. It was a bleak thought. He saw again the corpses littering the headland, and hoped he'd never have to see anything like that again. All his healer's instincts rebelled at such a horrible waste of life – which was made even more horrifying because he didn't understand what any of them were fighting *for*. What had caused the war? And why had it been raging for so long?

Such speculation was quickly put aside when his companions rose to their feet. Terrel realized that the meeting was breaking up, with officers heading in various directions, all filled with an obvious sense of purpose. The detailed preparations for the operation were evidently beginning.

Myrdal appeared in the wide doorway between the two rooms and beckoned the soldiers forward. Stykkis took hold of Terrel's good arm and dragged him to his feet.

'Time for you to meet the general,' he said.

CHAPTER TEN

Raufar went into the council chamber ahead of Stykkis and their prisoner.

'You still here, Captain?' Pingeyri sounded vaguely surprised.

'Yes, sir. I believe this could be important.'

'Very well.' The general glanced round; apart from Myrdal, only the brigadier remained from the meeting. 'What do you think, Eskif? Can you spare a few moments to take a look at this spy?'

The brigadier looked up from the map he was studying and shrugged, his indifference plain.

'Bring him in,' Pingeyri ordered.

At Raufar's signal, Stykkis marched Terrel forward, still holding his arm in a grip of steel. The senior officers stared, their interest piqued by the prisoner's misshapen limbs and crystalline eyes. Terrel met their gaze as steadily as he could, aware that these men held his fate in their hands. From close to, the general was a more impressive figure than he'd seemed at first. Pingeyri was a large man, but his bulk came from muscle, not fat. He was more than twice Terrel's age but his movements held the vigour of youth, and there was a shrewdness in his grey eyes that spoke of calculation rather than bluster. Even his voice seemed sharper now that he was not surrounded by so many of his colleagues, and Terrel wondered if the rather bluff character he'd seen earlier had been just an act.

'So, Captain, what makes this fellow so extraordinary?'

'It's a combination of things, General. But mostly it's the way we came across him. He climbed out of the top of Savik's Whale when its waterspout blew.'

Pingeyri was clearly astonished. He glanced at Terrel, then returned his gaze to Raufar.

'Great gods, man! Why didn't you tell me this earlier?'

The captain wisely chose not to point out that he'd been given no chance to do any such thing, and the general didn't seem to expect an answer.

'You'd better tell us what happened, and then we'll see what the prisoner has to say for himself,' he decreed.

'Yes, sir.' Raufar gave a brief but surprisingly fluent description of Terrel's appearance and his subsequent capture and interrogation. It was clear that he'd spent most of the enforced wait deciding exactly what to say. When he'd finished, Pingeyri and Eskif exchanged glances, then turned their attention to Terrel.

'Would you say that the captain has painted an accurate picture of what happened?' the general asked him.

'For the most part, yes.'

'You really expect us to believe you climbed the cliffs at Whale Ness?' the brigadier queried.

'Yes, because it's the truth. And if you send someone to Port Akranes, either Kjolur or any of the crew of the Skua will confirm it.'

'The ship will be long gone by the time a messenger could reach Akranes,' Pingeyri told him. 'Foreign merchants tend not to hang about.'

'Kjolur, then.'

'Even if we manage to locate him,' Eskif said, 'what are we supposed to do with you in the meantime?'

Terrel had no answer to that.

'I'm not a spy,' he stated instead.

'Simply a traveller?' the brigadier said sceptically.

'Yes.'

'One who just happens to come ashore at the right time and place to re-enact a scene from one of our best-known legends?'

For a moment the question baffled Terrel, and then he remembered the tale from Kjolur's book.

'I wasn't trying to re-enact anything,' he said. 'I was trapped and the blowhole was my only way out. And I didn't see a vision of the future, even though I was soaked through.'

'A vision?' the general queried.

'Isn't that what the legend says is supposed to happen?'

'That's one version,' Pingeyri admitted.

So what are the others? Terrel wondered, realizing now that Kjolur really *hadn't* told him the whole story.

'What puzzles me,' the general went on, 'is what you hoped to achieve by this charade.'

'Nothing. I was just following my own destiny.'

'You weren't trying to influence the progress of the battle?' Eskif asked.

'No. I was hiding.'

'And it didn't work anyway,' the brigadier commented, disregarding Terrel's denial. 'Captain Raufar saw to that.'

The soldier's description of events had emphasized the tactical nature of his company's withdrawal, drawing a veil over the panic that had accompanied their initial retreat.

'You were doing nothing,' Pingeyri said, 'and yet you claim to be a magian?'

'No. I don't even know what a magian is. I'm a healer.'

'But you've given us no proof of this claim.'

'I haven't been given the chance,' Terrel replied, glancing at Raufar. Two of his men had died from their wounds before they'd reached the healing pools. Terrel was convinced he could have saved their lives, but chose not to say so now in case he antagonized the captain still further.

'Such talent must surely have been learnt at the foot of a master,' Eskif declared. 'Which wizard trained you?'

'It was a gift I was born with,' Terrel said, shaking his head, 'and which I have learnt to use by experience. I've never been to Myvatan before, and I've never even met a wizard.'

'You claim to come from an island that floats upon an ocean none of us have ever heard of, and yet you speak our language,' the general observed. 'Who but a spy would need to learn a foreign tongue?'

'A traveller,' Terrel replied. 'How else am I supposed to make myself understood?'

'Myvatan does not welcome travellers.' The brigadier's views presented quite a contrast to Kjolur's, but Terrel saw no point in revealing that.

'Coming here was not entirely my choice,' he said.

'Ah yes, this prophecy of yours. Tell us more about that. No, wait.' Pingeyri held up a large hand. 'Myrdal, get Vatna up here, will you? I think he should hear this.'

The adjutant nodded and strode from the room.

'You think it's worth bothering him?' Eskif asked. 'This man's obviously a spy. His story is full of inconsistencies.'

'That's what intrigues me,' the general replied. 'For a spy, he's remarkably incompetent. I can't believe even the Gold would send someone as badly prepared as this. Reykholar's no fool.'

'You're not saying you believe him?'

'No, but Vatna will be able to put some of his claims to

the test. And if he fails, his end will be all the more unpleasant.'

Terrel did not like the sound of that. Whoever this Vatna was, he was in no hurry to meet him. However, a few moments later a commotion from the anteroom made them all turn to see what was happening. Myrdal had returned, accompanied by three men, but Terrel doubted that any of them was Vatna. Two soldiers were supporting the third newcomer, who was wrapped in blankets. His bare feet dragged across the floor and his head lolled from side to side. His lips were dark blue, as if they had been stained by ink. At the sight of him both Pingeyri and Eskif had risen to their feet, and the expression on the brigadier's face was one of shock and horror.

'I'm sorry to interrupt you, General,' Myrdal said hurriedly, 'but this may be urgent.'

'What happened to him?' Pingeyri demanded.

'He'd been captured by the Gold at Melrakka, sir,' one of the soldiers replied breathlessly. 'But instead of killing him they left him on the glacier, half naked. He was near dead when we found him.'

'Why didn't you take him straight to the pools?'

'He insisted on being brought here, General. Said it was vital he talk to you. But he passed out on the way.'

'He may have intelligence,' Myrdal guessed.

'Well, it's not going to do us much good if he dies before he can talk to us,' Pingeyri muttered. 'Where's Vatna?'

'He's on his way, sir,' the adjutant replied.

'He needs warmth. Bring some mitra. Quick!'

The sick man had been placed on a cushioned chair, and Terrel could see that he was in a very bad way. His nose, fingers and toes were all chalk white, and the rest of his skin had the greasy, pallid look of dead flesh. The cold had sunk deep into his body, right to the bones, robbing him of all but the last vestiges of life. When one of the soldiers brought a cup of steaming liquid, its fragrant herbal scent filling the room, the invalid was unable to swallow, the mitra running unnoticed down his chin. His eyes had rolled up so that they showed only white, making his appearance even more ghastly.

Belatedly, Terrel saw his chance.

'Let me help him,' he said loudly.

Everyone except the dying man turned to look at him.

'I'm a healer,' he added earnestly. 'I can help him if you let me.'

Pingeyri turned to the brigadier, who shook his head, his face a pale mask of grief.

'We'll wait for Vatna,' the general decided. 'Where is he?'

'Even Vatna may not be able . . .' Myrdal left the sentence unfinished. 'What have you got to lose?'

Pingeyri hesitated, indecisive for once.

'Please,' Terrel begged.

'Let the stranger try,' Raufar said, lending the healer unexpected support. 'If he fails, I'll kill him myself here and now.' The captain drew his sword.

The general looked to Eskif again. The brigadier seemed at a loss, but then nodded.

'Go!' Pingeyri commanded. 'Do what you can.'

Terrel moved quickly and knelt in front of the chair. He took one of the invalid's hands in his own, feeling the cold as a double shock. The skin was lifeless, but worse than that, the blood inside the fingers was frozen, turned to crystals of ice, and it was the same at the man's other extremities. Terrel found it hard to concentrate with Raufar standing right behind him, his blade at the ready, but the healer was determined not to let this chance slip away.

Closing his eyes, he let the outside world fade away and fell, unresisting, into the patient's waking dream. The cold had almost succeeded in shutting down the man's entire system, but he was clinging tenaciously to the last strands of internal warmth and strength. Terrel pushed and cajoled, feeding his own dream-heat into the void, at the same time trying to push back the twin invasions of pain and lethal indifference. If the mind and the body ceased to care whether they lived or died, the end would not be long in coming. He felt a glimmer of consciousness return, spreading light into the darkened dream and bringing new agonies with it. Terrel hurried to convince his patient that such torment was worthwhile – that it was a sign of returning life – but even the healer had rarely experienced such exquisite tortures. As he fought on, he was only vaguely aware of voices outside him, in another realm.

'He's got a little more colour.'

'His eyes! Look.'

'Is he coming round?'

Terrel knew that the man would not die now, that the energy he'd bequeathed him would be enough to prevent a total surrender, but he needed more than that. As the patient's own body began to fight for itself, Terrel was at last able to turn his attention to the frozen extremities, hoping that he could restore the ruined flesh before it was damaged beyond repair. Melting the malignant ice crystals proved easy enough, but the various balances within the blood were still all wrong, and he had to expend even more of his own reserves to try to put them right. If he failed, the fingers and toes would still rot and die even though they were attached to a living frame. He was just completing this painstaking task, coming close to exhaustion himself, when he was roughly shoved aside and the contact was lost. Sprawled on the floor, he tried to protest, but he didn't have the strength to speak and simply lay there, looking up at the man who had replaced him and who was now examining the patient's face and hands.

'Can you save him?' the general asked.

'That's already been done,' the newcomer replied, sounding puzzled. 'In fact, there's nothing wrong with him. As far as I can tell, he's just asleep.'

In the silence that followed this summation, several of those present looked at Terrel.

'Are you sure, Vatna?'

'Of course, General. What's going on here?'

'Kopak was near death when he was brought in,' Pingeyri explained. 'I'd swear that his hands and feet were already lost to frostbite.'

Others nodded in agreement.

'Well, there's no sign of it now,' Vatna said.

'But he was on the glacier . . .' The soldier's voice faltered, his incredulous expression mirroring the other faces in the group.

'Looks like Terrel really is a healer,' Raufar said softly.

All conversation came to an abrupt halt as the patient coughed. His eyes returned to normal and came into focus, and he looked down at his own hands and flexed his fingers carefully. The brigadier went to kneel beside him.

'Are you all right, Kopak?' he whispered.

'I'm fine, Father . . . I mean, Brigadier.' He looked round at the officers and tried to stand up, but Pingeyri pushed him back down. The patient accepted this indignity, looking very weary now but otherwise unharmed.

'You have something to tell us, I believe,' the general prompted.

Kopak looked bemused.

'Do you remember anything?' his father asked.

'I've just had the most extraordinary dream,' he replied,

speaking slowly and uncertainly, as he blinked and glanced around the group once more. 'But before that I—'

Terrel heard no more. He had fallen asleep where he lay.

CHAPTER ELEVEN

There had been other occasions when Terrel had woken up and not known where he was, but it had usually been an unpleasant and unnerving experience. On this occasion, however, he felt refreshed and invigorated by his enforced rest. Part of the reason for this was obvious as soon as he opened his eyes. He was lying on a comfortable mattress within a wooden box-frame, and covered with blankets that were both soft and warm. It had been a long time since he'd slept in such luxury.

The room was small and held little in the way of furniture – just the bed, a stool and a small table – but its whitewashed walls and brown stone floor were bright in the hazy sunlight that streamed in through the open window. The shutters had been thrown back and the door at the other end of the room stood ajar, so there was no question that these were lodgings rather than a prison cell.

The air that drifted in through the window was cool and crisp, scented with the now familiar tang of herbs, but also with something that made it seem pure and almost sharp, like the taste of underripe fruit. Without knowing why, Terrel had the impression that he was high up, above the busy and sometimes fetid domain of mankind, and this was confirmed when he got out of bed and hobbled over to the window. His room was near the top of one of the highest towers in the fortress, and it had a view over the upper part of the city and the snow-covered mountain beyond. Although the thin cloud of steam filtered the sun's brilliance, the panorama was breathtakingly beautiful.

Terrel shivered and realized he was wearing only a kind of shift, loosely tied with a cord at his waist. His pack and boots lay beside the table, but there was no sign of his clothes. He was debating whether to go exploring or to get back into bed when the door was silently pushed open and a woman's head peered around at him.

'Oh,' she said. 'You're awake! I was beginning to wonder.'

'Why?' Terrel smiled at her evident surprise. 'How long have I been asleep?'

'Almost a full day,' she told him as she came in. 'Can I get you anything? Are you hungry?'

'I'm famished.' He hadn't realized it until that moment, but now his hunger was almost painful.

'I'll bring you some mitra first,' she decided. 'Then food. Is there anything in particular you'd like?'

'Whatever you have.'

She turned to go, but in spite of the protestations of his stomach, Terrel didn't want to be left alone again so soon.

'Wait a moment,' he said, and she stopped in the doorway.

'Have I done something wrong?' she asked anxiously.

'No, of course not!' he replied, wondering why she should even think to ask such a question. 'I'd like to know your name, that's all. I'm called Terrel.'

'I know,' she said, looking shy now. 'My name is Latira.'

'Thank you for looking after me, Latira.'

'I'm only doing what I'm told,' she said, but she smiled anyway. She had a plain face and short mousy hair, but the smile lit up her pale blue eyes. She was the first woman Terrel had seen on Myvatan.

'Do you know where my clothes are?' he asked.

This time Latira averted her gaze and blushed, and Terrel realized that she must have been the one to undress him when he was unconscious. The thought embarrassed him too, though he wasn't sure why it should.

'They're back from the laundry,' she said, 'but they're not quite dry yet. I'll bring them up soon.'

'Thank you.' Terrel couldn't help thinking that in this climate a lack of clothes could imprison him as effectively as any iron bars, but he sensed no deception in her words.

'I'd better go,' she said. 'They wanted me to tell them as soon as you woke up.'

'They?' Terrel queried.

'The generals, of course,' she replied, and slipped away before he could ask her anything else.

His next visitor was Vatna. Fortified by a hot drink and a large meal, but still without his clothes, Terrel greeted him from his bed.

'Are you recovered?' Vatna asked as he drew up the stool and sat down, resting his elbows on his knees and looking at the healer intently.

'Almost.' In truth, Terrel still felt rather weary but, compared to the uncertainties that had plagued him for the last few days, he was in an excellent frame of mind.

'Good. Is there anything you need?'

'No. Latira is looking after me perfectly.'

'I'm sorry I treated you roughly yesterday. I didn't know then that we were brothers.'

'Brothers?' Terrel queried.

'You wear the marker of Jokulsa, the god of snow and rain. As do I.' Vatna rolled up his left sleeve and turned his shoulder towards Terrel, who winced involuntarily. Branded deep into the flesh of the islander's upper arm

were two vertical wavy lines and a small star. The scars
were old now, but Vatna must have endured terrible pain
when the wounds had been new. The healer did indeed
wear the same symbol, but his own marker had cost him
no discomfort. It was inscribed upon a small clay tablet,
which hung on a cord around his neck. He reached inside
the shift and pulled it out now, comparing the two designs.

'No one had seen your pendant,' Vatna explained. 'You
could have saved yourself a lot of trouble if you'd shown
it to us earlier.'

'I didn't realize,' Terrel said. 'I'm not familiar with your
gods. Where this comes from it's called "the river in the
sky".' He remembered the ceremony when it had been
presented to him by the desert nomads of Misrah. They
had named him 'the voice of rain' when he'd been
accepted into their tribe.

'The gods have many different names,' Vatna commented. 'But here, Jokulsa watches over us.'

Different and yet the same, Terrel thought. Some symbols apparently had a universal meaning. During all his
travels on Nydus, the same shapes and motifs had turned
up over and over again. He couldn't imagine two places
more disparate than Misrah and Myvatan, but even they
had such things in common.

'Your marker . . .' Terrel said awkwardly. 'What does it
signify?'

'That I am a magian,' Vatna replied, as if this ought to
be obvious. 'In name and rank, at least.'

'Does that mean you're a healer too?' Terrel asked,
hoping to clarify his thoughts.

'I have some slight skill in that way. We all do, but it's
nothing compared to yours. I might have been able to
save Kopak's life, but at the very least he would surely
have lost his hands and feet, if what the others have told

me is correct. He will remain a soldier, thanks to you. The Great Plain would have been denied him otherwise.'

Terrel wasn't sure what to make of this. He was simply glad that here – as elsewhere – his healing abilities had earned him respect and gratitude from the people he met. Now, perhaps, he'd be able to pursue his own goals without being threatened with torture or death. It had been some time since he'd even thought about trying to find the fourth elemental.

'You proved a couple of things there,' Vatna went on. 'Firstly, you obviously *are* a healer, and if that part of your story is true, then we have to take the rest seriously. A lot of people are going to want to ask you a lot of questions.' He grinned, and shrugged apologetically as Terrel looked pained. 'Secondly – and just as important – you demonstrated that you're not an enemy spy. You certainly wouldn't have kept Kopak alive if you'd thought he had vital intelligence about our foes.'

'And did he?' Terrel asked.

'Yes. He remembered it soon after you passed out.'

'What was it? What was so important that he should risk his life like that?'

'It's not for me to say.'

Terrel nodded, perversely glad that the soldiers were now keeping things from him. It meant they expected him to remain alive.

'Perhaps you could tell me something else, then,' he said.

'I'll do my best. What do you want to know?'

'General Pingeyri said that what I'd been told was only one version of the legend about Savik's Whale. What are the others?'

'I thought that might interest you,' Vatna said with a slight smile. 'You certainly made quite an entrance, didn't you? I wish I'd been there to see it.'

'It was all an accident, really. I had no idea what it meant.'

The magian eyed him speculatively for a few moments, then evidently decided to take Terrel's statements at face value.

'There are a lot of theories about who or what could emerge from the whale as you did,' he began. 'Some say he'd be half man, half fish, and would swim up from the sea. Others claim he'd be a messenger of the gods, or a phantasm created by wizards.'

'I'm sure I'm none of those things.'

'I don't see any gills or fins,' Vatna agreed, smiling, 'and you seem real enough to me. You could be a messenger and still be unaware of it, I suppose. The gods don't always tell us how they're using us. And they are meant to have built the whale.'

'I still don't think they'd have picked me,' Terrel said. 'Don't I have any other choices?'

'The only other version I know of is that the stranger is a man who's been enslaved by the monster who lives in the fires beneath the island. But that's just a tale for children. The old dragon of the volcanoes. My mother used—' He broke off, seeing the expression on Terrel's face. 'You look as if you know that story.'

Terrel had been doing his best to hide his reaction from the other man. The legend of a 'monster' underground was indeed familiar to him. He'd heard similar tales relating to the elementals in Vadanis and Macul – but he did not feel ready to reveal the true purpose of his journey to Myvatan yet.

'It's just that I was a slave myself once,' he said. 'Of a man, though, not a monster.'

'Raufar told us,' Vatna said, nodding.

'It brought back some bad memories,' Terrel improvised.

'Silly, really.' He did his best to smile, wondering if he really *had* been enslaved by the Ancients.

'Doesn't sound silly to me,' the islander said gravely. 'We're all free men on Myvatan.'

Terrel could have argued with that claim, but he had no wish to get into such a debate.

'Tell me about this monster,' he said instead.

'As I said, it's just a fable. Volcanoes played a big part in the creation of this land, and many of them are still active. When you're little it helps to have some explanation of what makes them erupt.'

'The dragon?'

'Just hope you're not too close when he sneezes,' Vatna advised with a grin.

'I'll try to remember that. Where is it likely to happen?'

'You mean where does the dragon live? No one knows. My mother used to say its lair was somewhere under the Lonely Peaks, but that it could travel anywhere by swimming down the tunnels of molten rock.'

Terrel wanted to ask more about the Lonely Peaks, but he was aware that he'd already shown rather more interest in the mythical monster than he could justify, so he just smiled and let Vatna go on with his retelling of the legends of Savik's Whale.

'That's all beside the point, really. The more interesting parts of the stories concern what the arrival of the stranger portends. The most common version in this quarter is that of a great fire – rain turning to burning tar, smoke and ash filling the sky and choking the life out of the land. Fortunately that hasn't happened yet.'

But it might explain the initial panic and retreat of the Black soldiers, Terrel thought. Had they really expected fire to rain down from the sky? It seemed ridiculous until he remembered the unnatural lightning that had played a part earlier in the battle.

'Alternatively,' Vatna went on, 'it's supposed to predict a terrible run of luck in the war, a series of defeats beyond our control. It's all nonsense, of course – Raufar and his men proved that – but soldiers can be a superstitious lot. Of course, for the Gold it means the opposite – a great victory, possibly the final decisive victory in the war as a whole, or at the very least, the return of the sculpture and the land it stands on to their "rightful" owners.'

'The Gold Quarter think it belongs to them?'

'Exactly. That's nonsense too. I can show you ancient maps and treaties, but good faith never meant anything to those scum.' For the first time Vatna's face showed traces of real anger and disgust. 'We'll never surrender what is rightfully ours.'

Terrel now had an explanation for the differing reactions of the two groups of soldiers. He also knew why Raufar and his men had found it necessary to return and kill all of the Gold troops. They couldn't allow any of them to go back to their own quarter with news that a legend had come to life. The propaganda value of such a story would have been enormous. By the same token, the soldiers would have wanted to keep the stranger's arrival from their own people, in case it was considered an ill omen. It was no wonder some of them had wanted to kill him on the spot.

'To be perfectly honest,' Vatna added, immediately contradicting Terrel's assumption, 'that's part of the reason Raufar chose to keep you alive. He wanted to prove you were just a man, not some fantastical creature.'

Terrel nodded.

'And the most rational explanation,' he said 'if I was an ordinary man, was that I was a spy.'

'Yes. Not that I'm saying you're ordinary.' The magian's lean face creased in another grin. 'But you could have been an impostor sent by one of the Gold wizards—'

'In order to fool people into thinking the legend had come true,' Terrel completed for him.

'That was certainly a possibility.'

'But you don't believe it any more?'

'No. Nobody does. What's happened since wouldn't make sense. And if you were one of Reykholar's people, you'd be trying to connect yourself *to* the legend, not denying any link.'

Terrel was glad now that he'd acted the way he had and hadn't tried anything more fanciful. Logic, it seemed, had proved his innocence.

'There are two more possible consequences to the appearance,' Vatna added. 'One is a vision of the future so powerful that it has to come true and there's nothing anyone can do to prevent it. That's the version you'd already heard, I gather.'

'Yes. But I certainly didn't see any visions.'

'So the final possibility is that it marks the beginning of a new era for Myvatan, a time of change.'

Terrel had come across that phrase before, in connection with the Dark Moon's suddenly erratic behaviour, but it seemed to have a more specific meaning here.

'What sort of change?' he asked.

'Who knows? It's so vague the inspirators can read whatever they like into it.'

'Inspirators?' Terrel queried.

'Storytellers,' Vatna replied. 'They're usually soldiers who've retired from active service. We use them to entertain the troops.'

'And to inspire them?'

'Perhaps. None of our men ought to need inspiration.

Our cause is just.' He sounded fierce now, and this made Terrel feel uncomfortable.

'So those are all the legends of Savik's Whale?' he asked.

'Not quite. There's one more thing,' Vatna hesitated, then smiled. 'You should be glad you're not associated with it, in fact.'

'Why?'

'Because in all the versions I've heard, the end is always the same,' Vatna told him. 'The man who comes from the whale dies.'

CHAPTER TWELVE

'So if Raufar had killed me,' Terrel said, when the implications of Vatna's words had sunk in, 'he'd have been fulfilling the legend, giving it credence.'

'That was probably part of his reasoning too,' the magian admitted. 'Contrary to what the general likes to tell people, you don't get to be a captain without having some brains.'

'How is the stranger supposed to die?'

'Think of something unpleasant and someone's suggested it. Fire, of course, a fall from the cliffs, being turned to stone, decapitation, or being struck by lightning. One way or another the stranger becomes a martyr or gets his just deserts, depending on your point of view. Raufar decided to let someone else take the responsibility for that.'

'Wise man,' Terrel commented.

'Of course, if you'd died from the cold anyway it would have made things a lot more complicated. Fortunately for us – and you – that didn't happen.'

'So what now?'

'We're considering that,' Vatna replied. 'You've got to admit, your appearing as you did was quite a coincidence, and we won't be able to keep it quiet for much longer. Some of the soldiers are bound to talk, so what we have to do is decide how to use these events to our advantage.'

'A new version of the legend?'

'It's been done before,' the magian agreed. 'Who knows? You might end up becoming a talisman for the whole army. Pingeyri's sent messengers to the other generals, and they'll put their heads together, ask the advice of anyone above a certain rank, and then come up with a plan.'

'Do I get any say in this?'

'That remains to be seen,' Vatna replied noncommittally.

'What rank are you?' Terrel asked.

'Technically I'm a colonel, but really it's just honorary. I act as liaison between the general's staff and Tofana's.'

'So will you be part of these discussions? Is that why you're here?'

'Yes. And partly. I have a professional interest in your healing. I'm a soldier *and* a magian. Having a foot in both camps can be difficult, but it has its advantages.'

'Tofana's a wizard?' Terrel queried.

'Yes. The best of them all,' Vatna replied proudly. 'I wouldn't be surprised if you get an invitation to the pyramid. Then you'll see for yourself.'

Their conversation was interrupted before Terrel could ask any more. Latira came into the room quietly, and although she was obviously afraid of Vatna, she was determined to say her piece.

'I think you've been here long enough, Magian.' The words came out in a rush, as if she was appalled by her own temerity. 'Terrel needs to rest.'

Vatna looked as if he were about to object, then thought better of it.

'You have your own dragon protecting you, it seems,' he remarked to Terrel.

'I'm only doing my job,' Latira stated defiantly.

'Indeed. It's good to know you're taking such good care of your patient.' Vatna turned back to Terrel. 'I can see you're tired. We'll talk again.' Standing up, he gave Latira a mock salute before striding from the room. Terrel smiled at his nurse.

'I hope you don't think . . .' she began. 'I was only . . .'

'I have no complaints,' he told her. 'I'm in good hands.'

'I'll bring you some more food,' she said, looking much happier now. 'Then you should rest.'

'Thank you.'

Terrel lay back as she left. He was indeed weary, and in one sense he was glad to be alone again. Vatna had given him a lot to think about.

As evening drew in, and with his stomach comfortably full once more, Terrel knew he ought to try to rest again, but while his body was tired, his brain was all too active. It kept returning to the problem of the riddle posed by Kjolur's role in recent events. As an educated man, it was reasonable to assume that the merchant would be aware of *all* the legends surrounding Savik's Whale, not just the one he'd told Terrel. So if that were the case, had he somehow been trying to use the mythology to take advantage of the superstitious nature of the people of Myvatan? Had he actually *wanted* Terrel to become a victim? Or a martyr? On the surface, that made no sense at all. Most of the tales pointed to outcomes that favoured the enemies of the Red Quarter, so to deliberately promote the possibility of them coming true was irrational. Unless, of course, Kjolur had lied about his real allegiance. Terrel only had the man's word for it – and he'd felt at the time that the merchant had been keeping something back. The red patch under his epaulet could easily have been faked. And yet the *Skua* had been heading for Akranes, which was in the Red

Quarter. Was it possible then that Kjolur was himself a spy? Given subsequent events, that would be ironic to say the least.

There were alternative explanations, of course. It was possible that Kjolur had genuinely been trying to help Terrel, and was either unaware of the dangers or had believed them to be irrelevant. The versions of the tales told in the Red Quarter might be very different to those Vatna had described. But the fact that Kjolur had not even admitted that he was responsible for Ostan's agreement to go to Whale Ness indicated that the merchant was unwilling to be associated with the stranger. That in itself cast his motives into question, and left Terrel more confused than ever.

In any case, the healer thought, even if Kjolur *did* want one of the legends to come true, how could he have possibly have predicted the events of that day? The presence of the two warring factions, Terrel's own decision to climb inside the whale's mouth, the rising wind – none of those things could have been known to anyone who had been away from the island for several months. It was a conundrum that had puzzled Terrel before, but he was no nearer an answer. Unless, of course, Kjolur was a prophet, and it was he, not Terrel, who'd had a vision of the future. Terrel's experiences in Misrah had convinced him that such things were possible, but he had no proof of it here. Either way, the chances were that he would never meet the merchant again. He wasn't even sure he wanted to. Although he didn't understand how or why, Terrel believed that Kjolur had used him for his own mysterious purposes, and he didn't want to risk it happening again.

The healer's thoughts were interrupted by the muted sounds of an argument outside the chamber. He couldn't hear what was being said until the end, when Latira's voice grudgingly conceded defeat.

'All right then. But only for a little while.'

The door opened and Eskif came in. The brigadier looked at Terrel, then hesitated, his deeply-lined face showing signs of strain.

'I wanted . . .' he began eventually. 'I wanted to apologize for misjudging you.'

'You don't need to apologize,' Terrel said. 'I'd probably have thought the same in your place.'

'Yes, but it would have been the greatest mistake I ever made if . . .' Eskif couldn't complete the sentence and instead looked down at his feet. A moment later he glanced up again and faced Terrel with a new determination. 'My son is alive and whole because of you. That is a debt I can never fully repay. If there is ever anything you need, you have only to ask.'

'Thank you.'

'That's all I wanted to say, really.'

'Good,' Latira said from the doorway. 'Off you go, then.' She stood outside to let the brigadier pass, then pointed a finger at her patient. 'You, go to sleep.'

Terrel copied Vatna's earlier salute and grinned. Latira smiled back, then closed the door. He lay down, thinking that now at least he had some allies he could count on.

The bitter scent of mitra followed him into his dreams. Among the images of ice and fire, of madness and blood, its soothing influence spread a calm detachment, so that Terrel was able to watch without pain or revulsion. It allowed him to be objective, to remain coolly observant, learning even from the images of a nightmare.

But such composure came at a price. An ominous presence hovered in the shadows, just out of reach – not that

Terrel had any wish to bridge the gap himself. If anything it was the other way round, with the interloper's frustration at not being able to do more spiralling into impotent anger. Terrel knew who it was. He knew he'd have to face his twin brother again one day, but he wasn't ready yet. He might never be ready. But he knew for certain that he didn't need Jax's interference now.

The dream changed then, twisting from the war in the night sky to the underground rivers of flame – where a dragon's eyes looked back at him with a crystalline stare that mirrored his own.

Terrel was woken by a loud rumble of thunder. Someone – presumably Latira – had closed the shutters while he slept, and a dull light filtered through the slats. A rattle of hailstones against the wood showed that the weather had taken a turn for the worse. In contrast to the previous day, the air in his chamber seemed thick and stuffy. The scent of herbs was stronger too.

Terrel found himself worrying that the mitra might have had an intoxicating effect. Its fumes seemed to be ever-present in the fortress, and had even filled the soldiers' tents on the journey to Saudark. There seemed to be no way to escape its influence, but if he was right, it was possible that Jax might be able to invade more than Terrel's dreams. In the past – in those extreme cases when Terrel had become drunk or had been incapacitated by the sharaken's potion – the prince had taken over his body too, with disastrous results. That was the last thing Terrel needed, and he made a mental note to ask Latira to take the herbs out of his room. He had no idea where they might be.

By the time his next visitor arrived, Terrel was up and dressed in his own clothes. Although wind-blown ice continued to batter against the shutters, the room was brighter now, thanks to an oil lamp Latira had brought in. His nurse had reacted strangely to his request about the mitra, claiming she couldn't smell anything, and for the first time Terrel had the impression that she was not being quite open with him. However, he didn't have much time to dwell on this before the arrival of General Pingeyri.

'Well, young man, you've created quite a stir.'

'That wasn't my intention, sir.'

'You're looking better than when I saw you last. Are we treating you well?'

'Yes. Thank you.'

'Good. Vatna's already been talking about his plans for you. Is there anything you'd like to do while you're here?'

'I'd like to see more of the city,' Terrel replied. 'I'm strong enough now.'

'I'd be glad to arrange that,' the general said, 'but perhaps you should wait until the weather improves. There's only so much the wizards can do about it this early in the year.'

'Your wizards are weather-mages?'

'I've not heard it called that before, but I suppose it's the same thing. The war wouldn't be half as interesting if all we had to fight it with were swords and arrows.'

'So the lightning at Whale Ness *was* deliberate!' Terrel exclaimed. 'The soldiers were using it as a weapon. Does that mean there were wizards there?'

'No.' Pingeyri laughed. 'Wizards are too valuable to risk in the field. That's what neomancers are for.'

'Neomancers are soldiers who use magic?'

'Didn't you know that?'

Terrel shook his head.

'Boys and young men who show a certain aptitude go to the wizards for training,' the general explained. 'When they're ready, they join the army. At least one to each company, sometimes more. They're vital to most operations, for attack and defence.'

'And your enemies do the same?'

'Oh, yes. Wouldn't be a fair contest otherwise, would it.' He laughed again. 'Our lads can use lightning, wind, hail – even storms and tornadoes – but they have to be able to protect their comrades from such things too.'

The whole process sounded horrifying to Terrel – an appalling misuse of magic – and it was impossible for him not to think of Jax. He too was a weather-mage, and if he was ever let loose in Myvatan, he'd be in his element. The consequences would not bear thinking about. It made Terrel even more determined not to give his twin such a chance.

'It's all part of the game,' Pingeyri added cheerfully.

The healer found this attitude hard to take.

'Doesn't all the killing bother you?' he asked.

Pingeyri frowned.

'Why should it?' he said. 'Our enemies deserve to die. That's the whole point, isn't it?'

'But what about your own men?'

'I'm sad to lose friends,' the general admitted, 'but what better way to die than as a warrior? To take your place in the march across the Great Plain? One day I shall do the same.'

'You don't direct operations from here, then?'

'What would be the fun in that? Or the glory?'

'So you really will sail with the fleet to Hofnar Fjord?'

'Of course. Did you doubt my intentions? This will be a major campaign. It's only right that I should be at the head of my army.'

Terrel was beginning to see why men would follow such a leader, but he still couldn't understand why the war seemed to be the only thing that mattered on Myvatan.

'Why are the springs at Hvannadal a worthy target?' he asked. 'It seems an enormous operation for such an objective.'

'The hot water springs are a powerful magical source for the White wizards,' the general replied. 'They also feed one of their main healing pools. To strike a blow there would demoralize the enemy forces, and boost our own.'

'Is that why the springs are considered sacred?'

'Of course. Their potency varies with the lunar sequence, but we can turn that to our advantage if Davik's plan works. You should come along.'

'Me?' Terrel wasn't sure if Pingeyri was being serious.

'Why not? Someone of your skills would be welcome in any company.'

Terrel didn't know how to respond. He didn't want to offend his hosts, but Alyssa's advice – and his own inclination – made him reluctant to get directly involved in the war.

'Think about it,' Pingeyri said affably. 'In any case, there's plenty for you to do before then.' He stood up. 'I'd better go. No peace for the wicked, eh?'

'How long has the war been going on?' Terrel asked quickly. It was one question he'd never got a straight answer to and it had been preying on his mind.

'Oh, I don't know. A long time. Hundreds of years, probably. But we'll win in the end. I'll see to that – with a little help from the gods, of course.'

The general strode out, leaving Terrel aghast. Hundreds of years of warfare? It was no wonder the entire island was insane.

'Tell me more about Kjolur,' Myrdal said.

'There's not much more I can tell you,' Terrel replied.

'What does he trade in?'

'I've no idea.'

After the general left, Terrel hadn't had long to wait for his next visitor. Pingeyri's adjutant had arrived carrying several scrolls, though he hadn't referred to them at all. After some initial pleasantries, the conversation had turned to Terrel's journey to the island – and to the merchant in particular.

'Why do you think he was so keen for you to go to Whale Ness?'

'I don't know for certain that he was. I'm just guessing that it was his influence that made Ostan change his mind.'

'But why would he have done such a thing?' Myrdal persisted. The adjutant was a young man, about the same age as Terrel. His serious face was framed by light brown hair which was short but thick, reminding Terrel of an animal's fur.

'Perhaps he was just trying to help a friend,' he said. It didn't sound convincing, even to him.

'Because of this prophecy of yours?'

'Maybe.' Terrel shrugged. 'I don't understand his motives, but he couldn't have foreseen what was going to happen.'

'Unless you'd agreed it between you beforehand,' Myrdal suggested.

'No. I—' Terrel faltered, realizing that he had not won the trust of *all* the Black officers.

'The general and his staff certainly seem to have taken a shine to you,' the adjutant remarked, his face displaying no emotion. 'Are they perceptive judges – or simply gullible?'

'I'm not a spy,' Terrel said. He had thought he'd put all that behind him, and discovering he'd been labouring under a misapprehension came as a blow.

'Perhaps I just have a suspicious mind,' Myrdal went

on. 'But this could be a plot to gain their confidence. Healing Kopak was a clever move, but it didn't necessarily prove your allegiance.'

'He was sick. I'm a healer,' Terrel said desperately. 'That's all I cared about.'

'Of course, you probably never anticipated ending up here. You wouldn't have expected *all* the Gold troops to be killed.'

'I never expected any of this,' Terrel protested.

'If even one of them had got away, you might have achieved your purpose.'

'No. That's not—'

'We only have your word that you arrived on a foreign ship, which – conveniently – was heading for Akranes, on the far side of the island, so there's no way of checking your story.'

Terrel was silent, unable to think of any plausible response.

'Of course, you may be the innocent you claim to be.' Myrdal's expression turned to a smile that was patently false. 'But I'm not as easily convinced as the others. I'll be keeping an eye on you, Terrel.'

With that, the adjutant turned and swept from the room.

CHAPTER THIRTEEN

So much for allies I can count on, Terrel thought ruefully. All of a sudden his room had begun to seem like a prison cell after all.

The encounter with Myrdal had shaken his new-found confidence. The adjutant's suspicions had been bad enough, but the prospect of his sharing them with his fellow officers was even worse. If that happened, all hope of co-operation would disappear and Terrel really would be a prisoner again. He wondered why Myrdal had kept his doubts to himself. Surely his duty to the general would have forced him to share his thoughts? Was it simply a case of his not being quite sure of his facts, and wanting to avoid the embarrassment of being proved wrong? Judging by the little he knew of him, Terrel thought the adjutant was probably someone who was used to keeping secrets. But might he have some hidden agenda of his own? If so, Terrel couldn't imagine what it was.

The other puzzle was why Myrdal had chosen to reveal his mistrust to Terrel. If he had been intent on unmasking him as a spy, then surely it would have been better for him to let the healer remain in ignorance. Then he could watch, and wait for Terrel to make a mistake. By warning him, he would have put any real spy on his guard. So what was he up to?

On reflection, Terrel realized that even those people

who seemed to be on his side had said nothing about granting him his freedom. They appeared to be more concerned with the various ways they could use him. Only Eskif had offered to help him, and as a result of Myrdal's visit Terrel was now wondering if he could take even that at face value. Did Pingeyri and Vatna really trust him, or were they playing roles in an elaborate game? They had both seemed perfectly genuine, but now Terrel was filled with doubt.

At the same time, the walls of his room seemed to close in upon him, and he felt a desperate need to prove he was not a prisoner. He went over to his pack and rummaged through its contents. The nomad dagger was still there, which made him feel slightly better. His hosts wouldn't have let him keep a potentially murderous weapon if he was considered an enemy. Unless that too was part of the bluff – hoping he'd try something stupid and give himself away.

Stop it! he told himself. You'll drive yourself mad if you go on like this.

He stood up, leaving the knife where it was, and walked over to the door. Hesitating for only a moment, he lifted the latch, opened it and stepped into the corridor. The passage outside was dark and narrow. At its midpoint, doors led off to either side, but they were all closed. At the far end, next to what Terrel assumed was a stairwell, Myrdal and Latira stood together. They appeared to be in an earnest conversation, but they fell silent, looking round, as Terrel emerged. Latira smiled. Myrdal didn't.

'You're looking better,' his nurse observed.

'I'd like to go out.' The weather had improved recently, and it had become very important to Terrel to prove that he *could* go out. 'I'd like to see something of the city,' he added. 'The general said I could.'

After a brief murmured exchange, Myrdal disappeared down the stairs and Latira came to join her patient.

'Colonel Vatna will be here soon,' she informed him. 'He's been wanting to show you around.'

Terrel would have preferred to wander off on his own – but he'd also realized that the chances of that happening were very slim.

'Is there anything you'd like before you go?' she asked.

'No. Thank you.'

'Are you going to help them?'

'Help who?' he asked. 'With what?'

'The war is all they think about.' Latira was the first person to show little enthusiasm for the fighting. 'With anything new, their first thought is how it – or he – can help them win.'

'I don't want anything to do with the war. I'm a healer.'

'Even healers are a valuable resource. The sooner the wounded get better, the more the army benefits.'

Terrel hadn't thought of it like that before. His healing had always seemed a good thing – and it still did – but if all he did was help men return to battle and get injured again – or even killed – then what had he really achieved? All he'd ever wanted was to reduce the amount of pain in the world.

'I'm sorry, Terrel,' she said. 'Don't look so worried. You're a good man, I'm sure of that. You don't need me to lecture you.'

Vatna came bounding up the steps before the healer could respond.

'You're ready,' he said breathlessly on seeing Terrel. 'Excellent. Let's go.'

A blustery wind was blowing down the street, but after his recent confinement, Terrel revelled in the freshness of the air. The hail had stopped, but high grey clouds moved swiftly across the sky – the protective layer of steam having been blown away – and the upper slopes of the mountain were no longer visible. The pavements were still wet, and it was cold enough to suggest that the puddles would turn back to ice by nightfall.

After their initial spiralling descent from the tower, their exit from the fortress had involved a labyrinthine trek through corridors and courtyards until they'd reached one of the lesser gates. The sentries there had saluted the colonel – and had tried not to make their interest in his companion too obvious. After that the two men had been the objects of many more curious glances. Inside the castle, almost everyone Terrel had seen had worn a military uniform, but the people in the city streets were the usual mixture of men, women and children. Yet even here there was a sense of orderliness, of purpose. Everyone seemed to be going somewhere or doing something specific. Terrel had never felt at ease in cities or large towns, avoiding them whenever he could, and Saudark was no different in that respect. However, he was observant enough to realize that it was like nowhere else he had ever been. No one loitered on corners, gossiping. If there was any trade going on, it was taking place indoors, out of sight. The cobbled lanes and alleyways were remarkably clean and quiet. Compared to the noisy, odorous chaos of somewhere like Betancuria or Qomish, Saudark was like a ghost town.

That thought brought a wave of longing to see Alyssa and her ghostly retinue, but there did not seem to be any animals about for her to occupy. No dogs or cats prowled the streets; no one rode on horses or mules; there didn't even seem to be any birds. Terrel knew that in a place this size there must be *some* animal life, but he had yet to glimpse any of it.

'Where are we going?' he asked, although he'd already guessed their probable destination.

'To the healing pools,' Vatna replied, confirming Terrel's prediction. 'I thought you'd want to start there, it being relevant to your line of work, so to speak.'

Having only seen the pools from the outside, and having observed the steam rising above the compound, Terrel had imagined them to be small, open-air lakes of hot water. But the reality proved quite different. After the guards at the entrance had let them through, Vatna led him into a windowless building and along a dimly-lit corridor.

'I'll take you to see the springs first,' he said, his voice echoing from the stone walls. 'That's where it all begins.'

They eventually emerged into a square courtyard surrounded by a cloistered pavement. The interior of the quadrangle was open to the sky and it was immediately clear that this was the source of the steam that lay over the city. Great white billows rose into the air from its centre, where water, half-hidden in the mist, gushed from the earth in undulating waves. From there it poured out in all directions, rippling over smooth mounds of multicoloured stone before dividing into separate streams. These in turn flowed into carved channels and eventually disappeared, still bubbling, into small holes that led beneath the pavement Terrel was standing on. Even from his position at the edge of the deluge, the heat was tremendous, and he knew without having to test the theory that the water would scald him if he allowed it to touch his skin. Near the centre, where it was literally boiling to the surface, it would kill him in moments.

'It's too hot to use it here,' Vatna said, as if he'd read Terrel's thoughts. 'That's why we siphon it off, and let some of the steam escape. The water cools as it flows through the pipes to the healing pools, so when it gets there it's just the right temperature.'

'Does it flow as strongly as this all the time?' Terrel asked, recalling the feeble springs of Misrah's desert.

'Without fail,' the colonel replied. 'The supply is constant. All we have to do is make sure the channels don't silt up.'

The water looked quite clear to Terrel, but he realized that Vatna had not meant the type of silt he was used to. There were presumably various minerals and salts dissolved in the liquid which would settle out as it cooled. That explained the weird mounds of grey-white stone, coloured with streaks of orange, blue and green.

'Are the springs at Hvannadal like this?'

'I've never seen them,' Vatna replied, 'but I suppose so, yes.'

'Have your enemies ever tried to destroy this place?'

The colonel shook his head.

'If they have, they never even got close,' he said dismissively. 'They'd be stupid to try.'

Does that mean your proposed raid on Hvannadal is equally stupid? Terrel wondered, but he kept the thought to himself. He simply stared at the massive spring, marvelling at the underground forces that brought such immense power to the surface. He would have expected the water to emerge with the roar of a mighty cataract, but in fact the outpouring was eerily quiet, punctuated only by the intermittent hiss of escaping steam and the gurgling of the lesser rivulets. The uncomfortably humid air was filled with smells that varied constantly, quite sweet one moment, sour or noxious the next, but there was something else in the atmosphere too, something Terrel could not explain. There was a vague sense of potency that impressed him but also made him feel uneasy. If this power was truly used for healing, it would dwarf his own meagre talent, but he couldn't escape the feeling that – in spite of appearances – it was somehow unnatural.

'We can go inside now,' Vatna said, obviously gratified by the foreigner's awe.

Terrel was led down another passageway, then through a side door. Leaving their coats on pegs provided in the vestibule, they went on into the lamp-lit warren beyond. The air here was very warm and thick with vapour, and Terrel was soon sweating profusely. The close atmosphere also held a new mixture of scents. Terrel couldn't hope to identify them all, but while some fragrances were flowery, others were bitter, and underlying them all was the herbal reek of mitra. He could only hope that he would not be overcome by the fumes.

'The magians work here constantly,' Vatna told him, 'making sure each patient gets the right mixture for his injuries, and checking that the water is aligned properly.'

'Aligned?' Terrel queried. 'What do you mean?'

'You really need someone better qualified than me to explain it properly. I can sense it, and use it to some extent, but I never really understood the theory.' Vatna sounded slightly ashamed of his shortcomings. 'The best I can do is say that water is a remarkable substance, and the elements that make it up can be aligned in various ways. To be effective for healing it needs to be in a certain pattern. It's the magians' job to make sure that the pattern's correct.'

Terrel was no longer surprised at learning something new and unexpected about a substance he had once taken for granted. Water was central to all life – his time with the Toma had taught him that – and as far as the Ancients were concerned, it was not only magical but also very dangerous.

By now the two men had reached a long narrow hall which had rows of small cubicles on either side, divided by plain stone walls. Inside each cubicle was a sunken bath, through which water bubbled, entering from openings at one end and exiting via drains at the other. In each pool of hot, swirling liquid floated a man. They were all naked, their eyes closed as if asleep. Each of them bore injuries of one kind or another. Although some of these appeared quite serious, none of the men was actually bleeding. Immersion in water would ordinarily have been the last thing Terrel would have recommended for open wounds, but what was going on here was clearly far beyond his expertise.

Seeing a man he recognized from Captain Raufar's company, Terrel stopped and stared. When he had last seen him, Kavika had been badly cut on his left arm and shoulder and his chest had been covered in a massive dark bruise. Terrel had suspected broken bones within, and had feared that the damage done would prove fatal before they reached Saudark. But the man had survived, and now it was hard to see anything wrong with him. There were only faint scars where his skin had been sliced open, and the discoloration over his ribs had vanished entirely. And all this had happened in less than two days.

'That's incredible,' Terrel breathed.

'He's ready to wake,' an unfamiliar voice stated.

The newcomer had approached silently, his bare feet making no sound on the warm tiled floor, and his words had startled Terrel. Turning now, he saw a young man dressed in a short grey tunic.

'Hello, Solva,' Vatna said. 'This is Terrel, the healer I told you about. Terrel, Solva is a magian whose talent far outstrips mine. He's in charge of the pools.'

Solva bowed his head slightly in acknowledgement, but

said nothing. After a moment he knelt down and dipped his fingers into Kavika's pool. He nodded, apparently satisfied, then stepped into the water. Supporting the patient's neck with one hand, he tapped his forehead gently with the other. The soldier's eyes opened and he took a deep breath, then sat up and smiled. Solva helped him to stand and when he had done so, retreated, letting Kavika come to terms with his new situation. The soldier stretched, then deliberately thumped himself on the chest with both fists. Terrel winced, but Kavika only laughed. He was whole again.

'What's *he* doing here?' he demanded, glaring at the foreigner.

'He's our guest,' Vatna replied. 'Terrel is a friend, not a spy. And he is a true healer.'

Kavika looked sceptical, but knew better than to argue with a superior officer.

'Could you have done this for me?' he asked.

'I doubt it,' Terrel replied truthfully.

'The difference is that he could have treated you in the field,' Vatna said, 'rather than having to wait until you got back here.'

The soldier did not seem overly impressed by this argument. He merely stood there, water dripping from his muscular frame, quite unabashed by his nakedness.

'You can return to your company now,' Solva told him. 'Come with me and get a new uniform.'

After the other men had gone, Terrel and Vatna continued their tour. The buildings on all four sides of the quadrangle were similar in design, and there were literally hundreds of pools, nearly all of them occupied. Terrel saw some invalids with quite horrendous injuries, but was assured that they would all recover eventually and return to active service. He was left with a deep sense of admiration for the work the magians were doing, and wished that it could be seen as an end in itself, rather than a means of helping the war effort.

'Could the pools be used to treat ordinary illness, rather than just wounds from battle?' he asked.

'I suppose so,' Vatna answered doubtfully. He had clearly never considered such an idea before. 'If the alignments were done properly. But all the resources here are needed for the army, so the question doesn't arise. If you've seen enough, I'd like to show you another part of the compound.'

'All right.' Terrel was beginning to feel rather light-headed now, and hoped that wherever they were going next was not so full of fumes.

Vatna led him back to the vestibule, where they collected their coats and went outside. The air felt very cold after the muggy atmosphere of the pools, and Terrel was soon shivering inside his damp clothes. Before long, however, he forgot all about his temporary discomfort. The colonel ushered him into a building a short distance from the springs. Inside was a dormitory, with rows of narrow beds, where a few dozen men lay perfectly still. Terrel knew what had happened to them even before his guide spoke.

'These are some we haven't been able to heal,' Vatna said. 'This ward is normally used for less urgent cases, who have to wait when the pools are full, or for those who've had to come out early to allow more serious wounds to be dealt with. But recently there's been a rash of injuries we can't explain. At first we thought they were just unconscious after a blow to the head, even though most of them showed no outward signs of that. But the healing pools didn't help them at all. They look as if they're dead, but they're not. If you watch closely, they're still breathing, although very slowly.'

'Sleepers,' Terrel whispered.

'That's what we call them,' Vatna said. 'How did you know?'

That's what everyone calls them, Terrel thought.

'I've come across this before,' he said aloud.

'Really! Can you cure them?'

'No.'

Vatna's disappointment was palpable.

'I'll try, just to make sure,' Terrel added hurriedly, 'but I'm reasonably sure that what's afflicting them is beyond my healing. Or anyone else's.'

'We had hoped—' Vatna began, then fell silent as Terrel went to one of the beds and took the hands of the comatose soldier in his own. The man's skin was cool, but not completely lifeless. The waking dream was still there, but so far away that Terrel had no way of connecting to it, let alone sharing it with the sleeper. His spirit was wandering elsewhere.

Terrel gave up the attempt and looked around. There were more sleepers here than he'd ever seen in one place. He had only ever seen isolated cases before. Alyssa had been the first, of course, at a time when he'd understood nothing of what was happening to her. Like all the other sleepers, she was somehow being protected, although that protection came at a price. He still found it hard to believe she had been in a coma for more than seven years now and, despite all the evidence to the contrary, even harder to believe that in all that time she had come to no harm. In fact, if her long sleep followed the pattern of others he had seen, she would hardly have aged at all since her dramatic collapse. Terrel had no idea what having so many sleepers here meant, but it confirmed that he had been right to come to Myvatan. Although he didn't understand it completely, there was undoubtedly a link between the Ancients and the sleepers.

'I'm sorry,' he said. 'There's nothing I can do for them.'

'Some of them have been here for months,' Vatna told him, 'but they don't seem to have come to any harm.'

'They won't,' Terrel assured him. 'I've seen sleepers who have hardly changed in ten years.'

'Ten years! We thought maybe their bodies had just got the signals for hibernation mixed up.'

'It's more complicated than that.'

'I see,' Vatna said, though clearly he didn't. 'Is it enemy sorcery?'

'I doubt it,' Terrel replied. 'Do you know if these men have anything in common?'

'Not that I'm aware of.'

'Did they fall asleep in any particular place?'

'No. Cases have been reported all over the quarter. Even one or two here in Saudark.'

'And they're all soldiers?'

'Yes. Of course.'

'Have any civilians become sleepers? Any women?'

'I don't know.'

'Who *would* know?' Terrel persisted.

'I think it's time you went to the pyramid,' Vatna decided. 'There's clearly a lot you need to discuss with Tofana.'

CHAPTER FOURTEEN

'Just ring the bell and give the doormen the password,' Captain Hosak repeated patiently. 'They'll let you in.'

'"Look into the ice-worm's eyes"?' Terrel asked doubt-fully.

'Yes. Think you can remember that?' The soldier sounded as though he was speaking to a small and stupid child.

'It's a strange password,' Terrel commented.

'That's the point. It's not going to just slip out in normal conversation, is it? Ice-worms don't even have eyes.'

The captain was in command of the eight-man patrol that had escorted Terrel from Saudark. Vatna had arranged the trip, but had been too busy with his own duties to accompany them. Hosak, like his men, had been generally uncommunicative during the two-day march, and had given the impression that he resented having to play nursemaid to a foreigner.

'Aren't you coming in with me?' Terrel asked. When he had first glimpsed the pyramid, he'd felt some initial stir-rings of unease, and now that it was only a short distance away he was unaccountably nervous.

'No. Tofana summoned you, not us.'

'But it would save you having to camp out in this weather tonight.' Snow had been falling intermittently for the last day and a half, and now lay ankle deep all around them. The soldiers had hardly seemed to notice this while they were on the move, but once they'd come to a halt their expressions had grown sullen, and they were stamping their feet impatiently. Terrel wondered which of them had been commissioned by Myrdal to watch over his progress – and who would take over that duty once he was inside the wizard's domain.

'We're used to it,' Hosak replied tersely. 'And if we stay here much longer they'll be using us for target practice. So get going.'

Terrel wanted to ask what he meant, but the captain's tone did not invite further curiosity.

'Thank you for escorting me here,' he said instead.

Hosak nodded but said nothing, and Terrel turned to look at the pyramid again. Its sloping walls were built of large slabs of warm, honey-coloured stone, which stood out from both the predominantly grey rock of the mountainous terrain and the pristine whiteness of the new snow. The triangular surfaces were quite smooth, except for incised symbols carved into some of the blocks. Terrel was not surprised to see that the carvings depicted familiar emblems. He had seen most of them, with minor variations, at different points on his travels. The most prominent was a large version of the design on his pendant and the brand on Vatna's arm – 'the river in the sky'. That was presumably Tofana's own marker. Terrel wondered if this was a good omen.

As he began to make his way towards the wizard's domain, Terrel heard some muttered comments from the soldiers.

'If an ice-worm *did* have eyes I'd bet they'd be just like his.'

'You really think he's never been inside a pyramid before?'

'He's in for a surprise then,' someone added, and Terrel could sense the smiles behind him.

He tried to set these remarks aside and trudged on, his boots sinking into the powdery crystals. The bell that Hosak had pointed out hung from a wooden frame that looked disconcertingly like a gallows. By the time Terrel reached it, he was only three or four paces from the lower edge of the pyramid itself, but he could still see no sign of a door, let alone any doormen. Reaching up, he grasped the clapper and pulled it against the bell. His nervousness made him tentative, and the resulting sound was dull and barely audible. Nothing happened. Overcompensating, Terrel yanked the clapper back and forth, setting up an ear-splitting clangour that he tried in vain to quiet. But still nothing happened.

As the last reverberations were dying away and he was steeling himself to shatter the peace of the mountainside once again, a movement caught his eye and he froze, his stomach tying itself in knots. A panel of stone had slid back and to the side in total silence. The opening this created was square, narrower than the width of his shoulders, and situated just above head height. This was obviously the doorman's window, not the door itself, but Terrel couldn't see anyone looking back at him. All he could see was the entrance to a small, dark tunnel.

Moments later he glimpsed movement within, and heard a faint pattering sound. First one, then several more pairs of small bright eyes emerged from the gloom, all of them fixed on him. As Terrel's unease turned to astonishment and then to laughter, a pack of furry rodents gathered in the opening, those at the back practically climbing over the others in their eagerness to get a better view of the outside world. To the healer they looked suspiciously like long-haired rats, but with their noses and ears twitching, their pink staring eyes and glossy coats, they seemed more like pets than vermin.

Apart from the scrabbling of claws on the stone floor as they competed for the best vantage points, the rodents watched Terrel in complete silence, until one of the larger animals, near the bottom of the shifting pile, opened its mouth. It chattered for a few moments, displaying some unpleasantly sharp teeth, then fell silent again. Terrel got the uncanny feeling that it had been speaking to him, but it was only when the performance was repeated – in a sharper tone – that he stopped grinning and realized what was happening. Even then he was not sure he believed it. Could these rats really be the wizard's doormen? There was only one way to find out.

'Look into the ice-worm's eyes?' Because he was feeling rather foolish, the password came out as a hesitant question. However, to his amazement, the creatures reacted instantly. As some of them trotted off back into the tunnel, their spokesman let out another series of squeaks, and then those that were left moved to one side of the opening, with several standing up on their hind legs and placing their forepaws against the inner wall. Terrel had no idea what they were doing, but then he heard a distinct click and felt some sort of mechanism grind into action. The rats had pressed a lever and were opening a door for him.

Although Terrel had come across invisible doorways before, that had been because the sharaken's dream-trading had hidden the truth from his sight. The door that was opening here was solid and real, sliding back and in as the portal had done, but this time with the slight grating noise of stone upon stone. However, Terrel knew he could have spent hours inspecting the sloping wall without finding the entrance. Whoever had built the pyramid had not only been a master stonemason but also a master of disguise.

The first thing Terrel noticed when he stepped inside –
apart from the welcome dry warmth of the air – was that
the interior walls glowed with their own pale light. Inside
the solid, windowless structure, day and night would mean
nothing, and but for the almost ghostly luminescence its
inhabitants would have been left in permanent darkness.
Burning torches or lamps inside such an enclosed space
would soon have made the atmosphere unbearable.

As the outer door closed behind him, with an ominously final clunk, Terrel threw back his hood and shook
the moisture from his coat. He stepped forward and was
immediately presented with a choice. Ahead of him was a
blank wall, but there were stairs to either side. Turning
left led downwards, into what was presumably a cellar. If
he turned right he would be climbing diagonally, travers-
ing one side of the pyramid. Just as he was debating which
way to go, and wondering whether he'd be given any further guidance, one of the rats popped out of a hole in the
right-hand wall and chattered at him. It had emerged just
above a thin stone shelf that ran along the wall at hip
height, parallel to the stairs, which Terrel realized was a
walkway for the rodents. With an imperious swish of its
tail, the small creature began trotting up the slope. Taking
this as his cue, Terrel followed.

The passageway wound up and around the perimeter of
the pyramid in a triangular spiral. Terrel and his companion passed several open doorways to the interior, but
although he looked into several of them, he couldn't see
anything. He wasn't sure whether this was simply because
the light was too dim, or whether there was something
obscuring his view. At times it almost seemed as though
there was something wrong with his eyes. But he somehow
felt that he was not meant to explore those avenues yet –
and this was confirmed by his guide, who was still pattering

uphill, pausing every so often to glance back and make sure that Terrel was following.

Eventually, after a number of traverses and turns, and what felt like hundreds of steps, they rounded the final corner and saw another doorway – this time not shadowed but brightly lit. By then Terrel was breathing quite hard. Far from being stuffy, as might have been expected, the air was fresh, though much warmer than it had been outside. There was also a tang to it, which made the healer's tongue and lips tingle, but – thankfully – he could detect no trace of mitra. However, as he made his way into one of the most peculiar rooms he had ever seen, the air seemed almost to crackle against his skin, and the small hairs on the backs of his hands and his neck stood on end.

The triangular room was huge – the size of a large barn – but because the walls leaned inwards to form a pointed roof within the apex of the pyramid, it felt claustrophobic. This was emphasized by the extraordinary amount of clutter inside. Terrel only had time to get a vague impression of several tables – which were all covered with forests of bottles, jars and bowls, numerous parchments and lumps of rock, as well as a mass of quite unrecognizable paraphernalia – before his attention was drawn to the people in the room. They were all – both male and female – dressed in a variety of black tunics, and they all seemed quite young, from about ten to twenty years old – with one notable exception.

Terrel guessed the woman's age to be around forty, but that was not the only thing that set her apart. Her black tunic was more like a robe, reaching down to her ankles, and her skin was paler than any Terrel had seen since he'd left the sunless world of the fog valley in Macul. Her cheeks were ghostly white and made a startling contrast with her bright green eyes and rich brown hair. Even in isolation, her hair was extraordinary. It seemed to consist entirely of corkscrew curls, which sprang out from her head in all directions as if trying to escape.

All the others had stopped what they were doing when Terrel entered the room, but she was still striding between the tables, gesticulating wildly with her thin hands and talking to nobody in particular – in a piercing, high-pitched voice that could have sharpened steel.

'We've got the shapes backwards, my little snowflakes. Backwards! Hah!' Fingers so pallid that the nails seemed almost blue weaved patterns in the air to emphasize her speech. 'You can't have chains without links, so you can't have a chain reaction without a means of forging those links. Like putting the sled before the dogs, eh? Do you think I don't see what you're doing?'

This last remark came out as a screech, and appeared to be addressed to a line of buckets which stood at the base of one of the walls.

'What do you take me for?' she demanded shrilly. 'A frostbitten old baggage?' With that she turned round and faced the room again.

In a rare moment of silence, Terrel's furry guide squeaked as if to announce their presence, and the woman finally noticed what everyone else in the room was looking at. During her almost hysterical monologue, the visitor had had a hard time stopping himself from laughing. He couldn't imagine what this madwoman was doing in the wizard's lair, but when she fixed her emerald gaze upon him he forced himself to keep a straight face. He gave a small bow in greeting, but before he could speak the woman transferred her regard to the rat.

'Not now, Bezylum,' she groaned. Although she was speaking more quietly now, her voice still grated in Terrel's ears.

The rodent chattered again.

'Yes, I can see that,' the woman snapped. 'But I don't need a healer at the moment. Terrel will have to look after himself for a while.'

Terrel gaped. Not only had it not been necessary for him to introduce himself, but unless he was very much mistaken, the woman had understood what the rat had said. In that instant he knew who she was. He had imagined the wizard as a grey-bearded old man, rather like some of the seers in his own homeland. It had never occurred to him that Tofana might be a woman – and certainly not one as eccentric as this.

'No, I'm not angry with you,' she said now, waving an expressive hand. Then she set her teeth together and uttered her own series of squeaks. Bezylum immediately turned tail and disappeared through another small hole in the wall. Terrel was impressed. The wizard could speak to rats, and in their own language.

'Talk to her,' Tofana said, pointing to one of the young women. 'I have work to do.'

She turned away, leaving Terrel in no doubt about his dismissal. He glanced at the girl who had been chosen – apparently at random – to take charge of him. She hadn't moved, and was looking rather bemused, so he walked over towards her. As he got closer, his first impressions were confirmed. She was perhaps a couple of years younger than himself and she was beautiful, with straight blonde hair, blue eyes and a delicate, heart-shaped face. Terrel smiled.

'Hello. I'm Terrel. I—'

'I know who you are. I am Magian Tegan.' Her response was slightly haughty, as if he ought to have known who she was. Terrel got the impression that she had no wish to act as his nursemaid and felt the task to be beneath her. This suspicion was confirmed when, having introduced herself, she turned away and called to one of the younger boys.

'Yarek, come here!'

The boy arrived quickly, with every appearance of eagerness.

'Take the healer to the guest quarters,' Tegan instructed. 'See that he has everything he needs.'

'Yes, Magian,' Yarek replied, then turned to the visitor with an earnest expression on his youthful face. 'Come with me, sir.'

Terrel was about to thank Tegan but she had already turned away and was engrossed in a manuscript that lay on a nearby table.

'Please don't call me sir,' the healer said quietly as he followed the boy out. 'My name's Terrel.'

'Yes, s—, Terrel.' Yarek gave him a hesitant smile.

On their way to the door, they walked past some of the buckets Tofana had addressed earlier. They were full of water. At the same time, Terrel heard voices muttering.

' . . . bitten old baggage . . .'

' . . . sled before the dogs . . .'

' . . . now Bezylum . . .'

If it hadn't been such a ridiculous idea, Terrel would have sworn that the mutterings were coming from the buckets themselves.

CHAPTER FIFTEEN

Yarek led the healer down the same stairs he had climbed earlier and, like the rat, he glanced back every so often to make sure his charge was still following. On several occasions Terrel had the feeling that the boy was about to speak, but each time he seemed to think better of it, and went on in silence. For his part, Terrel's mind was teeming with questions, but he wasn't sure Yarek was the right person to ask. He didn't want to get the boy into trouble, or offend his peculiar hostess, so he too remained quiet.

Eventually they came to the short tunnel where Terrel had entered the pyramid, but they didn't stop there. Yarek went on down, taking the visitor into unexplored territory. If it hadn't been for his prior knowledge, Terrel would not have been able to tell that they were now below the surface of the ground. The quality of light didn't change, and the design of the corridor was the same as the others, with more passages leading to unseen rooms in the interior. The traverses became longer, with the sharp corners now further apart, indicating that the pyramid extended outwards as well as down.

'So the guest quarters are underground?' Terrel ventured, thinking that this should be a safe enough topic to begin a conversation.

'All the living spaces are,' Yarek replied. 'And the store-rooms, kitchens and wash-houses. The pyramid's like an

iceberg.' Seeing the visitor's blank expression, he added,
'When you see an iceberg floating in the sea, the part
above the water is only a small fraction of the whole thing.
There's much more beneath the surface.'

'I see.' Terrel understood the comparison now.

'I would have thought you'd have known that,' his guide
remarked. 'You must have seen some from your ship.'

'Yes, but I don't know much about this part of the
world.'

Yarek nodded, accepting the explanation easily.

'Is it true you came up out of Savik's Whale?' he asked.
Now that the silence had been broken, he seemed eager to
talk.

'Yes,' Terrel said, wondering what else this apparently
lowly member of the wizard's household already knew
about him. 'But there was no magic involved. It was just
a strange coincidence.' Even as he spoke, he wondered if
he believed what he was saying.

'You were supposed to have died,' Yarek commented.

'According to the legends. Yes, I know.' Terrel didn't
want to discuss that any more. 'Does Tofana really talk to
the rats?' He hadn't seen any more of the creatures, but
their walkways ran alongside all the staircases, and there
were holes every so often.

'They're not rats!' his guide exclaimed, and Terrel
couldn't tell whether he was offended or amused. 'They're
mustelas. The Wizard can talk to them, but only a few of
them are clever enough to be able to talk back properly.
Like Bezylum. They're all completely loyal to her,
though.'

'And some of them can understand human speech,'
Terrel said.

'Not really. They respond to her vibrations, the tone of
her voice, things like that. Oh, you mean the passwords?

They can recognize patterns of sound even if they don't know what they mean.'

'Remarkable.' Terrel had talked to a lot of animals, but only when a human spirit was inside them, and their conversations had been silent, using psinoma rather than speech. Tofana's achievement in being able to communicate with the mustelas was extraordinary, but it was obviously only one of her talents.

'Tofana's the most powerful sorcerer on all Myvatan,' Yarek said, reinforcing the point. It didn't sound like a boast, more a simple statement of fact.

'I hadn't realized Tofana was a woman,' Terrel said, then – seeing the boy's puzzled glance – he hastened to explain. 'I mean, the army seems to be in charge of everything here, and all the officers are men. So I thought—'

'Oh no, all the wizards are women,' Yarek cut in.

'*All* of them?' Tofana's sex had been a surprise, but the idea that, in what had seemed an entirely male-dominated society, the most powerful – and secretive – occupation of all was reserved for women came as a shock.

'I thought everyone knew that,' Yarek said. 'Women can't be soldiers, can they? So this is how they fight in the war. With magic.'

Something in the boy's tone made Terrel hesitate before asking his next question. He couldn't quite pinpoint what it was, but Yarek didn't seem quite so sure of himself any more.

'Are you here to train as a neomancer?'

'I suppose so.'

'You don't sound very sure.'

'I thought once—' Yarek began, then shook his head. 'There are some things you can't change, no matter how hard you try.' This time his air of disillusionment was easy to recognize.

While they had been talking, they had been tunnelling deeper into the underground warren. Now at last Yarek turned into one of the inner doorways and led Terrel along a level corridor. The healer was glad of that – his mismatched leg muscles had been complaining about all the steps for some time – but he didn't want the conversation to end just yet. Before he could say anything, however, his guide pushed open a door and ushered him inside.

The room was triangular, with the walls leaning inwards only very slightly, and had a flat, luminous ceiling. The furniture consisted of a narrow bed, a small table, a stool and a storage chest. Empty shelves lined part of one wall.

'This will be your private room for the length of your stay,' Yarek informed him. 'When the door is closed no one will disturb you unless you want them to. The nearest wash-house is just a little further along the corridor. Meals are usually taken in the refectory, but you can ask the servants to bring food to you here if you prefer. Is there anything you'd like now?'

'Perhaps later,' Terrel replied, tossing his pack on to the bed and slumping down next to it. 'Why don't you sit and talk to me for a while?'

'I ought to be getting back,' the boy said doubtfully. He was clearly tempted by the invitation, though, and Terrel sought to reassure him.

'You can blame me if anyone complains about you being late. I'm a stranger here and there are a lot of things you can help me with. Tegan did say you were to make sure I had everything I needed.' He smiled encouragingly, and after a few moments the boy grinned back, a new excitement in his pale blue eyes.

'What do you want to know?' he enquired pulling out the stool and sitting down.

'Are all the rooms in the pyramid the same shape?' Terrel asked, beginning with something that couldn't possibly be forbidden.

'Yes. They all fit in that way. The triangle is the most stable and strongest geometric shape there is,' Yarek explained. 'And a pyramid is easy to defend from above as well as from the ground. Not that anyone would dare attack this place.'

'That's true,' Terrel remarked, with a wry smile. 'Even your own soldiers seem afraid of it.'

'I'm not surprised,' Yarek said, and once again the healer sensed an undercurrent of disenchantment.

'Why do you say that?'

'It's just . . .' the boy began, then faltered. 'I think you'd better talk to one of the magians about that.'

'Is it because of the work you do here?'

Yarek nodded, but did not elaborate.

'I already know that Tofana trains neomancers,' Terrel went on, 'so they can use weather-weapons in the war. What's the difference between them and the magians?'

'Nothing to begin with. It's just a matter of how they use the skills they learn here. Neomancers use theirs directly for fighting. The others do . . . different things.'

'Like the people who look after the healing pools?'

'Yes. Is it true you can heal people without using the springs?'

'Sometimes, yes.'

'How do you do it?'

'I'm not really sure. It's just a gift I was born with.' Not that I knew that for a long time, Terrel added to himself.

'But you must use the water-lines somehow.'

'I'm not sure what you mean.' He didn't really want to talk about himself, and sought to return their exchange to life within the pyramid. 'Water's important here, isn't it?'

'It's central to everything we do,' Yarek confirmed.

'When we left Tofana, I thought I heard voices coming from some of the buckets of water there. Is that possible?'

'Oh, yes! The chains are the Wizard's special—' He broke off once more and looked down at his feet. 'I shouldn't really . . . This is . . .'

'I should wait to talk to Tofana herself?'

'Yes,' Yarek agreed gratefully.

'Will you tell me a little about yourself, then?' Terrel asked. He was intrigued by the way the boy veered between eagerness and reticence.

'If you like. What do you want to know?'

'Oh, how old you are, how you came to be here. That sort of thing.'

'I'm fourteen. I came here when I was ten, because I'd shown enough talent to earn a sizarship and become an apprentice. I would've been training for the army by now if I hadn't.'

'And you'd rather be a magian than a soldier?'

'I'd rather be—' Yarek hesitated again. 'Yes.'

Terrel knew he'd been going to say something else, but decided not to push him.

'What did your family think of your choice?' he asked instead.

'My father was already dead,' Yarek replied bluntly. 'I think my mother was pleased. I'm not sure about Takkara. He's my grandfather,' he added, by way of explanation.

'Was your father killed in the war?'

'Yes. He walks the Great Plain now.'

This last sounded like an oft-repeated refrain, and Terrel couldn't tell whether Yarek believed it or merely hoped it was true.

'Do you miss him?' he asked quietly, thinking of his own father, a man he had never met.

'Yes. No. Not really.' The boy looked completely flustered now. 'I was too young to remember him properly, but sometimes I think . . . No. It's silly.'

'What is?' Terrel prompted gently.

'I dream about him sometimes. He shouts, trying to tell me something, but I can never hear him. He doesn't seem very happy.' Yarek paused. 'You won't tell anyone about this, will you?'

'No, of course not,' the healer promised. Although he was surprised that the apprentice had chosen to unburden himself to a stranger, on reflection perhaps it was *because* he was a stranger that Yarek had revealed his secret.

'Can I ask *you* something now?' the boy ventured, obviously wanting to change the subject.

'All right.'

'Have your eyes always been like that?'

The question took Terrel by surprise. He'd been aware of the boy's fascination with their unusual coloration, but few people expressed their curiosity so directly.

'Yes. They were like this when I was born.'

'They're beautiful. Like ice,' Yarek said, then blushed and stammered. 'I . . . I mean . . .'

'Some people find them unnerving,' Terrel said, remembering the horrified reactions his unveiled eyes had sometimes caused, 'but I can change them if I like.' He blinked, summoning the glamour, making his companion believe that a lie was the truth. When he next looked up, Yarek saw eyes that were the same shade as his own, and he gasped in astonishment. At the same time, warning signals flashed through Terrel's mind, and he felt a dark presence stir and look around. He quickly released the spell, allowing his eyes to revert to their true appearance, but it was too late. His demonstration had been a mistake and he knew it. A door had opened and he was powerless to close it again. As Alyssa had reminded him on numerous occasions, all magic exacted a price, and using it for such a frivolous end had been stupid.

'That was amazing!' Yarek breathed. 'Can you show me how to do it? Can you do it again?'

'Not now,' Terrel replied firmly, regretting his impetuous action even more. 'I—'

He was interrupted by a strange, almost musical buzzing, which made the air in the room shiver and seemed to vibrate through the floor and walls.

'What was that?'

'Just an earthquake,' Yarek replied casually. 'It's all right. You're quite safe here.'

'Does Myvatan get a lot of earthquakes?'

'I suppose so. We generally know when they're most likely to happen, but it's more difficult to be precise now that the moons are behaving oddly.'

Terrel nodded, having heard that explanation elsewhere on his travels. But he was confused by the fact that he'd received no internal warning of the tremor. For several years a trembling deep inside him had preceded quakes, allowing him to predict their arrival – albeit by only a few moments. But on this occasion he had been taken quite unawares. The only other time that had happened had been in the fog valley in Macul, and for the life of him he couldn't see any connection between that place and the pyramid.

'That wasn't a very big one,' Yarek was saying, 'but even the largest of them don't affect us. The pyramid is self-contained and adjusts to cope with any external forces.'

'That's good to know,' Terrel murmured, for want of anything better to say.

'I should be going,' Yarek said, standing up. 'Would you like some food now?'

'Yes, please.'

'I'll tell the servants. Or I could bring it myself if you like,' he added hopefully.

'That would be good. Thank you.'

'Is there anything else?' the boy asked, eager again now. 'Do you need writing materials, or something to read?'

'I'd like to read, but I'm not familiar with your written language.'

'I could read to you,' Yarek suggested. 'The library has lots of books on legends and so on.'

'I might take you up on that some time,' Terrel said. 'But for now, do you think you could bring me a map of Myvatan? I'd like to get my bearings.'

'I suppose so. There must be one somewhere.'

After Yarek had left in search of food and a map, Terrel lay down on the bed and stared up at the ceiling, lost in thought. At one point he closed his eyes, and sensed that the room immediately became darker. Opening his eyes again made the ceiling grow in brightness once more. He tried this again a few more times, with the same results. When his eyes were closed for any length of time, the light in the room responded, apparently trying to lull him into sleep. It was uncanny, feeling all that magic responding to his needs and knowing that it was only a tiny fraction of the power contained within the wizard's domain.

Half an hour later, when Yarek had still not returned, weariness overcame Terrel's awe and he closed his eyes with a greater sense of purpose, deciding that a nap would do him good. A few moments later, he fell into a nightmare he would have given anything to escape.

CHAPTER SIXTEEN

The full Red Moon was alone in the night sky. There weren't even any stars to set against its dominance. Fire, love and violence, Terrel thought, wondering which of these portents held true this time.

In the blink of an eye his vision changed. The sky was now made of ice and the moon was a sword, its blade running with blood. Moments later he was looking down, not up, into the terrible chaos of war. As he watched, men were engulfed by flame and clouds of sulphurous steam. Gouts of boiling mud sent great swathes of different colours splashing out over the snow, and stripped flesh from bone. Elsewhere, hailstones the size of fists battered limbs and crushed skulls, freezing rain turned soldiers to icy statues, and then avalanches buried them in wintry graves. A river of fire, where dragons swam, ran across the battlefield, its two banks sliding sideways but in opposite directions, as if the land itself was being torn apart. And everywhere men screamed in agony, disfigured by hideous injuries, burns, frostbite and gangrene – but the fighting went on, driven by a relentless hatred that had crossed the border into madness.

The carnage made Terrel feel sick to his stomach, his revulsion stemming not just from a healer's sensibilities but also from simple human compassion. He had lost the cool objectivity of his dream in Saudark, but he was trapped by his own visions, unable to look away.

Just when he thought it couldn't get any worse, he saw
the wizard. The black-robed figure stood on a hilltop,
facing away from him. As a pale finger pointed, an entire
city was destroyed by an icy deluge, the glittering water
ripping buildings apart. Another gesture, and a whole
mountain was torn to shreds by an explosion of flame
hurling boulders as big as houses high into the smoke-
filled air. The wizard turned to look at him then, but it
was not Tofana's face that Terrel saw. Yarek stared back at
him in triumph, with the eyes of a dragon. Eyes that
matched the healer's own.

The dream changed, lurching from the crowded horror
of battle to an empty, featureless plain of bare earth and
parched grass. The war had gone and all that was left was
the endless desolation of this fearful place. The sense of
loneliness and grief was overwhelming, but there was no
one to be seen.

Terrel struggled to escape and succeeded, only to find
himself somewhere even worse. The room was dark, but
he knew the walls were closing in on him and he felt himself suffocating. There was no way out. The door he had
inadvertently opened earlier only let others in. The ominous presence was close now, hovering in the shadows.
Waiting.

The red sword appeared again, above him, bright against
the pitch black.

I see you've found a new plaything, a familiar voice
remarked. *I'd be careful if I were you. It looks dangerous.*

Well, you're not me, Terrel replied.

No, Jax conceded, laughing. *But I could have been.
Have you ever wondered what would have happened if you'd
been born first? Would our roles have been reversed, do you
think?*

Leave me alone. Terrel still couldn't see his twin.

Now why would I want to do that? This is too much fun.

You think this is fun? the healer gasped, feeling the last of his breath being squeezed out of him.

I think I'm going to like this place.

Terrel was seized with the desire to see his brother, to confront him face to face. It was an absurd, irrational impulse, but he could no more control it than he could tell his heart to stop beating.

Where are you? he shouted.

Are you afraid? Jax taunted. *And you with that great big sword.*

It's not mine.

I'll show you how to use it some day.

Why not now? Terrel demanded. *You're the one who's afraid. Come in here and show me!*

Not this time. I—

'Get in here!' Terrel yelled.

Light flooded his senses as he returned to the waking world with a rush. Blinking away the nightmare, he found that he was sitting up on the bed and that the door to his room stood open. Yarek was waiting there, holding a tray, a terrified expression on his young face.

'You did say to come in, didn't you?' the boy asked nervously.

'Yes, yes. I'm sorry. I fell asleep.'

'But you were shouting. I thought . . .'

'It's all right. I'm glad you woke me up.'

Yarek relaxed visibly, then came in and set the tray down on the table.

'I'm sorry I was so long,' he said. 'It took me a while to find the map.'

Terrel glanced over and saw the rolled parchment that lay beside the food, but he was distracted by the familiar scent filling the room. Even though he would have welcomed a calming influence just then, he knew he couldn't afford to have any of his senses dulled.

'Is that mitra?'

'An infusion, yes.'

'I don't want it. Take it away, please.'

Yarek looked surprised but obeyed, picking up the steaming cup and taking it out into the corridor. As he went, Terrel thought he detected a faint smile on the boy's lips and wondered why his refusal had prompted such an intriguing reaction. Without any way of answering that question, he moved to the table, set the map aside for later and began to eat. In spite of his recent experiences he was hungry – and he needed the reassurance of ordinary activity to distance himself from the nightmare and its possible interpretations.

When Yarek returned, he was obviously nervous once more.

'Is your meal all right?' he asked tentatively. 'I wasn't sure what you liked.'

'It's very good.' Terrel had not taken much notice of what he'd been eating, but now that he thought about it, it was excellent fare. The pyramid's storerooms were clearly well supplied. Yarek looked pleased.

'Most people would be glad of mitra,' he remarked with studied nonchalance. 'Why don't you like it?'

The ingenuous question seemed natural enough, but Terrel had the feeling there was more to it.

'It's too bitter for me,' he said.

'It would help you sleep better.'

'I'd rather sleep naturally.'

Yarek nodded, apparently approving of this sentiment.

'The soldiers drink a lot of it, don't they?' Terrel prompted.

'Almost everyone does. The war would be much harder to cope with if they didn't.'

Terrel was about to follow this up when there was a knock on the door.

'Come in,' he said.

Yarek, who had been perched on the end of the bed, stood up as the newcomer entered.

'Do you have everything you need for the moment?' Tegan asked Terrel.

'Yes, thank you.'

'Then you may go, Yarek.'

The apprentice accepted his dismissal meekly, slipping out into the corridor and closing the door quietly behind him. Tegan remained standing, watching over the table, her face as expressionless as it had been earlier. Terrel found her presence vaguely menacing, like that of a bird of prey.

'Why are you here, Terrel?' Her tone was faintly accusatory.

'I didn't have much choice,' he replied. 'Tofana summoned me, and the generals decided I should come now.'

'I didn't mean why are you at the pyramid. I meant why did you come to Myvatan in the first place?'

'I don't mean to be rude,' Terrel said, deciding he'd had enough of answering this particular question, 'but I'd rather discuss that with Tofana.'

Tegan accepted the implied rebuke impassively.

'Are you going to help us win the war?' she asked.

'I've no reason to fight for one side or the other,' he told her. 'I would rather help *end* the war.'

'The generals will tell you that the only way to end it is to win.'

'And do you believe that?'

'What else can I believe? The gods would not have granted me such talent as I have unless it was for a purpose.'

'So you're trying to become a wizard.'

'Less than one in a hundred magians go on to become wizards,' she replied. 'I'm under no illusions about my chances of going that far.'

'So what will you do with your talent?'

'The same as almost all the other magians. Learn how to find, channel, store and release magical powers.'

'For Tofana to use?'

'And the neomancers.'

'Of course.'

Tegan paused, apparently waiting to see whether the healer wanted to continue their conversation. When he said nothing, she broke the silence herself.

'It's late and we have an early start tomorrow, so I'll leave you to rest. Has Yarek explained the way things work around here?'

'Yes. He's looked after me very well.'

'It seems to me he's done more than that,' Tegan remarked, looking at the map. 'But for one so young he has remarkable talent, so we forgive him a few indiscretions.'

'Are there secrets on this map I'm not supposed to see?' Terrel asked, half smiling.

'I don't mean to be rude,' she replied, mimicking the tone of his earlier words, 'but can we be sure you're not an enemy spy?'

'You must have been talking to Myrdal,' he muttered.

'Who?' she asked, looking puzzled.

'He's General Pingeyri's adjutant,' Terrel told her. 'There's no reason why you should know him.'

'Actually, I think I do. We grew up in neighbouring villages, but I haven't seen him in a long time.' There was an odd inflection in her voice now that Terrel couldn't identify.

'Since you came here?'

Tegan nodded.

'When was that?'

'Three years ago. My talent developed later than most.'

'And yet you're a magian already, rather than an apprentice.'

'The Wizard is a good teacher,' Tegan said, her serenity restored. 'And she is generous with her knowledge.'

'Will I meet her again tomorrow?'

'I can't say.'

'What's the early start for?' he asked, trying another line of questioning.

'We're conducting some new trials.'

'Weather-weapons?'

'Yes.'

'Excellent,' Terrel said, rubbing his hands together in mock glee. 'Something interesting for me to spy on.'

Tegan actually smiled. It didn't last long, but it transformed her beauty from that of a porcelain doll to that of a real person. Then she became serious again.

'You know,' she said, 'if you *are* a spy, you'll never leave this pyramid alive.'

CHAPTER SEVENTEEN

The first thing Terrel noticed when he'd made his way back up to Tofana's room was that the top of the pyramid was no longer there. The wide triangular floor was as it had been before, the cluttered array of tables and equipment were much as he remembered them, but the inward sloping walls that formed the roof were gone.

The entire scene was now open to the air, and Terrel stared in disbelief at the sky above – which for once was a cloudless blue – and at the mountains that surrounded them, the dark rock of the steeper slopes contrasting with the dazzling white of the snow that lay everywhere else. Such was his astonishment that it took him a few moments to realize that, although they were supposedly exposed to the elements, there was no wind and the air was as warm as it had been before. Even on a calm sunny day it ought to have felt much colder.

He made a more detailed inspection of his immediate surroundings then, and saw what he had not noticed before. On closer inspection, the roof *was* still there, but it was just a ghostly shadow of its former self, a faint outline of light almost invisible in the brightness of the morning. If he concentrated hard and squinted, he could trace the angles of the corners leading up to the apex of the pyramid. Elsewhere, he could just make out the spectral shapes of several markers that had been carved into the *outside* of the walls. Otherwise the solid blocks of stone had become invisible.

Instinctively, Terrel knew that the walls remained in place. Tofana would never leave herself open to attack by having them moved. Logically, therefore, it must be that some form of sorcery was being used to enable him – and presumably everyone else – to see past them for the moment. For a brief instant he wondered whether it might be some extreme form of the glamour, but he soon rejected that idea. The technique Babak had taught him helped him to make people believe they were seeing things that weren't there – or were different in reality – but he didn't think it could be used to make people see through something that *was* there. There had to be more to it than that.

No one else seemed surprised that their place of work was now open to the sky. Terrel was the only one looking at the spectacular scenery around them. The magians and apprentices were all busy with various tasks, and Tofana was striding among them, her shrill voice cutting through the silence like a knife.

'No, no. That way. *That* way!' she chided one unfortunate. 'Look at the chart, my little icicle. Only the *Gold* Moon is waning. Look at the chart.' A white finger stabbed at a parchment covered in spidery script. 'There are rules to the dance,' she added, hopping and spinning around as if to demonstrate the principle, her black coat swirling out and then becoming tangled around her legs. She stumbled and half fell before righting herself, shooing away the assistants who had moved to help her.

Shaking her head so that her unruly hair bounced and swayed, the wizard moved on. Coming to the table where Tegan was stationed, Tofana picked up a clear glass phial and held it up to the light, inspecting the contents.

'Excellent. Excellent!' she exclaimed, glancing back at

the magian. 'We'll make a real sorcerer out of you yet, my pretty one. In spite of your foolish qualms.'

'I—' Tegan began, her usually placid face looking alarmed.

'Don't look so worried,' Tofana said, cutting off her feeble protest. 'You think I don't know? As long as you do work like this, it doesn't matter what you think in your more sentimental private moments.' With that she casually tossed the stoppered phial into the air and turned away, leaving Tegan to lunge forward and try to catch it. She did so easily enough, but Terrel had seen the momentary terror in her eyes, and wondered what would have happened if the container had fallen to the floor and broken. He found that his heart was beating fast – and guessed that Tegan's was too. Looking at her now, she seemed calm enough, but her cheeks had a little more colour than usual and her embarrassment was plain. Several of her companions were glancing at her curiously.

Tofana had continued on her way, and now came to a halt in the middle of the room, directly under the ghostly apex. Raising her arms, she performed a sort of jig on the spot, laughing quietly to herself as she stared up at the sky.

'What better day to challenge the gods?' she cried suddenly. 'Do you hear me, Jokulsa? Will you bless our efforts? Or curse them?'

The wizard looked down again and spun slowly round on one heel, so that her emerald gaze passed over everyone in the room. Terrel thought she looked demented, but more like a clown than a true lunatic. He found it difficult to reconcile her fearsome reputation with her eccentric behaviour and appearance.

'Just as long as he's not indifferent, eh?' Tofana declared. 'That would be an insult.' She caught sight of the healer and smiled. 'Ah, the child of the whale is here, so we have Savik watching over us too. I think it's time we began, don't you, my little snowflakes?'

The previous night had done little to prepare Terrel for the experiences of that morning. After Tegan had left him, he'd found he had neither the willpower nor the energy to study the map, and had decided to leave it for another time. He'd had no way of telling how late in the evening it was, but judging by his own weariness, night must have fallen some hours earlier. Even so, it had been a long time before he could bring himself to lie down and close his eyes. After the magian's parting words, darkness had not seemed a welcoming prospect. And since his earlier nightmare, the idea of going to sleep hadn't been too enticing either.

The curious thing was that in spite of Tegan's suspicions, and Yarek's part in his dream, Terrel found that he was drawn to them both. It was as he considered this anomaly that he remembered Alyssa's advice about not trusting his instincts, and this was enough to make him doubt his own feelings. Tegan's attitude to him had been vaguely antagonistic, and even though Yarek was just a boy, the dream might have meant that he was destined to become a wizard whose power would add to the misery of the war. It was becoming clear that no matter how hard Terrel tried to distance himself from the conflict, it was going to affect him – and his own mission – whether he liked it or not.

These musings had kept him awake for a while, but eventually he'd been unable to put off the inevitable. In the event his slumber had been undisturbed, and he'd woken refreshed, wondering what the new day would bring. Light had filled the room when he'd opened his eyes, but he'd had no idea of the time. Getting out of bed, he had dressed, and then wondered whether to go exploring. Reluctant to disturb the deep silence – and not wanting to make anyone think he was sneaking round like a spy – he'd chosen to study the map instead. Soon after that he'd been alerted by a sonorous tolling, which apparently marked the beginning of the day within the pyramid. Yarek had arrived, bringing the visitor some breakfast, but the boy had had no time to talk and had scurried off again. Shortly after Terrel had finished eating, the apprentice had returned and ushered him up to the wizard's workroom.

Showing unexpected agility, given her earlier performance, Tofana jumped up on to one of the tables and swung her arms wildly. It took Terrel a moment to realize that she was waving everyone else forward, but at a nudge from Yarek he went with the others as they crowded close to the northwest-facing wall – the wall that was now transparent. He found himself standing next to Tegan and Yarek, and wondered if this was by accident or design.

'What's happening?' he whispered.

'There's going to be an imaginary battle fought across that escarpment over there,' Tegan replied, pointing to a ridge running down from one of the mountains. 'The soldiers' positions are set by were-marks, and their subsequent movements will be based on observations of what happens in real encounters, both for our own men and the enemy.'

'But there's really nobody there?' Terrel guessed.

'Only our three trainee neomancers,' she told him. 'They'll take it in turns to assist our troops, then see if they can work as a team as well, both in attack and defence.'

'Defence against what?'

'The Wizard will be supplying the enemy magic to counteract our own.'

'That doesn't seem fair.'

'She'll only use the strength enemy neomancers would have,' Tegan explained. 'Together with a few tricks. The test will be to see if our neomancers can still win, and destroy the enemy while neutralizing their magic. It's the sort of thing they have to learn before they can be entrusted with the lives of real soldiers.'

'And Tofana will do all that from here?'

'Yes.'

'How will we know what's going on?'

'Just watch,' the magian said shortly, her patience evidently having run out.

Terrel did as he was told, but he didn't see how it was going to do him much good. As far as he could judge, even the nearest slopes of the battlefield were well over a mile away, and he had no idea where the were-marks – whatever they were – or the three would-be neomancers might be.

Another bell rang then, its deep note rolling out over the intervening crags even as it made the stone beneath his feet vibrate. Terrel assumed that this was the signal for the trials to begin, and was wondering what would happen next when his legs almost buckled under him. The air shivered and distorted as he found himself flying. He swayed backwards, thinking he was about to topple over the side of the pyramid, but then felt a steadying hand grip his arm. As his reeling senses recovered a little, he watched the escarpment come towards him at an alarming rate, growing bigger with every moment until it seemed to fill the whole horizon. Details of the terrain that had been quite indistinguishable were now plain to see, including the areas designated as military positions. The were-marks were faintly glowing outlines of men, some yellow, some grey.

When the landscape finally grew still, Terrel understood that the movement had been an illusion. Neither he
nor the escarpment had gone anywhere, but something had
happened to make their observation possible. He suspected
that the properties of the invisible wall that separated him
from the outside world had been altered once more. Now,
in addition to being transparent, it also magnified whatever
was on the other side. He remembered the telescope he'd
found in Muzeni's abandoned observatory at Havenmoon,
and guessed that this was a vastly more sophisticated and
powerful way of bending light.

'You could have warned me,' he breathed, but neither of
his companions took any notice. The first of the neomancers had set to work.

The mist rose from a patch of snow in an irregular
spiral, swirling into the sky and then moving quickly
across the ridge. Behind him Terrel heard Tofana mutter
something, and in an instant the new-born whirlwind flew
apart and evaporated. However, it was immediately clear
that this had merely been a diversion. The real threat
came from another emerging cloud that had drifted
serenely from a narrow defile much higher up the mountainside. The cloud was thick and grey, its bulges
concealing another source of power. Lightning flickered
and a sudden sheet of rain lashed down, but neither was
aimed at the enemy positions. Instead they were used to
set off an avalanche from a large snowfield above them. As
the boom of thunder reached the spectators, the first
cracks appeared in the hard-packed surface, and soon after
that the loosened snow began to slide in great waves,
exploding into powdery billows in places, flowing like
water in others. In spite of Tofana's efforts – which
managed to divide and divert part of the deluge – some of
the enemy locations were inundated. Murmurs of approval

rose all around Terrel.

After that, battle was joined in earnest. As each neo-mancer tested his skills against his mistress, the weather on the side of the mountain became a chaotic mixture of miniature tornadoes, sudden cloudbursts, blizzards and squalls. Drifting snow blocked some routes and made others treacherous; abrupt shifts in temperature added to the pitfalls a real army would have faced; lightning cracked and rocks split asunder; and pounding gusts of hail pelted the enemy to protect the movements of their own troops. At the same time, Tofana – in her role as the enemy neo-mancers – did her best to counter such attacks and launched some of her own, testing the defences of her pupils. Shields like the one Terrel had seen at Whale Ness sprang into life to protect what was beneath, while other more subtle methods were used to divert further forms of attack.

Tofana muttered constantly to herself, sometimes sounding annoyed, sometimes disappointed, but more often than not simply reacting to the drama unfolding before them with satisfaction and even a little excitement. Finally, however, when the three prospective neomancers were acting as a team and the mock battle was at its most intense, the wizard grunted, then spoke aloud.

'No, Dayak, you idiot! You're not ready for that. Leave it alone!'

Terrel was sufficiently distracted by the harsh words to notice that both Tegan and Yarek had glanced round uncertainly. Before he could ask what was happening, Yarek had turned and slipped away. Terrel would have followed him, but his attention was caught by a huge sheet of flame that shot out of the ground, splitting the escarpment in two. The fire was so intense that he stepped back, unable to believe he could not feel the heat of it.

'Fool!' Tofana shrieked. 'You go too far. Don't try to help him! Don't! It will only—' Her words were lost in the sudden hubbub as the view disappeared. The stone wall was back in place, as solid and impervious as it had first appeared – and the room was in pandemonium. The centre of the commotion was further back, near where the wizard had been standing. Following Tegan, Terrel pushed his way through the gathering crowd and saw Tofana kneeling over a prostrate figure. When she stood up, her face was contorted by fury, but it was Yarek's appearance that shocked Terrel to a much greater extent. The boy lay on the floor, gasping for breath. His lips were dry and cracked, his eyes feverish and staring. Huge angry blisters were rising on his hands and face, growing larger and more livid even as they watched.

A few moments earlier, the boy had been perfectly healthy. Now he looked close to a brutal and particularly painful death. It made no sense. Terrel remembered what had happened to Kalkara, a desert nomad girl, when she had thought – wrongly – that she'd seen a creature of fire and light called a tiarken. But her injuries had been real enough at the time – and Yarek's were even more serious.

'This is what happens when you interfere in the magic of others,' Tofana growled, glaring round at all her magians and apprentices. 'Dayak will not thank him for this, and Yarek himself has already paid the price for his stupidity.' She paused, her flashing green eyes coming to rest on the foreigner.

'Well, now!' she intoned, a faint smile replacing her frown. 'This gives us an opportunity to see our legendary guest in action. Come on, Terrel. Let's see you heal *that*.'

CHAPTER EIGHTEEN

The first thing Terrel felt when he came to was the water lapping gently at his face. For a moment he was seized by panic, which overcame the pleasant lethargy that pulled him down, and he tried to sit up. But he could only flail wildly and ineffectually, as warm liquid splashed over his face and chest. He spluttered, thinking he was going to drown, unable even to open his eyes.

'Be calm and still. Nothing can harm you here.'

The gentle voice floated out of the scented darkness, and Terrel found reassurance in its solicitous tone. He tried to do as he was told, and found it surprisingly easy. Taking a deep breath, he willed himself to relax – at least until he understood what was going on. Very deliberately, he took stock of his situation. He was lying on his back in water that supported him easily and in perfect comfort. There was clearly no danger of his sinking, let alone drowning. He was naked, but he felt warm and safe. What was more, for the first time he could ever remember, there was no pain in his crooked leg. Nothing at all, not even the smallest twinge. He flexed it now, hardly believing that it could be true, and felt the joints move slowly and easily. Then he grew still again, enjoying the wonderful sensation of being totally at ease. Sleep beckoned once more, and he gave into it contentedly. It

had been a very long time since he had felt so tranquil, so
free from any responsibility.

When he next awoke, it was to a vague feeling of disquiet.
He was still very comfortable and relaxed, but something –
perhaps from an unremembered dream – was nagging at
the back of his mind, telling him that all was not well. He
tried to ignore it, and to simply take pleasure in doing
nothing, but the annoying presence would not go away.

Opening his eyes with reluctance, he saw in the faint
glow of subdued rooflight that he was in a small cubicle.
He had already worked out that he must be in a healing
pool, and assumed that it was somewhere in the pyramid –
although for all he knew, he could have been taken back to
Saudark. He closed his eyes again, having seen all he
needed to see.

'That's right,' the unknown voice soothed. 'You've no
need to struggle. Your treatment's almost over.'

Part of Terrel didn't want it to be over. He wanted to
stay there for ever, cocooned in this artificial womb of
comfort and safety. But another part of him was struggling
to assert itself, reminding the healer that – for him – his
mother's womb had been anything but safe.

Memories, as unwelcome as they were necessary, began
to return in fragments. He saw Tofana dancing amongst
the cluttered tables. The shape of Whale Ness on the map.
A glass phial sailing through the air. The ghostly outlines
of the vanished pyramid walls. An avalanche. The vertig-
inous sensation as the escarpment rushed towards him.
Fire bursting from the mountainside. And Yarek, writhing
in agony.

He could not make sense of all the images, nor put them
in sequence, but each one increased his sense of unease.
Once again he fought against himself, simultaneously

wanting to hide the memories away and yet needing to explore them, like a tongue returning to a broken tooth.

He kept seeing Yarek's tortured face, and finally Terrel knew that he could not deny what had happened. Tofana's challenge had left him with no choice. Just as the neomancers had had to endure their trials, so he'd had to face his own. Kneeling beside the stricken apprentice, he had taken the boy's burning, blistered hand in his own, and had fallen into the hidden realm. He would normally have been able to seek out the pain and illness, in order to repel it, but on this occasion the experience was unlike anything he had encountered before. This waking dream had originated *outside* his patient. Terrel had to do more than heal Yarek; he also had to trace and remedy the *cause* of his ailment. And that had been far away, in another dream. Terrel had traced the links back to their source, and set aside their malign influence, before dealing with the boy's own pain and distress. He *had* been able to heal Yarek – but only at great cost to himself. He'd been engulfed by a black wave of exhaustion, and the next thing he could remember was waking up in the healing pool.

'Easy now.' A face wavered into view. 'We don't exactly know what you did, but it left you very weak.' Her eyes were kind, matching her voice. 'The pool will have restored what was necessary, but it might take you some time to adjust, so take things slowly.' She was gentle but strong, far stronger than he was. One arm was around his shoulders, each hand supporting him under his arms. 'Ready?'

Terrel nodded. He seemed to have lost the use of his voice.

'All right. Up on your feet.'

He moved, pushing down with his legs until they

encountered stone and driving himself from the warmth at the same time as she lifted him. Water ran from his body in rivulets, and even though the air was balmy, he shivered, feeling the loss of his cocoon.

'Don't worry if you feel wobbly at first,' she said, still holding his arms. 'I'm here, and even if you fall the water will protect you. How's that?'

Standing upright seemed alien, and Terrel felt slightly light-headed, but otherwise he was fine. It was even easier than normal to balance on his upturned right foot.

'I'm all right,' he whispered.

'Excellent. We'd better get you dressed, then. The Wizard's waiting to talk to you.'

Once Terrel was able to put on his own clothes, and his specially crafted boots, he became prey to mixed emotions. Although physically he felt fine, better than he had done for some time, several matters were now weighing heavily on his mind. But the servants who attended him barely spoke, and the magian who had helped him from the pool had left before he was able to formulate any questions, so he had to school himself to patience.

Outside the pool section of the pyramid, the air seemed fresher as well as cooler and less humid, and he realized that the air he'd been breathing while he was healing – and perhaps the water he'd been lying in – had been suffused with mitra. This made him feel even more uneasy, but as he left the fumes behind his head cleared, and he began to look forward to meeting Tofana and getting some answers from her.

He managed the long climb easily, but when he reached the wizard's workroom, he was glad to see that all the walls were firmly in place. On this occasion Tofana was the sole occupant of the top floor of the pyramid. She was bent over something on one of the tables, murmuring to herself, and either did not hear him come in or pretended not to. Terrel waited, not wanting to disturb her, while the servants who had escorted him retreated down the stairs. At one point he heard low voices coming from another part of the room, but he couldn't tell what the muttering buckets were saying, and so decided to ignore them as best he could.

Eventually the wizard straightened up, with a small groan, then turned and faced her visitor. Terrel had to stifle a smile; an optical instrument had been fixed over her left eye, which made it appear huge, several times larger than its twin. The monstrous green orb blinked, then widened in surprise. The wizard stretched her face, allowing the eyeglass to fall out into her hand, and gave Terrel a measuring look.

'So, you've recovered again?'

'Yes.'

'Well, come here then,' she commanded impatiently. 'Or are you going to stand there all day like a ten-year-old apprentice?'

Just at that moment Terrel felt as if he *were* about ten years old, and he moved forward like a reluctant pupil meeting his tutor. He had to remind himself that he was a grown man now, and even if he didn't feel comfortable as the wizard's guest, he ought to act as though he did.

'Think you can stay awake this time?' Tofana enquired.

This time? Terrel wondered, enduring her scrutiny with difficulty.

'I hope so.'

'Good. I was enjoying our talk earlier. Have you any more tricks you'd like to show me?'

Terrel's bewilderment must have shown, because she decided to explain further without any prompting from him.

'You could show most neomancers a thing or two. Even the good ones. Your handling of that tornado was particularly impressive.'

'I don't know what . . .' Terrel began, but a truly horrible suspicion was growing in his mind and he faltered, aware that Tofana was still watching him very closely. 'How long was I in the healing pool?' he asked at length.

'Three days the first time, two the second.'

It took a few moments for the significance of her answer to finally sink in.

'And it was the time in between when I controlled the tornado?'

'You don't remember?'

'Not really. It's all a bit like a dream.' He was improvising now. In fact it was only his imagination that was filling in the gaps in his memory. But that was bad enough. 'What happened, exactly?'

'Does this mean you *don't* have anything else to show me?' Tofana asked, ignoring his question.

'I'm a healer,' he replied awkwardly. 'I could—'

'I've seen that for myself,' she cut in. 'I'm more interested in the talents you *weren't* prepared to admit to when you got here.'

'I don't know what . . . Something must have happened. I'm not really a weather-mage.'

'Well, you were doing a pretty good impression of one two days ago,' the wizard remarked. 'Not feeling yourself then, eh?' A slow smile spread across her face.

She knows, Terrel thought. She may not know it was Jax, but she knows it wasn't me.

'Interesting,' Tofana said, as if the healer had spoken aloud. 'I thought there was something different about you then. Your lines had changed.'

The irony was not lost on Terrel. In the past, whenever

Jax had taken over his body, no one had been able to tell
the difference between them, and so he'd been blamed for
the prince's misdeeds. This time, when claiming to be
responsible for his actions might actually have gained him
some respect, the only observer who mattered *could* tell the
twins apart. Terrel didn't know what the lines she had
mentioned were, but he was willing to bet they had nothing to do with his physical appearance.

'Does this often happen to you?' Tofana asked. 'This
switch from one personality to another?'

'No,' he replied, deciding there was no point in trying to
deny that such a change had taken place. 'It's very rare.'

'What brings it on?'

'I've no idea,' Terrel lied. 'I think it just happens at
random.'

Tofana nodded, although her expression remained
guarded and he wasn't sure whether she believed him or
not.

'Does he have a name?'

'Jax.'

'I should like to meet Jax again sometime,' the wizard
said, confirming Terrel's fears.

'It's not something I can control.' He had no wish to
reveal his particular vulnerability to his brother when his
mind was affected by something like alcohol or mitra.
'Will you tell me what I – I mean Jax – did?'

'Oh, I haven't had so much fun in years!' Tofana
exclaimed, waving her arms in the air in one of her expan-
sive gestures. 'It's a shame you missed it.' She giggled,
suddenly sounding like a much younger woman. 'He came
up here, all pink-faced and bright-eyed from the pools, and
looked around as if he'd never seen any of this before –
which makes sense now. He was particularly fascinated by
the various samples of water. From that, the obvious next

step was the way such things translate to the outside world, and we ended up showing each other some tricks, as I said. He went a little too far in the end, of course, which was why he collapsed and was taken back to the pools.'

Terrel wanted to ask whether Jax had run out of strength or had simply become bored and decided to abandon his usurped body, but there was another possible interpretation of the wizard's words, and this made him hesitate. Had Jax and Tofana become embroiled in some sort of contest with their tricks? And if so, had his brother 'gone too far' by opposing the wizard in some way? It would have been a battle the prince was bound to lose. But he wouldn't have minded that; he'd have known he could leave at any time, and that he would not be the one left behind to face the possible consequences. And making trouble just for the sake of it would be the sort of thing Jax enjoyed.

'This is the first time I've seen either of you since his relapse,' Tofana added. 'Are you telling me you remember absolutely nothing about what happened?'

'I'm afraid not.' Terrel was glad to know that even Jax had his limits. Whatever the reason for his return to the pools, it had eventually enabled Terrel to reclaim his own form.

'Perhaps we should work at helping you call on the talents of this other self,' the wizard suggested. 'They could prove a valuable asset.'

Terrel was surprised by the way Tofana had simply accepted the presence of a second person within him – and he wondered whether she had come across something similar before. For himself, talking openly about Jax with a relative stranger had been an unnerving but strangely liberating experience. However, he'd had enough of it now.

'I don't think I want to do that,' he said. 'In any case, you might not want to make me too powerful. Some people in the Black Quarter still think I'm a spy.' This was not something he'd have chosen to bring up, but he was so anxious to change the subject that he'd jumped at the first thing that came to mind. He achieved his purpose, but Tofana's reaction was not what he had expected.

She laughed.

'I don't really care if you are,' she said. 'What are you going to do? *Heal* our armies into oblivion?'

'I could send information back to your enemies,' he argued, wondering why he was advancing such theories.

'If you do,' she replied cheerfully, 'it'll just be what we want them to hear. You really think you'd be allowed to betray anything important? You're simply another part of the game. We just have to decide how to use you.'

'You think the war's a *game*?'

'What else can it be? Boys will be boys. We just make the toys they play with a little more interesting.'

'But that's—' Terrel stopped. He'd been about to say 'insane', but had thought better of it. 'Have you ever considered all the wonderful things you could achieve if you put your magic to use for good? For peace?'

'Peace!' Tofana exclaimed derisively. 'You might as well go looking for Akurvellir. No one wants the war to stop. Why should they? If they weren't fighting, they wouldn't know what to do with themselves.'

Terrel found he had no way of countering that argument. Even though it was insane, it was the truth. All the soldiers he had met, from the general to patrolmen, appeared to be afraid of nothing and actually seemed to revel in the carnage. Their bloodthirsty enthusiasm and eager, even cheerful attitude to the conflict had been demonstrated often during his time on Myvatan.

'Nor would I, come to that,' Tofana muttered. 'My work is fascinating. You'll see that soon enough, even if the neomancer trials didn't convince you.'

Mention of the trials reminded Terrel of Yarek and his dreadful injuries.

'Is the boy all right?'

'He made a remarkable recovery. None of my magians could have done as much for him.'

'Could you?'

'Perhaps. But I don't waste my energies that way. That's what the pools are for.'

'What happened to him?'

'Ah, so you *are* interested,' Tofana said, chuckling.

'I've never come across such injuries before,' Terrel said. 'At least none that were inflicted in such a way.'

'Dayak made the first mistake,' the wizard explained. 'He's too clever for his own good. He'd make an excellent neomancer if he applied his talent wisely, but he overreached himself, tried to make use of power he couldn't hope to control. Earthquakes and volcanic activity *can* be used as weapons, but only under certain conditions, and under the supervision of very experienced people. Armies usually just try to take advantage of such things when they happen naturally.'

'Did Dayak try to *create* such an upheaval?'

'He nearly succeeded too,' Tofana replied, nodding, 'but he used too much of himself, left his defences open. Such power is not bought easily. Dayak's own lines became distorted and broken. He'd probably have died if Yarek hadn't intervened.'

'Yarek was trying to help him?'

'Exactly. I believe he and Dayak consider themselves friends. The boy is certainly talented, but this was beyond him. In trying to disentangle Dayak's lines, he disrupted his own – and suffered the consequences. He's lucky you were there to help him, or he'd still be paying for his error.'

'You think trying to help a friend is an error?'

'In this case, yes. And a potentially deadly one. I'm grateful to him, though. His efforts provided some insights that may well help my own research. Now, tell me about your healing. How do you do it?'

Terrel was wondering how best to answer this question when he was saved from having to respond by the unexpected arrival of another visitor. The mustela emerged from one of the holes in the wall and scampered across the floor, its claws skittering on the stone.

'Bezylum?' the wizard queried. 'What are you doing here?'

The rat-like creature answered with a nervous chattering, then – showing unexpected agility – it leapt up on to one of the tables, skidded on the wooden surface and scattered pieces of paper and stone in all directions. Coming to rest amid the debris, it stood up on its hind legs and chattered again. Its fur appeared to be standing on end, making it seem twice its normal size.

'Don't be silly, dear,' Tofana said. 'No one can do that. Not even me. And anyway, why would anyone *want* to?'

The animal shook itself and clicked its teeth, looking about with wild eyes. Tofana looked puzzled.

'We're busy here,' she pointed out. 'I'm sure you'll feel better soon. Now scram!'

Bezylum did not react well to the reassurance. Although the wizard clearly expected the mustela to leave, it did nothing of the sort. Instead it suddenly seemed quite demented, leaping to and fro as if trying to evade an invisible foe, and sending various objects flying over the side of the table.

'Bezylum!' Tofana shrieked, angry now. 'Stop that at once!'

But the rodent paid her no attention. In fact, its manic exertions became even wilder, until it misjudged one particular twisting leap, slid over the edge of the table and fell directly into a bucket full of water below. Tofana exclaimed in annoyance, but Terrel couldn't help laughing at the ludicrous spectacle. A moment later the laughter died in his throat as the mustela laboriously dragged itself over the rim of the container, flopped to the ground with a squelch and then shook itself vigorously.

'Perhaps that'll teach you not to be so stupid,' the wizard muttered.

Terrel didn't think so. But then he knew something Tofana did not. The spiky, bedraggled creature was no longer Bezylum. It was Alyssa.

CHAPTER NINETEEN

There's something really peculiar about this thing, Alyssa complained, still shaking water from her borrowed fur.

That's probably because— Terrel began, then saw Tofana glancing back and forth between the two of them.

Who's she? Alyssa asked. *A friend or an enemy?*

I'm not really sure, he replied truthfully, *but she's a wizard and—*

A wizard? Alyssa sounded understandably alarmed.

Yes, and there's—

Their silent exchange was interrupted by a fierce chattering from Tofana which was clearly directed at her strangely unbiddable doorman. Alyssa tensed at the sound, her damp fur becoming even more spiky.

Am I supposed to understand that? she asked.

Yes. She must be telling you to do something.

What?

I've no idea, but you ought to do something, even if it's the wrong thing. She was telling you to go away earlier.

But I've only just got here, Alyssa objected. *You've no idea how—*

'What's got into you, Bezylum?' Tofana grumbled. 'Get out of here before you make me really angry.' She added a further comment in the squeaking language of the mustelas, and ended in an unpleasant hiss.

You'd better go, Terrel said. *She might suspect something, and in any case, we can't talk here. I'll catch up with you as soon as I can.*

'I don't know why you're so fascinated with Terrel,' the wizard said, confirming the healer's fears. 'He's not the one who trained you. Or the one who feeds you.'

Go, Terrel urged. *There'll be another chance to talk later.*

We may not get another chance, Alyssa replied. *The window was only open a crack this time.*

Her cryptic comment dismayed Terrel. He'd waited a very long while to be able to talk to Alyssa, and the thought of missing this opportunity was appalling. But he knew their present situation was hopeless

You have to go, he told her. *I'll follow you.*

Finally bowing to the inevitable, Alyssa turned tail and scampered off, skirting around the edge of the room until she came to one of the rat-holes. As she disappeared inside, Terrel hoped she'd retained enough of Bezylum's memories and knowledge to find her way about in the dark maze of tunnels. If she got lost, she might not be able to locate him again before the window closed and she had to leave.

'That's not like him,' Tofana muttered. 'He's usually the most reliable of them all.'

'Perhaps he's ill?' Terrel suggested.

'It's lucky the alignment-potency of that meltwater wasn't too great,' the wizard added, glancing at the puddles around the bucket. 'Or he wouldn't have recovered so quickly.'

Her comment raised Terrel's level of unease another notch. He could only hope that, whatever the water might have done to Bezylum's body, it would not have affected Alyssa's invading spirit.

'I should leave you to get on with your work,' Terrel said as Tofana stooped to pick up some of the fallen objects and replaced them on the table.

'Right now you *are* my work,' she replied. 'You were going to tell me about your healing.'

'I'm not sure there's much I can tell you,' he said quickly. 'And I'd like to go back to my quarters now.'

'Not yet. You have to earn your keep first.'

'But—'

'It's not much to ask, is it?' Although the wizard had spoken mildly, there was a stubborn glint in her eyes and Terrel realized he had no choice.

Reluctantly, he launched into a hurried account of his progress as a healer, but the wizard would not allow him to rush his explanation, and demanded further details and examples of the experiences he was describing. Terrel eventually tried to curb his impatience, realizing that haste would only make the examination last longer. He wondered briefly what Tofana would do if he simply walked out, but he didn't have the nerve to try it.

Towards the end of the discussion, Terrel realized that he too was learning something new. The 'waking dream' that he used when healing was similar in concept to the 'lines' that — according to the wizard — lay inside everyone, and which were utilized in many of her magical processes, including the healing done in the pools.

'Of course, the lines aren't just confined to our bodies,' Tofana went on. 'They're everywhere, and they can be used for destroying things as well as mending them. Obviously, the more violent a tornado you can bring down upon your enemies, the more proof you have that the gods are on your side.'

Terrel couldn't tell whether the wizard was being sarcastic or serious. He wanted to know more about her work — but not now. He was desperate to get away and talk to Alyssa.

'Of course, the gods are supposed to be above such

things,' the wizard added, with a wry smile, 'but if that's the case, then why did they cause the Lunar Schism in the first place?'

'What's that?' Terrel asked, unable to restrain his curiosity.

'It all goes back to the last Great Conclave,' she replied. 'At Akurvellir, three hundred and seventy years ago. During a debate in the Circle of Truce, a dispute arose over Bvandir's comet and whether it could materially affect the orbits of the moons. That was easy enough to resolve, of course, but the more important aspect of the argument, the one that caused the divide, was whether Bvandir and all the other gods could arrange such things to suit themselves, or whether they were as much the victims of fate as we are.'

'And that caused the schism?'

'Yes. Black and Red against White and Gold.'

Terrel blinked, hardly believing the implications of what he was hearing.

'You mean that was the start of the war?' he exclaimed.

Tofana nodded.

'A point of philosophy?' Terrel was half shouting now. 'You've been fighting for hundreds of years over a tiny philosophical disagreement?'

The wizard shrugged.

'Such matters of theology were important then,' she said. 'Now it's just history.'

'Then why don't you *stop*? Thousands of people have died – your country is literally being torn apart – and all for nothing!'

'The hatred is sufficient reason now,' she explained. 'It's unquenchable. We just have to go on until we gain the victory we deserve.'

'That's insane,' Terrel declared, his earlier inhibitions swept aside by sheer horror.

'Hardly that. The gods themselves sanctioned the conflict.'

'How? What did they do?'

'Nothing.' Tofana smiled at the healer's astonishment.

'Then how . . .'

'The leaders of the four wizardly orders set out a covenant. The dispute would be settled by a sign from the gods. But none came.'

'They did nothing.'

'Exactly. Which proved our side of the argument, as far as I'm concerned. Of course, the White and Gold didn't see it that way at the time.'

'And the fighting began,' Terrel whispered.

'Yes,' Tofana admitted cheerfully.

'That's the most—' Terrel began, then stopped. He felt a mixture of outrage and revulsion at what he'd learnt, and knew that he couldn't stand to be in the wizard's presence a moment longer. Heedless of her attitude, he swung round and strode blindly towards the door. Once there he hesitated, glancing back. Tofana had already returned to her solitary pottering amongst her documents and samples, and appeared to have accepted his abrupt departure easily enough. Looking at her now, she seemed to be nothing more than an ineffectual eccentric, but Terrel knew better. Tofana and her kind were responsible for the continuing madness of all Myvatan.

As he turned to leave, hoping to find Alyssa, Terrel was halted by another, quite different voice – but one he knew just as well.

'You can't hide from your dreams,' one of the water buckets whispered. 'You never could.'

It was something Jax had said to him before Terrel even knew who he was, and to hear his brother's mocking tone coming from a supposedly inanimate object was doubly unnerving.

'And now you can't hide from me either,' the bucket added ominously.

CHAPTER TWENTY

The stupid thing even tried to drown itself rather than let me take over, Alyssa declared. *When it realized it couldn't stop me, it went beserk.*

All the mustelas are trained to be completely loyal to Tofana, Terrel pointed out. *Taking orders from anyone else must have been horrifying for him.*

It wasn't much fun from my point of view. I've never met such resistance before.

That's probably Tofana's doing. She can talk to them – not like this, but so they can understand each other. They must have a very strong link.

Which might make them wise to what I do, Alyssa concluded.

Terrel nodded.

Are you all right now?

Yes. I'm in control – for the moment, at least. He . . . what's his name?

Bezylum.

He's lying low, but I can't help feeling I'm being watched.

You think he might remember? Terrel queried. The only aftereffect shown by the other creatures Alyssa had inhabited had been a short-lived puzzlement.

I hope not. That could make things awkward for you.

I'm glad you're here, anyway.

To Terrel's immense relief, the mustela had popped

out of one of the rat-holes just as he was nearing his own room. No one had seen them go inside, and once the door was closed they had been able to relax in the knowledge that their privacy would be respected.

I didn't have any choice, Alyssa added, obviously still worrying about the possible consequences of her host's connection to the wizard. *There aren't any other animals in here.*

I'm just happy you were able to stay this long, Terrel said. After her earlier warning, he'd been afraid that she would be gone when he finally managed to get away from Tofana.

Sometimes, when the windows aren't open wide enough, it's necessary to break a few, Alyssa replied, sounding grim.

You haven't put yourself in danger, have you? he asked, not liking the tone of her voice. *You know that's the last thing I'd want. I mean—*

You're not the only one who needs these meetings, she said, cutting off his protest. *I have to keep an eye on you, don't I? What's the point of loving someone unless you try to look after them?*

For a few moments, Terrel was unable to respond. He'd known for a very long time that he loved Alyssa, and knew that the feeling was returned, but each time he was reminded of this fact he was swept by a wave of longing to see her in her own shape. Her presence in spirit, and the familiar sound of her voice, had been of great comfort to him during their years apart, but he wanted more. Even in his dreams he was denied the sight of the real Alyssa.

I'd look after you too if I could, he said quietly.

Someone else is doing that, she replied. *But don't worry, Terrel. I know what's in your heart.*

Moons! Are you two getting all slushy?

Elam's ghostly figure had materialized in a corner of the room, sitting cross-legged on the floor. Apart from being transparent and faintly luminous, he looked exactly like the fifteen-year-old boy he'd been when the warden of Havenmoon had stabbed him to death, and the expression of mock disgust on his urchin face was one Terrel remembered well. Since that time – over seven years ago – the boy's appearance hadn't changed at all. Had he lived, he'd have been a full-grown man by now, just like his friend. Setting aside that melancholy thought, Terrel grinned.

It's good to see you, he said.

At least you've got some decent accommodation for once, Elam remarked, looking around. *Even if it is a bit weird.*

All the rooms in the pyramid are this shape, Terrel told him.

Are the others with you? Alyssa asked.

They'll be along soon, Elam replied, his expression turning sour. *Let's just enjoy our time together first. I'm sick of having to be serious all the time. You're still not much good at cutting your own hair, I see,* he said, looking at the mustela.

The animal's fur was dry now, but it had set in clumps that gave it an uneven, unkempt look. The same had been true of Alyssa's own blonde hair, which she used to crop herself, careless of her appearance. The memory of it now almost overwhelmed Terrel. He thought back to the last time he had seen her – lying unconscious in a dungeon cell, a pale shape in the darkness as she began her long dreaming. Everything he had been doing since then was worthwhile in part because he believed he would get back to her eventually. Without that hope, he would have given up long ago.

Animals don't cut their hair, silly, Alyssa said, her laughter making the mustela chatter softly.

I've always wondered about that, Elam went on, grinning again now. *Why is it only human hair that keeps on growing? And why only on our heads?*

It could get a bit embarrassing if it happened anywhere else, Alyssa commented.

And I don't suppose you'd get too many people wanting to be barbers, Elam added.

Terrel found that he was blushing – which was mortifying – while laughing at the same time – which felt wonderful. There hadn't been much laughter in his life recently. It was good to have the three of them together again, even if they could never go back to the way they'd once been.

Almost like old times, isn't it? Elam said, echoing the sentiment. *Except that unlike the rest of us,* he's *growing up.* He peered closely at Terrel's face. *What* is *that?*

Terrel rubbed his chin, knowing that his recent attempts at shaving had been only partly successful.

My Aunt Melia had a better beard than that, Elam declared. *She was someone you wouldn't want to meet on a dark night, I can tell you.*

Terrel had never heard his friend joke about his family before. He had always referred to them in resentful terms. The fact that – like Terrel's parents – they had abandoned him to a madhouse had been one of the similarities that had drawn the two boys together in the first place.

Do you suppose I have aunts somewhere? the healer wondered.

When your father has seven wives, you're bound to have quite a few, Elam commented.

I don't know that I want to meet any of them – even in daylight, Terrel added. *I have all the family I need right here.*

A rat and a ghost? Elam exclaimed. *You're not fussy, are you?*

I'm not a rat, Alyssa stated haughtily. *I'm a mustela.*

I'm sorry, your ladyship, Elam said, bowing. *At least you should feel at home here. This whole island is mad.*

You felt that too? Terrel queried.

It would've been hard to miss. It's stronger in some places than others, mind you.

This was something Terrel hadn't known, but now Elam had mentioned it, it seemed to tie in with his own experiences. Just as he was about to ask how the newcomer knew so much about Myvatan, the air shivered and two more ghosts appeared. As they did so, Elam's smile turned to a resigned frown, and Terrel remembered the disquiet he'd felt at his friend's earlier comment. He'd been aware of friction between his spectral allies for some time, and the last thing he needed now was for that to get worse. The expressions on the faces of the latest arrivals did little to quell his anxiety.

How long do we have? Shahan asked quickly, looking down at Alyssa.

I'm not sure, she replied. *Long enough not to have to rush, I think.*

Good. With his great beak of a nose, his straggly beard and grey hair, Shahan looked just like the common perception of an imperial court seer – which had indeed been his role in life. *Hello, Terrel. It's good to see you again.*

And you. Do you have news for me?

We've a lot to tell you, but much depends on what you already know, Muzeni replied.

Even though his image was less sharp than that of the other ghosts – because he had died peacefully, centuries before them – the old man was an instantly recognizable figure. His colourful, outlandish clothes were unlike any Terrel had ever seen on anyone else, and his eyes still shone with heretical zeal. *So it would probably save time if you fill us in on what you've been up to since you got here.*

Terrel could see the logic of this argument and, in any case, he knew that was the way things always worked during their infrequent meetings. So he set aside his own impatience and tried to put his thoughts into some kind of order. His voyage on the *Skua* seemed a long time ago now – even though in reality he'd been on Myvatan for less than a month – and so much had happened since then that it took him a while to think back. Presenting his experiences in chronological order was the only sensible way to proceed, so he began with his conversations with Kjolur and the subsequent arrangement for him to go ashore at Whale Ness. Muzeni and Shahan were obviously pleased that the local legends seemed to be linked to their earlier discoveries, but they were clearly as uncertain as Terrel himself about the reasons for Ostan's change of heart.

Have you seen this Kjolur again since then? Shahan asked.

No. And I'm not likely to. The Red Quarter's on the opposite side of the island. Look, I'll show you. Terrel pulled out the map and pointed to where they were, then to Port Akranes. *And this is Whale Ness,* he added. *You can see why the whole peninsula is a forbidden zone. Most of it's in the Black Quarter because it's to the west of the dividing line, but because it's such a long spit of land, the only way to reach it from the main part of the island is to go into the Gold Quarter and double back.*

Unless you approach from the sea, as you did, Muzeni said, nodding.

That's right. I climbed the cliff directly below Savik's Whale, Terrel told them with a touch of pride. He went on to describe the sense of madness he'd encountered, the crystal city dream that had reinforced his sense of foreboding, and his adventures inside the stone whale. His audience remained attentive as he told them about the battle, his eventual capture and the journey to Saudark. With the benefit of what he had learnt more recently, he was also able to tell them something about the background to the war and its cause.

The war is everything here, he added. *No one alive has ever known anything else. The hatred is inbred. The wizards think of it as an elaborate game — with the soldiers as their willing pieces. Everyone else just goes along with it. It's awful.*

Does anyone here still think you're a spy? Muzeni asked.

A few of them are still suspicious, Terrel admitted, *but there's not much I can do about that. I keep telling them I don't want to get involved, but no one seems to be able to accept it.*

You're right to do so, Shahan muttered. *This isn't your war. Go on.*

Terrel obediently related his exploits in Saudark, describing the various people he had met and the things he had seen after he'd been accepted as a healer. The healing pools and the hall full of sleepers were singled out for particular mention.

After that I was brought here, he continued. Providing a description of the pyramid and its inhabitants took quite a while and, naturally enough, some of his recent discoveries were the subject of considerable interest.

Magic seems to be very important on Myvatan, Muzeni hazarded.

Yes. It runs through everything here. And it's all connected to water.

Alyssa gave a small chitter and Terrel sensed her discomfort.

No wonder . . . Muzeni began. *That would mean—*

That the elementals' belief is true, Terrel completed for him. *Water is a magical substance, at least in the hands of Myvatan's wizards and their neomancers.*

So this island is the worst possible place for one of the Ancients, Shahan concluded.

Exactly. There's so much water here, in every one of its forms – snow, ice, liquid, steam. And they make use of it all.

That explains a lot, Elam said grimly.

Terrel wasn't sure what to make of this comment, but his friend did not elaborate.

That's not my only problem, Terrel added, and told them about the time he'd lost when Jax had taken over. *He's a weather-mage, don't forget. He's in his element here.*

You'd better make sure you don't give him another chance then, Muzeni advised.

Which means avoiding this mitra stuff, Elam put in.

That could be tricky, Terrel said. *It's everywhere.*

Everywhere? Shahan queried.

Yes. It's not just in the pools, it's in every building I've been in – except this one – and even the soldiers' tents were full of the smell of it.

I wonder whether that might have anything to do with the general attitude to the war? Muzeni mused.

This idea made perfect sense to Terrel. The detachment he'd felt while under the herb's influence had dulled his outrage at the violence, as well as ultimately leaving him unable to defend his own body. In that moment he became determined to find out more about mitra and its effects.

You'll have to watch your step with Tofana, Shahan said. *She's probably going to want Jax to take over again sometime, so they can compare notes.*

Terrel hadn't considered that possibility.

You'll have to be on your guard, Muzeni agreed.

Are you a prisoner here? Elam asked. *Could she force you to inhale the stuff?*

I haven't actually been told I'm a prisoner, Terrel replied. *There's just no way to leave. It's as if the thought that anyone would ever want to is beyond belief. As far as I know, there's only one door to the outside, and the mustelas control that.*

So if you ever need to get out, Alyssa could occupy one of them again and help you to leave? Elam concluded.

I suppose so, Terrel replied, glancing at the quiet creature. *But she might need some of the others to go along with her and—*

If they're all as stubborn as this one, that could be a problem, Alyssa completed for him.

So if you're stuck here, Muzeni said, *could Tofana make you take mitra?*

My guess is that inside this pyramid she could do anything she wants. I'll just have to try to persuade her not to. She's preoccupied with a lot of other things at the moment. Terrel paused. *That's just about it, really,* he concluded, hoping they'd give *him* some news now.

As I see it, Shahan said slowly, *apart from the indications that brought you here in the first place, the only real corroboration that the fourth elemental is on the island is the presence of the sleepers.*

There's my dream too, Terrel said cautiously. *The crystal city is linked to the Ancient somehow – as well as to the sleepers.*

You said it was in pieces? Muzeni queried.

Yes. He'd been reluctant to talk about it too much in front of Alyssa, but as desperately as he needed her help and companionship, he did not want to endanger her – and the least he could do was warn her. *It was all fractures. The original structure was unrecognizable.* He'd known at the time that there was no chance of his being able to heal the shattered city.

And you think this could mean the Ancient here is either sick or mad? Muzeni said.

Yes. It might even be infecting the whole island. Terrel

looked at Alyssa again, hoping she'd be able to reassure him that her protection was still intact, but she remained silent, the rodent's hooded eyes giving nothing away.

Then it seems imperative that you locate the elemental as soon as possible, Shahan commented.

If it's as bad as I think, I'm not going to be able to heal it, Terrel warned.

Well, you've got to try.

No one else would even have a chance, Muzeni added. *And we'll do all we can to help you.*

Elam made a derisive snorting noise. Psinoma did not allow for genuine sound, of course, but the silent link could be just as eloquent as the human tongue.

What? Terrel asked. *What is it?*

Our friend here has been feeling a little low recently, Shahan said quickly.

This extended stay in your world isn't easy for any of us, Muzeni explained.

Oh, come on! Elam snapped. *That's not the problem. You know as well as I do that we're not* meant *to be here.*

As if to punctuate this emphatic declaration, someone knocked sharply on Terrel's door.

CHAPTER TWENTY-ONE

Everyone froze in place, the same thought running through each mind. Apart from Terrel, only a very few people had ever been able to see the ghosts, and they had usually been young children. But because so many of the pyramid's inhabitants had some sort of magical talent and training, it was possible that they'd be able to see into the spectral world. It was even possible that Tofana herself was outside – and Terrel doubted whether they could hide anything from her.

'Who is it?' he called out, nervousness making him brusque.

'I've brought your evening meal, sir. Shall I bring it in?'

With some relief, Terrel recognized the voice as belonging to one of the servants.

Shall we go? Shahan asked silently.

No. We'll risk it, but you'd better hide, Alyssa. Quick.

The mustela scampered across the room and disappeared under the bed.

'Come in!' Terrel called.

The girl entered with a tray, putting it down on the table in front of Terrel at his signal. She gave no sign of noticing the three ghosts, who remained quite still, watching her closely, and after Terrel thanked her she hurried out, closing the door behind her.

Definitely better accommodations, Elam said. *You've never had service like this before.*

Nobody responded to the light-hearted remark and, in truth, Elam's habitual flippancy had seemed forced. Terrel ignored the food. He had no stomach for it now.

What did you mean, you're not meant to be here?

Just that, Elam replied dourly, unable to meet the healer's gaze.

We don't have any choice, Shahan said.

You think I don't know that? Elam exploded. *But just by being here we're going to make things worse. You know we are.*

Make what worse? Terrel asked.

You wouldn't understand.

This dismissive comment was so unlike Elam that Terrel was hurt, and shocked into silence.

If we can keep the disruption to a minimum— Muzeni began.

How? Elam demanded. *Just because we're in this triangular box, it doesn't mean they're not aware of our presence.*

No, but—

Who are they? Terrel cut in.

This has nothing to do with your task, Shahan said.

You can't fob me off like that! On too many occasions in the past, Terrel had discovered – too late – that his ghostly allies had not told him all they knew. Their excuses – that they had done it for his own good, or because the information had seemed irrelevant – had already worn very thin.

And anyway, how can you be so sure? Elam asked belligerently. *What if this is another test?*

It goes way beyond that, Muzeni answered. *And besides, why should Terrel still need to prove his worth? Time and again he's—*

Not here, Elam countered. *Not to these gods.*

You have *to tell me what you're talking about!* Terrel shouted.

We can't, his friend replied, sounding wretched now rather than angry. *It would only make it worse.*

Then talk about something that is *useful. Otherwise we're just wasting time.*

The ghosts were obviously shaken by Terrel's unaccustomed venom.

I'm sorry, Shahan said eventually. *You're right. We should not be burdening you with our problems.* The seer glanced at Elam, who was hunched over, looking down at the floor.

I'm sorry too, the boy said quietly.

Reluctantly, Terrel accepted that he was not going to learn any more. Even so, he was still feeling both distressed and indignant, and he was glad when Muzeni took the lead in bringing up a topic relevant to his own progress.

Assuming they're going to let you out of this place eventually, the heretic began, *and regardless of the elemental's state of health or mind, you're going to have to try to track it down. Do you have any idea where it might be?*

No, not really, Terrel replied. *The one in Misrah settled in the most remote place possible, but that was because it was also the driest place it could find. The trouble with Myvatan is that there's water everywhere.* He pulled the map out from under the tray and pointed to the middle section. *The central part of the island is furthest from the sea, but it's covered by an enormous permanent ice field, so it's not likely to be anywhere there. But there are rivers, springs and other glaciers spread all over. I just don't know where it could have gone to escape the water.*

Do you think that's why it's gone mad? Shahan asked. *Because it couldn't find a safe resting place?*

I doubt it. If what I saw and felt in the dream was accurate, then I think it must have been caused by something worse than that. Even the Ancient in Talazoria was nowhere near as bad, and it was surrounded by a moat.

Which doesn't get us very far, Elam concluded, rejoining the discussion. *Have you heard any rumours or gossip that might help you?*

Not that I can think of.

What about local legends? Muzeni asked.

Nothing that seems relevant.

After a few moments, Shahan pointed out another problem.

If the war is going on all the time, it's going to make travelling difficult, let alone tracking the creature down.

The war doesn't go on all the time, Elam said. *Perhaps Terrel could use the period of hibernation, when everyone else is asleep.*

Maybe, the healer responded. *But what if I fall asleep too? There's no way of knowing how I'll react when the time comes.*

And it will be horribly cold then too, Shahan added. *It might be hard for Terrel to survive on his own.*

Anyway, that's months away. It would mean me having to stay here almost a year. I'd rather get on with the search sooner if I can. Terrel paused. *Wait a moment. Surely you can find out roughly where the Ancient is! All you have to do is to travel round the island with Alyssa and find out where the wind comes from.*

In the past, each of the elementals had been surrounded by a power that could not be felt by anyone in Terrel's world, but which had repulsed the ghosts with the force of a hurricane. The trouble was that with each successive discovery, the distance at which they were held had increased. If the same thing happened this time, they wouldn't be able to pinpoint the strange entity's exact position but they *could* confirm its presence.

When none of the ghosts answered immediately, Terrel was worried.

What's the matter?

We've already tried that, Shahan admitted. *It didn't work.*

You didn't feel it at all? But that means the Ancient can't be here!

The ghosts glanced at each other.

It's not as simple as that, Muzeni said. *We* did *feel something, but . . . it was so erratic it was impossible to draw any conclusions.*

It's as though it's there sometimes but not at others, Shahan added.

At first we thought it must be moving around, the heretic went on, *but the fluctuations are too chaotic for that. Nothing is consistent – the strength of the force, its direction, even the places it affects. So we can't be any help, I'm afraid.*

The only thing we can say for sure is that the elemental here – assuming that really is what's producing the wind – is different from all the others, Elam said.

It's lined up differently, Terrel murmured.

What?

Nothing. He didn't want to articulate his fears. *It sounds as though this isn't the first time you've been to Myvatan.*

We've been here several times, Shahan confirmed. *Whenever we could. But it's always been the same. You'll have to trace the Ancient by some other means, I'm afraid.*

Fishing for treasure, Terrel whispered.

In the meantime, Muzeni said, sounding a little more positive, *there are aspects of our own researches at home that may be useful.*

Tell me. In the past, such guidance as Terrel had received from the seers had proved confusing and dangerous at times, often only becoming clear in retrospect. Nevertheless, one way or another it had usually led him closer to his eventual goal, and in his current situation it was certainly better than nothing.

We're short on specifics as yet, Shahan began, sounding uncharacteristically apologetic, *but the background's becoming a little clearer at least. The seers are still monitoring the changes to the Dark Moon, but it took them longer than it should have done to realize that the orbits of the other three are now being affected too.*

Most people know that, Terrel claimed. *The sailors who brought me here were certainly aware of it.*

Yes, well, Kamin and the other court seers aren't exactly quick on the uptake, Muzeni commented, with a return to his normal disdain for Shahan's former colleagues.

To be fair, the seer commented, *the changes were quite subtle to start with. They still are, in fact.*

Are the changes because of the Dark Moon, or is something affecting each moon separately? Terrel asked.

It almost certainly stems from the Dark Moon, Muzeni replied, *but no one's been able to prove that conclusively yet. What it has done is make the calculations for predicting the next confluence fearfully complicated.*

Even we've had trouble with it, Shahan admitted, *and with Lathan still a sleeper, there's no one in Makhaya who's really up to the task. As it is, the one thing we can definitely say is that it keeps getting earlier.*

There are several different possibilities, Muzeni went on, *depending on whether the changes continue, and at what rate, but the most likely projection now puts it between ten and twelve years from now. That's only thirty-two to thirty-four years after the last one, rather than the seventy-five it's always been before.*

Terrel and Jax had been born on the night of the last

four-moon conjunction, which was why their lives had always been under particular scrutiny.

That's less than half the previous cycle, Shahan pointed out.

But it's still a long way off, Elam said.

It's not going to take me ten years to find the last elemental, Terrel agreed. *Wherever it is.*

Perhaps it's not the last one, Elam suggested.

The healer frowned at this idea. He had assumed that once he'd completed his task on Myvatan, he'd be free to start the long journey back to the Floating Islands. But if there was yet another Ancient, the nature of his bargain would force him to seek it out before he could go home.

Even if this is the last one, Alyssa said, *it's still going to take you some time to get back to Vadanis. That's where the circle closes.*

Not that long, I hope! Terrel exclaimed. He wanted to talk about the prospect of seeing her again, but he felt awkward about expressing such a sentiment in the presence of the others — and then he was distracted by the mustela's odd behaviour. Unnoticed by any of the others, she had crawled out from under the bed and was now lying on her back in a most unratlike pose, with all four legs in the air. *Are you all right?*

I'm fine. Keep talking.

Are we running out of time?

No. I just need to concentrate.

Concentrate on what? Terrel wondered, but he knew he'd get no answer. Turning back to the others, he found Elam grinning, his eyebrows raised.

Practising her backstroke? he suggested.

Terrel smiled. Alyssa had always refused to join the boys when they swam in the lake at Havenmoon. She hadn't even liked getting splashed.

The Tindaya Code still seems to indicate that this is the last one to be found, Muzeni said, returning the discussion to its original course.

And in any case, we're getting ahead of ourselves, Shahan commented. *Until Terrel renews his bargain with the Ancient here, this is all speculation. In that sense, it doesn't matter if there are any more.*

It matters to me, Terrel thought, but didn't say anything.

Have there been any new developments with the Code? he asked instead.

Actually, quite a lot, the seer replied. *There's been a huge increase in the scope for new research recently.*

Really? Why?

You might find this hard to believe, Shahan answered, *but it's because of Jax.*

You mean he's actually been helpful for once?

Not deliberately, I'm sure, Muzeni remarked, *but his actions certainly led to the new discovery.*

What did he do?

He came across a reference to a spring at Tindaya, Elam said. He had made it his duty to keep an eye on the prince ever since the allies had discovered that Terrel's destiny was linked to his brother's.

On top of the mountain? the healer enquired.

That's what surprised everyone. It made no sense to take it literally. Interpreters had always assumed it was just a poetic notion — a fount of knowledge, or some such phrase — but Jax insisted on an expedition to find the source of what he called the 'sacred water'.

And because almost everyone there still thinks he's the Guardian, Muzeni put in, *no one was prepared to argue with him. The extraordinary thing is, he was right.*

He told them where to dig, Elam said, taking up the story, *and they discovered an underground chamber, a cellar no one had even known existed. When they finally broke through, the workers were almost swept away. The entire room had filled up with water. After it emptied out, they found a small spring bubbling up from a hole in the floor – but that wasn't all. The walls and even the ceiling of the chamber were covered with writing and signs.*

It's another part of the Code, Shahan said, *one that no one's ever seen before, and it's provided a whole new field for study. For us, as well as for Kamin's people.*

Jax wasn't much interested in that, though, Elam nodded. *He just wanted the water. He insisted on taking samples of it back to Makhaya, and building a system of channels and reservoirs so that in future supplies would always be available when he needed them.*

This was beginning to sound unpleasantly familiar to Terrel, and he understood now that there had been another reason for the ghosts finding Myvatan's link between magic and water so disturbing. The prospect of Jax as a wizard did not bear thinking about.

Has he done anything with the samples yet?

Not as far as I know, Elam replied. *But two days ago he left for Betancuria, taking some of the water with him.*

Terrel was unable to conceal his dismay. Betancuria was the mining area near the centre of Vadanis where he had encountered the first of the Ancients. It had made its lair in the disused workings, and part of his initial bargain with the creature had been to promise that it could remain in the mines undisturbed. Jax had already broken that promise, and now seemed to be intent on doing so again, but this time he might be armed with a magical weapon that would terrify the elemental. The possible consequences of that were too appalling to contemplate.

I wasn't able to follow him there, of course, Elam added regretfully.

We just have to hope Kamin doesn't let him do anything too stupid. Shahan did not sound very confident. *In the meantime, we're left with the new section of the Code.*

Does any of it apply to what's happening here? Terrel asked, trying to rid himself of the dread he felt at this latest news of his twin.

We think so, yes, Muzeni replied. *For a start, there's mention of a group of creatures — some people say snakes — who eat ice and possibly even live inside ice.*

Ice-worms? Terrel wondered, remembering the soldiers' comments about his eyes.

Could be. Have you seen them?

No. And I don't think I want to. How do they fit into the prophecy?

Believe it or not, Shahan told him, *they're supposed to become bodyguards to the Guardian.*

They're protecting the Ancient?

It seems like it, but it's hardly going to need protecting from you, is it? The Guardian and the Mentor are allies.

It hasn't always felt like that, Terrel muttered.

The central premise of the Tindaya Code was that a hero, known as the Guardian, who had been born — or perhaps awoken — on the night of one lunar confluence, would fulfil his destiny at the time of the next four-moon conjunction, and in doing so prevent an upheaval that would destroy most of Nydus. The other main figure in the prophecy was the Mentor, described as a go-between, or translator, who was supposed to teach the Guardian to distinguish between good and evil. The ghosts' latest thinking was that the entity was the Guardian, and that Terrel, as the link between them and humanity, was the Mentor. Everything they did was based on that assumption, even though – like most oracles – the Tindaya Code was frustratingly ambiguous.

The same section of inscriptions also describes a 'city drowned beneath the sea', where a 'sacred flame burns even in the darkness', Muzeni stated. *Have you heard of anything like that? In one of the legends?*

Terrel shook his head. A vague memory nagged at the back of his mind, but he couldn't place it.

Well, see what you can find out, Shahan suggested. *It could be important.*

And there's another passage that's interesting, Muzeni went on. *Do you remember the inscriptions at Y-Harah?*

I never saw them myself. Terrel had been blind at the time. *But I remember being told about them.*

Well, one of the carvings there referred to a pendulum. The same motif is repeated at Tindaya, but this time it seems to imply that the pendulum is not swinging through the air but through water, possibly the sea, until it becomes fixed in place.

By a curse? Terrel asked.

I don't remember anything like that, Muzeni said, glancing at his colleague for confirmation. *Why do you ask?*

Because one of the legends here describes how Myvatan travelled back and forth across the ocean, as a floating, mobile fortress, until it was set in place by their enemy's curse.

Interesting, Shahan responded. *So you think Myvatan might be the pendulum. We'll have to look at that section again. It also contains an obscure reference to the Dark Moon, just as the one at Y-Harah did, so I'm sure it's connected to your task.*

None of this really helps me, though, Terrel said.

I suppose not, but it might be useful later as we learn more. Is there anything else?

There's a very strange reference to a family becoming starlight, but we can't make head nor tail of that.

Could it be anything to do with my star? Terrel glanced at his left hand. That was where, under special circumstances, the invisible amulet that he carried within him appeared. He had captured it at Tindaya during the first total eclipse Nydus had ever experienced. The Ancients referred to it as his 'spiral', but to human eyes it looked just like a miniature star.

It's possible, Shahan conceded, *though I don't see how.*

Are there any eclipses involving the Dark Moon forecast some time soon? Terrel asked. In the past, he'd been able to make remote contact with the elementals during those rare and awe-inspiring events.

None here that we can foresee, Muzeni replied at once, as if he'd been expecting the question. *But if the orbits keep changing, you never know.*

The only other translations we've managed so far are some lines about 'crossing a bridge between the clouds', and a warning to 'beware the fire within', Shahan added.

And I don't suppose you know what they mean either? Terrel remarked resignedly.

Don't eat too much spicy food? Elam suggested.

I don't suppose the people who built the temple were too concerned about our digestion, Terrel replied, grinning nonetheless. *It's frustrating, though. I keep getting warnings I don't understand. When I saw Alyssa on the* Skua, *she told me not to trust my own instincts.*

The ghosts all looked at the mustela.

I don't remember much about that visit, Alyssa said, rolling over on to her stomach and then squatting up on her hind legs.

We were trying to warn you about the perils you were facing, Muzeni told Terrel. *We couldn't come ourselves, and Alyssa offered to act as messenger. It seems she got a little confused.*

As it turned out, things went as well as we could have hoped, Shahan added, *but it might have been very different. Playing with legends can be a dangerous business.*

But you wanted Terrel to do it all the same, didn't you? Elam's faintly accusing tone was not lost on the seers.

We had little choice, Shahan argued. *He had to come ashore somewhere, and his exploits* have *given him access to much more than any orthodox arrival would have done. It led him here.*

The fact that the seer had bothered to defend his own actions to the boy was another sign of the change in the relationship between the ghosts. When Terrel had first come to know them, both Shahan and Muzeni had regarded Elam with an amused tolerance that was not far short of contempt. It was very different now – almost as though the boy was the one who held the reins of power within the trio. In the ghosts' world, it was possible that Elam *had* grown up.

CHAPTER TWENTY-TWO

There's no point worrying about the past, Terrel told them, as anxious as ever to avoid any disputes among his friends. *It's what happens next that's important. Is there anything else I should know?*

You've moved again as far as the predominant lunar alignments are concerned, Muzeni said. *You're in the sphere of the Red Moon here.*

Fire and violence, Terrel thought. That's appropriate for Myvatan. And love, he reminded himself. Don't forget that. Unconsciously he glanced at Alyssa before returning his attention to the ghosts.

I've lost track of the cycles since I've been in here. What is the Red Moon now?

It'll be full in six days' time, Shahan replied.

And the others?

The Amber was new two days ago, the White will be full tomorrow night and the Dark Moon was full yesterday.

Everything changing, Alyssa remarked.

The wizards here know that their respective powers alter according to the relative strengths of their moons, Terrel said. One way or another, everyone on Nydus was in thrall to the moons.

Shahan and Muzeni nodded, apparently having come to the end of what they wanted to say.

There's something else you can tell me, Terrel said. *Apart from anything Jax might do with what he's learnt here, is there anything on Vadanis that's being affected, or is likely to be affected, by what I'm doing on Myvatan?* Much to his dismay at the time, the earlier threats that he'd had to deal with had expanded to include his homeland, regardless of how far away he had been. The last thing he needed now was to have to worry about the safety of the island where Alyssa still slept.

Not as far as we know, Shahan answered.

Good.

But ultimately, all of Nydus will be affected, Muzeni pointed out.

He knows that, Elam snapped irritably. *And so will—*

What's she doing? Shahan cried in sudden alarm.

Terrel swung round to look at the mustela. It was holding one of its forelegs up to its mouth and was gnawing at something in the fur. At the seer's cry, it looked up, its beady eyes flaring, and Terrel saw that the rodent's teeth had been chewing on Alyssa's ring.

What are you doing? he gasped, his heart pounding at the thought of what might happen if that precious link was destroyed.

I . . . I . . . Alyssa sounded bewildered.

Is it all right? Terrel asked, getting down from his stool to inspect the animal's forepaw. To his great relief the ring was still intact, if a little frayed. *What were you trying to do?*

It wasn't me, she muttered angrily. *This . . . this thing keeps trying . . .*

I think we should leave, Shahan offered. *She obviously won't be able to take the strain for much longer.*

No, Alyssa responded. *I'm all right now. You can go on.*

Terrel was just as concerned as the seer, and he was about to tell her that when something happened to throw all his thoughts into confusion. Although Terrel couldn't feel anything, it had suddenly become clear that the ghosts were being affected by a strong, blustery wind blowing across the enclosed room. Their clothes and hair were flapping wildly, and Muzeni was having difficulty keeping himself upright. From the expressions of panic on their faces, Terrel guessed that they were terribly afraid – and knew that the meeting was finished now, no matter what Alyssa thought. He had never seen the ghosts in this state before.

We . . . have . . . to . . . Shahan gasped.

Go! Terrel shouted, making it an order.

The three ghosts vanished instantly, and the room was still once more.

Did they get away safely? Terrel asked.

I think so.

You think *so?*

I couldn't exactly follow them, could I?

Terrel calmed down, recognizing the sense of her argument.

That was the elemental, wasn't it?

Yes.

Is it still blowing?

Yes. It's even stronger now. I won't be able to leave for a while yet.

But you're all right?

Of course. As long as I'm in the shape of an animal, there's no problem.

Even this one?

He is giving me more trouble than usual, but I'm still in control.

Can I do anything to help you?

Just keep talking to me, Alyssa replied. *Did you manage to discuss everything you wanted?*

I wanted to tell them that I feel the other three elementals

*were somehow guiding me on the journey here. That's a good
sign, don't you think?*

*You mean there was a link between them and the one here
even before you arrived?*

*Yes. It might be that they're aware their 'brother' is sick,
and they want me to help him.*

*Let's hope so. I have the feeling you're going to need all the
help you can get this time.*

*Do you know what's happening with the other elementals
now?*

*No, but I know Shahan and Muzeni have a theory that
they only came up to the surface of the planet recently – in
their terms, at least. When you're as old as they are, a few
years, even decades, are the mere blink of an eye.*

Terrel considered this. He was quite willing to believe
the theory because it coincided with his own impressions.
It would surely have been impossible for the Ancients to
remain undetected for so long unless they had been buried
deep within the rock and fire at the heart of Nydus. But
quite why they should have chosen to rise now – and thus
unknowingly disrupt so much human activity – was still a
mystery. As yet, all Terrel knew for certain was that it
must somehow be connected to the changes in the course
and size of the Dark Moon.

What are they trying to do? he wondered.

I've no idea, Alyssa confessed. *But I guess we'll find out
at the next four-moon confluence.*

Whenever that is, Terrel agreed, nodding. All their fates
seemed to be leading up to that one shifting point in the
future.

The mustela began to fidget, and Terrel quickly began
to speak again. They had already been talking long into the
night, but he wanted to keep her mind alert in case
Bezylum tried to reassert himself again.

Do you know why they were arguing? What's the problem they wouldn't tell me about?

They won't talk to me either, she replied, rather resentfully. *I can only think there must be something wrong in their world.*

Is it because they can't 'move on', that they're still stuck here helping me?

No, I don't think so. That is affecting them, Elam most of all, but this is something different. Maybe I should ask some of the ghosts here.

There are ghosts on Myvatan?

Too many, Alyssa replied mysteriously. *They're everywhere.*

I haven't seen them. Terrel had no idea what she was talking about.

You haven't been looking, she told him. *The corners are different here.*

Alyssa had always seen ghosts – even back at Havenmoon, where the dead were often just as insane as the living inmates. She had told Terrel that ghosts 'walked differently' and that, for most people, they were always 'just around the next corner', but after the adventures of the last few years, Terrel had come to believe that this was a corner he could now see around. Apparently that was not always true.

Are there any here now? he asked.

Of course not. The wind is blowing. But when it stops you won't have to look far.

Really?

I told you about them earlier.

You did?

You'll find out soon enough. Although ... She broke off, and the mustela cocked its head to one side as if listening to something.

Although what? Terrel prompted hopefully.

The palace builders have lots of names, Alyssa remarked obscurely. *If I can't rest, I'll sleep here.*

Is that wise? Won't Bezylum—

He can share my dreams if he wants to, she decided, with a touch of mischief in her voice. So saying, she jumped up on to the bed and curled into a ball. Almost immediately her breathing slowed to the rhythms of sleep, and Terrel was left alone.

He spent the next hour revising everything he had learnt, and picking at the food that had been left for him. He hadn't expected to have much of an appetite, but when the mustela finally stirred, he was surprised to see that the plates were all empty.

The trouble with breaking windows, Alyssa remarked drowsily, *is that you sometimes get hurt.*

Are you hurt? Terrel was used to her abrupt way of starting conversations in the middle, and was only concerned with the implications of her words.

No, but then I haven't tried to close it again yet.

I don't want you taking any unnecessary risks.

Too late for that now, she told him. *The wind's stopped, and I have to go.*

Terrel had been expecting this.

Goodbye, he said quietly, trying to hide the sadness he felt at her impending departure. *You'll come back soon, won't you?*

Of course. There are a lot of twists and turns ahead of us. She was referring to the unknown road that Terrel had been following for the last seven years, and to the critical points along the way where she had been able to join him.

Good.

Aren't you going to open the door? she asked patiently.

Why?

Because if Bezylum comes to in here, he's going to know you've been up to something – even if he remembers nothing of the last few hours.

Terrel nodded, feeling stupid. He got up and opened the door, peering both ways down the dimly-lit corridor.

All clear, he reported.

Alyssa jumped down from the bed and rubbed briefly against his ankle on the way out. Terrel watched her scurry away until she disappeared into one of the rat-holes, then he went back inside and lay on the bed, feeling the small patch of warmth where she had just been sleeping. For some reason it made him want to cry.

A short while later, he felt a tiny wrench inside his heart and knew she was gone. He was truly alone once more.

CHAPTER TWENTY-THREE

The sound of bells invaded the end of Terrel's formless dream, so that when he awoke he imagined he could still hear the last echoes of their tolling. Opening his eyes so that the ceiling brightened into life, he wondered how long he'd been asleep, and whether it was the next day or still the middle of the night. Then he realized that the bells in his dream had almost certainly been prompted by a real one – the one that roused the inhabitants of the pyramid from their beds. He was in no hurry to confront a new day – he was still struggling to come to terms with everything that had happened the day before – but a knock on the door made it clear that he was to have no choice in the matter.

'Come in!' he called, assuming it would be a servant with his breakfast. But when the door opened he saw that his visitor had come empty-handed. There was a look of serious determination, mixed with a little trepidation, on Yarek's face as he came forward, making it obvious that this visit was an onerous duty rather than a social call. The apprentice showed no sign of his earlier injury. His skin was smooth and unmarked.

'I came to thank you,' he blurted out. 'I would've come sooner, but I only just found out you were back from the pools.'

'You've no need to thank me,' Terrel replied, sitting up

and smiling at the boy's earnest expression. 'I'm a healer. It's what I do.'

'But you didn't need to. It was my own fault.' Yarek almost faltered then, but forced himself to go on. 'If you hadn't been there, I could have died. I brought it on myself, and I deserved—'

'No one deserves to suffer like that,' Terrel cut in. 'Especially not for trying to help a friend.'

Yarek looked up, meeting the foreigner's gaze for the first time. What he saw there seemed to calm him a little.

'Even when it's forbidden?' he queried. 'When I knew it was wrong?'

'Forbidden, maybe,' Terrel replied. 'Wrong, no. You can't measure friendship in that way.'

'I *did* save Dayak,' the boy stated quietly.

'Then you have no reason to regret what you did.'

'I don't. I never even thought about what I was doing. It just happened. But you didn't have to help me. You used up a great deal of your strength.'

'Actually, Tofana didn't give me much choice, but I hope I'd have acted on instinct anyway, just as you did.'

'Does that mean you're my friend?' Yarek whispered.

'I'd like to be.'

Terrel's words were rewarded with a shy smile from the boy, which faded quickly as something else occurred to him.

'Even when what I did meant that you were left . . . vulnerable?'

Terrel surmised that the news of Jax's appearance had become common knowledge in the pyramid.

'That's gone and forgotten,' he lied. 'I'm fully recovered now – and even Tofana seemed pleased by the eventual outcome. In some ways, at least.'

'She was very angry with me and Dayak,' Yarek admitted.

'Still is, in fact. But she *did* learn something from it. I'm not sure what it was, but she's been quite excited these last few days.' He fell silent then, perhaps aware that he should not be discussing the wizard's business so freely.

'Has Dayak recovered?' Terrel asked.

Yarek nodded.

'He had to spend a day or so in the pools after they brought him back, but he's fine now.'

'Then all's well that ends well.'

'I should go. Thank you again.' The apprentice's eyes were downcast, and he looked so meek that the image from Terrel's earlier dream – of the boy as an insane sorcerer with the eyes of a dragon – seemed ludicrous.

'Do you have to go? I'd like to talk.'

'What about?' Yarek asked, unable to keep the eagerness from his voice.

'What can you tell me about the ice-worms?'

If Yarek was surprised by the question, he gave no sign of it, and at Terrel's suggestion he settled himself on the stool.

'I've never seen one myself, but I'm told they can grow up to six paces in length, and the biggest ones are much thicker than a man's body. They're mostly white, but sometimes you can see right through them, as if they're made of living crystals. They live in all the glaciers.'

'*In* the glaciers?' Terrel queried. That tallied with what the ghosts had told him, but he still didn't see how it could be possible. 'You mean actually inside the ice?'

'Yes. They tunnel through it.'

'How do they do that?'

'No one knows for sure. Some people say they melt the ice and swim through it before it freezes again behind them. Others say they *eat* their way through.'

Neither method sounded at all plausible, but Terrel knew that these creatures were unlike anything he'd come across before, so he was in no position to dispute the theories.

'Do they live in groups?'

'No. They usually travel alone.'

Terrel frowned, sure that Muzeni had referred to a *group* of animals.

'Do they ever come to the surface?'

'Only rarely. The best way to see them is from above, where the ice is clear enough. Some prospectors follow them that way. They believe the worms will lead them to mineral deposits.'

'Really?'

'There's all sorts of things embedded in the glaciers,' Yarek explained.

Terrel nodded, wondering how creatures who lived in an environment so hostile to the elemental could possibly act as its bodyguards.

'What made you ask about them?' Yarek enquired.

'The soldiers who brought me here told me about them. They said my eyes reminded them of the ice-worms.'

'I can see what they mean,' the boy said, 'but ice-worms don't have eyes. They don't have any features – apart from a mouth, of course.' He shuddered slightly.

'Are they dangerous?'

'Not usually. They keep to themselves most of the time. But I wouldn't want to pick a fight with one.'

'Neither would I,' Terrel agreed. 'At the moment I don't think I'd even like to *meet* one. Can I ask you something else?'

Yarek nodded.

'Is there a drowned city somewhere off the coast of Myvatan?'

'I don't think so.' The boy was obviously puzzled.

'There's supposed to be a sacred flame burning there,' Terrel went on.

'Oh, you must mean Akurvellir. That wasn't drowned, it was lost. But it's just a legend. Most people don't think it ever existed in the first place, and even if it did, it disappeared hundreds of years ago.'

Belatedly, Terrel realized where he'd heard the name before, and understood why Tofana's inference had been that 'looking for Akurvellir' was a hopeless task.

'How did it come to be lost?'

'It apparently happened during a hibernation. The city was there when people went to sleep, but when they woke up it was gone.'

'Even for a legend, that doesn't make much sense,' Terrel commented.

'Not many of them do. And as you may have noticed, we have a lot of legends here.' Yarek's timid smile reappeared briefly.

'So you've no idea where it is?'

'I wish I did. The Circle of Truce is there – that's where the flame is supposed to be – and it's said that it needs to be relit before the war can end.'

'You want the war to end?' Terrel asked, surprised.

'I want us to win,' the apprentice said, looking nervous again.

'That's not what you meant, though, is it? The Circle of Truce is a place of peace, isn't it?'

'I'd better go,' Yarek mumbled, standing up. 'The Circle of Truce never existed. It's just a silly idea.'

'Do you really believe that?'

The boy nodded, but didn't speak.

'Why did you really come here?' Terrel asked. 'To the pyramid, I mean.'

Yarek didn't answer, and it seemed to the healer that he was engaged in some sort of internal debate.

'I can keep a secret,' Terrel told him softly.

'I wasn't like the other boys,' Yarek whispered. 'I didn't want to fight, so they laughed at me. I had to lie about it to everyone. I thought if I could use magic, I could . . . But it's all the same. In some ways it's worse. The neo-mancers don't even have to look into the eyes of the men they kill.'

'Some magians do good, though,' Terrel pointed out. 'In the healing pools, for instance.'

'I know. That's what I'd like to do, if they let me.'

It came as a great relief to Terrel to find someone on Myvatan who found the endless warfare abhorrent. He'd begun to despair of the entire country, but Yarek had restored his faith a little. And he couldn't help feeling sorry for the boy. Having his romantic notions about wizardry dashed by experience must have been a painful process.

'You won't tell anyone what I said, will you?' Yarek pleaded.

'No, of course not,' Terrel promised. 'But surely there are others who think like you. You could—'

'No! The war is everything. If Tofana knew . . .' The boy shrugged helplessly, unable to bring himself to complete the sentence, then started violently at a knock on the door.

'It's all right,' Terrel hissed, then raised his voice. 'Who is it?'

'Tegan. May I come in?'

'Open the door for her,' he told Yarek.

The boy did as he was instructed, and the magian glanced at him in surprise.

'Yarek came to thank me for my healing,' Terrel explained.

'That was courteous,' she responded, nodding her approval to the apprentice. 'You may go now.'

Yarek ran off instantly.

'He's a strange one,' she murmured thoughtfully.

'I don't think anyone here is *ordinary*,' Terrel remarked.

'Perhaps not,' Tegan conceded, unsmiling. 'The Wizard wants to see you.'

This was clearly a summons, not a request, and Terrel's heart sank.

'Do you know why?'

'No. I'll wait outside while you dress.'

After Terrel had made himself presentable, he came out to find the magian leaning against the wall. She set off immediately and he hurried to fall into step next to her.

'Do you still think I'm a spy?'

Tegan glanced at him suspiciously.

'I'm not sure,' she admitted. 'What you did with Yarek was remarkable, but . . . I don't know what to think.'

Terrel found her candour endearing.

'What *do* you think in your private moments?' he asked.

'What?' She glanced at him sharply again.

'I remembered what Tofana said to you,' he explained. '"It doesn't matter what you think in your more sentimental private moments".'

'She was just teasing me,' Tegan claimed, but the touch of colour in her cheeks told another story.

By now they were climbing the steps that led up to the wizard's workroom.

'There's not much room for sentiment in war, is there?' Terrel remarked, probing gently.

'No.' Her voice was flat, expressionless.

'Is that what your "foolish qualms" are about?' he asked, quoting Tofana again.

'It's none of your business,' she snapped.

They walked on in silence for a while.

'I'm sorry,' Terrel said. 'I didn't mean to pry.'

'I'm sorry too,' she replied. 'I'm just a bit tense at the moment. Some soldiers arrived during the night, with messages from Saudark, and there are all sorts of rumours flying about.'

'What sort of rumours?'

'You'd better ask the Wizard that. She's the only one who really knows what's happening.'

'Perhaps she's planning to find the Circle of Truce,' Terrel suggested innocently.

This time the look she gave him was one of frank astonishment.

'That's just a dream,' she said, then corrected herself. 'A legend, I mean. It doesn't exist.'

'Legends have to start somewhere.'

'If you're a foreigner, how do you know so much about our myths?'

Terrel realized that she was trying to change the subject, and decided to ignore the question.

'And sometimes dreams are meant to tell us something,' he added quietly, but Tegan did not rise to the bait. She remained resolutely silent for the rest of the way up to the top of the pyramid.

At the entrance to the apex room she stopped abruptly, and Terrel looked past her to see that Tofana was not alone. Standing talking to her on the far side of the room was a military officer. After a moment he realized who it was, and also became aware that Tegan had recognized him too. However, the magian stood where she was, making no attempt to make the others aware of their presence.

'Excellent, excellent!' Tofana was saying, her unruly hair bobbing in emphasis. 'That fits my plans perfectly. The timings will have to change, of course.'

'I'm not sure the generals will—' the envoy began.

'They will when they hear what I've got to say,' the wizard stated confidently. 'Hvannadal will be protected by magical forces as well as military, but we can find ways round that. This is going to be the greatest, most decisive campaign of the war. When we all get to Saudark, I'll explain why.'

'You're coming to the city in person?' the soldier exclaimed.

'Actually, I – and quite a few of my magians – will be coming all the way to Hvannadal,' Tofana replied, enjoying his astonishment. 'This is one operation I must supervise personally.'

'But it's unheard of,' the envoy spluttered.

'Exactly! You said yourself that this expedition needs the element of surprise. Well, it's going to have it by the bucketful.' The wizard laughed at her own witticism, then saw the newcomers for the first time. She beckoned them over in her usual extravagant style.

'You already know our foreign healer, I believe,' Tofana said, nodding at Terrel. 'This is Tegan, one of my best magians. Tegan, this is Adjutant Myrdal.'

'It's a pleasure to meet you, Magian,' the soldier said as they shook hands in greeting.

Tegan simply nodded, but her face betrayed rather more. Terrel suspected that she did not trust her own voice at that moment. Although Tofana seemed quite oblivious, Terrel could see that Tegan's earlier explanation – that she and Myrdal had grown up in neighbouring villages – fell short of the whole truth. Although they looked calm enough, neither of them could quite hide their inner turmoil. This meeting might have been foreseen, but no amount of prescience could have prepared them for the feelings it evidently aroused.

'I'll have something very exciting to show you later, Adjutant,' Tofana said, still unaware of the undercurrents in the room. 'But until then I think our business is complete, and I need a word with Terrel here. Tegan, perhaps you could see that the Adjutant and his men are given a meal in the refectory. They've been travelling all night and must be in need of sustenance as well as rest.'

'Of course,' Tegan replied. 'Please come with me, Adjutant.'

Terrel watched as the soldier followed her from the room, wondering what would happen once they were out of sight of the wizard. He had a feeling they might well end up in each other's arms. Alternatively, they might come to blows. He couldn't be sure whether the spark he had seen between them had been lit by love or hate, but either way, there was no doubting its power.

'That's one thing soldiers are always good at,' Tofana remarked. 'Obeying orders.' She turned back to look at Terrel, and at the same time Bezylum emerged from a nearby rat-hole and hurried up to his mistress.

Terrel felt as if a lead weight had just been deposited in his stomach.

'Well now, healer,' the wizard said. 'You just keep getting more and more interesting.'

CHAPTER TWENTY-FOUR

'Can you show me how you did it?' Tofana asked. At her feet, Bezylum chittered nervously.

'Did what?' Terrel replied.

'Come now, don't be coy,' the wizard chided him. 'Usurping the mind of one of my little friends is an admirable achievement. I didn't think it was possible. But it was also rather impolite. The least you can do is tell me how the process works.'

Terrel had no idea how to respond. He desperately wanted to find out how much Bezylum had remembered – and passed on to his mistress – but Tofana hadn't given him enough to go on yet. Although she clearly knew that *something* had happened, Terrel needed to tailor his story to exactly what she knew – and what she didn't.

'I'm afraid I can't,' he said cautiously. 'I don't know how it works.' That was at least partly true.

'You just happened to kidnap him?' the wizard responded sceptically. 'What did you hope to learn?'

'Nothing,' Terrel replied, before the implications of her question sank in. If Tofana was inferring that his motive had been to learn from the mustela, it was unlikely that the creature had been aware of the ghosts' presence, or of his conversation with them.

'Then what was the point of the exercise?' Tofana asked.

'There *was* no point. These things just happen. I can't control them.

'I don't believe you.' The wizard paused, then smiled. 'It wasn't you, was it? You were here with me when Bezylum was first affected.'

Terrel said nothing, uncomfortable with the fact that Tofana was edging closer to the truth.

'Was it Jax?' the wizard asked, excited now. 'Is this how you talk to him?'

Once again the healer did not reply, hoping in this case that his silence would be taken for assent. It was as plausible an explanation as any he was likely to come up with – unless he told the whole story, and that was something he wanted to avoid at all costs.

'What did you learn from him?' Tofana asked. 'Did our ideas work?'

'What ideas?' Terrel said, instantly worried.

'So he didn't tell you much,' the wizard reasoned. 'A pity.' She glanced down at the mustela. 'You see, little one. You have nothing to fear from our guest. And now that I've shown you how to protect yourself, you've no need to worry about his friend either.' She looked up at Terrel to make sure he'd got the point.

Bezylum chattered briefly in response, and Tofana laughed.

'You could say that,' she replied, but chose not to translate the mustela's remark for Terrel's benefit.

The animal trotted off, apparently satisfied, and Terrel watched it go with a mixture of relief and foreboding. In all Alyssa's previous visits, not only had the various creatures she had inhabited seemed to dismiss the missing parts of their lives almost instantly, but they had not been able to tell anyone about the experience either. This time it was different, and if Alyssa tried again there was no telling what the consequences might be. Terrel found himself hoping that she would stay away while he was still in the pyramid. Borrowing the shapes of animals outside the wizard's lair would be considerably less risky.

'You disappoint me, Terrel,' Tofana remarked. 'You claim not to be a foe of our quarter, yet your actions are more like those of a spy than a friend. As allies, you and I might make a formidable team, but you would not want me as an enemy. You'd be much better off being honest with me from the start.'

'I've no wish to be your enemy,' Terrel replied. 'But I have no enthusiasm for this war. I've made no secret of that.'

'The war is going to end soon,' the wizard claimed, a visionary gleam in her eye. 'I'm going to see to that.'

Terrel thought that if Tofana got her wish, he wasn't going to like the way the war ended, but he saw no point in telling her that.

'You can choose to play a part in our victory,' the wizard offered. 'Your talents are great, but at present they are limited by your ignorance. I could teach you how to make the most of them.'

'How would you do that?'

'Conventional wisdom tells us that in this phase of history the Red Moon is dominant, but that doesn't take into account the signals the Black Moon – our moon – is sending. You know as well as I do that this is a time of change. The skies themselves tell us so. And a time of change is also a time of opportunity. *Our* time.'

'I still don't see—'

'Your arrival here is no coincidence. It was a sign. You're an innocent, Terrel. A natural.'

'An innocent spy?'

'You're confusing politics and magic,' she muttered

impatiently. 'Your healing uses principles of magic even though you don't understand the theory behind them. Just think how much more powerful you could be if you had that knowledge ingrained in your mind, your fingertips.'

'Why would I want to be more powerful?'

Tofana waved his question aside as irrelevant.

'You don't even know where it comes from, do you?' she said. 'Your mind only shapes the magic, it doesn't create it. The source of all such power is deep within Nydus, contained within forces we can't imagine. A little of it is released every time the planet's core is breached, and even then it's useless unless you can control it. I've spent my life learning to do just that. And the oldest secret of wizardry is also the most extraordinary. Water, that common, ordinary substance, is uniquely suited for storing such power.'

Terrel already knew this, but there was no need for him to respond. Tofana was talking as much to herself as to him, lost in a world of her own.

'It's not only the moons telling us it's a time of change. A few years ago, a volcano erupted under the central glacier. It thawed an enormous section of ice, creating vast mud slides and flash floods, as well as the usual ash and smoke. Of course this event caused the level of magical potency to rise dramatically − something we've all taken advantage of − but the most remarkable aspect of the eruption was that so much of the meltwater was lined up naturally. It was already full of latent sorcery − without any of us having to do a thing!'

'Where was the volcano?' Terrel asked.

'Among the Lonely Peaks,' Tofana replied, 'but its location is of no consequence now.'

Terrel disagreed. He already knew he was going to have to go and see this volcano for himself.

'The point is,' the wizard went on, 'that that was the beginning of the change, the first signal. There have been others since, but your arrival has marked the latest stage.'

'Why do you think that?' Terrel asked, though he wasn't really sure he wanted to know the answer.

'You've given me the last great secret of wizardry,' Tofana replied. 'And later today I'm going to demonstrate it to everyone here.'

This time Terrel was ready for it. As the invisible wall distorted, and brought the distant mountain into immediate focus, he was able to accept the transformation without feeling too dizzy. He was back in the wizard's workroom, several hours after his last visit, and this time the place was crowded. All the magians and apprentices were present, and their numbers had been swelled by additional observers – Myrdal and several other members of the military. Everyone was waiting to see what was about to happen outside, but as yet there seemed to be no movement there, and Tofana reclaimed their attention when she climbed up on to one of the tables and spoke to the assembly.

'We have long used water-lines to create what are commonly known as weather-weapons. Lightning clouds, avalanches, freezing rain, acid lakes . . . all these things are commonplace on the battlefield now. But there are other lines, lines that stretch far beyond the boundaries we set. It took a foreigner to show me how to use them – and even then it came about by accident.'

Terrel listened uneasily, aware of several sidelong glances directed towards him.

'Such are the quirks of fate, the jokes that the gods like to play on us. The seeds of our victory lie within this bucket.' Tofana pointed to the container that sat on the table beside her. 'As you will soon see for yourselves.'

With that she turned away from her audience and faced the magnified image of the outer world. A bell rang out, and a man soon appeared in view, scrambling over the ridge. He was looking around anxiously, perhaps expecting a new trial.

It was with some disquiet that Terrel recognized the man as Dayak, Yarek's friend. He wondered whether the magian was being given the chance to redeem himself, or whether Tofana's choice had a more sinister motive. Glancing across at Yarek, he saw that the apprentice looked pale and worried.

Tofana made a small gesture, and a swirl of cloud began to form above the mountainside. Dayak spotted it immediately, and responded. The cloud dispersed before it could take proper shape, but as it did so the neomancer clutched at his chest, his face contorted in sudden agony. A moment later he fell to his knees and then, to the consternation of all the onlookers except one, bright flames burst from his mouth and eyes. In the next instant, the fire erupted from his rib cage and belly, spilling out of his scorched flesh and searing away his clothes. By then Dayak was clearly dead, but his body continued to burn fiercely even after he had collapsed to the ground, until – an incredibly short time later – all that was left of him were his hands and feet. Everything else, including his bones, had been reduced to a pile of grey ash that even now was blowing away on the wind.

At first the audience was stunned, but then they burst into rapturous applause and cheering. Tofana beamed as they congratulated her, basking in triumph, and some of the soldiers were almost dancing with glee.

Terrel watched the celebrations in horror. He felt sick, especially when he remembered that he had been partly responsible for the repulsive spectacle. He could not believe that human beings – any human beings – could react with joy at such a nauseating sight, and yet this was what was happening. There were a few notable exceptions. Tegan's smile was forced and, for a moment, Terrel saw his own disgust reflected in her eyes. Myrdal too appeared more subdued than his colleagues, while Yarek was hiding in a corner, being quietly ill. A few others seemed a little uncertain, but the vast majority were obviously delighted by the wizard's latest demonstration.

'You have seen the fate that awaits our enemies!' Tofana declared, her voice rising above the hubbub and silencing the room.

Terrel remembered the words from the newly-discovered section of the Tindaya Code. 'Beware the fire within' now had a meaning that was all too clear. And if Tofana was prepared to do this to one of her own people, the thought of what she might inflict upon her enemies did not bear thinking about. If Terrel had ever thought of the wizard as a figure of fun, that idea had been completely eradicated now.

'Dayak would have been useless as a neomancer,' Tofana added. 'This way he goes to the Great Plain as a hero, his sacrifice pointing the way forward.'

It was a revolting piece of self-justification, but everyone except Terrel seemed to accept it readily.

'Earlier today, Dayak drank some of this water,' Tofana went on, indicating the bucket again. 'Once those lines were set up, the reaction was ready to be triggered. As soon as he tried to use any form of water-magic, the water inside his own body responded. Quite literally, he burned himself up from within.' She paused, looking around the room. 'This will be our final vengeance on our foes!' she cried. 'We are ready. We leave for Saudark tomorrow!'

PART TWO

THE ICE ROAD

CHAPTER TWENTY-FIVE

Ten days after he had left Saudark, Terrel found himself back in the city, installed once more in his tower room high above the generals' fortress. The journey from the pyramid had been achieved with the help of several sleds, pulled by willing teams of dogs – a novel form of transport that Terrel had never encountered before. During his time in the enclosed realm of the wizard's lair, a lot of snow had fallen in the outside world, which would have made the trek both arduous and dangerous had it been undertaken on foot. As it was, with the short spring season now well under way – a prelude to the long light of summer – the large party had travelled swiftly and in relative ease.

Forewarned by a messenger sent ahead by Myrdal, the citizens of Saudark had come out in force to witness the arrival of the wizard and her entourage, greeting them with a mixture of enthusiasm, awe and a little trepidation. Tofana had not ventured from her home for several years, and she had never brought so many people with her before. Everyone knew that something important was afoot, and because the wizard had been in conference with the generals since then, with no public announcement of what was being discussed, it was inevitable that rumour would fill the void left by the lack of any real news.

One hotly disputed piece of gossip maintained that Tofana intended to accompany the army on its next campaign. Some people argued that this was why she'd brought so many of her magians and other followers with her, while others refused to believe that she would do any such thing. The idea of a wizard risking her own life on the battlefield was unprecedented. Another popular line of speculation concerned a wondrous new weapon that Tofana was supposed to have devised, one that would finally enable the Black Quarter and their allies to win a decisive victory in the war. But this was not the first time such stories had been circulated, and most people were inclined to dismiss the rumour as wishful thinking. However, it was beyond dispute that the discussions taking place within the fortress must be of unusual significance, not least because Tofana and her company had not been the last to arrive. Three other wizards – two Black and one from the Red Quarter – had also come to Saudark, and they too had been accompanied by a larger than usual number of magians and neomancers. Military envoys from other parts of the quarter and from the opposite side of the island were also in attendance. Strangest of all, the city had also witnessed the arrival and subsequent incarceration of a sizeable group of prisoners. Enemy soldiers were usually executed on the spot, or left to die on the frozen battle-grounds. Although some would occasionally be held for interrogation in the field, it was unheard of for them to be transported all the way to a city like Saudark. Their unexplained presence added fuel to the fires of gossip.

'They'll have to tell us what's going on soon, surely,' Latira reasoned.

Terrel could only shrug. In the five days since his return to the city, he had relied on Latira to keep him up to date with the gossip. The fact that he knew more about what had happened at the pyramid – and was thus in a position to make a more educated guess about what the wizards and generals were discussing – did not mean that he had no interest in the latest rumours. He still was not sure whether he was considered a guest or a prisoner. He'd been granted a relative amount of freedom within the castle, but knew he was unlikely to be allowed to go anywhere he pleased. When he did go somewhere he was either accompanied, or watched over by the numerous sentries on duty. His uncertain status had made him wary of revealing what he knew of Tofana's plans, even to Latira, and she had been tactful enough not to press him on the subject.

'I've never known a time like this,' the maid went on. 'Don't you wish you could listen to what Tofana and the generals are saying?'

'This isn't my war,' Terrel replied. He did indeed wish he could be privy to some of the discussions, but of even greater concern just now was his own lack of progress. Being stuck in Saudark was not getting him any closer to finding the elemental.

'No, I suppose not,' Latira said quietly. Her expression was wistful now. 'Sometimes I think . . .' She was silent then, and shook her head.

'What?' Terrel asked, wondering what had prompted her sudden melancholy.

'I used to be married,' she told him, after a pause.

Almost at once Terrel could imagine the rest of the story, but the details of her tale went beyond what he had foreseen.

'His name was Hallen. He looked a lot like you – except his limbs were straight and his eyes were blue, just like mine. We used to joke that they matched because our souls were intertwined. He was the love of my life.' She paused again, evidently gathering enough resolve to continue. 'I was pregnant when they brought me his tag and told me he'd died a hero. I wanted to be proud that he'd gone to the Great Plain, but all I could think about was that he'd never see his child. In the end it didn't matter, because a few days later I lost the baby too. I've always wanted children.' Her voice had been growing quieter as she spoke, until now it was little more than a whisper. 'Always.'

'I'm sure it's not too late,' Terrel said sympathetically. Latira was older than he was, but only by a few years.

'The magians told me I'd probably never be able to conceive again,' she told him bleakly. 'Besides, I'll never find anyone else like Hallen.'

Terrel wanted to reassure her, but as he thought of the way he felt about Alyssa, and realized what his own reaction would be if the prospect of their being together was taken away from him, he found he had nothing to say. He couldn't ask Latira to settle for second best when he would not be willing to do so himself.

'I know I'm not the only one it's happened to,' Latira added. 'And I don't regret a moment of our time together, but sometimes it's hard not to think about what's been lost. I know the war is more important than anything else, and our cause is just, but . . .'

'Do you really believe that?' he asked.

'Of course,' she said, but there was no conviction in her voice.

'I know I'm a foreigner, and that it's none of my business,' Terrel went on, 'but I don't think this war is just at all. It's insane – and quite unnecessary.'

'No.' Her pain was obvious now. 'No, you can't say that. You *mustn't*.'

'It's the truth, Latira. Surely there must be *some* people here who can see that?'

She shook her head, but Terrel couldn't tell whether

this was in denial or from the desire to avoid even thinking about such things.

'You deserve better,' he said.

'Me?'

'All of Myvatan. But you in particular.'

'Why me?'

'Because you're kind and decent and hard-working and beautiful—'

'Beautiful?' she exclaimed, her eyes glittering with unshed tears. 'Now you're mocking me.'

'I'm not,' he stated earnestly. 'You think I can afford to judge people solely by outward appearances, when I look the way I do? You *are* beautiful, Latira, because you're a good person. Hallen saw that – and so would a lot of men if you gave them the chance.'

Latira looked so distraught then that Terrel instinctively took her in his arms. She cried quietly on to his shoulder for a while as he held her, then she drew back and tried to smile.

'You're a remarkable man, Terrel. I wish there were more like you here.'

'Are you sure there aren't?' he said. 'You don't have to be a healer to dislike the suffering of others.'

She didn't respond, and something else occurred to him.

'I *am* a healer. Do you want me to look at you, to see if the magians were right? I might even be able to do something about it.' He was remembering Ysatel, who had finally become pregnant with her husband's child after Terrel had inadvertently healed her. That she had subsequently become a sleeper – and still was, as far as he knew – was a matter for sorrow, but the fact remained that she *had* conceived, against all expectations.

Latira's reaction was to pull away slightly.

'I wanted Hallen's child, not yours,' she whispered, then – realizing what she had said – she blushed.

'I didn't mean . . .' Terrel began, feeling his own colour rise.

'I know you didn't,' she said hurriedly. 'I'm sorry. Thank you, but . . .' She fled from the room without finishing the sentence, leaving Terrel in a state of some confusion.

Terrel's restlessness increased over the next few days. He took to wandering about the fortress, testing the boundaries of his freedom. He twice tried to leave the castle, but on both occasions he was turned back. By then he had learnt from Vatna that the sleepers he'd seen on his previous visit had first started falling into their comas after the eruption of the meltwater volcano. This reinforced his opinion that the elemental must somehow have been involved, and increased his frustration at not being able to go and seek it out. Vatna had also told him that although only a few sleepers had been reported during the early years of the phenomenon, the majority had been overcome only the previous year. Neither man had any idea why that should have been. What was more, beyond the fact that the volcano was centred somewhere within the area known as the Lonely Peaks, Terrel was unable to discover any more about its exact location. Everyone he questioned seemed very vague on the subject, and it soon became clear that the site was so inaccessible that travelling there was considered out of the question – and apart from the healer, no one had any reason for making such an attempt. It was a depressing thought that the natives of Myvatan, who were presumably hardened to the island's harsh conditions, seemed unwilling to venture into that part of the interior. If that was the case, Terrel did not rate his own chances of making the journey very highly — always assuming that he was ever allowed to leave Saudark. He was certainly going to need help, but he had no idea who to ask. The generals were too preoccupied with their own agenda to even talk to him — and in any case, he wasn't sure how he could phrase his request.

With the continuing high-level talks within the fortress, it had become obvious that Tofana had vetoed the original timing of the raid on Hvannadal. Even Terrel could work out that if the army had not moved by now, there was no chance of them completing their mission by the date Colonel Davik had proposed. However, the healer did not know what had caused the delay — and he could find no one who was able to tell him. He was thus left in limbo, half hoping that the operation would begin so that he could volunteer to go with the soldiers, while also wishing that further bloodshed could be avoided.

News of some distant battles filtered through to him, but it was clear that these were comparatively minor border skirmishes. Opinion seemed to be that both the White and the Gold were puzzled by the Black forces' lack of action, and were trying various sorties in an attempt to determine what their enemies' plans might be. Everyone on both sides knew that something big was coming — but only a very few people had any idea of what it actually was.

Late one afternoon, Terrel stood shivering in one of the larger courtyards. He was wearing all the clothes he owned, together with some Latira had found for him, so that he looked rather like some kind of overweight, bulbous animal — but he was still cold. He had taken to spending as much time out of doors as he could stand, because the enticing, bitter scent of mitra was everywhere within the fortress and, while he tried to avoid the worst concentrations, he still feared being overcome by fumes whenever he was in an enclosed space.

On this occasion he was watching a group of young boys, who were playing with toy sailboats on a shallow pond which was already encrusted with ice around its edges. It seemed an innocent scene, out of keeping with the generally tense mood of the castle, but the boys – and their tutor – were evidently taking the game very seriously. While they occasionally shouted in triumph or despair, most of them were concentrating fiercely.

'Think you could do any better?' Vatna asked, coming up beside Terrel.

'At sailing boats? I doubt it.'

'It's an important part of their early training,' the magian explained. 'At least some of the boys here will go on to command real boats, ferrying soldiers around the coast. This is where they first learn the ways of wind and water – and how they can be manipulated by neomancers like Atha there.' He nodded in the direction of the boys' tutor.

'So it's not just a game,' Terrel said. He was disappointed, but not surprised.

'It is,' Vatna replied, 'but it has a serious purpose too.'

Even children are preparing for their part in the war, Terrel thought dismally.

'However,' Vatna went on, 'that's not why I came to find you. The generals want to see you.'

'Now?'

'Now,' the magian confirmed.

As the healer was escorted into the campaign room, he realized that several conversations were going on at once. The only voice he could pick out was Pingeyri's.

'Capital, capital!' the general boomed. 'An excellent suggestion, Colonel. Make the legends work for us, as you say.' His remarks were addressed to a thin man – whose uniform sported a red epaulet – who was standing with his back to the newcomers.

A hush fell upon the room as those present noticed Terrel's arrival.

'Ah, Terrel,' Pingeyri said. 'I think you know most of the people here, but there are some of our allies you won't have met.'

The colonel from the Red Quarter turned then. Terrel struggled to match the other man's calm gaze, but inwardly he was reeling.

'Terrel, this is Colonel Jarvik. Colonel, this is the healer we've been talking about.'

'Good evening, Terrel,' Jarvik said.

'Hello,' the healer replied, wondering how he was supposed to respond to the slight smile on the colonel's face. In the end he did and said nothing, still trying to collect his wits. He had met Jarvik before, but on that occasion the colonel had claimed to be a merchant named Kjolur.

CHAPTER TWENTY-SIX

Afterwards, Terrel was never quite sure why he did not confront Jarvik about his imposture. At the time it was an instinctive reaction. Initially, he was too astonished to do anything. And then he realized that the colonel must have foreseen the possibility of their meeting – his own lack of surprise indicated that he knew Terrel had survived his adventure at Whale Ness – and would therefore have been ready to counter any accusation. And what, if anything, was Terrel to accuse him of? For all the healer knew, it might be common for military officers to play other roles in life, and there could be any number of legitimate reasons for his adoption of a different name and identity. Pingeyri and the others might well be aware of Jarvik's trading voyages, and challenging him would serve no purpose. In the end Terrel did nothing, but decided to wait and see what happened.

Apparently unaware of the foreigner's internal quandary, Pingeyri had gone on to introduce several other soldiers. In his preoccupation, Terrel instantly forgot all their names, but he did note that neither Tofana nor any of the other wizards were present. He wasn't sure whether to be relieved or disappointed about that.

'Tell me, Terrel,' the general said once the preliminaries were over, 'how would you like to become one of the greatest heroes of our time?'

'Me?' The offer rang alarm bells in the healer's head.

'The gods brought you here,' Pingeyri claimed. 'That's true, whether you believe it or not. You have a role to play.'

'In the war?'

'What else?' the general responded, sounding as enthusiastic as ever.

Terrel wanted to reject the idea outright, but he held his tongue, wanting to know more before committing himself. He was not surprised when Jarvik entered the conversation.

'I'm told you're familiar with some of the legends surrounding Savik's Whale,' he said, with an ironic smile. 'What you may not know is that those tales are connected to another, equally ancient set of prophecies concerning the Peacemaker.'

For a moment Terrel thought that sounded more hopeful – but then he discovered what the Peacemaker was, and how it was destined to bring peace. As Jarvik explained about the legendary sword, and the way it would make whoever wielded it invincible, Terrel saw that such peace would be won only by wading through another sea of blood.

'Legend has it that the blade can only be found on the very rare occasions when the Red Moon is full and all the other moons are new,' the colonel went on. 'But there's another possibility, one that is linked to the whale. The reason this is not generally known here is because the tale originates in the Gold Quarter, and the omens within it are usually thought to favour them. However, with careful study, the original texts can be interpreted in several ways.'

Where have I heard that before? Terrel thought wearily.

'In essence,' Jarvik went on, 'it seems possible that whoever arrives in the way you did has a particular advantage in trying to locate the sword, in that you'll be able to see it whenever the Red Moon is full, regardless of the phases of the others. You would do this, and I'm quoting the actual text here, by "reading the far crystals" with "eyes like slivers of ice". That seems particularly appropriate to you, don't you think?'

Terrel now understood some of the comments that the Gold soldiers had made at the time of his emergence from the stone whale. To them he had indeed been a figure from legend.

'A convincing case can be made that whoever helps you find the Peacemaker will be victorious in the war,' Jarvik added. 'And now that you're one of us . . .' The colonel spread his hands in a gesture that said he didn't need to spell out the implications.

'I'm a practical man by nature,' Pingeyri declared. 'Normally I'd be wary of such fantastical notions, but even I can see the possibilities here. Sometimes the best weapon a soldier has is his mind – and sometimes it's his greatest weakness.'

'That's absolutely true,' Jarvik said. 'Although Raufar and his men performed their duties with admirable efficiency when they rescued you, in retrospect it's a pity that one or two of the Gold soldiers didn't escape from Whale Ness. Then they could have been rejoicing at your arrival, believing it to be an omen of their forthcoming victory – and when we revealed the true relevance of your coming, the effect upon their morale would have been devastating. As it is, we'll have to start from scratch. But the beauty of it is, we'll be using the Gold's own revered sources to make our case.'

'But none of it is true,' Terrel objected.

'Are you sure?' the colonel asked.

'Even if it isn't, enough of the enemy will believe it to *make* it true,' Pingeyri added.

'But the way I arrived was an accident,' Terrel said. He was no longer sure that he believed his own claim, but he was horrified by the thought of being the catalyst for another round of violence.

'From what I've heard, it was a remarkable set of coincidences for a simple accident,' Jarvik remarked.

'The gods don't always make it easy for us, eh?' the general rumbled, provoking smiles from several of his fellow officers.

Terrel didn't know what to think now. Remembering Kjolur's role in the events leading to his arrival at Whale Ness gave the colonel's words a double-edged meaning – while his motives remained as obscure as ever.

'How do you know so much about the Gold legends?' he asked.

'Such things predate the war,' Jarvik replied. 'If you know where to look, the references are easy enough to find. Most wizards keep libraries of books and documents, the contents of which are better kept from the public until the right time.'

It was a plausible answer, but could just as easily be yet another lie.

'How will you plant the story with your enemies?'

'There are always ways of allowing information to leak out,' Pingeyri answered. 'You needn't worry about that.'

'When they find out what's happened, won't the Gold try to take me back?' Terrel asked. This disturbing idea had just occurred to him.

'We'll make sure that doesn't happen,' the general assured him. 'You'll be protected until it's time for you to play your part.'

'And afterwards?'

'Afterwards, no one is going to threaten you,' Pingeyri declared confidently.

'What exactly are you expecting me to do?'

'Come with us to Hvannadal. And then on to the Lonely Peaks.'

Terrel had been expecting something of the sort. The fact that the general was intent on going to the one place on the island that the healer needed to reach might represent his only opportunity of heading towards his own goal.

'Why there?'

'The legends all agree that that is where the Peacemaker lies,' Jarvik replied. 'Buried deep within the ice.'

'Then how . . .'

'We may have little chance of actually retrieving it,' the colonel cut in, 'but just the idea that we might – especially after what will have happened at the springs – will be more than enough to strike fear into the hearts of our enemies.'

'And who knows,' Pingeyri said, 'you might even succeed. And then there'd be no stopping us.' The gleam in the general's eyes betrayed the fact that he was probably imagining wielding the sword with his own hand.

'There'll be no stopping us either way, General,' Jarvik said. 'We have the chance to lay all the heresies to rest, to prove to the gods that we are worthy of claiming the final victory. We must not waste such a chance.'

Pingeyri nodded, then turned to the healer.

'So, Terrel, are you with us? Will you lead us to the Lonely Peaks?'

Terrel could see no alternative. This was *his* chance.

'Yes, General,' he replied. 'I will.'

To Terrel's frustration, he was not told anything more about the forthcoming operation or, more importantly, about when they were due to leave. As soon as he'd agreed to the general's request, an attendant had escorted him from the castle's central complex, leaving the soldiers to

continue their planning. However, the prospect of being
taken to the Lonely Peaks, even if the circumstances were
less than ideal, had given Terrel a little hope. But he was
still bothered by the many unanswered questions about the
enterprise, especially about the mystery over the dual identity of Kjolur or Jarvik – or whoever he really was. His
true purpose – and the motives behind it – was now even
more obscure than when Terrel had thought he was just a
merchant. There were many legends connected with
Savik's Whale – and the colonel seemed to be an expert on
such things – so had his supposed help had a specific goal
in mind? Did he really think that Terrel would be able to
find the mythical sword? And none of this explained how
Kjolur could have foreseen what would take place at Whale
Ness. Had he just been taking the chance that *something*
would happen, hoping to take advantage of it later, whatever it was? It would have been a huge gamble – but one
that seemed to have paid off after all.

Terrel wanted to be able to talk to Jarvik on his own,
but he knew this was unlikely to happen unless the colonel
himself decided upon a meeting. As Terrel had already
discovered during his unsuccessful attempts to locate
Tofana and others, when someone did not want to be disturbed, there were plenty of places within the vast fortress
that could be made inaccessible. Indeed, the only person
he could be reasonably sure of seeing whenever he wanted
was Latira. Since her emotional confession, they had been
a little wary of each other, their friendship kept at a super-
ficial level. But she was still his best informant, and the
obvious person to ask whenever a new question occurred
to him.

On this occasion he found her in her own domain, the
kitchen located at the base of his tower. She was preparing
food which would provide him – and several others – with

their evening meal. His offer to help was politely refused, but she didn't seem to mind his watching as she worked.

'Has something happened?' she asked. 'You look puzzled.'

'I was called to see the generals,' he told her. 'They want me to go with them on the campaign.'

'I thought they probably would. Do you mind?'

'I don't think I have much choice. I can't stay here for ever.'

Latira nodded, but said nothing.

'Do you know anything about a man called Jarvik?' Terrel asked.

'No,' she said, then frowned. 'Who's he?'

'He's a colonel from the Red Quarter.'

'There are a lot of them here now. Everyone thinks it's because the generals want to co-ordinate a big campaign this season, across the whole island. But I haven't met any of them.'

Some time later, Terrel couldn't shake his impression that there had been something slightly odd about her response – the initial denial, then the question as an afterthought, followed by vague generalizations. Yet logically there was very little chance of her knowing anything about a newly-arrived soldier from the far side of the island, and he told himself that he was imagining things.

One of his other unanswered questions was about what the wizards had been up to recently, but the next day, during one of his aimless walks around the castle, Terrel happened upon a scene that told him more than he really wanted to know.

Entering a courtyard he had not visited before, he saw a party of servants – wearing stained clothes and with masks covering the lower part of their faces – busy collecting a large amount of ash that had been scattered over the paved yard in separate heaps. The debris was being swept into buckets or sacks and then transferred to a wooden-sided cart. When Terrel peered in to the cart he felt bile stinging his throat, and he broke out in a cold, queasy sweat. Mixed with the pungent grey ash were several human hands and a few boots, with stumps of blackened flesh protruding from them. It didn't take much imagination to realize what must have happened to the enemy prisoners who had been brought to Saudark.

Tofana's experiment had obviously been repeated many times, and if she was allowed to get her way, the gruesome results would soon be duplicated all over Myvatan – and presumably on an even greater scale. This thought kept Terrel feeling nauseous for several hours.

Much later in the day, after a number of futile attempts to find someone he might be able to talk to about the wizard's vile research, Terrel was returning to his own lodgings when he was met by a somewhat flustered-looking Latira.

'There you are!' she gasped, sounding relieved. 'Vatna wants to see you.'

'Good.'

'You're to meet him on the ground floor of Well Tower as soon as you can.'

'All right.' Terrel hesitated, trying to remember which of the many towers this was.

'Go across the West Courtyard, past the kennels, then take the corridor that has the carving of Jokulsa's marker in the lintel stone,' she told him. 'That will lead you to the tower.'

'Why there?' Terrel wondered aloud.

'I don't know. I'm just passing on the message. I got it some time ago, so you'd better hurry.'

Terrel followed her directions, and entered the tunnel below the sign that matched the pendant he wore – and the brand on Vatna's arm. He surmised that the Well Tower – presumably named for a source of water – was probably connected to the magian's art, but he hadn't been this way before and didn't really know what to expect.

The passageway was only dimly lit, and the paving underfoot was rough and uneven, suggesting that it was little used. At one point, Terrel stumbled and almost fell. Recovering, he couldn't help noticing that it was very quiet here, with no sign of the bustle that characterized much of the castle. Even the dogs, many of whom had been barking when he'd passed their compound earlier, were silent now. Then, somewhat to his relief, he heard Vatna's voice from up ahead.

'Come on, Terrel. You're late. You're going to want to see this.'

The healer hurried on, stepping into some shadows that created a patch of darkness in the corridor. He knew at once that something was wrong, and tried to pull back, but his limbs would not obey him. It was like walking into a blanket of cobwebs. The thick grey mass filled his eyes and throat, making him blind and dumb. His head swam. And then everything went black.

He woke to find himself tied to a chair, his arms and legs strapped tight. As he blinked, trying to clear the cobwebs from his mind, fear stabbed through him. He had no idea who had done this to him, or why, but being so helpless was terrifying.

The only light in the room came from a small high window. Late afternoon sunlight was falling from it directly on to his face, half blinding him, and making the rest of the chamber all but invisible – an arrangement that was obviously deliberate.

Terrel sensed movement in the shadows. There were several people in the room with him, but he couldn't see any of them. He tried to speak, but his tongue felt as if it was made of coarse wool, and no sound emerged from his lips. Before he could try again, a woman's voice drifted out of the darkness.

'Welcome back, Terrel. You do realize that if you ever look likely to actually find the Peacemaker, we're going to have to kill you.'

'I've no wish to find the sword,' Terrel stated truthfully. 'This war is not my concern.' His voice was no more than a croak, but he was rapidly recovering his wits. His captors' threatening statement meant that they knew what the generals were planning. So who *were* they?

'Then what is your reason for being here?'

'I'm just a traveller.'

'You're also a liar.' The accusation was made with complete confidence. 'What's the real reason?'

'Sometimes you can't avoid your destiny,' Terrel said.

'That's closer to the truth,' his interrogator conceded, 'but it's not exactly very informative, is it? Does your destiny tell you there's something you must do on Myvatan?'

'Yes.'

'What?'

'I don't know yet.'

'Don't lie to us, Terrel. It's pointless.'

'I'm not lying.'

'Yes, you are,' she insisted, with a touch of anger. 'You give yourself away every time. What is it you're here to do?'

Terrel didn't answer, wondering if he was truly as transparent as his adversary claimed.

'Are you a spy?' she asked abruptly.

'No.'

'Does your task have anything to do with the war?'

'No.' His answer provoked an exchange of whispers, though Terrel couldn't hear what was being said.

'Then what *does* it concern?'

'You wouldn't believe me if I told you,' he answered wearily.

'Try us.'

'You want the truth?'

'Of course.'

'All right,' Terrel replied, making up his mind, and finding an almost vindictive pleasure in the thought of sharing what he knew about the island's strangest resident. 'I came here looking for a creature that by any normal standards doesn't exist, but which is nonetheless enormously powerful. And unless I *do* find it, the consequences could be disastrous, not just for Myvatan but for all of Nydus.'

There was a prolonged, expectant silence after he stopped speaking. Terrel guessed that the others in the room were waiting for his interrogator to pass judgement on his claim.

'He's telling the truth,' she said eventually, barely able to conceal her astonishment. 'Or at the very least he believes what he's saying. Tell us more about this creature.'

Having begun, Terrel saw no point in refusing to elaborate. They could either decide that he was telling the truth or that he was quite mad. Either way, it would hardly make his current predicament any worse. He described the elemental's peculiar appearance as best he could, then explained something of the incredible powers it wielded. There was a lot more he could have told them, but he stopped there, knowing that even his brief introduction had given his invisible audience a lot to take in.

'So you've met its kind before?' his questioner asked.

'Yes. Three times. On each occasion I was able to make a bargain with the Ancient which prevented a serious upheaval.'

'And you need to do this again here?'

'Yes.'

'Because of the prophecy?'

'Yes.' Terrel couldn't recall mentioning the prophecy during his questioning, but he'd spoken about it several times since he'd arrived in Myvatan, and his captors clearly had access to a great deal of information.

'Do you know where the creature is?'

'The only clue I have is that it may have been responsible for the volcanic eruption near the centre of the island a few years ago.'

There was another silence as the implications of his statement sank in.

'So you wish to go to the Lonely Peaks?' his interrogator said, sounding oddly pleased.

'Yes. That's why I agreed to go with the army. It's my only chance of getting there. But I have no interest in finding the sword.'

This comment prompted another whispered conference between his captors. The sun was slightly less bright now, and he could just make out several shadowy figures, huddled together.

'Can we trust you, Terrel?' their spokeswoman asked as they drew apart.

'You tell me,' he replied. 'You seem to know whether I'm telling you the truth or not. The real question is, why should I trust *you*? You've kidnapped me and tied me up, and you don't even have the courage to show your faces.'

The woman laughed uneasily.

'Of course we could just kill you now and be done with it,' she remarked.

'What purpose would that serve?' he shot back. 'I've already told you I've no interest in finding the sword, if that's what you're afraid of. What do you *want* from me?' He was aware of being under intense scrutiny, but he also sensed the group's uncertainty. He wondered again who he was dealing with, and what they hoped to achieve.

'That's not an easy question to answer,' their leader said eventually. There was an odd inflection to her words, and a new suspicion grew in the healer's mind.

'That's not your real voice, is it?' Terrel had used the glamour to enhance his own voice in the past, but that had simply been to make it sound louder or more impressive. He had never thought to use it to disguise his voice or imitate someone else.

'It wasn't Vatna who called me, was it?' he asked. 'Who *are* you?'

There was no response. He had not really expected any, but now something else occurred to him. In the past he had limited his use of psinoma to learning new languages. Prying into another person's mind had always seemed an unforgivable breach of privacy, but on this occasion he felt it could be justified. He might at least learn the identity of the people who had abducted him, and thus alter the balance of power a little.

Initiating the telepathic contact was easy enough. It was simply a matter of intent. Reaching out with his own thoughts, he began to delve into the other consciousnesses in the room.

There was an instant response.

'What are you doing?' a different woman cried out in alarm. At the same time Terrel felt his questing thoughts turned back, blocked by a shield he could not penetrate.

Knowing that his efforts had been discovered, he stopped, feeling guilty.

'What's going on?' the first woman asked.

'Nothing,' the other replied quietly. 'Nothing. I'm sorry. Forget it.'

So, Terrel thought, these people have someone who can not only detect psinoma, but also prevent its use. They have an interesting range of talents between them.

'I'm sorry,' he said, then decided to turn the tables on his captors if he could. 'I've answered all of your questions as best I can. It's time you answered some of mine.'

'We can't tell you who we are. Not yet, at least.' His original interrogator had taken charge again.

'Then at least tell me what it is you want from me.'

'Very well.' She seemed to have come to a decision of her own. 'The generals want to use you as a weapon. That's the only thing they understand. In a way we want to do the same, but with a very different end in mind.'

'What end?'

'This war has gone on long enough. We want peace.'

'Peace?' Terrel queried incredulously. This was not the response he had expected.

'For everyone,' she confirmed. 'Regardless of their allegiance.'

Terrel looked down at his bound wrists and flexed his muscles against the straps.

'For people who are so peaceable,' he remarked, 'you have a funny way of treating someone who's on your side.'

'*Are* you on our side?'

'Yes. This war is an abomination. I would gladly work with anyone who genuinely wants to put a stop to so much pointless bloodshed.'

His words provoked another series of whispered exchanges, then his interrogator spoke again.

'You have to remember that our aims are considered treasonous. We'd all be executed if we were discovered. We have to be sure of you.'

'Will you help us?' the second woman asked. Her voice sounded familiar.

'Why should I believe you?' Terrel asked. 'This could all be a trick.'

'The generals would not bother with such subterfuge,' the first woman said. 'If they even suspected you of betrayal, you'd be dead by now. As it is, they might find your presence useful. On the other hand, we *need* you.'

'Why?'

'Not all legends are steeped in blood. You can help us write a different ending. Your presence signals a time of change, hopefully for the better. If you agree to assist us we'll do all we can to make sure that comes true.'

'I only have your word for that,' Terrel pointed out. 'You seem to know when I'm telling the truth. I don't have that skill.'

'Perhaps you do,' the second woman put in.

'What do you mean?'

'Look into my mind. That's what you were trying to do earlier, wasn't it? I'll let you this time. You'll find the truth there.'

'He's a mind-reader?' her companion asked.

'Of a sort. Though he seems ashamed of it.'

'Are you sure this is wise?'

'No. But I'm willing to give it a try. He has a point, you know. Why should he trust us? This would at least show that we're being honest with him.'

'But won't it tell him who you are?'

'He already knows. Don't you, Terrel?'

'Yes,' he admitted. He had suspected it for a while, and the recent exchange had confirmed his impression.

'So I have nothing to lose,' she concluded. 'He could betray me now if he wants to, unless we convince him otherwise.'

'Or we make sure of his silence another way.'

'No! I won't have another death on my conscience.'

'Even if that death saves thousands of lives?'

'Even then. Besides, as you said yourself, we need him to have a chance of saving all those lives.'

There was a long pause.

'All right,' the interrogator said at last. 'But be careful.'

Terrel felt the barrier around one of the group dissolve. Very gently, he began to search for the truth in Tegan's mind.

He was so engrossed in trying to pick his way through the labyrinth of the magian's thoughts that when something thudded against the door of the room and pushed it open, Terrel was unable to understand what was happening. Half-seen movement, several shouts and a ferocious growling all combined to disorientate him completely.

Moons, this feels good! Alyssa declared. *Whose throat do you want me to rip out first?*

No one's! Terrel replied hurriedly, seeing for the first time the large dog that contained her spirit. *They're friends.* He had seen enough in Tegan's mind to be sure of that now.

Friends don't tie you to a chair, she responded. She was standing foursquare to the group, her hackles bristling as she displayed a fearsome set of teeth. Having been taken completely by surprise, Terrel's captors were cowering against the wall of the room. However, it would surely not be long before they realized the intruder was alone, and that together they should be able to overcome a dog. As if in response to that thought, Terrel caught the glimpse of a knife blade being drawn from its scabbard.

'The dog won't hurt you unless you try to harm her or me,' he told them.

I wouldn't be too sure of that, Alyssa said, anger pulsing through her words.

Sit down, Terrel pleaded. *This is important.*

With every sign of reluctance, Alyssa lowered herself onto her haunches, although she still eyed Terrel's captors suspiciously, and a deep growling rumbled in her throat.

'Is this Jax?' Tegan asked. She was clearly aware of Tofana's mistaken impression concerning the time Bezylum's body had been usurped.

Alyssa snarled angrily at the suggestion.

'No, it's not,' Terrel said.

'You have some interesting allies,' his interrogator commented.

'I do, don't I,' the healer agreed, feeling a little more at ease now. 'But don't annoy her. She's not always so obedient.'

Very funny, Alyssa grated.

'I think this meeting has served its purpose,' the woman said. 'We should be going.'

'How do I contact you again?' Terrel asked, knowing they still had much to discuss.

'You don't. We'll be in touch with you. Don't approach Tegan unless you have a good reason for doing so.'

'Fair enough. Are you going to untie me now?'

'The rest of you should leave,' Tegan said decisively. 'That way I'll still be the only one at risk if we're wrong about him. I'll set him free once you've all got away.'

There was a pause while the others considered her suggestion.

'What about the dog?'

'She won't be any trouble.'

Don't bet on it, Alyssa muttered venomously. *Are you just going to let them walk away?*

They're acting honourably.

Now, maybe. But not earlier. Tying you up wasn't—

It's all right now, he cut in, sensing the pent-up fury in her waiting to be unleashed.

'Go on,' Tegan urged.

There was a shuffle of movement as the others left. After a while, the magian stepped forward into the light, looking understandably nervous under Alyssa's feral glare. She loosened the straps and retreated into the shadows. Terrel freed himself, stretched painfully and rubbed his aching limbs.

'I'm sorry it had to be this way,' Tegan said.

'It's all right. I understand.'

'I'll go now. Will you wait here until I've had time to get clear?'

Terrel nodded.

'Thank you. Go carefully, Terrel,' she said in parting. 'You hold my life in your hands now.'

CHAPTER TWENTY-EIGHT

The ghosts need to see you, Alyssa said as soon as they were alone.

Terrel was delighted by the news – and relieved.

So they got away all right, he said, remembering the abrupt end to their last visit.

Yes. Alyssa seemed unconcerned. *Is this a safe place? Or should we move?*

I'm not sure where we are. Terrel explained how the dark cobwebs had enveloped him.

More magic?

I can't think what else it could have been.

It's interesting that Jax didn't try to take over when you passed out, don't you think?

I hadn't even thought of that, Terrel admitted. *Maybe he did. I mean, how would I know?* The idea horrified him.

The people who tied you up would've noticed, Alyssa pointed out. *I'm sure Jax was never here, so don't worry about it. Let's just be thankful for small mercies. Now, are we staying or going?*

Terrel moved the chair over to the barred window, then climbed on to it so that he could look outside. They were not in Well Tower itself, but in a nearby annexe built against the outer wall of the fortress. It was a part of the castle he had not visited before. Stepping down, he went to the door and peered out into the corridor. It was empty and utterly quiet.

I didn't see anyone on my way in here, Alyssa volunteered. *They hadn't even set a lookout.*

It seems deserted, Terrel said. *Perhaps no one uses this section.*

Why not? It seems sound enough.

Maybe it's haunted, he suggested with a grin.

Then it's just what we need. The dog growled in what Terrel hoped was its equivalent of laughter.

It's as good a place as any, he agreed. *What about you, though? Will anyone notice you're not in the kennels?*

Don't worry about that, she said dismissively. *I can take care of myself.*

You like being a dog, don't you.

They're stupid, but trained to obedience, so it's easy for me. And having the strength of this brute suits me at the moment.

You really would have torn their throats out, wouldn't you?

Oh yes, she replied enthusiastically. *If you hadn't been such a spoilsport.*

Terrel wasn't sure how serious she was. In her own body, Alyssa had been the most gentle of beings, delicate and otherworldly, but whenever she took on the form of an animal she also inherited some of their characteristics. Even so, such eager belligerence made him feel uneasy. Was it possible that she had been infected by Myvatan's warlike obsession? He knew she would do anything she could to protect him, but her rage and readiness to resort to violence had seemed out of proportion to the situation. Terrel had the feeling that it had been touch and go as to whether she heeded his warning not to attack.

Well? Alyssa asked, impatient now. *Do I call them here or not?*

Go ahead. I need to talk to all of you, especially about what just happened.

The three ghosts flickered into existence before he had finished speaking. They all looked slightly flustered, as if they'd been taken unawares, and Muzeni even seemed to be out of breath.

A little notice would have been appreciated, my dear, the heretic grumbled.

Stop whining, Alyssa growled. *Just get on with it before you're all blown away again.*

Muzeni looked taken aback by her aggressive tone, but he did not respond.

You're in a good mood, Elam remarked *Shall I fetch you a bone to chew on?*

Not unless it's one of yours, she retorted.

There was never much meat on my bones, Elam said, unabashed. *Even less now, I should think.*

Terrel felt a sudden pang when he realized that his friend had been dead a few months short of eight years, and that his bones presumably lay in an unmarked grave somewhere within the grounds of Havenmoon. The fact that Elam could talk about such things with his usual flippancy was a good sign, but with Alyssa in her present mood the ghost was playing with fire.

Let's get on, then, Shahan said quickly, evidently recognizing the situation.

There are people here who want the war to end peacefully, Terrel began. *I've just met some of them, and—*

Never mind that, Muzeni cut in tetchily. *Have you been able to establish where the Ancient is?* Alyssa's criticism seemed to have made the old man grumpy.

Not for certain, Terrel replied, *but it seems it might be in the central ice-field.*

I thought you said— Shahan began.

Let him finish, Alyssa snapped.

That area of the glacier is called the Lonely Peaks, Terrel went on, uncomfortable with the obvious tensions within the group. *The main reason I think it's there is because a volcano erupted in that region a few years ago, and that's when the sleepers here first started appearing. What's more, the meltwater from the eruption was very potent magically.*

But the elementals hate both water and its magic, Muzeni objected, glancing at Alyssa to see if she was going to tolerate this interruption.

I know, Terrel said. *Here's what I think happened. Alyssa told me your theory about the Ancients moving up towards the surface of the planet quite recently – in their terms, at least. Isn't it possible that in doing so, this one actually caused the volcano to erupt? The problem was, it didn't know it was underneath a huge quantity of ice. The fires would have melted a vast amount, and the elemental itself may have been inundated. It could be that in trying to protect itself, it inadvertently lined up the water, in the way that the wizards do here.*

But it failed, Shahan suggested, *and that was enough to make it ill, or drive it mad.*

It sounds plausible, Muzeni conceded.

But not very encouraging, Elam added.

There's one more thing, Terrel said. *You remember you told me about some creatures who were supposed to act as bodyguards to the Guardian?*

The ice-worms?

Yes. I've found out a little more about them. They really do live inside glaciers – and if they're supposed to protect someone, he'd have to be near a glacier too. The only thing is, ice-worms usually travel alone and you said they were in a group.

That's what the text indicated, but it's a minor point, Muzeni decided. *This is certainly the best evidence we've come up with so far.*

So how are you going to get to these Lonely Peaks? Elam

asked. *I don't suppose they have a Race of Truth here, do they?*

There is a way, Terrel replied. *It's not ideal, but as far as I can see, it's my only chance. The army here is going to mount a campaign soon to some springs at a place called Hvannadal, then push on to the Lonely Peaks. They want me to go with them.*

Excellent! Elam exclaimed.

Why? Shahan asked.

This is where it gets complicated, Terrel said. He went on to tell them about various legends, and about the fact that he was supposed to be the one to find a mythical sword. *It's called the Peacemaker, which is a bit of a sick joke, because—* He stopped, aware of the strange expressions on the faces of the two seers.

The Peacemaker? Shahan queried.

Yes. Why?

That name's mentioned in the new part of the Code, Muzeni explained. *We thought it referred to a person.*

If it's a sword, it puts a completely different complexion on several passages, Shahan added.

Why did you think it was a person?

Because the text tells of him speaking to the whole island, Muzeni replied.

Which doesn't make a lot of sense if it's a sword, Elam added helpfully.

The wording is ambiguous, but I never expected this, Shahan admitted. *When you mentioned the people here who wanted an end to the war, we assumed the Peacemaker was one of them.*

No. In fact, the last thing the people I just met want is for me to find the sword. They threatened to kill me if I did.

Not very friendly of them, Elam commented.

Tell us about these ... what do we call them? Muzeni asked. *Rebels?*

The Holma, Alyssa said, making one of her rare contributions. *It means the underground. That's what they call themselves.*

Terrel glanced at the dog, wondering how Alyssa could know that when he didn't. It had not been one of the things Tegan had allowed him to see in her mind.

Well? Muzeni demanded irritably.

They want me to help them too, but for a different purpose, Terrel began, then went on to tell his allies all he knew about the underground – which turned out to be remarkably little.

So you don't know who these people are? Shahan said when he had finished.

Apart from Tegan, no.

More to the point, you've no idea how they plan to achieve their goal of a just peace, Elam commented, his scepticism plain.

No, I don't, Terrel admitted. *But they have to be a better bet than the generals!*

Did they believe you when you told them about the Ancient? Muzeni asked.

I think so. They seemed to know when I was telling the truth. The curious thing was, I got the impression they were pleased that I wanted to go to the glacier – and yet it certainly wasn't because of the sword.

And you don't know how they want you to help them? Shahan queried.

No. They said they'd be in touch.

The real question, Muzeni stated dogmatically, *is whether co-operating with them will give you a better chance of reaching the elemental. You'll be playing a dangerous game.*

You might find yourself caught between them and the generals, Shahan agreed.

Given the choice, I'd rather go with the underground,

Terrel said. *Tegan at least seems genuine in her desire for peace, and I have to assume the others are too. But I know what my priority has to be.*

Good, Muzeni said, dismissing the subject. *Do you have any other news for us? Have any of the clues from the Code become any clearer?*

At least one of them has, Terrel replied grimly. *I'm pretty sure I know what 'beware the fire within' means.* He went on to tell them about Tofana's demonstration, and about his more recent discovery of the gruesome remains in the castle courtyard. As he spoke he was aware of some surreptitious glances between the ghosts. He kept expecting one of them to say something, but no one did. *The worst thing is,* he concluded, *I think I was the one who showed her how to make someone burn up from inside.*

Why should you think that? Shahan asked.

Tofana said that the first great secret of wizardry was recognizing the magical potential of water, and it seems the last great secret was the way in which all *water — even that inside people — can be linked up. Apparently, something I did showed her that.*

That's an unfortunate coincidence, Muzeni said heavily.

Now are you going to tell me what's going on? Terrel said, dread coiling in his stomach like a malevolent snake.

There have been some unexplained deaths on Vadanis, Shahan revealed. *From what you've told us, the cause was the same as those here.*

The snake wriggled, making Terrel nauseous.

Only the extremities were left, the seer went on. *All the rest was reduced to ash.*

Was it Jax?

There's no proof, Muzeni replied, *but I don't see how there can be much doubt.*

Terrel swore in dismay. It was clear now what ideas Tofana and Jax had discussed.

There have always been legends about fire-starters, the heretic added. *People who could make their enemies' hearts burst into flame inside their chests . . . but until now it's been no more than that.*

No one knows who the first victims were, Elam said, taking up the story, *but they died in Betancuria while Jax was there. And there were some earth tremors in the region at the same time. As far as we know, Jax didn't interfere with the Ancient on his latest visit, but we can't be sure because we're having to rely on second-hand gossip. In any case, he's been back in Makhaya for several days now.*

The latest victim was anything but anonymous, though, Shahan said.

Who was it? Terrel asked.

His name was Remi. He was the Empress' chamberlain.

As always, the mention of his estranged mother made Terrel prey to several different emotions – all of them unpleasant.

It caused quite a sensation in court, Shahan added. *Adina was wild with rage and grief.*

There were rumours that Remi was rather more than her servant, Elam said.

No one was able to explain the fire, the seer went on. *His body was completely destroyed, yet when they found him in his apartment, nothing else was damaged. Even the furniture next to his body was barely scorched.*

Do you think Jax killed him deliberately?

It's possible, Muzeni replied. *It was common knowledge that the two of them didn't always see eye to eye. But it's also possible it was just a random act, to prove he could do it under everyone's noses and get away with it.*

Terrel thought that both explanations sounded plausible. The prince was vindictive, but he was also vain, and delighted in proving his superiority to those around him.

The healer already knew his twin to be capable of murder.

It's like another plague, he groaned. Against all the odds, his homeland was being affected by the events in Myvatan.

Not really, Shahan said. *This is Jax's doing, not the elemental's. It's spread there because of his link, nothing else. If we stop him, the threat goes away.*

Unless he teaches others how to do it, Terrel pointed out. *Like Tofana's doing here.*

I don't think he'll want to do that, the seer argued. *He'd rather keep the fun for himself.*

I don't see him being much good as a teacher, Elam concurred.

So how do we stop him? Terrel asked.

No one had an answer to that.

We'll work on it, Elam promised eventually.

It wasn't much, but Terrel knew it was all he could expect. The ghosts were very limited in the ways they could affect his world.

Do you think it's connected to the 'sacred' water he took from the spring at Tindaya?

Probably, Shahan answered.

Could you or any of the other sleepers help? Elam asked Alyssa.

Some parts of the palace are forbidden to us, she replied, *but I'll see.*

We're getting off the point again, Muzeni muttered. *As long as Jax doesn't interfere with the elemental, what he does is of limited concern. There are more important matters to deal with here.*

Terrel loathed the idea of his malignant brother having access to such lethal power, but he had to grant that the heretic was right. That was a problem for some time in the future, and he tried to bring his thoughts back to the present. The mention of Tindaya inevitably reminded him of the Code, and of the lines the ghosts had quoted on their earlier visit.

You remember the inscription about a city beneath the sea? he said. *Well, it features in local legend too. It's called Akurvellir, and it wasn't drowned, it's just lost.*

Careless of them, Elam remarked.

Something called the sacred flame went out at the same time as the city disappeared, Terrel went on, ignoring the interruption. *It was in a place called the Circle of Truce, and it needs to be relit for the war to end.*

But no one knows where it is, Elam responded. *Brilliant.*

Unless the underground think they've found it, Muzeni suggested.

Could it be near the Lonely Peaks too? Shahan said. *Under a sea of ice?*

If it is, there's no way anyone could find it, Terrel replied. *The glacier's been there for hundreds of years.* He remembered Tegan saying 'That's just a dream', and wondered what she had meant.

We'll look at the text again, Muzeni promised. *And see if we've missed something. Is there anything else?*

Just one curiosity, Terrel answered. *The merchant who sailed here with me is also a colonel from the Red Quarter, under a different name. He's the one who suggested I went to look for the Peacemaker. I've no idea what he's up to.*

It was clear from the ghosts' expressions that they were none the wiser.

Have you got any news for me? Terrel asked.

We've covered most of it, Shahan replied, *but there is one other thing we found in the new section of the Code. It seems to indicate that either the Guardian or the Mentor will be helped by a wizard.*

I can't see how it could be Tofana, the healer said.

It's connected somehow to the starlight family, the seer

added. *I don't suppose you've learnt anything more about that?*

Terrel shook his head.

How clear is the translation? he asked. *Could it be 'magian' instead of 'wizard'?*

It's possible, Muzeni conceded. *You think it could be Tegan?*

Yes. Or maybe the other woman in the Holma, the one who questioned me.

Well, it's worth bearing in mind, Shahan said. *It's possible that not all the wizards are potential enemies.*

They were silent for a while.

Are . . . Are things any easier here? Terrel enquired tentatively. *For you, I mean.*

We may have overcome some of our difficulties, Shahan replied. *Our opportunities are still limited, but—*

At least we don't seem to be making things worse now, Elam completed for him.

Thanks to you, Muzeni said, nodding at his young colleague.

I do what I can, he declared.

But you're still not going to tell me what it is? Terrel asked.

We can't.

Some things you have to discover for yourself, Alyssa said.

Terrel glanced at her.

Do you *know what it is?* he asked suspiciously.

Hedges look different from the inside, she replied.

What? Even for her, this reply was unusually bizarre.

You need to go soon, Alyssa told the ghosts.

Is the wind coming? Muzeni's concern was obvious.

Yes.

Then we should go while our dignity remains intact, the heretic said. *Goodbye, Terrel.*

Good luck, Elam added, as all three faded into thin air.

Do you have to go too? Terrel asked Alyssa.

No. In fact, I won't be able to for a while. I'll come back to your lodgings.

Are you sure? he asked in surprise.

Alyssa bared her fangs.

Who's going to stop me? she asked.

CHAPTER TWENTY-NINE

It was growing dark by the time Terrel got back to his own tower, Alyssa trotting at his side. He'd made a half-hearted attempt to find Vatna – and had failed – but in any case, he was reasonably sure that the magian had not been involved with his abduction. During his wanderings, Terrel had received a few odd looks, but no one had challenged his right to be accompanied by a hound. Most people had merely given the pair a wide berth.

Just as they were about to start the long climb up the stairs, Latira came out of her own quarters. When she saw the dog she flinched, her eyes wide with fear.

'It's all right,' Terrel said. 'She won't hurt you.'

Alyssa sat down, and let her tongue hang out of the side of her mouth, her head tilted slightly. Latira edged forward again, reassured by the dog's apparently placid demeanour.

'Where did she come from?'

'I've no idea. She's just adopted me. You don't mind, do you?'

'No. No, of course not. The handlers might be puzzled, though. Do they know she's gone?'

'I'll explain in the morning if there's a problem,' Terrel assured her. 'When Vatna sent for me, did he give you the message himself?'

'No. It was a soldier. I didn't know him.'

Terrel was not surprised.

'I thought it was unusual,' Latira added, 'but the magians do use Well Tower sometimes. Did you find him?'

'No. He wasn't there.'

'Perhaps he was called away on military business.'

'I expect so.'

'Have you been to see the generals today?'

'No.'

'So there's no news, then? About when you'll be leaving, I mean.'

'Not yet,' Terrel confirmed. 'I'd like to know that myself.'

Latira nodded.

'I'd better get back to work,' she said, glancing uncertainly at the dog again.

As the maid returned to her own domain, Terrel and his companion set off up the stairs.

She's a good actress, isn't she? Alyssa commented.

What do you mean?

She was one of the people in the room. One of the Holma.

Are you sure? Did you see her?

Not very well, Alyssa admitted, *but I'd have known it was her even if it had been pitch black. This nose works even in the dark, and all you humans have a different stink.*

Terrel was still digesting this news when they reached his room.

Would you be able to tell me who the others were? he asked as he sank down on the bed.

If we meet them again, yes.

That could be very useful.

Glad to be of service, she said, though she sounded dispirited.

Are you all right? Terrel asked.

This place puts a strain on me, she admitted. *Never quite knowing when I'll be able to come or go.*

Well, I'm glad you're here.

Me too. Do you mind if I sleep for a bit?

Of course not. He was disappointed, and would have preferred to talk, but he knew she had to husband her resources whenever she occupied an animal.

Terrel watched her as she rested. Every so often the hound's body would twitch slightly, and he wondered what images were being conjured up by a brain that had been possessed by another spirit. Alyssa claimed never to remember her own dreams, even though she could often 'see' other people's, but would that still hold true while she was a dog? He kept hoping that she just needed a short nap and would wake up soon, but Alyssa drowsed on, and Terrel eventually began to speculate on his latest discoveries – running through the events of the day and then re-evaluating some of his earlier conversations with Latira. Now he knew she was a member of the Holma, it seemed clear that she had been feeling him out, testing him in some way. Right from the first she had probably been trying to assess whether he'd make a suitable recruit for her cause. There were so many questions he wanted to ask her, but he recognised the need for caution. He considered her a friend now, and the last thing he wanted was to put her in any danger.

Then Terrel wondered about who else might be involved in the underground movement. He had his suspicions, but unless he could arrange for them to meet Alyssa's latest host, he had no proof. The one thing he was sure of – despite Muzeni's attitude – was that he would help them if he possibly could. It felt right.

It was only when he recalled Alyssa's earlier advice

about not trusting his own instincts that his doubts
returned.

The dog woke up briefly when Latira arrived with the
evening meal. She wolfed down the food that had been
brought for her, and then – to Terrel's disappointment –
lay down again and seemed to go straight back to sleep.

'She was hungry,' Latira exclaimed, glancing at the
empty dish. 'Unlike some people, I see. Is something
wrong?'

Terrel had not touched his own dinner.

'No, it's fine.'

'You haven't tasted it yet.'

'You're an excellent cook, Latira,' he said. 'Among other
things.'

'What other things?' Her smile seemed a little forced.

'I don't know what I'm talking about. Ignore me.' He
began to eat.

'Let me know if there's anything else you want,' Latira
said, then left the room.

The hound opened one eye.

I see you're working your charms on older women now,
Alyssa teased him.

Don't be ridiculous! he shot back. *There's nothing between
me and—* He fell silent, aware that this time Alyssa really
was asleep.

A small part of Terrel remained aloof from the dream,
watching as if it were an episode from someone else's life.
Outside his room he knew that the Red Moon was several
days past its peak, but here it shone in its full glory.
When it shifted into the shape of a sword – as he had
known it would – he saw it through the eyes of a warrior.
What else could this be but the Peacemaker, a weapon

forged by the gods? He saw it cut a swathe through a human field, harvesting lives as though they were no more than ears of wheat, a crop of blood and pain. But this time, even as they fell, the bodies of the slain burnt away to ash.

The endless bare plain came next, as it had done before. It was just as bleak and joyless, but it was no longer empty. The vast space was crowded now, not with people but with swirls of light. Terrel soon realized that these twisted shapes were ghosts, and he knew they were the spirits of dead soldiers. This was the Great Plain – but it was not a place of ease and plenty where heroes took their well-earned rest. This was a realm of torment and hopeless regret.

Why are you wasting time here? Go back to the battle. I was enjoying that.

This is not your place, Jax.

Oh, it is now, the prince replied casually. *I can do anything I want. And you can't stop me. I know I'm playing with fire,* he added, laughing. *That's what makes it so much fun.*

No good will come of this, Terrel told him.

Good? Spare me the lecture, please.

Being a fire-starter will rebound on you in the end.

A fire-starter? Jax mused, trying the word out for size. *I like that. It has a nice ring to it.*

I'm serious, Jax. This isn't just fire you're playing with. It's evil.

Yes, the prince agreed happily. *I know!*

A sound from the outside world intruded then, breaking the hold of the dream.

Until next time! Jax called cheerily.

The noise was repeated as Terrel opened his eyes, shrugging off the miasma of sleep as best he could. The dog also raised her head and looked at the door. The knocking came again, louder this time.

'Come in!' Terrel called, rubbing his eyes. He expected it to be Latira, and was wondering why she was rousing him so early, but it was not the maid who entered.

'I'm sorry to wake you,' Yarek said, 'but I need to talk to you and there isn't much time.'

'Why? What's happening?' the healer asked, wondering if the long-awaited campaign was finally about to get under way.

'Tofana's scheduled some new tests for this morning, and I'm supposed to take part.'

Terrel did not have to ask what sort of tests the apprentice was talking about.

'You don't want to?'

'No! It's horrible. You saw what happened to Dayak. How can I do that to anyone?'

'They can't force you to take part,' Terrel said, sympathizing with the boy's distress. Asking anyone to become a fire-starter was bad enough, but at Yarek's age it was barbaric.

'But if I don't, she'll send me home. I'll have to become a soldier, and then ...' He faltered, momentarily distracted by the presence of the dog. Alyssa had just risen to her feet and was staring at the newcomer. When she didn't do anything else, Yarek found his train of thought again. 'I was hoping you could help me ... find a way to make it ... impossible for me to do it.'

'How? I don't know enough about the process.'

'But you were the one who showed Tofana how it was possible,' the boy pleaded. 'You must have *some* idea.'

'Couldn't you pretend to be ill?'

'The magians would know I was lying.'

'Perhaps I could say I need you to help me with something,' Terrel ventured.

'That's good,' Yarek responded, brightening a little. 'What?'

'I don't know yet.'

What about long-distance healing? Alyssa suggested silently. *The army would have to be interested in that.*

Go on, Terrel said, pretending to think.

If fire-starters can harm people from a long way away, why shouldn't you be able to heal them?

Yes! And Yarek's the obvious one to help me because I healed him before. Perfect. You're a genius.

As well as mad, Alyssa agreed modestly.

'Have you thought of something?' Yarek asked hopefully.

'I think I have,' Terrel replied.

After the apprentice had dashed off to ask permission to join Terrel, the healer sighed.

Do you think distant healing is really possible?

That was an unpleasant dream, Alyssa said, ignoring his question.

I know, he said, thinking back. *I had a similar one not long ago.*

Not yours, she corrected. *The boy's.*

It hadn't blown away? Terrel knew that the afterimages of a dream – which only Alyssa could see – faded after a while, like clouds dispersed by a breeze.

No. It must have been very vivid.

What was it about?

There was a soldier shouting at him – I think it might have been his father – but his voice didn't make any sound so Yarek couldn't hear what he was saying. It made them both very unhappy.

He's had that dream before, Terrel said.
Does it always end with the boy killing himself in a huge explosion? Alyssa asked.

Terrel spent the time before Yarek's return thinking about his own dream. If his vision had not stemmed purely from his own imagination, and thus bore some resemblance to the reality of the situation, then the Great Plain was far from being the idyllic afterlife imagined by the people of Myvatan. It was a place of endless grief and agony – and in that world there was no mitra to dull their perceptions. But if this was true, he couldn't tell anyone. The only consolation for people like Latira was to believe that their loved ones were at peace. The truth would be too cruel. However, it made Terrel more determined than ever to bring the war to an end.

He also realized that there had been something missing from the dream, and it took him a while to work out what it was. When he did, he wasn't sure what it meant. In the earlier version, the one he'd had at the pyramid, the battle had involved not only the Peacemaker but also a wizard – a wizard with Yarek's face. He had not appeared this time. It was also a curious coincidence that on both occasions the boy had been the one to wake him from his nightmare.

Belatedly, he thought to ask Alyssa if Yarek was a member of the underground.

No, she replied. *At least, he wasn't there yesterday.*

He'd be an ideal recruit, Terrel thought. And the Holma must need all the help they can get – especially if it comes from someone with magical talent. Nevertheless, he decided not to broach the subject directly, but to wait and see if it arose naturally.

He's dangerous, Alyssa added unexpectedly.
Dangerous? Why?

He has more power than he can control, she answered simply, and Terrel could not persuade her to explain further.

Yarek returned, flushed and breathless, obviously overjoyed that their ruse had worked and that he'd been given permission to miss the trials.

'Where shall we start?' he asked eagerly.

Terrel was taken aback.

'I didn't really mean . . .' he began. 'It was just an excuse to keep you away from the tests.'

'But it *could* work, couldn't it?' the boy asked, obviously disappointed.

'I've no idea. And I'm not sure—'

What else have you got to do today? Alyssa asked, cutting him off. *There's no harm in trying. It might even come in useful one day.*

Terrel gave in.

'I suppose the first thing we should do is find someone who's sick,' he said aloud.

'We can ask Latira,' Yarek said. 'She knows most of what goes on in the outside world.'

Latira directed them to one of the servants' quarters, where a cook was suffering from a fever. Once they'd located the dormitory where she lay, they stayed outside while Terrel tried to contact the woman's waking dream. He met with no success, so they tried a different approach. Yarek went in to see the patient, holding her hand, and Terrel attempted to complete the link through him – again with no success. Finally Terrel went in to visit her himself. At the touch of her hot skin he was immediately aware of the problem, and knew he could cure her of the infection easily enough. He held himself back, however, and went outside again to repeat the attempt now that he had a feel for her dream. This time there was a fleeting contact, but he couldn't achieve anything worthwhile from even that modest distance. Disappointed, he went back inside and became a normal healer again.

It was only when he had finished, and the cook was thanking him profusely, that Terrel realized – to his dismay – that at some time during the morning the dog had left him. Alyssa had not said goodbye, and he couldn't believe that she'd just go without a word. But if she still inhabited the hound, why had she wandered off?

Knowing that the trials would be over now, Yarek left Terrel to his own devices that afternoon and the healer resumed his aimless existence, walking around the castle whose outer regions were becoming more and more familiar. He felt restless and dissatisfied, and longed for something to happen to point him towards the future – while at the same time dreading those developments. A dull, cold rain began to fall, matching his mood and driving him to seek shelter. Eventually, feeling chilled, tired and hungry and with no sign of Alyssa – either at the kennels or anywhere else – he returned to his own tower. Once there, enticed by the smells of cooking, he looked into Latira's quarters. She saw him and beckoned him inside.

'Why don't you eat here with me this evening?' she said. 'It'll save me having to carry it all the way up to your room. And you look as if you could use some company.'

Terrel accepted the invitation gratefully, wondering whether she would try to get him to talk about the underground. He was half inclined to tell her that he knew of her involvement, but decided to keep that knowledge to himself for the time being. As it turned out, Latira showed no interest in talking about the war – or peace – and was more curious about the healer's day. They chatted amiably about trivial matters and, for the first time in a long while, Terrel began to relax, enjoying her company and the comfortable surroundings. The meal increased his feeling of wellbeing – Latira was indeed an excellent cook – and even Alyssa's continued absence no longer bothered him quite so much. After all, he told himself, she had always been a law unto herself, and on Myvatan her movements were circumscribed by other factors too. She would return when she could.

When they had eaten their fill, Latira produced a jug of hot liquid. The steam rising from it was fragrant with spices and honey.

'Would you like some?'

'What is it?'

'Melcras. My grandmother used to say that after a cup of this you could crawl through a snowdrift and not feel the cold. I still make it using her recipe.'

'There's no mitra in it, is there?'

'No, nothing like that.'

'No alcohol?'

'No,' she replied, with a touch of impatience. 'Do you want some or not?'

'Yes, please.'

Terrel's first cautious sip convinced him of one thing. Melcras was delicious. The next increased his admiration for Latira's grandmother. It was only after he had finished his second cup that he realized he'd made a terrible mistake.

Terrel woke the next morning in unfamiliar surroundings. He had a dull headache, a raging thirst and a queasy feeling of uncertainty in the pit of his stomach. He shifted slightly in the bed, realizing he was naked beneath the sheets – and then saw that he was not alone. Latira lay beside him, still sleeping peacefully.

As he was struggling to grasp what had happened, a dog appeared in the doorway of the bedroom.

Do you still claim there's nothing between the two of you? Alyssa asked bleakly.

CHAPTER THIRTY

It wasn't me! Terrel cried, sitting up in bed. *It was Jax!* But the hound – and Alyssa – had gone.

Terrel stared at the empty doorway in an agony of indecision. Surely she couldn't believe . . .

'It wasn't me!' he called aloud, hoping the dog's keen ears would pick up his plea.

Beside him, Latira stirred in her sleep at the noise and Terrel froze, not wanting her to wake. Alyssa did not come back.

After a certain point Terrel could remember nothing of the events of the previous night, but he was in no doubt as to who had taken advantage of his insensibility – and some of his dismay turned to anger. Jax had already cost him the full use of his limbs and, although his twin had not been directly responsible for the loss of his birthright, his injuries must surely have been part of the reason for his parents abandoning him. The prince had also made Terrel's life difficult on several occasions during his travels. But if his brother caused him to lose Alyssa's love, that would be an act of malice far worse than anything that had gone before. The twins' mutual enmity had never been in doubt, but until that moment Terrel had not actively hated Jax. He found himself clenching his fists, the good hand curled into a ball, the crooked fingers of the right twisting into a rigid claw. For all that Terrel loathed violence, if Jax

had been in front of him at that moment, he knew he
would have tried to kill him.

And then the healer remembered when, a very long
time ago – in another life, it seemed – he'd had a vision of
his own death. Terrel had been on the top of Mount
Tindaya, the sacred site at the heart of Vadanis, when a
second world had been superimposed upon his own. In
that world he had seen himself, several years older, with
another man, who wielded a sword. The fatal blow was
about to fall when the vision ended but now, at last, Terrel
knew who the malevolent presence was. If the chimera had
been genuinely prophetic, he would meet his twin one
day – but it would be Jax who would do the killing.

For a few moments the cold remembered dread of that
meeting overwhelmed him, but then he forced himself to
set such thoughts aside. As he had told himself many
times before, the future would have to take care of itself.
He had to deal with the present.

You haven't lost Alyssa yet, he assured himself, hoping
this was true. *She'll understand once you explain what
happened. But what if she never comes back?* a smaller,
traitorous part of his brain added.

Whatever had happened in the night, Terrel had not
been responsible. But he *had* been the one foolish enough
to drink too much melcras. After his experiences in the
past, he should have known better – in spite of Latira's
assurances that the drink would have no intoxicating
effect. That was just one of the mysteries he was faced
with now. Glancing at the woman in the bed, Terrel was
filled with a mixture of emotions. He had begun to think
of her as a friend, and although he already knew she was
keeping a secret from him, there had seemed nothing
false about her kindness and generosity the night before.
On the other hand, the suspicion remained that she had

done this deliberately. But if that was the case, *why* had she done so?

During the course of his travels, Terrel had occasionally found that some younger women – those close to his own age, like Esera and Ghadira – thought him attractive, although he still didn't understand why. His strange eyes and crooked limbs were more often a source of fear or revulsion, but the women had seemed to overlook his odd countenance. After all, that was only his outer physical appearance, and Terrel was wise enough to know that there were other factors involved in human attraction. He just wasn't sure what they were.

However, no one of Latira's age had ever shown any signs of a romantic attachment to him. Could she really have plied him with melcras with the intention of seducing him? Might she have had some ulterior motive? Had she even known about Jax? And if so, what had she hoped to achieve by giving the prince the chance to take over? Perhaps the whole thing had just been an accident. Part of Terrel wanted to wake Latira and ask her all these questions, but part of him also wanted her to stay asleep so that he could avoid the one question uppermost in his mind. What exactly *had* happened between them?

In theory Terrel knew the ways of men and women, but in practice he was still an innocent. The guilt that was consuming him was based on guesswork. It would be ironic if he was technically no longer a virgin but couldn't remember anything about the experience. It hadn't been him. And yet, if – as seemed likely – something had happened, it *had* been his body. As far as he could tell, nothing felt different, but he had no way of knowing whether this was significant or not. As a healer, he had never been able to explore his own waking dream, so there were no discoveries to be made that way. He knew the only solution was to find the courage to talk to Latira.

And then he remembered an earlier occasion when Jax had been able to usurp his consciousness, and Ghadira's response to his question. 'You don't remember?' she had teased him. 'That's not very flattering, you know.' Terrel had found the nomad girl's romantic interest in him both awkward and perplexing, but at least he had been aware of it. With Latira he'd had no inkling of any such involvement – beyond Alyssa's earlier jibe about 'older women', which now haunted his thoughts. Had he really done anything to encourage Latira to believe that he'd wanted this?

Then an even more bizarre – and mortifying – thought occurred to him. If, as a result of their encounter, Latira became pregnant, who would be the father – him or Jax? That was something he didn't even want to think about.

'Moons!' he breathed, holding his head in his hands. 'What a mess.'

Beside him Latira shifted, then sighed, and he tensed, wondering if she was waking up. A moment later her eyes opened and she looked at him. For a few heartbeats her face was a mask of incomprehension, and then something in his expression must have amused her, because she laughed briefly. Then she became still, her gaze unreadable once more, and Terrel had no idea what she was thinking.

Without a word, she slipped from under the bedclothes. Terrel looked away quickly when he saw that she too was naked, but Latira took no notice. Pulling on a robe, she walked from the room.

'Latira?' he said awkwardly. 'Please, wait. I—'

She did not even pause in her stride and, for the second time that morning, Terrel was left staring at an empty doorway. No one wants to talk to me, he thought dismally. He looked around and realized that he had no idea where his clothes were. He couldn't see them anywhere. By this time he was so unnerved that he simply stayed where he was, pulling the blanket up around him as the chill of the morning seeped into his flesh. He heard various noises coming from the kitchen, and then there was a period of quiet before Latira eventually returned to the bedroom door. Her face had a pinched look now, and her gaze was cool, measuring.

'Do you want some breakfast?' she asked.

The mundane nature of her question made Terrel want to laugh, but he controlled himself and shook his head.

'What happened last night?' he asked before she could leave again.

'You tell me,' she replied shortly.

'I don't remember,' he admitted, feeling the colour rise in his cheeks.

'Oh, very funny,' she muttered sarcastically. 'You didn't have *that* much melcras.'

Terrel couldn't tell whether Latira was offended or simply irritated by his query.

'Why did you let me drink that stuff?' he asked. 'I asked you if—'

'It's only honey and a few herbs,' Latira exclaimed. 'It keeps you warm and helps you relax. I thought you'd enjoy it. How was I to know . . .' There was no mistaking her annoyance now.

'What?' Terrel prompted.

'Nothing,' she snapped. 'Are you going to stay in bed all day?'

'I don't know where my clothes are,' he told her, knowing how pathetic he must sound.

Latira sighed, her exasperation plain, and disappeared. When she returned, she tossed the healer's clothes on to the bed and withdrew at once.

'I see you've made yourself at home,' Vatna remarked, replacing her at the entrance to the room. The magian was grinning. 'If I'd known, it would have saved me a climb up the tower.'

Terrel's humiliation was complete.

Vatna had been sent to inform Terrel of a meeting with Pingeyri. As the magian led the healer into the general's staff room, Terrel saw at once that it was an important gathering. Not only were all the senior officers present, but they had been joined by Tofana and three other robed figures – who he assumed were wizards – and a number of their attendants. Captain Raufar and several of his lieutenants were also there, standing stiffly to attention. And in another corner of the room, Jarvik stood with a group of soldiers whose uniforms identified them as coming from the Red Quarter.

'Gentlemen . . .' Pingeyri began, then corrected himself. '*Ladies* and gentlemen, this is Terrel, the seeker of legend, who is to lead us to the Peacemaker.'

Terrel's thoughts were still in turmoil from the events of the previous night, and finding himself the centre of intense scrutiny only increased his unease.

'He's also the one who enabled me to trace the lines used by the fire-starters,' Tofana added, glancing round at her colleagues. 'We may need his help to identify the specific pattern sequences once we get to Hvannadal.'

'I thought such things were within the competence of your magians now.' The woman who spoke wore a scarlet cloak, marking her as a visitor from the other side of the island. She was older than Tofana, but her mist-grey eyes were shrewd and the tone of her voice was faintly accusing.

'For simple chains, yes,' Tofana replied, unperturbed. 'But the springs will present a far greater challenge. It will require a combined effort. That is why you and I – and our esteemed colleagues – must accompany the expedition, Varmahlid.'

The Red wizard nodded slightly in acknowledgement, but her expression remained neutral. Terrel wondered briefly whether there was any rivalry between Tofana and her counterpart.

'Can he protect himself on the battlefield?' one of the other wizards asked.

'We wouldn't want such knowledge to fall into the hands of the enemy,' the fourth added. Both women wore black, but their deference to Tofana was clear when she answered their joint query.

'He will be protected,' she stated confidently. 'By magic, and by force of arms if necessary.'

'Captain Raufar and his men have been assigned to escort him,' Pingeyri said, rejoining the conversation. 'That seems appropriate, as they were the ones who rescued Terrel from the Gold when he first arrived on Myvatan. I have no doubt that they are up to the task, especially now they're to be joined by your own trainees.'

'Which of the fire-starters will accompany them?' Varmahlid asked.

'Hraun and Jauron,' Tofana replied, beckoning to a group of men who stood behind the wizards. Two neomancers stepped forward. Terrel thought that they looked perfectly ordinary, and it was hard to imagine them killing in such a horrific manner.

'If all goes according to plan,' Tofana added, 'they'll be among the first to put the new process into effect at Hvannadal.'

'What exactly are we going to do there?' Terrel asked, finding his tongue at last. 'Why are the springs so important?'

'In order to destroy his victim, a fire-starter must first establish some sort of contact with him,' Tofana explained. Her expression was almost rapturous now, and she was clearly enjoying the opportunity of displaying her ingenuity to such an audience. 'Water provides the easiest way of forging such a link – you've seen that for yourself – but at least some of the patterns have to be known in advance. A certain amount can be learnt from observation and experience – our neomancers have made considerable progress even in the short time we've been in Saudark – but the advantage of a place like Hvannadal is that the lines within the water there are distinctive, extending beyond the normal spheres of influence. Once we've been able to study the springs at first hand, and identified these unique patterns, it will be possible to create the greatest chain any of us has ever seen. Every man who has ever used the healing pools there – virtually all the White Quarter's soldiers – will be linked to it, and when we set the fire in motion it will be passed from one to the next until every one of them is destroyed.'

The enormity of such a massacre rendered Terrel speechless with horror, but Tofana's evident delight was mirrored on almost every other face in the room. Even Varmahlid was smiling now. Glancing at her and the other wizards, Terrel could not imagine any of them helping him, but the hint from the Tindaya Code would have to be followed up if possible.

'The great adventure is about to begin,' Pingeyri declared. 'We march north at first light tomorrow!'

CHAPTER THIRTY-ONE

The castle was in ferment as the army prepared to leave, and Terrel felt like a piece of driftwood, floating aimlessly upon a sea of human endeavour – not part of the enterprise, but not wholly separate from it either. Like it or not, his fate was entangled with that of the soldiers now.

He had begun by looking for Alyssa in the kennels. The hounds had been in a state of high excitement, perhaps sensing that they too would soon be needed. Their barking had lessened slightly when Terrel was nearby, but his search had been fruitless. So many of the dogs looked the same, and the healer couldn't tell if the animal Alyssa had occupied was back among them. He'd questioned some of the handlers, but they were too busy to pay him much attention, and their answers were of no help.

Still hoping that Alyssa had not abandoned him, Terrel had then begun a haphazard search of the rest of the fortress, even returning to the empty section near Well Tower, but there was no sign of her. Eventually realizing that if they were to meet again it would be by *her* choice, Terrel returned – with some reluctance – to his own quarters. Though he dreaded the prospect, he knew he must talk to Latira. He owed her an explanation, and he was hoping that in return she would answer some of his questions.

When he reached her apartment at the base of the

tower, he found the outer door standing open. He went in, hoping to find her in a better mood than when he'd last seen her, but the woman sitting alone at the kitchen table was not Latira.

'I thought you'd come back here eventually,' Tegan remarked. 'Shut the door, will you?'

Terrel did as he was told, feeling a mixture of nervousness and excitement. Now that the long-awaited campaign was about to get under way, it made sense for the Holma to contact him again. He took the chair Tegan indicated.

'I don't think we need to tie you to it this time,' she commented with a slight smile.

'I prefer it this way,' he replied. 'I don't—'

'Will you betray us, Terrel?' she cut in abruptly.

'What possible reason could I have for betraying you?'

'Just answer the question. Please, it's important. Would you ever knowingly betray us?'

'No.'

'And do you genuinely want peace for Myvatan?'

'Yes.'

Tegan twisted round in her seat and addressed the apparently empty room.

'Well?'

For answer the slatted door to Latira's pantry was pushed open from the inside. Colonel Jarvik emerged from his hiding place and nodded to the magian.

'He's telling the truth,' he stated. 'You were right to trust him.'

Terrel was not entirely surprised that the soldier who was also a merchant was playing yet another role. It made perfect sense that the underground would need informants within the military hierarchy, and Jarvik was clearly a man used to subterfuge. The fact that he had now chosen to display his own trust in a foreigner by revealing his secret allegiance was a promising sign – and a list of questions was already forming in Terrel's mind.

'What's your real name?' he asked, picking the first one that had occurred to him.

'Jarvik is the name my parents gave me, but I've had several others in my time.'

'What would you have done if I'd told the generals about a merchant called Kjolur?'

'My twin brother, you mean?' the colonel answered with a smile. 'He's the black sheep of the family. No one's quite sure what he'll do next.'

Reminded of his own twin, Terrel wondered briefly whether Jarvik was telling the truth, but soon dismissed the idea. The soldier's smile told its own story.

'Why do you travel?'

'For the same reason you do.'

Terrel thought about that for a few moments.

'Because you had no choice?'

'That's how it felt to me,' Jarvik confirmed. 'I knew there was something out there, waiting for me.'

'And have you found it?'

'Perhaps.'

'Something to help your cause?'

'Actually, before I started travelling I didn't *have* a cause. Before I set sail I never questioned the war. I didn't even know there were people here opposed to it, let alone an organization like the Holma. Leaving Myvatan helped me to clear my mind – and in the process I discovered some things about myself, as well as the outside world. My hidden talents came to the fore, so to speak.'

'Was one of these talents the ability to tell whether someone's lying or not?' Terrel asked, wondering at Jarvik's earlier certainty.

'No. I have that ability, but there's nothing strange

about it. It's the result of many hours of study and training. Anyone can do it if they have the patience to learn, and eyes that know what to look for.'

'You can see the truth in someone's face?'

'And the lies,' the colonel said. 'It's all there in the minute changes in their expression, their gestures and mannerisms. Some are better liars than others but no one can hide such changes completely. Most are entirely involuntary.'

'You're trusting me with your life on the basis of tiny signals in my face?' Terrel said, finding it hard to come to terms with this idea.

'I'm very rarely wrong,' Jarvik told him. 'Especially when someone is confronted with a direct question, as you were just now. But I have to admit, it wasn't my judgement alone. When Tegan allowed you to look into her mind, it was not entirely a one-way process.'

Taken aback, Terrel glanced at the magian. She kept her eyes lowered, as if she was ashamed of her actions, and when she spoke her voice was quiet.

'I didn't mean to trick you,' she said. 'I can't initiate such contacts, but I can sense them and block them if necessary – and once one is made I can see a little . . . of your thoughts.'

'She saw nothing to make us doubt you are genuine,' Jarvik concluded for her. 'The little test today was just for confirmation. We have to be careful, you understand.'

Terrel nodded. He had felt nothing during the contact with Tegan, had not been aware of any probing into his own mind, and he could not help wondering how much she had discovered. He was very glad now that he had chosen to tell the truth during his interrogation.

That memory triggered another realization.

'Is one of your talents the ability to change your voice?' he asked Jarvik, who smiled but said nothing. 'It was you who mimicked Vatna, wasn't it? And you were the woman who questioned me. Do you use the glamour?'

'I don't know it by that name, but I can disguise my voice. It's an ability I was born with, apparently, but it took the teaching of an old man to make me realize it.'

'An old man?'

'Yes. He was a pedlar I met on my very first trip abroad.'

'Was his name Babak?' Terrel asked, remembering his own mentor in such matters.

'No, it was Kaisek. It's a word from an ancient tongue no one speaks any more. It means—'

'Let me guess,' Terrel cut in. 'It means "the king"?'

'You *are* a scholar,' Jarvik exclaimed in surprise. 'How did you know that?'

'Intuition,' the healer replied. 'I . . . Never mind, it's not important. Is changing your voice your only talent?'

'No. It seems I am also a prophet. Of a sort.'

With those words, several things began to fall into place.

'You knew that if I went to the sculpture I'd be seen by the soldiers there.'

'I knew it was a possibility,' the colonel admitted. 'I can't control what I see. The visions come upon me in flashes. It was frightening at first, but I've learnt to accept them for what they are – glimpses of things that will happen, or might happen.'

'Othersight,' Terrel whispered.

'What?' Jarvik looked puzzled.

'Do you know what prompts these visions?'

'Not really. I think the lunar alignments play a part, but there's more to it than that. They only started once I left the island.'

Terrel was forming his own theory about that, but for the moment he wanted to return to more personal concerns.

'So you're the one who persuaded Ostan to take me to Whale Ness?'

'Yes.'

'Why?'

Jarvik and Tegan exchanged glances.

'You expected me to die, didn't you?' Terrel said. 'You sent me there, knowing that!' The realization made him doubt the worth of his new allies.

'I did,' the colonel admitted. 'It was a mistake, and I'm sorry for it . . .'

'Thanks a lot,' Terrel muttered.

'He didn't have all the facts,' Tegan explained, 'and his vision hadn't told him the whole story. He saw it as an opportunity for peace and acted accordingly.'

'Peace? By getting me killed?'

'But you *weren't* killed,' Tegan pointed out. 'You're here now, and we all have an even greater opportunity because of it.'

Terrel couldn't argue with her logic, though the earlier deception still rankled.

'And I'm supposed to trust you now, am I?' he said. 'Or are you planning to get me killed the next time an opportunity arises?'

'You're worth a lot more to us alive now than you would have been dead,' Tegan told him earnestly.

'I don't blame you for being angry,' Jarvik added. 'I'll try to explain if you'll let me, then you can judge for yourself.' Taking Terrel's silence for assent, he went on. 'As you know, I've always been fascinated by legends, and one of the tales that's always been associated with Savik's Whale is that an arrival such as yours would be a harbinger of a time of change. Interpretations vary, but I'd always hoped it meant there'd be an end to the war.'

'And you were prepared to sacrifice me for that?'

'Yes,' the soldier replied bluntly. 'The death of an inno-cent martyr would have been a very powerful symbol on which to build our case for peace.'

'Then why did you try to deny your involvement in my going ashore there?' Terrel asked, more curious now than angry.

'I had to distance myself, in case you were captured rather than killed. I didn't want Kjolur to become too well known.'

Terrel digested this argument, finding that he could accept it with relative calm.

'A time of change could mean anything,' he said. The phrase was already familiar to him from other occasions in his travels, and he had found Jarvik's use of it oddly reassuring. 'What made you think it would be your interpretation that was believed?'

It was Tegan who answered.

'That's where the Holma comes in. We've been waiting a long time for the chance to send a message to all Myvatan – and this was the starting point.'

'One legend among hundreds?' Terrel queried scepti-cally.

'Yes, but a very powerful one,' she replied. 'All four quarters have their own versions.'

'And we had something else to lend credence to our message,' Jarvik put in. 'Something more than just an old story.'

'And what was that?'

'This.' The colonel took something from his pocket and held it up between his thumb and forefinger. 'It may not look like much, but it's the last part of a puzzle I've been trying to put together for a long time.'

The object he was holding was a slim metal cylinder, no bigger than his little finger. The surface had the dull sheen of much wear and tear, but as Terrel peered at it, he could see faint markings that seemed familiar. He picked out representations of a fish, a whale, a bird, and a bolt of lightning, and he had no doubt that somewhere he would find the other three symbols the nomads had used for their oracle, and which he had also seen elsewhere. He felt a tingle of excitement, certain that this must be part of his own quest too.

'What is it?' he asked quietly.

'It's a container,' Jarvik replied. 'The vial is important, but only because it's proof that what's inside is genuine.'

'And what's that?'

For answer, the colonel unscrewed the top of the cylinder, then tipped the contents out onto his palm. A translucent red stone slid out. It was faceted like a crystal, tapering slightly towards one end before coming to a sharp angular point. Within its delicate, jewelled depths, something small and bright glowed like a trapped snowflake.

'This is the last and most important stone in the circle of flame,' Jarvik said reverently. 'It's said that it was made from a drop of the moon's blood that fell to Nydus from Bvandir's comet and then froze within the ice. With this, you have a chance to rekindle the flame that once burned within the Circle of Truce.'

'Me?'

'Yes. You were the one whose arrival signalled the time of change.'

'Can I hold it?' Terrel asked, wondering how so small a stone, no matter how curious or beautiful, could be so powerful.

'Of course.' Jarvik handed the crystal over, then watched as Terrel's expression changed from interest to astonishment. Tegan cried out a moment later and the colonel's mouth fell open in disbelief.

As the fingers of the healer's good hand had closed around the stone, the small imperfection at its heart had begun to shine more brightly than before. In the space of a heartbeat the glare became so intense that it was hard to look at it directly, and the whole room was bathed in a brilliant, rose-coloured light.

CHAPTER THIRTY-TWO

Terrel was so mesmerized that he hardly felt the internal trembling, but in the next moment, when everything in the kitchen began to shake, he recognized it for what it was. In a reflex action that he could not have explained rationally, he put the crystal down on the table, where its light faded instantly, but the vibration went on.

Even though it was clearly a relatively small tremor, the earthquake raised the usual primeval fears in Terrel, and he was very glad when it died away. Both Jarvik and Tegan seemed to have taken the disturbance in their stride, and Terrel reminded himself that such things were common enough on Myvatan. What had happened with the stone was not. The islanders were both staring at the crystal. In the still silence, their faces shone with the memory of its brief radiance.

'How did you do that?' Jarvik breathed.

'I didn't *do* anything. It just happened.'

'But ...' The colonel was staring intently at Terrel now, his expression betraying utter astonishment. The healer could understand the other man's amazement. He didn't know what had happened either. He wondered whether the invisible star he carried within him had somehow reacted with the stone, but he couldn't see how or why it should have done so. There had been no eclipse — and he certainly wasn't inside an elemental.

'It's a sign!' Tegan declared, her eyes bright.

Jarvik shook his head, and for once Terrel thought he glimpsed a little of the truth within the soldier's eyes. It was a truth that made what had happened all the more surprising.

'It *was* a sign,' Tegan repeated, eager now. 'We're going to find it. The real one!' She glanced at Jarvik, and Terrel saw the hope in her face – and knew that neither he nor the colonel would say anything to crush her newborn faith. Tegan had just moved one step closer to the fulfilment of a dream.

'I think you should put the stone away,' Terrel said. He had presumed all along that Jarvik and Tegan would have a plausible reason for the three of them to be meeting like this, but it would be better if their alliance remained known only to their friends – and he was worried that the burst of light might have attracted some unwanted attention.

Jarvik picked up the crystal and held it for a moment before sliding it back into the metal container and stowing it away in his pocket. His face still betrayed his confusion, but he was trying to hide it now.

'It *is* a sign, isn't it?' Tegan asked, sensing the uncertainty around her. 'We were right about Terrel. This proves it.' She turned to the healer. 'Did you see anything? Were you able to read the far-crystals?'

Terrel shook his head.

'I don't know what you mean. All I saw was this room.'

The magian looked disappointed, but then seemed to convince herself that all was not lost.

'It's not time yet,' she said. 'And we're not in the right place.' She looked to Jarvik for confirmation.

'You're right, of course,' he said, recovering his composure.

'How did you come to have the stone?' Terrel asked.

'I came across it on my latest trip abroad,' the colonel replied. 'At the time it seemed just like a chance encounter, but I think there was more to it than that. Fate – or perhaps the stone itself – was guiding me.'

'So you had it with you on board the *Skua*,' Terrel said, remembering the casket in the merchant's private cabin.

'Yes. I would have shown it to you then if I'd known . . .'

'Why was it in a foreign land when it was supposed to have fallen on Myvatan?'

'Long ago, the guardians of the Circle of Truce saw that war had become inevitable,' Tegan replied. 'They thought the only hope for the future was to hide the sacred artefacts so that they would not be tainted by the madness of the conflict. So some of them travelled from these shores.'

'And neither they nor any of the things they took with them were ever heard of again,' Jarvik said. 'Until now.'

'It's strange,' Tegan went on. 'When Kjolur sails to the south, it's under the pretence of looking for new weapons for the war. What he's actually brought back could bring peace.'

'And the sooner the better,' the sometime merchant declared. 'You heard what Tofana's planning to do. It's appalling.'

'We can't let her do this!' the magian exclaimed, her own revulsion clear.

'The springs at Hvannadal, you mean?' Terrel queried.

'Gods, yes!' Tegan cried. 'What she's done already is bad enough, but that would be catastrophic.'

'You'd better tell Terrel what's been happening,' Jarvik said.

The magian took a deep breath, preparing to relive unpleasant events. When she began speaking she kept her voice neutral, as if she could only bring herself to talk about such things by shutting down her emotions.

'As you know, the Wizard has been busy training fire-starters. At first she was hoping they'd be able to use the water inside any human body to kill from within. That way, the neomancers would be able to pick their targets at will. But it didn't work, because the chains weren't always complete and the lines weren't accurate enough. There were some dreadful accidents, where the whole process reversed itself and it was the fire-starter and not his intended victim who burned. At other times they killed the wrong targets, and sometimes the experiments spiralled out of control so that everyone close by was in danger. Even when the fire-starters were unharmed, some of them have been driven half mad by what's going on. The gods know what would happen if we ever let such men loose on a real battlefield. They could just as easily end up slaughtering their own comrades as the enemy.'

'Which is why Tofana reverted to an earlier plan,' Jarvik put in.

'The worst thing is that this plan might really work,' Tegan went on. 'If we *do* manage to get hold of Hvannadal's secrets, the chain will almost form itself. Any magic nearby will start it off and trigger the internal fires. In effect, the White neomancers will kill themselves and all their companions. It's a nightmare, the ultimate perversion of wizardry.'

'And if it works at Hvannadal,' the colonel added, 'there's no reason to suppose it won't work at any of the other enemy water supplies.'

'That's what Tofana intends,' Tegan confirmed. 'The problem is, the wizards on the other side aren't stupid. They're bound to find out what she's doing, and try to use the same thing against us. Imagine the pools here being turned into a deathtrap.'

The horror of such an enormous increase in the scale of violence was not lost on any of them.

'Tofana claims that if we time it right, we can wipe out all the enemy wizards and magians before they realize what's going on,' Jarvik said. 'Or at least before they get the chance to retaliate.'

'*All* of them?' the magian exclaimed in disbelief. 'She can't possibly believe that. By its very nature, the process will go out of control as soon as it's initiated. We won't be able to tell *where* the chains will lead.' Tegan's forced calm had deserted her now.

'I'm not defending Tofana,' Jarvik told her. 'I'm just reporting her reasoning.'

'And the generals believe her?'

'They believe her because they want to. If she's right, and they take Hvannadal, they'll become the last great heroes of the war, the ultimate victors. Who's going to argue with the chance of having such a place in history?'

'Even if it comes at the price of thousands dying, in the most horrible manner imaginable?'

'They're the enemy. They deserve to die.'

Tegan's disgust at such justification almost overwhelmed her. Controlling herself with some difficulty, she went on, enunciating her words with unnatural precision.

'It could be even worse than that.'

'What do you mean?' Terrel asked.

'Ultimately, all the water sources on Myvatan are linked. If the subverted lines spread, we could *all* end up burning. Every man, woman and child on this island would be destroyed.'

They were silent for a while, each of them contemplating the prospect of Myvatan being turned into a gigantic funeral pyre.

'So the question becomes, how do we stop all this from happening?' Jarvik said eventually.

'Is there any way you could sabotage Tofana's efforts?' Terrel suggested.

'I've done what I can to slow her progress down,' Tegan replied, 'but it's not enough. And if I do anything too obvious, she'll just get rid of me – probably in the next round of tests.' She shuddered at the thought.

'No,' the colonel decided. 'We must stick to our original plan.'

'What's that?' Terrel asked.

'The underground has been working towards a single goal for several years now. The only way we can see any hope of peace returning to Myvatan is if we rebuild the Circle of Truce – a place where old enmities can finally be set aside. If we do that, Tegan and her colleagues could turn all their magical resources to doing good, rather than finding ways to promote destruction. If that happened, the benefits would soon become clear to everyone. But to persuade people to give it a fair chance, we need them to believe it's what the gods want, what is meant to be. That's where the legends come in.'

'It's not going to be easy to overturn centuries of hatred.' Terrel had seen the vile results of other, much shorter wars, in other lands, and knew the terrible difficulties the Holma faced.

'We know,' Jarvik admitted. 'The war is so entrenched in our way of life that it's going to need something spectacular to change the way everyone thinks.'

'And that's where you want to use the Circle of Truce?'

'Exactly.'

'But I thought Akurvellir has been lost for generations.'

'It has,' the colonel conceded 'but we don't really need to find the city. The flame is all we need. That was – is –

the true heart of the place. Then we can build a *new* Circle of Truce.'

'But wasn't the flame extinguished?'

'That's what most people think. We're going to prove them wrong.'

'How?'

'By finding it in the ice and lighting a new torch,' Tegan replied. 'Bringing it out into the open again.'

'But—'

'The whole thing may just be a myth,' Jarvik explained, 'but it's a myth a lot of people *believe*. Whether we find the real thing or not is almost irrelevant.' He glanced at Tegan, but she remained silent. 'The flame will be a tangible sign that the war is *supposed* to end, that the ancient schism can be healed. Why should it matter where it comes from? In this case, the end really will justify the means.'

It was the kind of dishonesty Terrel could approve of, but he still didn't understand how it could be done.

'Can you really do it?' he asked.

'With your help, I'm sure we can,' Jarvik replied. 'The problem is, we have to do it *before* Tofana's let loose at Hvannadal. Anything else is just too appalling to contemplate.'

'So we have to get Pingeyri to change the order of the campaign?'

'Precisely. That's where you and the Peacemaker come in. It gives us the perfect excuse to go to the Lonely Peaks and "discover" the flame. We have to convince the general that it would be worth his while to have the sword before he goes to the springs. Any ideas?'

'Not at the moment,' Terrel said, beginning to consider the problem. 'It's hard to see how one weapon could make much of a difference.'

'It doesn't exist, of course,' the colonel said. 'At least I hope it doesn't.'

'And if it did, we certainly wouldn't want anyone to find it!' Tegan added fervently.

'But its mythical status would make the man who wields it invincible, because all his comrades – and his enemies – would *believe* that he was. The sword's attraction for Pingeyri is not in doubt.' Jarvik smiled ruefully. 'What we need is an excuse to go looking for it first. Then we'll just happen to find something else.'

'Do you know the timing of the campaign?' Terrel asked.

'Nothing's been set in stone yet,' the soldier replied. 'There are just too many unknown factors in a military operation of this size. The only thing I know for sure is that Tofana wants to be at Hvannadal when the White Moon is at its strongest. That's the opposite of normal tactical logic, but it means that the magic of the springs will be at its most potent – and so the chain reaction will be even more powerful.'

'On the other hand,' Tegan said, 'if you're going to pretend to look for the Peacemaker, you'll need to be on the glacier at the full of the Red Moon.'

'So where does that leave us?' Terrel realized he had taken little notice of the lunar configurations recently. This was unusual, and he wondered at his own indifference.

'At present, the White Moon is three days short of new,' the magian told him. 'So it will be full nineteen days from now.'

'That's probably too soon,' Jarvik stated. 'We'd never be able to get there in time, unless the White choose not to defend their territory at all. And that's hardly likely.'

'So we should have until the next full, at least,' Terrel concluded.

'Yes,' Tegan agreed, 'and in the meantime, the Red Moon will be full some seventeen days before that.'

'Then it fits,' Terrel said. 'From a logistical point of view, it *would* make sense to go to the Lonely Peaks first.'

'You can argue that way,' Jarvik conceded, 'but Pingeyri seems set on Hvannadal. We need to persuade him to change his mind. I'll do my best, but he's stubborn when he's got his heart fixed on some great adventure, so if there's any other avenue you want to pursue, do whatever you can.'

The colonel was about to say something more when he was interrupted by a sharp double tap at the door. All three of them froze. After a short pause, the knocking was repeated, first three times, then twice again. Tegan and Jarvik relaxed at what was obviously a prearranged signal, and the magian hurried across to let the newcomer in. It was Myrdal, and as soon as he was inside, the adjutant and Tegan embraced. Such was the intensity of their kiss that, as far as they were concerned, there might as well have been no one else in the room. Terrel found himself staring, then grew embarrassed at his own curiosity and looked away. On the other side of the table, Jarvik smiled and gave an apologetic shrug.

'They're not the only ones who have given up a great deal for the cause,' he said quietly, 'but in the end not even war or magic is going to keep those two apart.'

Terrel nodded, but he couldn't find the words to express what he was feeling. He could imagine much of the couple's story now, but his thoughts had flown to Alyssa – and whether they would ever experience such a reunion. Seeing Tegan and Myrdal together made his memory of the events of the previous night even more bitter.

'Enough, you two,' Jarvik called amiably. 'You're embarrassing our guest.'

After a brief exchange of whispers, the lovers disentangled themselves and crossed to the table.

'Are you going to help us?' Myrdal demanded without preamble.

'Yes. I'm going to do everything in my power to help you.' As he spoke, Terrel couldn't help wondering what the reaction would have been if his answer had been different. He knew too much to remain free – unless they trusted him.

'You know all my secrets now,' Tegan said, emphasizing this point.

'But you're still going to search for this elemental of yours?' the adjutant queried.

'Yes, I have to.'

'You think it's become an ally of the old dragon of the volcanoes?'

'Perhaps it *is* the old dragon,' Tegan suggested. 'That would explain a lot.'

Terrel was considering this idea when Myrdal spoke again.

'The general wants you,' he told Jarvik. 'One last meeting to discuss strategy.'

'I'd better go, then,' the colonel decided. 'We're pretty much done here for the time being. We'll be in touch, Terrel.'

'Good luck.'

'Thanks. We may need it.'

After Myrdal had snatched another kiss from Tegan, the two soldiers left together. For a few moments the magian looked bereft, then she turned back to Terrel, a determined smile on her beautiful face.

'Latira will be back soon. She's one of us too.'

Terrel nodded, not wanting to reveal that he already knew this.

'It's good that the two of you have been getting on so well,' Tegan remarked.

'She's made me very welcome,' Terrel replied awkwardly.

'I should go,' the magian said. 'Tofana might be wondering what I'm up to.'

'Can I ask you something first?'

'Of course.'

'Is Yarek a member of the Holma?'

'No. Not yet, at least. I know how he feels about the war, but he's too unreliable.'

'I think he could help us.'

'We'll see,' she said. 'Don't tell him anything, will you?'

'No. I can keep secrets too.'

'I'm sure you can.' Tegan walked over to the door, put her hand on the latch, then hesitated. 'You *will* find the flame, you know. The real one. Jarvik was just trying to make sure . . . Never mind.'

'I'll do whatever I can,' Terrel promised.

'Once you're at the Lonely Peaks, you could even ask your elemental to help us.'

'I'm not sure that would work,' he replied, 'but if I get the chance, I'll try.'

'Having a dragon on our side could be useful,' Tegan added, and smiled.

CHAPTER THIRTY-THREE

The three newest recruits to Raufar's troop were staked out naked on the half-frozen ground. To Terrel, who was watching with a mixture of distaste and morbid fascination, they looked very young, no more than boys. Their bodies were pale in the flickering torchlight, and they were shivering as much from fear as from the cold. Far above, the White Moon, almost full, silvered the scene with its frigid radiance.

The initiation ceremony was almost over now. The young soldiers had already been forced to endure various humiliations in silence, and this was their final test – though neither they nor Terrel knew exactly what it would entail. The rest of the onlookers did, however, and their sadistic amusement was plain. They had all had to undergo the same sort of trial on the eve of their first trip into an enemy quarter – and having survived the experience, and been accepted into the warriors' brotherhood, they saw no reason why others should not have to do the same.

Terrel could only be glad that he had not been included in the evening's entertainment. He was effectively a member of their company now and, apart from a brief incursion into the Gold Quarter on the way back from Whale Ness, he had not ventured into enemy territory either. However, no one had suggested that he join the initiates, either out of respect for his supposed talents or uncertainty about his standing within the troop, given that he was not a proper soldier – and a foreigner to boot.

Captain Raufar had not taken an active role in the proceedings, and had just watched impassively as his lieutenants went about their business. Terrel had gathered that the military authorities officially disapproved of such rituals, but were prepared to turn a blind eye to them as long as they remained private, within the various units of the army. No outsiders would be allowed inside the troop's section of the camp until the ceremonies were over.

Terrel watched as Pjorsa poured a sticky brown mixture from a bucket, covering each of the trio in turn. The healer had no idea what the noxious substance was, but he did not have to wait long before its purpose became clear. The circle of spectators parted and Narvat and Stykkis returned, each leading several of the dogs that were used to pull the baggage sleds. The hounds were straining at their leashes, eager to start, and as soon as they were released they leapt forward and began to eat the mixture, licking it from the novices' skin with long, rough tongues. The snuffling noises they made were horrifying in themselves, and the expressions on the victims' faces revealed their terror, especially when the dogs' fangs moved close to the more tender parts of their anatomy. Yet still none of the initiates made any sound. At first they could not help squirming, trying to avoid the hounds' attentions, but eventually they realized that their ordeal would be over more quickly if they kept still. And so they lay rigid, eyes screwed shut, breathing in erratic gulps, while the onlookers laughed and shouted out various helpful comments.

Finally, when the last specks of food had been licked clean, the dogs were led away. The three young men were untied and helped to their feet, amid much laughter, backslapping and words of congratulation. They were allowed

to dress, and steaming cups of melcras were pressed into
their trembling hands. All three recovered their spirits
quickly, soon joining in with the good-natured banter and
smiling with relief. The gathering dispersed to make
preparations for the evening meal, for the night's rest —
and for the next day, when the serious business would
begin.

The huge encampment was situated close to the border
with the White Quarter. It had taken more than half a
median month to get there — much longer than Terrel had
expected — because an army of such size was a cumber-
some entity, and could only move at a fraction of the
speed a single company could have managed. In all that
time Terrel had hardly seen anyone outside the company
to which he'd been assigned — and had found this increasingly frustrating. There had been no further contact from
the Holma, and no one in Raufar's troop had given any
sign that they might be a member of the secret organization. Terrel understood that as they moved into enemy
territory the various units would split and go their separate
ways, and he knew he was running out of time. Nor had
there been any sign of Alyssa or his ghostly allies, and this
left him feeling more alone than ever. He could not believe
that Alyssa would really have abandoned him — but if she
had, she couldn't have picked a worse time.
    Adding to his anxiety was the fact that General Pingeyri
had proved intractable about his plan of campaign, and
would soon take his land-based forces into the mountain
passes that led to Hvannadal. That he would do so on a
day when the White Moon was full was an act of bravado
of which the entire army seemed to approve. The very fact
that they were to scorn the chance of waiting a mere two
days until their own Dark Moon would be full was in itself

a challenge, both to their foes and to their own warrior mentality. Terrel felt sick at the thought of the violence to come, but there seemed to be nothing he could do to prevent it. He just had to go where fate took him, and keep his own goals in mind. It seemed that if he were ever to reach the glacier – and the Ancient – he would have to go to Hvannadal first.

His last night in Saudark had been a confusing time. After Tegan had left him he had waited for Latira, but she hadn't returned, and eventually Terrel had gone out on an errand of his own – reasoning that he would be able to talk to her later in the evening. He had gone to see Eskif, hoping that the brigadier's promise of help still held good. It had taken him some time to track his quarry down, but after several arguments with harried adjutants, he had finally been ushered into the room where the senior officer and his son were poring over several maps.

The two men had smiled when they saw their visitor, and made him welcome, but as soon as Terrel raised doubts about the wisdom of the military operation, the brigadier had become as stubborn as the general would subsequently prove to be. Once the matter of the lunar configurations had been dismissed as irrelevant, Terrel had not been able to give any plausible reason for them going to the Lonely Peaks before Hvannadal, and Eskif had informed him – with feigned regret – that even if he wanted to change Pingeyri's mind, he would not be able to do so.

Terrel had then tried to point out some of the possible dangers of Tofana's intended course of action. This had met with a more sympathetic response – with Eskif admitting that he didn't really like the plan, because it relied on 'too much wizardry and not enough soldiery' – but in the end the conclusion had been the same. When Terrel had asked if the brigadier would at least try to get Pingeyri to question the true nature of Tofana's new magic, Eskif had pointed out that the general was his commanding officer, and Tofana the most powerful wizard on Myvatan. Only a fool would try to come between those two. It seemed that everything had been decided.

Returning to his own tower, Terrel had again waited for Latira, but she had been nowhere to be seen and so he had climbed the stairs to his own room, and finally, late into the night, fallen into a restless sleep. His mental turmoil over what Alyssa had seen – and what she might believe had happened – made it impossible for him to relax, and his dreams were a mixture of fragmentary and disturbing images.

The next morning there was still no sign of Latira, and Terrel had begun to worry about her mysterious absence. But then he had been swept up in the preparations for his own departure, and kitted out with new, warm clothes and a backpack containing the equipment he would need – to which he had added his own few belongings. Before he had known it, he had been leaving Saudark, wondering whether he would ever see Latira again. Having no command of Myvatan's written language, he hadn't even been able to leave her a note, and he fretted about all his unanswered questions.

A few days later, he had discovered – quite by chance – that she was in fact travelling with the army. The unprecedented presence of various wizards and their retinues had meant that unusual measures had had to be taken for the provisioning of the army. To that end, various servants were travelling with the soldiers. It was possible that Myrdal had been in charge of such arrangements, and had chosen Latira in order to have another member of the

Holma on hand, but Terrel had no way of knowing this for sure. He had made several attempts to locate her during the march north, but he had not even caught a glimpse of her.

The journey itself had been an extraordinary experience, and if he hadn't been so preoccupied with other matters, Terrel would have wondered at the things he had seen. Travelling with the main army – a second force had headed southwest from Saudark to the ports, whence they would complete the journey to the White Quarter by ship – their route had taken Terrel through a landscape that he could only ever have dreamt about. He'd trudged across vast snowfields, some of which would not melt even at the height of summer. He had seen vast glittering mountains in the distance, and walked beneath great cliffs of blue-white ice as the troops skirted the edges of the glaciers. He'd crossed ravines that he had first thought to be rivers, but which he had discovered were fissure lines, where the skin of the planet was thin and cracked, revealing some of the power within. In places steam rose from these fissures, while in others there were bubbling masses of scalding mud, and he had even seen one place where the underground heat had produced small lakes of hot water inside caves made entirely of ice. Most surprising of all were the many small settlements that clustered around these fissures, taking advantage of the energy within and defying the dangers of living on such unstable land. In times of earthquakes it was not uncommon to see flames and smoke rising from the crevasses, and the opposite banks often shifted, so that any bridges and crossing places had to be repaired almost constantly.

Terrel had also seen many strange rock formations, with several enormous boulders balanced with seemingly impossible precision on top of much smaller stones. This had reminded him of Savik's Whale, and he wondered whether it had been carved from one such formation. In other places, outcrops of bare rock were scored with straight lines, which he had been told always ran precisely north-south, and were thus a useful aid to navigation in open country. At first he'd assumed that these were man-made, even though it had seemed a huge and, for the most part, pointless undertaking to carve so many lines. However, Raufar had told him that the marks had been made by the gods – to show that even the land beneath men's feet was theirs to do with as they wished.

Elsewhere there were signs of mankind's influence on the terrain, including some that appeared to be almost unimaginably ancient. The jumbled, eroded ruins of long-dead buildings – it was impossible to tell whether they had been fortresses, temples or mere dwellings – lay at various points along the route. When Terrel had asked about them, he'd been told that no one knew who had built them or what had happened to the builders. None of the soldiers seemed to care one way or the other, but the healer had seen similar evidence of vanished civilizations during his other travels on Nydus, and the implications of their existence continued to intrigue him.

Something else preyed on his mind as they travelled, and that was the sense of madness and evil that seemed to pervade the entire island. As Elam had pointed out, it was stronger in some places than in others – for no discernible reason – and in a way, that made it harder to bear. If it had been constant, like an unvarying background noise, it would have been easier to ignore. As it was, Terrel would often find himself feeling better or worse without knowing why, and it seemed that even staying in one place was no guarantee of constancy. The strength of the invisible forces also varied with time – and Terrel couldn't help wondering

whether it was fragmented in the same way as the 'wind'
that made it impossible for his spectral allies to remain
with him at times. If that was the case, it would be another
indication that the insanity of Myvatan was linked to – or
even caused by – the elemental.

Once that thought had become fixed in his mind, Terrel
had begun to notice something else. At the times when the
madness was at its lowest ebb, he had become aware of
other presences in the air. Initially, these had been no
more than half-seen flickers at the edge of his vision, but
as he'd grown accustomed to them he had begun to see
them a little more clearly. Even so, it had taken a long
time before he was able to convince himself that they
really were what they seemed. These ghosts were not like
his allies from home, but were twisted, malformed shapes
that were only occasionally recognizable as human forms.
None of their features were ever clear, but their torment
was. They writhed and gesticulated, often close to some of
the soldiers, as if they were trying to get the living to listen
to them. If that *was* the case, they were failing. It was
obvious that Terrel's companions could not see them, and
even he could hear nothing of what he imagined were the
ghosts' shouts and screams. If these tortured wraiths had a
purpose in pursuing the people of the healer's world,
then – like Yarek's father in the boy's dream – they were
meeting with a complete lack of success.

At times they seemed to be everywhere, clamouring
silently for attention or just drifting hopelessly by on an
invisible breeze, and Terrel had to try to block them from
his vision to keep from being driven to distraction. The
phantoms were superimposed on the real world but separate from it, and he found their presence unnerving. He
understood now why Alyssa had said that there were 'too
many' ghosts on Myvatan. The fact that they matched the

images from his own dream about the Great Plain – and the futility of that dreadful place – convinced him that they were the spirits of soldiers, but there was no way to help these lost souls, or even to make contact with them.

Terrel's new awareness made him long more than ever to talk to his own allies again. He was reasonably certain now that this must have something to do with the problem in the ghosts' world – the reason for Elam's insistence that they ought not to be on Myvatan. But if that was the case, why would their presence have made the situation worse? And if that *was* true, how had Elam solved their dilemma?

'You've done well,' Raufar said as they ate their evening rations. 'Some of my men didn't think you'd be able to keep up.'

'Some of them resented having to watch over you, is what the captain means,' Pjorsa put in.

'I can be strong when I need to be,' Terrel said.

'So we've seen,' Raufar conceded. 'But the real test starts tomorrow.'

'It's been pretty easy going up to now,' Stykkis observed with a grin.

'And this is the last night the army will be together,' the captain said. 'Is there anyone you want to see before we go?'

There were a few smiles and sidelong glances exchanged between the soldiers then, and Terrel realized that his liaison with Latira must have become common knowledge. There were other people he dearly wanted to see as well, but she was the only one he could admit to.

'You mean I'm free to visit whoever I want?' Until then, Raufar and his men had taken their bodyguard duties very seriously. Terrel had never been left alone, and had not been allowed to move outside the company.

'For tonight,' the captain confirmed. 'Just make sure you're back by the last bell.'

Terrel got to his feet at once.

'He's in a hurry!' Narvat remarked, provoking some ribald laughter.

'Need someone to hold your hand?' Pjorsa enquired. 'We wouldn't like you to get lost on such an important mission.'

Terrel realized that he did indeed need some guidance. The camp was huge; he could wander around for hours without finding the person he was looking for.

'Latira's assigned to the wizards' caravan,' Raufar said, taking pity on him. 'Over there, on the other side of that ridge.'

'Thanks.' Terrel set off, trying to ignore the advice that was shouted after him, and began to thread his way between the rows of tents. However, he had not gone very far before he felt a hand on his arm.

'I was just coming to see you,' Jarvik remarked casually. 'We need to talk.'

CHAPTER THIRTY-FOUR

'Is it safe to talk here?' Terrel asked, glancing at the various groups of soldiers they were passing. Some of the men were boisterous while others were quiet, their faces showing no expression.

'Everyone reacts differently to the prospect of battle,' Jarvik replied, 'but I doubt any of them will be paying us much attention. Some of us find it hard to keep still, so walking round the camp is natural.' They had set off again, though with no particular destination in mind.

'You're not afraid we'll be overheard?'

'Not really. We should try not to say anything . . . foolish. But if we keep moving no one will hear too much anyway. As I said, they have their own concerns at the moment. If anyone saw us trying to hide away somewhere, that *would* look odd, but like this we're just part of the crowd.'

Terrel still felt nervous, but he had little choice but to heed the colonel's advice. They *did* need to talk, after all.

'Is the general still determined to stick to his plan?'

'Yes. We've tried everything we can to persuade him otherwise, but he won't be budged. Tofana's eager to get to the springs and test her theories, and together they've got their minds made up.'

'So what are we going to do?'

'We have some ideas,' Jarvik told him, 'but it's probably best if you don't know the details just yet.'

'But—'

'There's still a chance we'll be able to change things,' the colonel said, cutting off Terrel's objection. 'But if we can't, and we have to go to the glacier after the springs, then we'll just have to make the best of things.'

'It might be too late then.'

'Let's hope not. In any case, I don't want you to worry about that. Your job is to make sure that whenever we *do* get to the Lonely Peaks, you make the discovery we need.'

'Should I try to persuade Raufar to go there instead of Hvannadal?'

'No. The good captain would never disobey a direct order from the general. And besides, we need your discovery to be witnessed by as many people as possible, not just one company. The more public the event, the more weight it will carry. There'd be little point in you going off on your own. You see what I mean?'

Terrel nodded.

'We have to put on a show,' he said.

'Exactly.'

'And that's all it will be, isn't it? A show.'

'Perhaps,' Jarvik admitted. 'Does that bother you?' When Terrel did not answer, he went on. 'Whatever the reality, it's the effect that's important. I thought we agreed on that.'

'We do. It's just . . .'

'You can't afford to be half-hearted about this,' the colonel said earnestly. 'None of us can. Too much depends on it. So, are you with us?'

'Yes,' Terrel replied, pushing his doubts aside. 'Of course.'

'Good. Then you'd better take this.'

Terrel felt the cold metal of the cylinder being pressed into his hand. He took it and quickly slipped it into a pocket, out of sight. He couldn't help glancing around to see whether anyone had noticed the transfer but, true to Jarvik's prediction, no one was paying them any attention. Even so, it was a while before his racing heartbeat returned to normal.

'You're the one who's going to have to use it,' the colonel said. 'I'll be there with you if I can, but who knows what'll happen between now and then, so it's best if you keep it. Just don't open it until the time is right.' This last instruction was accompanied by a grin.

Although he had no intention of doing so, Terrel couldn't help smiling at the thought of the stir he would cause if he removed the stone now and filled the night with its rose-tinted radiance.

'I'll save it for the show,' he promised.

'Good decision,' Jarvik commented.

'I can't guarantee it'll work again, though,' Terrel added. 'After all, it's a fake, isn't it?'

The colonel's stride faltered momentarily, and he didn't answer straightaway.

'What makes you think that?' he said eventually.

'There are some lies even I can see on your face.'

Jarvik considered this statement for a while, then evidently made his decision and became businesslike once more.

'The container is genuine,' he said. 'I'm certain it came from . . . the right place. I was drawn to it by forces I don't understand even now, and you can't imagine the joy I felt when I found it – or my disappointment when I realized it was empty. Try as I might, I couldn't trace the stone. The trail had gone cold and I was running out of time.'

'So you found something to replace it.'

'Yes. I bought the stone you have from a market trader

in Barkarillia. It's just a pretty bauble roughly the right size and colour. At least I thought it was, until . . . That's why I was so surprised when you . . . did what you did.'

'Thank you,' Terrel said.

'What for?'

'For trusting me with the truth.'

'Promise me you'll keep this to yourself,' Jarvik pleaded. 'We're dependent on faith if we're to succeed – and it can be a fragile thing sometimes.'

Terrel was aware of that, just as he was aware that faith could also be incredibly strong at times. Given the right circumstances, belief could overpower truth. Even so, he was worried about the way the falsehoods seemed to be multiplying. The stone was false; the underground had no genuine expectation of finding the real Circle of Truce; and the flame they were to rekindle would in fact have little in common with the original fire. And they were going to the Lonely Peaks under the pretence of looking for something else entirely. Out of such base components, Terrel was supposed to construct a 'show' that would bring peace to a land ravaged by a bitter civil war for nearly four centuries.

'I won't tell anyone,' he said, thinking of the hope he'd seen in Tegan's eyes.

Jarvik looked relieved.

'Do you really not know why we saw what we saw?' he asked.

'I've no idea.' This was only a half-truth, but it seemed to satisfy the colonel.

'Do you think it might have absorbed power from the vial somehow?' Jarvik asked.

The same thought had occurred to Terrel, but he had no way of telling if it might be true. And that still wouldn't explain why the stone had reacted to his touch and no one else's. The healer had wondered about the fact that the burst of crystal light and the barely acknowledged earthquake had occurred simultaneously. If the glow *had* been connected to his amulet, then it was possible that both phenomena were linked to the elemental – and that the timing had been anything but coincidental. But quite what that would mean was beyond him.

'It's possible,' he said. 'Let's hope so.'

'I should get back to my own unit,' Jarvik said as the first of the three signal bells rang. 'Is there anything else?'

'Are you aware of the effect mitra has?' Terrel asked.

'Yes. It wasn't a coincidence that my abilities came to the fore when I left Myvatan. After I returned it wasn't hard to work out why.'

'Is there any way to counteract it?'

'Some of our friends are working on a solution, but it's everywhere. You've seen that for yourself.' Jarvik waved a hand at a steaming cauldron, from which the unmistakable scent of the herb was drifting into the night. 'It actually does do some good – helping people to breathe more easily when the air is thin, combating the effects of cold – but no one seems to realize the effect it has on people's minds. I'm surprised you picked up on it so quickly. We can't destroy the stuff. There's just too much of it. And breaking the habit of its use will be a long-term project. We can't afford the time. For now we'll just have to avoid it as much as possible.'

Terrel wondered if the friends Jarvik had mentioned were magians like Tegan, and whether their solution would involve magic, but that was something he didn't feel able to discuss in the open. For the moment, it was enough to know that the Holma were aware of the problem.

'One last question,' he said. 'Is there a wizard among our friends?'

Jarvik shook his head.

'I wish there was,' he said, 'but that's the last place we should be looking for help.'

After he and the colonel had parted company, Terrel resumed his search for Latira – but was intercepted once more. Initially he did not recognize the captain who was pacing up and down, but as he passed by, the soldier looked up and his face betrayed first surprise then an eagerness the healer didn't understand.

'Terrel! I didn't expect to see you again here.'

'Hello, Kopak. Are you well?'

The brigadier's son glanced at his fingers.

'Very well, thanks to you, but . . .' He hesitated.

Terrel could see that his former patient wanted to talk, but time was getting on, and if he wanted to see Latira and still keep his promise to Raufar, he had no time to waste.

'There's something I have to do,' he said. 'I'd like to stay and talk, but—'

'Please, I've got to tell you something,' Kopak said urgently. 'It won't take long.' And then, as if to contradict himself, he fell silent.

'Well?' Terrel prompted. 'What is it?'

'Something's changed inside me,' the captain whispered. 'Ever since you healed me. For the first time in my life I've been having doubts about the war and the reasons for it. Nothing makes sense any more.' His eyes were haunted now. 'When you came to ask my father for help, I found myself agreeing with everything you said, and since then I've been trying to persuade him to change his mind. I haven't been able to, but I'm still trying. I think in his heart he knows you're right, but he won't admit it, even to himself. If only he'd go to Pingeyri, I think it would have some effect. He's one of the few men whose opinion the general respects. Do you still think using magic at the springs will lead to disaster?'

The confession had come out in a rush, as if it had been bottled up for too long, and Terrel was intrigued now.

'I'm sure of it,' he replied. 'Thank you for trying to help me. Do you think my healing was somehow responsible for your own change of heart?'

'It must have been,' Kopak said, his eyes flicking from side to side as he tried to check that they weren't being overheard. 'I can't believe I risked my life for what turned out to be a useless piece of intelligence. I was lucky you were there to save me.'

'Maybe it wasn't luck. Maybe it was meant to happen.'

'And that's not all,' the captain went on. 'Ever since then, I've found the taste and smell of mitra revolting.'

'Really?'

'Yes, it's odd. Do you know why that's happened?'

'I'm not sure. But you're right to avoid it. And keep working on your father.'

'I will,' Kopak promised. 'Is there anything else I can do . . . to help you, I mean?'

'Not that I can think of at the moment.'

Some of the soldier's fellow officers were approaching now, and it was clear their conversation would have to end. In any case, Terrel was not prepared to reveal the existence of the Holma, and decided instead to tell one of the underground that the brigadier's son might be a suitable recruit.

'I hope we get the chance to talk again,' Kopak said quickly.

'Me too,' Terrel agreed. 'Good luck, Captain.'

'And to you,' Kopak replied, then turned to his comrades.

Terrel went on his way, wondering about what he had

learnt. If his efforts really had been responsible for the changes in Kopak's attitude – and for his aversion to mitra – then there had to be a chance that he could use his healing again to the same end. He had no idea how or why it had happened, but the possibilities it raised were interesting. For instance, what if Pingeyri was to fall ill and Terrel was called upon to heal *him*?

He was still speculating on this when he found himself entering the wizards' section of the campsite.

'I didn't think I was ever going to see you again,' Latira said.

'I haven't had the chance to contact you,' Terrel replied. 'I thought you were avoiding me . . . after what happened.'

'I was at first,' she admitted. In the pale moonlight Terrel could see that there was no anger or resentment in her eyes, just a deep and weary sadness.

'Will you tell me about that night?'

'You really don't remember?'

'No.'

'That's hard to believe, you know.'

'It's true, though. In a sense I wasn't even there.'

Latira nodded, apparently accepting his claim.

'I know about Jax,' she said. 'I didn't then, but I do now. Tegan explained it to me. It was him, wasn't it?'

'Yes. I'm sorry.'

'I'm sorry too. I shouldn't have given you the melcras. I didn't think—'

'That doesn't matter now,' he cut in. 'Will you tell me what happened between you and Jax?'

'It wasn't *all* Jax though, was it?' she asked. 'Earlier on, when we were just enjoying ourselves, you were comfortable with me, weren't you?'

Recognizing he need for reassurance, Terrel smiled.

'Too comfortable, as it turned out,' he said ruefully. 'You're my friend, Latira. Whatever happened, that hasn't changed. I hope you can still think of me in the same way.'

'I can. I mean, I do.' She looked embarrassed now. 'There was a time when I thought you might become more than that.'

'I love someone else,' he said gently. 'She's a very long way from here, but I'm going back to her one day.'

'So now you want to know if you've remained faithful to her?'

Terrel was about to object, to argue with her assumption, but the question had an awkward ring of truth to it that he could not deny.

'Yes.'

'Will you answer me one question first?'

'If I can.'

'Did you know then about my real allegiance?' She lowered her voice as she spoke, even though there was little chance of their being overheard. They were sitting together on one of the rocks on the ridge that Raufar had pointed out earlier, and the nearest tents were some distance away.

'Yes,' Terrel said. 'Is that important?'

'It is to me,' she replied softly. 'Not to anyone else. We were playing an elaborate game with each other, weren't we?'

Before Terrel had a chance to answer, the second of the evening's bells rang out, piercing the night with its clear call.

'Not all of it was a game,' he said as the reverberations died away.

'You certainly seemed willing enough to come to bed with me,' Latira said, 'but I suppose that was Jax, not you.'

'Yes. I'm sorry. What happened next?'

'Nothing.'

'Nothing? We didn't sleep together?'

'Sleeping was all we did – apart from talking, of course.'

A great weight seemed to lift from Terrel's shoulders. No matter how much he had told himself that what Jax had done with his body was not relevant, he had known that it *was*. He tried to hide his relief, not wanting to hurt Latira's feelings any more than he already had, but it was obvious that he was only partially successful.

'Happy now?' she asked. The melancholy in her voice made him feel ashamed of himself.

'No,' he said. 'I mean ... I'm glad Jax didn't take advantage of you.'

'I wanted him to, you idiot!' she exclaimed. 'Being rejected like that doesn't feel nice, no matter who you're with.'

Terrel didn't know what to say to that. In the end all he could do was apologize again.

'I'm sorry,' he said. 'I'm not very good at this.'

'Ah, well. At least you can tell your girl that you're still as pure as freshly fallen snow.'

'I'm surprised Jax didn't ...' he mumbled awkwardly, stung by her dismissive sarcasm.

'I don't suppose I was up to his standards.'

'That can't be true. You're beautiful—'

'Don't insult me by lying, Terrel,' she snapped. 'We've had this argument before. Remember?'

'I'm not lying. Beauty isn't just what's on the outside. Look at me. I'm hardly the world's most perfect man, and yet—'

'I wanted you,' Latira finished for him. 'Point taken. But you weren't there, remember? Some of the things you – he – said weren't very nice, and some were down-right bizarre. I thought at one point you were going mad.'

'Can you remember what he said?'

'Do I have to?'

'It would help me understand, but if you'd rather not . . .'

'Now that I've told you this much, I might as well tell you the rest,' she said resignedly. 'He was keen enough to start with, but then something changed. I've no idea what. He said, "Get away from me. Leave me alone." At that point we'd already got undressed and got into bed, so I was very confused, as you can imagine. I asked what he meant and he said, "Not you. Him." Was he talking to you?'

Terrel shook his head.

'No,' he said. 'I think it was someone else.'

'Someone else? Gods! How complicated does it get in there?' she responded, gesturing at the healer's head.

'It's a long story,' Terrel replied. He was now reasonably sure that it was Elam who had somehow prevented Jax from following his natural instincts. 'Go on.'

'By then I didn't know what to think, and he wasn't paying me much attention. We'd drawn apart. He muttered something like, "Leave her out of it", then glanced at me and made a horrible face, as if I was something that had floated up from the bottom of a pond when the spring ice melts. I got quite scared and asked him what was going on. He told me it was nothing, but then he said, "I'd kill you if someone hadn't already beaten me to it." I'd have run away then, but he reached out and caught hold of my wrist. The last thing he said was, "I can't do this. I'm going to sleep now." And that's exactly what he did.'

'I'm surprised you stayed,' Terrel commented.

'So am I,' she said, shaking her head. 'I probably should have gone, but once you were asleep you looked so harmless and I felt safe again. I was tired, and I'd had quite a lot of melcras too. It just seemed like too much effort to get out of bed. My bed. The next thing I knew it was morning and, well, you know what happened then.'

Yes, Terrel thought, but you don't. Once again he saw Alyssa looking at him through the dog's eyes and then walking away. Latira had been asleep at that point, and he wished he'd had the courage to wake her so that Alyssa could have heard the truth.

'What are you thinking?' Latira asked.

'I'm just sorry you had to go through all that,' he replied, evading the question.

'I've had better nights,' she admitted.

They were both silent for a few moments.

'While we're on the subject of Jax,' she said eventually, 'I gather he has some skill as a weather-mage. Is that right?'

'Yes.'

'But you don't?'

'No.'

'Tegan wants to know whether you'd be willing to let us use Jax's power against Tofana if it becomes necessary.'

'Let him in deliberately, you mean?'

'Yes.'

'I'm not sure about that.' In truth the prospect was horrifying. 'How would you control him?'

'Tegan thinks she might be able to guide him.'

'But when he tried to oppose Tofana before, he came off worst,' Terrel pointed out. 'She sent him back to the healing pools.'

'Yes, but he was on his own then. There'd be others helping him next time. What do you think?'

'I don't like the idea at all,' he stated truthfully, 'but I might consider it as a last resort.'

'Fair enough. I'll tell Tegan.'

'Will you tell her something else?' Terrel said, and went on to describe his encounter with Kopak. 'He might be a useful contact.'

'He might at that,' Latira said, nodding.

There was another pause then, with each of them wondering whether they should return to their respective tents. But there were still some unanswered questions between them.

'When you told me about your past,' Terrel began hesitantly. 'About Hallen and the baby . . . was all that true, or were you testing me?'

'I lost my husband and our child exactly as I told you,' she replied bleakly. 'But it's true, I was hoping to find out what you thought, to see if we could risk trusting you.' She laughed without mirth. 'It's funny, really. If you'd made love to me, at least you wouldn't have had to worry about becoming a father. But then you already knew that.'

In fact Terrel had forgotten that the miscarriage had left her barren.

'Do you still want a child?' he asked softly.

'You have to find a man first,' she said caustically. 'That's how it works.'

'But if you did,' her persisted, 'would you want a child?'

'What's the point of wishing for something you know you can't have?'

'Perhaps you can.'

It took a few moments for the implication of his words to sink in.

'You could really do that?' she asked eventually. 'Are you *that* good a healer?'

'I've done it before,' he replied. 'And my healing skills are stronger than they were then.' In fact, when he had made it possible for Ysatel to conceive Kerin's child, he had not even been aware of what he was doing. It had been an instinctive, unconscious act.

'I'm not sure,' Latira said.

'It's up to you.'

'What would I have to do?'

'Just let me hold your hand for a while,' he said, and left it at that.

After a few moments, without another word being spoken, Latira stretched out her hand. Terrel took it in his own, and fell into the waking dream. As he had hoped, the problem was easily solved – a simple matter of moving various lines and shadows back into their proper pattern – and after only a short time, he released her fingers.

'Now what?' she asked.

'It's done,' he told her, smiling at her evident disbelief. 'And for what it's worth, I believe you will find someone worthy of loving and being loved by you.'

There were tears brimming in Latira's eyes.

'If you'd talked to me like that in bed,' she said softly, 'things would have gone rather differently.'

'Can we still be friends, even so?' he asked, smiling.

'Yes. Though after tonight I don't suppose we'll ever see each other again.'

'You're not coming with us?' he guessed.

'No. I'm going back to Saudark with the rest of the servants. The army will cater for itself from now on.'

'So this is goodbye.'

'Yes. Farewell, Terrel. You're already a hero in my eyes. By the time this is over, all Myvatan will be looking at you the same way.' With that she kissed him lightly and vanished into the night.

Terrel watched her go with a lump in his throat, but content in the knowledge that their reconciliation was complete. As he walked across the camp, the third bell rang, as if to remind him that it was now time to look ahead, not back.

CHAPTER THIRTY-FIVE

'I can't hold it,' Hraun reported breathlessly.

'Keep trying,' Raufar ordered. 'Where's Jauron?'

'I don't know.'

'He's wandered off again,' Narvat said disgustedly.

Raufar swore under his breath. Above them the sky crackled and sparked, dark swirls of cloud rolling back and forth.

'How long before Stykkis gets there?' the captain asked, raising his voice over the increasing tumult.

'Too long,' Narvat replied, glancing first at the human battle on the slope of the pass, then at the magical conflict overhead.

'Shield roof!' Raufar yelled, and the men around them reacted in unison, leaving their various positions and gathering round their commander. 'On the ground, Terrel. Now!'

The healer did not need telling a second time. He had seen the troop perform this manoeuvre before, and knew that his role was simply not to get in the way. Flinging himself down, he felt the darkness close in around him as the soldiers moved to their assigned places – kneeling for the most part, their shields held above their heads to form an overlapping shell that covered them all like the carapace of a giant reptile.

Their defences were in place just in time. As Hraun's efforts were finally overcome by the enemy neomancers, hailstones the size of a man's fist plummeted from the

storm clouds, crashing into the shield roof, which shook
and almost buckled under the assault but did not break.
The noise below was almost deafening.

'Let me know when you can do something!' Raufar
called to Hraun. The neomancer was lying on the ground
close to Terrel, recovering from his earlier efforts.

'Does this count as an emergency?' Narvat asked.

'Not yet,' the captain replied.

The significance of the question was not lost on Terrel.
The fire-starters – like Hraun – had been ordered not to
use the new technique in battle until they reached
Hvannadal. The only exception would be in a dire emergency – anything that threatened Terrel's life or his
capture. The general was determined not to give the
enemy any warning of what was coming, and as a result,
the neomancers in Raufar's company had only used conventional magic so far.

'They won't be able to keep this up for long,' the captain added, 'and in any case, Stykkis may well interrupt
them soon. We'll stick it out for now.'

Raufar's assumption was proved correct shortly afterwards. The barrage of hail relented, and he was able to
give the order to break ranks and resume the ground
attack. However, as had happened several times before, the
enemy forces chose to withdraw rather than fight a pitched
battle – and this left the Black troop with no way of vent-
ing their frustration. Even the sortie led by Stykkis had
only managed to engage a small number of the opposing
troops, and casualties on both sides had been light. Terrel
was grateful for that, but he shared the soldiers' misgivings
about the progress of the campaign.

'They seem to know what we're doing before *we* do,' Raufar
grumbled. 'They're one step ahead of us the whole time.'

The captain and his lieutenants, together with Terrel and the two neomancers, were gathered round the camp-fire that evening.

'Then why aren't they trying to stop us?' Pjorsa asked. 'All they do is harry us for a while, then run away.'

'Perhaps they're just trying to annoy us,' Narvat suggested.

'In which case they're succeeding,' Pjorsa growled. The war of attrition was not what the soldiers were used to, and it had been grating on their nerves for some days now.

'But we must focus our anger,' Raufar warned. 'We don't want to do anything stupid just because the White are behaving like cowards.'

'We might have been able to have a decent fight if we'd all been doing our jobs properly,' Stykkis said. He did not look at Jauron, but everyone knew who his remark was aimed at. 'As it was, we didn't have time to get to them and they were able to take cover.'

'What exactly were you doing at that point, Jauron?' the captain asked.

'Weakening the were-cloud,' the neomancer replied wearily. 'Do you think your shields would have held against it if it had struck at full force?'

'You were supposed to be making it possible for us to break through to their positions,' Stykkis said.

'Those were your orders, neomancer,' Raufar concurred. It was not the first time Jauron had disobeyed a command, but he always seemed to have a good reason for his actions. Nevertheless, his waywardness had not endeared him to his comrades.

'I understood that the healer's safety was paramount, Captain,' he replied, with the habitual touch of arrogance that had done nothing to curb the resentment the soldiers felt towards him.

'So it is,' Raufar responded, 'but it's not for you to decide how best to do that. I command this company, and the next time I tell you to do something, you do it. Understood?'

'Yes, sir.'

'Good. We all have to work together. It's not going to get any easier from here on. We'll hit the ice road tomorrow.'

The captain was referring to the high point of the mountain pass which had been chosen as their route into the interior of the White Quarter. Apparently this was not a true glacier but an area of highly compacted but unstable snow, which grew in size each winter as another layer was added to its depth. However, in spring some of these layers were prone to shear off, creating explosive avalanches and patches of a type of snow – like a frozen quicksand – called skelf. The prospect of entering such a region was unnerving, and the soldiers were well aware of the challenges they would face there.

'You think we'll come under attack?' Narvat asked.

'We have to be prepared,' Raufar answered, 'so we'll pick our route carefully, but my guess is no. The terrain will be as difficult for the White as it is for us, and the only way they could set up an effective ambush would be to camp there overnight. I don't think that's something they'd be prepared to do.'

'What about magic?' Stykkis asked. 'They could have left traps for us.'

'We can take care of that,' Hraun stated confidently. He had clearly been embarrassed by the behaviour of his fellow neomancer, and wanted to demonstrate that they were still a valuable part of the team. 'There are always telltale signs left by residual magic.'

'Good,' Narvat said. 'The ice road is not a place where you want to spend too much time.'

'It could be worse,' Pjorsa remarked. 'We could've been assigned to the ships in Hofnar Fjord.'

There were nods of agreement all around, and even a few grim smiles. Terrel knew that operations by sea were not popular with most soldiers – who were reluctant to trust themselves to the unpredictable mercies of the wind and tides. He had been treated to several gruesome tales – vast blocks of ice collapsing into the water from glaciers, swamping any boats nearby, or miniature icebergs called ivu that propelled themselves from the sea and flew through the air at random, and of dark whirlpools pulling sailors down to an icy death.

Such prejudices had not been helped by rumours that the troops who'd been sent into Hofnar had been driven back or even annihilated. Since they had entered the White Quarter, news from other parts of the campaign had been infrequent and probably unreliable. It came in the form of messengers from units in neighbouring regions, whenever their commanders wanted to co-ordinate their tactics, and as a result any reports from as far away as the northern coast were necessarily several times removed from their original source – and thus quite possibly inaccurate.

'We don't know for sure what's happened there,' Raufar pointed out. 'What we *do* know is that the Red army will be well inside the quarter by now, so the White aren't going to be able to concentrate all their efforts on us.' The invasion from the east was not directed towards Hvannadal, but was supposed to create a diversion, allowing Pingeyri and his forces to converge on the springs. 'As far as we know,' the captain went on, 'we'll be meeting up with our other units near the target soon enough. Then the fun will really start.'

'Let's hope so,' Pjorsa muttered.

'Have you thought that the White might *want* us to go

to Hvannadal?' Stykkis asked. 'That could be the reason they keep using these hit-and-run tactics.'

'We're being led into a trap, you mean?'

'It would explain a lot.'

'Even if that's true,' Raufar said, 'and I don't believe it is – we have a few surprises for them, don't we? Let's just do our job, and let the generals worry about stuff like that.'

The discussion ended on that decisive note, and the soldiers dispersed to make their preparations for the night. Terrel made his usual rounds, tending to any of the company who had been injured or who were ill. Although many of the men had been suspicious of him at first, his attentions were always welcome now, and Raufar's troop had adopted him as one of their own – which was a singular mark of honour for a civilian. They were under orders to keep Terrel safe, and they had all realized that he had an important role to play in Pingeyri's strategy. But it was the fact that he willingly used his talents for their benefit that had done the most to hasten his acceptance. The novelty of having many of their ailments cured in the field had earnt him the soldiers' gratitude and respect. And regardless of the fact that he hated their bloodthirsty attitude to both the enemy and to the war in general, Terrel had come to admire the company, both for its discipline and its camaraderie. He'd already been impressed by several acts of selfless bravery that seemed to come naturally to the warriors, and he knew that, should the necessity arise, they would risk life and limb to protect him. He was grateful for this knowledge, but it made him feel uneasy when he thought about his true intentions, his real reasons for being there – which the soldiers would have considered treasonous. Terrel was still hoping that there might at least be one member of the Holma in the company, but if there was, he hadn't given the healer any sign of his presence. Ever since the campaign had begun in earnest, Terrel had – in one sense, at least – been on his own.

Crossing the unmarked border had been a strangely anticlimatic event, but now, after several days in the White Quarter, it had become clear why the frontier territory had been undefended. The enemy had evidently preferred to wait and fight at places of their own choosing. Of course the movements of such a large army could not be kept entirely secret, but the worrying thing was that, as Raufar had pointed out, it did indeed seem that their foes were able to anticipate the invaders' every move. If their own progress was anything to go by, the campaign as a whole would be moving much more slowly than expected. On the other hand, because of the defenders' tactics, casualties had been fewer than forecast – much to Terrel's secret relief.

Now, for the first time, it occurred to him to wonder whether the underground had members inside the White or Gold Quarters. If so, what lengths would his own contacts be prepared to go to in order to avoid a magical catastrophe, and to gain their own objectives? Would they really betray their own side in the war? And if that were the case, how would it affect what was going to happen at Hvannadal? This was another aspect of his situation over which Terrel had no control. Together with the constant uncertainty about what each day might bring, it meant that he spent his time living on a knife-edge.

As he curled into his bedding, sheltered beneath the canvas of his tent, Terrel knew he would have to set all such considerations aside. Whatever else lay ahead, the one thing he knew for sure at that moment was that he needed the solace and restorative powers of sleep.

The whale was the size of an entire country. As it swam it piled up waves as big as mountain ranges, the foam at their crests mimicking snow. Water spouted from its blowhole in a massive fountain, reaching towards the stars, but its eyes were fixed straight ahead, its cavernous jaws opening . . .

Terrel tried to scream as he was sucked into that monstrous darkness, but choking liquid filled his mouth and throat, flooding his lungs with an acid chill.

In the silence the night turned red. Bodiless now, he looked around for the sword, but it was nowhere to be seen. This time it remained hidden, even in his dreams. Yet it was still a malevolent presence, waiting to be brought to the surface.

Abruptly, Terrel found himself looking down from the sky as the great pendulum swung across the ocean, marking time in the slow heartbeats of the world. Was it Myvatan or Vadanis? He couldn't tell the difference any longer. He looked more closely, peering inside the skeleton of stone, and saw an entire city frozen in ice: palaces and castles, towers and warehouses, walls and streets, all held captive by the unyielding magic. All movement, all warmth extinguished. How could a flame, any flame, burn in such a place?

Terrel fell back into the red gloom – and then he was in the ocean again, left in the churning wake of the great whale, just as he had been left behind by his homeland when he'd been exiled from Vadanis.

CHAPTER THIRTY-SIX

Terrel woke feeling utterly homesick, but he had no time to indulge in self-pity. The nights were short now, and the troop was already gearing up for the next stage of their journey. The healer stirred himself into action, even though his sleep had afforded him little rest. Not wanting to dwell on the dream, he pushed his thoughts in the direction of the day ahead, only to find that this made him nervous. Despite what Raufar had said, Terrel thought that the ice road sounded like the perfect place for an ambush.

The first sign that anything was wrong came when one of the scouts flanking the main party broke the silence. The order for quiet had been imposed because – as Raufar had explained – under certain conditions, any loud noise might set off an avalanche. The company were adept at moving by stealth when necessary, and were able to communicate by sign language. But circumstances sometimes dictated a more immediate response. The lookout's cry brought no movement of snow, but although the bitter wind carried his words away, the urgency and fear in his voice were unmistakable.

Terrel knew that Raufar and his lieutenants routinely studied and analyzed whatever terrain they were passing through, noting possible places of shelter and defensive positions, as well as identifying natural dangers and the most likely spots for their enemy to be hiding. However, on the ice road there appeared to be little or nothing to see. The white plain was virtually featureless, stretched out in a wide saddle between two jagged peaks of broken, impassable stone. Any irregularities were confined to gentle undulations – where the wind had sculpted hump-back drifts – and minor changes in the texture and luminescence of the snow. The snow itself varied from a coarse granular crust that seemed quite dull to a smooth, shiny surface that was as hard and as brittle as glass – but as yet there had been no sign of the dreaded skelf.

As usual, Narvat had been in command of the scouts. He had been leading the main party himself, and as soon as he heard the warning cry, the lieutenant began directing the people around him. Raufar deployed men as best he could until they were able to discover the nature of the threat. Pjorsa, who was Terrel's self-appointed protector, pulled the healer down so that they were kneeling in the lee of one of the drifts. The expression on the soldier's scarred face was serious as he scanned the plain, but there was also a glint of anticipation in his eyes.

'Don't worry, healer,' he whispered. 'There's no way they can get to us without us seeing them first.'

A few moments later, the enemy came hurtling over the curved horizon ahead of them. But it was not soldiers Raufar's troops were about to face. It was a fast-moving wave of dense and blinding fog.

'Together. Spear length!' the captain yelled, heedless of the dangers of avalanches now. His more pressing concern was to prevent his entire company from becoming dis-persed in the mist. As a group they could still defend themselves. Apart, they could be picked off one by one by enemy raiders.

For Terrel, everything after that happened in a disorientating blur. As the fog enveloped them, all but his
closest companions became invisible, and even those
nearby were little more than shadowy outlines. Raufar's
voice drifted out of the murk.

'I thought you said you could deal with this sort of
thing.'

'This is different,' Hraun replied. 'Something's . . .' The
rest of the neomancer's response was lost as shouts were
heard in the distance, followed by the clash of steel. The
fighting had begun.

'Stay here,' Pjorsa ordered, then disappeared in the
direction of the noise.

A moment later Stykkis loomed up out of the mist, his
sword in hand.

'This way,' he hissed. 'Follow me.'

'Pjorsa told me to stay here.'

'You can't,' Stykkis stated flatly. 'We're moving. Let's
go.'

Until then Terrel had had no trouble with his footing
but now, as they set off, his boots seemed to slide or sink
unpredictably with each step. It was as if the water vapour
in the air was also making the snow beneath his feet slippery. He was part of a silent phalanx of soldiers, each man
keeping the distance between him and those to either side
to a minimum, while still giving themselves space to use
their weapons if necessary. The sounds of combat were
coming from several different directions now, but as yet
the actual fighting remained invisible. It occurred to Terrel
that in the severely reduced visibility it would be difficult
to tell friend from foe, and in such confused conditions it
would be easy to panic. But Raufar's men were better dis-
ciplined than that. They moved on steadily and with
purpose.

Thunder crashed overhead, its rumbling echoes shaking the ground, and then, without warning, the fog lifted, swept away by a sudden gust of wind that shredded the layers of mist and scattered the remnants over the mountainside. After the grey gloom, the daylight was almost blinding, even though a thick blanket of high cloud shrouded the sky.

The soldiers exploded into action, sprinting in different directions in response to their officers' commands, or reacting to the obvious needs of their comrades. Terrel found himself more or less forgotten, left to fend for himself, and in the blur of activity he didn't know which way to turn. In the end he simply crouched down, hoping to make sense of what was going on about him.

Although it soon became clear that this was the most serious encounter of their campaign so far, Terrel was at a loss to tell how the Black troops were faring. He could already see places where the snow had been stained red with the blood of the fallen, but it was impossible to know which side was winning the fragmentary battle. The very fact that their foes had prepared such an ambush – both magical and military – in such a place was an indication of their serious intent, and they had had the element of surprise on their side. But Raufar's men were seasoned warriors for the most part, and Terrel was in no doubt that they would prove difficult to overcome. Until then he had not considered what he would do if he was captured by the White forces – and even now, when the possibility was rather more immediate, he was no closer to a decision. In any case, his first priority was simply to stay alive. Ultimately it did not matter who won Myvatan's war; it was his own mission to find the elemental that was paramount.

A series of urgent shouts drew his attention to the fact

that four miniature tornadoes – each one whirling snow up into its twisting, cone-shaped vortex – were weaving their way down the slope from the northwest. Their progress was erratic, and even though the danger they presented was obvious, Terrel couldn't see how any of the neomancers – on either side – could hope to use such inaccurate weapons effectively. Soldiers of both sides were running to avoid them, with a few of the more unfortunate being caught and flung aside as if they were rag dolls. It soon became clear that staying where he was was no longer an option. Although the whirlwinds were constantly veering in different directions, the general line of their progress was towards Terrel. Just as he had reached this conclusion, and was wondering which way to go, Stykkis reappeared at his side.

'We've got to get you out of here,' he said, breathing hard. Blood stained the sleeves of his uniform as well as his blade.

'Are the tornadoes ours or theirs?' Terrel asked.

'Theirs. Come on.'

They ran, crouching in case they became targets for any enemy archers, and reached a hollow whose only occupants were dead. The two men had evidently killed each other with simultaneous spear thrusts. Stykkis ignored them, allowing himself only a few moments to study the latest developments of the battle, but Terrel couldn't help staring. The White soldier could not have been more than nineteen years old, and the expression frozen on his face was one of surprise rather than pain. His opposite number was Kavika, the man Terrel had met at the healing pools. He had been restored to health in an almost miraculous fashion then, but there would be no way back from this injury. His enemy's spear had buried itself in his heart. His end had been quick – he had hardly bled at all – but the frost that was already forming on his eyelashes and on his beard made Terrel shiver, sickened by the senseless waste of young life.

'This is a mess,' Stykkis muttered. 'I can't tell what's going on. What do Hraun and Jauron think they're doing?'

The four tornadoes had now coalesced into one much more powerful entity. Everywhere it went – and its movements were still wholly unpredictable – the tornado whipped up a series of miniature blizzards, filling the air with spikes of flying ice. Such was the disruption it had caused that the fighting between the two forces had taken second place to the soldiers' efforts to avoid the howling menace.

'Raufar's trying to regroup our men,' Stykkis said. 'We'll circle round . . . Let's go.'

Terrel followed the lieutenant, happy to leave the macabre tableau of the hollow behind. They skirted round the area where most of the fighting had taken place, climbing on to a slightly higher level of the plateau. In doing so, they were coming closer to their objective of rejoining the main body of the company, but they had also exposed themselves to view from the entire battlefield. That fact had deadly consequences a moment later when a volley of arrows whirred through the air around them. Terrel threw himself to the ground and escaped unscathed, but one of the bolts caught the lieutenant in the side, burying itself deeply in the flesh beneath his rib cage. Terrel crawled to his aid.

'You have to go on,' Stykkis gasped through clenched teeth.

'I can't leave you like this. Let me—'

'No. This . . . is not . . . good.' The soldier's strength was fading fast. 'If you stay here all you'll do . . . is get . . . yourself killed.' As if to emphasize the point, another arrow thudded into the ground nearby, but the healer still hesitated. 'Go,' Stykkis whispered, then fell silent, his eyes already filming over.

Terrel got to his feet and ran. At the same time he became aware that the tornado was no longer screaming, and that the battle had been rejoined in earnest. However, he also saw that a group of his comrades were making their way towards him, and was heartened both by that and by the fact that no more arrows were coming his way.

His feet thudded against hard-packed snow, his lop-sided gait propelling him towards at least some measure of safety, but in the next step he overbalanced and fell head-long, only to land on snow softer than any pillow. He skimmed along the surface, white crystals flying up around him, blind once more. When he came to rest, he tried to get up, but there was something wrong with his limbs. None of them could get any purchase on the snow beneath him. He felt himself sinking, and fear jolted through his entire body as he realized what had happened. He had stumbled into a patch of skelf.

Petrified now, he tried to remember what the soldiers had told him to do if he ever found himself in such a predicament. Keep still. Don't struggle. But that was easier said than done. Moving will only make you sink faster. He concentrated simply on breathing, blowing flakes of snow from his nose and mouth. The white stuff around him was like nothing he had ever come across before. It was incredibly fine, almost powdery, and it was dry – except where a few grains had melted against his skin. It supported his prone body, but he couldn't feel it. It was as if he were weightless, floating on some sort of liquid rather than lying on the ground. Perhaps I can *swim* out, he thought, but as soon as he tried to move, the skelf shifted and slid around him, making him think of quicksand. You couldn't swim in that.

His only hope was that the soldiers would recognize his peril and come to the rescue. The last thing he wanted was for any of them to blunder into the same trap and be sucked down too, but perhaps they'd be able to reach him from the edge with a spear, or throw a rope to him. He tried to see where they were, but his eyes were too close to the surface, and he couldn't see much. He tried to call out, to attract their attention and to warn them, but he was lying face down; the powder muffled his voice, and the movement of his chest set the snow quivering again. There was no response. All he could hear was the soughing of the wind. Even the sounds of warfare seemed to have been silenced now.

Then, at last, he glimpsed someone walking towards him. He was about to cry out in warning again when he realized it would not be necessary, and his relief turned to amazement. The skelf would present no threat to this visitor – because he was a ghost.

Elam glided effortlessly over the treacherous surface and looked down at his friend with a slight smile on his face.

What are you doing down there?

This isn't ordinary snow. It's like quicksand. I can't move.

Elam laughed.

Really? You get yourself into some awkward spots, don't you?

It's not funny, Terrel said, angry now. *Is anyone coming to help me?*

The ghost looked around.

Not that I can see.

Where's Alyssa?

Who? Elam asked, then grinned. *Oh yes, the one you always dream about. I don't think you'll be seeing her any more.*

What do you mean? Terrel was both confused and

alarmed now, not only by what Elam had said, which didn't make much sense, but also by the way he'd said it. His voice didn't sound right.

They've stopped fighting, his friend reported, glancing round again. He sounded almost disappointed. *Perhaps I should start another set of tornadoes.*

Another set? Terrel wondered, then the truth came crashing into his brain like an avalanche. In spite of appearances, this was not Elam. It was Jax.

CHAPTER THIRTY-SEVEN

The implications of his twin's presence made Terrel's head reel. Jax was obviously now capable of travelling independently, and of changing his appearance – but the healer was too preoccupied with his own situation to dwell on what that meant. He had realized that in spite of his efforts to keep still he was sinking gradually, so that now he was having to crane his neck back in order to breathe. He kept hoping the soldiers would come, but there was no sign of any of them. What had happened to the men who had been heading towards him?

The cold was beginning to seep through his thick clothing, but there was nothing he could do about that. He was about to drown in snow – and he was effectively alone. There was nothing Jax could do to help him, even if he'd wanted to – which was in itself very unlikely. But he was currently Terrel's only link with the outside world, and perhaps he could somehow use him to attract the attention of his human companions.

What are you doing here, Jax?

No fooling you is there, brother? the prince responded sarcastically. *And I thought this was such a clever disguise.* He was not looking at Terrel as he spoke, his attention focused elsewhere.

Are you watching the soldiers?

Jax didn't answer, but a small shiver ran through his spectral frame and his borrowed eyes shone with delight.

What next? he asked himself.

An ominous rumbling sound reached Terrel's ears, and the skelf around him trembled. He felt his hips sink a little deeper, his legs submerged now. Soon, as the angles changed, his whole body would begin to slide into a frozen grave.

Will you help me? he asked desperately.

That did get Jax's attention.

Help you? he said incredulously. *All this time you've been trying to keep me away, and now, when you can't stop me, all of a sudden you want my help? That's rich.*

Why are you here? Terrel asked. *Why here exactly?*

I've got to keep an eye on you, haven't I? the prince replied. *I must give you some credit, brother. I wouldn't have even known about this place if you hadn't come here. You've no idea how much fun I've had.*

Terrel could believe it. As a weather-mage, Jax was, in effect, a natural neomancer. He was, quite literally, in his element – and Tofana's tuition had evidently made the place even more attractive. But something he had said had given the healer an idea.

I was the one who led you here, he said, grasping at the flimsiest of straws. *If I die, that link will be lost, won't it?*

Jax shrugged, apparently unconcerned, but there had been a flicker of uncertainty in Elam's eyes.

I don't think so, he said. *Tofana—*

But you can't be sure, can you? Terrel persisted, cutting him off. *Do you want the most exciting part of your day to be your studies at court?*

At least I won't have to listen to you moaning any more, Jax muttered, but there was no conviction in his tone.

Terrel was still sinking, albeit very slowly. Only the

upper part of his head was now completely clear of the surface. His mouth was already blocked, and he was having to breathe through his nose.

Last chance, Jax. I haven't got long.

What am I supposed to do, anyway? The prince sounded petulant now.

Terrel was seized by a sudden, terrifying inspiration.

Start a tornado, he said. *Right here.*

For a few moments Jax just stared at him.

Do it! Terrel ordered.

After a moment, he sensed the first few wisps of powdery snow being picked up by the nascent spiral breeze, and then felt the wind grow rapidly in strength. After that he had no time to speak, or even think, as the world around him went mad. Even if he'd been able to keep his eyes open, there would have been nothing to see except a white blur. The noise levels rose to a howl that made him think of the karabura – the black sandstorms of the Binhemma-Ghar – and primeval forces robbed him of any control over his own body. He had hoped that he'd simply be thrown aside, out of the skelf, but in fact he'd been caught up in the heart of the maelstrom, surrounded by swirling powder, buffeted and twisted this way and that. At times he seemed to be turning cartwheels, at others he spun round like a top, and all the while he had no idea which way was up or down. It was like being punched by a hundred fists all at the same time, while his limbs were almost wrenched from their sockets by invisible hands and his clothes were nearly torn from his back.

At last the tornado abated a little, but to Terrel's dismay he felt himself not being tossed clear but falling. It seemed that Jax's efforts might succeed only in burying him even deeper. Then he landed with a jarring thump that knocked what little breath he had left out of him, and he realized that he was now lying on solid ground. When he was finally able to open his eyes, he found he was at the bottom of a deep hollow. The sky above was cross-hatched with streamers of white as the tail end of the tornado blew itself out. The whirlwind hadn't moved him at all, but it had emptied the skelf out of the depression he had stumbled into, dispersing it to fall as a harmless dusting of snow across the whole expanse of the ice road. Terrel was gasping for breath, battered and bruised, and it felt as if he had strained every muscle in his body – but he was alive.

He looked up to see Jax smiling down at him from Elam's face. He tried to stand up, but his legs gave way beneath him and he sat down again with a bump, groaning as pain shot through his whole body. He decided to stay where he was for the time being. Now that there appeared to be no immediate danger to his life, he decided to try to persuade Jax to answer a few questions.

Why did you choose to look like that? he asked.

He's been annoying me for a long time now, the prince replied. *And I thought it'd be a good joke.*

Terrel recalled the last time Elam had 'annoyed' his twin, and was grateful to his friend.

I can choose what I look like in this form, Jax nodded, *but it's easier if it's a shape you know.*

Where's the real Elam? Terrel asked, wondering whether the prince's borrowing of the ghost's shape had had any effect on his friend.

How should I know? his brother replied with a touch of irritation.

Did Tofana teach you how to do this?

She gave me a few hints, but I worked most of it out for myself.

So you can come here any time you want to?

Yes. Does that bother you? Jax's malevolent glee was plain to see.

Not at all, Terrel lied. *I was hoping you could.*

Why? his twin asked suspiciously.

There'll be an opportunity soon for you to have some fun and help me at the same time.

Why should I help you? Isn't saving your life enough? Jax asked. *What more do you want?*

Tofana's planning to do something at a place called Hvannadal, and I want to stop her.

Magic? the prince queried eagerly.

Of course. What else would a wizard be doing?

Then why should I want to stop her?

Because if she succeeds it will mean the end of the war, the end of everyone on Myvatan – and quite possibly the end of all magic here. There won't be any left for you to use then. He was exaggerating the risks – or at least he hoped he was – in a deliberate attempt to worry Jax. The prince would not care about the people of the island, but any threat to his own pleasure might spur him into action. *Of course, I'll understand if you don't want to oppose her,* he added.

What do you mean?

She beat you last time, after all.

She did not! Jax stated angrily.

Then why did you end up back in the healing pools?

I just got tired. That happens after a while.

If you say so, Terrel goaded him. *Still, as I say, it's no disgrace to be afraid of her.*

I'm not afraid, Jax claimed. *I'll show you.* Then his expression changed, becoming arrogant again. *I know what you're doing.*

What? the healer asked.

Trying to trick me. We're so alike sometimes.

Terrel wanted to deny that assertion, but he had more

important things on his mind. All he could hope was that
his twin would respond to the challenge he had thrown
down, even though the prince had discerned his motives.

It's strange that all the wizards here are women, he
remarked, hoping to play to Jax's misogyny, but his twin
was no longer paying any attention. He had suddenly been
surrounded by the flickering shapes of wraiths who had
arrived silently and unannounced. Their intentions were
far from clear. At first Terrel thought they were attacking
the foreign ghost, and indeed Jax was flailing about, trying
to ward off their unwanted attentions, but they seemed to
be doing him no harm. After a few moments of this
ungainly dance, Terrel began to suspect that the wraiths
did not regard the newcomer as an enemy, but simply as
an object of curiosity, perhaps even of hope. They continued to cluster round the prince, distracting and annoying
him.

What is this? Jax muttered. *Go away!*

Terrel remembered Elam's comments about the ghosts
'just being there' making things worse on Myvatan, and
wondered whether Jax was unwittingly doing the same
thing. The wraiths were clearly drawn to him, but now
they seemed to be becoming more and more agitated.

I have to go, Jax stated abruptly. He sounded weary as
well as frustrated now, and Terrel guessed that his earlier
exertions had used up most of his strength – and that he,
like Alyssa, would need to return to Vadanis to 'rest'
before long. It was reassuring to know that there were
limits to his brother's power. However, thinking of Alyssa
prompted another memory, and there was a question
Terrel needed to ask before Jax left.

What did you mean about not seeing Alyssa again? he said
hurriedly.

Oh, it seems she's got the idea that you betrayed her, the prince replied, with a malicious grin. *Can't imagine why. I think this one's been trying to tell her the truth, but he can't find her.* He was still waving his arms at the wraiths, but his image was fading now, his voice growing fainter.

As Terrel watched his brother leave, he almost wished he hadn't asked the final question. The answer implied not only that Alyssa was still angry with him, but also that there was more trouble between his allies. It had always been Alyssa who found the ghosts before – or at least Terrel had assumed it to be that way round – and the fact that she had chosen not to contact them raised the awful possibility that she did not intend to lead them to his aid. And that meant she really might have abandoned him – which was the worst punishment Terrel could imagine.

He was still considering this dreadful prospect as the wraiths drifted away and a new set of visitors took their place. Raufar and Pjorsa came scrambling down the side of the hollow, while several other soldiers watched from the rim.

'Gods, he's alive!' Pjorsa exclaimed.

'Are you hurt?' the captain asked as he came to a slithering halt beside him.

'A bit,' Terrel replied. 'Nothing serious.'

Pjorsa shook his head in amazement.

'You have a charmed life, healer,' he said.

Terrel was not sure he agreed. At that moment it felt more as if he was cursed.

'It was odd,' Raufar said thoughtfully. 'The White didn't seem to know what was going on either. Their neomancers must have produced the whirlwinds, but it didn't seem to do them much good.'

'It was a mess,' Narvat agreed. 'Both sides lost a lot of men.'

Terrel was listening to the discussion, but not taking an active part. He could have told them who had really been responsible for the tornadoes, but to do so would have raised more questions than it answered, and he did not feel up to that. He was in pain and very weary, having dragged himself to the other side of the ice road along with what remained of the company. They were still high enough in the mountains for there to be snow lying in places, but for the most part there was solid earth beneath their feet now – and everyone was thankful for this. But the mood in the camp was sombre. They had left over twenty men behind, including Stykkis, and quite a few more were struggling with injuries. Terrel had used the last of his flagging energies to do what he could for them, until Raufar had ordered him to stop, pointing out that they still had a long way to go and he did not want Terrel exhausting himself.

'After the whirlwind died away,' the captain was saying now, 'the White were about to renew their attack when one of them burst into flame. After everything else that had happened it was just too much for them, and they ran off. Then the avalanches started, which meant we couldn't pursue them.'

'It also cut us off from where you were,' Pjorsa added. 'Or we'd have been with you a lot sooner. Not that I'd have been too keen to end up where you did.'

'I've never seen anything like it,' Narvat said, his amazement still obvious even some hours after the event. 'Are you sure you're not a neomancer?'

Terrel shook his head, but said nothing.

'Well, whoever or whatever was responsible, it probably saved your life,' Raufar said. 'I'm not sure we'd have been able to pull you out of the skelf in time, especially after the avalanches had made so much of the terrain treacherous.'

It was clear that, for the soldiers, the whirlwind that had surrounded Terrel was just one more inexplicable event in a day that had contained several, but none of them mentioned having seen any ghosts or wraiths.

'Did one of our fire-starters kill the White soldiers?' Terrel asked quietly. He had noticed the deep hole in the snow, which had been melted by the heat of the deadly fire. Where it had refrozen it was discoloured with ash, but there was nothing left of the man except for a few scorched fragments at the bottom of the pit. He still found it hard to believe that any human being could be reduced to such insignificant remains.

'I presumed they must have done,' Raufar answered. 'And I tore them off a strip for disobeying orders, but they both swear blind it wasn't their doing.'

'Can you believe them?' Pjorsa asked. 'Jauron's not exactly reliable, is he?'

'No,' the captain agreed, 'but on this occasion I think he's telling the truth. It's a mystery.'

Terrel's suspicions were confirmed. Jax had been responsible for this as well. He wondered whether the victim had been chosen specifically, or simply picked out at random.

'Who else can it have been, though?' Narvat asked. 'Unless the enemy have worked out how to do it too.'

'If they have, they're not very good,' Raufar said. 'It was one of their own men that burned.'

'Maybe it was a mistake,' Pjorsa suggested. 'I've heard rumours of things like that happening to some of our neomancers in Saudark.'

'Yes, well, we shouldn't pay too much attention to rumours,' the captain said. 'We've got a job to do. If all goes according to plan, we should meet up with the units from the Krafla Pass tomorrow, or the day after at the latest. After that it's an easy run to Hvannadal.'

'Let's hope it's easy,' Pjorsa said.

'We're through the worst now,' Raufar assured him. 'After today we ought to be able to cope with anything, eh, Terrel?'

The healer could only nod absently. His heart was so full of foreboding he couldn't bring himself to speak.

CHAPTER THIRTY-EIGHT

Things did not go according to plan. After several unintentional detours, the troop finally reached the agreed rendezvous point, but there was no one there to meet them. Narvat swore they'd got the right place this time, but there was no sign of any of the other units.

'Could they have got here earlier and gone on?' Pjorsa asked.

Raufar shook his head.

'They'd be disobeying orders if they did,' he said.

'Not if there'd been a signal.'

'We'd have seen it too,' the captain replied. 'Besides, there'd be some sign of a camp here. No one's passed this way recently.'

'You think they've been driven back?' Narvat said.

'All of them?' Raufar muttered. 'I doubt it. It's more likely they've been delayed like we were.'

Listening to him, Terrel wondered if their commander's response was genuine or simply expedient. The idea that all their nearest allies had been defeated would be bad for morale. No one had mentioned the other possibility – that the other units had been massacred – but he could tell by the expressions on the soldiers' faces that the thought had occurred to them.

'I'll send scouts to the entrances of the other passes,' Narvat said. 'See if we can find out what's going on.'

'Do that. In the meantime, we wait and make the best of this.' Raufar looked around. 'We should investigate that valley down there.'

'I'll go,' Narvat said.

'Go carefully,' the captain advised. 'If it's as fertile as it looks, they're not likely to have left it undefended.'

The lieutenant went to organize the various scouting parties, and left Raufar and Pjorsa to oversee the setting up of the camp. They had chosen the spot for its defensive advantages – the approaches could all be guarded by a relatively small number of sentries – but the position offered little comfort. Set on a small triangular plateau, and surrounded by boulder-strewn escarpments, it was exposed to wind and rain. Even though there were only a few hours of darkness now, and the snowfields were behind them, it still promised to be a cold night.

Since their last encounter, three days earlier, they had seen no sign of any enemy forces, but they were alone in unfamiliar territory, and the future of the campaign was uncertain. Even for men hardened by many years of war, it was a nervous time.

As the sun set, Narvat returned with news that seemed too good to be true, and Terrel was not surprised when Raufar treated it with some suspicion.

'There is a village,' the lieutenant reported, 'but it's been abandoned. Not a single person to be seen. At first I thought they'd retreated to the tower – it's a good one, solid stone, no windows until the third floor – but that was empty too.'

'You're sure?'

'Absolutely. The ladder was still in place. We were able to walk right in. They'd even left some grain and other stores inside.'

'This doesn't sound right,' Raufar declared. 'It must be a trap.'

'If it is, I don't know how they're going to spring it. We checked all the approaches and they're clear. Even if the White *did* reappear, we'd be able to get away in plenty of time.'

'Magic?'

'Hraun was with me, and he says there's nothing unusual.'

'Poison, then?' the captain suggested, still looking for the danger he felt sure was there.

'Hraun checked the well and some of the other stuff,' Narvat replied. 'He says it's clean. Most of the crops haven't even been harvested, so it's difficult to see how they could have been poisoned. There are even some goats and pigs still in their pens. Give me a foraging party first thing tomorrow and we can be feasting by midday.'

'This is insane,' Raufar grumbled, still not convinced. 'What are they playing at?'

'Maybe the White army's already retreated,' Pjorsa said, 'and the villagers knew they wouldn't be able to defend themselves, so they left in a hurry.'

'Without their livestock? Or their stores?'

'Perhaps they were *ordered* to leave,' Narvat suggested.

'That would only make sense if it *was* a trap,' the captain said. 'But from what you tell me, there's no indication of that.'

'And if it isn't, we'd be fools not to take advantage,' Pjorsa commented. 'The men would feel a lot better for a bit of roast pork in their bellies.'

Raufar could not deny the truth of that. The campaign had already lasted longer than anyone had foreseen, and a chance to replenish their dwindling supplies was unquestionably attractive. Even so, his doubts persisted.

'What do you think, Terrel?' he asked, turning to the healer.

'Me?' Terrel couldn't hide his surprise at being consulted. 'I've no idea.'

'You don't have any feeling about this? One way or the other?'

'No.' He wasn't sure what Raufar was getting at.

'All right,' the captain said, turning back to Narvat. 'I want a close watch kept on the valley through the night. Tell the lookouts to report anything they see. Anything at all. I'll decide in the morning.'

'I'll organize it,' the lieutenant replied. 'Are any of the other scouts back yet?'

'No,' Raufar answered. 'Which means no one else is close. For the time being, we're on our own.'

The next day brought more definite news. Narvat and his foraging party had a successful – and uneventful – return to the valley, and the food they brought back was very welcome. After the short rations of the previous few days, the midday meal did indeed seem like a feast. While he still couldn't fathom the reasons behind the villagers' actions, even Raufar was now prepared to enjoy the benefits of their withdrawal.

They were still savouring the meal when one of the scouts returned from a neighbouring pass with the news that another company would be joining them soon.

'Did you make contact?' Raufar asked.

'Yes, sir.'

'Whose troop is it?'

'Captain Hosak's.'

The name sounded familiar to Terrel, and he remembered that Hosak had commanded the squad that had escorted him from Saudark to Tofana's pyramid.

'Casualties?' Raufar asked.

'About the same as us, as far as I could judge.'

'Did you see any enemy activity while you were out?'

'No, Captain. Not a thing. And Hosak's men hadn't seen any sign of the White for the last three days either.'

'Good man. Get some food and rest. You've earnt it.'

'This is the strangest campaign I've ever known,' Hosak concluded. 'What the White are doing makes no sense.'

The two captains, together with their respective lieutenants and neomancers, had spent some time discussing their progress. The newcomers' story matched Raufar's in most respects. Although they too had been harassed and delayed by their elusive foes, there had been no serious engagements. Even though the enemy seemed to be aware of what the Black forces were intent on doing, they had made no concerted effort to stop them.

'Their tactics are strange,' Raufar agreed. 'Have you had news of any other units?'

'Not for some time, and what we heard wasn't much better than rumour. According to some of the troops to the west of us, the landing at Hofnar didn't go well, but I've no confirmation of that. And some of the units we're supposed to meet up with have apparently got themselves lost or turned back.'

'I find that hard to believe.'

'Me too,' Hosak said. 'I'm just reporting what we were told.' He paused, apparently weighing up his next words. 'The only other thing we've heard sounds even more dubious. There've been some rumours about treason — that someone has told the White exactly what we're planning to do.'

'That's ridiculous!' Raufar exclaimed. 'No one would contemplate such a thing. And in any case, it would make what the enemy have been doing even more absurd.'

'Agreed. It's probably just a stupid joke that someone took too seriously.'

Terrel wasn't ready to dismiss the idea so readily. He was still wondering whether the Holma might have betrayed Pingeyri's plans for reasons of their own. If they had, he wished they'd let him in on the secret – and on what such a move was supposed to achieve.

'There's another reason why this campaign is different from any we've been on before,' Narvat remarked, when it became clear that the captains had completed their initial discussion.

'What's that?' Hosak asked.

'We've got wizards with us this time.'

'Surely you're not suggesting that *they're* responsible for any of our misfortunes?' Hraun gasped.

'I'm not suggesting anything,' Narvat replied, remaining calm in the face of the neomancer's outrage. 'I'm just stating a fact.'

'The lieutenant has a point,' Hosak commented.

'And the White must know about it by now,' Raufar added. 'Perhaps they're waiting until they can get their own wizards involved.'

'They *want* us to go to Hvannadal?'

'Yes, but at a time of their choosing. That would explain why they've been trying to delay us rather than drive us back.'

'If that's the case,' Narvat put in, 'then I can't help wondering what they might have waiting for us there.'

'Whatever it is, they'll be no match for Tofana,' Jauron stated with a confident smile. 'Get us there and we'll finish the job.' Unlike his fellow neomancer, he had not been angered by the captain's theory.

'Are you sure of that?' Pjorsa asked. 'If they *do* know what we're planning, then their wizards will have made arrangements to counter our magic.'

'Not *this* magic,' Jauron claimed.

'We saw one of them burn, don't forget,' the lieutenant persisted. 'That means they must know *something* about it.'

'Not necessarily,' Hraun said. 'That could just have been a random chain. Their neomancers were clearly incompetent. They couldn't even control their own whirlwinds.'

'Are you telling us you can become a fire-starter by *accident*?'

'You wouldn't mind them having some fancy new sort of crossbow if all they could do was shoot themselves with it,' Jauron remarked.

'They could get better,' Pjorsa pointed out. 'It took your lot a while to get the hang of it, so I've heard.'

Hraun's face darkened at the suggestion, but Jauron merely smiled.

'Don't worry,' he said. 'When we're done, this is going to be the end of the war.'

'Just as long as it's not the end of us too,' Pjorsa replied. 'I can face a warrior's death, but I don't want to get turned into a pile of ash.'

'Then you'd better make sure you stay behind me.'

'Enough!' Raufar declared, as the two men locked stares. 'We're soldiers. We'll follow orders. That's an end of it.'

The ensuing silence was finally broken by Terrel.

'There is an alternative,' he said tentatively.

'What's that?' Raufar demanded.

'If you're in doubt, we could go to the Lonely Peaks before heading for Hvannadal.'

Although the soldiers were obviously shocked by this idea, no one spoke, and Terrel seized his chance.

'We're among the units furthest to the east, aren't we? So we're closest to the glacier. If we were to find the Peacemaker *before* we got to the springs, no one would be able to stand against us.'

'We could only do it if we don't get the signal to advance,' Raufar said after a few moments.

'You're not seriously considering this?' Hosak exclaimed. 'It would be tantamount to desertion!'

'Not if it leads to victory,' Terrel said.

Hosak looked at him, measuring the foreigner anew.

'You've made quite a reputation for yourself since we last met,' he said. 'But you're wrong about this.'

'How can you be so sure?'

'The Red Moon was full last night.'

Terrel had been hoping that no one would point that out.

'Even so—' he began, but Hosak cut him off.

'And there's no guarantee you or anyone else will ever find the sword.'

Terrel was about to say something more, even though he already knew the cause was lost, but their discussion was interrupted by the hurried approach of one of the sentries.

'There's movement in the valley, Captain,' he reported breathlessly.

The soldiers instantly set about readying themselves for battle, all thoughts of future plans set aside. However, an hour later, the news came that the latest arrivals were their allies. Two more companies of the Black Quarter were now close by, and the tension in the camp eased once more.

Terrel was woken during the night by the sound of another report being made to Raufar.

'Sorry to wake you, Captain, but the sentries have seen a signal flare over to the west.'

'What colour?' Raufar asked quickly.

'They think it was green, but it was too far away to tell for sure.'

'Then there'll be another. Get more men on watch now. We need to be certain.'

Terrel crawled out of his tent and looked around to see that Raufar had done the same. He was wrapping himself in a cloak while watching the western horizon. Not wanting to disturb him, Terrel found a vantage point on a nearby rock and waited.

A short time later, the healer saw a small flame rise into the sky, trailing a faint line of sparks. It was much closer than the earlier one had been – as the various units passed the message along the line – and when the flare exploded, the vivid green colour was unmistakable.

'That's our answer,' Raufar told the soldiers around him. 'We've got the go-ahead. We begin the final push for Hvannadal tomorrow.'

Chapter Thirty-Nine

It was the size of a mountain, but it wasn't like any mountain Terrel had ever seen. He stared in amazement, as did everyone around him. And like everyone around him, he wondered what it meant.

The way it shimmered in the air, the way it was there and not there at the same time, reminded him of the dome over the doomed palace in Talazoria. But this was a quite different shape. It was a glittering, three-sided pyramid – like the upper level of Tofana's home when she had made it transparent in order to watch the neomancer trials. But this pyramid was *huge*; it covered an entire city and a good part of the plain around it. The walls and towers of Hvannadal were visible inside, but they looked as if they were being seen through a thin layer of sunlit gauze. It made the place seem otherworldly, as though it was an image from a dream.

The awed silence of the soldiers with Terrel was an indication that they were as unnerved and as mystified as he was. No one had ever seen anything like this before, and to have come so close to their objective only to be faced with such a vast and unknown power had rendered them all speechless. Glancing at his companions, Terrel saw that even Raufar was temporarily at a loss. The captain clearly knew that he ought to be doing or saying something – to reassert his authority, and to remind his men of their military discipline – but, like all the others, he was too surprised to do anything but stare at what lay ahead of them. In the end it was Pjorsa who broke the silence and the spell that had been cast over them.

'Savik's teeth,' he growled. 'They must be terrified of us if they've gone to the trouble of building that thing.'

With those words the mood began to change. To Terrel's amazement the soldiers became warriors once more, their confidence renewed and their fears forgotten. Raufar snapped out of his reverie and began to issue orders. Before long, jokes and laughter were being exchanged, and the pyramid was being viewed as just another challenge in the war that was the all-consuming passion of their lives.

It had taken them almost half a median month to complete the journey to Hvannadal. They had met with little or no resistance from enemy forces, with the White defenders apparently melting away before any serious fighting could take place, but this had only reinforced their suspicions that they were being lured into a trap. Because of this, Raufar and the other commanders had proceeded cautiously. They had all been aware that they were supposed to launch the final assault on the springs at the full of the White Moon. This gave them plenty of time, and they did not want to make a mistake at this stage. They had made contact with other units as they'd gone, taking satisfaction in the evident success of the generals' plan, until they'd arrived at the present positions with two days to spare before the date set for the attack on the city.

Terrel had been aware of the army massing all around, but as yet he hadn't seen anyone other than the men from Raufar and Hosak's companies. He had hoped to be able to talk to some others – especially to Jarvik, Tegan or

Myrdal – but he had no idea where they were, and he couldn't just wander around what might soon become a massive battlefield. Raufar had sent messengers to General Pingeyri, requesting orders and hoping for news, but that had been before the ghostly pyramid had formed – spreading up and out from its apex as though it had been buried beneath the plain and then raised into the air by some unimaginable force. As yet there had been no response and, in the absence of any other duties, Raufar had set his men to making their camp as secure and comfortable as possible. The soldiers had been in the field for a long time now, and although the fighting had not been as fierce as might have been expected, the journeying and constant watchfulness had taken their toll. They were all glad of a chance to rest for a while.

Eventually, in the long twilight that preceded the few hours of true night, a deputation arrived from Pingeyri. A colonel Terrel did not recognize called Raufar and Hosak together for a briefing. The other newcomer was Vatna, who evidently had plans of his own.

'It's good to see you again,' he told the healer. 'Are you well?'

Terrel nodded. He was about to say more, but the magian was clearly in a hurry.

'Good,' he said. 'Come with me.' He set off again without waiting for a response.

'Where are we going?' Terrel asked as he fell into step beside him.

'Pingeyri's summoned a council of war,' Vatna replied. 'He wants you there.'

The general's command centre was based in the largest tent Terrel had ever seen. It was bigger even than Algardi's family home. This reminder of the nomad elder who had died while Terrel had been in Misrah made him wonder briefly how things were going in that beleaguered land, but he was given no time to dwell on it now.

Pingeyri acknowledged their arrival, and waved the newcomers to one of the unoccupied rugs that were laid out on the floor. Other members of the council of war – most of whom were familiar to Terrel – were already seated in a ragged circle. Junior adjutants were moving among them, serving drinks, but apart from that little seemed to be happening. The general himself was engaged in a quiet conversation with Myrdal – one of the faces Terrel had been glad to see – who was kneeling behind his master. The expression on Pingeyri's face was a mixture of concern and displeasure, and the exchange ended with him dismissing his adjutant with an angry gesture. As Myrdal stood up, he caught Terrel's eye and nodded almost imperceptibly. Terrel returned the greeting in a similar manner, then looked away quickly.

As he sat down, he scanned the other faces in the tent. Tofana sat next to her fellow wizard, her normally expressive face now impassive. Varmahlid had her crimson cloak wrapped around her bony shoulders, and was staring into space, ignoring everyone around her. Several magians were hovering behind their mistresses, but to Terrel's disappointment Tegan was not among them. Flanking Pingeyri were Eskif and Davik, and there were several officers the healer did not recognize. Although two of them wore the insignia of the Red Quarter, Jarvik was not present.

The general cleared his throat.

'Now that we're all here,' he said, 'we can begin again.'

Again? Terrel thought. He found it hard to believe that the discussion had been delayed for his benefit.

'I want to know what that *thing* is,' Pingeyri stated forcefully, as he turned his gaze on the wizards. 'What it means

for us. And I don't want any high-flown theories. I want
facts.'

'I've already told you—' Tofana began.

'Then tell me again,' the general said belligerently. 'But
this time in words I can understand.'

The wizard's emerald eyes shone menacingly in the lamp-
light, but Pingeyri was clearly in no mood to be intimidated.

'It's a projection of Onundar's pyramid,' Tofana replied
tersely. 'A simulacrum. It has no substance, but it has
power. It's similar to the shields your neomancers use in
the field.'

'Similar, but not the same?'

'Correct, General,' the wizard conceded. 'This is different not just in scale but in scope. The screen here not only
offers physical protection against invasion or weather-
weapons, but it also has magical potency.'

'Are you telling me magic can't get in either?'

'That's a somewhat crude way of putting it,' she told
him, 'but in essence it's the truth.'

'Magic can't get out either,' Varmahlid put in before
Pingeyri had the chance to react to the jibe. 'While it's
there, you need not worry about being attacked by
Onundar or any of the enemy's neomancers.'

'Then what good does it do them? Why lure us here
just to create a stand-off?' The idea that they were being
led into a trap had obviously occurred to Pingeyri, as well
as to his company commanders, but the general's bewilderment made Terrel wonder whether this might be what
the underground wanted. Had they somehow arranged a
situation where the conflict at Hvannadal turned into a
stalemate, hoping that Pingeyri would give up and head for
the Lonely Peaks instead? If that really was the case, it
must mean that they had influential friends among the
people of the White Quarter.

'There is something my colleague hasn't mentioned,' Varmahlid said, looking at the general and studiously ignoring Tofana's warning glance. 'It's possible the shield is designed not only to stop magic but actually to repel it, so that any assault upon it would rebound on the attackers.'

'You have evidence of this?' Pingeyri demanded.

'Yes. In—'

'It was an aberration,' Tofana cut in impatiently. '*My colleague* is wrong to draw such an inference from an isolated case.' The friction between the two wizards was obvious now.

'What happened?' the general asked bluntly.

'While we were investigating the shield, one of our fire-starters spotted a group of enemy soldiers spying on us from within, and he reacted like a soldier, not a magian. He thought he had isolated the chain that would destroy them, but instead he destroyed himself.'

'He burned?'

'Yes,' Varmahlid confirmed. 'As did three more of our neomancers who were nearby.'

'He made a mistake,' Tofana admitted. 'The pyramid may well be distorting chains, but it proves nothing.'

'It's not exactly encouraging, though, is it?' Pingeyri snarled.

'We need to investigate further,' the wizard muttered.

'Rather more carefully,' Varmahlid added.

'Is that why the White kept retreating?' Eskif asked. 'Do you think they're expecting us to defeat ourselves by pointless attacks on this thing?'

'If they are, they're seriously underestimating our intelligence,' Davik commented. 'How long did they think it would take us to stop once we realized the risks?'

'Which brings me back to my original question,' Pingeyri said. 'What good does this shield do them?'

'Their generals aren't stupid,' the brigadier replied. 'They must be planning something else, or they'd never have left so much land undefended.'

'What can they do from inside that thing?' another officer asked.

'It's not just that,' Pingeyri went on. 'They won't be able to feed themselves for much longer. All their summer provisions are out here – with us! We can supply ourselves indefinitely, but they'll starve by the autumn.'

'That raises the question of just how many people really are in Hvannadal,' Davik said. 'I've had reports that some White units haven't retreated, but slipped between our lines and let us go past.'

'Yes, yes, I've heard the same thing,' the general snapped. 'A few small companies may well be behind us, but we *saw* most of them heading for the city. They still won't be able to survive a siege of more than a short month.'

'So they must be planning something else,' Eskif repeated.

'Not necessarily,' Tofana responded. 'If they've found out about our new magic, this could be a desperate attempt to avoid a catastrophic defeat, to buy themselves a little more time.'

'Time for what?' Pingeyri asked.

'Reinforcements from the Gold Quarter?' Vatna suggested.

'No. We have that covered,' Davik replied. 'If they were going to send a force big enough to make any difference, we'd have known about it by now. As it is, they couldn't get here in time.'

'Unless Hvannadal has already been prepared for a long siege,' Eskif put in. 'They may have been stockpiling supplies.'

'You saw their fields,' the general exclaimed, waving a large hand to indicate the plain around them. 'The crops weren't even harvested. They'll have to come out and fight eventually. All we have to do is starve them out.'

'Just how long are we prepared to wait?' the brigadier asked.

'How long do you think they'll be able to maintain the pyramid?' Davik asked, looking at the wizards. 'It must be a huge drain on Onundar's resources.'

'Undoubtedly,' Varmahlid agreed, 'but the structure appears stable. Maintaining it now it's in place may be relatively easy – and Onundar has a ready supply of power in the springs.'

'I'm confident we'll find a way to break it down eventually,' Tofana added stiffly.

'And in the meantime, our enemies inside will be growing weaker,' Pingeyri concluded. 'It looks as though we could be here for a while, gentlemen.'

'We do have an alternative course of action.'

The voice had come from the shadows behind the general, who frowned at the interruption. Myrdal stepped forward, his face drawn and pale. Terrel had the feeling that the adjutant had already raised this alternative and been rebuffed, but the Holma must be desperate by now, and the young man was risking the general's wrath in order to try once more.

'I've already told you that's out of the question,' Pingeyri said angrily.

'With respect, General, all I'm suggesting is switching the order of our plans. We can't do anything here as long as the pyramid is in place, but there's nothing to stop us searching for the Peacemaker now.'

'Myrdal has a point,' Eskif said quickly, before the general could respond.

Pingeyri glanced at his colleague in surprise.

'If the army sits around for too long, waiting for something to happen, morale will suffer,' the brigadier went on. 'At least going on to the Lonely Peaks would renew their sense of purpose.'

Terrel was delighted by this turn of events. It seemed that Kopak might have finally persuaded his father to change his mind. Nevertheless, it was soon evident that it was going to take more than this to convince Pingeyri.

'We have all the purpose we need right here,' he stated firmly. 'We didn't come all this way just to give up at the first obstacle.'

'Then perhaps we could send a separate party to the glacier,' Myrdal persisted. 'That way—'

'No!' the general roared. 'I've had enough of this, Adjutant. Do I make myself clear?'

'Yes, sir.'

'Good. We're here now, and we'll *stay* here. All of us. Hvannadal is our primary objective, and I have no intention of setting off on what may prove to be a wild-goose chase. Nor do I intend dividing our forces again. We've learnt that lesson.' The vehemence with which he spoke silenced any opposition and quashed Terrel's hopes. Pingeyri looked around at everyone in the tent, his gaze finally coming to rest on the healer.

'What do you think about all this?'

Terrel had been wondering why Vatna had brought him to the meeting, and was taken aback by the sudden question. He had never understood why Raufar had sought his opinion – and now the general was doing the same. The healer had the feeling that the consequences of his words might be far-reaching.

'I believe I ought to go to the Lonely Peaks,' he said carefully. 'That's where my destiny lies.'

Pingeyri's face darkened at this, but he kept his temper in check.

'I think you have a part to play here too,' he said, watching Terrel closely. 'Do you have any feelings about the pyramid?'

'It's as much a mystery to me as it is to you,' the healer replied.

'So you've no—' the general began, then broke off abruptly and glared at the nervous-looking soldier who had just entered the tent. 'What do you want?'

'I'm sorry to interrupt, General, but I think you ought to come and see this.'

'Now?'

'Yes, sir.'

Muttering darkly to himself, Pingeyri got to his feet and followed the man outside. Everyone else did the same, and Terrel was one of the first to join the general in the open air. The sun had just set, leaving the cloud-patched sky a deep shade of cobalt blue – but there was something strange about the stars that shone faintly in the heavens. It took Terrel a while to realize what was amiss, and when he did he could hardly believe it. The stars were the wrong colour – flecks of gold rather than silver – and some of them were *beneath* the clouds. And there were lines . . .

By then, Terrel – along with most of the others – had recognized the truth. A second, even more colossal pyramid was now in place, its outer edges extending well beyond the plain on which the army was camped. Even though it was dwarfed by the new structure, Onundar's shield was still there. And they were trapped between the two.

CHAPTER FORTY

During the next two days the atmosphere among the soldiers grew increasingly tense. While the wizards, together with every magian and neomancer, were fully occupied in investigating the pyramids, there was little anyone else could do. The officers tried to maintain a sense of purpose by enforcing sentry rotas, and by despatching men to forage – plundering the abandoned fields and farms – but such tasks offered little distraction. The general preoccupation with what was happening about them was natural enough, and rumours spread rapidly through the ranks.

The results of the wizards' enquiries became common knowledge almost as soon as they confirmed them for themselves. There were no official announcements, but in so fraught a situation there was no way such things could be kept secret. In any case, most people were quite capable of guessing the results. Everyone assumed that the inner pyramid was Onundar's creation, and it didn't take much of an intuitive leap to predict that the larger shield stemmed from Reykholar, the Gold Quarter's most powerful wizard. Her whereabouts were unknown, but the flecks of colour in the massive structure were almost as good as a signature.

Details of the exact nature of the pyramids were harder to come by, and so the gossip was often vague and sometimes contradictory, but some facts did emerge clearly.

Both barriers were physically impassable, which meant that the army was effectively imprisoned. Retreat – or a diversion to the Lonely Peaks – was no longer an option. It also meant that a military attack on Hvannadal was impossible, and that the enemy forces within the city were similarly restricted. Excavations soon established that the shimmering planes extended below the ground, so it was impossible to tunnel their way out.

Of even greater significance was the fact that the pyramids also formed barriers to magic. After the earlier misfortune of one of their number, the fire-starters had been forbidden to use their deadly skills. Although several other neomancers had made cautious efforts to employ more conventional weather-weapons, their experiments had been unsuccessful. The space behind the two shields remained unaffected, and on several occasions the destructive forces had been turned back on their creators. Swirls of snow, whirlwinds and bolts of lightning had caused havoc, and all such attempts had quickly been halted. As far as anyone could tell, magic did indeed rebound from the screens, but it did so in an almost random manner, striking anywhere within the area they enclosed. Not only that, but in a few instances the spell somehow repeated itself without any further prompting from the neomancers, so that its influence spread far and wide. What was more, even when it splintered in this way, each separate occurrence – each freezing downpour or crash of thunder – seemed to be just as violent as the original. It soon became clear that the release of any substantial quantity of magical energy would be potentially disastrous, possibly even to the point of destroying everything and everyone trapped between the two pyramids.

Terrel took no part in these investigations, and no one came to tell him anything about the results. Like the

soldiers around him, he had to rely on gossip and intuition. But there was one indisputable fact that soon became
obvious to everyone. No magical skill of any kind was
necessary for this; simple observation was enough to see
that the white pyramid was growing larger while the gold
one was shrinking. This meant that, at ground level, the
two impenetrable shields were moving closer together.
Although the movement was ponderous, no more than a
few paces per hour, the Black army was slowly being
squeezed into a smaller and smaller area – and if the
process continued they would eventually be crushed in a
gigantic vice. The trap they had walked into was being
sprung.

Terrel woke to his third day outside Hvannadal. He had
slept for only a short time, and his slumber had been too
full of dreams to grant him much rest. As far as he could
tell, there had been nothing significant in his visions, and
the vague but disquieting images soon slipped from his
mind as he looked up to the sky, and then towards the
city. Both pyramids were still in position.

   All around him men were talking in whispers, and
although their military training was preventing a complete
breakdown of discipline, it was obvious that an air of fear
was beginning to dominate the general mood. Panic lay
just below the surface.

   The night that had just passed had seen the full of the
White Moon, marking the time when Tofana had planned
to attack the springs. That was impossible now, of course,
but there had been some hopeful speculation that the
enemy forces might choose to take advantage of this
favourable alignment to launch an attack of their own. To
do so, they would have had to lower their shield – but
nothing had happened, and the soldiers' hopes had been

dashed. All they could do now was wait, and pray that the gods – or their own wizards – would help them to find a way out of the mess they were in.

Naturally enough, Terrel shared their concerns – his life was at stake, after all – but he had an additional set of worries. Apart from the fact that he was unable to make any progress in his own quest, he was desperate to know when – or if – he would see Alyssa again. Even discounting Jax's assertion that she would not be returning, Terrel was convinced that she would be unable to get through the outer pyramid. And this meant that the ghosts – the advisors he'd relied upon at crucial moments throughout his journeying – would not be coming either. Any perils he was about to encounter would have to be faced alone.

Terrel was looking around the encampment, thinking that he ought to get some breakfast, even though he had little appetite, when his attention was caught by a disturbance some distance away. A group of soldiers had gathered, and the sound of their voices drifted over the sluggish, early morning air. They seemed to be asking a series of questions, the volume rising as they competed to make themselves heard. Terrel finally realized that their increasingly vociferous demands were being directed towards an outsider, someone who had just arrived, but he couldn't see who the newcomer was. More soldiers were heading towards the spot now, while others were watching the scene with some interest.

Eventually the situation was resolved when Raufar strode across, shouting with the voice of authority. His men fell silent and parted to let their commander through, and then Terrel saw who had caused the commotion. He got to his feet at once and moved closer.

'I don't *have* any news for you, Captain,' Tegan was saying when Terrel came within earshot. 'You will be told of any developments through the normal chain of command. And I don't appreciate being jostled in this manner.'

'I'm sorry, Magian,' Raufar replied, motioning his men to move a little further back. 'It won't happen again.'

'Thank you.' Tegan's expression softened. 'I wish to speak to Terrel, the foreign healer. He was assigned to your company, I believe. Is he here?'

Raufar glanced round and saw Terrel, who had stopped a few paces away.

'He is,' he said, pointing.

Tegan nodded and made her way towards the healer. Raufar went with her, and when several other soldiers moved to join them, the magian stopped in her tracks.

'It will be a *private* conversation, Captain,' she stated, employing her haughtiest tone.

'As you wish,' Raufar said, and turned away. 'Give them some space,' he ordered.

The soldiers obeyed, and Tegan joined Terrel. They sat down next to the nearest campfire, far enough from the rest of the company to be sure of not being overheard. Even so, Terrel was uncomfortably aware that they were the subject of a number of sidelong glances. Tegan did not speak immediately, and the expression in her clear blue eyes was bleak.

'Is this as bad as it seems?' Terrel ventured.

'It's worse,' she whispered, then seemed to make a determined effort to pull herself together. 'How much do you know about what's been happening?'

'Only the common gossip.'

Tegan nodded, taking a deep breath. Her hands were shaking slightly.

'For once the rumours are probably right,' she said. 'All the chains and lines between the two pyramids are getting increasingly twisted and distorted. If we're not careful, the water could even become too dangerous to drink soon. And we can't do anything at the moment without making things worse. What little we *are* trying is just making it more and more dangerous.' She paused for breath, trying to calm herself. 'We've made some progress in slowing down the movement of the shields, but we're a long way from being able to stop them altogether. The pressures that build up between them are just too great. The only other slightly more encouraging news is that we've discovered some possible weaknesses in the structures – at their corners. We may eventually be able to exploit this, but even if we *do* manage to break through, Tofana is still intent on corrupting the springs. We can't let her do that. It'll be the end of everything.'

'Can't you make her see the risks she would be running?'

'She won't listen. I've tried and tried, but ...' Tegan shrugged.

'Then can you stop her?'

'Not on my own, no. But I may have help.'

'Who from?'

'I haven't had a chance to talk to her directly, but I know Varmahlid is worried. She may well have been looking into the same theories I have.'

Terrel immediately wondered whether this might be the wizard who – according to the Tindaya Code – was supposed to help him. It seemed like a distinct possibility.

'Of course the whole thing is academic unless we get out of here,' Tegan added. 'I don't suppose you have any ideas about that?'

Once again Terrel was surprised by someone asking for his advice.

'I haven't a clue,' he replied. 'A lot of people seem to think I know what I'm doing, but this is all new to me.'

'You see the future.'

Terrel was bewildered by this response.

'That's what everyone thinks, anyway,' she told him. 'Ever since you emerged from Savik's Whale—'

'I didn't see any visions then, and I haven't since,' he protested.

'Are you sure?'

'I think I'd have noticed.'

'Perhaps,' Tegan conceded, then lowered her voice. 'Do you still have the stone?'

'Of course.' Terrel was tempted to tell her that the crystal was a fake, but something made him hold back. Belief might still be important to the Holma's cause.

'Let's hope you get a chance to use it,' Tegan said.

Not knowing how to respond to that, Terrel remained silent.

'I don't know what to do,' the magian whispered, the depths of her misery suddenly apparent. 'Everything is so . . .'

'You could talk to Jarvik,' he suggested. 'Do you know where he is?'

'Jarvik was killed three days before we got to Hvannadal.'

It took Terrel a few moments to recover from the impact of her words. The underground were effectively leaderless now.

'I'm sorry,' he said, knowing it was an inadequate response.

'That's not all,' Tegan added, her voice almost cracking. 'I can't find Myrdal.'

'What do you mean, you can't find him? Surely—'

'I can't get in to see the general, and his staff are all tight-lipped. No one seems to know anything.' She was trying to keep her feelings under control but it was costing her a great deal. 'Something's wrong.'

'We don't know that,' Terrel said. 'He could have been sent out on a mission.'

'Where to? No one can get out of here, remember? He's vanished. After all this, if we . . .' She looked down, unable to complete the sentence.

Terrel wanted to reassure Tegan, but he knew that anything he could say about Myrdal would only provide false comfort.

'The person I love is on the other side of the world.' He wasn't sure why he'd said that. The words had simply formed themselves in his head.

Tegan looked up, fighting back tears.

'But I've never doubted that I will see her again one day,' Terrel said, with as much conviction as he could muster.

'I have to keep believing,' Tegan whispered after a while.

'It's all we have,' Terrel confirmed.

They sat quietly for a while, watching the flames of the fire.

'I should get back,' the magian said eventually. 'Tofana will be wondering where I am.' She got to her feet.

'Keep trying to change her mind,' Terrel advised as he too stood up.

'I'll do what I can.'

'There's no love lost between Tofana and Varmahlid, is there?' he added. 'That could be your opportunity to—' He broke off as Tegan suddenly glanced up into the sky, the expression on her face changing from surprise to horror in an instant. Following the line of her gaze, Terrel saw that a patch of the gold pyramid far above them was glowing rather more brightly than the rest of the shield around it.

'What is it?' he asked.

'A fire-starter,' Tegan breathed. 'Some idiot is trying to . . . He could kill us all.'

A scream split the air then, followed by several panic-stricken yells. Looking for the source of the noise, Terrel saw a bright flame in the distance – and knew that this was no ordinary campfire.

CHAPTER FORTY-ONE

'Come on,' Tegan said, tugging on Terrel's arm. 'We've got to get away from here.'

'I thought it could rebound anywhere,' he said as they began to run.

'It can, but the most likely place is close to the source.'

'Shouldn't we try to stop them?'

'Too late for that.'

Ripples of terror were flowing through the encampment now, and Tegan and Terrel were not the only ones running. Most of the soldiers were trying to get as far away from the fire as possible, but the magian was cutting across their paths, angling towards the inner pyramid.

'Where are we going?' Terrel gasped.

'The pattern was high up,' Tegan replied. 'That means it's most likely to strike nearer the outer wall. The further in we go, the safer we'll be.'

Eventually they came to a halt, only a few paces from the shimmering white plane. When Terrel had taken a close look at it on a previous occasion, he had been almost mesmerized by the complex swirls within the transparent gauze, but this time he could see that the movement had become more agitated, making the patterns impossible to follow.

They were both breathless as they turned to look back. Almost immediately they spotted two more unnaturally

bright fires, and dark wisps of smoke. There was movement everywhere, though much of it seemed to be without
purpose. The panic that had been simmering beneath the
surface of the camp was out in the open now.

'Gods!' Tegan breathed, looking up.

Four new patches of light were blossoming on the outer
pyramid. Terrel stared at them in horror, knowing that the
fire-starter's magic was dividing and spreading.

'It's being amplified with each reflection,' Tegan whispered. 'I knew this would happen eventually.' The dread
in her voice chilled Terrel to the core.

'I don't understand.'

'The lines are so distorted now, they're beginning to
double back on themselves. The magic's feeding on itself.'

Terrel was still not sure he understood, but the consequences were becoming more apparent by the moment.

'How do we stop it?'

'We can't.'

'There must be something—' He was silenced by an
enormous crash of thunder from high above them.
Looking up, he saw storm clouds gathering under the
apex of the outer shield, lightning flickering within the
ominous mass. Down on the ground, more flames were
burning. Squalls of hail and sleet battered men and
uprooted tents, whirlwinds shrieked, and the ground
seemed to shake beneath their feet.

'It's set them all off,' Tegan explained miserably. 'All
the spells we tried to use earlier are coming back at us, but
stronger than ever. If the fire-starter's chain doesn't kill us,
the other weapons will.'

'Can't you do *anything*?' Terrel asked, terrified by the
resignation in her voice.

'Anything we do to try to counteract it will only make it
worse,' she explained, 'multiplying the effects even faster.

As it is, we haven't got long. The two pyramids are acting like mirrors, reflecting everything back and forth, over and over again. Sooner or later everyone in here will be caught up in one strand or another. This whole area will be pulverized.'

Fire burst in the air above them and the ground shook again, emphasizing the magian's point.

'It's just a matter of time now.' Tegan's expression was desolate as she turned to look at Terrel. 'There's nothing we can do. I'm sorry it had to end like this. The only thing I can hope is that the war truly will be over now. That way, at least our deaths won't have been in vain.'

The healer stared at her, then at the appalling scene all around them. It reminded him once again of Talazoria, where he and Aylen had been trapped inside the dome as the palace tore itself apart. But this time there would be no giant bird to rescue him. Even so, he could not afford to give up hope as Tegan had done. He knew that even if this catastrophe did end the war on Myvatan, the consequences of his failure to reach the elemental would eventually have far greater and more disastrous results for the whole of Nydus.

'We can't let this happen,' he muttered.

Tegan shook her head, but could not speak. She was crying now, and Terrel knew that she was bidding her own farewell to the world, and to Myrdal. He was about to try to shake her out of her morbid acceptance of fate when a soldier came running over to them.

'What do you want us to do?' Pjorsa rasped.

At first Terrel thought he was speaking to Tegan, but the lieutenant was looking directly at him.

'I don't know,' he said helplessly, his mind returning to Savik's Whale, and to the moment when the leader of the Gold troops had asked him the same improbable question. 'Do you know who started this?'

Pjorsa's scarred face distorted into a scowl.

'That filthy idiot Jauron,' he replied. 'Raufar got to him fast enough, but it was already too late.'

'Is he dead?'

'I'm not sure. The captain flattened him all right, but he might just have knocked him out.'

Terrel turned to Tegan and took her arm.

'If we can get to Jauron, would you be able to read the lines? Reverse whatever he did?'

The magian shook her head.

'It's too late. There's nothing we can do now. Look.'

Chaos was engulfing the entire region, growing more violent with every moment.

'Then we'll have to break the mirrors,' Terrel said. 'So the magic isn't contained.'

'There's no way to do that. We've tried everything.'

'Are you sure? What if we were able to attack one of the wizards responsible for the pyramids?'

'They're on the other side,' Tegan said wearily. 'There's no way of reaching them.'

'Have you thought of something?' Pjorsa asked hopefully. 'I can get some men—'

'This isn't a job for soldiers.' The first inkling of an idea had indeed just occurred to Terrel, sparked off by the reminder of his arrival on Myvatan. 'Stay here with Tegan, will you?'

Pjorsa nodded, though he and the magian both looked confused. Terrel knew he had no time to explain now, even if he could. He had not seen into the future when he'd been at Savik's Whale, but it was possible that he had *heard* it. He turned and walked towards the barrier, sensing its pulsating power. There was no way he could pass through it, but someone with a little less *substance* might be able to. And there was one 'ghost' who might be able to come to him without Alyssa's help. The thought of what he was about to do made Terrel feel sick, but desperate measures were called for. More people were dying as every moment passed, and the situation was deteriorating rapidly. *Do it!* he told himself.

Summoning the glamour to no purpose was something he would not have dreamt of doing in any other circumstances, because it left him vulnerable. But that was precisely what he wanted now. Turning his eyes blue was something he had done many times before, but this time, just to make sure the invitation was received, he turned his hair green as well. He heard Tegan gasp and Pjorsa swear explosively, but he paid them no attention because a spectral figure had just materialized next to him. Although at first glance it looked like Elam, the healer knew it was Jax. The prince had made some changes to the image, giving his muscles greater bulk and making himself a hand span taller. His clothes were much finer too, and a sword in an ornate scabbard hung from his belt.

You called, master? Jax said, in his habitual mocking tone, then looked around at his new surroundings. Immediately his eyes lit up and he laughed. *Now this looks like fun!*

Hello, Jax.

Need my help again, do you? the prince asked, eyeing the mayhem all about them.

You could say that.

Why should— Jax began, then stopped. *What's this?* He was staring at the transparent wall of the pyramid. Before Terrel could answer, Jax stuck out a hand and pushed it into the barrier. To the healer's delight it passed through without any apparent harm. The prince shivered, then laughed. *That tickles.*

Can you go all the way inside?

Jax stepped through the shield as though there was nothing there, his passage simply leaving a few ripples in the flecks of white light.

Interesting, he muttered. *What city is that?*

It's called Hvannadal. There's a wizard there who's more than a match for you, so you'd better not go too close.

Another dare? Jax asked, smiling. *I've learnt a few things since the last time, you know. Tofana won't get the better of me now.*

It's not Tofana. Her name's Onundar.

You want me to stop her too?

Yes.

Why?

Because if you don't, everyone here will die. Including me.

Jax thought about that for a few moments, then grinned. Seen through the shield, his ghostly face was even paler than before.

Do you know where she is? he asked. *No, don't bother. I'll just destroy the whole city.*

No! Terrel cried. *There are thousands of people in there.*

But it was too late. Having accepted the idea, there was no stopping Jax now. Even as Terrel watched, the first swirls of dark cloud began to form inside the white pyramid, and streaks of lightning crashed down on the tallest towers of Hvannadal. Several small whirlwinds sprang up, each growing rapidly as they moved towards the city until they struck with the force of a tornado.

Jax! Stop this. You only need— Terrel fell silent, realizing that his twin was not listening. He could only stare in awe at the forces he had unleashed.

'You have the gods on your side, healer,' Pjorsa commented, coming up beside him.

'How did you do that?' Tegan exclaimed.

It was clear that neither of them could see Jax, but

Terrel guessed they might have seen the shift in patterns as the prince moved through the barrier.

'I don't know,' he said, unable to think of a plausible explanation.

'You must have opened a portal somehow,' the magian reasoned, 'and some of the magic here leaked through.'

'What happens now?' Pjorsa asked.

Inside the white shield, the storm was growing in size and intensity with extraordinary speed. The violence of Jax's assault was so strong that some buildings were already collapsing.

'I don't understand how it's happening so fast,' Tegan replied, 'but the pyramid's reflecting the magic inside over and over again. Onundar will have to release it or the whole place will be destroyed.'

'Then we'd best be ready for a fight,' Pjorsa concluded eagerly, and ran off.

Terrel was still watching Jax, who was adding to the tumult and almost dancing with glee. The lightning strikes were coming in clusters now, shattering roofs and setting parts of the city on fire, even as deluges of rain and ice flooded other sections. It was a scene from darkest nightmare, from the end of the world.

Guilt threatened to overwhelm Terrel, and he could only hope that Onundar would recognize the inevitable and dismantle the pyramid before everyone in the city was killed. Hundreds of people must have died already, and the fact that he was responsible for their deaths weighed heavily on the healer. Even if he had been able to persuade Jax to stop, the weather-weapons he'd invoked had taken on a life of their own now, feeding on their own devastating power.

Beside him, Tegan had been rendered speechless by the spectacle, but a scream from nearby – on their side of the barrier – made them both realize that their situation, while not as bad as that of the citizens of Hvannadal, was still grave.

'She has to—' Tegan began, then gasped as in the blink of an eye the inner pyramid vanished.

In the next instant the storm within spread out, freed from its unnatural constraints. This added another ferocious element to the chaotic ferment beneath the outer shield, but Terrel saw that the gold barrier was shifting and weakening too.

'It's going!' Tegan exclaimed, confirming the healer's impression. 'You did it!' She flung her arms around him, even as thunder echoed above them and an icy wind tore at their clothes.

'It'll dissipate now,' she said as they drew apart. 'All of it. It may take some time, but . . .' She broke off once more, no longer staring at the tortured sky, but at what was happening on the ground.

Terrel soon saw what was alarming her. All that was left of the Black army was now on the march towards Hvannadal – at the same time as huge numbers of people were pouring from the city. The soldiers were back to a world they understood, and the massive pitched battle that Pingeyri had always wanted was about to take place. But as it turned out, this was not the most pressing of Tegan's worries. Her magian's senses had warned her of something else.

'Tofana's going to do it!' she gasped, sounding distraught once again. 'After all this, she's still going to do it. She's insane!'

'The springs?' Terrel asked.

Tegan nodded.

'How do we stop her?'

Want me to do it? Jax asked, appearing at Terrel's side.

His face – Elam's face – was flushed with an unholy pleasure.

Can you?

'Can I what?' Tegan asked.

'You heard that?' Terrel said in amazement.

'What?' she mumbled, looking confused. 'I thought . . .'

There's another wizard trying to stop her, Jax commented. *Varmahlid?*

Stupid old crone's doing it all wrong though, the prince added. *She doesn't stand a chance.*

'What's happening?' Tegan cried, putting her hands over her ears. 'I keep hearing things.' Fear sparked in her eyes.

'It's me,' Terrel told her. 'My thoughts. Shut them out, like you did before.'

'But . . .'

'Please, Tegan. This is too complicated to explain now.'

'There's someone else, isn't there?' she said, then nodded and turned away.

Tofana killed her, Jax said, his tone betraying doubt for the first time.

Tofana's the one I really need you to stop, Terrel said. *Can you—* But he got no further, because just at that moment his internal trembling began. The tremor struck a few heartbeats later, but it was like no earthquake the healer had ever experienced before.

Wide cracks split the entire plain, quickly widening into deep, jagged trenches that belched clouds of steam and smoke. Tegan and Terrel had both been thrown to the ground by the initial impact, but now, as the earth shook and growled beneath them, they recovered sufficiently to be able to look up and see the first of the walls of flame burst from the newly-formed ravines. The conflagration spread rapidly until the whole area was divided by sheets of orange fire.

As Terrel watched, beyond terror now, the old dragon
of the volcanoes rose from the flames of the nearest fissure
and looked directly into the healer's eyes.

CHAPTER FORTY-TWO

The sense of madness in the dragon's eyes was over-whelming, and Terrel felt all the boundaries of reality slipping away from him as he stared into the smouldering fires of those twin orbs. It took a considerable effort of will to stop himself from falling into a dream from which there would be no escape.

Wings of flame rose and fell, a cavernous mouth opened in a volcanic roar, and talons of fire gripped and shook the banks of the ravine. But it was the eyes that told the story. Terrel had seen their like before – and he knew who had made them. The realization triggered a remote contact, real but fleeting, and he sensed the Ancient's surprise. But the link was lost before he could even attempt to use it – and in any case, there was nothing he could have said. In the face of such demented fury, his healing skills were useless.

The dragon slid back into the crevasse, and was lost among the flames and the lava that bubbled and flowed in its depths.

'Did you see?' Tegan yelled over the roar of the con-tinuing earthquake. 'Was it real?'

'Real enough,' he replied, wondering if she'd been shown the same thing he had.

He was watching the progress of the lines of fire now, as they burned their way across the landscape. He wasn't sure what the elemental was trying to do, but it was obvious that its actions were out of control. There was no pattern, no purpose to the latest devastation. It was the reaction of a madman — of a madman with more power than sense. The existing fissures were still widening, and more were opening all the time. Terrel had no doubt that the upheaval was spreading far beyond the plain. Myvatan was literally tearing itself apart.

'Did *he* do this?' Tegan asked. 'The other person, the one I can't see?'

'No. This came from the creature I told you about, the one I'm supposed to find.' He looked around, wondering what had happened to Jax, but his twin was nowhere to be seen.

'Why's it doing this?'

'I don't know.'

'Perhaps it wanted to help you,' she suggested. 'Perhaps all this was meant to stop Tofana.'

Terrel was on the point of denying her assertion, but then it occurred to him that the elemental might have taken such drastic action in part because of Tofana's magic and its intimate connection to water. However, he couldn't afford to spend much time analyzing the motives of a being who was undoubtedly insane. His more pressing problem was how to ensure that he and Tegan survived.

The ground was shaking less now, and the healer managed to get to his feet. He was about to offer his companion his hand when he saw one of the soldiers' sled dogs racing towards him, trailing a broken leash. Its fangs were bared and its eyes shone red — giving it an almost demoniacal look — but something stirred deep within Terrel at the sight, and his burdens suddenly all seemed lighter.

Alyssa? he called tentatively, as the hound covered the

last few paces in a series of athletic bounds before coming
to a slithering stop.

Shape it, Terrel, she responded. *Shape it!*

What? He had no idea what she was talking about.

Hurry! There's a reason for this. Change the pattern!

What pattern!

The fire, the tremor, all of it, Alyssa urged. *You can shape it.*

I don't know what you mean.

Make it work for you, she snarled, angered by his hesi-
tancy. *Separate the things you need from those you don't.*

*You're the only one who can trace the patterns from the
elemental,* Elam added. *You can shape them too.*

The ghost had appeared next to the panting dog.

Is it really you? Terrel asked, staring.

Who else would it be? Elam replied, with a puzzled frown.
*You haven't got any time to waste. The Ancient's already
done most of the work for you. You just have to finish the job.*

I don't— Terrel began, then was struck dumb as Jax
reappeared in his amended version of Elam's shape.

The two phantoms stared at each other. Elam's face
registered stark astonishment, while the prince burst out
laughing. Alyssa growled deep in her canine throat.

What happened with Tofana? Terrel demanded quickly.

Oh, I don't think you need worry about her any more, Jax
replied casually.

The springs are safe?

I'm not sure I'd go that far, the prince said, glancing at
the nearest flame-filled crevasse, *but Tofana's not going to
touch them. In any case, she can't even get to the city now.*

What's he *doing here?* Elam asked, recovering from his
shock.

Saving everybody, Jax replied smugly. *It's a tough job but
someone has to do it – and none of you were faring too well,
were you?*

Terrel! Alyssa screamed in his head. *Stop wasting time. This was the pendulum. You've got to—*

But the rest of her words were lost in an unearthly howling. Both Elam and Jax – who until that moment had been unaffected by any of the storms raging about them – were suddenly caught in a strong wind, their clothes and hair flapping.

That's not meant to happen, Jax exclaimed. *What's—*

We have to go! Elam shouted above the gale. *Do what you can.*

The two spectral figures vanished, blown away by the elemental wind, and the dog, its fur standing on end, ran away, barking furiously.

Alyssa? Terrel called, stumbling after her. *Alyssa!* But it was no use, and he knew it. Alyssa had gone.

'Are you all right?' Tegan asked. 'Was that the dog from Saudark?'

Terrel didn't answer. He was too busy wondering just what it was he was supposed to do. Alyssa and Elam had evidently risked a great deal to pass the message on to him, but what they wanted him to do seemed impossible. Even if the earthquake *did* originate from the elemental, how was he supposed to influence it?

'It's like a wind,' Tegan murmured. 'Do you feel it?'

Terrel glanced at her.

'What?'

'There's a force here, pushing . . .'

'There is,' he told her, 'but not in this world. Can *you* feel it?'

'Something.' She had climbed to her feet now, and was looking around. 'In here.' She tapped the side of her head.

'Will you let me . . .' He hesitated.

'Look inside?'

'Yes.'

'Will it help?'

'It might.'

Tegan held out her hands and Terrel took them in his own, smiling in an attempt to reassure her. He didn't really know what he was looking for, but the magian's waking dream was a strange and wonderful realm, and he fell into it easily. The ghost wind was a moving shadow, an ephemeral presence that neither he nor Tegan could grasp properly. He had to make do with fleeting glances whenever it slowed down enough to become visible.

'The Black Moon,' Tegan whispered, her voice echoing in a distant world.

Terrel saw it then – the Dark Moon that had always haunted his dreams and his daydreams, his birth and his destiny. It was the ultimate source of the wind, the end of all the strands. And he could see them clearly now.

Delusions clawed at him with a dragon's talons. But he could see past them. The pattern was clear because there *was* no pattern. No reason, no order, just fury and the need to lash out. But even though the dragon was insane, it was nonetheless learning from these events. There was cunning within the madness.

He could see now.

In the world of men, Terrel recognized what was needed – the roads and barriers, the swords and shields, the magic and the chains. He saw how to treat them, how to expel the diseases, cauterize the wounds. He was a healer again.

He heard a scream and then Tegan's voice, but he couldn't understand what she was saying. He had done all he could. Darkness claimed him.

It was dark when Terrel awoke, but this time the darkness was outside him – and it was not complete. The bloody crescent of the Red Moon floated overhead, encircled by a necklace of stars. Love or war? he wondered. Waxing or waning? He felt too weary to even think about it.

And then he remembered. Alyssa had come back to him. They may not have had any time to talk, but she had not abandoned him. That simple fact flowed within him like a beacon, illuminating other, less welcome memories.

She had risked a lot simply by being there. In spite of her protestations about being protected, Terrel knew that sleepers *could* die. He had seen Vilheyuna's life end at the shaman's stone in Qomish. Certain kinds of magic could make them vulnerable, and there had been so much magic all around the pyramids. The fact that she had come to him anyway was proof of the importance of the message she had brought, but it must also have meant that she thought him worth the danger. That meant she still loved him. Didn't it?

He slept again, hoping. And dreamt about walking down a corridor of fire.

'He's coming to.'

The voice was familiar, but it didn't belong in his dream. Terrel opened his eyes and saw Yarek looking down at him.

'Did I help?' the boy asked eagerly.

'Help?' Terrel rasped.

'I was trying to help you get better,' Yarek explained. 'Like you showed me. But I'm not sure I was doing it right.'

Terrel was too confused to know how to respond, but he was saved from having to answer by the arrival of Tegan and Vatna.

'How are you feeling?' Tegan enquired solicitously. 'Is there anything you want?

Terrel sat up. He'd been lying in the open, wrapped in blankets. He asked for and was given a drink, which hurt his parched throat but made him feel as though he were at least partially alive. Looking around for the first time, he saw the rough terrain on which they were camped, and the mountains beyond.

'Where are we?'

'The Grundar Hills,' Vatna replied. 'About six miles north of Hvannadal.'

'North?' Terrel queried, struggling to make sense of this development. It was the last direction he would have expected them to take, leading them even further away from their home quarter.

'We didn't have much of a choice about the way we went,' Vatna explained. 'The earthquake saw to that.'

A corridor of fire, Terrel thought, as he felt other memories stirring into life.

'How much do you remember?' Tegan asked.

Terrel saw the dragon's eyes again, and decided there were some things he did not *want* to remember – but there were some gaps he needed filling in.

'Most of it,' he said. 'What happened after I collapsed?'

'We all got out of there as quickly as we could,' Vatna replied.

'The earthquake ended the battle before it began,' Yarek added, not bothering to hide his satisfaction at this outcome.

'The curious thing was that the fissures could almost have been designed to separate the opposing forces,' Vatna went on. 'Hvannadal is cut off now, and our army's been split into sections. Most of them were able to head back south, though, so they should be able to get home. Unlike us.'

Did I do that? Terrel wondered, recalling Alyssa's frantic

advice. Was it possible that he'd directed the course of the fissures to prevent the battle taking place? He couldn't believe it, but nor could he quite rule it out. He glanced at Tegan, whose insight had guided his efforts, but she just smiled, saying nothing.

'Not that I'm complaining, mind you,' Vatna continued, oblivious to the silent interchange. 'The fact that so many of us got away at all was a miracle.'

'There's never been a tremor like that before,' Yarek put in, clearly eager to join the conversation. 'No one knows why it happened, but it must be some new sort of volcano. You can see lava flowing in the bottom of most of the ravines.'

'And it's extended way beyond the plain,' Vatna added. 'The mountains haven't been so badly affected, but the upheaval even got as far as the sea.' He pointed to a nearby hilltop. 'You can see out over Hofnar Fjord from up there. There's a new volcanic island growing off the coast.'

'As far as we can tell,' Yarek said, 'Hvannadal was the centre of the earthquake, but it probably spread over all of Myvatan.'

'For a while it was as if the whole island was trying to tear itself apart,' Tegan remarked.

Does she know? Terrel asked himself. Does she think *I* stopped Myvatan from being destroyed?

'As it is, it's just even more divided than usual,' Vatna said. 'It's settling down a bit now, but most of the fissures are still impassable – and probably will be for some months at least.'

'Did any of you . . . see anything in the flames?' Terrel asked tentatively.

His three companions exchanged glances.

'What did *you* see?' Vatna asked.

'A dragon.'

'So did I!' Yarek burst out. 'It had black scales that reflected the flames like armour, and its eyes were yellow. But no one believed me.' He subsided abruptly then, glancing at Tegan as if wondering whether he'd gone too far.

'It's not that we didn't believe you,' she told the apprentice, 'but it was difficult for any of us to tell *what* we were seeing in all that confusion.'

'I could have sworn I saw a flock of geese at one point,' Vatna said, nodding. 'Which makes no sense at all.'

'Everyone saw something different, it seems,' Tegan concluded.

Like Mlicki's darkness, Terrel thought. The nomad boy, who was to become a shaman, had enveloped two warring tribes in his vision. What they had seen had reflected their own concerns – and their own futures. An elemental had had a hand in that encounter too.

'What did you see?' he asked Tegan.

'Just flames,' she replied, but her eyes would not meet his, and he didn't need Jarvik's special skills to know that she was lying.

Thinking of the dead colonel reminded Terrel of the underground, but Vatna's presence meant he couldn't discuss such things with Tegan yet.

'What happened to Tofana?' he asked instead.

'Something very strange,' Vatna replied. 'She and Varmahlid were in dispute about what they intended to do once the pyramids collapsed, and apparently the argument got out of hand. The only thing we know for sure is that Varmahlid is dead.'

Terrel frowned at this confirmation of the news Jax had brought. If Varmahlid *had* been the wizard who was supposed to help him, she hadn't done much good.

'By then everyone was turning against Tofana,' Vatna went on. 'Even her own magians were shocked by what she'd done, and Eskif finally persuaded Pingeyri to forbid her to corrupt the springs. But she was determined to go ahead anyway, on her own if necessary. She would have done so too, I think, if it hadn't been for the tornado.'

'It was blue, and it gave off sparks!' Yarek exclaimed.

'Strange as it may seem, that's what I saw too,' Vatna admitted. 'No one had ever seen anything like it before, but everyone assumed it was some sort of new weather-weapon. I mean, if they could produce those pyramids . . .' He paused, as if trying to organize his thoughts. 'No one's really sure what happened after that, but Tofana definitely didn't get the chance to go to Hvannadal. And soon afterwards the fissures cut the city off from all of us.'

'Is she dead?'

'Probably,' Vatna replied, 'but no one's seen her since then, alive *or* dead. Either way, she'll have been completely humiliated. She was supposed to be the most powerful wizard on Myvatan, and yet she was swallowed up by another's tornado. I don't think we need worry about her any more.'

This repetition of Jax's words ought to have been reassuring, but Terrel did not find it so. It was yet another reminder of the terrible price that had already been paid for their escape. He tried to tell himself that the eventual outcome had been the best he could have hoped for, and that many lives had been saved, but it still didn't assuage the guilt he felt about all those who had died.

'How do you know all this?' he asked.

'I was in the wizard's company,' Vatna said. 'So were most of the command staff.'

'Then how did you get here?'

'Captain Raufar is a very resourceful officer. He and his

men pulled most of us out of there when the rest had
turned and run. He saw the way out when no one else
could. I'd be dead now if it weren't for him. And then we
found ourselves with no choice but to retreat up here.'

'Who else is here?'

'Pingeyri, but he's wounded.'

'When you feel up to it, you might be able to help
him,' Tegan put in.

'Eskif is here, and his son,' Vatna went on. 'Davik. A
few magians. Most of the rest are men from Raufar's company. There are about a hundred of us in all. Not much if
the White ever regroup and decide to attack, but I think
we're safe enough for the time being.'

'Any fire-starters?' Terrel asked.

'Not that I know of. Why?'

'Just wondering.'

'You should rest,' Tegan said, looking concerned. 'All
this talking is wearing you out again.'

Terrel did indeed feel very weary, but he didn't think
he could sleep now.

'Are there any dogs with us?' he asked.

Vatna and Yarek were obviously puzzled by his question, but Tegan answered at once.

'A few. Shall I bring them to you?'

'No. Not now.'

Alyssa would come to him when she was ready. He had
to believe that.

Terrel had been wrong about his ability to go back to
sleep. He sank into a dark void, and left even his dreams
behind.

CHAPTER FORTY-THREE

Once word got around that the healer had recovered consciousness, he received several visitors, but the one constant in his world was Yarek. The boy seemed to have adopted the roles of nurse, servant and protector. He tended to Terrel's needs, brought him food and drink, and made sure that he was not disturbed when he needed to rest. He also acted as his patient's informant, telling him about the latest news in the camp.

Terrel learnt that Yarek had played no active part in any of the battles around Hvannadal – either military or magical – and that he had been terrified throughout. His depiction of the fire-born dragon was nothing like the healer's recollection, while others had apparently seen completely different visions. These included flying fish, giant insects, and a ship under full sail – all of them composed of flame. Although Terrel had no doubt that the elemental had been involved in creating these illusions, he was also certain that their form had been shaped by the minds of the people who had seen them. What he couldn't understand was just what the Ancient was trying to achieve with such displays.

Having been concerned with local matters for so long, the contact had forcibly reminded Terrel that he had to concentrate on his own goals now. His impression that the elemental had been learning from their previous encounters was worrying, because there was no telling what it might do next. With apparently unlimited reserves of power at its disposal, almost any knowledge could be turned into a weapon to be used against humanity. In some ways the earthquake had been a crude method of attack, but Terrel had unwittingly shown it how such things could be targeted with more precision. If the creature ever felt threatened again, its response might well be more accurate and deadly. Given that Terrel still had the journey to the Lonely Peaks ahead of him, this was not an encouraging thought.

Time became a blur. Terrel did not want to sleep, but he had little choice in the matter. Days seemed to run into one another – in part because the night had now been reduced to a short period of twilight. The season of light would begin soon, when the sun would not set at all for two median months. For a foreigner like Terrel this was a disconcerting prospect, but it had the advantage that the temperature remained relatively high. The soldiers had only been able to bring some of their supplies and equipment with them on the retreat from Hvannadal, and if the weather had been colder, it would have meant even greater hardships.

'We're doing all right,' Raufar said on one of his visits. 'The foraging's not as easy as it was down on the plain, but we won't starve. And if we have to defend ourselves we have a good position here. The magians ought to be able to cope with most enemy magic, even if they're not trained neomancers.'

'What happened to them?' Terrel asked.

'Hraun was killed. Jauron's missing, but we're pretty sure he's dead too. In any case, after what happened down there I don't think any of us are too keen on using magic at the moment. If we can defend ourselves, that'll be enough for me.'

'It was a mess, wasn't it?'

Raufar laughed.

'That's putting it mildly,' he said. 'From a military point of view it was very nearly a disaster. If the pyramids hadn't come down when they did we'd have been wiped out. As it is, the army's been split up and forced to retreat in a dozen different directions. My guess is that most of them will be heading for home by now – and we'll follow eventually. Then we can get ready for the next campaign.'

Terrel couldn't believe that the captain was thinking about returning to the war after everything that had happened.

'We might have to wait until next year,' Raufar added resignedly. 'Mind you, the White can't be in much better shape. The quake stopped us from getting to Hvannadal, but the storm and the fires did most of the job for us. My guess is the springs won't be much use to them now, even though Tofana got herself killed.'

'It's just a scratch,' Pingeyri muttered impatiently, trying to shake off Terrel's attentions. 'Go and help someone who needs your skills.' The general waved at the other men in the tent.

'I will,' the healer replied. 'Just as soon as I'm sure it's not infected.'

The jagged gash ran from behind Pingeyri's left ear, down his neck and shoulder, and into the flesh of his upper arm. The encrusted wound looked hideous, but as far as Terrel could tell, it was healing as well as could be expected. The general's helmet, which was topped with metal bat wings, lay beside the bed. It was severely dented, and Terrel suspected that if it had not absorbed a good part of the blow that had injured its owner, Pingeyri would have been among the dead on Hvannadal plain.

'You'll do.'

'Thank you,' the general said gruffly. He was too stubborn to admit that the healer's ministrations had eased his pain, but the relaxation in his face told its own story. 'Now go and make yourself useful.'

Terrel did as he was told, moving among the wounded who were lodged together regardless of rank in the best of the salvaged tents. He had taken up such duties as soon as he was physically capable of doing so, and even now Yarek trailed around after him, making sure he did not overexert himself.

That night, Terrel found himself alone with Tegan for the first time since they'd fled into the hills. She was in a sombre mood and it wasn't hard to divine the reason.

'No news of Myrdal?'

'Actually there is,' she replied, 'but not the sort I wanted.'

'Oh. I'm sorry.'

'He's not dead,' Tegan said, correcting Terrel's natural assumption. 'Or at least not as far as I know.'

'Then what's happened to him?'

'I finally got Kopak to talk to me. Myrdal was arrested before the battles even began.'

'Arrested? What for?'

'Treason.'

Terrel quickly looked around to make sure that they could not be overheard.

'No one here knows what happened to him,' Tegan added, 'but if he's caught now, the chances are they'll execute him on the spot rather than bother with a court martial.'

'Do you think he told the White what we were planning?' Terrel asked quietly.

'I don't know. It's possible. It's also possible he just said some stupid things to the wrong people. He couldn't stand the way the war just kept on getting worse. Having to play a part in it was tearing him apart. Still, I can't worry about that, can I? If we're ever to achieve peace, we've got to carry on with whoever is left.' Her brave words were hardly convincing, but Terrel admired her for remaining resolute.

'Are there any other members of the Holma here?' he asked.

'A few, but no one who can exert much influence. You and I are the best hope.'

'What about Eskif? I get the feeling he might be open to persuasion, especially if Kopak's on our side.'

'I'm not sure. They're still soldiers, don't forget, and you know what they're like. Most of them are looking forward to getting back to some proper fighting.' Tegan shook her head in disbelief.

'You still think finding the Circle of Truce will do the trick?' Terrel asked.

'It's our only hope.'

'Then we'd better persuade the general to head for the Lonely Peaks.'

'Easier said than done right now. No one's going anywhere for a while yet. But you're right,' she added. 'It's what we should be working towards. And you need to go there for your own reasons, don't you?'

'It's what I have to work towards,' Terrel agreed.

Tegan nodded. They had not discussed everything that had happened on the plain, and Terrel had the distinct impression that the magian didn't want to. Her life was already complicated enough, and there were some things she simply preferred not to know.

'But you will still help us, won't you?' she queried anxiously.

'If I can, yes.' He wished he could just have agreed, but he was too honest for that – and Tegan accepted his answer in the same spirit.

'None of us can do the impossible,' she said.

'What will happen now that Tofana's gone?' Terrel asked.

'One of the other wizards will take over her role.' Tegan didn't sound as if she cared very much about that. 'They'll go on as best they can, just as the army would have gone on if Pingeyri had been killed.'

'You're not looking for a promotion yourself, then?'

The magian glanced at him quickly, then laughed when she saw his deliberately innocent expression.

'No,' she replied, with heavy emphasis. 'I'm not.'

Terrel was pleased to see her smile. It might only be a brief light moment in the midst of such horror, but it was worth a great deal nonetheless.

'Can I ask you something else?' he said, hoping to take advantage of the lift in her mood.

Tegan nodded absently.

'What did you really see in the flames?'

'Nothing,' she replied immediately, then amended her answer when she saw that he did not believe her. 'It's not important.'

'Tell me. Please.'

Tegan looked at him as if weighing up her options, then sighed.

'It was a sword,' she said. 'As tall as a castle tower, and made out of flames the colour of blood.'

The visitor Terrel had most wanted to see came to him after they'd been in the Grundar Hills for several days.

She had taken the form of a merlin, a small falcon, that
skimmed over a nearby ridge and landed neatly – with a
rapid flickering of wing feathers – on a pointed rock. Once
the bird was no longer in motion, its hunched stance and
blunt, curved beak gave it a pugnacious look, while its
mottled plumage helped it to blend in with the upland
landscape. But Terrel, who had been dozing after another
healing session and had only seen the last part of her
approach, was not concerned with outward appearances.
Even if he hadn't been able to see the ring – which was
looped around one of the merlin's legs – he would have
known that Alyssa's spirit was contained within the bird's
slight frame.

Can you stay this time? he asked quickly.

I'm the wrong person to ask, she replied. *I'll stay as long
as I can.*

Until the elemental makes it impossible, Terrel thought,
resolving to make the most of whatever time they were
granted.

Then we can talk, he said. *I need to explain.*

Explain what?

Terrel couldn't tell whether she genuinely didn't know
or was simply trying to punish him.

About what happened with Latira, he said.

Oh, that, Alyssa said dismissively. *Forget it.*

Once again Terrel was unable to fathom her attitude.

Don't you want me to tell you what happened?

You're growing up, Terrel. Things are bound to happen.

But it wasn't me! he burst out, alarmed by the resignation in her tone. *It was Jax. And even he didn't make love
to her.*

I know.

For a few moments Terrel was too stunned to respond.

You know? he said eventually.

Yes.

Have you always known?

No. Elam told me some time later. I'm sorry I misjudged you.

When he had imagined this conversation, it had never occurred to Terrel that it would include Alyssa apologizing to him – and now that it had happened he felt horribly guilty.

I'm sorry I let you down, he said. *I should never have let myself get into such a mess.*

Even as Jax, there's a part of you that's still you, she told him. *That's why Elam was able to intervene successfully.*

Terrel heard her words, but they did not register immediately. When they did, he didn't want to believe them. If Alyssa's assertion was correct, it meant that he was at least partially responsible for some of the things his twin had done – or could perhaps have prevented them altogether. It was another heavy weight for his already overburdened conscience.

It won't happen again, he said quietly.

It doesn't matter.

Yes, it does! he exclaimed. *It's you I love, Alyssa. You know that, don't you?*

Yes.

I was miserable when I hurt you, when I thought you weren't coming back.

You really thought that? she asked, sounding genuinely surprised.

Yes.

Then we're even, aren't we? Alyssa told him coolly. *Don't we have anything else to talk about?*

How can you be so calm about this? Terrel demanded.

She did not answer immediately. When she did, her words brought him a mixture of pleasure and pain.

I love you, Terrel. Never doubt that. It's just that in our current situation I'm not sure love is enough.

Don't say that! he cried. *It has to be. We haven't got anything else. And we will be together again one day, I swear it.*

This time it was Alyssa who paused before responding.

I have to keep believing, she said at last, unknowingly repeating what Tegan had said a few days earlier.

We both do, Terrel said. *Don't give up on me, my love. None of this would make any sense if you did.*

I'm not sure it makes much sense anyway, she commented, but there was a lighter note in her voice now, and Terrel's spirits began to rise. It was time to move on.

Are the ghosts coming? he asked.

The merlin glanced about, apparently testing the air. Then, without another word being spoken, three spectral figures appeared, glowing faintly in the thin sunlight. They too looked around quickly, taking in their new surroundings, before Elam broke the silence.

Jax isn't here, is he?

No.

That's a relief. I nearly died of shock when I saw my face on that slimy little worm. Elam grinned, letting Terrel know that his choice of words had been deliberate.

What was he doing here? Shahan asked.

It was the only way to break through the pyramids, Terrel replied. *We could all have been killed otherwise. I didn't have any choice.*

Are you sure? Muzeni queried.

What else was I supposed to do? Terrel asked, feeling defensive now.

There's always a price to be paid for such aid, the heretic informed him.

I'm aware of that. I just couldn't think of any alternative. And I didn't see you rushing in to help.

What's done is done, Shahan said placatingly. *What's important is where we go from here.*

You haven't made much progress towards the Lonely Peaks, Muzeni observed.

You think I don't know that? Terrel declared angrily. *I can't just march up there on my own.*

It's possible you may have to.

Thanks a lot. Is all your advice going to be so useful?

Calm down, both of you, Shahan told them forcefully.

In the silence that followed the seer's intervention, the merlin chattered softly.

Sorry, Terrel said quietly.

I apologize, Muzeni said. *We're all a bit on edge at the moment.* He glanced round again, and Terrel wondered what he was looking for.

Tell us what's been happening since we last met, Shahan said.

The healer did his best to describe his recent exploits in as succinct a manner as possible. He told them about the Holma's plans, confirming their speculation about Akurvellir and the Circle of Truce in the process, about the campaign – including the time when Jax's uninvited arrival had saved his life – and about the various battles at Hvannadal. The ghosts were obviously relieved that Tofana's plans for the springs had been foiled, and were very interested in the fact that, with Tegan's help, Terrel had been able to sense the elemental wind and, through that, influence the creature's other actions.

I'm still not sure I really did change the direction of the fissures, he concluded, *but it felt as if I did.*

Maybe Tegan's the wizard who's supposed to help you, Shahan argued.

Either way, I think you should persuade her to stick around, Elam commented. *That sort of talent could be very useful.*

The real question is how soon you'll be able to persuade the people here to go to the central glacier, Muzeni said, single-mindedly pursuing their main aim.

I'm not even sure it's possible yet, Terrel replied. *The fissures are still burning. We may be stuck here for some time.*

Let's hope not, Elam said. *Everyone seems to have a reason to go. Pingeyri wants to find the sword, and the Holma want to rediscover the Circle of Truce.*

Or pretend to, Terrel corrected him. *All they need is to make people believe the flame's been rekindled. But they've suffered a lot of setbacks, and I'm not sure they're ready to go through with it at the moment.*

Show us the stone Jarvik gave you, Muzeni requested.

Terrel looked around to make sure no one was watching, then slipped the metal cylinder from his pocket.

The container's genuine, he said as he held it up for them to see. *But the stone's a fake.*

You told us that already, Elam said. *I'd like to see it anyway.*

I'd rather not. If it glows again, someone's bound to notice.

Fair enough, Shahan said, and Terrel hid the vial away again. Elam frowned, but said nothing.

What's going on in Vadanis? Terrel asked. *Has Jax killed anyone else there?*

Not that we know of, Muzeni replied.

He's probably getting enough excitement on his trips here, Elam remarked. *He hasn't been back to Betancuria either, which is good.*

What about the Code? Have you been able to make sense of any more of it?

Not really, Shahan admitted.

We're getting nowhere, Muzeni said, his frustration plain. *It's all so vague and contradictory.*

The only new thing is a reference to something that 'blinds the eyes from within', the seer added. *We think it might refer to mitra. Apparently there is a way to counteract its effects, but we can't work out what it is.*

Something about mud, if you can believe that, Muzeni said, shaking his head.

But we can't find anything that seems to be connected with the Ancient here, or the Lonely Peaks, Shahan concluded.

Don't forget the pendulum, Alyssa put in.

What about it? Muzeni asked. *Those passages make even less sense than the rest.*

It's important, that's all, she said, sounding defensive.

Why?

Alyssa did not answer, and the merlin seemed to hunch even lower on its perch.

They're coming, Elam warned.

Who?

Elam moved his head slightly to indicate what he meant, and Terrel turned to look.

Wraiths? A group of the tormented phantoms were drifting up the slope below them.

If that's what you want to call them.

You can see them? Alyssa queried.

Terrel nodded.

We can hide ourselves better now, Elam told him, *but they always find us in the end.*

Can they harm you?

No, but we can harm them.

In that moment Terrel understood what Elam had meant when he'd said that the ghosts shouldn't be on Myvatan.

We make things worse for them just by being here, his friend added, confirming the healer's intuition.

Even though they hadn't 'moved on', Elam and the seers were still whole, recognizably human and with the ability to act purposefully – unlike the wraiths.

We should go, Shahan said sombrely, watching the approaching company.

Goodbye, Terrel, Muzeni said. *Get to the Lonely Peaks as soon as you can.*

I will.

And don't let Jax make you do anything stupid, Elam added with a grin.

The ghosts vanished before Terrel had a chance to respond to that. He looked at Alyssa, wondering how she was feeling now.

I'll keep believing, she said quietly, answering his unspoken question. And then, to Terrel's great disappointment, the merlin flew away.

To Terrel's immense frustration, it proved impossible to keep his promise to Muzeni. By the time it was determined that the company was fit enough to move, Raufar's scouts had discovered that all routes out of the hills were blocked by fissures. These were not burning as fiercely as they had done at first, but they still presented a formidable barrier to progress, especially for a large group of people. Although they could go a certain distance in several directions, they'd soon be forced to turn back, and so it was decided that they should stay where they were for the moment. The land around them was reasonable for foraging and hunting, there was no danger of their being attacked, and during the continuous daylight of summer the weather was mild. After several discussions, most of them instigated by Terrel, the group came to the conclusion that – if there was time, and when a route became passable – they would head in the direction of the central glacier. But no one other than the healer seemed in any hurry to set off.

A month passed, and during that time Terrel saw nothing

of Alyssa and the ghosts. He hoped this was a good sign. If they'd been desperate, he told himself, they would at least have tried to visit him again. Even so, his own impatience was building to an almost unbearable level, and on several occasions he considered simply heading east on his own. But his nerve failed him each time – and common sense allowed him to justify his decision to stay. But then news came that was to change the attitude of his companions.

Pingeyri had been up and about for a while now, but Terrel still went to check on him every other day, and the healer was with him when the messenger arrived. The soldier was filthy, his uniform torn and scorched, and he was clearly close to exhaustion, but he would let no one tend to him until he had made his report.

'I'm not sure what to make of this, General, but I thought you should know. Tofana was seen in Nordura a few days ago. She was heading towards the Lonely Peaks.'

'What in the blazes would she be wanting there?' Pingeyri responded.

The Peacemaker? Terrel thought. Or Akurvellir?

'Well, whatever it is,' the general went on, 'I'll wager she's up to no good.' The wizard's mutinous behaviour at Hvannadal had soured his opinion of her.

'That's not all, sir,' the soldier went on. 'There's also a report that a company of the Gold are already on the glacier.'

'Right,' Pingeyri said, his decision made. 'Can you show us the way you came?'

'Yes, General. It'll mean going a long way round, and it's difficult in places, but it should be possible.'

'Good man. It's time we started getting active again.' Pingeyri began bellowing orders to various officers, then turned to Terrel. 'Well, healer,' he said. 'It seems you're going to get your wish after all. We're going to the Lonely Peaks.'

PART THREE

THE LONELY PEAKS

'Look out!' Even as he yelled Raufar was running, reaching Terrel in two long strides, and the two of them went down in a heap just as a boulder that would have crushed the healer bounded past. The fall knocked the wind out of Terrel and he lay there gasping, his heart hammering against his rib cage as he watched the rock tumbling down into the gully below.

'That must have been a mistake,' Raufar muttered as he scanned the ridges above them.

Even Terrel could see that they were in a terrible situation. The entire company was trapped on a rough trail halfway up one side of a ravine, and if their enemies held the high ground then they would be vulnerable. Everyone was crouching now, making the most of whatever cover they could find. Voices echoed across the canyon as sightings were reported – confirming that their foes held the advantage.

'Pjorsa!' Raufar called, beckoning to his lieutenant. 'Get over here.'

The soldier arrived, moving rapidly in a crouched position.

'Take some men and see if you can get around their flank,' the captain said, pointing up the valley. 'If we have to stay here they'll pick us off one by one. We need to keep them occupied while we try to move.'

Pjorsa nodded and scuttled off.

'Thank you,' Terrel whispered, having finally managed to get his breath back.

'Don't thank me,' Raufar replied, still looking up the steep slope. 'If you get yourself killed, even by accident, we're all dead.'

'What do you mean?'

'It's you they want,' the captain told him. 'Haven't you worked that out yet? They could have overrun us several times if they'd been prepared to slaughter anyone in their way. They didn't, because they want you alive. But if you get killed anyway there's nothing to stop them massacring the rest of us.'

Terrel wasn't sure he could believe what he was hearing. He'd been aware for some time that the soldiers were especially protective towards him, but he'd assumed that this was simply because, as an adopted member of their company, he was one of those least able to look after himself in battle.

'Why me? How do you know this?'

'I don't *know* it,' Raufar answered, 'but it's the only thing that makes any sense – and it does make sense when you think about it.'

'Not to me it doesn't.'

'Look. Ever since we left the hills, they've been dogging our footsteps. That's not surprising, given that we're in enemy territory, but they've missed several chances to kill us all – and that's not like the White.'

'But they did kill some of us,' Terrel objected. To his distress, Lieutenant Narvat, Colonel Davik and the magian Vatna had all been among the recent casualties.

'Yes, but only those who were isolated,' Raufar said. 'When they could pick their targets and make sure they weren't killing the wrong person.'

'Me?' the healer queried, still finding it hard to accept.

'Yes. And it's not just the White we're facing. Every unit we've come across has had someone from the Gold army with it. According to *their* legends, the man who comes from Savik's Whale is a harbinger of their great victory. In their eyes, you're a prisoner here and they're trying to rescue you. They're quite prepared to get rid of the rest of us, or capture us if it's easier, or split us up and drive us away – just as long as you end up with them. It's the only thing that explains their tactics.'

'But why me?' Terrel persisted. 'What am I supposed to do for them?

Raufar shrugged.

'Perhaps they want you to find the sword – if that's really what you're planning to do up there.'

The doubt inherent in the soldier's words gave Terrel pause for thought. He didn't see how Raufar could know the truth, but he was an intelligent man, and in this war everyone's motives were suspect.

'I don't really care,' the captain added. 'The fact that they want you is enough for me. Whatever it is, we're going to make damned sure you don't fall into their hands.'

This sounded ominously like a threat, and Terrel wondered what lengths Raufar would be prepared to go to in order to keep his word.

'How do they even know I'm here?' he asked, still trying to find a fault in the captain's theory. 'You killed all their soldiers at Whale Ness.'

'I'd like to know the answer to that myself,' Raufar said grimly. 'The White seem to have known far too much about all our plans.'

'You really think they're after me?'

'Yes.'

'If you're right, then you'd better get as many people as

close to me as possible,' Terrel said. 'If the White won't risk killing me, then it'll provide some protection for the rest of you.'

'I'm aware of that, but it's difficult in this terrain.' The company was strung out along the trail, with little room for manoeuvre. 'For the time being, we stay here. And keep your head down.'

Their journey from the Grundar Hills had been beset by troubles right from the start. At first Terrel had been tempted to compare it to the Race of Truth – a voyage into the most inhospitable regional imaginable – and crossing various fissures had reminded him of the Valley of the Smokers. But he had soon been forced to revise his opinion. This trek was no mere race; there was no code of honour among these adversaries. This was war, and the perils they faced were not just the natural dangers of climate and land-scape but also the murderous efforts of other men.

Although there had been several battles, their losses had never been serious and they had always been able to move on. They had faced both White and Gold forces, and because the enemy had neomancers among their number, Pingeyri and his men had often been at a considerable dis-advantage. The magians among them, including Tegan, had done their best. In theory they knew how to defend against weather-weapons, but in practice they lacked the instincts and reactions of trained warriors. Terrel had wit-nessed heroics and tragedy, savagery and sorrow. He hated the violence as much as ever, but he'd learnt an even greater respect for Raufar and his company. The constant daylight had at least allowed the soldiers to keep watch even during the quiet hours, but the season of light was coming to an end now, and the possibility of night raids would soon become an additional worry.

On top of that, they were moving through unfamiliar country, with all the pitfalls that entailed. The land itself was in turmoil, and there were tremors nearly every day. Most of them were minor, and none seemed to be directed at the travellers, but they all represented new dangers — especially when the group was close to any of the fissures that ran across the landscape at irregular intervals. In all, the delays had been so bad that after almost a median month they had still not reached the edge of the central glacier. Under any other circumstances, going on with their quest would have been regarded as madness, but Terrel had no choice in the matter, and for the rest the situation was normal. The war *was* mad.

Their journey had been beset by troubles, but now it looked as though it might be coming to a premature end. It was clear that on this occasion their enemies had an almost overwhelming advantage in both manpower and position. However, the Black forces were not about to give up without a fight. From their own position, Terrel and Raufar had difficulty following what was happening elsewhere, but occasional glimpses of movement allowed the captain to make an educated guess.

'Pjorsa's almost there,' he said with some satisfaction, 'and the rear group are climbing too.' His expression changed as he squinted into the distance. 'Gods, Pingeyri's leading them himself!'

Terrel knew that the general was not the type of man to issue orders from a position of safety if he had any choice in the matter, but this latest exploit seemed particularly foolhardy. The route his party was taking was steep and difficult, and led straight towards the enemy position on the rim of the gorge.

'What's he trying to do?'

'I'm not sure,' Raufar replied, 'but they'll provide a diversion if nothing else.'

'Even if they all get killed?'

'Even then,' the captain confirmed. 'And it'll give us a better chance to avenge them. Time for us to move. Come on.'

Terrel followed as Raufar ran along the trail, directing the others who were left in the main group. Their enemies made no move to attack, but before long sounds of fighting could be heard from above – both ahead, where Pjorsa was, and from the general's sortie. The remainder of the company was urged to move faster, in the hope of being able to escape from the ravine and negate their foe's advantage.

As he stumbled over the rough terrain, Terrel saw that Raufar and several other soldiers remained between him and the enemy at all times, and he felt both grateful for and guilty about their vigilance. Without knowing where they'd come from, Terrel then found Tegan beside him, and Yarek at their heels.

'Do you know what's going on?' the magian asked breathlessly.

'Not really.' He still couldn't accept that so many people were taking such terrible risks simply to protect him. 'I'm just doing what I'm told.'

They ran on until a shout from behind made them hesitate and glance round.

'Keep going!' Raufar told them, then peeled away, calling orders to his men. The sounds of fighting came closer.

The decisive moment in the battle came not because of some clever strategy or any special display of courage or tenacity, but from the intervention of blind chance. Unlike any of his companions, Terrel knew that the tremor was coming before it struck, but he was unable to do anything about it, and his warning cry was lost in the uproar of combat.

The earthquake put a stop to the fighting because it suddenly became difficult for anyone to keep their feet, let alone swing a sword, but within moments everyone was aware of a new danger. Boulders like the one that had nearly hit Terrel, and a host of smaller stones, began tumbling down the sides of the gully, crashing and splintering as they went. Most people tried to find a sheltered place and crouched down, hoping to remain safe, but Terrel and his companions were a little way ahead of the main group now, and in a relatively exposed position halfway across a small ledge. All three of them were terrified, not knowing what to do for the best, when Kopak appeared in front of them, waving urgently.

'There's a cave up ahead!' he yelled. 'Quick!'

The urgency in his voice broke the spell that had paralyzed them and they ran on, following him up a small scree slope and into a dark opening. Almost as soon as they were inside, a great roar of stone deafened them as an avalanche swept over the ground they had just crossed.

'That was close,' Kopak gasped, his face sheened with sweat.

The other three could only watch in awe as the landslide rumbled past them. They knew that if they'd been only a few moments later, they would have been crushed to death.

'Did it hit the others?' Tegan asked, trying to see through the cloud of dust that was rising into the air.

'I think most of them are on the far side,' Kopak replied. 'Let's hope so, anyway. There are some falls over there, but nothing compared to this.'

'Will they be able to reach us?'

'There's no telling yet. We'll know once this has calmed

down.' Although the tremor was over now, rocks were still falling, and the air was full of debris.

'How did you know the cave was here?' Terrel asked.

'I was with Pjorsa when he went forward. We spotted it on the way. I was going back to report to Raufar when the quake hit.'

A red glow filtered through the dust that now filled the valley.

'What's that?' Terrel wondered.

'The quake's reopened the fissure at the bottom of the ravine,' Yarek guessed. The boy sounded afraid, and Tegan put an arm round his bony shoulders. He looked up at her in surprise, but didn't move away.

'It's a pity you couldn't have given us a bit more warning,' the magian said to Terrel. 'If we'd been in the right position, we could have used this to get away.'

'You knew it was coming?' Kopak exclaimed.

'Yes, but only a few moments before. There wasn't time to do anything.'

'So the legends were right,' Yarek concluded. 'You *are* a seer.'

'No, not really.'

'You came from Savik's Whale,' the apprentice said, as if this proved a point. 'Are you really going to find the Peacemaker?'

'I've no idea,' Terrel said, conscious of the different attitudes to their mission within the small group. 'Right now I'd be glad just to see our way out of this cave.'

By the time the dust settled, the enormity of what had happened had slowly become clear. The avalanche had gouged out a new ravine and cut them off from the rest of the company. Its sides were sheer, and around the edges and at the bottom it looked treacherous, with many smaller rockslides still tumbling down the slopes. Although they could see some movement at the far side, it was too far away in the misty atmosphere to tell who it was or what they were doing. No one wanted to risk calling out in case they gave their position away to the enemy.

'Even if it *is* our men,' Kopak said, 'there's nothing much they can do.'

'They probably think we were killed by the avalanche,' Tegan said quietly.

'There must be a way round it,' Terrel said.

'Yes, at the top,' Kopak agreed, 'but it would take a long time, and we've no idea what's happened to the White troops.'

'Then what are we supposed to do now?'

'Go on?' Tegan suggested tentatively.

'Just the four of us?'

'Perhaps some of the others will catch up eventually,' she said. 'And we do have a job to do.'

'I don't see that we have much choice,' Yarek stated. 'Waiting here won't do us any good, and the trail's the only route out. We have to go on, for a bit at least.'

Kopak nodded, approving of the boy's common sense.

'We can review the situation once we're out of this place,' he said, looking down at the smoke and occasional bursts of flame coming from the bottom of the canyon. 'The sooner the better, I'd say.'

No one argued. They set off, scrambling down to the trail and continuing along it to the head of the valley. They made good progress for a while, but then – as they emerged from a narrow defile – they found the path blocked by a patch of rubble. Climbing over the heap was a frustrating business, and when they finally reached the other side and regained solid ground, they took a moment to catch their breath. It was then that a sharp noise made them all jump.

'Don't move!'

The unfamiliar voice cracked like a whip, and all four of them froze. Several soldiers with white epaulets stepped out from their hiding places. All but one carried crossbows, which were trained on the quartet. The exception was the man who had spoken, and who was clearly in charge of the group.

'Now this is a surprise,' he said as he studied his prisoners. 'We—'

Kopak yelled something unintelligble and his hand went to his sword as he began to charge. The blade was only halfway out of its scabbard when the bolt thudded into his chest, sending him sprawling to the ground. By the time the sound of Tegan's scream faded away he was dead.

'Anyone else want to be a hero?' their captor asked, then looked directly at Terrel, his expression changing rapidly.

'Is it him?' one of the other soldiers asked.

'Look at those eyes,' the officer replied. 'What do you think?'

CHAPTER FORTY-FIVE

Tegan moved forward slowly, and the bowman who was covering her tensed.

'What are you doing?' their leader snapped.

'I'm collecting his tag, Captain. You'll allow me to do that, surely?'

After a moment he nodded and she knelt to retrieve Kopak's chain. When she stood up there were tears in her eyes, but they were given no time to mourn the brigadier's son. Under the watchful eyes of the soldiers, they were taken up a path that twisted its way to the top of the incline. There they were met by a much larger group of men, who regarded the prisoners with a strange mixture of curiosity and antagonism. Almost immediately the captain ordered the entire company to move off, but one of his lieutenants queried the decision – pointing out that many of the Black soldiers were still at large in and around the ravine.

'Forget them,' the captain replied. 'They're not important. He's what we came for.'

'Then do we need the other two?'

'A woman and a boy in a war party? I think they might be of interest too, don't you? Let's move!'

'Where are you taking us?' Terrel asked.

They had been walking for over an hour now. All his

earlier questions had been ignored, but this time the captain turned to look at him and grinned.

'Nordura,' he said. 'There's someone there who wants to meet you.'

'Who?'

'You'll find out soon enough,' the soldier replied, and then returned to his former obdurate silence.

Terrel remembered that Nordura was where Tofana had been seen, and he wondered if perhaps she hadn't made it as far as the glacier after all. But he couldn't understand why the White forces would be co-operating with an enemy wizard. He glanced at Tegan and saw that she was frowning, perhaps considering a similar puzzle.

At their camp that night, the three prisoners sat a little way apart from the soldiers as they ate the food they were given. During the march they had been watched closely, by neomancers as well as by ordinary guards, and the soldiers had not relaxed their vigilance once they'd come to a halt. One of the neomancers – who, unlike the rest of the company, wore the colours of the Gold Quarter – sat staring at the trio with an almost manic intensity.

'What's he doing?' Terrel asked quietly.

'I've no idea,' Tegan replied.

Once the meal was over, a soldier came to collect their bowls. He displayed the now familiar combination of interest and enmity when he looked at them, but he flinched slightly when he took Terrel's dish, and the healer saw another emotion flicker briefly across the young man's face before he moved away. Why should he be afraid of us? Terrel wondered. What did he think I was going to do?

He was distracted then as he saw that the sky had

turned a pale shade of green. At first he thought he was hallucinating, and wondered if their food had been poisoned, but then he realized that he and his two companions were now imprisoned beneath a magical pyramid, a miniature version of the structures at Hvannadal. Instinctively, he glanced over at the Gold neomancer and saw that the man's eyes were closed, his head bent forward in concentration.

'They're not taking any chances, are they?' Tegan commented. She nodded in the direction of their guards. In spite of the barrier that enclosed their charges, the soldiers were still watching them closely, their bows close at hand.

'It's like a tent,' Yarek remarked, studying the faintly glowing shield. 'A magical tent.'

'Well, at least we shouldn't get wet if it rains,' Terrel said.

Tegan smiled.

'Could you break us out of here?' she asked softly. 'If you needed to?'

'I doubt it,' Terrel replied. 'And I don't think we'd get far even if I did.' He indicated the bowmen.

'They wouldn't kill you. Not after going to so much trouble to capture you.' She had obviously reached the same conclusion as Raufar.

'But they might not have the same scruples about you two, and I'm not prepared to risk that.' Then, wanting to change the subject, Terrel asked, 'Who do you think it is who wants to meet us?'

'It could be Onundar,' the magian surmised. 'Or maybe some of their generals.'

'Or Tofana?'

Tegan shook her head.

'No,' she said. 'I know she was supposed to be in Nordura, but that wouldn't make any sense.'

'Unless she's changed allegiance.'

'Never.' Tegan sounded absolutely certain. 'It would make a mockery of her whole life's work.'

'That sort of hatred doesn't just change sides,' Yarek added.

They both looked at the boy.

'She wanted all the White to *burn*,' he explained. 'There's no way she'd work with them now.'

'He's right,' Tegan said.

'I suppose we'll just have to wait and see,' Terrel concluded. 'Do you know anything about Nordura?'

'Just that it's a city about the same size as Saudark,' the magian replied. 'It's important because it's the furthest inland of any major town in the White Quarter.'

'So it's near the glacier?'

'Yes. And it's also quite close to the Red border. Hence its strategic importance. That's all I know about it.'

'They have mud baths there,' Yarek told them. 'For healing.'

'Really?' Terrel said, his interest piqued.

'How do you know that?' Tegan asked.

'It was in one of the old books at home. I mean, at the pyramid. The real one. Tofana's.' He was becoming increasingly flustered.

'I didn't know you had access to the wizard's library,' Tegan remarked.

'No one minded,' Yarek said defensively.

'Because no one knew?' the magian queried mildly.

The boy didn't answer.

'What else did you find out?' Terrel asked, remembering his own voyages of discovery in the old library at Havenmoon.

'About Nordura? Not much.'

'What does this mud do?'

'It's like the pools. Only . . .'

'Only thicker?' Terrel suggested.

Yarek smiled.

'I suppose so.'

'Do the White soldiers use mitra?' the healer asked Tegan, who looked surprised by this sudden change of topic.

'Yes. Everyone in Myvatan does. Why?'

'Just thinking. It's not important. What do you suppose will have happened to Raufar and the rest?'

'We know that some of them survived, at least,' Tegan said.

'Do you think they'll come after us?'

'That depends on whether they know *we* survived. If they do, it's possible they might follow our trail, but if they think we're dead they'll probably head for the nearest friendly territory – which would be the Red Quarter – or try to make it back over the mountains and home.'

'I suppose us getting caught was a good thing in one way,' Terrel reasoned.

'They let the others go,' Tegan agreed, nodding. 'Doesn't help us much though, does it? The gods know when we'll ever get the chance to go to the Lonely Peaks now.'

When they reached the city of Nordura three days later, a strange, faintly sulphurous smell hung in the air. Outwardly the buildings looked very similar to those in Saudark, and the fortress – which stood on a hill, with a commanding view over the town and the surrounding countryside – could almost have been built from the same plans as its counterpart. Terrel was not surprised when they were led in through the castle's main gates.

'I guess we'll find out who wants to see us soon now,' he said to Tegan as they entered the courtyard.

Time would prove him wrong.

Terrel had been imprisoned before, but never in such luxurious circumstances. In all but one respect he and his two friends were treated like honoured guests, with servants to bring them food and tend to their needs. The three captives were housed in quarters built round a quadrangle that was open to the sky, and where a few small fruit trees and some flowers grew. All they lacked was any news of the outside world – and the freedom to leave their lodgings. Armed guards patrolled both entrances to the enclosed garden, and the doors and windows of their rooms all faced inwards. However, the main obstacle to their freedom was the transparent screen of a pyramid that enclosed the entire complex except for brief periods when the servants needed to enter or leave.

As hours turned into days and still nothing happened, Terrel's frustrations grew. He spent a lot of time talking with Tegan and Yarek about what they ought to do, but they weren't able to come up with any solution to their problem. The only people they saw were their attendants, who were obviously under strict instructions not to talk to the prisoners about anything other than their household duties. Terrel persisted in trying to get some news of events beyond the gold-flecked pyramid, but he got nowhere – and short of threatening them with physical violence, he didn't know what else to try. At Tegan's suggestion he tried to initiate contact through psinoma, but the servants' minds were shielded somehow, and he soon gave up the attempt – feeling shame as well as annoyance at his failure.

A month passed and night returned to Myvatan,

although true darkness only lasted a short time. And still nothing happened. No one came to see them, and no one would even tell them who they were supposed to be waiting for. Although they were living comfortably, Terrel thought that if this went on for much longer he would go mad. Increasingly drastic ideas filled his mind as he dreamt about escaping, but he knew they wouldn't work. Even if he summoned Jax again, and succeeded in removing the pyramid, the chances of their finding their way out of the castle and the city were slim. The White soldiers might not have wanted to kill him, but if he and his companions tried to escape there was no telling what could happen. As Tegan pointed out, their best chance of leaving was to do so with their captors' permission.

'You never know,' she said. 'They might send you up to the glacier with one of their own companies.'

'To find the sword?'

'Why not? Pingeyri thought it was a good idea. Their generals might too.'

'So we just find the Circle of Truce with them instead,' Terrel said hopefully.

'*You* do,' Tegan corrected him. 'I don't think Yarek and I would be allowed to go with you. We're the enemy, don't forget.'

'I'm not going without you.'

'We'll see. It may never happen, anyway.'

'If they *do* want me to do something like that, why are we being kept waiting here?'

'I've no idea,' the magian admitted. 'I'd still like to know *who* we're waiting for.'

'I think I could dismantle it,' Yarek said.

'The pyramid?' Terrel exclaimed.

'Yes.'

'Really?' Tegan queried. 'How could you do that? Whoever's producing it is outside.'

'It's not a question of who, it's *how*,' the boy replied. 'I think I can match the pattern and then unravel it from within. Do you want me to try?'

Terrel and Tegan looked at each other, both wondering what Yarek's efforts would achieve. Even if he were successful, they would still be inside the fortress, with guards all around them. And beyond that lay a hostile city. Any freedom that they might gain would probably be short-lived at best, and if their captors realized that it was Yarek who had destroyed the shield, the boy might suffer as a result.

'We'd need to know what would happen after the pyramid was gone before we try anything,' Terrel said eventually.

'I agree,' Tegan said. 'We must think about what we want to achieve, make a plan.'

'So, no, Yarek,' the healer concluded. 'Don't do anything yet.'

Disappointment warred with relief on the apprentice's face. Terrel guessed that formulating a theory and actually putting it into practice were two very different things. Yarek looked frail enough as it was, and the effort involved in what he was proposing might well exhaust him and make his own escape impossible. And Terrel had meant it when he'd said that he was not going to leave his companions behind.

'I'm very impressed, though,' Tegan added. 'How did you work out what you needed to do? Will you show me?'

'If you like,' Yarek said, looking pleased now.

Terrel left them talking, and walked around the courtyard. Looking up, he saw a bird circling high above the pyramid and wondered – for the thousandth time – when he would see Alyssa again. She had not appeared at any time during the journey, and now that he was hidden behind another magical screen he wasn't even sure that she'd be able to locate him. It was one more frustration among many.

Telling himself to put such negative thoughts aside, he tried to think of ways that Yarek's new discovery might be useful. For instance, if he spotted Alyssa outside the barrier, could the apprentice open a gap for her to come through? It would be worth asking him, just in case. And if—

The healer's musings were interrupted then by an internal trembling that he had come to know all too well over the last few months. He yelled a warning to Tegan and Yarek, but they were already out in the open, sitting near the centre of the garden, so that when the tremor struck they were in no immediate danger. The earthquake was a minor one, shaking the fortress for no more than a few moments, and Terrel remained on his feet throughout. However, at the end of it, an image had been seared into his memory, and it was this that made his legs give way beneath him.

He found himself sprawled on a paving stone, with his head spinning and his stomach churning. He tried to fight back the nausea and work out what had happened. It had been a message, he had no doubt of that, and he was almost certain it had come from the Ancient. But he couldn't decide why the elemental had chosen to contact him, or how it had managed to do so. In the end, though, none of that mattered. What *was* important was to know whether it had been real or not. He tried to tell himself that it was just an illusion, but he had seen too many instances where glimpses of the future *were* possible to discount the notion of prophecy out of hand.

'Are you all right?' Yarek asked, coming up beside him. 'You look very pale.'

'I'm fine,' Terrel lied. 'It was just the tremor.'

The boy nodded, but did not seem to be wholly convinced. Tegan joined them.

'That was odd,' she remarked.

'What?' Terrel asked, looking up. He still didn't trust his legs enough to stand.

'The tremor made the pyramid flicker. Why would it do that?'

'I don't know.'

'Maybe whoever built it was caught off guard,' Yarek suggested. 'Their concentration might have slipped.'

They couldn't come up with a better explanation, and Tegan and Yarek soon forgot the incident. Terrel speculated privately about whether it might have been the elemental's influence that had caused the shield to tremble, but once again he was unable to come to any conclusions.

That night, Terrel fought against his need for sleep for as long as possible. He knew that as soon as he closed his eyes he would once more see the imagery that retained the power to terrify him. He had seen himself writhing in agony as flames poured out of his body, first from his chest and then from his mouth and eyes.

CHAPTER FORTY-SIX

Terrel was lying on his back in the garden, gazing up at the unnatural colour of the sky, when it turned blue again for a few moments. He assumed that a servant was coming in, but a gasp of surprise from Tegan made him look round. The newcomer wore an ornate cape that glittered in the filtered sunlight, and there was an aura of power about her that left Terrel in no doubt as to her status. He stood up as the wizard walked over to him. On the other side of the quadrangle, Tegan and Yarek had also got to their feet, but their visitor ignored them, her liquid brown eyes fixed upon the healer.

'My name is Reykholar,' she announced.

'I'm Terrel.'

'I know who you are,' she replied. 'But I'm curious about *what* you are.'

'I'm a healer,' he said, giving the only answer he felt comfortable with.

'For a healer, an awful lot of death and destruction seems to follow in your wake.'

'That's not my doing. Or my intention.'

'What *is* your intention?'

'I have none.'

'You don't talk to dragons, then?'

Terrel didn't know how to respond to that.

'I've been told a great deal about you,' the wizard said,

'but little that makes any sense. One of the things I've heard is that you were responsible for what happened at Hvannadal, and that you enlisted the dragons to help you do it.'

'Dragons are mythical creatures. They're not real.'

'Oh, I wouldn't say that,' Reykholar remarked casually. 'What *did* you do at Hvannadal?'

'I tried to stay alive. Like everyone else.'

'Is that all?'

'Yes.'

'Well, then, you succeeded. Unlike many others.' Her steady gaze did not disguise the fact that she knew he was lying, and Terrel began to feel uncomfortable, wondering if she could read his thoughts.

'So you weren't responsible for breaking the pyramids?' she asked.

'No.'

'And you didn't cause the earthquake?'

'I'm a healer. I can't command that sort of power. Do you think I'd still be a prisoner here if I did?'

Reykholar nodded, acknowledging the point.

'I think you'll find you're being treated rather better than most prisoners,' she said.

'I'm aware of that,' Terrel responded. 'Everyone here seems to think I'm some character out of a legend.'

'The child of the sea,' the wizard said quietly. 'Born of Savik's Whale.'

'Something like that.'

'But you don't think so.'

'I've no interest in your war.'

'Then why have you been fighting with the Black army?'

'I haven't. I've been travelling with them. They gave me no choice.'

'Why was that?'

'They had the idea that I might be able to help them find a sword called the Peacemaker.'

'And can you?'

'How should I know? I'd never heard of it before I got here.'

'Why *did* you come here? Not many foreigners risk approaching our shores.'

'I'm a traveller. I go where I like.'

'And where destiny takes you?'

'Perhaps. We could all say that, couldn't we?'

Reykholar smiled for the first time, the skin around her eyes crinkling into a hundred tiny lines. It made her seem more human, a little less intimidating. Her hair, appropriately enough, was the colour of pale gold, and was cut quite short. She could not have been much more than thirty years old, but her eyes seemed considerably older, and the mind behind them was clearly formidable.

'You took a long time to get here,' Terrel remarked, feeling it was time he asked some questions of his own. 'Why was that?'

'Travelling on Myvatan has been difficult since the Hvannadal earthquake.'

'Even so, we've had to wait over a month.'

'Was there something you would rather have been doing?' she asked innocently.

'I don't like being cooped up.'

'That's understandable,' the wizard conceded, 'but I didn't want to entrust the job of talking to you to anyone else. And I needed time to recover my strength.'

'You were responsible for the outer pyramid at Hvannadal.' It was a statement rather than a question, and Reykholar nodded her head in acknowledgement. 'I can see how that would have exhausted you,' Terrel said. 'Is that why Onundar hasn't come to see us?'

'My colleague has been in a coma since the city was attacked.'

Terrel didn't even attempt to conceal his surprise.

'I don't believe it was the storm that caused her downfall,' the wizard went on. 'What happened to the springs must have affected her deeply. They were her pride and joy, after all.'

'What did happen to them?' the healer asked quickly, hoping that Tofana's efforts had not been successful.

'You don't know?'

Terrel shook his head.

'There was so much magic all around them that the waters became corrupted,' Reykholar said, and the healer's heart sank. 'The balance of such things is delicate.'

'The pools don't work any more?'

'No. In fact, the waters now harm anyone who immerses themselves.'

'How are they harmed?' he asked, fearing the worst.

'They don't burn, if that's what you're wondering,' she said, surprising him again. 'They simply develop fevers, and their wounds become infected.' The wizard looked at him thoughtfully. 'We know about the fire-starters. You can't keep that sort of thing secret for long.'

'They're nothing to do with me. They're Tofana's creatures.'

'Really? I was told you were the one who showed her how to use the technique.'

'No! Such things are hateful to me.'

'Your friends have no such scruples,' Reykholar said, glancing over at Tegan and Yarek, who had kept their distance but were watching the encounter closely.

'Some of them,' Terrel conceded, 'but not these two. They feel as I do.'

Reykholar looked doubtful, but did not question his claim.

'Do you have any news of Tofana?' Terrel asked.

'Why would you be concerned with her now?'

'Because she may still be trying to initiate a further stage in her magic, one that would be catastrophic for all Myvatan.'

'Tell me more.'

Having raised the subject, Terrel did not feel he could stop there, so he explained as much about Tofana's plans – and their possible repercussions – as he could.

'You think she might begin these chains from another location now that Hvannadal's no longer an option?' the wizard asked.

'It's possible. Do you know where she is?'

'She's made herself a little nest, an eyrie really.'

'Where?'

'Among the Lonely Peaks.'

'Reykholar said that Tofana's set herself up *inside* the glacier,' Terrel reported later. 'In a cave or something. And the place is well protected, apparently.'

'But how can she survive there?' Yarek asked.

'No one knows.'

'More to the point, what is she *doing* there?' Tegan said. 'Do you really think she's still working on the firestarter chains? I know she can be pretty single-minded, but this is extreme, even for her.'

'There are lines in ice,' Yarek reminded her. 'Perhaps she's hoping to use them.'

'Turn the whole glacier into a weapon, you mean?' the magian exclaimed. 'Gods, what an appalling thought. What's Reykholar planning to do to stop her?'

'She didn't say,' Terrel replied. The Gold wizard had left without giving him any clue as to her intentions, and without answering any of his questions about the prisoners' fate.

'My guess is she's going to consult with the generals here before she decides what to do next.'

'Do you think their plans will include you?' Tegan asked. 'Or us?'

'I expect so. They wouldn't have waited so long for her to see us if they didn't think we were important.'

'So we may yet get to go to the Lonely Peaks,' Tegan surmised.

'What are you really planning to do up there?' Yarek asked.

Terrel and Tegan looked at him in surprise.

'I'm not stupid,' the apprentice added. 'I know you don't really plan to look for the sword. That was just a story to tell the generals. So what's the real reason?'

Terrel nodded, tacitly agreeing that the boy deserved the truth, and Tegan told him about the Holma and their plans. Yarek could hardly contain his delight.

'I'll do anything I can to help,' he said eagerly.

'There's something else I have to do there,' Terrel added, then told his own tale – or part of it at least. By the time he had finished, Yarek was practically bursting with excitement.

'This is like something out of an old book,' he exclaimed. 'And I'm in it!'

'Real life is a lot more dangerous than books,' Tegan told him.

'I know, but this *is* amazing. I never thought I'd get the chance to do anything important in my life. Do you really think we could put a stop to the war for ever?'

'I do,' Tegan replied firmly, smiling at his eagerness.

'And help Terrel at the same time?'

'I don't see why not.'

'Do you think I'll get to see the Ancient?' Yarek asked, returning his attention to the healer.

'I can't tell you that,' Terrel said. 'Before we can do any of this, we have to get out of here.'

Although they all hoped Reykholar would return with more news, she did not come that day, or the next. Or the next. Terrel fretted, though he tried to remain outwardly calm for the benefit of his companions.

'Something should be happening by now,' he muttered. 'They can't still be talking.' Knowing that the wizard was there had stripped away the last of his patience. 'What are they waiting for?'

'I wish I knew,' Tegan said.

The two friends lapsed into a pensive silence. They were sitting in the room where the magian slept.

'You're thinking about Alyssa, aren't you?' Tegan said eventually. Now that they had grown comfortable in each other's company, they could often read the other's mood.

'Yes.' Terrel had told her about his love, but not about the way she visited him during his travels.

'It must be hard, being so far away.'

'There are harder things,' he said, thinking of Myrdal and the uncertainty surrounding his fate.

Tegan nodded solemnly.

'Tell me about the two of you,' Terrel said quietly.

The magian didn't need to be told who he was referring to.

'We've known each other since we were children,' she began. 'We were both different, and we knew it. I think that's why we became friends, to avoid the ridicule of all the others. I'm not sure when friendship turned into something more. It just happened. One day we were playing games, the next we . . .' She paused, her pale skin darkening a few shades. 'I'll never forget the first time he kissed me. It seemed to last for ever.' She smiled at the memory, her eyes seeing another time, another place. Then she came out of her reverie and glanced at Terrel. 'He was due to go into the army soon after that, and so we spent every moment we could together. And then my talent was discovered, and it became inevitable that we would both be going away. So we made a pact, to get ourselves into positions where we might be able to do some good, to seek out other people who thought like us, but most important of all, to remember that we would be together again one day.' There were tears in her eyes now.

'You will be,' Terrel said.

'How can you be so sure?'

'I can see the future, remember?'

'You don't believe that.'

'In this case I do. If—'

He was interrupted by an excited cry from the courtyard. Moments later Yarek burst into the room.

'The pyramid's changed!' he declared. 'There's all sorts of ripples in it.'

'Do you know what's happening?' Tegan asked, wiping her eyes.

'No, but there's something else too. The guards outside the entrances are lying on the floor. They look as if they're asleep.'

'All of them?' Terrel queried. 'In the middle of the day?'

'Come and see for yourself.'

A few moments later, all three of them were looking out through the tunnel that led to the outside world. On the other side of the magical barrier that blocked the far end, two soldiers lay sprawled on the ground. A little further away, one of the servants was also lying on the flagstones.

'What's going on?' Tegan whispered.

'I don't know,' Terrel said, 'but I think we ought to find

out, don't you? Yarek, do you still think you can break through the pyramid?'

'Yes,' the apprentice said confidently. 'It's already becoming unstable. It should be easier now.'

'Then go ahead.'

Yarek closed his eyes and held his body perfectly still. In front of them the shield shimmered and buckled, then simply vanished. Tegan cried out in astonishment and Yarek opened his eyes.

'I did it,' he murmured, then swayed on his feet. His companions moved quickly to support him, but after a few moments he shrugged them off. 'I'm all right,' he said.

'Well done,' Tegan said. 'That was incredible.'

'Ready to go?' Terrel asked.

'What are we waiting for?' Yarek replied, grinning weakly.

They went forward, and Terrel knelt beside one of the fallen guards.

'This isn't natural sleep,' he reported, once he'd had the chance to investigate the man's inner dream-world. 'I'm not sure what it is.'

'Some sort of sickness?' Yarek suggested.

'Is it like the sleepers in Saudark?' Tegan asked.

'It's like that, but not the same. I can't put my finger on it, but . . .' Terrel stood up and looked around. He couldn't see any movement anywhere. 'I wonder how many others have been affected like this.'

An hour later they had at least a partial answer to that question. As they made their way through the fortress, everyone they saw was fast asleep.

CHAPTER FORTY-SEVEN

'It's as if the time of hibernation came upon them unexpectedly,' Tegan said, 'so they had no time to prepare.'

'But there's still almost three months to the time of darkness,' Yarek objected.

Having discovered that there was no one to stop them, Terrel and his companions had climbed on to the outer battlements of the castle, and were now looking out over the rest of Nordura. An unnatural stillness enveloped the scene below, and they could see people lying in several of the streets. Nothing moved, and the only sound was the gentle wuthering of the breeze. The entire city was asleep.

'What if the whole island's like this?' Yarek whispered. 'What if we're the only ones left awake?'

While they'd been exploring, they had discussed the reason for their being the only ones unaffected by the bizarre occurrence. The obvious answer was that the pyramid, which had until recently imprisoned them, had also protected them somehow – which implied that whatever had induced the mass sleep had been magical in origin. The question of who was responsible was less easy to answer. The similarities with the sleepers led Terrel to wonder whether the elemental had been involved, but he couldn't work out how or why its interference should have taken such a strange form. The other leading candidate was Tofana, of course, but Tegan didn't know of any magic commanded by her former mistress that could have produced such an effect. A third possibility – and one which brought Terrel out into a cold sweat – was that the Ancient and the wizard were somehow working together. The idea of the creature's almost limitless power harnessed to Tofana's malevolent designs was almost too appalling to contemplate, and yet there was some evidence to suggest that this might be the case. Much earlier, Terrel had sensed that the elemental had learnt from events at Hvannadal, and the 'message' it had sent the healer implied that it knew about fire-starting. The inner dreams of the people of Nordura, and the fact that Tofana was now on the glacier – in reasonably close proximity to the creature – also pointed to a possible collaboration. But there was no way of telling whether such an alliance had been agreed upon willingly by both parties, or whether one was taking advantage of the other. Either way, Terrel knew he had to put a stop to it.

'When do you think they'll wake up?' Tegan asked.

'I don't think it'll be any time soon,' Terrel replied. 'All those I've tested are deeply unconscious.'

'But whatever caused it is no longer happening,' the magian reasoned. 'Otherwise we'd have fallen asleep ourselves as soon as the pyramid was gone. So presumably it'll wear off eventually.'

Terrel nodded.

'We'd better take advantage of the time we have, then,' he said. 'Let's gather what we need and get out of here.'

After such a long period of enforced idleness, it took Terrel a few days to get used to travelling again. Although he was able to ease the stiffness in his companions' limbs each night, Yarek's tentative efforts to do the same for the healer failed, and so Terrel was forced to bear his aches and pains on his own. He did this gladly enough – it was something he was used to, after all – because it was the price he had to pay to be moving closer to his goal.

However, Yarek did succeed in another enterprise which made their progress rather more comfortable. With Tegan's help and encouragement, he developed his own technique for building a protective shield over them, creating this magical 'tent' whenever they were in need of shelter from the weather, and thus allowing them to sleep at night in reasonably secure circumstances. Once it was set up, he could maintain the barrier even when he was asleep, but the price he paid was to wake the next morning feeling weary and uncomfortable. Because of this, they usually tried to find other means of ensuring their safety, taking advantage of whatever refuge the countryside offered.

For the most part, they avoided any human settlements. Once they had got a few miles away from Nordura, it had become clear that other parts of the island had not been affected in the same way, and they'd seen the locals going about their normal business. They had even spotted a company of the White army on the march, but had managed to remain undetected. There was no way of telling whether their escape had been discovered, and therefore whether anyone was looking for them, but as fugitives they could take no chances.

Eventually they reached the rim of the giant glacier, only to be faced with the problem of how best to go about climbing on to that forbidding expanse of blue-white ice. The frozen cliffs that they first came to were too high and too sheer to scale, so they had to move around the border, looking for an easier approach. In this way they discovered a 'valley' between two vast protrusions of ice, which enabled them to walk several miles closer to the heart of the glacier while remaining on solid ground. The gently sloping defile narrowed to a point as it climbed, but at the far end the buttresses of ice seemed smaller and less steep than any they had seen before, offering the hope of access to the Lonely Peaks.

That night they camped near the foot of the glacier in a small rock cave. They had not seen another human being since the previous day, and in such a remote spot they decided that it would be safe to light a fire. Now that they were almost surrounded by ice, the air was permanently chill, and the warmth from the flames was welcome. They ate some of their carefully rationed food, and then settled down for the night.

'Do you want the shield?' Yarek asked.

'No,' Terrel replied. 'We're sheltered enough here. Save your strength for tomorrow.'

Tegan nodded her agreement, then glanced at the healer.

'Do you still have the stone?'

'Of course.' Terrel took out the metal vial and showed it to her.

'Do you think it'll lead us to the Circle of Truce?' Yarek asked.

'I hope so.' Terrel was more concerned with finding both the elemental and Tofana, but he wasn't ruling anything out.

'Not going to be much of a show though, is it?' Tegan commented. 'With just the three of us there to see it.'

'That doesn't matter,' Yarek claimed. 'Once the flame is relit, no one will be able to deny it.

The magian smiled at the boy's earnest confidence.

'Whatever happens, it will make a difference,' Terrel agreed, as he wrapped his blanket around him and tried to find a comfortable position on the uneven floor of the cavern.

'There's something odd here,' Tegan said a little while later.

'What?' Terrel asked anxiously.

'Like the wind I felt at Hvannadal.'

So Alyssa and the ghosts won't be coming to help us, Terrel thought. He'd been hoping to see them again at some point during their journey, but if Tegan's intuition was correct, they would not be able to reach him. The elemental wind wasn't going to hurt them, though, so his fears subsided.

'That won't bother us,' he assured her. 'Let's get some rest.'

The last thing Terrel saw before he fell asleep was the slim crescent of the Amber Moon, only a few days old, framed in the entrance to the cave.

It was still dark when Terrel woke. While he'd been asleep, the cold of the glacier had seeped into his limbs and he sat up, shivering, and rubbed his arms to warm them. The fire had gone out, and its ashes gave off no heat. Even though he had only slept for a short time, his brain felt dull and foggy, and it was a few moments before he was able to make out a faint red light coming from outside the cave. He assumed that this was the first pale glimmer of dawn, and wondered about waking his companions so that they could be ready for an early start. But Tegan and Yarek were still fast asleep, and he didn't have the heart to disturb them. Terrel was so cold now that going back to sleep himself was out of the question. He yawned and stretched painfully, still feeling less than fully alert. Outside the cave's entrance the sky was full of dark clouds, but a wind-blown gap allowed him to see a few stars, and then revealed the Amber Moon. Terrel blinked, knowing that something was wrong, but even as clouds obscured his

view again, he was certain he had not been mistaken. The
Amber Moon had been full.

I must still be dreaming, he thought. But if he *was*
dreaming, then it was in an uncomfortable realm that
mimicked the real world with uncanny accuracy. He
decided to wake the others, to see if they were part of the
illusion, and he was on the point of reaching over to shake
Tegan's shoulder when he stopped short. What if he
wasn't dreaming? What if the Amber Moon really had
been full? That would mean he'd been asleep for nine
days, which wasn't possible. Unless . . .

Fear trickled into Terrel's heart like icy water. He got to
his feet, pulling the blanket around him, and tiptoed over
to the mouth of the cave. The Amber Moon chose that
moment to reappear, sliding majestically into another gap
within the fast-moving stream of cloud. It was indeed full,
and it looked *real*. What was more, the scene illuminated
by its soft light had changed almost beyond recognition.
The valley was now coated with a thick layer of snow that
glistened like pale gold in the moonlight. In addition, both
sides of the valley were blanketed by a dense veil of fog,
and the red glow he had seen earlier was coming from
these mist banks.

Terrel's fears froze into icy certainty. There was no way
these changes could have occurred during the course of
one short night. The mysterious malady that had been
inflicted upon Nordura had claimed them too.

'This is crazy,' Tegan muttered. 'The sun should have
risen by now. The night is lasting way too long.'

'And it shouldn't be this cold,' Yarek said.

Terrel's companions had woken of their own accord
about an hour after the healer. At first they had dismissed
his theory that they had been asleep for nine days, but

when they'd been presented with the evidence of their own eyes, their certainty had crumbled – and now they were being forced to consider an even more outrageous possibility.

'What was the Red Moon's aspect when we fell asleep?' Tegan asked.

'Just past full,' Yarek replied. 'About three days past, I think.'

'And what is it now?'

The boy glanced up again. They had been watching the heavens for a long time, but the clouds granted them only fleeting glimpses of the sky above.

'It's in the last part of its cycle,' he said. 'It'll be new tomorrow, probably.'

'And the White?'

'It'll be new in a few days.'

All three were capable of the calculation that followed, but it was Tegan who put the inevitable conclusion into words.

'The Amber Moon has been through another two cycles,' she said. 'We haven't been asleep for nine days. We've been asleep for two months.'

Later, when the sun finally rose, they discovered that it was not just the snowfall that had transformed the valley during their long slumber. New fissures had opened up on either side, with lava flowing silently in their depths. This was what was producing the clouds of steam, as the ice and snow around them melted in the heat.

'It must have been quite an earthquake to produce this,' Tegan said, looking down into the red glow of one of the crevasses. 'How could we have slept through it?'

They moved away from the edge, and trudged back through the snow towards the cave. As they did so, the day's cold reasserted itself.

'It's as if we've missed autumn and gone straight from summer to winter,' Terrel grumbled.

'It's always a short season,' Tegan said, 'but it's never gone by *that* fast before.'

'We'll have to look for a place to sleep soon,' Yarek said.

At first Terrel didn't understand what the boy meant, but then he realized that the time of Myvatan's hibernation – the two months when the sun never rose – was only a few days away. It made the tasks that still lay ahead of them more urgent than ever.

'Do you think it was deliberate?' Tegan asked.

'What?'

'Us sleeping for so long, the fissures, all of this. Do you think someone was trying to delay us? Or have we just been unlucky?'

'I've no idea,' Terrel admitted.

'Was it the elemental?' she went on. 'I remember feeling something just before we went to sleep.'

'If it is, the chances are we've just been unlucky. Its power is erratic,' he replied, thinking of the unpredictable nature of the wind that blew the ghosts away, and of the tremors at Hvannadal. 'But if Tofana's got something to do with it, she might have been trying to target us specifically.'

'You think it's her doing?'

'It could be.'

'Then why let us wake up again now?'

'Maybe she's done all she needs to do. Or perhaps she can't control the spell all the time. I don't know. Anyway, this is all just speculation.'

'If it was all accidental,' Yarek put in, 'the pattern of the fissures is quite a coincidence.'

'Why?' Terrel asked. 'What do you mean?'

The apprentice pointed to the upper end of the valley, where steam rose from the base of the glacier.

'Unless I'm very much mistaken,' he said, 'the two fissures intersect up there. There's only one way out of here now, and that's to go back the way we came.'

Terrel and Tegan stared, but they both knew that the boy was right. They had been cut off from the Lonely Peaks by a moat of fire.

'Unless you fancy wading through molten rock, of course,' Yarek added.

CHAPTER FORTY-EIGHT

'We have to go back,' Terrel said.

They had returned to the cave and were packing up their supplies. Although some of their food had gone mouldy, most of it still seemed edible.

'If we retreat now, we'll never get up there in time,' Tegan said. 'The dark will be here.'

'We haven't got any choice,' Terrel said. 'There's no way to cross the fissures.' They had climbed to the top of the valley to see the point where the two lava flows split apart. The rivers of fire emerged from beneath the glacier in a smooth, continuous stream, then divided to run down both sides of the valley.

'I know,' Tegan muttered, her frustration plain. 'I just wish we knew what Tofana was doing. If we have to wait till next year to get up there, we could be too late.'

'Having slept so long now, maybe we won't need to hibernate,' Yarek suggested.

'I wouldn't like to stake my life on that,' the magian replied.

'I might not be affected by the hibernation,' Terrel said. 'Perhaps I could go on alone.'

Tegan frowned, but before she could say anything more they were interrupted by a muffled roar from outside.

'Earthquake?' Yarek queried doubtfully.

'I don't think so,' Terrel replied. He hadn't experienced any internal trembling.

The rumbling continued, and the three friends went outside.

'There,' Yarek said, pointing to the glacier above the steam clouds at the head of the valley.

'The heat's melting the outer edges of the cliff,' Terrel decided. 'It's falling into the fissure.' As they watched, more huge chunks of ice broke away and disappeared into the mist.

'Could it fill the gap?' Yarek asked hopefully.

'No,' the magian answered. 'You saw how hot it was down there. The ice will melt almost at once.'

Vast billows of steam were erupting now, emphasizing her point and obscuring the view even more.

'Maybe if enough ice fell in, we might be able to get across,' the boy persisted. 'Could we use magic to increase the size of the avalanche?'

'We could try,' Tegan said, 'but I still don't think it would do us much good. The fallen ice would still be much too unstable for us to use.'

Listening to the crash and roar of the exploding cascade, Terrel was forced to agree with her.

'Come on,' he said. 'The sooner we start, the sooner we'll have a chance of finding another way in.'

He set off, his boots sinking into the ankle-deep snow, only to come to a halt a few paces later. A large animal was bounding across the valley towards them. It looked like a cat, but it was huge, and its powerful legs propelled it along at breathtaking speed. Its fur was pale cream with grey markings, like smudges of ash.

'It's a snow leopard,' Yarek breathed, caught between terror and awe.

'Don't move,' Tegan said quickly. 'If we run, it'll chase

us down easily. Our best chance is to shout as loud as we
can. We might be able to frighten it away.'

'It won't attack us,' Terrel stated calmly, his spirits rising.

'How do you—' Tegan began, then stopped.

You're going the wrong way, Alyssa told him. *They won't
be able to keep the bridge in place for long.* She came to a
skidding halt, her large paws scattering snow.

A bridge?

*At the head of the valley. Can't you see? But you must
hurry.*

'Come on,' Terrel said to the others, who were still
staring at the beast in silent amazement. 'Yarek was right.
We *are* going to get across.' He began to run, and after a
moment's hesitation, his companions followed. The snow
leopard padded alongside, matching their pace with ease.

Who are they? Terrel asked as he ran.

What?

You said they won't *be able to keep the bridge in place.*

Does it matter? she asked impatiently. *They're risking
their lives to help you. Isn't that enough? Just make sure
their efforts aren't in vain.*

Terrel stumbled on, the weight of his pack making him
even more clumsy than usual. Ahead of them they could
hear – but not see – more ice falling. He plunged into the
cloud. To begin with it felt both cold and clammy, but it
rapidly grew warmer. Half blind now, they slowed their
pace until they came out above the rim of one of the fissures. Below them the lava was still flowing, red hot, but
there were darker patches within the stream now, marking
the places where some of the rock had solidified once
again. Further up the crevasse there was an area where ice-
boulders were falling continuously, hissing as they crashed
into the fire. The lava flow there was darker in colour and
moving sluggishly.

'This way,' Terrel gasped, following the snow leopard.

Looking across at the glacier wall, he thought he saw movement within the ice, but assumed this was either meltwater or a trick of the light. However, the illusion persisted, becoming more noticeable as they drew closer to the site of the avalanche. Something was loosening the ice deliberately, causing huge blocks to break away and tumble down into the fissure. He could pick out several of them now, each one glittering like moving crystal, half hidden beneath the surface of the glacier – and Terrel suddenly realized that he knew what they were. The ice-worms had come to his aid.

'It's working!' Yarek shouted. 'The gap's filling up!'

Terrel peered ahead through the mist and saw that the boy was right. At the point where the avalanche had been at its heaviest, not all the ice was melting instantaneously. Some huge blocks lay across the ravine, forming a jagged, shifting causeway across the blackened and smouldering lava. It was still impossible to imagine crossing such dangerous terrain, but as he watched, even more ice landed on top of the pile, adding another layer to the frozen pontoon. Moments later there was movement *inside* the fallen boulders as the ice-worms burrowed into their construction. As they did so, the various sections of ice seemed to shift and coalesce, freezing together into a single, continuous span that linked the two mist-enshrouded banks.

Now? Terrel asked silently.

Now, Alyssa confirmed.

Following the snow leopard, Terrel set out to cross the bridge between the clouds.

'No going back now then,' Tegan remarked, looking down from the top of the glacier.

Far below them, the valley was still wreathed in fog, but

they could see enough to know that the bridge had melted and fallen into the fissure again. The ice-worms were nowhere to be seen, but their efforts had served their purpose. The glacier seemed quite stable again, and although the climb had been arduous, it had been relatively straightforward.

The snow leopard was still with them, and although both Tegan and Yarek glanced at it warily every so often, they seemed to be getting used to the creature's presence. For once, Terrel found that he didn't need to talk to Alyssa immediately. He was still thinking about what had happened, and relating it to the various prophecies in the Tindaya Code. According to that ancient text, the ice-worms were supposed to act to protect the Guardian – which implied that having Terrel and his friends reach the glacier somehow worked to the Ancient's advantage. This was encouraging, if a little hard to fathom. And now that they had crossed the bridge between the clouds, Terrel was in no doubt that he was on the right path.

He turned round to look out over the seemingly endless expanse of the glacier. It was a frozen sea that stretched to the horizon, broken only by a few distant mountains that jutted up from the plain like isolated ships adrift on a great ocean. It was his first view of the Lonely Peaks, and he understood now how they had got their name.

'You have some strange allies,' Tegan remarked. 'Few people have ever seen a snow leopard this close, let alone been led by one.'

'Don't forget the ice-worms,' Yarek added. 'What you made them do was incredible.'

'It wasn't my doing,' Terrel said, glancing at Alyssa.

'Well, they don't usually behave like that for their own amusement,' Tegan commented.

Are you going to spend the whole day talking? Alyssa

enquired. *Or are you going to do something useful?*

    Thank you for getting us across, Terrel said.

    It was their idea, not mine.

    The ice-worms?

    The sleepers here.

    Understanding dawned with her words. Just as Alyssa had commandeered the snow leopard, so the sleepers of Myvatan had taken over the bodies of the ice creatures – and come to the travellers' rescue.

    'We have more allies than you know,' he said aloud. 'Let's go.'

Contrary to Terrel's first impressions, the surface of the glacier proved to be anything but flat. It was pitted and uneven, with moulds and hollows, ridges and grooves, and occasional deep cracks running down into the ice that glowed with an eerie blue light. Some of these crevasses were large enough to force the travellers to make detours, and their progress was slow and erratic. When they had been collecting their equipment in Nordura, Tegan had insisted on taking some curious implements which could be fitted on to the soles of their boots, surrounding them with jagged teeth, and Terrel had now begun to appreciate their value. Without the extra purchase on the ice, he would have been slipping and sliding with every step.

    'Where are we heading?' Yarek asked.

    'I don't really know,' Terrel replied. 'Just towards the mountains.'

    The snow leopard was still keeping pace alongside them, and Terrel took comfort from her presence, but in contrast to most of her visits, neither of them felt the need to talk all that much. Alyssa's mood was tense and serious, and it seemed that she had seen little of the ghosts since the last time she had joined him on the unknown road – and as a result she had brought no news or advice from Elam or the seers. She also appeared to know what had happened to Terrel recently, even before he told her about his various adventures. But all she seemed to care about was the fact that they were finally on the glacier now, and that the end of their quest was in sight.

The day proved to be very short, with the sun barely rising above the horizon, and so they were forced to carry on walking long into the deepening twilight. Finally, when constant flurries of snow began to make their progress even more hazardous, they called a halt. The snow leopard loped off into the gloom. Alyssa's parting words had re-assured Terrel that she would rejoin him as soon as she could, but he still hated to see her go. He watched the animal until it was out of sight, then turned and saw that Tegan was looking at him.

'Will it come back?' she asked quietly.

'I hope so,' Terrel replied. Alyssa had been with him during all his previous encounters with the elementals, and he certainly wanted – and needed – her to be there this time.

Without waiting to be asked, Yarek created a pyramid around them, and they settled down to wait out the darkest hours and the storm that was brewing. A blizzard was soon whipping past their camp, but the magical shield kept the travellers dry and relatively warm. It even provided a little illumination in an otherwise pitch-black night.

'I hope this eases before morning,' Tegan said, watching the swirling snow. 'Or we'll be stuck here.'

'How long can you keep the barrier going?' Terrel asked.

'As long as we need,' Yarek declared confidently. 'All the work is in setting up the patterns. After that, maintaining it is easy. There's a lot of power here to draw on.'

'In the ice?'

'Yes.'

'Do you think you could maintain the pyramid all the way through the long dark?' Tegan asked.

The apprentice looked rather less sure now.

'Maybe,' he said cautiously.

'It's just that I'm not sure we'd survive up here if we were forced to hibernate without some sort of protection,' the magian explained. 'And we've no idea how long this is going to take.'

'Let's deal with that when we have to,' Terrel said. 'Right now we need to get some sleep.'

The storm blew itself out during the latter part of the night, and left the sky clear. First the stars and then the Amber Moon cast their beguiling radiance over the scene, reminding Terrel of a very different desert. The baking sand and dust of Misrah had often appeared beautiful in the varied moonlight, but, like the ice, they could be deadly too.

The improvement in the weather made all three of them eager to push on, and they set out as soon as the pre-dawn glow gave them enough light. They had gone no more than a mile when Terrel came to an abrupt halt and stared ahead. Beside him, both Tegan and Yarek let out gasps of surprise. A few hundred paces away, a black pyramid was growing out of the ice. It rose and expanded just as the shield had spread out to cover Hvannadal, but this structure was opaque, its lustrous surfaces reflecting the light of the newly risen sun.

'Tofana!' Yarek whispered.

'It has to be,' Tegan agreed.

For a few moments none of them moved, but just stared at the wizard's eyrie.

'What should we do?' Tegan asked. 'Try to go around, or face her?'

'If she can do that,' Yarek said, 'we can't match her magic.'

'And I don't think she's going to let us just slip by,' Terrel said.

He yawned suddenly, then glanced at his companions. Yarek's eyes were already closed, and Tegan was swaying unsteadily on her feet. Terrel tried to call out, to tell Yarek to build their own pyramid, but his tongue would not work, and then he realized that it was already too late. The boy had slumped to the ground.

The last thought that passed through the healer's beleaguered mind before sleep engulfed him was that they were going to have to face Tofana now whether they liked it or not.

CHAPTER FORTY-NINE

When Terrel awoke, he had no idea how he had come to be where he was or how much time had passed. But as soon as he was able to look around he was certain of two things; he was deep beneath the surface of the glacier, and he was inside the black pyramid.

He was alone in a chamber of ice, its walls sculpted into smooth curves by the passage of meltwater that had long since flowed away, leaving behind an underground labyrinth of sinuous beauty. It ought to have been dark, but the walls glowed blue with an inner luminescence. It ought to have been deadly cold, but although everything around him was indeed frozen, the air within was mild enough for Terrel to know that he could survive in such an atmosphere. Which made it all the more surprising that the only sound of running water came from some distance away. The walls of his cavern were dry.

Although it seemed that he was in no immediate physical danger, and there was nothing to stop him from leaving the chamber by any one of the three narrow passageways that led from it, he was under no illusions about his situation. He, and presumably Tegan and Yarek, were Tofana's prisoners. This was her lair, and within its boundaries – as at the stone pyramid near Saudark – she could do anything she liked. However, there was no point in simply staying where he was and waiting for her to decide his fate. In such a predicament, doing something – anything – was better than remaining passive.

Terrel stood up and listened for any sounds of activity. He heard nothing except the muffled drip and splash of water and so, on impulse, he chose the tunnel that seemed to lead towards that. In places the winding corridor was so narrow that he had to turn sideways in order to slide through, and at one point he had to duck his head to avoid a cluster of icicles that hung from the ceiling. When he brushed against one of them it rang with a pure musical note that seemed to reverberate throughout the maze of ice. The frozen world was a place of extraordinary complexity and a strange, hypnotic beauty, and under any other circumstances Terrel would have been lost in wonder. But he was too concerned with finding his companions – and with the inevitable confrontation with Tofana – to appreciate his surroundings.

Eventually he came to a much larger cavern, and the end of his search. Tegan and Yarek were sitting meekly on the floor near the centre of the echoing chamber, and Tofana – resplendent in a black cloak that was rimed with glittering frost – stood over them, obviously in complete control of the situation. At the far end of the cave a cataract of water fell through a wide opening in the roof and disappeared into a hole in the floor that plunged even deeper into the glacier. From where he stood, the noise of its passage made it impossible for Terrel to hear what the wizard and her former assistants were talking about.

All three of them turned to look at the newcomer as he stepped forward. A small measure of relief showed on Tegan's face, but Yarek's expression remained taut and fearful. Neither of them spoke, and it was left to Tofana to greet him.

'Come and join us!' she called above the hiss of the

waterfall. 'Now that you're all here we can begin properly.' She sounded eager, almost gleeful, and even from a distance Terrel could sense the madness in her emerald eyes. As he moved towards her, he felt a mixture of dread and determination. He swore to himself that, even if the wizard was invincible here, he would not go down without a fight. He could only hope that both Tegan and Yarek would show the same resolve.

'Sit down,' Tofana commanded when he reached the others.

'Are you all right?' he asked his travelling companions as he obeyed.

'I'm fine,' Tegan replied, with a welcome touch of defiance in her tone.

Yarek just nodded.

'I have no intention of harming them,' Tofana assured him. 'They may be misguided, but their talents are too valuable to waste. As are yours, Terrel.'

'You really think we would use our talents to help you?' he said.

'You won't have any choice,' the wizard replied, with a smile as cold as her new home.

Terrel's dread intensified. Tofana might be insane, but that did not mean she was without intelligence. Although her logic might be skewed, her cunning was undiminished.

'You've all learnt some new tricks since we last met,' she remarked. 'But you're no match for me. Please remember that.'

Her captive audience remained silent, and Tofana's thoughts seemed to be wandering as she gazed up at the arch of ice far above them.

'I do miss the mustelas,' she murmured eventually. 'Especially Bezylum.'

Tegan and Terrel exchanged a glance, wondering if there was any way they could take advantage of the wizard's evident distraction, but before they could do anything their captor looked down again, businesslike once more.

'I should have come here long ago. You don't need things like this.' She gestured contemptuously towards the travellers' packs, which lay at her feet. 'All you need is magic, and this place is the source of the greatest power I've ever encountered. And here, at this very spot,' she added, stabbing a finger towards the floor, 'is the most potent concentration of all. From here I can do anything.'

Terrel recalled Yarek saying that there was a lot of power in the ice, and if a mere apprentice was able to draw upon it, it was hardly surprising that a wizard could do so too.

'Soon it will be lined up,' Tofana went on. 'All the chains, all the patterns. And all at my command.'

The whole glacier as a weapon, Terrel thought, remembering an earlier conversation. It had been a nightmarish possibility then; it seemed it was a reality now.

'So what are you going to do?' Tegan asked.

'End the war.'

'How?'

'My plan at Hvannadal was a good one,' Tofana said. 'It just didn't go far enough. I can command *all* the chains from here. I simply have to separate out those that lead to our enemies. Then they'll burn – all the soldiers, all the wizards and magians, everyone.'

'Everyone?' Terrel queried in horror.

'The entire population of the two quarters,' she confirmed enthusiastically.

'That's barbaric!'

Tofana shrugged.

'They'd do the same to us if they had the chance,' she said. 'It's the nature of war.'

'That's not the point,' Terrel began, but Tegan overrode him.

'You'll end up killing your own people too,' she declared.

'Nonsense, my dear.'

'Chains within water can't be divided so neatly,' the magian persisted. 'Varmahlid knew that. That's why she opposed you.'

'She was a foolish old woman,' Tofana stated complacently.

'No. She was right. If you do this, every person on Myvatan will burn. It won't just be the end of the war. It'll be the end of everything.'

'You're being tiresome now, child,' the wizard said. 'I don't expect you to understand. Just watch and learn. It's Terrel who'll be helping me.'

'Me?'

'I'm just going to borrow a little of your mind to guide the chains. I could do it myself, but this will be so much more elegant. And please don't think you can resist,' she added, as the healer shook his head. 'I can do it after sending you to sleep if necessary. It's just that you'll miss all the fun that way. Jax wouldn't want you to do that, now, would he?'

Mention of his twin confused Terrel for a moment, making it impossible for him to think clearly.

'Will he be coming back any time soon?' Tofana asked. 'He'd enjoy this, don't you think?' Without waiting for an answer, she reached inside her cape and took something from a pocket. 'Before we start, there's just one question I'd like an answer to. What's this?' She held up a small metal cylinder.

Reflexively Terrel's hand went to his own pocket, but of course the vial was gone. Beside him, Tegan let out a cry of dismay.

'The container is interesting,' Tofana commented. 'Quite old, I think, with some residual power. But this . . .' She tipped the crystal out on to her palm. 'This is just a worthless trinket. So why were you carrying it with you?'

Terrel chose not to answer.

'Perhaps you can show me,' she suggested, and tossed the stone to Terrel, who caught it in his good hand.

Immediately the pale speck within the red began to glow, becoming brighter by the moment until the entire cavern was stained pink.

'Very pretty,' Tofana observed, her disdain obvious. 'Is that supposed to prove anything?'

But then a deep growling, that seemed to come from the ice all around them, made her hesitate. The floor of the cave shook as the tremor passed, and the glacier rang like a giant bell. Terrel was suddenly aware of another presence in the chamber, remote but watchful, and from her expression, he guessed that Tegan felt it too. Whatever else it had done, the crystal's display had attracted the attention of the elemental.

Although Tofana had seemed to regard the interruption as irrelevant, evidently used to the pyramid protecting her from earthquakes, she had lost her train of thought. She stared at the ceiling again, muttering unintelligibly to herself, reminding Terrel of some of the lunatics who had been incarcerated with him at Havenmoon. He looked round at Tegan, hoping that they could use the wizard's reverie to their benefit, when he was distracted himself by yet another unexpected occurrence. Several wraiths were drifting into the cavern, apparently drawn to the light that was still streaming through his fingers. It was clear that none of the others could see them, but one of the ghostly figures seemed more interested in Yarek than in the crystal.

'What's going on?' Tegan whispered.

'I'm not sure.'

The independent wraith wrapped itself around the boy, and as it did so Yarek's expression changed from fear to amazement. He still couldn't see the phantom presence, but something had obviously told him it was there.

'We should begin,' Tofana announced, her voice sounding very loud in the echoing space.

At the same time another voice, much quieter and sometimes indistinct, was sounding inside Terrel's head, but he knew at once that it was not speaking to him.

You were never a coward. Don't even think ... could not have come this far ... time to believe ...

Terrel realized belatedly that he was overhearing the wraith as it spoke to Yarek, and a glance at the boy confirmed that he was hearing it too. Tears were filling his eyes now, and sadness combined with joy on his young face.

'What's the matter with him?' Tofana muttered, glaring at the apprentice. 'Never mind. He's not important.' The wizard turned back to Terrel. 'Now, are you going to cooperate, or must I destroy you too?'

'Why should I help you?' the healer asked, stalling for time.

'Because it'll be much easier for you if you do, and the end result will be the same in any case.'

... can't let her do this ... all be in torment ...

The words flitted through Terrel's mind even as the other wraiths clustered silently around him, seeming to bask in the rose-coloured light.

'Come, Terrel,' Tofana said impatiently. 'The White

Moon is beginning a new cycle. This is a time of change. Shall we play our part?'

'No. I want nothing to do with your vile schemes.'

Tofana frowned, then shrugged.

'That is regrettable. You had interesting potential, but if that's the way you choose to go, so be it.'

Arcs of silver-white light crackled through the air between them, like miniature streaks of lightning, and Terrel felt pain searing through his head and heart. There was nothing he could do, no way to defend himself. Tofana had been right; he was no match for her. She would use whatever she wanted and then discard him like an empty husk. He was blind to all but the pain now. Far away, he heard Tegan screaming, and beyond that another voice, calm but insistent.

. . . *you did it before . . . don't be afraid . . .*

The wizard's sorcery was burning Terrel from the inside, and he realized that that would be his eventual fate. Once his usefulness was over, he too would become a victim of the greatest fire-starter of them all. He struggled against a power too strong to comprehend, knowing that his resistance was merely a futile gesture, but unwilling to yield. His agony grew worse.

Tofana laughed.

'It begins!' she cried.

'No!' Yarek's voice cut through the spell, and Terrel forced himself to open his eyes.

'Oh, please,' Tofana exclaimed scornfully. 'What do you think *you're* going to do?' She tried to swat the apprentice aside as if he were a troublesome insect.

But Yarek would not be dismissed so easily. He had stepped between the wizard and Terrel, disrupting the pattern of white light. It danced around him in swirls and jagged shards, but instead of simply trying to divert the link, Yarek had *accepted* it, drawing it into himself. Terrel felt his own torment lessen, then fall away.

'You made this mistake before, boy,' Tofana snarled. 'Would you destroy yourself in trying to save another?'

'To save a friend,' Yarek whispered, 'yes, I would.'

'This is pointless,' the wizard told him. 'All you can achieve is a slight delay – and your own death.'

'So be it,' the boy grated, his voice thick with pain.

The silver inferno redoubled in ferocity, and once again Yarek made no effort to avoid it. Instead he seemed to reach out to Tofana, almost in supplication.

'What are you doing?' Tegan screamed. 'You'll—'

The rest of her words were lost as Yarek yelled, a wordless howl of agony and triumph. The lightning was flaring back and forth between him and Tofana now in an unbreakable loop. And it was growing more powerful with every repetition, spiralling out of control.

For the first time, uncertainty registered on the wizard's face, and as the realization of what was happening came to her she was caught between fury and fear. She increased her efforts, trying to destroy her enemy, but that only accelerated the process, turning the centre of the cavern into a coruscating storm of magical energy. She tried to pull back, but it was too late. She was trapped in her own web now.

'Fool!' she spat. 'You think this will save your friend? It will kill us all unless—'

'Be quiet!' Yarek roared, then turned to look at Terrel with the eyes of a dragon. 'I can start it, but you and Tegan have to maintain it. Can you do that?'

'Do what?' Terrel asked, squinting into the blaze.

'I can do it,' Tegan said. 'You were an excellent teacher, Yarek.'

'Good.' The apprentice turned away.

Amid all the chaos, a small oasis of calm sprang into being as a miniature pyramid formed, enclosing Terrel and Tegan. The magian took Terrel's hand in her own, and closed her eyes in concentration.

'Help me,' she whispered.

The healer sank into her waking dream, hoping that she'd be able to take whatever she needed from him. He had no idea what was going to happen, but it was clear that they needed the pyramid in order to survive. Outside its walls, the magic was spiralling to greater heights of frenzy, still feeding on itself.

'What about Yarek?' he asked.

Locked in her own battle, Tegan didn't answer. Leaving himself open to her, Terrel turned his attention to the outer world and saw that both Tofana and Yarek had become creatures of flame, each shining like a miniature sun. Alyssa had once told the healer that Yarek had 'more power than he can control', and what was happening now was proof of just that. The former apprentice might well have found a way to defeat his one-time mistress by using the wizard's own sorcery against her, but he was going to pay a high price for his victory. In trying to save Dayak he had made himself ill. This time he would die. And what was more, the boy knew it – and was going ahead anyway. Of all the acts of courage Terrel had ever witnessed, this was the most selfless, and he could only watch in awe and admiration – and anguish. Now he knew the identity of the wizard who had been destined to help him. His own dream had been prophetic – but in a way no one could have foreseen.

Outside their shield, the focus of the battle shifted. Entangled in a trap of her own making, Tofana was still struggling, but to no avail. She had staggered towards the far end of the cavern, trying to distance herself physically from her tormentor, but he had simply followed her – and so had the magic.

... come with me ... this is just the beginning ... a release for both of us ... together ...

The faint voice drifted from the maelstrom, and even though Terrel could no longer see the wraith, he knew it was there. And he knew who it was.

'Now!' Yarek cried, and launched himself at Tofana. 'Welcome to my dark dreams!'

Their collision created a new whirlwind of fire and light, but it also took them both to the edge of the precipice where the waterfall disappeared into the lower reaches of the glacier. As Terrel watched, aghast, they toppled over the rim and vanished amid the cascade. The brightness of the magic went with them, leaving the cavern in relative gloom, and it took the healer's eyes some time to adjust.

'Is it over?' he asked, his voice hoarse.

'No,' Tegan whispered, her hand still gripping Terrel's. 'It's out of control. When the end comes, you'll know it. Yarek took them down there in the hope of protecting the rest of the island, but I don't think it's going to work.'

'What do you mean?'

He was answered by the glacier itself, as all around them the ice cracked and shattered and then hurled itself into the sky.

CHAPTER FIFTY

It was like a dream of flying, but this was happening in the waking world. The pyramid was spinning into the sky with the frozen debris from the explosion, while inside, still clinging to each other, Terrel and Tegan were tossed from side to side. Although the experience was disorientating, they were weightless, moving so slowly that no harm came to them. Terrel had long since given up trying to understand what was going on around him. He could no longer tell which of the pyramid's four sides were the roof and which the floor, and he didn't know whether they were going up or down or sideways. All he could do was watch the chaos beyond the magical barrier and hope that Tegan could somehow keep them safe. She still had her eyes shut tight, in her own sleep-like trance, but through the link between them Terrel knew that she was awake — and lost in the demands of the task Yarek had bequeathed her. He lent what support he could, but did not interfere in case he disturbed her concentration.

It was hard to believe the scale of the devastation that the magic had caused. Terrel saw irregular blocks of ice, some of them the size of a small house, go sailing by, turning lazily in the air as if they weighed no more than a bird's feather. Elsewhere, smaller shards moved faster, flashes of blue or white, or flurries of tiny pellets like hail. Occasionally the scene glittered with a brief crack of lightning or a glimpse of sunlight, but for the most part it was like being at the centre of a giant storm, marooned in its dark and relentless fury. Without the barrier, they would have been torn to shreds in moments.

'I can't do this any more,' Tegan gasped. 'The patterns are unravelling.'

'Keep trying,' Terrel urged. 'Take whatever you need from me.'

'We don't have the strength,' she whispered. 'It's hopeless.'

The pyramid bucked and swayed, and Terrel saw ripples in the surface where impacts from the ice were testing the shield.

'Don't give up,' he said, and reinforced the message through the link between their dream-worlds even as he sought ways of bolstering her fading resolve. 'Yarek sacrificed himself for us. We can't let that have been in vain.'

'It's no good,' Tegan groaned. They had both reached the end of their reserves now, and even Terrel was forced to recognize that fact. But he fought on, railing against fate, determined to resist to the last. Outside the pyramid the ice storm battered at their sanctuary, its clamour rising to a howl of victory as the shield buckled and began to collapse.

'I'm sorry,' Tegan breathed.

But in the next moment they were wrapped in a cocoon of silence. The walls of the pyramid were strong again, and the storm's rage was impotent once more. Terrel was stunned by what had happened, and when he glanced at Tegan he saw that she was wide-eyed, as shocked as he was by their reprieve. It was only then that he realized where the new source of power had come from. In contrast to all its earlier actions, the elemental was now helping them – feeding a tiny fraction of its own limitless strength into the shield and protecting them from harm.

'Why's it doing this?' Tegan asked. She too was obviously aware of the Ancient's intervention.

'I've no idea.' Terrel didn't know whether their rescue had been a deliberate act or simply an accidental by-product of the elemental's whim. He wasn't even sure if it had fed its power directly into the pyramid or if he and Tegan had 'shaped' the energy to their own purpose, as they had done at Hvannadal. 'But I'm not going to argue. Can you make sure the patterns don't unravel?'

Tegan nodded.

'It's easy now,' she said. 'Yarek really was an excellent teacher.'

And his sacrifice won't have been in vain, Terrel thought, hearing the catch in the magian's voice.

'Is this really happening?' Tegan whispered, staring for the first time at the tumult outside their refuge.

The healer knew that she neither needed nor expected an answer to her question. He shared her amazement, and when at last a space began to open up around them – so that they could make some sense of their surroundings – the sight that greeted them was even more incredible.

They were floating on the wind, far above even the tallest mountains. All about them the ice was still flying, spreading out into a fragmentary roof that covered the whole island before plummeting back towards the land. The impact of the larger boulders would be violent, but most had broken up now and would fall as hail. Directly beneath the pyramid the air was clear, and the two friends could see that a huge area of the glacier had simply been torn away and hurled aside, leaving only the bare rock that had lain beneath it for centuries – and it was towards this that they were slowly descending.

'The lines are still there,' Tegan said.

'What?'

'In the ice. The chains that Tofana was going to use are still there, even though it's all in pieces now.'

'Could what she started still work?' Terrel asked in alarm.

'No. She's gone. No one will burn. But *we* could use the lines.'

'What for?'

'Healing. The ice is going to fall over every part of Myvatan. You could use it to break their reliance on mitra – like you did with Kopak.'

'I can't do that,' Terrel protested. He was already weary beyond belief.

'Maybe you can,' the magian told him. 'There's more than enough power here. Use that.'

Terrel hesitated, recalling Alyssa's advice that long-distance healing 'might come in useful one day' – and also remembering the reference in the Tindaya Code to something that 'blinds the eyes from within'. When the ice melted, even if that was not until the following summer, some mud was bound to be formed – and sooner or later everyone would be affected by the water.

'I don't know how,' he confessed.

'See through me,' Tegan said. 'Like you did before.' Their hands were still clasped together, a mutual anchor in this strange, shifting realm.

Terrel closed his eyes and slipped into her waking dream, instantly sensing the Ancient's immense influence. He followed its trail – and saw the chains, each drop of water linked to the next, each ice crystal joined to an infinite array of others within the expanding remnants of the glacier. For the first time he knew what the links were, what they *meant*, and he saw how to use them. From that moment on, his healer's instincts took over, shaping the patterns within the ice as he did within his human patients.

Images filled his head – of mudslides, pools and newly formed streams, of water being drawn from a well, crops growing – and he felt a sense of release, of fulfilment. He withdrew, utterly spent. He had done all he could.

When he opened his eyes again, the pyramid was still drifting down towards the area from which the glacier had been cleared. It was several miles across, and most of it was simply bare rock, but there was something at its centre.

'What's that?' he asked, fighting vertigo as he looked down.

'The ruins of a city,' Tegan replied, her voice a reverent whisper. 'It's Akurvellir.'

The closer they came, the more detail they could make out. The pyramid's unnatural flight was gradually taking them to the centre of the ruins. The sky was darkening now, and they could see a light burning in the heart of the city.

'It never went out,' Tegan breathed. 'All we had to do was bring it back into the open.'

The joy and wonder in her voice left Terrel with nothing to say, and so he simply watched. The flame was still far below them when it suddenly flickered. For a while it was impossible to tell what had happened, and they waited nervously, but then it became clear that the flame was still burning and that there was now a *second* light, rising up towards them like a stream of tiny white sparks. As it came closer, Terrel saw that the radiance consisted of two intertwined spirals, like twin galaxies. As they passed by the pyramid and continued up into the night sky, a voice sounded in Terrel's head.

. . . *make use of the far crystals* . . . *bring the sword to its resting place* . . .

And then another voice, younger than the first.

My dark dreams were right, Yarek said. *For just a little while I was the greatest wizard in all the four quarters. Farewell, Terrel. Farewell, Tegan. Remember me.*

And then they were gone, their starlight dwindling into the infinite darkness. Terrel watched until they were lost among all the other constellations – starting a journey he could not even begin to imagine. He wished them well, and knew he would have no trouble obeying the boy's final request. Reunited now, Yarek and his father would be in the sky for ever, and whenever he looked up, the healer would see them and remember.

It was only when he glanced at Tegan and saw the tears running down her cheeks that Terrel realized he was crying too. They smiled briefly at each other, dabbing at their eyes, before another matter demanded their attention.

'Look,' Tegan said hoarsely, staring down at the city below. 'It's the Circle of Truce.'

At the centre of the ruined city lay an amphitheatre, and at the centre of that lay a large uneven boulder. It reminded Terrel of the shaman's stone in the Great Circle at Qomish. Did this rock fall from the sky too? he wondered.

The flame they had seen earlier was burning at the top of the boulder, and now that they were only a short distance above it Terrel could see thin veins of colour in the rock. But here they were red, not green as they had been in Qomish.

With the gentlest of bumps, the pyramid finally came to rest on flat ground next to the boulder. A moment later it vanished, leaving Terrel and Tegan to struggle to their feet. They were no longer weightless, and the simple act of standing up was almost beyond them. After all their exertions – and now that the elemental was gone – they were sorely in need of rest, but for a few moments they just stood and stared at the flame. They understood now why Tofana's caves had been at the centre of the glacier's potency. They had been directly above the sacred site, a focus for all the magic of the centuries. To be standing in such a place was awe-inspiring, even for Terrel, and he could only imagine what Tegan must be feeling. She was looking at her dream made real.

'Jarvik always said he wouldn't live to see this,' Tegan said quietly. 'It was one of his premonitions, I suppose. But it didn't stop him working towards it.' She continued to gaze at the serene white fire. 'I can hardly believe it's happened.'

'He knew you wouldn't let him down,' Terrel said. 'And wherever he is now, he knows about this.'

'On the Great Plain?' the magian said. 'I hope so.'

Terrel could have said more, but he chose not to. It was obvious that Tegan could not see the ghost who stood beside them, transfixed by the flame. His shape was slightly distorted, but he was still recognizable. Jarvik had been right. He had not lived to see the Circle of Truce. But he was seeing it now anyway, and the healer and the ghost exchanged the briefest glance of understanding. That was all they needed.

'Come on,' Terrel said. 'We'd better find shelter and get some rest.'

'But we have to—' In the act of turning to face him, Tegan staggered and almost fell.

'It can wait. You won't do anyone any good if you collapse from exhaustion.'

After a moment's hesitation she nodded, her shoulders sagging, and the two friends helped each other from the amphitheatre, leaving the Circle of Truce to the guardianship of a ghost.

Neither of the travellers knew exactly how much time passed before they were able to recover their strength, but several short days and long nights went by in a haze of utter weariness. They woke every so often for just long enough to force themselves to eat a little food from their packs before succumbing to sleep again. Eventually, when they were able to leave the stone-built cellar that had been their refuge, Tegan studied the sky and groaned.

'The sun's going down already. That means there's only a day or two left before the long dark. We'll have to hibernate here.' She had been hoping to spread the news about the re-emergence of the Circle of Truce before the island's winter sleep, but it was too late for that now.

'I may not have to sleep,' Terrel said. 'If I can stay awake, I'm going back to the glacier once you're settled.'

'In the dark?' Tegan queried, obviously horrified by this idea. 'On your own?'

'I have this,' Terrel said, holding up the red crystal which still glowed every time he touched it with his left hand. 'I won't have to worry about meeting any soldiers. And I still need to find the elemental.'

'And the Peacemaker?'

'No one's going to need that now, are they?'

'I suppose not, but didn't the voice say—'

'I heard it,' Terrel cut in. 'But this is a place of peace, not war.'

Three days later the sun failed to rise, and Tegan could not stay awake any longer.

'I'm never going to see you again, am I?' she said, her eyelids drooping.

'Maybe not,' he replied. 'That's one part of the future I haven't seen.'

'The legends were right. You brought a time of change.' Her eyes closed.

'Goodbye, Tegan. Good luck.' Terrel kissed her cheek gently, but she didn't seem to notice.

'Goodbye, Terrel,' she murmured.

Once he was satisfied that the magian was fully asleep, and as well protected as possible, Terrel hefted his pack and set out into the darkness. So far, it seemed that he was not affected by it as the islanders were. In fact he felt wide awake, refreshed by his long rest and eager now to resume his quest.

He made the most of any moonlight, and used the crystal only when he had to. Long before he reached the new boundary of the glacier, he was aware that he was being followed by a shifting number of wraiths, and he was reasonably certain that it was the stone's light that drew them to him. Although they did not interfere with his progress in any way, their presence made him nervous.

Climbing up on to the ice proved less hazardous this time, but once he was on that frozen plain, his self-imposed task seemed daunting. The Lonely Peaks were only shadows in the far distance, and even with spikes on his boots the footing was often treacherous. What was more, he dared not ever risk sleeping in case he was caught by the need to hibernate. If that happened, he would surely freeze to death. As it was, as long as he kept moving, he was comfortable enough. The crystal seemed to give off heat as well as light, warming him from the inside. He suspected that the stone had somehow rekindled the star he carried within him – and he hoped that this would lead to some form of communication with the elemental, as it had done in the past. He sometimes felt as if the Ancient was watching him as he crept ever closer to its lair, but he was never able to establish a direct link.

For all his efforts, the mountains never seemed to get any closer. By now he was light-headed from lack of sleep, and his provisions were about to run out. How close do I have to get? he wondered despairingly as he trudged on.

As far as he could judge from the passage of the moons and stars, four days passed in this manner. And then he began to hear voices. At first he thought it was a delusion, brought on by the darkness, the gnawing cold and his own exhaustion, but the sound persisted and he was eventually forced to admit that it was real. As he came closer, he recognized it as a man's voice, raised in song. The words sounded like gibberish to Terrel, but that was insignificant compared to the fact that someone else on Myvatan was still awake. Could it be another foreigner? And if so, what were they doing on the glacier?

Drawn by the need for answers, Terrel headed towards the source of the noise. When he found him, the man was sitting with his back to the healer, rocking to and fro as he sang the same phrase over and over again, varying the tune and his inflection each time.

'And *so* the comet sailed away. And so the comet sailed *away*. And so . . .'

The refrain halted as the singer became aware of Terrel's faltering approach. He turned round and looked at the healer with the red-rimmed, hollow eyes of a madman.

'And so the *comet* sailed away,' Jauron sang.

CHAPTER FIFTY-ONE

'Are you from the comet?' Jauron asked.

Terrel shook his head, not knowing how to respond to such a question – or how to react to the neomancer's presence.

'What are you doing out here?'

'I'm still awake,' Jauron stated proudly.

'I can see that. Don't you want to sleep?'

The neomancer's mouth worked, and he blinked several times, but instead of answering he pulled up the left sleeve of his jacket. For once the sky was clear and the White Moon was just past full, giving enough light for Terrel to see the puncture marks on Jauron's forearm. Several of the wounds were scabbed over but others were still fresh, with blood oozing out. It didn't take much imagination to work out how the neomancer had been keeping himself awake.

'I'm waiting for the comet,' Jauron said, pulling his sleeve down again and glancing up at the sky. 'Wrong one,' he added mysteriously. 'Not ready yet.'

Something had happened to the neomancer. His incoherent ramblings, and the fact that he showed no sign of recognizing Terrel, made that obvious. The healer's best guess was that the perils of becoming a fire-starter, combined with the traumatic events at Hvannadal, had unhinged his mind. Lack of sleep had probably completed

the process. The rather pathetic creature Terrel saw before
him now bore little relation to Jauron's former self. The
man Terrel had known previously had been confident to
the point of arrogance, and dangerously self-centred.

'It's here somewhere,' the madman said, waving his
arms about vaguely.

What is? Terrel wondered, then realized that he knew
the answer. But before he could say anything, Jauron gestured towards the large pack that lay beside him.

'Do you want some food? I have plenty.'

It was the first coherent thing he'd said so far, and the
offer was tempting, but Terrel still hesitated. He didn't
want to get involved with a lunatic, and yet his own supplies were running very low. Jauron waited, then smiled
suddenly.

'I could make a fire,' he said. 'If we had anything to
burn.'

'No,' Terrel said quickly, 'but I would like some food.'
He moved closer and sat on the blanket that was already
spread out on the ice.

Jauron watched as Terrel ate, but did not join him. Now
that he had stopped moving, the healer had begun to feel
the bitter cold sink into his body, but he was reluctant to
use the crystal to warm himself because he wasn't sure how
the neomancer would react to its light. In the end he slipped
his hand inside his pocket and held the stone there, hoping
that the thick material would conceal the glow. Jauron
sighed then, but gave no sign of noticing anything unusual.

A little while later, feeling better for both food and
warmth, Terrel became aware that there were wraiths hovering all around – keeping their distance so that they were
only on the edges of his vision, but filling the night with
a nervous watchfulness. Jauron seemed quite relaxed now,
and was clearly unaware of the phantoms' presence.

'I have to go. Thank you for the food.' Terrel got to his feet and shouldered his pack. Jauron got up too, hurriedly stuffed the blanket into his own pack, and looked at Terrel expectantly.

'Which way?' he asked.

'Are you sure you want to go with me?' Although the healer had anticipated this development, it was still unwelcome – complicating his already unpredictable situation.

Jauron nodded eagerly.

'The Red Moon will be here soon,' he said. The sly look in his eyes indicated that he thought he was being clever.

'I'm not—' Terrel began, then changed his mind. 'I'm going to the Lonely Peaks.' He set off without further ado, knowing that he could not stop the neomancer from following him, but hoping he'd either lose interest or fall behind. Jauron did neither, matching the steady pace that Terrel set and seeming quite content.

They walked in silence for the most part. Terrel was in no mood for conversation, and although Jauron glanced up at the sky occasionally and made a few remarks about comets and the moons, he didn't seem to expect any response. However, Terrel was aware of a growing sense of excitement in the neomancer, and when a faint red sheen covered the glacier, he understood why. The Red Moon had risen, and it was full.

After a while, as the moon rose higher into the sky, Jauron became agitated. Eventually he could contain himself no longer.

'Why don't you look?' he burst out.

Terrel ignored him.

'Why don't you look?' he repeated more loudly.

'What for?' the healer asked, feigning ignorance.

'The sword! The Red Moon is full now.' Jauron gestured at the sky.

'But none of the others are new,' Terrel replied. 'Isn't that what you need to find the sword?'

'Not for you. You came from the Whale. You have a piece of the comet. Use that.'

So he does recognize me after all, Terrel thought, realizing that Jauron might not be quite as mad as he seemed.

'The war is over,' he told him. 'No one wants the sword.'

'The Wizard does. She told me. If I bring it, I'll be her favourite.'

'No.'

'Yes I will!' Jauron shouted, stamping his foot like an angry child.

'Tofana's dead,' Terrel stated bluntly.

The neomancer screamed then, hurling imprecations at the healer and shaking his fists. Terrel did his best to ignore him, and simply trudged calmly on across the ice until eventually the tantrum subsided. A mass of thick cloud was now streaming in from the southwest, smothering the moon and turning the dark day almost black. Terrel was forced to move more slowly, but he refused to stop altogether. Some time later Jauron spoke again, and this time his voice had lost its aggressive tone and become an ingratiating whine.

'Use the stone. Why won't you use the stone?'

Terrel had been wondering about doing just that, and realizing that his unwelcome companion already knew about the crystal made the decision easier. Practical considerations overrode his instinctive reluctance and he took the stone from his pocket, bathing the surrounding area in light that mimicked the recently shrouded moon.

'Comet light,' Jauron said approvingly.

Moving ahead more easily now, Terrel once again noticed that there were wraiths nearby, matching his course. He remembered Elam's reaction to being told of the crystal, and the fact that he had seemed to be worried about it. Could it be that the stone somehow harmed the wraiths? Terrel had only begun to see them after he had made it glow for the first time, so it seemed possible that there was some connection, but he had no idea what it was.

He was still wondering about this when a gap in the clouds allowed the Red Moon to illuminate a small patch of ice ahead of them. As they moved towards it, the two sources of red light came together. But instead of coalescing, they seemed to be in conflict, producing a rippling pattern of intersecting curves which gradually resolved into a series of concentric circles, spreading out from a point like the ripples from a pebble thrown into water. Terrel was mesmerized by the spectacle – but then he was seized by a sudden dread. His immediate reaction was to put the crystal away, but it was already too late for that. Jauron was running ahead, tossing his pack aside as he headed for the centre of the circles.

By the time Terrel caught up with him the neomancer was on his knees, clawing at the glacier with his bare hands, although the healer could see nothing within the ice to warrant his efforts. And trying to dig in such a manner was the mark of a man who was truly insane.

'What are you doing?'

'It's here. It's in here. Down there.'

'There's nothing there. And even if there was you're never going to reach it.'

'It's here,' Jauron insisted. 'I have to.'

Terrel shrugged.

'You do what you like. I'm going on.'

The expression in the neomancer's eyes changed then, a new and evil cunning rising to the surface, and in the next

instant Terrel felt his skin crackle, his hair begin to stand
on end. He felt a burning sensation deep inside him as his
blood began to simmer. Belatedly, he cursed himself for
eating the other man's food. That had provided the link
the fire-starter needed. As Terrel instinctively resisted the
assault, he saw Jauron's ability to inflict pain and death on
others as a kind of sickness. And he knew how to deal with
sickness. But although he was able to halt the progress of
the destructive reaction inside his own body, to hold it in
abeyance, his adversary showed no sign of relenting, still
pressing home his attack.

'Stop this, Jauron,' Terrel gasped through the pain.

The neomancer did not reply. Far from stopping, his
efforts grew more feverish in their intensity, and Terrel
had to fight even harder. His heart felt as though it was
about to explode, and his skin was radiating heat into the
cold air, drenching him with sweat as waves of agony
washed through him. At last, realizing that he couldn't
continue like this for much longer, Terrel admitted to
himself what he had subconsciously known all along. The
only way to stop Jauron, to heal his sickness, was to turn
the magic back upon its creator – just as Yarek had done
with Tofana. The link worked in both directions.

'Last chance, Jauron,' Terrel grated. 'I don't want to
hurt you.'

But the madman paid him no attention and so, fighting
back his horror, Terrel turned the fire-starter's fury on
himself. Jauron's face registered momentary surprise
before he screamed. Fire burst from his chest, incinerat-
ing his clothing in an instant, and a moment later flames
poured from his mouth and eyes. Terrel's own torment
died at the same time as the neomancer. As Jauron fell
forward, his body continued to burn from within, the
intense heat making the ice crack and spit. Steam rose

along with foul-smelling smoke, and Terrel turned away
in disgust.

Appalled at what he had done, even in self-defence, he
staggered a few paces and then sank to the ice, holding his
head in his hands. I'm a healer, he told himself. Not a
murderer. The fact that he'd had no choice, that he would
have died if Jauron had not, didn't lessen his guilt or his
revulsion at the abuse of his gift.

'I'm a healer,' he said aloud, talking to the air. 'A
healer.' And I'm the only person awake on this entire
island, he added silently, suddenly overwhelmed by loneliness.

There was an eerie stillness all around him, as if the glacier was waiting for something. Still adjusting to the
after-effects of the fire, the ice cracked loudly, the only
sound now that the wind had died away. Terrel stood up
and forced himself to go and look at the body of the vanquished fire-starter. All that was left was a shallow pit
containing a thin pile of wet ashes. As always, it was hard
to believe that such pitiful remains had once been a human
being.

Fractures in the ice radiated out from the scene of the
blaze, and refracted in one of these Terrel saw a blur of
colour that looked out of place. As he peered more closely,
the image slowly resolved itself into a recognizable shape.
Jauron had not been completely insane after all. The
Peacemaker *was* there, still buried deep, but just visible.

Terrel told himself that the sword was irrelevant, that it
was a relic from a time of war that he hoped was over now,
and he was about to turn away and continue his journey
when the internal trembling warned him that an earthquake was on its way. On the glacier there was nowhere to
hide, so he just braced himself as best he could and waited.
He could see it coming towards him like a solid wave, the

surface of the ice buckling and throwing small chunks into the air as it passed. The vibration reached him through the soles of his boots well in advance of the main tremor, and as the rumbling grew ever louder, he knew he was in trouble. He was unlikely to escape such violence without injury – and in his situation, even a twisted ankle could prove fatal. He was just beginning to panic when he heard Alyssa's voice again. *Shape it! Change the pattern. You can shape it.* But he didn't have Tegan with him to guide his efforts this time – and the Dark Moon was as remote as ever. He tried to remember what he had done at Hvannadal, tried to recapture his understanding. It was there in places, fleeting glimpses of the truth, but there were too many shadows now. I'm a healer, he thought, but it was hopeless.

The earthquake struck.

When Terrel came to, he was lying on his back with one leg twisted under him. Every part of him seemed to ache, but when he gingerly tested his limbs, nothing seemed to be broken or sprained. He had survived. He had no idea whether his faltering efforts had achieved anything, or whether he had just been lucky, but he didn't really care. All that mattered now was that he could go on.

As he picked himself up, he saw that his immediate surroundings had been drastically altered by the quake, making his own escape even more remarkable. Jagged boulders of ice had been piled up in places, while crevasses had opened in others. There was no sign of Jauron's remains, and Terrel decided that the fire had probably weakened the structure of the glacier, making the disruption in that spot much more severe.

He was looking around for his pack when his eye was caught by something at the bottom of one of the newly opened cracks, and he knew at once what it was. What should I do? he thought. If I leave it here, someone else might find it. Now that the Peacemaker was at least partially exposed, anyone might stumble across it, even without the assistance of the Red Moon. In due course, the glacier would probably close over it again, but Terrel wasn't sure he could risk that. Jauron had hoped to use fire to reach it. Others might have different ideas, and the spot was marked now.

After deciding that rather than leave the sword where it was, he would take it himself, Terrel clambered down into the narrow crevasse. It was a tight squeeze, but he was determined, and forced himself on until his target was in reach. I can destroy it in a lava flow, he thought. Or hide it at the bottom of the ocean. But when he finally grasped the hilt of the Peacemaker, all such ideas vanished in an instant.

In that moment he felt the towering strength of a thousand men, and a righteous fury arose in him that scoured away all doubt. He was invincible. He wanted to march out against his enemies, to the glories of battle. He wanted to feed his ravenous hunger for blood. He wanted to kill.

A small voice of reason urged him to release his grip on the sword, but the pull of its spell was too powerful. His fingers tightened in place as he dragged the rest of the blade from the ice, and struggled back up to the surface of the glacier. He held the sword aloft in triumph, saluting the Red Moon – and then found himself at the centre of a swirling tornado that came from another world.

The wraiths had converged upon him, flocking around him in a silent, multi-coloured storm. There were hundreds, thousands of them – and they were no longer content to keep their distance. Terrel struck out at them with the sword, flailing wildly and pointlessly. He could not harm them, and the movement only seemed to agitate them even further. At length, driven wild by their unwanted attentions, Terrel had enough sense to realize that it was not him they were drawn to. It was the sword. He flung it to the ground and stepped back. Sure enough, the wraiths clustered round the blade, fighting to get close to it.

The healer was himself again, only half remembering the thoughts and desires that had ruled him while he held the sword, but appalled nonetheless. He knew now that he should never have touched the Peacemaker, never brought it out into the open.

The wraiths were still mobbing the sword, like a swarm of bees round a particularly fragrant flower, but as Terrel watched he noticed something extraordinary. Each one dipped towards it only once and then floated away, leaving the frenzy behind. The contrast between the nervous agitation of those who were still arriving and the calm, almost languid movement of those who had had their turn was marked.

Terrel sat down to watch, bewildered by the performance. He had no idea what their actions meant, but he couldn't look away. He was transfixed, his own problems forgotten, and so failed to see the gyrfalcon until it landed next to him on the ice. Startled, he looked at the newcomer, then saw the ring around one of its powerful talons and knew that he was no longer alone.

Alyssa! he exclaimed joyfully.

This isn't a game, she said, and something in her voice made him suddenly afraid.

I know that. Are you all right?

I will be when we're finished here, she replied.

But you're not at the moment? he queried anxiously.

This time Alyssa ignored his concern, turning predator's eyes to watch the wraiths.

Do you know what's going on? Terrel asked.

It's in the world again, she replied. *You have to take it with you.*

The sword? No. It's horrible—

It was, she cut in. *Not any more.*

With a final flurry, the last of the wraiths had touched the Peacemaker and were drifting away into the darkness. A sense of peace descended on the scene.

Go and take it, Alyssa said. *We have to get going.*

Terrel did as he was told, reluctantly wrapping his fingers around the hilt. He braced himself for the assault, which duly arrived – but it was different now. This time he saw the entire history of the war, the reality of it, from the pain of every wound to the grief of every widow and orphan. There was no glory in this picture of battle, no heroes, just the enormity of its evil and injustice. The images were so powerful and so numerous that he was completely overwhelmed. For a few moments – which felt to him like several hours – he was held captive, and when he was released Terrel felt his heart swell with sorrow, even as he began to understand what had happened.

With no mitra to repress them, all the memories, all the feelings of an unjust and pointless war had returned to mock the spirits of the dead soldiers, turning them into wraiths. The Great Plain was indeed a place of endless torment. But now the phantoms had found a use for the Peacemaker, infusing it with all their pain, their guilt and longings. In doing so they had not only eased their own tortured existence, but had changed the sword from the ultimate weapon of war to an instrument of peace. The irony was that now the blade really did deserve its name and reputation. The man who wielded such a sword would never be defeated in any battle, because no man who had touched it would ever go into battle again. Any man who had seen what Terrel had seen would look for another way to settle his differences with his enemies.

Terrel knew now what he had to do with the sword, but he had another duty to fulfil first. The gyrfalcon flew up into the air in readiness, and Terrel turned to look out over the red glacier before setting off towards the Lonely Peaks.

CHAPTER FIFTY-TWO

Terrel found that time seemed to be travelling even more slowly than he was. Although he had not yet been affected by the need to hibernate, he hadn't lost his fear of it completely, and for that reason he had allowed himself to doze for only a few minutes at a time, secure in the knowledge that Alyssa would wake him if necessary. In effect he had been awake for several days now, and the lack of sleep was making him desperately weak. He was dragging himself over the glacier by pure willpower, and mentally he felt dazed and almost delirious at times, close to the madness that had claimed Jauron. On top of that, the constant darkness was grimly depressing. Terrel longed for sunlight, to feel its warmth upon his face and to be able to see clearly once again. He felt trapped in a never-ending night, which seemed to close in upon him with every step he took.

The only reason he was still able to summon up the strength to go on was because Alyssa was with him. Without the continued presence of the gyrfalcon circling above him, he would almost certainly have given up. Whenever he faltered, she would fly down and chivvy him out of his stupor, renewing his resolve simply by being there. Yet even in their companionship there were moments of unease. Once again, Alyssa was less talkative than usual, and Terrel worried that she might be ill. She refused to discuss it, and this left Terrel to speculate – and worry – on his own. Thinking back, he realized that it had been the same when she'd been in the snow leopard, which meant that if she *was* ill, she could have been sick for some time. Terrel's healing instincts made him want to tend to her, but she wouldn't let him, and so there was nothing he could do about it.

At the beginning of their journey he had talked a good deal, telling her about everything that had happened to him recently. She had listened, apparently taking it all in, but had not really offered any comments of her own or answered any of his questions. She hadn't even seemed particularly interested in the Circle of Truce, and when Terrel expressed the opinion that at least now there was a chance of peace on Myvatan, and asked whether she thought it might have been one of the 'tests' that he'd been expected to pass every so often, her response had been evasive and noncommittal. When in turn he *had* coaxed her to talk to him, she'd had little to tell him, and what news there was did nothing to raise his spirits. She had confirmed that the ghosts wouldn't be able to join them – something Terrel had already guessed – because as they drew closer to the elemental the dangers to his allies became ever greater. There were gaps between the gusts of alien wind, but these were too erratic to be used safely, and if the ghosts were caught unawares, the consequences would be horrible.

The only other information she gave him concerned further unrest on Vadanis. The Emperor had apparently fallen ill with a mysterious fever – some said he had never fully recovered from an earlier brush with plague – and Jax was now ruler in all but name, to the dismay of most of the court. The Empress Adina was openly at odds with the prince, and loyalties were divided in the council of seers.

As always, hearing about his estranged family stirred mixed emotions in Terrel, but on this occasion such distant events seemed irrelevant, and he was able to view them without undue anxiety. The Floating Islands were a long way away, and it was the fate of Myvatan that concerned him now.

Terrel wanted to stop and rest. His pack had been replenished from Jauron's supplies, and because the sword was strapped to it too, it was much heavier than before. He allowed himself to set it down on the ice every few hours, but whenever he came to a halt, the thought of sleep became desperately tempting, and the unrelenting cold began to stiffen his limbs and make his thoughts even more sluggish. He knew this was another reason why he couldn't afford to go to sleep properly. Even if he did not fall into the hibernation, an ordinary night's rest could still prove fatal if his blood began to freeze as Kopak's had done. Terrel might simply fail to wake up – and even if he did, he would not be able to heal his own maladies.

He looked up, taking comfort from the sight of Alyssa's wings slicing through the gloom, then turned his gaze ahead once more. In front of him, still several long miles away, was the largest of all the Lonely Peaks. It had the same conical shape that Terrel had seen from the *Skua*, but this volcano was much bigger and much older than those newborn islands. From afar, the top of the mountain looked flat, but the healer knew that he was actually seeing the rim of a huge crater. Even in the subdued moonlight, it was possible to see smoke rising from the peak, and occasionally a dull red glow gave testament to the fires that were raging within its massive walls.

How close do I need to get? Terrel wondered, gazing at the forbidding scene. If this truly was the home of the elemental – and both he and Alyssa were certain that it was – communicating with it was going to be incredibly difficult. All three of his earlier meetings with the creatures had involved being taken *inside* them, but he didn't see how that could be possible here. The volcano would surely kill him even if the Ancient did not. How *was* he supposed to make contact? Could he do so from a distance? He knew that this might be possible during an eclipse, but there was no chance of that happening here. The sun wasn't even going to rise for the next two months.

There were times when Terrel felt some sort of fleeting connection through the star that he carried inside him. He was using the red crystal almost all the time now, both for light and warmth, and it seemed to react with the amulet sometimes, adding its radiance to the stone. The other elementals had been fascinated by his talisman, which he had carried with him all the way from Tindaya. They referred to it as 'the spiral', and it was one of the reasons he had eventually been able to win their trust. However, the contacts here were so brief and so uncertain that they were effectively useless. Terrel was about to ask Alyssa whether she had any ideas, hoping to draw her into conversation at least, when all action, all thought, became meaningless.

Even by the standards of Myvatan's interminable night, the darkness that enveloped the healer now was profound. The elemental had come to him.

Terrel had encountered various forms of insanity on many different occasions, but there had never been anything that even came close to the horror of the world he entered now. His previous meetings with the Ancients had all begun in an atmosphere of suspicion and doubt, even enmity, but had then changed over a period of time to gratitude and even to a type of friendship. With *this* entity there was no chance of any such conclusion. The creature was consumed by rage, boiling over with malice and a vindictiveness that went beyond all reason. Terrel's initial entreaties were swept aside with swift and brutal contempt, leaving him stunned and terrified, defenceless against the violent barrage of images that crashed down upon him.

He saw the Ancient rising towards the ice-bound surface of the planet, finding what it thought was a safe haven within the heart of a dormant volcano, only for its luck to run out when an eruption melted the glacier above it, inundating the entire area with meltwater, steam and silt mud. As the ghosts had surmised, it was this water that had driven the elemental mad, distorting its energy patterns to such an extent that Terrel knew he would never be able to heal them. To make matters worse, its futile attempts to protect itself had unwittingly provided the wizards of Myvatan with fresh sources of the magic that the Ancients abhorred – and their subsequent use of this power had confirmed and strengthened the elemental's hatred of mankind. Terrel was shown several atrocities from the war, simultaneously experiencing both human terror and the entity's revulsion.

The healer had no idea how long the bombardment went on, but it felt like a lifetime. And even when it ended he was granted no relief. All the earlier encounters had been, in essence, an exchange. The Ancients had tested him, probing him in ways that seemed almost gentle now. But this one had attacked him with its own history, and now, rather than seeking out the healer's truth, it was simply taking what it needed, ripping memories and knowledge from Terrel's mind. Images flickered briefly,

many of them going by too quickly for him to comprehend. But, with dizzying speed, he did glimpse water
gushing from the blowhole of a stone whale, the ghosts,
Dayak burning, Latira's room bathed in pink light, several
battles, Tegan cowering amidst the storm at Hvannadal,
the explosion in the ice-caves, and Jauron's eyes as they
burned. And then it was over and he was back in the
moonlight, standing with shaky legs on a frozen sea.

I didn't have the chance to do anything, Terrel said. *There
was no question of it even listening to me.*

You've still got to try again, Alyssa told him.

Terrel was sitting on the ice, leaning against his pack,
with the gyrfalcon standing in front of him. After his
recent experience he'd had no choice about resting – his
legs had no longer been capable of supporting him. He
wasn't sure he'd ever be able to walk again. The exhaustion he felt was both physical and mental, but it was the
utter hopelessness of his task that caused him the most
anguish, and Alyssa's insistence that he carry on took him
close to breaking point.

I can't heal that! he cried. *It's impossible.*

Maybe not, she conceded, *but there's something else you
have to do.*

What?

*I think the Ancient learnt more from the events at
Hvannadal than we realized.*

What do you mean?

*Yours may not have been the only mind it was interested in.
Tofana was there too, don't forget, and it's my guess it went
on learning from her afterwards.*

And in return it gave her access to some of its powers,
Terrel reasoned, nodding. *But she's dead now. That threat's
gone, at least.*

I'm not so sure. What if the elemental decides to do some fire-starting of his own?

You think it can? he asked in alarm.

I'm sure it can, she replied, *but I'm not sure it knows exactly how to go about it yet. Which is why it needs you.*

Me?

It could have killed you just now, Alyssa pointed out. *But it didn't. I think it's still learning.*

From me? But—

Tofana got the idea from you.

Yes, but I'm a healer, not a fire-starter.

They're the opposite sides of the same coin. I think the elemental knows that, and is going to combine its own power, Tofana's ideas, and your knowledge of the lines inside human beings to get rid of them.

That's terrible! Terrel exclaimed – and then remembered the 'message' he'd been sent while he was imprisoned in Nordura. *I saw myself burning*, he whispered. *I thought it was a threat, or a warning. But perhaps it was a sign of intent.*

Maybe it was a trial run, Alyssa suggested, *testing how you reacted, trying to learn your secrets before the real attack.*

I don't know what my secrets are!

Perhaps that's a good thing.

That's why I'm still here?

That's why I think it still needs you, Alyssa confirmed.

Belatedly, Terrel realized why the elemental had saved him and Tegan by reinforcing their failing shield as it protected them in the explosion above Akurvellir. It wasn't because it thought of them as allies, or from some intimation of friendship, but because it knew it wanted to *use* Terrel – as Tofana had tried to do – to build the chains that would allow all the people of Myvatan to burn. Alyssa's theory suddenly made a lot more sense.

So the threat hasn't gone away? he said, feeling sick now. *Myvatan might still become a giant funeral pyre.*

It's worse than that.

Terrel stared at the bird, wondering what could possibly be worse than the annihilation of an entire race.

The chains don't stop at the coast of Myvatan, Alyssa told him.

CHAPTER FIFTY-THREE

It took a little while for Terrel to absorb the significance of what Alyssa had said.

You can't mean . . . he began, then fell silent.

Think about it, she went on. *The oceans are made of water. And there are all sorts of other links if you know where to look. Through you, through me, even the ghosts. Everyone who ever came to Myvatan from another land. Jax has even taken fire-starting back to Vadanis. And then there's the elementals themselves. They're the greatest links of all. If the Ancient here gets its way, all of Nydus will be doomed. So you have to stop it.*

But how? The dismay Terrel felt at the realization that his homeland was under threat once more made it difficult for him to think straight. The sheer scale of the impending massacre was almost impossible to comprehend, and the fact that his own life was one of those under threat hardly registered at all.

There's a chance it might listen to you, Alyssa told him. *You may not be able to heal it completely, but your bargain with the others must surely count for something.*

Terrel knew she was right. No matter how reluctant he was to admit it, he had to go on – even though the enormity of the task ahead threatened to overwhelm him.

Good and evil, Terrel thought as he trudged on towards the volcano. How do you explain the difference between them to a creature who's insane? And how am I even supposed to get close enough to try.

It occurred to him then that one possibility might be to leave his body behind, as he had done when he'd become the double-headed man at Makranash. But there was no cliff here for him to jump off, and even if there had been, he was far from sure that this Ancient would save him. Besides, he'd been guided by an oracle then, and he'd had Alyssa and Vilheyuna to advise him. He had none of those things now. Alyssa had been silent since they'd resumed their journey, even though he'd tried to talk to her several times. For a moment he thought of trying to kill himself another way, trusting that Alyssa had been right – that the elemental still needed him, and so would prevent his death. Although the idea appalled and terrified him, how else was he supposed to separate his spirit from his physical form?

He was about to put the idea to Alyssa, hoping to coax her into responding, when a fluttering in the darkness above him made him look up. It was immediately obvious that there was something wrong with the gyrfalcon, and the sight of its uneven, laboured flight made Terrel's heart lurch.

Are you all right? he called.

It's beginning, she said, her voice made hoarse by pain. *Don't wait. You have to do it now.*

Do what? he asked, teetering on the edge of panic.

Their magic doesn't vanish just because they're asleep, she told him as the bird struggled to remain aloft. *We've been doing this all wrong. You can use the dark dreams.* A last convulsive effort from the gyrfalcon's broad wings only succeeded in slowing its descent a little. The bird crashed on to the ice, skidded, then came to rest, lying on its side.

'Alyssa!' Terrel screamed, running towards her.

You need to sleep, she murmured as he reached her. *I can't help you any more.*

Terrel knelt by the crumpled form and stretched out a hand. But before he could touch her the ring vanished, and the bird, fully revived, rose in alarm and flew away – shrieking its protest as it went. The healer watched its powerful flight with a heavy heart, distressed by this proof that it was Alyssa who had been suffering, not her host.

Truly alone now, he stood up and saw that long tendrils of white light were snaking out from the sides of the mountain. They moved liked tentacles, searching in wide sweeps, and he knew that he was their prey. *Don't wait.* He also knew that if they found him, he would be helpless to prevent the massacre. *We've been doing this all wrong.* But there was nowhere for him to hide, nowhere to run. It was just a matter of time. *You need to sleep.*

Terrel lay down on the ice and closed his eyes, wondering if he would ever open them again.

He knew in the next instant that he was no longer alone. There were dreams upon dreams upon dreams here, all separate strands of the same whole. At first it was overwhelming, and he could make no sense of anything, but he was gradually able to pick out individual threads within the gigantic tapestry, and to see which would be useful. But that, he knew, was for the future. Right now he had work to do.

He moved without effort into the heart of the volcano. All around him, molten rock bubbled and spat. The air was full of smoke and poisonous gases, and the heat and noise were terrifying. But none of these things touched him. They could do him no harm. He had entered the dragon's lair. Now all he had to do was face that fearsome beast.

The elemental's initial reaction to his presence was one of surprise, followed quickly by pleasure, then confusion. As the shifting darkness swallowed him, Terrel felt the Ancient testing this new, disembodied form of life, searching for the things it wanted. For his part, the healer simply waited, knowing that his own beliefs, his memories and knowledge, would be there when needed. He couldn't hide anything, and there was no point in trying. All he could hope to do was persuade the elemental that its intentions were wrong, based on false premises, and that his own convictions were genuine.

He sensed the frustration around him, and knew that even in spirit he was a healer first and foremost. The Ancient was looking for a way to use him to kill, for the opposite side of the coin – and it couldn't find it. Without his physical body there was nothing for the fire-starter's chains to latch on to, no starting point for the lines of death. Frustration grew into anger, and the demands upon Terrel's strength became more acute. His thoughts were shredded before he could assimilate them, his dream-vision blurred, and a great roaring thundered in his ears. And yet he held firm, knowing that this was now a battle of wills, not strength.

Abruptly, the dream shifted, and Terrel saw the crystal city so familiar to him from many previous nights. As he expected, it was smashed, almost unrecognizable, reflecting the madness he knew he could never heal. But he looked for a way to do something anyway, to make his point, and found an even greater opportunity. He recognized one of the formations within the broken structure. It bore the imprint of Tofana, of the knowledge she had bequeathed to the Ancient. His first instinct was to smash it, to destroy it as so much else had been destroyed, but he held back, unable even now to deliberately harm a patient. I am a healer. He concentrated, gradually restoring that small part of the city to the way it had been before, erasing the wizard's influence from the elemental's memory. He met no resistance – probably because his actions were so completely unexpected – but he knew there would be a reaction once his meddling had been discovered. When he'd finished he drew back, hoping that what he'd done was enough – and found himself in the midst of an inferno.

He was back inside the volcano, where great plumes of fire were being hurled into the sky. The Ancient had realized, too late, what Terrel had done, and because it had been robbed of its ability to destroy its tormentors, its fury had turned inwards. It was still irretrievably insane, but it had lost the skill of fire-starting – and with Tofana dead, there was no way it could ever learn it again. Terrel's knowledge, such as it was, was useless by itself, and the elemental knew it. All it had left now was revenge.

Terrel had thought that the barrage he'd endured during his first encounter had been bad enough, but this time it was a hundred times worse. Images of unbelievably gruesome violence were piled one on top of the other, so that he could not escape or even try to lessen their impact. Sickened and despairing, his mind reeled under the onslaught, as he wondered whether it would ever end. He knew that he was being shown humanity at its most depraved, the natural world at its most deranged. Everything here was corrupted, everything was vile. And just at the point when he was thinking that it couldn't possibly get any worse, the elemental sought to drag him down into the pit of madness with an image from his own personal nightmare.

Alyssa stood before him in her own form – something he'd been longing to see for more than eight years – but this was not the girl he remembered. This Alyssa was shrunken and wrinkled, drained of water and life, her sunken eyes like smouldering coals. As Terrel watched in horror, she crumpled even further, then burst into flames, screaming in agony. Within moments, the image of his love had been reduced to a mere pile of ash. Although he told himself that this was just an illusion, it still filled him with despair, and he couldn't help believing that some part of it must be true. He wondered if the elemental here could use its lunacy, its evil, to affect the real Alyssa back on Vadanis. Such thoughts were an invitation to madness, but there was no way he could avoid them, no way to forget what he had seen. It was the Ancients who protected Alyssa and the other sleepers in their seemingly defenceless state, and if that protection had not only been withdrawn, but turned to such terrible enmity, then the prospects for all of them were bleak.

Unexpectedly, Terrel found refuge in another dream-world. He didn't know who was responsible, but the islanders were with him again, allowing him to recover a little of his strength and composure. The elemental sensed their presence too, and hesitated, watchful now.

I am a healer, Terrel said, taking advantage of this brief respite. *I can help you.* Even as he spoke, he knew his own certainty of failure made the plea pointless. In spite of its deranged state, the Ancient could tell that he was lying. But now, instead of renewing its frenzied assault upon his mind, it turned back to the physical world. Robbed of its weapon of choice, it was reverting to another – one that it needed no help in understanding.

The mountain growled and shook.

Intolerable forces were building up within and below the volcano. Terrel knew that when the eruption finally came it would be vast, so violent that it might devastate all Myvatan and wipe out the entire population. Even if it didn't, it was certain to melt most, if not all, of the glacier. The water that produced would undoubtedly drive the elemental even deeper into insanity – and he dreaded to think what might happen then. He would not be there to see it, of course – his own body would be the first to be destroyed – but at that moment he was not thinking of himself. He couldn't bear the thought that now, when for the first time in centuries the island had a genuine chance for peace, all their efforts might have been in vain. Something had to be done to stop the elemental, and because it was clearly beyond reason, it would have to be done from the outside.

Their magic doesn't vanish just because they're asleep. You can use the dark dreams.

He felt them, waiting, uncertain. In a sleep so deep that no dreams would normally come to the surface, he was an interloper, his spiral light a focus of attention. They were all aware of him. All he had to do was tell them what was needed, shape their dark dreams to his own purpose.

The wizards stepped forward first, then the magians and neomancers, all working in unison for once. As the volcano exploded, spewing lava and deadly clouds into the air, the pyramid formed. It was flecked with all the colours of its creators – black and white, red and gold – so that it shimmered with the light of all the moons. The shield was in place only just in time. Still caught in the centre of the mountain's rage, Terrel saw a fountain of fire streak past him only to meet the impenetrable barrier above. Infernal forces rebounded upon themselves, destroying the volcano's massive walls and turning the entire area into a chaotic blizzard of flying rock, searing flame, and great surges of lava and smoke. But it could not escape, confined by the pyramid – which not only refused to let the fire out but also prevented any water from going in.

The dream ended for Terrel as he opened his eyes. He was back in his own body, on the open glacier again, but the pyramid was still there. He stared at it in awe, unable to believe that such primeval fury could have been contained by such a seemingly flimsy structure, or that he had been inside its walls. The eruption flared and shuddered, pulses of orange, red, grey and black swirling across the triangular surfaces, marking the patterns of the incredible turbulence within.

Terrel had no idea whether the volcano was now simply reacting to the forces that had been released, or whether the Ancient was driving the process on to even greater extremes of violence. But there was no sign of it stopping or even slowing down. Time passed, and Terrel remained hypnotized by the spectacle, wondering which side would yield first. He got his answer when cracks began to appear near the edges of the pyramid, and its sides began to bulge slightly towards the centre. It seemed that Myvatan's magic was not equal to the sustained rage of the elemental. It would surely not be long before the Ancient broke out of its prison and unleashed its fiery venom upon the world.

Terrel was at a loss, exhausted, knowing that he'd done all he could. The cracks spread out further, in jagged orange lines. The ice beneath his feet shook, as if in anticipation, and the healer was certain this was one tremor he would not be able to control. He found himself clasping the red crystal in his hand, willing the amulet into life. He didn't understand what he was doing; he had just acted on instinct. But then the air was filled with a vast, wordless rumbling that made the noise of the eruption seem feeble by comparison. It was a sound Terrel had heard before, at

Tindaya, when he had been no more than a boy. But on this occasion, as then, it shook him to the core, leaving him breathless and deafened. And now, as then, a second, less cavernous note was added to the roar, as if in response to the first. However, this time a third voice was added to the ear-splitting chord. And then a fourth.

Terrel had no idea what it meant until he saw the spiral light blazing from his clenched fist. Then he knew that he had called upon the greatest link of all. The other elementals had come in answer to his silent plea. And they had come not to save him, but to protect their sick brother.

The pyramid became stable once more, reinforced by power beyond imagining, and then the monstrous noise died away, and the amulet's glow faded. Inside the magical shield the eruption also declined rapidly, until it was as dark inside the pyramid as it was outside.

Terrel knew it was over at last. The eruption had been contained, the elemental had come to no further harm because no ice had melted, and even though he had not been able to heal its sickness, Terrel had ensured that it could not take its revenge on humanity by using Tofana's repulsive methods. The healer had not been able to renew his bargain with Myvatan's Ancient, but it seemed that it still held good with the others, and that would have to be enough. This stage of his quest was complete.

And then he remembered the gryfalcon's fall and Alyssa's tormented farewell, and all his relief turned to doubt and grief. Even without the grotesque vision he had been shown, he knew that she was seriously ill. It was possible that she was dying, or even dead, and if that was the case, there was no point in his going on. After all these years, Terrel's main reason for surviving, for fulfilling his quest, seemed to have gone. Utterly exhausted, and depressed beyond belief, he simply had no resolve left. *I can't help you any more.* His job was done. The Guardian would have to do without the Mentor's services from now on. It was over.

Terrel lay down where he was and did not even feel the deadly cold of the ice against his cheek. In the next moment he was alone in a dark and dreamless sleep.

He woke to see a dozen Amber Moons floating in the sky above him. He blinked, but they remained, each one a perfect glowing circle. Memories filtered back into his consciousness and he groaned, wondering if he had died and was in another world. He felt comfortable and warm, but if he was a ghost that might not mean very much.

He moved a little, encountering more resistance than he'd expected, and the Amber Moons shifted and jumped, some of them breaking apart and then reforming. There were even more of them now. Shaking his head as if to clear it, Terrel discovered that he was lying on something soft and pliable. Looking round, he could see nothing except a dark mist, which seemed to swirl in a peculiar manner as he moved. There was obviously something wrong with his eyes.

He stretched, trying to get up, only to find that he was surrounded by the same peculiar substance that he was lying on. It hemmed him in on both sides, and lay as a ceiling only a little way above him. Here and there it caught the light of the moons, so that it shone like transparent crystal.

Terrel began to struggle wildly, panic making him imagine that he was in some kind of bizarre grave, that he'd been buried alive – and his movements produced a most startling and terrifying effect. The ceiling and walls of his coffin began to move too, sliding in different directions as though they were alive.

A moment later the healer felt a draught of freezing air on his face, and his eyesight came back into focus. There was only one Amber Moon in the sky now, and he was still in his own world. Then the surface he was lying on began to move again and he sat up, thoroughly unnerved. What he saw then was almost beyond belief.

He was surrounded by ice-worms. Two of them had burrowed beneath him so that they were providing him with a living mattress, while others – those who had now glided away – had covered him like a blanket, leaving only enough space between them for him to breathe. When he'd first woken up, he had been looking at the sky *through* one of these creatures, and its crystalline form had broken the light of the moon into several different images. The most surprising thing was that, in spite of their icy appearance, the worms were not cold. Their outer skins gave off an appreciable amount of heat, and the flesh beneath, while being firmer and more elastic than human muscle, was still very much part of a living creature.

Terrel's first thought was that they had been taken over by sleepers again, in order to help him, but he realized almost immediately that this was not the case. The ice-worms were themselves, nothing more. Quite why they had chosen to protect him like this – to save his life – was a mystery.

Clambering off his living bed, Terrel saw that his pack and the sword were still there. He also saw that the mountain had been blasted out of existence. Only a blackened plateau remained, from which a little smoke was rising. The pyramid had gone. Perhaps it *wasn't* over yet.

It seemed that, whatever Alyssa's fate, his own road was not being allowed to come to an end. He had to go on, to be with her again, whether she was alive or dead. He had to know for sure. And in the meantime, he had other tasks to complete.

The ice-worms seemed to be in no hurry to leave him, and he sensed in their presence an unspoken question, an offer of further assistance should he need it. He shouldered his pack, then placed a tentative hand on the nearest creature. Sensing its eagerness, he threw a leg across its broad back, sitting astride it as if it were a horse.

The worms began to move even before he told them where he wanted to go.

EPILOGUE

In one of the last of her dark dreams, Tegan saw a man with strange eyes and a light in his left hand. He came and looked at her, gently kissed her forehead, and then vanished. She wanted to speak to him, to ask him who he was and what he was doing there, but then the dream moved on and she forgot all about him.

The flame-bright sword was taller than a dozen men. It shone like a beacon in the darkness, waiting to greet a new dawn.

When Tegan woke, the sword was still there. It towered over her, a beacon not just for her but for all the people of Myvatan. She stared in wonder, seeing that the burning image stemmed from a real sword, a blade of solid, burnished metal which was now embedded in the sacred rock, next to the rekindled flame. She knew then that they would have the 'show' that Jarvik had wanted, and even though she did not yet know how it would work, she understood that the Peacemaker would play a central role in the event. Unaware of the multitude of ghosts who waited all around the Circle of Truce, and of one of their number in particular, she wished that her friend and former comrade could have been there to see the drama unfold.

*

The generals came first, together with all their senior officers. Pingeyri was one of those Tegan recognized, but
there were others too, from all quarters of the island,
watching each other warily. The beacon had vanished by
then, its purpose achieved, and the real sword was lit only
by the newly-returned sunlight and by the flame that had
always burned at the heart of the Circle of Truce. All the
soldiers saw it, but none dared approach – until finally
Eskif strode forward and climbed up on to the rock. In one
hand he held a tag that had been given to him by Tegan,
the magian who was already been called the Priestess of
Akurvellir, and with the other he grasped the hilt of the
Peacemaker. Conflicting emotions ran across his face, but
he seemed moved rather than surprised by the experience.
The sword did not budge, and the brigadier stepped away
with tears in his eyes. As he did so, there was movement
in the great unseen gathering of wraiths that had clustered
around the amphitheatre. One of their number changed
shape a little, and then faded away beyond any sight.

One by one, all the soldiers approached the sword. Each
one tried to pull it from the stone, but it was immovable,
as if the blade had fused with the rock itself, and each one
of them returned, defeated – and a different man. As they
did so, more and more of the wraiths regained their human
form. They were still ghosts, but they were whole again,
and free to move on from the world. The Great Plain was
no longer their prison.

This process went on for several days, and the sun rose
higher and shone brighter with each passing day. Just as
the Tindaya Code had predicted, the Peacemaker was
speaking to the whole island. And when the procession
finally came to an end, everyone knew that Myvatan's
seemingly endless war truly was over.

*

The sword was not the only thing that affected the atmosphere of change. All over the island, most mitra plants had died during the winter, and those that had survived were soon dug up and destroyed, now that everyone had developed an inexplicable aversion to the herb.

It had also been discovered that the healing pools no longer worked, and so the magians were using their talents to find other methods of healing people. Some of the wizards had begun to devise ways of making people's lives better, rather than inventing new means of destruction. And, for the first time in three hundred and seventy years, a Great Conclave was convened.

Myrdal came last, after all the fuss was over and the peace confirmed. He came to Akurvellir, guided not by any beacon but by love. His reunion with Tegan was perhaps the most joyous moment among many inside the Circle of Truce, and everyone who witnessed their embrace understood that destiny had brought these two together – and that now nothing would keep them apart.

One of these onlookers was unseen by anyone else there. He was the last of the ghosts, and he had been waiting just for this moment. Jarvik smiled then, and turned away to begin his own journey.

The most notable absentee from the Circle of Truce during all these events was the one who had done most to bring them about. By the time Tegan and Myrdal were locked in each other's arms, and Jarvik was on his way to another world, Terrel had embarked upon a voyage of his own. His ship was already some days out of Port Akranes, on its way south. He had not waited to see the results of his efforts for one very good reason.

He was going home.

ICE MAGE

Julia Gray

The remote and wild land of Tiguafaya is on the edge of
chaos. The menacing volcanoes that dominate the landscape
grumble and threaten destruction. The repulsive fireworms,
the marauding pirates and the ancient dragons grow bolder
by the minute. The corrupt and ineffectual government
is paralysed and helpless in the face of all the dangers.

The country's only hope for survival lies with a group
of young rebels known as the Firebrands. Led by the
lovers, Andrin and Ico, and the half-mad musician, Vargo,
the Firebrands are desperately fighting back. Using the
once-revered but now lost arts of magic against the
overwhelming odds, they are all that stand between
Tiguafaya and total destruction.

Rich and exciting, powerful and engrossing, *Ice Mage* marks
the arrival of a thrilling new voice in fantasy adventure.

'All the ingredients of great fantasy . . . If you enjoy moments
of terror and moments of delight, with a handful of firecracker
surprises along the way, this is the book for you'
Maggie Furey

FIRE MUSIC

Julia Gray

In the Firelands, music is the ultimate magic.

The new government in Tiguafaya has finally brought
peace to a people long suppressed by its tyrannical rulers.
But it may not last, for now a much greater power threatens
the Firelands – the mighty Empire to the north, whose
Emperor will not tolerate the Tiguafayans' heretical belief in
magic. Attempts to resolve the dispute by diplomacy will all
count for nothing, however, if the fire and lava shaking
the ground cannot be controlled.

Passion, politics and magic collide in *Fire Music*,
the magnificent sequel to *Ice Mage*.

Orbit titles available by post:

☐ Ice Mage	Julia Gray	£6.99
☐ Fire Music	Julia Gray	£6.99
☐ Isle of The Dead	Julia Gray	£6.99
☐ The Dark Moon	Julia Gray	£6.99
☐ The Jasper Forest	Julia Gray	£6.99
☐ The Crystal Desert	Julia Gray	£6.99
☐ Transformation	Carol Berg	£6.99
☐ The One Kingdom	Sean Russell	£6.99
☐ A Cavern of Black Ice	J.V. Jones	£6.99

The prices shown above are correct at time of going to press. However, the publishers reserve the right to increase prices on covers from those previously advertised, without further notice.

orbit

ORBIT BOOKS
Cash Sales Department, P.O. Box 11, Falmouth, Cornwall, TR10 9EN
Tel: +44 (0) 1326 569777, Fax: +44 (0) 1326 569555
Email: books@barni.avel.co.uk

POST AND PACKING:
Payments can be made as follows: cheque, postal order (payable to Orbit Books) or by credit cards. Do not send cash or currency.

U.K. Orders under £10	£1.50
U.K. Orders over £10	**FREE OF CHARGE**
E.C. & Overseas	25% of order value

Name (BLOCK LETTERS) . . . .

Address . . . .

. . . .

Post/zip code: . . . .

☐ Please keep me in touch with future Orbit publications

☐ I enclose my remittance £ . . . .

☐ I wish to pay by Visa/Access/Mastercard/Eurocard

☐☐☐☐ ☐☐☐☐ ☐☐☐☐ ☐☐☐☐

Card Expiry Date ☐☐☐☐

A Spo

Roland was furious. That slut Maggie had turned him down the previous evening so she could hang out with the team. His team. She and Troy were far too interested in each other for his liking. They'd probably been screwing all night. And now his star player's performance was suffering. She was nothing but trouble: using him to get free tickets, manipulating people and interfering with players' training. She would have to go. 'You'll rue the day you turned me down, you little whore,' he muttered to himself.

A Sporting Chance

SUSIE RAYMOND

BLACK
lace

First published in 2000 by
Black Lace
Thames Wharf Studios,
Rainville Road, London W6 9HA

Reprinted 2000

Typeset by SetSystems Ltd, Saffron Walden, Essex
Printed and bound by Mackays of Chatham PLC

ISBN 0 352 33501 7

Chapter One

While Maggie was waiting for her friend to return she glanced around at the posters on the walls. One in particular caught her attention:

THE BRISTOL HUMMINGBIRDS
V THE FAIRWOOD TROJANS
6 MARCH FACE-OFF: 7.30 P.M.

She moved over to examine the poster more closely. It was going to be a crucial match. If the Trojans could just beat the 'Birds, they would be in with a real chance of going through to the finals. What she wouldn't give to see the game live! She glanced at the squad photograph and ran her eyes hungrily over Troy, the tall, dark-skinned ice-hockey player of her special fantasies.

It was a great picture of him: his raw sexuality was practically oozing out of the poster at her. She pictured him skimming effortlessly across the rink with the perspiration beading on his forehead and running down his chest. The image was so vivid that she could almost smell the masculine odour of his body radiating towards her. Ebony and ivory. Fire and ice. What a combination.

1

Involuntarily, Maggie rested her hand lightly on the poster with her fingers covering his hard, lean stomach. She was surprised and slightly shocked at the strength of her yearning to caress all that hot flesh and feel it pressed up against her.

'Maggie? What are you staring at?' The voice came from behind and made her jump. She removed her hand guiltily from the poster and spun round. Her friend was just coming out of the ladies room. 'Come on. If we don't get a move on we'll miss the start of the film.'

Thirty-two-year-old Janet Nichols tossed her head so that her shoulder-length blonde hair fanned out attractively around her pretty, heart-shaped face. She hurried across the cinema foyer to where Maggie was standing and peered curiously over her friend's shoulder.

'Oh. It's the Trojans. I might have guessed. Don't you get enough of them at work every day?' Jan rolled her eyes expressively and licked her lips. 'Will you just look at the size of Pele's shoulders!' She pointed to a blond-haired, blue-eyed giant with biceps like watermelons. 'Can't you just imagine that giving you a good-morning hug?'

Maggie couldn't help smiling. She and Jan had been friends ever since Jan had helped her to find her flat on behalf of the estate agents where she worked. When Maggie had started working as a receptionist at the Fairwood ice rink, the two of them had also become avid fans of the local ice-hockey heroes, the Trojans. Arguing over the players was a favourite pastime.

'I still prefer Troy,' Maggie maintained loyally, as she thoughtfully traced his outline with her fingertip. She wondered if she would ever get the chance to really know him.

Jan laughed. 'I bet they're the only reason you stay on at the ice rink,' she accused her friend. 'The pay's lousy and the hours suck, so it has to be them.' She squinted at the photo again and then removed her glasses to give them a quick wipe with her sleeve. 'Unless it's because of Justin? As a close friend of the management, I suppose you'll automatically get a ticket to the game?' she teased.

'I doubt it. A home game is one thing, but this match is down in Bristol.' Maggie hoped that Jan wasn't about to start trying to make something of her on–off relationship with the ice rink manager, Justin Edwards – again. It wasn't a subject she enjoyed discussing.

She thought about her friend's comment and wondered if she was right. She did enjoy working for Justin most of the time, and she liked the idea of being near the Trojans even if she never saw much of them. The truth was, it didn't really matter to Maggie where she worked. A job was just a job to her, a way to pay the bills. She certainly wasn't as career-minded as Jan. In fact, she couldn't understand why her friend put so much effort into her work or why she was so ambitious to get on; perhaps even open an estate agents of her own one day. Maybe, if Maggie had done better at school and gone on to college – like her friend – but she had been too impatient. At the time, a steady wage had seemed much more attractive than another three years of study. With plenty of work available, qualifications had seemed superfluous.

Jan was still staring intently at the poster. 'Well, I confess that I wouldn't mind going, but I can't see Marcus being very enthusiastic. You know what he thinks of my interest in the Trojans.'

'Didn't you say that Marcus was going to be away next weekend anyway?' Maggie reminded her. Jan's current live-in lover was in computer sales and often travelled away on business. At least, so he said. Privately, Maggie had her doubts. Jan could be a bit domineering at times and she suspected that sometimes Marcus just needed a break.

Jan nodded. 'You aren't actually thinking of buying tickets are you? Won't they all be sold out by now?'

Maggie shook her head. 'I don't know.' She ran her eyes over the Trojans again. 'I don't think I can afford it anyway. I'm flat broke at the moment. Besides, we'd have to stay the night somewhere, unless you fancy driving back after the match.' She shrugged. 'I guess we'll just have to make do with watching it on your TV.' Maggie couldn't afford satellite or cable. She glanced at her watch. 'Come on. The film's about to start.'

The following morning Sara Williams arrived at the ice rink to start her next shift in the café and stopped by the front desk to examine the large poster. The rink was justifiably proud of their home team's success and never missed an opportunity to promote the star attraction. She was still staring when Claire, who worked part-time as a cleaner, also arrived. Claire stopped and peered over Sara's shoulder.

'I wish I could go and watch,' she commented somewhat wistfully. 'It should be one hell of a game.' Sara turned and smiled at Claire's long, honey-blonde hair and lithe dancer's figure. Even though she was a good ten years younger than Sara or Maggie, the three of them were firm friends and united in their support of the local team. Mind you, it had to be said that they had never had the chance to be quite as supportive as they would have liked! In fact, since the Trojans usually trained early in the morning, before most of the staff arrived, or late at night, after everyone had left, they didn't even get much opportunity to see them other than at a game.

'It's bound to be live on Sky,' she consoled the younger woman.

Claire snorted rudely. 'It's not the same.' She stared intently at the poster and then heaved a theatrical sigh. 'I'd do anything for an evening out with any one of them,' she continued dramatically. 'Especially Pary. He could do whatever he wanted with me.'

Sara's grin broadened. Knowing Claire, she would

probably die of fright if any of the Trojans so much as looked at her. She was terribly shy with the opposite sex. Perhaps it was because she was so young? Sara examined the photo again and began to wonder just what it would be like to actually meet her heroes in the flesh. Every one of them had a body to die for. If their stamina under the sheets was anything like their stamina on the ice . . . Her cheeks began to glow. Truth to tell, Claire probably wasn't the only one who would turn into a quivering wreck in their presence!

She focused her gaze on her personal favourite. As part of their image they all had silly Trojan-sounding names. The one who was known as Ean, short for Aeneas, sort of reminded her of Mark, an old boyfriend. They shared the same dark-brown hair and almost black eyes. Mark's body had never been quite that perfect, of course.

Claire glanced round at the clock and sighed even more dramatically. 'Shit. I'll have to go and get started or Justin will flay me alive. He hates it if the locker rooms aren't swept out before the public arrives.'

Sara smiled indulgently after her friend's retreating figure before returning her gaze to the poster. What would Mark be like now, she wondered.

'It should be a terrific match.' A man's voice just behind her took Sara by surprise. She turned round quickly.

Justin Edwards, the rink manager, was immaculately dressed, as always, in a dark suit and crisp white shirt. His longish blond hair was tied back in a ponytail and his pale-blue eyes seemed to sparkle with mischief as he casually appraised her trim figure.

'Are you going?' he questioned, with a nod at the poster.

Sara flushed under his gaze and unconsciously fingered her short silvery-blonde hair. She knew Justin's reputation only too well. She was flattered by his interest

5

but didn't take it all that seriously. Everyone knew about him and Maggie, although that didn't stop his eyes from roaming when given half a chance. Or his hands.

She shook her head. 'I try to get to all the home matches,' she explained softly, 'but, I haven't got the time or the money to go to the away fixtures.' Sara backed away and walked off quickly. The early morning staff would be in for their breakfast soon and she was already running late. Besides, being Saturday, the rink would be packed with kids later, all starving and with money to burn. As usual, she and her fellow workers would be flat-out serving burgers, fries and hotdogs. Sara took her responsibilities very seriously. She might be only an agency canteen assistant, but that didn't mean she could afford to be slipshod.

Maggie finished her own shift on the reception desk just after midday. It had been a particularly hectic morning and she was feeling exhausted. Shortly after they had opened, a little girl had fallen on the ice and sprained her ankle. It hadn't been a particularly serious injury, but it was rink policy to play it safe, so the child had had to be taken to the local A&E for an X-ray. The girl had been terrified so, when her parents could not be contacted, Maggie had volunteered to go with her and see her safely home afterwards. Although he was irritated by the inconvenience, Justin had been forced to see the sense of this.

Once she had got over her shock, the child had proved to be an endearing little thing, shyly admitting her secret ambitions to be a professional skater. ''Cos, it's only a dream. I'll never be half good enough.'

'Nonsense,' Maggie told her. 'If that's what you really want then you can do it.'

'Do you really think so?' asked the child and her tear-stained eyes had shone with excitement.

'Of course,' Maggie insisted. When she had been about the same age, she had dreamed of becoming a doctor, but everyone had laughed at her. Perhaps, if someone had encouraged her and given her confidence in herself . . . 'You can do anything you put your mind to,' she declared firmly. 'And don't ever let anyone tell you differently.'

By the time Maggie had returned from A&E, her shift was almost over and it was hardly worthwhile relieving her replacement. After picking up her coat from the staff room, she walked back through to the main entrance and gave the Trojans' photo another long, lingering look. If only. As she was turning to leave, Justin came through the door from the rink. His eyes brightened when he spotted her.

'Maggie. I was hoping to catch you before you left. Is the kid OK?'

Maggie nodded. 'Fine. Just a simple sprain. I drove her home and made sure everything was OK with her mum.'

'Good. Thanks. Look, I'm finishing here early tonight. Do you fancy a meal at the Cellar?' The Cellar was the restaurant-cum-nightclub attached to the flashiest hotel in Fairwood. It was so popular that it was almost impossible to get in without a reservation – unless, of course, you had influence.

'We could go back to my place afterwards,' he added meaningfully.

Maggie hesitated. She just couldn't make her mind up about Justin. He was great fun to be with and he could be so sweet and attentive, when it suited him. He could also be totally faithless and unreliable. Their last row had been about him standing her up, supposedly for a business client.

It wasn't that Maggie minded him dating around. She wasn't looking for a permanent relationship with him or anyone else. It was just the way he went about it. In her books, there was nothing more insulting than being stood up; it was as if she were nothing more than some kind of reserve option.

'Oh, I don't know, Justin. The Cellar can be so loud and crowded. I'm not sure I'm in the mood.' Besides, she had already half-promised Sara that she would go with her to an exhibition of local artists' work at the town hall. Sara was a bit of an amateur artist herself and was always talking one or the other of them into visiting galleries or attending evening classes. Unfortunately, she was the only one of the four with any real talent. Maggie's recent attempts at pottery had left a lot to be desired. She had managed to get more clay in her hair than on the pottery wheel.

Maggie stared back up at the Trojans' poster. She wouldn't say no to a night at the Cellar with one of them – or going back to one of their places afterwards! She felt a rush of warmth to her loins. An evening with Justin certainly held more potential than traipsing round the town hall. Jan had agreed to go with them anyway, so she wouldn't really be letting Sara down.

Justin moved up closer behind her. 'I don't understand why you women spend all your time drooling over those boneheads,' he commented dryly. 'Don't be fooled by all the padding. They haven't got anything I haven't got.'

Maggie grinned.

'I suppose you've already bought your ticket?' Justin continued.

Maggie shook her head. 'I'm broke,' she explained ruefully. 'It must be something to do with the terrible wages you pay me.'

Justin's face took on a crafty look. 'If you really want to go, I might be able to rustle you up a couple of tickets.' He put his hands on her shoulders. 'If you play your cards right.'

Maggie stared at him in surprise. Was he offering to get her some tickets if she went out with him tonight? How could she possibly refuse an offer like that? Besides, after her thoughts about the Trojans, she was more than

8

ready for whatever else Justin had in mind back at his flat.

'I can't afford a hotel, either,' she explained cautiously.

Justin's hands slipped down her body and cupped her breasts. 'I think I could sort that too, if you want,' he whispered, as he started to kiss her neck before moving up to nibble her earlobe. His fingers began to tease her already enlarged nipples through her bra. Maggie shivered with pleasure, but said nothing.

Justin snorted contemptuously at her silence. He pushed her body round and pulled her hard against him. 'Well? Do you want to go or not?' he demanded.

Maggie wasn't entirely sure if his question referred to going out with him or going to see the Trojans. Or, were they one and the same? 'Are you saying that if I want some tickets, all I have to do is go to dinner with you?' she challenged him.

Justin nodded. 'And then back to my flat.' He ran his hands down her back and squeezed her buttocks possessively. 'And stay the night,' he added softly.

Maggie hesitated. He was always asking her to stay the night with him. So far, she had always resisted.

'We could discuss it better in my office,' he suggested as his left hand slid down inside the waistband of her skirt. Maggie gritted her teeth as she felt his fingers gliding over the thin material of her panties. He pulled her even harder against him so that his erection was pressed urgently into her flat stomach. She felt her own breathing quicken in response.

'Let me get this straight. If I let you have your wicked way with me, you'll get me the tickets and fix me up with some accommodation?' she teased him. Maggie's blouse was completely untucked now and she could feel his hand creeping back up her body, his fingers drawing intricate and tantalising patterns on her sensitive skin. She melted against him and savoured the little tremors of passion already rushing through her. She felt his other hand leave her buttocks and begin a slow and exciting journey around her hip towards her already damp and swollen sex. She shuddered with delight.

'If you come to my office with me, we can talk about dinner and about you spending the night with me at my flat. Then, we'll see.' Justin pulled his hands free of her clothing, twisted her round and started to guide her towards the door to the manager's office on the far side of the corridor. Without removing his hands from her waist, he kicked the door open with one foot and steered her inside. He let her go while he pushed the door closed behind them and Maggie heard the gentle click of the lock.

'I'll need two tickets,' she pushed him. 'One for me and one for my friend, Jan.'

'I'm sure that could be arranged –' Justin grabbed her from behind and pushed his hand back inside her waist-band '– if you please me.' His other hand glided down her leg and his fingers started to gather up the hem of her skirt. Maggie glanced across the room and saw herself clearly reflected in the glass front of a trophy cabinet. She thrilled at the sight of his hand revealing first her stocking top and then the lace of her panties. She trembled as his fingers slowly disappeared inside them, and her breathing again quickened as he began to caress her neatly-trimmed mound.

'Twice,' he added hungrily.

'Oh please Mr Edwards, sir, do I have to?' Maggie put on her innocent-virgin act. She enjoyed playing roles and Justin was always quick to catch on to her games and play his own part superbly. It was one of the things she most liked about him.

'Yes, my girl. You do. If you want those tickets, you will have to do whatever I tell you.' His finger pushed down between her sex lips and unerringly sought out her hardened bud. The palm of his hand began to squeeze her mound rhythmically. 'Everything I tell you to,' he added softly.

Maggie took a deep breath. 'What do I have to do?' she whispered, hoping that he would be explicit. It always drove her wild when a man told her exactly what he was going to do to her.

'First, I'm going to finger you until your juices run down your legs, then you're going to strip naked for me.' His finger started to probe deeper into her and Maggie could feel his pelvis thrusting into her buttocks. She shivered again and closed her eyes.

'You are going to pose for me in every position I can think of, so I get to see you in all your naked glory.' She could hear his breathing getting heavier as his own imagination ran away with him. His hands squeezed her even harder and another tremor of longing shot through her.

'Then, you'll have to touch yourself while I watch you.' He tweaked one of her nipples painfully. 'I might even have to spank you for being such a naughty girl.' He pinched her nipple again and grinned as she cried out. 'Or, maybe I'll hand you around to all my friends? Better still, maybe I'll invite them all to come round and watch you play with yourself? After you've stripped off for them, maybe I'll hire a girl so that the two of you can entertain us?' He was really getting into his fantasy now. Maggie felt herself becoming ever wetter.

'How would you like to sit on their laps and rub yourself on their hard pricks until they lose it inside their pants? Oh yes, you'd enjoy that, wouldn't you?' he emphasised the question by squeezing her mound even harder with the palm of his hand.

Maggie pretended he was talking about the Trojans. 'Yes,' she gasped, helplessly. 'Yes, I'll do whatever you want.'

'Perhaps I'll sell your body to them. Then you'd have to do whatever they wanted, wouldn't you?' His breathing was almost as ragged as her own now, and his cock was as rigid as an iron bar against her buttocks.

'First, you're going to kneel in front of me, with your knees apart, and unzip me,' he continued hoarsely as he gave her mound another hard squeeze. 'You're going to drop my trousers and pants and take hold of my cock.' He emphasised each word carefully. 'You're going to take me in your mouth and suck me dry.'

Maggie half-opened her eyes and again looked at the reflection in the glass. 'No. Please sir, don't make me suck your cock,' she pleaded softly.

'Worse than that, Maggie. You are going to put your hand between your legs and finger yourself. Right in front of me so that I can watch you.' He pushed his finger deeper into her. 'I don't want any faking, Maggie. I want to see you climax.'

His voice was becoming more and more strained as his arousal deepened. Maggie felt him tug her panties down to her knees and pull her skirt up. As he guided her back against him, she discovered that he had also unzipped himself. She couldn't contain the soft moan as she felt his burning cock nestling between the cheeks of her buttocks. What if somebody came looking for him? Well, it was a bit late to worry about it now; she doubted if she could stop him even if she wanted to.

'Oh yes,' she whispered, as he began moving up and down against her. She tightened her muscles around his hardness and stared at the reflection as he tugged her skirt even higher, exposing her mound. She glanced up and saw him watching her watching them both. His face was flushed with excitement and the memory of his words made her clit tingle even more urgently.

Justin pushed her forward and thrust harder against her. 'When I'm finished with you, I'm going to pass you around to all my friends,' he breathed softly. 'Women as well as men. You'll have to please them all.'

'Oh please, no,' she whispered. 'Not women, too.'

Maggie felt his movements grow more urgent at the sound of her pleading, and her own breath caught in her throat. 'I'll do anything you want if you just promise not to give me to your female friends,' she begged.

'You're already doing what I want,' he whispered. 'Maybe I'll make a video of you screwing my friends. Would you like that? A film of you going down on another woman?'

'No. Yes.' Maggie felt faint as she gave in to the images he was conjuring up in her mind. She imagined a room full of men and woman all running their hands over her naked body at the same time, while Justin watched and wanked himself. Her legs trembled and she felt another trickle of lubrication run down her thighs.

'You'll let me watch you licking another woman. Yes?'

'Yes.' She would too. She knew she would. What she really wanted was to be made to do it, so that she had no choice. It was one of her darkest fantasies to be virtually raped by a whole group of men and women.

Justin groaned helplessly as the first burst of his climax splattered across her lower back. Maggie felt him spurt again then again, directing his flow over her buttocks and thighs. She could hear his laboured breathing and see the wild look in his eyes as she stared round at him. She pushed her mound hard on to his hand and let her own pleasure engulf her.

Spent, Justin pulled her limp body up and pushed her over the chair. She felt his hands smearing his spunk all over her buttocks and thighs. She lifted her skirt higher to make it easier for him.

'It is supposed to be good for the skin, isn't it?' He smiled cheekily at her as he stood up and began to tug his clothes back on.

Maggie started to get up. 'I think I need a shower.'

'I'll see you tonight then. About eight o'clock?' Justin started towards the door, then stopped and turned his head to whisper in her ear. 'You can keep yourself hot and juicy for me,' he commanded softly, 'but you're not to climax until I say you can.'

Later, as she brushed her short brown hair and pondered over what to wear, Maggie contemplated how much she had enjoyed earning her tickets. The whole concept of virtually selling herself like that thrilled her. Maybe she could acquire a couple more tickets this evening. She knew that Claire and Sara would both love to go to the match too.

Maggie threw the dress she was holding to one side and picked up another one. It was short and tight fitting with a slit up one side and a low V-neck. The soft, silvery-grey material matched her eyes perfectly and gave her skin a warm, healthy glow. She remembered how Justin's eyes had bulged the last time that she had worn it.

Maggie slipped the dress over her head and pushed her feet into matching silver sandals. As she gave her face a final quick scrutiny in the mirror, the doorbell buzzed. One thing you could say for Justin: he was always punctual. Unless, of course, he failed to show at all. Remembering his unforgivable sin of standing her up, Maggie resolved to give him a hard time that evening. Given the way she was feeling, she decided, that shouldn't be too difficult. Smirking to herself, she picked up her jacket and bag and hurried to the front door.

'Ready?' Justin eyed her up and down and whistled softly. 'Very nice.'

Maggie smiled and gave him a swift kiss on the cheek. She caught a whiff of his expensive aftershave. 'You don't look so bad yourself,' she told him generously. It was true. Justin might not be a Trojan but his body was in pretty good shape and his silk shirt and well-tailored trousers fitted him like a second skin.

She savoured her memories of what he had done and said to her in the office and wondered what he had in

14

store for her later. Would he dare keep any of his threats? If so, would she go through with it? She'd never been with another woman before. Well, not properly, only the sort of adolescent playing around most young girls experimented with at some stage. Still, she knew that a lot of men fantasised about it. Now that she thought about it, it was perfect for her. She'd always been a natural tease and, although men thought they controlled her, it was usually they who ended up desperate and panting for it by the time she was done. This, of course, was just the way she wanted it.

'Is that all I get?' he complained. 'A peck on the cheek?' Justin put his arms around her and pulled her closer to him. He put his lips against hers and forced them apart with his tongue.

Maggie snuggled tightly against him, savouring the moment. She put her hands behind his head and ran her fingers along his ponytail. She loved long hair on men. It was so sensual. Her pelvis was hard against his groin and she could feel the outline of his cock through the tight material of his trousers. She closed her eyes and conjured up an image of the dark Trojan who was never far from her mind. She hadn't forgotten Jan's words and the thought of pushing herself against Troy's huge prick caused a sudden rush of moisture between her thighs.

With a soft moan, Maggie plunged her tongue deep inside Justin's mouth. She wriggled her hips, pushing herself eagerly against him. Justin's body stiffened slightly and she felt his penis twitch against her as he started to respond. His hand slipped down to the small of her back, pulling her body even harder on to him and she felt her breasts flattening against his broad chest. She marvelled at the sheer strength of his arms.

'You're a bit overdressed for what I've got in mind,' he told her, as he pulled his lips from hers and started to nuzzle her neck in a way that was guaranteed to drive her insane. Her legs started to tremble and a flame of lust ignited like a pilot light in the pit of her stomach. She could see the longing in his eyes and hear his breath rasping as he struggled to keep himself under control.

'Take your knickers off,' he ordered her, as he released her body and stepped back to watch.

Maggie put a look of fear and disdain on her face. Slowly, as if reluctant to comply, she pulled her hem up to her waist and spun round on her heels. She leant forward and slipped her fingers through the elastic. Gradually, she slid her panties down over the bulge of her buttocks, taking care to ensure that the hem of her skirt remained well up out of the way. She straightened slowly, sliding her fingers round over her hips and on round towards her mound as she turned back towards him.

Justin was watching her avidly, his face frozen and his eyes unblinking. As she grasped the elastic at the front and began to roll the material down over her crotch, she heard his urgent sigh.

'Now your bra,' he demanded hoarsely.

Maggie stepped out of her panties and tugged the shoulders of her dress down. As she undid her bra, her breasts dropped free and Justin bent his head forward and nipped her right nipple with his front teeth. Immediately, she felt both nipples harden. Maggie had big nipples and she knew from experience that they would not go down again for ages now. What's more, Justin knew it too.

Grinning, Justin nibbled her other nipple and then pulled her tight against him again and started squeezing her buttocks. She could feel his cock straining against his clothing. If she didn't stop him soon, it would be too late. Teasingly, she pushed him away. She didn't want things to go too far, just yet. She wanted to tease him until he was horny and desperate. They had the whole evening in front of them. She certainly didn't want him sated so soon.

16

'Come on,' she whispered. 'I'm starving. I haven't eaten anything since breakfast.' Her voice sounded shaky, even to her own ears. She realised that she was more turned on than she had been for a long time. She loved this game, loved it when a man lusted after her like this. She watched his face as he tried to cover his disappointment. His breathing was fast and erratic and she examined the longing in his eyes anxiously, wondering if she had already gone too far. She heard him swallow as he regained his self-control.

'OK then. Let's get going before you get me too excited.' Justin tugged at the crotch of his trousers to loosen them and Maggie felt another erotic thrill at the thought of what was causing his discomfort.

Outside, Justin helped her into the passenger seat of his almost-new MGF, and Maggie savoured the way his eyes darted up her skirt as she swung her legs in, and sank back on the soft leather.

For once, he drove slowly, only lifting his hand from her thigh to change gear. Maggie could see that his trousers were still too tight across the groin area: a situation she did her best to encourage by placing her hand in his lap and gently tracing the outline of his zip with one fingertip. By the time they reached the club, they were both flushed and breathless and she could feel her heart thumping erratically in her chest.

Justin parked the car in one of the very few remaining slots and moved slowly round to open her door. Maggie noticed that he was having trouble walking and that he had to stop to adjust his trousers again. This vivid reminder of his physical arousal made her squeeze her own thighs together tightly. She took her time climbing out, deliberately smoothing her skirt over her thighs to remind him that she wasn't wearing any underclothes.

As they headed for the door, Maggie could see Justin glancing repeatedly at her still-swollen nipples poking proudly through the thin material of her dress. She shivered with a mixture of excitement and cold as the raw February wind cut through her clothing and chilled the dampness between her legs.

As they passed a convenient clump of spindly bushes, he grabbed her arm and tugged her into the scant seclusion provided. His tongue found her mouth again and his hands were soon all over her naked thighs and buttocks. She could sense an unaccustomed intensity to his caresses that made her weak with longing as she eagerly curled her tongue around his. It was only when she heard the sound of his zip opening that she found enough will-power to push him away.

'Behave yourself,' she whispered shakily, as much to herself as to him.

When they pushed through the Cellar door the heat hit them like a wall. As they stumbled down the narrow stairwell, blinking in the subdued lighting, Justin gripped her tightly round the waist with his fingertips teasing one of her nipples. Maggie clamped her thighs together, as tightly as she could, and hoped no one would look up her skirt as they descended the stairs.

Although it was still quite early, they soon discovered that the popular club was already packed and humming. Justin forced a path through the swaying bodies on the dance floor as he led her over to the tiny 'reserved' table in the far corner. A perspiring waiter appeared almost immediately, and he and Justin exchanged a few friendly words before Justin ordered two glasses of white wine.

Maggie was acutely aware of the way the waiter was staring at her, almost as if he could see her nakedness under her dress. She wondered if Justin had said any-thing about her to him. They obviously knew each other. The neckline of her dress was low enough to give him a good view and she made a conscious effort to stop herself from crossing her arms to cover up. He must have been able to see her nipples. She examined his crotch surreptitiously, wondering how he would react if she let her hem slip up any higher over her naked thighs.

As the waiter left, Justin sat back and opened the menu.

'What do you fancy to eat?' he asked. 'Maggie? Wake up!'

'What?' The sound of her name pulled her back from her fantasies. 'Sorry. I was miles away. What did you say?'

'Food. You said you were starving. What do you want to eat?'

Maggie realised that the waiter had already returned with their wine and was hovering over them expectantly, his eyes everywhere. Her stomach was doing little flips as the after-effects of her arousal still coursed through her veins. 'Eh, um.' She glanced down at the menu and remembered the blue-black sheen of Troy's skin. 'Stuffed aubergine with cheese sauce.'

Justin raised one eyebrow, then looked up at the waiter. 'And I'll have a steak and salad. Rare, with lots of mushrooms.'

While they waited for the food, they sipped their wine and chatted about work. Justin, who was a dynamic and ambitious manager, had recently introduced a new quality management programme at the rink. He was anxious to discuss ways in which he could encourage the casual staff to get more actively involved.

Maggie tried to show some enthusiasm, but her heart was not really in it. Although she could appreciate what he was trying to achieve, it was harder to imagine how casual part-timers like herself and Claire could be motivated to give the same dedication to their work as Justin did to his. Jan would appreciate his point of view, but then Jan was as ambitious, maybe more so, as Justin was.

Besides, Justin wasn't exactly making it easy for her to concentrate. Her mind was far too engrossed in the feel of his hand – which had somehow contrived to find its way on to her thigh under the table – to worry about anything else. She marvelled at the casual way in which he managed to carry out a perfectly normal conversation while his fingers crept relentlessly up her leg. By the time the food arrived, she found that she was no longer hungry – at least, not for food. She pushed her fork around her plate, absent-mindedly tracing suggestive patterns in the thick white sauce. The purple-black skin of the aubergine seemed to taunt her.

'I didn't think that was really your sort of thing,' Justin said and nodded towards her plate. 'Do you want to try something else?'

'No. This is fine, honestly. I guess I'm just not as hungry as I thought.' She gave up on the meal and pushed the plate away from her.

Justin finished polishing off his steak and took a swig of wine. He stood up. 'Well then, since you won't want a sweet, how about a dance?'

'Why not?' Maggie greeted the idea enthusiastically. She was still feeling keyed-up and restless. Dancing would be a great way to burn off some of her excess energy. She stood up slowly, carefully rearranging her dress, and took his outstretched hand.

The dance floor was now so crowded that it was virtually impossible to do anything more than stand in one spot and sway in time to the music. Justin pulled her against him and slipped his hands down on to her buttocks. Maggie sensed that he was keen to recreate the thrill of their earlier embrace. That was just fine with her.

She hugged him tight, her own passion quickly mounting at the feel of his cock pressed into her stomach. Her head was reeling with the effects of the wine, the heavy atmosphere and the unsettling images in her mind. She was practically willing him to lift her hem and expose her nakedness to everyone. Excitedly, she thrust her crotch harder against his, grinding her hips against him in an effort to provoke him still further. She felt an uncharacteristic urge to behave both impulsively and dangerously.

Before she could stop herself, Maggie slipped her hands between their bodies and took hold of the catch at the waistband of his trousers. She eased it open and started to slide the zip down.

Justin tensed and pulled her tighter against himself, trying to trap her hand. 'What are you doing?' he whispered anxiously.

'I'm sorry? Is something wrong?' she questioned innocently as she finished undoing the zip and pushed her fingers inside the opening. 'Don't stop dancing.'

'Jesus, Maggie!' Justin jumped violently as her hand slipped down the top of his pants and closed around his expanding penis. He lost his balance and they stumbled against the couple next to them. 'Sorry,' he muttered awkwardly, as he pulled her even closer against him. His hands slipped around her hips to try to hide what she was doing. He was holding her so tightly that her fingers could barely move.

Maggie drew her stomach in and pulled back slightly to create some space in which to work, then slid her fingers gradually down his burning shaft. Justin immediately pushed hard, trying to pin her hand, and Maggie's whole body began to tingle with the erotic stimulation of what she was doing to him. He had a problem. He couldn't back away from her or he would expose himself to everyone. She pushed his pants down and tucked them under his balls so that his cock was even more exposed.

'Stop struggling or everyone will see,' she threatened softly, as she gave his genitals a warning squeeze. Justin gasped and relaxed his body slightly. Maggie smiled and wrapped her fingers round his cock again. Despite his shock, Justin was still swelling rapidly beneath her fingers and she could feel his body trembling as she tightened her grip and began to pump him slowly.

'Shit. Don't. Oh God, woman! What are you trying to do to me?' His voice was no more than a feeble squeak. He tried to pull her even closer against him and she felt his hands tightening on her buttocks. She shivered again and began to pump him harder. His cock twitched in her fingers and she felt the first drops of moisture dribbling from the tip.

A surge of lust shot through her, so powerful that she almost fell over. Her breasts began to tingle and her own lubrication was making a rapidly expanding damp patch between her legs. His cock jerked again and she heard him draw a sharp breath.

'Why don't we go back and sit down?' he hissed through clenched teeth as he tried to guide her back towards their table. Maggie shook her head.

'Not yet,' she told him softly. 'I'm just getting into the rhythm.' She increased her movement still further, so that she was pumping him rapidly. She heard him gasp again as he tried to jerk his hips back from her.

'For God's sake,' he pleaded, 'I won't be able to hold it if you keep doing that.'

'Try,' she breathed, kneading him mercilessly with her fingertips and marvelling at the way he seemed to be still growing. 'You're always preaching about self-discipline. Practise what you preach.'

Perversely, her words seemed to steady him a bit. He took another deep breath and pushed his tongue into her ear. Maggie whimpered and almost lost her balance again as a cold shiver ran down the back of her legs. Justin started to pull the front of her dress up and Maggie stumbled against him.

'What's the matter?' he whispered as he steadied her swaying body with his strong arms. 'Where's that self-control you were talking about?' He nibbled her earlobe and squeezed her tightly.

Maggie realised that Justin was fighting back. He put his hand on the small of her back and pulled her tight. His other hand moved on to her breast and she felt his fingertips caressing her exposed nipple. She was squeezed so tightly against him that, as she moved her fingers up and down his cock, she was rubbing herself as well. The pang of desire in the pit of her stomach was so strong, so intense, that it was making her head spin. She couldn't remember ever feeling quite so desperate. It was all she could do to stop herself ripping his clothes off him in front of everyone. Her fingers clasped his cock so hard that he grunted in pain.

'Christ. Be careful what you're doing,' he gasped as he jerked his hips back. 'What's got into you tonight?' He moved his hand so that it was resting on her bare thigh, then slipped it up under the back of her skirt so that his fingers were lightly brushing the curve of her left buttock. Maggie felt the hem of her dress lifting.

What indeed, Maggie asked herself as she thrust her breasts urgently on to his chest. Her nipples were now so hard that they were almost painful. She thought about her nakedness under her dress and wondered if she could lift the material even higher so that she could feel him directly against her burning skin without anyone noticing. She forced her hand deeper into his trousers again and cupped his balls with her palm. Her fingers started to caress the soft, sensitive skin just behind them.

Justin's body shuddered violently and she felt his cock lurch against her arm. 'Oh Jesus. Let's get out of here,' he whispered urgently.

Maggie nodded silently, not trusting herself to say anything. She started to withdraw her hand, enjoying the feel of his burning erection as she ran her fingers slowly up him. When she reached the top, she started to tease the damp tip with tiny circular movements of her fingers. The trembling of his body and his ragged breathing in her ear told her how much he liked it, and his reaction fed her own passion so that they were both shaking as if consumed with a raging fever.

'Please Maggie. We have to go. I swear I can't take much more.'

His words were almost more than she could stand. Her clit was so hot and sensitive that she was half-afraid just the touch of her dress rubbing across it would be enough to bring her off. She knew that she would shout out loud when she came. Justin was right. They had to leave, fast.

Maggie pulled her hand out of his trousers and tried to force the zip back up. He was so hard that she couldn't close the material across him.

'Leave it. I'll do it.' Justin moved his hands up between their bodies. His knuckles pressed hard against her and she raised herself on tiptoe so that she could press her mound on to his hand. Her movements made his task even more difficult but, finally, she felt the zip close. Justin slipped his arm around her waist and, walking just behind her, began to guide her through the gyrating bodies surrounding them.

Maggie's legs felt weak and wobbly and she took small, careful steps; her hands were clasping his so hard that her knuckles whitened. We must look as if we're both drunk, she realised, as they weaved and swayed awkwardly across the dance floor. Justin was hunched over, trying to hide his obvious arousal and she could feel her dress sticking to the patches of damp sweat down her back and between her thighs. The soft material rubbed teasingly across her oversensitive clit, so that she could hardly think about anything else.

She had no idea where they were going. She didn't care. Just so long as he got them out before the heat, noise and excitement overcame her completely. She half-closed her eyes and allowed him to push her along in front of him until they were practically running. The tingling between her legs continued to torment her.

Justin steered her swiftly along a dim corridor that led

to an emergency exit at the back of the club. When he let her go to lift the bar handle, she swayed awkwardly and had to put her hand against the wall to steady herself. What was wrong with her? She had only had one glass of wine.

Maggie heard Justin sigh with relief as the door opened. He grabbed her arm almost roughly and pushed her through. As he slammed it closed behind them, he was already ripping at his tie. Dropping it to the ground, he unzipped his trousers and let them fall to his ankles.

She breathed in deeply. The air was sharp and cold after the intense heat of the dance floor and she felt the goose bumps rising on her skin. Apart from the faint boom of the disco music, the hotel grounds were quiet and deserted, save for a slight creaking of the branches in the surrounding trees.

Justin grabbed her again and pushed her round so that her back was up against the door. With one quick move-ment, he pulled her dress up over her head, trapping her arms and blinding her to the world. His strong hands began kneading her aching breasts and she felt his warm, damp tongue running across her stomach.

'Oh my God!' she cried out, as she felt one of her nipples sucked into his mouth. Another surge of animal lust tore through her. Almost unaware of what she was doing, she struggled one arm free and tugged her dress off her, leaving her naked but for her sandals. She reached out desperately to grab his pants. As she ripped them down, she felt his cock burst out and rub across her bare flesh. He groaned loudly. He grabbed her left leg and lifted it up round his hip, exposing her hot dampness.

Maggie dug her heel into his thigh and leaned back hard against the door to stop herself falling. She felt his arms lifting her up so that she was almost off the ground and she whimpered softly as his prick slipped effortlessly into her. Instinctively, she pushed her hips forward,

25

pulling him in even deeper. She hooked her right leg round his other thigh so that she was totally impaled on him.

'God, woman. You've been asking for this all night.' Justin started to thrust roughly in and out of her and she felt her buttocks and thighs banging rhythmically against the door. Nearby, she heard the sound of another door opening and muffled voices carried clearly through the still night air as a couple of kitchen staff sneaked outside to enjoy a quick smoke. They sounded very close. What if they heard and came to investigate?

Maggie started to struggle, wiggling from side to side as she attempted to escape. Her movements only seemed to excite Justin further. She could sense that he was now so far gone that nothing would stop him. He probably wouldn't care if the entire kitchen staff stood round shouting encouragement.

Despite her fear, the thought of being caught only served to fuel her own passion. As she felt Justin lean forward and suck her nipple into his soft lips, Maggie gasped aloud and ground her clit desperately against him until she felt her long-overdue orgasm finally explode inside her. Sobbing almost incoherently, she sagged limply against him, then gasped again at the feel of his cock juddering violently as he, too, started to climax.

'Oh yes,' he groaned loudly, as the pleasure of his release overwhelmed him.

Totally spent, Maggie sank back against the wall and felt his cock slipping softly out of her. The kitchen door opened and closed again as the workers finished their cigarettes and returned to work. In the distance, through the heavy door behind them, Maggie could still hear the thumping rhythm of disco music. The cold night air caressed her naked body.

'I think that was probably worth at least four tickets, don't you?' she whispered huskily, as she reached out for her crumpled dress.

Chapter Two

Maggie struggled to appear nonchalant as she waved the coveted match tickets under her friend's nose. Jan's eyes widened when she realised what they were.

'Where the hell did you get those?' She snatched at the tickets. 'Four of them! I heard that there weren't any left to be had anywhere.' She grinned meaningfully. 'I said it was useful to have friends in high places, didn't I? Good ol' Justin. What did you have to do to get them?'

Maggie looked smug. 'Oh just be my normal, irresistible self,' she said, laughing.

Jan stared at the tickets again. 'It's a pity Marcus isn't going to be around. Mind you, I don't suppose he'd go. He's becoming so lazy, it's as much as I can do to get him to take me out for a meal these days.'

Maggie grinned to herself. No matter what Jan said, everyone knew who wore the pants in their relationship. If Jan really wanted Marcus to take her anywhere, then Marcus would take her. Secretly, Maggie found Marcus rather pathetic. She had always preferred her men to be a bit more forceful. Not too forceful, mind you. It was fun to take the dominant role sometimes, too.

'So, who else are you going to invite?' Jan questioned. 'You can't let these go to waste. They're like gold dust.'

'I've already asked Sara and Claire,' Maggie replied quickly. Jan and Claire did not always get on that well. They tended to argue pointlessly about the most stupid things while Sara and Maggie did their best to keep the peace. It was probably because Claire was even more flighty than Maggie was. Jan seemed to feel a kind of personal responsibility to set Claire straight on almost everything, from politics to fashion. Still, it couldn't be helped. She had four tickets and, if anything, Claire was a bigger Trojan fan than Jan was.

'What about accommodation? I don't fancy the idea of driving back afterwards and I can't afford anything too pricey. I've just paid out a small fortune to have the bedroom redecorated.' Jan was always redecorating one room or another. It was an obsession with her.

Maggie breathed a mental sigh of relief that Jan had not made a fuss about her inviting Claire. 'No problem,' she replied. 'Justin has promised to fix us up at a B&B he knows. It won't cost much.' Her smile broadened as she prepared to spring her other surprise. 'He's even hinted that he might be able to get us invited to dinner with the Trojans after the game.'

'You're kidding?' Jan grinned knowingly. 'That must have been some night.'

Maggie thought about what she had done to Justin in the Cellar. 'You could say that I found his weak spot,' she replied with a giggle.

The day of the match was dull and wet and the traffic on the motorway was even worse than Maggie had anticipated. Despite setting out mid-afternoon, by the time they reached Bristol and found the accommodation that Justin had arranged for them, it was already growing quite late.

Maggie was feeling tired and grumpy from the drive. No one had offered to help her navigate and the Saturday

28

traffic through the centre of Bristol had been so heavy and erratic that she had had trouble finding her way. Several times she had missed a turning and been forced to double back.

While she had been concentrating on reading road names and dodging suicidal shoppers, the others had all been laughing and chatting excitedly as they discussed the match and the possibility of dinner afterwards. For once, even Jan and Claire seemed to be getting on, and as Maggie watched her three friends talking and joking together as they filed into the boarding house and began squabbling over who was going to sleep where, she felt a little excluded. She quickly dumped her overnight case on a bed by the window and then excused herself to go and freshen up.

As she stared at her flaming, angry face in the mirror above the basin, Maggie's bad temper melted away. Why spoil the weekend by sulking? The drive might have been awful but they were there now. In just over an hour they would be watching the game and, if Justin kept his word, afterwards they would actually get to meet the players in person.

Seeing that there was no shower attachment and deciding that she did not have time for a bath, Maggie stripped off to her lacy bra and matching thong and gave her body a quick sponge down. Then she splashed a little cool water on her cheeks and repaired her make up before hurrying back to the room to change.

The others were already unpacking their things. Maggie pulled on a long-sleeved jumper and wrapped her favourite calf-length tartan skirt around her slim waist. The players might be dripping with perspiration during the game, but it could be quite cold for the spectators. Normally, she would have worn trousers like the others, but the skirt was more flattering to her figure and she wanted to look her best.

* * *

29

The 'Birds' home rink was packed to capacity. Maggie was surprised at how many Trojan supporters were among the excited throng and delighted to find that the seats Justin had got for them were in the front row, right in the centre of the neutral zone. Maggie scanned the crowd, searching for Justin, but couldn't spot him anywhere. She could see the Trojans' coach talking earnestly with the team manager and another important-looking businessman, probably one of the sponsors. The coach's face looked strained and he seemed to be arguing with the manager about something.

The clock moved towards 7.30 p.m. and the four women quickly stocked up with popcorn and fizzy drinks from the kiosk. As they hurried to get seated before the face-off, Justin suddenly appeared, grinning excitedly.

'Hi Mags.' He kissed her cheek in an almost brotherly fashion. 'Sorry not to have caught up with you earlier. The coach was in a flap about something or other. Is your accommodation OK?'

Maggie smiled up at him. He was looking even smarter than usual in a beige-coloured suit and black silk shirt. His pale blue eyes were flashing with excitement.

'It's fine, thanks. And the seats are great.'

'Yes. Thanks Justin,' Jan added. 'I don't know what you made Maggie do for them, but whatever it was, it was worth it.' She gave them a sly grin.

Maggie glared at her friend, but Justin just chuckled. Sara smiled awkwardly and Claire giggled.

'Oh, by the way –' Justin gave Maggie one of his most dazzling smiles, '– the Trojans' manager hopes that you and your friends will join us for dinner afterwards.' He manoeuvred himself between Maggie and Jan as he ushered them towards their reserved seats. Maggie found herself on the end of the row, up against a partition, with Justin on her other side.

As they sat down there was an increased buzz of

excitement and the two ice hockey squads entered the rink, waving their sticks enthusiastically in the air to the delighted roaring of the fans. The first twelve players took up their positions and one of the referees held up the puck between the two centre ice players.

Justin leant forward and reached under his seat. 'We wouldn't want you to catch cold now, would we?' he explained cheerfully as he produced a quilted blanket and started to spread it out to cover their legs. It was just wide enough to cover Jan's knees as well.

'Thank you.' Maggie was touched by this unexpected consideration.

There was a yell from the crowd as the puck dropped to the ice in the centre of the face-off circle. The Trojan centre player was on it immediately. With an elegant and skilful flick of his stick, the puck went spinning across the ice into their attacking zone, with one of the Trojan's forwards in hot pursuit. It was difficult to see who was who under the helmets and heavy padding but Maggie had no trouble picking out Troy as he neatly intercepted the pass and spun round to try for a shot at goal.

The 'Birds' closest defender zoomed into action, barging full speed into Troy in an attempt to knock him off-balance. His stick passed in front of Troy's legs, just below the shins, and Troy went flying.

'Penalty,' screamed the Trojan supporters, as Troy struggled in vain to regain his balance and keep possession of the puck.

The whistle blew. 'Two minute hooking call against the 'Birds. Power-play to the Trojans.'

The crowd roared and Maggie's heart thumped with excitement. The 'Birds would be at a real disadvantage for the next couple of minutes while they were a defender down. She watched breathlessly as the two sides vied for possession of the elusive puck and the precious seconds ticked by. 'Come on, Trojans!' she muttered over and over. Suddenly, the puck shot across the ice, deep into the attacking zone, where it was neatly intercepted by Bri. With a deft flick of his wrist, the young Trojan forward sent the puck careering wildly towards Troy on the far side of the goal.

The 'Birds remaining defender sprang into the fray, skimming over the ice to barge heavily into Troy's broad back. Troy stumbled and the spectators gasped then cheered as he regained his balance and drove the puck relentlessly on towards the goal. Suddenly, the 'Birds' defender barged him again, whisking the puck away from under the blade of Troy's stick before he had time to react.

Maggie and her friends groaned in dismay as the puck flew back over the blue line and into the neutral zone. Maggie glanced at the clock. The power play was almost up. Another twenty seconds and the second defender would be back in play. The advantage was getting away from them. Justin's hand slipped on to her knee under the blanket and Maggie stiffened. She turned her head and saw that he was cheerfully discussing the 'Birds' checking skills with Jan. His hand crept up her leg.

Damn! She could be so naïve sometimes. The blanket wasn't meant to keep her warm at all: it was to hide what he was up to. She glanced nervously at Jan, wondering if her friend knew what was going on, but all three women seemed to be totally engrossed in what Justin was saying. She shifted her buttocks awkwardly, wishing that the seats were not so small and cramped.

'So, tell us more about some of the players,' Claire begged Justin. 'Like, what do they do when they're not skating? I mean, I've never seen any of them out clubbing or anything.'

Justin smiled indulgently. 'They don't have much time for clubs during the season. They have to train hard. Besides, a lot of them don't come from round here. When the season's over, they usually go home.'

'What about Pary?' asked Claire '– does he, like, have

a girlfriend or anything?' Maggie had been wondering how long it would take for her to get round to that question; she could be so transparent sometimes.

'I've no idea,' Justin replied. 'You can ask him yourself later.'

Claire reddened visibly.

'I've heard rumours that Pele is thinking of not renewing his contract next season,' Jan commented. 'Do you know why?'

Justin shrugged. 'There are always rumours at this time of year. It's all part of the game of negotiating new contracts for next season. I guess it depends if we win the cup or not. Pele's also a skilled mechanic. So far as I know, he plans to set up in business for himself when his hockey days are over.'

'Really?' Jan responded thoughtfully. 'Still, it would be a shame to lose him. He's the best goalkeeper we've ever had.'

'Net-minder, not goalkeeper,' Claire interjected scornfully. Maggie sighed, praying that she and Jan were not about to get into one of their stupid scraps. She felt Justin give her leg another gentle fondle and quickly squeezed her thighs together.

'At least you'd know where to take your car for servicing,' Maggie commented pointedly, knowing that it wasn't her car Jan was thinking about. Sometimes, Jan could be nearly as transparent as Claire.

There was another scream of anticipation from the fans and a sudden flurry of activity on the ice as the Trojan centre lunged madly to intercept the speeding puck. The crowd groaned as he overshot, crashed into the side of the rink and fell heavily. Immediately, a substitute rushed out on to the ice. It was the Trojans' newest recruit, Tor, and Maggie held her breath again as he expertly whisked the puck out from under his opponent's nose and sent it gliding back towards the Trojan attacking zone.

The penalty period came to an end and the 'Birds' second defender rushed back into the game. He was too late; Troy had timed the speeding puck perfectly. As it reached the blade of his stick, he whirled it round and sent it skimming straight into the goal. It was so fast and so precisely timed that the 'Birds' net-minder never stood a chance.

'One, nil!' Jan, Sara and Claire roared with delight as the scoreboard registered the Trojans' success and the fans all jumped to their feet to cheer and clap. Maggie took advantage of the situation to push Justin's hand away and leap up herself. Now that she was wise to him, she would be more careful when she sat back down.

Justin flashed her another beguiling smile. 'Enjoying yourself?' he whispered innocently as he helped her back into her seat and carefully rearranged the blanket over her legs before she could protest. Within seconds, his probing fingers had found the split in her wrap-around skirt and started pulling it clear of her clamped thighs. Maggie clenched her teeth as his hand began to slide higher and higher up her now bare thigh.

Out on the ice, the pace of the game intensified. The 'Birds' fans were screaming for blood and there were definite signs of panic in their ranks as their two forwards struggled to level the score. Substitute players were rushed on and off in a seemingly senseless frenzy, as if the 'Birds' just couldn't settle on a coherent line up, and a vicious fight broke out between one of their burly def-encemen and a Trojan winger. Inevitably, this resulted in both players being banished to the penalty box for rough-ing, and another exciting double power-play struggle ensued.

Maggie crossed her legs and tried her best to follow the frantic action. Without being too obvious about what she was doing, she tried to tuck the material of her skirt back between her thighs, while Justin remorselessly pulled it clear again with his fingers. Before she realised

34

his intentions, she felt him fiddling with the skirt pin at her thigh. With a deft flick of his fingers, the pin came undone and Maggie tried to grab his hand before he could remove it. She was too slow. As he withdrew his hand, she felt her skirt falling away from her legs, so that all she was wearing under the blanket was her lacy thong and her stockings. Feeling incredibly exposed, she gripped the blanket tightly with both hands, holding it up over her nakedness.

Justin triumphantly examined the pin then slipped it into his far pocket, where she could not hope to reach it. 'Yes. Go for it!' he called excitedly, as Pary made a surprise attack on the goal that almost got past the skilful 'Birds' defence. His hand began to explore Maggie's legs once again, and she was surprised at the strength in his fingers as they forced their way between her tightly clenched thighs, obliging her to expose herself even further to his demanding caresses. Her knuckles had turned white with the effort she was putting into gripping the blanket up over her. If she had dared to let go of it, she would have slapped his face. Except, of course, she wouldn't really. If she did, then everyone would know what he was doing to her.

'Stop it!' she hissed at him as his probing fingers began gliding up her thigh towards her mound. His touch was now so light that she could barely feel it and goose bumps were making the little hairs on her thighs stand up. Another shiver of anticipation and longing trickled down her spine as his fingers drew ever closer to her tingling clit. She sighed with disappointment as he stopped and retraced his journey back down her leg and over her stocking top. Despite her discomfort at her predicament, her treacherous body was already responding enthusiastically to his caresses, and part of her was willing him to move back up.

Out on the ice, the battle continued. Despite their obvious panic to score, the 'Birds were not letting up on their relentless defending for one second. They were famous for having the best defensive play of any team and, no matter how hard they struggled, the Trojan's couldn't seem to get through their two defenders a second time.

Justin, on the other hand, was having a much easier time of it. As if sensing her growing arousal and wavering resistance, he intensified his assault. Maggie yelped softly as his hand glided up her leg and moved over to the other one, so that his knuckles skimmed lightly across her sex. She reddened and looked around quickly to see if anyone had heard her, but everyone seemed to be engrossed in the game, even Justin. She frowned at the innocent expression on his face and took a deep breath to calm her thudding pulse. As she struggled to return her concentration to the ice rink, she felt his knuckles return. She bit her lip to stop herself whimpering as his fingers started to grope under the elastic of her panties.

'Yes! Well played!' yelled Jan as Troy made another magnificent pass to Bri and the 'Birds' defenceman lost his balance and mistimed his attack. Maggie felt her panties starting to slip down her thighs.

'No!' She grasped his hand through the blanket.

'Yes!' Justin began to pull the blanket away with his other hand, so that Maggie was obliged to let go of him to pull it back over her. Immediately, she felt him resume his efforts. She pushed her bottom down hard on to the seat, but it was no use. Either the elastic was going to snap or her skirt was going to slide right off her with her panties. As she raised her buttocks in surrender, she glared angrily at his enigmatic smile and contemplated scratching his eyes out.

Justin's smile widened as he continued to lower her panties down her thighs. As soon as they were clear of her buttocks, Maggie sat back down quickly to stop her skirt disappearing as well. She could hide the fact that her knickers were missing, but she wouldn't be able to move out of her seat if her skirt fell right off too.

Out on the rink, another fight had broken out in the neutral zone between the two centre players, and the crowd was roaring and booing as the referee hurried to intervene. Justin had left Maggie's panties halfway down her thighs and was now using his fingers to prise her legs open even wider. She shivered and tried to wiggle her panties down further. Somehow, leaving them half-way down her legs seemed worse than if he had taken them right off. She shivered as he began to lightly caress her outer sex lips with his fingertips. She could feel the telltale dampness of her increasing arousal and was certain that he would notice it too.

'Popcorn?' Maggie jumped as Jan leant over Justin and waved the tub under her nose.

'No thank you,' she muttered stiffly, as she did her utmost to ignore Justin's insistent caresses. Part of her wanted to beg him to stop, part of her wanted to urge him on. She was growing more and more aroused by the second and was becoming desperate to feel his fingers inside her. Every time he touched her, she tensed her body and tried to hint what she wanted by pushing herself on to him. What was wrong with him? He wasn't usually so slow to catch on. Finally, it dawned on her.

Bastard! Maggie sank down on the seat and closed her eyes. He knew perfectly well what she wanted him to do. He was playing with her, trying to make her beg. This must be his revenge for what she had done to him in the Cellar. She opened her eyes again and stared deter-minedly at the game, fighting not to twitch as he parted her labia and started to tease her swollen clit. She shifted back in her seat to make it harder for him to reach her.

'Not too warm, are you?' he questioned innocently as he began to lower the blanket again.

'No! I'm fine.' Maggie grabbed the blanket quickly. Checkmate. If she didn't do exactly what he wanted, he would pull the blanket away and expose her. She watched without comment as he withdrew his hand and deliberately licked his fingers before slipping them back under the blanket.

Maggie glanced anxiously at the clock. There were only a few minutes to go before the end of the first period. She pushed her own hand under the blanket and tried to wriggle her panties down further. If she could just get them off, she could kick them under the seat before anyone noticed. Justin yanked at her arm.

'I'm taking them off,' she whispered, thinking that he had misunderstood her intentions.

Justin shook his head and resumed his relentless attack on her outer lips. Now what? Maggie sat there helplessly, watching the seconds tick by, while he continued to torture her; his caresses just enough to drive her mad but not enough to do any real good. She sighed with frustration and tried to tighten her thighs around his hand without him noticing. She almost jumped out of her skin when the hooter sounded. It was the end of the first period. Jan, Claire and Sara all stood up.

'I need another drink after all that shouting,' Jan announced, as she looked down at Justin and Maggie. 'Are you coming?' She started to pull the blanket off them.

Maggie slammed her arms down to cover herself. 'No!' she exclaimed loudly. Jan stared at her in surprise.

'Sorry. I only asked.'

'Shall I get you something Maggie?' Justin questioned as he slipped out from under the blanket and stood up.

Maggie nodded mutely.

'Pepsi?' he enquired. She nodded again.

'Come on then, Jan.' Justin took Jan's arm as they turned to follow after Claire and Sara who were already heading for the kiosk. 'Leave everything just as it is, Maggie,' he whispered, over his shoulder, as they left.

Maggie watched in silence as Justin and Jan moved off.

She glanced down at the blanket and realised that she could clearly see the ridge of her rolled-up panties underneath it. Quickly, she scrunched the blanket up so that it was not so obvious, then sat with her legs slightly apart so that she could feel the cold air from the rink rushing up between her naked thighs. Her legs kept twitching as if his fingers were still playing with her. She kept her face turned to the front, half-afraid to look round in case anyone had been watching what was happening.

Had anyone seen anything? Closing her eyes, Maggie started to imagine that the man sitting behind them had been watching it all. She pictured how excited he would have become. Was he still there, or had he rushed off somewhere private to relieve his frustrations? The idea of some strange man wanking in the loo because of her was so exciting that it was all she could do to stop herself from pushing her own hand down between her trembling thighs.

'Sorry to have been so long.' Justin's cheerful voice broke into her fantasy. 'The queues were awful.' He flopped down beside her and, before she could react, lifted the blanket up in the air to spread it back out over his and Jan's legs. Maggie felt the blood rushing to her cheeks again as she hastily yanked it back down over herself. She shot a quick glance out the corner of her eye to see if Jan or the others had noticed anything and was relieved to find that they were looking the other way.

Although she was anticipating Justin's hand under the blanket again, she wasn't prepared for the shock as he slipped a can of ice-cold Pepsi between her thighs and pushed it up hard on to her hot sex.

'Oh!' Maggie gasped aloud and doubled over, trying to push the can away. 'You bastard!' she hissed as the numbing cold began to spread over her mound and down her thighs.

Justin gave her a crooked smile and retrieved the can. Quite deliberately, he licked the side of it before handing it to her. 'Here's your juice,' he told her innocently. 'You taste better than what's inside it,' he added in a whisper as she snatched the can from him.

Her hands shaking, Maggie pulled the ring and took a long gulp of the fizzy liquid to ease her parched throat. She could still feel the numbing cold where it had rested against her and realised that she was tensed – ready for the warmth of his hand.

Jan, Claire and Sara were all chatting excitedly about the first period play, but Maggie refrained from joining in the discussion. Apart from being fairly certain that the Trojans were a goal up, she realised that she couldn't actually remember much of what had taken place. Although she clapped her hands enthusiastically as the players reappeared to start the second period, she remained firmly in her seat.

As the two teams started to race back and forth across the ice, Maggie fidgeted impatiently, longing to feel Justin's hand between her thighs again. What was he waiting for? She glanced round suspiciously to make sure that he wasn't doing anything with Jan and was relieved to see that Jan had not bothered to replace the blanket over herself when she had sat down.

From time to time, Justin patted Maggie's legs affectionately through the blanket, but she had the feeling that this was only to check that she hadn't pulled her clothes back on. For some perverse reason, his lack of attention seemed worse than his caresses had been. Her clit was still tingling and her preoccupation with her semi-nakedness made it extremely difficult to concentrate on anything else but her burning need to be fondled.

A roar from the fans directed her attention back to the ice, just in time to see their defenceman, Ean, expertly knocked off-balance by the burly 'Birds right winger. It was a superbly executed check. Before he could recover, the left winger has scooped up the lost puck and sent it spinning powerfully towards the Trojan net. Pele almost turned himself inside out trying to stop the shot but he was just not quick enough.

'One all!' screamed the ecstatic 'Birds supporters as the buzzer sounded to acknowledge the goal.

'Damn it!' Jan and Sara cursed in unison, while Claire groaned and wrung her hands together in despair. Maggie shifted awkwardly and pretended to look suitably upset. It was the first time she could ever remember being totally unaffected by a game.

Finally, with over half the second period gone, Justin seemed to remember her again. He slid his hand slowly down her back, neatly unclipping her bra on the way, then forced his fingers between the small of her back and the seat. Maggie leant forward so that his hand was resting on the top of her buttocks and Justin gave her a gentle push to tell her that he wanted her to lift herself up.

Maggie wriggled awkwardly, trying to cross her legs, but her panties were making it difficult to manoeuvre. She shifted her weight on to her left cheek, raising her right one, and gritted her teeth as she felt his hand slip underneath her. Without taking his eyes off the game, Justin began to casually caress, pat and even gently pinch her buttock between his fingers, causing little tremors of desire to race up and down her spine, and her pussy to grow damper and damper.

'Good, isn't it?' he murmured with a nod towards the ice rink. Before Maggie could respond, he slipped his hand further underneath her and she felt him deliberately collecting her juices with his fingertips. As he moved his hand back, Justin turned his head so that he could stare into her flushed face.

'Yes. Very good.' He ran one damp finger up her arse crack and round the hole. Maggie gasped and clenched her muscles, pushing him away. She tried to thrust herself back down on to the seat but that only seemed to make it easier for him. As she felt his fingertip beginning

41

to slide in, she lifted up again so that he slipped back out.

'Two-minute slashing call penalty. Power-play to the 'Birds.' The jeers from the crowd quickly drowned out the rest of the announcement. Justin gave Maggie's hole another gentle probe and then withdrew his hand and winked at her.

'You've got a great arse, Maggie,' he told her. 'Very fuckable.' He watched her expression carefully. When she said nothing, he continued, 'Yeah, I think I might bend you over later and give you a good buggering. You'd like that, wouldn't you?'

Before Maggie could think of a suitable reply, Justin suddenly got up and, pushing past the other women, disappeared up the steps and out the exit tunnel. Maggie sat back on the seat and tried to stop her muscles twitching. She was very aware of the strange tingling in her back passage, as if his finger was still exploring her.

Jan moved across into Justin's vacated seat and gave Maggie a hard stare. 'Just what have you two been up to?' she whispered accusingly. 'Justin's cock was so hard when he left that I thought it was going to split his trousers.'

Maggie grinned feebly, not daring to answer. There was another yell from the crowd and Jan and Maggie turned back to the match. The 'Birds' wingers were making the most of their remaining advantage. As the left winger sent the puck gliding over the ice towards the goal, a Trojan defender was homing in to retrieve it. Before he reached it, however, the second winger knocked him flying, scooped up the puck and blasted it so hard at the Trojan net that Pele only just saved it. The crowd howled their approval as the teams repositioned themselves for the face off. Soon the desperate battle was once more in progress as both sides fought for supremacy.

Justin returned just as the hooter went for the end of

42

the second period. As Jan moved out to make way for him, he calmly sat down and began to rearrange the blanket.

'Where have you been?' Maggie demanded softly.

'Washing my hands,' he replied. 'Why? Did you miss me?'

'Liar,' she hissed. 'It doesn't take that long to wash your hands.' She was almost certain that she could smell his guilt. 'You've been wanking, haven't you?' she accused him.

'Tut, tut. Such language.' His grin seemed to grow to match her rising temper. Maggie wished that she had been able to relieve her own frustration while he was away but, with Jan sitting beside her, she had hardly dared to move. Even if Jan hadn't seen the way her clothing was rucked up under the blanket, she must have spotted that Maggie's bra was undone at the back. She'd certainly noticed the state Justin was in.

While they waited for the final period to start, the five of them remained in their seats, continuing their conversation about the players. Once again, Maggie took little part in the discussions, although her ears pricked up when Jan started to question Justin about Troy.

'He's a bit of an enigma, that one,' Justin told her. 'The coach once told me that he's got a first-class honours degree in maths or something. He's always been into sports of all kinds. Nearly chosen to swim for England in the Commonwealth games once, I believe. Anyway, he somehow got into ice hockey and here he is. I guess the money's better than teaching or whatever else he might have done.'

Maggie's heart sank. If Troy was such an intellectual he'd hardly be interested in her, would he? She'd only just scraped through her maths GCE at the second attempt. Jan was probably much more his type. It was a good thing that Jan had always seemed more interested in Pele. Besides, Jan already had Marcus, didn't she?

Maggie pretended to study a brochure about the teams while her mind raced. Every time she felt the blanket move she tensed her body, waiting for the feel of Justin's hands. The anticipation of what he might do was driving her crazy. By the time the players trooped back to resume play she was in such a state she couldn't think straight.

For a while, Justin took no further notice of her, directing all his attention to the game. Gradually, Maggie began to calm down and started to think about how she was going to make herself decent before she had to stand up.

'Drop your knickers to your ankles and open your legs wide,' Justin whispered suddenly, as if remembering how he had left her.

'No way,' Maggie responded coldly. He'd had more than enough fun at her expense already.

Justin tugged on the blanket, exposing the top of her thighs. Maggie grabbed it quickly. 'All right,' she agreed. After all, she had to do something about her knickers before the game finished. As casually as she could, she worked the offending garment down her legs and off over her ankles. Glancing round to make sure her friends were not watching, she pushed her hands up her sleeves and carefully removed her loosened bra, too.

'Very neat!' Justin grinned as he reached under the blanket to retrieve it. 'Give me your knickers as well,' he commanded, as he stuffed her bra into his pocket.

Maggie reached down and scooped up her panties from under the seat. She glanced at the clock and saw that there were only a couple of minutes of play remaining. The score was still even and, thankfully, everyone was riveted to the battle on the ice. Maggie did what she could to straighten out her skirt. She would have to try and hold it closed around her until she could get to the ladies room and do something about the missing pin. Sara might have something she could use. She was always prepared with a spare of everything.

44

As if reading her mind, Justin grinned and produced the skirt pin from his pocket. He waved it under her nose. 'Would you like this back?'

Maggie stared at him in silence.

'No? OK. I just thought I'd ask.' He went to put the pin back in his pocket.

'Yes, of course I want it,' Maggie snapped.

Justin held the pin up again. 'Only if you make me a promise.'

Maggie nodded mutely.

'I want you to promise me not to masturbate tonight. I want to think about you lying there, all hot and juicy and desperate, longing for me,' he told her.

Maggie frowned. It was all right for him, nipping off to the loo like that. She remembered that she was sharing a room that night anyway. 'All right,' she muttered. 'I promise, if it makes you happy. Now give me that pin.'

The clock moved into the final sixty-second countdown and the crowd leapt to its feet as the Trojans made one last, desperate bid for victory. Maggie thankfully pinned her skirt closed round her nakedness and, for the first time since the start of the game, stood up with the others to urge her heroes on.

As Troy scooped the puck from under the opposition's blade and bore down on the 'Birds' goal, Justin stood up beside her and she felt his hand creep in through the slit in her skirt. As he cupped her naked mound in his palm, she pushed herself down hard on to his hand, savouring the renewed tremors of passion rushing through her.

Troy seemed to move as if inspired. His stick flew over the ice and the opposition fell aside against his onslaught as though he was protected by an invisible force field. As he took his shot at goal, the whole rink fell silent, as everyone their breath. The puck skimmed effortlessly across the ice and into the net just as the hooter sounded for end of play. Two–one. The Trojans had won.

Maggie cheered with the others and then sighed with

regret as she felt Justin's fingers give her clit one final, lingering caress before it slipped away.

'Game over,' Justin whispered regretfully. 'And not a single interference penalty.'

She honestly couldn't decide whether to laugh or slap his smug face.

Maggie followed behind Justin's car to the restaurant the Trojans' manager had booked for their after-match celebrations. She drove silently, ignoring the conversation of her friends, with her thoughts in a whirl. Her body was still tingling from what Justin had done to her, and her imagination was fired-up by the realisation that she was finally about to meet the Trojans in person. She did her best to not even think about her lack of underwear.

By the time they arrived at the restaurant, the whole squad was already there, as well as their triumphant manager and the equally delighted coach, Stephen Jackson. There was also a pretty young brunette called Gemma, who was introduced to Maggie and the others as the Trojans' personal physiotherapist. Maggie instantly felt a pang of envy and admiration for the young woman. Now that was what she called a career! Imagine having a legitimate excuse to run your hands over all those divine bodies whenever you felt like it.

Maggie and her friends were introduced to everyone personally by Justin and her legs started to wobble when she finally found herself standing in front of Troy. She raised her head slowly, her eyes devouring his hard stomach and smooth, sleek chest. He had changed into an immaculate cream-coloured suit that fitted him to perfection. His neck was as thick and solid as a tree trunk and his chin was as square as if it had been carved from a block of solid granite. He was so close to her that she could see the gleam of perspiration on his brow and smell the strong masculine odour of his body.

Their eyes locked and, to her consternation, she

46

realised that he had been watching her careful appraisal of his assets. His eyes were jet-black and glistening like bullets. She blinked and tried to turn her head but his gaze was too commanding, almost hypnotic. She could not pull away. She felt her cheeks flame.

'Do you like it?' Troy murmured softly. His voice was almost as hypnotic as his eyes. She felt his warm breath across her burning cheeks and saw his gaze drop down on to his groin. She only just stopped herself from gasping.

'The suit. I've been told the colour compliments my skin.' His voice was filled with amusement and she was certain that he was playing with her. Maggie had the uncanny feeling that he could read her every thought and she remembered what she had just learned about him. Definitely not a man to be trifled with. She gulped hard and forced herself to find her voice.

'It does,' she croaked softly. Her eyes scanned his crotch again. Was it tighter than it had been a few seconds ago?

Troy laughed and put one huge hand on her arm. His touch burned like fire. 'I imagine you're thirsty after all that cheering and clapping. Can I get you a drink?'

Maggie nodded her head, not trusting herself to speak again. Her legs were now so wobbly that she was half-afraid she would fall over when he let go of her arm. She rolled her tongue around her mouth, trying to stimulate some moisture. It was ironic that her mouth should be so dry while the area between her legs was growing damper by the second.

By the time Troy reappeared with a glass of white wine in one hand, everyone was starting to move into the dining area to eat. In a daze, Maggie allowed herself to be guided to her place. She found herself sitting between Justin on one side and the physiotherapist, Gemma, on the other. She could just see Troy sitting down the far end of the table between one of the other forwards, Bri, and the Trojans' newly acquired Canadian centre, Tor.

Jan was sitting opposite her and Maggie noticed that her friend seemed to be watching the handsome new centre ice player with more than a passing interest. Tor was certainly worth looking at, with his close-cropped fair hair and big silver-grey eyes. Maggie grinned. Was Pele forgotten so soon? She realised that she felt a bit like a small child let loose in a sweet shop, surrounded as they were by so many desirable men.

As the first course was being served, Justin put his hand under the table and placed it casually on her thigh again. It occurred to her that he might be feeling a bit under threat with so much competition around. Perhaps he was subconsciously reminding her of his prior claim? She almost giggled aloud at that thought. It made her sound like a piece of real estate or something. She gave him an encouraging grin. A bird in the hand and all that. Still, if she were being completely honest with herself, should Troy indicate that he was interested all thoughts of Justin would be vanquished in a flash.

The Trojans' coach, Stephen, leant across the table and engaged Justin in a petty argument about the use of the ice resurfacing machine while Maggie supped her soup and tried to ignore the effect of Justin's hand burning into her leg. Hearing excited laughter on the other side of her, she turned her head to see what was going on.

Gemma was in full flow about something, and judging by the pink faces of her audience, her topic of conversation was nothing to do with the weather. Maggie leaned over slightly so that she could hear what Gemma was saying. She was talking to Claire and a couple of the younger players, and Maggie's ears pricked up when she realised just what the conversation was about.

'So, anyway,' Gemma continued her tale, 'it turned out that he was really into the S&M scene. You know: leather, rubber, whips, chains. The whole bit. He even had this

48

special whipping stool back at his flat,' she continued enthusiastically, 'with a chain and handcuffs attached. I couldn't believe my eyes.'

One of the young ice hockey players turned red and squirmed uncomfortably in his seat and Claire looked stunned as if she couldn't believe her ears. Maggie suppressed another grin. Although she had never been all that actively involved, she had dabbled on the fringes of the scene once or twice and Gemma's tale, true or not, brought back some amusing and erotic memories that she had almost forgotten. She smiled cheekily at Justin and settled back to enjoy the rest of her meal.

After the final course had been cleared away, Maggie ordered a coffee while Jan and the others indulged in a colourful variety of liqueurs. She had never been fond of liqueurs, finding them much too sweet and sickly for her liking. Abandoning the remains of their feasting, the Trojans and their guests gradually began to wander back into the lounge area, where further drinks were being served.

The Trojans' smarmy-faced, middle-aged manager edged closer to her with his right hand outstretched eagerly. 'It's Maggie, isn't it? I've seen you around the rink. A real pleasure to meet you.' He took her hand in his own sticky paw and began shaking her arm up and down enthusiastically while his eyes devoured her breasts. 'As you probably know, I'm Roland Donaldson, the Trojans' manager. I do hope you enjoyed the match?'

'Yes, thank you.' She withdrew her hand and tried to resist the urge to wipe it down the side of her skirt. 'It was very kind of you to invite us.' Roland's pungent aftershave was turning her stomach and she tried to step back and away from him.

Her body bumped against a solid thigh and she looked round quickly. It was Troy. She hadn't even realised that he was anywhere nearby. Just for one delightful moment, she could actually feel his genitals pushed up against her, and a sudden pang of lust tore through her. Maggie casually put her hand down by her side and pretended not to notice as her fingers brushed against his crotch. She heard Troy's breathing deepen and was delighted as she felt him edging even closer to her.

Roland beamed at him. 'Here's our hero of the match.' He thumped Troy on the back. 'That was a splendid effort this evening. Really splendid. I expect you will sleep well tonight, eh?'

'I don't feel much like sleeping at the moment,' Troy muttered softly in Maggie's ear. Maggie felt herself tremble at his words and the touch of his breath on her neck. In her imagination, she could picture him guiding her away alone somewhere and taking her up against the wall the way Justin had. Her stomach started doing flip-flops at the idea of his huge hands caressing her burning flesh.

'A toast!' Roland yelled. 'Bring another tray of champers someone. Let's drink to the success of tonight's match and to the continued good health of all.'

A young waitress hurried into the room with a tray of drinks and Troy moved away from Maggie to reach for a glass. Maggie swayed slightly and steadied herself against Jan. When Troy handed her a drink she took a quick gulp and grimaced as the bubbles stung her nose.

The next twenty minutes passed in a blur of laughter and jokes, and an almost indescribable atmosphere of sexual tension. Although Maggie had now regained her composure, she was feeling hornier than ever. She glanced around the room and saw that her companions were all supping the champagne freely and becoming increasingly relaxed and abandoned as the time passed.

She noticed Roland was leaning back against one wall, ogling all the women intently. As she watched, he sidled up towards Claire and draped his arm around her shoulders. Claire leaned her body against him, her face flushed with too much champagne and excitement and, with a flash of insight, Maggie realised that Roland was using the Trojans to get the women worked up before he made his move on them.

Roland's hands started to paw Claire's breasts and Maggie grimaced. What a bastard. She moved quickly across the room and guided her friend from his embrace on the pretext of asking her something. Claire seemed too fuddled and bewildered to realise what was going on.

Troy had wandered over to stand beside Gemma and, as Maggie moved closer to them, she could hear Troy chatting to the pretty physiotherapist about water sports. Maggie felt a twinge of jealousy as she watched Gemma responding to Troy's deep sexy voice and natural charm. As she began searching for a way to interrupt them, she couldn't help wondering just how well they already knew each other.

'Sorry to spoil everyone's fun, but we really will have to be on our way soon. We have to be off the premises by midnight,' Roland announced suddenly. Maggie glared at him silently, wondering if that were true or if he just wanted to spoil everyone else's fun since he didn't seem to be getting anywhere with any of the women himself.

As Roland began to round up the squad, Maggie kept an eye on Troy who, with two other Trojans, was now busy talking to Justin. At least Gemma wasn't swooning all over him anymore. She glanced surreptitiously at Troy's fabulous body and felt more than a tinge of regret for what might have been.

Roland seized her arm and pulled her to one side. 'Perhaps I can arrange for you to join us again?' He ran his finger down her arm suggestively. 'I'd be delighted for you to be my personal guest sometime.' His eyes devoured her breasts, leaving no room for doubt about what he actually had in mind. Maggie turned away from

51

him in disgust. For some reason, he really made her skin crawl.

Justin finished his conversation and came over to her. 'I have to get back to Fairwood tonight,' he told her. 'Stephen needs a lift back so that he can supervise the junior team's friendly match tomorrow afternoon.' He slipped his arm around her waist. 'If I were going back on my own, I'd take you with me,' he muttered.

She grinned. 'What, and abandon both my car and my friends? Thanks for arranging everything, Justin. I'll see you at work on Monday.'

'Dream of me?' he suggested.

'Of course.' Maggie saw Troy turning to leave and smiled to herself. Her dreams were already booked for the night.

'Don't forget your promise, though,' Justin added softly as he walked away.

Ten minutes later, with the noisy farewells and good wishes of the Trojans still ringing in her ears, Maggie unlocked the door of her car and slipped in behind the wheel. She was still feeling tense and excited. Over her shoulder, she could hear the exuberant chattering of the other women as they clambered inside. Although their jumbled conversations made Maggie smile, their words also served to remind her of her own thoughts about Troy.

She shifted her buttocks uncomfortably on the driving seat as she remembered the touch of his hand on her arm and the feel of his crotch pressed against her. She could smell the warm, sweet scent of perspiration and female arousal wafting through the car. There probably wasn't a dry pair of knickers among them!

'Fasten your seatbelts,' she called. 'If everyone's ready, we'll get on our way.' She put the vehicle into gear and let the clutch out slowly. Her fingers lingered on the gear stick, fondling the knob as another shiver of longing ran down her spine. She had been right about Troy. He was everything she had expected him to be. And some. She eased the car out the car park and turned left towards the B&B.

As the journey progressed, the others gradually stopped chattering and fell into a kind of dreamy silence, while Maggie found herself wide awake and restless. She drove the vehicle automatically, with all her spare concentration focused on Troy. Her thoughts did little to help her unwind.

To calm herself down she switched her mind back to the Trojan's creepy manager. He had made it more than clear that he fancied her. What a revolting thought! Not even the chance of free tickets to all the Trojan matches would induce her to hop into Roland's bed.

They arrived back at their accommodation just before 12.30 a.m. and crept up to their rooms, giggling foolishly at every creaking floorboard and squeaking door. As Maggie snuggled down under the duvet, her body was still tingling with excitement and pent-up desire. What with Justin fondling her all through the match and then her thoughts about Troy, she seemed to have been in a permanent state of semi-arousal all evening. Through the wall, she could hear Sara and Claire whispering to each other in the next room and guessed that they would be talking about the players. Maggie remembered Sara had once let slip that Ean reminded her of someone special from the past. Sara never spoke about her son Kevin's father, but Maggie was certain that was who she was thinking of when she looked at the handsome young defender. Across the room, Jan muttered softly to herself and rolled over restlessly.

'Are you still awake?' Maggie whispered. There was no reply. Lucky Jan. She must already be lost in her dreams. Maggie was feeling more wide awake than ever. She stared up at the dark shadows on the ceiling and listened to the sound of a dog barking somewhere in the distance. Gently, she ran her fingers over her breasts and felt her nipples spring up under her thin nightie. Her thighs prickled with renewed lust.

Maggie rolled on to her side and curled her legs up. As she tightened her thighs, she could feel the urgent tingling deep within her. She clamped her legs tighter together, savoured the pleasurable pressure on her sensitive clit, and thought about her stupid promise to Justin. Not that she would dare break it anyway: she had never mastered the art of coming quietly. If she masturbated now, she was bound to cry out when she came. What if she woke Jan?

Sighing with frustration, she rolled over on to her stomach and pummelled the pillow with her hands, trying to make herself more comfortable. She screwed her eyes up tightly and tried to picture Troy in his tight-fitting suit. A smile played across her lips as she remembered the way he had teased her about its colour.

She awoke later with a sudden start and stared around her, trying to remember where she was. Her body was damp and cold with perspiration and she could smell the harsh, musky odour of her arousal under the duvet.

She had been dreaming about Troy. They had been alone on the ice and Troy had been holding her tightly in his arms as he glided gracefully around the rink. She had been snuggled tightly against him, enjoying the warmth of his body and the pressure of his hard cock pushed into her stomach.

Somehow, she was suddenly naked and Troy had been rubbing his hands all over her body. He no longer seemed to be wearing any trousers and his erection had been caressing her bare flesh as he hugged her to him. Urgently, she had reached down to take his cock in her hands. She was going to impale herself on him; bury his hot shaft deep inside her.

Sod it! Maggie sat up and looked across the room. Jan still appeared to be fast asleep. Now what? She couldn't masturbate in case she disturbed Jan and she couldn't even manage to satisfy herself in her dreams. What a time to wake up! Just a few more seconds and she would have felt Troy rammed deep inside her dripping cunt. It was no good. She'd never get back to sleep now.

As quietly as she could, Maggie climbed out of bed and peeled her sodden nightie off her damp body. Shivering, she tugged on some underwear and slipped into a skirt and blouse. Pulling a jacket around her shoulders, she tiptoed silently out of the room. Maybe if she went out for a walk, the fresh air would help calm her down a bit.

Chapter Three

Maggie let herself out through the back door of the B&B and made her way down a narrow path. Clambering up on to a small gate, she sat astride it and surveyed her options. To the left, the pathway appeared to lead back on to the lane that passed round the front of the B&B. To the right, it disappeared into nearby woods. Maggie wiggled her buttocks; she was acutely aware of the hardness of the gate pressed up between her thighs. She remembered her promise to Justin and almost began to wish that she hadn't been so hasty in turning Roland down. The way she was feeling right now, any prick would do. She laughed to herself. Roland was definitely one of the biggest pricks she'd ever met – next to Justin! She didn't dare let herself think about what she'd like to do to Justin right now.

God, she was feeling horny. Although she normally prided herself on keeping her promises, she was beginning to admit to herself that this one might be the exception. She had the urge to do something totally daring and reckless. For once, her fantasies and her nerve were in perfect harmony. If it hadn't been so cold she would have ripped all her clothes off and run naked down the lane, yelling with frustration. She pushed her-self harder on to the gate and savoured the tantalising pressure against her mound.

'Damn Justin!' Maggie ground her teeth together and slid off the gate on to the path. Hesitating momentarily as she gazed towards the dark privacy of the woods, she sighed heavily and started left towards the lane. With every step, she felt more wide awake than ever. She was very aware of the cold dampness between her thighs and thought longingly about her obliging vibrator lying alone at home, waiting for her.

Maybe she should just give in and take care of herself? Maggie stopped walking and felt a sudden shiver of excitement run down her spine as she glanced around. There was certainly no one about now to see or hear what she was doing. She shut her eyes and summoned up an image of Troy, naked but for a thong. She put her hand on her thigh and started to move her fingers slowly up under her skirt.

As her fingertips began to make slow, teasing move-ments around her already hardened sex bud, Maggie imagined herself peeling Troy's thong down over his rampant erection. Nearby, an owl hooted mournfully; she pictured herself lying naked on the grass with the moon shining down on her and Troy kneeling beside her with his cock in one hand, fondling her aching breasts. The image was so strong and powerful that she could almost smell the sweet scent of the grass. She wanted to feel the breeze on her bare skin. She was consumed with a crazy urge to pleasure herself naked with her body bathed in the moonlight like a Greek goddess.

Sod Justin and his stupid promises! How would he ever know anyway? Besides, a promise made under duress wasn't really a promise. Maggie peered down the lane ahead. Maybe there was a way into the field round the next bend? She started forward again eagerly.

As she walked, Maggie glanced around at the dark

shadows of the hedgerows on either side. The soft caress of the cool breeze on her damp underwear only added to her mounting arousal. Her whole body was tingling with anticipation. She increased her pace.

When she rounded the bend and saw a light ahead of her, she almost groaned aloud with shock and disappointment. There was some kind of van parked in a gateway just ahead. Images of a courting couple seeking privacy in the back of the van filled her mind and added to her fury. There was no way she could risk sneaking past them. What on earth would she say if anyone saw her? Her fantasy was disintegrating before her eyes.

As she stood, cursing her luck, the van door opened and a tall, dark shape climbed out and began to move towards her. Maggie froze as she was caught in the powerful beam of a torch, like a fly trapped in a web. She heard an exclamation of surprise and saw a second figure climb out of the front of the van.

'It's a woman.' The voice was deep and distinctly masculine. His words were as incredulous as if he had said: 'it's a Martian.' Maggie felt her temper flare. She put her hand up to protect her eyes.

'Would you mind pointing that somewhere else?' she called angrily. 'I can't see a damn thing.'

'Sorry.' The light moved to one side and Maggie blinked her eyes to clear the afterglare.

She couldn't decide whether to stand her ground or run away. She was acutely aware of her vulnerability but, at the same time, still keyed up enough to relish the titillation of this strange encounter. Perhaps this was the very opportunity she was seeking? She took a few steps forward and peered into the darkness. Two tall and heavily built men were standing just in front of the van, peering back at her. Through the windscreen, she could see several others moving about and realised that there was something familiar about them. No. Impossible. It couldn't be. She gasped as realisation dawned, then gasped again as her foot slipped on some loose gravel and she stumbled forward.

The man with the torch rushed forward and grabbed her arms to steady her. 'Hey. Take it easy. What's up? Have you been in an accident?'

Maggie gazed up wordlessly at the Trojans' new centre ice player, Tor. She blinked and shook her head to clear it. How could it possibly be him? Her overexcited imagination must be playing tricks on her. She heard the other men moving around inside the van and the side door began to slide open.

'What's happening? Who is it? What's going on?' Their questions were a confused jumble in her ears.

Tor stared at her in surprise. 'Wait a minute. Don't I know you?' Suddenly, he began to chuckle. 'Yeah. You were at the game tonight.' He grinned. 'Guess what guys?' he called over his shoulder. 'It's one of those babes that came to dinner with us after the match. The ones that gave us such a hard time,' he emphasised.

Maggie felt herself blushing from head to toe. 'What on earth are you doing here?' she stammered in confusion.

'We're supposed to be heading for our hotel,' he replied. 'Roland's got us booked into some fancy place way out in the country somewhere. But the stupid bastard put his foot down and left us behind.'

The dark shape in the night that was Troy stepped closer to them, so that Maggie could see his teeth and eyes gleaming with amusement in the light from the van. He always seemed to be smiling. She stared at him in shock. He was so close to her that she could feel the warmth of his body radiating from him. Her knees began to tremble.

'Hello Troy,' she muttered stupidly, as if there were nothing strange about her being out walking on her own at this time of night.

Troy stepped closer. He raised his hand and let his

finger trace the outline of her cheekbone. 'I think maybe you and I have some unfinished business,' he whispered suggestively.

Maggie's head started to swim. She felt remote and distant, as if she were in someone else's body, looking out. None of this was real. She was dreaming again, letting her fantasies run away with her. He couldn't possibly be out here, in the middle of nowhere. She felt the same as when she had unzipped Justin in the Cellar. Crazy and reckless. Horny. She lowered her eyes and stared hungrily at his groin. If it were only her imagination, it was the most realistic fantasy she'd ever had. Please God, don't let me wake up, she begged silently.

Tor followed her gaze. 'You know, I think she's curious to see just how big you really are without all the padding,' he sniggered. Maggie could smell the drink on his breath and realised that they were probably all slightly pissed.

Troy's grin widened. 'No problem.' His hand dropped from her cheek and started to explore the outline of her left breast. Apart from a sharp intake of breath, Maggie did not react. As he started to undo the buckle of his belt, she drew another deep breath. Casually, he flipped the button open and slid his zip down.

His trousers dropped to his ankles, revealing a pair of light-coloured boxer shorts. His legs were so dark that she could barely see their outline, so that his torso almost seemed to be floating in mid-air. Slowly, he put his hand between the opening of his shorts and peeled the material back. Maggie gulped and finally let her breath out.

'Well?'

She swallowed again and nodded her head. 'Very nice,' she croaked feebly without taking her eyes off his already expanding cock. Now she knew that she had to be dreaming.

'It gets bigger if you stroke it,' he promised crudely.

Maggie heard the sound of the van door opening

again. She glanced up at Tor, who was still holding her arm, then turned her head to look at four other Trojans who had now piled out of the van to gather round them. She could smell the alcohol on them too and wondered just how drunk they were. Obviously drunk enough to have got themselves lost in the middle of nowhere.

One of the other forwards, Bri, grinned at her and gave her an exaggerated wink.

'Go on, love. Make his day,' he encouraged her.

Make *his* day! Maggie remembered how desperately she had wanted him earlier and what she had been planning to do to herself before she had bumped into them.

Tor took her hand and guided it over Troy's groin. Although she could hardly believe what she was doing, she still made no effort to resist. She jumped as her fingertips made contact with his flesh. It seemed so hot in the cool night air. Totally unable to restrain herself, she closed her fist around his hardness and started to slide her hand up towards the tip.

He still wasn't fully erect and, as she began to move her hand back down towards the base, she could feel him expanding in response to her caress. She looked up into his face and noticed that his jaw was tightly clenched. Her stomach flipped and she felt a deep tingle of urgent arousal burning within her. Slowly, she slid her fingers down to the base of his stem and lightly caressed his balls. She felt his body stiffen as she pushed her fingers into the tight pubic curls and squeezed him gently.

'That's it, give him a good grope,' one of the other Trojans encouraged.

Maggie licked her dry lips and moved her hand back up to enclose his stem. At least he wasn't too drunk. His cock was now as hard as any vibrator and she could feel his pulse thudding as the blood surged through his swollen veins. Another stab of longing tore through her. She opened her fist and stepped back, straight into Tor.

'You know, Troy, you shouldn't go around exposing yourself like that. Should he lads?' Tor reprimanded him as he put his arms around Maggie's waist.

'You suggested it,' Troy protested.

'No I didn't. I just said that she was curious. I didn't mean for you to scare her like that. The poor girl's trembling with shock.' He squeezed her more tightly.

She was certainly trembling, but she wasn't sure shock was the most appropriate word to describe her emotions. Her whole body felt as if it was on fire and she was acutely aware of Tor's body pushed up hard against her.

'Get him guys. Troy needs to be taught a lesson,' Tor continued.

Two of the others grabbed Troy from behind and pushed him up against the side of the van. Chuckling sadistically, they whipped his boxer shorts down round his ankles. Maggie felt herself being herded up against his hard buttocks until she was pushed between the two men like the filling in a sandwich. Instinctively, she placed her hands on Troy's thighs and squeezed the taut flesh with her shaking fingers. It didn't matter what you did in a dream, did it? It wasn't real so it didn't count.

Troy grunted and began to roll his hips suggestively, pushing his cheeks back hard against her already over-sensitive mound and sending little tremors of pleasure coursing through her body. She squeezed him again and felt his muscles twitch in response. Tor thrust himself against her from behind and she could feel his own excitement hard and urgent through his clothing.

Suddenly, she felt herself being pulled back and she watched in silence as the other men continued to strip Troy's clothes off him. She almost giggled at the way he struggled and cursed furiously as he tried to break free. Three against one, it was hopeless. As soon as his shirt was removed, they spun him round and lifted him up as easily as one might lift a doll.

'Pull his trousers off,' one of them commanded her.

Needing no further urging, she bent down and ripped his trousers and shorts off his flailing ankles. Her eyes were fixed almost hypnotically on his massive penis and her fingers itched to stroke it again. Tremors of excitement and lust shot through her body and her mouth was so dry that no matter how often she licked her lips, no moisture seemed to stay on them.

'Shit! That's enough. A joke's a joke.' Troy strained against them so hard that his muscles bulged.

Tor chuckled. 'Bend him over,' he commanded mercilessly.

The two men spun Troy back round and pushed him over against the van. Maggie couldn't take her eyes off the sight of his buttocks twitching angrily as he struggled against their hold.

'Six of the best.' Tor took Maggie's hand and motioned for her to whack him. Troy twisted his head round to glare over his shoulder.

'Get off, you bastards!' he yelled and renewed his struggle as another of the players grabbed him and pushed his head back round. 'When I get free, I'll break your frigging necks.'

'Hang on. We don't want her to hurt her hand.' One of the defenders, whose name Maggie suddenly couldn't recall, climbed into the back of the van and rummaged around. A few seconds later he reappeared with a jubilant expression on his face. He was holding a hockey stick in his left hand.

'Here you go, love.' He handed her the stick. 'Six strokes. He has to learn more self-control or, next thing you know, he'll be getting a hard-on during a game. That would never do.'

'No, I can't.' Maggie's eyes were gleaming with anticipation as she slipped her jacket off and took hold of the stick.

'Yes you can,' Tor contradicted her. 'Otherwise, we'll let him whack you. After all, it's your fault he's got so excited.' He grinned. 'Not that I blame him. Hell, a sexy woman like you is enough to get anyone hot.'

Maggie was already moving into position. 'OK.' She gripped the stick firmly and lifted her arm. Thankfully, no one tried to stop her. She was so excited that it would probably have taken all of them to prevent her now.

'For fuck's sake, let me go. Ahh!' Troy's words were interrupted by the thud of the stick on his left buttock. He grunted with shock and renewed his attempts to wriggle free. 'Ow!' Her second hard whack was followed rapidly by two more on the other cheek.

'Bend him right over,' Maggie heard herself whisper, 'make him touch his toes.'

As Troy's buttocks were raised even higher into the air, Maggie dropped the stick and spat on her palm. 'I'll use my hand,' she added as she landed yet another resounding whack on his right buttock. Leaving her hand on his skin, she rubbed the flesh gently with her fingers then quickly raised her arm and planted another slap on his left cheek.

Tor laughed. 'Well, I guess that's taught you a lesson, eh, Troy?'

'Jesus, that stings,' Troy muttered softly as his three friends finally released their grip and allowed him to straighten up.

Rubbing his buttocks tenderly, Troy turned round to face her. His erection seemed bigger than ever and, without even stopping to think about it, Maggie wrapped her fingers round his cock and pulled him closer so that her body was rubbing against him. She slid her fist up and down, pumping him gently.

'You don't seem to have learned your lesson though, do you?' she whispered derisively.

'No ma'am,' he mocked her in return, 'and, since it's your fault you're gonna to have to take care of it.' He placed his hands on Maggie's shoulders and began to push her down in front of him. Excitement raced through her. He wanted her to suck him in front of everyone!

As she lowered her mouth over him, Tor put his hands round her and pulled her back, forcing her to bend at the waist to reach Troy. She slipped her hand between his legs and pushed against his thigh. Obligingly, Troy spread his legs further apart and Maggie placed her right hand on his prick to hold him still. The fingernails of her left hand started to trace soft patterns on his upper thigh.

As her tongue shot out to lick his swollen cock, Maggie felt his whole body shudder and saw his muscles tense. She could sense the other men gathering closer to watch. She turned her head slightly and saw one of them pulling at the front of his trousers to try and make himself more comfortable. Her smile widened as he gave up and pushed his hand down the waistband. She watched, fascinated, as he struggled under his clothing. When he finally pulled his hand back out, his cock was a hard bulge up the front of his fly.

Enflamed, Maggie started to run her tongue down Troy's shaft. She had no idea what was going to happen next. She had never sucked a man in front of an audience and the idea appealed to her more than she would ever have believed. She bent lower and wrapped her tongue around his balls. As she pulled them towards her, she slipped her hand further between his legs and used his buttocks to steady herself. She dug her nails into his flesh and felt him squirm in response.

Her body felt as if it were engulfed in flames. She was sensitive to every sound and every movement. She could feel the cold night air creeping up the back of her short skirt and caressing her thighs and she imagined the other men staring at her exposure. Were they all getting excited? Her mind filled with delightful images of them all stripped and wanking as they feasted their eyes on the curve of her buttocks. Maybe they hoped that she would take care of them all?

Exhilarated, she took Troy's full length into her mouth and sucked as hard as she could. Slowly, she slid her lips up his long thick shaft, allowing her teeth to graze lightly over the sensitive flesh. When she felt his muscles tensing still further, she put her hand between his buttocks and began to run her finger around his arsehole. He gasped with pleasure and her searching fingers felt his balls swelling and tightening.

Not wanting things to end too soon, Maggie took her hand away, pulled her head back and gripped him tightly between her fingers. Only when she felt him relax slightly did she replace her tongue on his hot tip.

Troy sighed and groaned with the agony and ecstasy of her deliberate teasing as, time and time again, Maggie brought him to the brink of his climax and then drew back, squeezing him with her fingers until his immediate urgency passed. His whole body was visibly trembling with the effort and his knees were shaking so much that he could barely stand. Each time she held him back it took longer to get him under control and each time she resumed her torment his desperate arousal seemed swifter.

Maggie could sense the other men moving in closer and closer. She could feel their body heat radiating from them and, when she swayed her hips, she felt her buttocks brush against a huge erection. Its owner placed his hand on the small of her back and gradually moved his fingers down over her bottom. As they moved back up under the hem of her skirt his fingertips caressed the bare flesh of her inner thighs so that it took all of her self-control not to clamp her teeth together. She parted her legs to encourage him further.

She began to knead Troy's cock even harder, trying to distract herself from the fingers creeping closer and closer to her sex. Gradually, she became aware of more hands touching her body. Sure fingers expertly unclipped her bra and she felt the ping of the elasticated straps springing open. A hand crept up the slit at the side of her knickers and started to caress her left buttock while another hand pulled her blouse free from her skirt.

Maggie shuddered again as a gentle kiss on the back of her knee drew her attention to the Trojan crouching behind her. His tongue ran down her leg and his hands guided her ankles further apart. She quickly smothered a groan of delight by sucking Troy back into her mouth. As she pumped him up and down with her lips, she watched the droplets of sweat running down his body. Unable to resist, she ran her tongue up his lean stomach muscles and licked the sweat from him.

Another sigh burst from her as someone opened her blouse. Her loosened bra had ridden right up and she felt a huge hand cup one of her breasts while another peeled the blouse back over her shoulders and halfway down her arms. Soft lips kissed her back and probing fingers flicked her rapidly hardening nipples. She gasped again and tightened her mouth round Troy's cock so that her teeth were pressed into his flesh.

There was a shuffling of feet as the other men moved back to stand behind her. She jumped as a hand lifted the hem of her skirt and started to lower her knickers. Maggie heard several sharp whistles as her buttocks came into view.

As soon as her knickers were down to her ankles one of the men lifted her foot and made her step out of them. Everyone cheered and she felt a hand slipping up between her thighs. Another shudder raced through her as she tightened her lips on Troy's cock and pumped him rapidly in and out. In her excitement, she misjudged his control and pushed him too far.

With a deep groan, Troy exploded. As his stream of hot spunk pumped out of him he grasped her head, forcing his prick further and further into her mouth and thrusting back and forth desperately until he was utterly spent.

Maggie heard his gentle sigh of release as he finally pulled back and leaned his drained body against the side of the van. Gradually, he slid down until he was resting on his heels. Still breathing heavily, Maggie stood up and watched silently as his cock gradually began to soften and relax.

A pair of hands snatched her from behind and began to slide up her stomach and on to her breasts. She felt her loosened blouse and bra slipping down over her arms and saw them drop to the ground beside her knickers. The man pulled her back hard against him, all the while squeezing and kneading her aching breasts. Her skirt began to drop over her hips and down her legs.

At the sound of a zip opening she glanced over her shoulder and saw Tor. He eased his cock free of his jock strap and Maggie bit back a moan as it sprang hard against her thigh. With a powerful thrust of his hips, she felt him nuzzling it deeper into her crack. Trembling with excitement, Maggie pushed back against him until she could feel his thick pubic hairs tickling her skin and the smooth tip of his cock was hard up against her anus. She looked down and saw Troy watching them silently.

'Bring me some oil,' Tor commanded hoarsely as he moved himself gently up and down her crack. He pushed her forward until she was balanced over Troy with her hands resting on the side of the van. Troy lifted his head and started to lick her breasts and, with a whimper of pleasure, Maggie lowered herself a little more so that he could suck her nipples into his mouth. His wide lips were as soft as silk, soothing her burning flesh.

Tor stepped back and tugged the remainder of his clothes off. He stood beside her, waiting for the oil and she turned her head to gaze hungrily at the massive erection standing out proudly from his groin. The glistening whiteness of his skin there was in sharp contrast to the darker area of his stomach and thighs.

She gritted her teeth against the teasing caress of Troy's soft lips and watched avidly as Tor took the baby oil from his friend's hand and carefully unscrewed the top. He stepped forward and she felt a few drops of the warm, sticky fluid dribbling down between her buttocks.

Tor smoothed the oil into her crack with his finger, passed the bottle down to Troy and slipped a condom over his cock. Troy tipped some of the oil into his hand and started to rub it gently into her breasts and stomach. Maggie moaned with pleasure at the unexpected massage then jumped as she felt Tor pushing his oil-covered finger gently into her back passage.

Dear God in heaven! Maggie shivered from head to foot as she watched Tor slowly and deliberately spread some of the oil down his shaft. He was intending to take her anally. She shivered again with a mixture of fear and excitement as he pushed her down until her hands were resting on Troy's shoulders. Tor moved round behind her and put his hand between her legs; he lifted her up until her toes only just touched the ground and her bottom was stuck up in the air.

She whimpered softly as she felt him opening her cheeks. She had never had anal sex before, although earlier Justin had made it clear he wanted it. Now, this man she had only just met, this virtual stranger, was about to take her virginity. Involuntarily, she clenched her buttocks. Should she tell him it was her first time and beg him to be gentle with her? She shivered again. Everyone was watching her. After what she had already done, how could she now simper like a teenage virgin? She bit her lips and tried to relax her muscles, giving herself up to the sensation of his finger slipping unresisting into her back passage.

Gradually, as she abandoned herself to the pleasure, she forgot her fear. Her clit was prickling as much as if he had been taking her from the front and she could already feel the little ripples of her building orgasm. She closed her eyes and pushed back against him.

'Go on. She's ready for it. Shove it in and fuck her.'

Maggie started at the words and opened her eyes. She had almost forgotten the other men. Now, she could feel them swarming round her, with their eyes and hands everywhere. How could all this possibly be happening? She took a long, deep breath then let it out again in a sharp whoosh as Tor pulled his finger out, yanked her backwards and thrust his slippery penis hard against her.

'Oh, Jesus!' she cried as his cock rammed into her and his hand slid round her thigh to squeeze her mound. She whimpered again as, with apparent ease, he lifted her bodily off the ground so that she was impaled on him. With the palm of his hand pressed hard on to her mound and his middle finger massaging her swollen sex bud, Tor swung her away from Troy and moved her closer to the van.

Maggie instinctively raised her arms to try and steady herself, but Tor used his other hand to brush them aside. Stepping forward, he pushed her breasts hard on to the side of the van. The metal felt as cold as ice on her burning flesh and a shiver ran through her body as another gasp burst from her lips. She felt his cock pull out slowly, then thrust back in again in time with his insistent caressing of her tortured clit.

'You should see the view from here,' a voice beside them muttered hoarsely.

The words seemed to enflame Tor. With a loud grunt, he thrust himself hard into her again, deeper and deeper; further than she would have ever dreamt possible. His thighs slapped against her buttocks and she moaned as she felt her tightness resisting him. She struggled to relax and felt a brief rush of surprise that what he was doing to her did not really hurt.

She relaxed further and felt the pleasure of the sensation increasing as her fears finally receded. Another tiny whimper escaped her lips as his hand pushed up between her and the van to squeeze her nipple. The combination of being simultaneously stimulated in three places at once was driving her wild, so that her breath was coming in short little pants and she could feel the perspiration dripping from her.

'I bet this is her first time,' another voice called.

'Nah. How could an arse like that escape for so long?'

'Is this your first time, love?'

Maggie had no voice to answer. Tor was pumping her harder and faster. His finger was pushed up inside her and his thumb was rhythmically massaging her clit. She was only seconds away from her climax. She pushed her body back against his chest and twisted her head round so that she could lick his ear.

Tor grunted and thrust into her again and Maggie cried out, biting his lobe in her overwhelming excitement. She leant back even harder against him, so that he was trapped inside her, then tightened her anal muscles round him as if trying to crush him. She could feel his sweat pouring down his body and mingling with her own. She bit his ear again and increased the pressure of her muscles.

'I'm coming,' he gasped. 'Oh Jesus, I can't . . .' He pushed her savagely forward, so that she almost lost her precarious balance. Quickly, she raised her hands and pressed her palms hard against the side of the van. Tor grabbed her round the waist and drew himself back for one final thrust. As he pushed into her, he pulled her body back on to him and they both cried out as she felt the urgent judder of his impending explosion. He moaned again.

'Oh yes,' Maggie whimpered as her own orgasm ripped through her body and they both collapsed forward against the van. With a final grunt, Tor climaxed, his whole body tensing as his fluid burst from him. He gradually began to pull back out of her.

When he released his grip on her waist, Maggie discovered that her legs were too weak to support her and she only just managed to catch herself with her arms before she fell. Dimly, she became aware of the other players cheering and whistling their performance.

'Phew!' Tor exclaimed as he wiped the sweat from his eyes. 'That was incredible.'

'I'm next,' cried a voice in her ear. 'You can go on top and I'll just lie back and let you fuck me.'

Two down and four to go, Maggie thought to herself with a shiver of anticipation. This was some fantasy!

'Nah, I'm next.'

Maggie looked round and saw Ean's huge dark eyes staring down at her. 'What she needs right now is a long, slow screw, don't you love?' He licked his lips. 'I'm just the man for that.'

'You'd better get in quick Pary,' Tor laughed. 'After Ean here has finished with her there won't be much left.'

Maggie leant back against the van and watched as Ean pulled his shirt over his head without undoing the buttons, slipped out of his shoes and whipped his trousers down. She was astonished at how casually she was taking all this. She wasn't normally quite so free and easy. But then, there was nothing normal about any of this. It wasn't even really happening. It was just some crazy, erotic dream. Any moment now the alarm clock would ring and she would wake up in her own bed, alone. She fixed her eyes on Ean's rampant cock and felt another shudder engulf her as he slipped a condom on and took her by the hand.

Ean led her over to the grass verge and gently helped her down on to her back. As before, the others gathered round to watch and Maggie was amazed to see that Troy was already beginning to recover. Ean lay down beside her and snatched a handful of her breasts.

'Come on, get on with it,' Pary moaned. 'I can't wait all night. You can play with her tits later.'

'OK, keep your pants on,' Ean laughed as he opened her legs and knelt between her thighs.

'That's just it. I don't want them on,' Pary complained as he massaged his groin. 'They're much too tight.'

Everyone roared with laughter as Ean pushed his hand between her legs and prised her sex lips apart. She quivered as she felt his fingers playing with her dampness. He shuffled closer and allowed his tip to rub against her teasingly. She immediately thrust herself against him, forcing him up into her. She lifted her legs and wrapped them round the back of his thighs, then pushed herself on to him. He groaned and pushed his hands under her. As he started to pump her, he used his strong arms to lift her up off the ground and on to his lap.

Maggie leaned forward and rested her hands on his shoulders, pushing herself up and down enthusiastically. She squealed as his finger slipped into her crack and penetrated her recently deflowered anus. Enflamed, she thrust her breasts forward on to his mouth, urging him to suck first one nipple then the other. All around them, the enthusiastic audience shouted encouragement and muttered obscenities.

'Do you think she'd do it with other women, too?' a voice questioned.

'Of course she would.' She recognised Troy's deep voice. 'She'd screw anything. Look at her go.'

Maggie found that their comments were only adding to her stimulation. Every word, every suggestion, seemed to push her closer and closer to the edge. Frantically, she matched Ean's movements thrust for thrust; her hands dug into his back as she tried to pull herself even harder and deeper on to him.

'What a goer. I'm beginning to wonder if we're enough for her.'

'Don't worry. I've got what she needs.'

73

Their words danced and swirled in her head. If there were any other women present she felt sure that she would do it with them, too, so that anal sex wouldn't be her only first of the night. She was beginning to understand just what a turn on it was for a man to watch two women together. She was starting to find the whole concept more and more intriguing.

Ean placed his hands back under her buttocks. He lifted her effortlessly up and down so that all she needed to do was to steady herself as he slid her up and down his hard shaft. She deliberately tightened her vaginal muscles around him so that she was squeezing him in time with his thrusts. She could hear his breath rasping urgently and imagined the thoughts of the other men as they watched his cock pumping in and out of her.

'Yes,' she cried as her climax engulfed her. 'Oh God, yes.' Another sob burst from her as she felt Ean start to come. She relaxed against him, hugging his chest as she savoured every burst of his own violent and powerful release.

Gradually, she became aware of the cold touch of the breeze against the dampness of her bare skin. Goose bumps covered her body. She could feel Ean shrinking away inside her. Someone took her arms and lifted her up off him and she could see the dumb smile of satisfaction on his face.

Tor produced a towel and started to dry her and one of the others handed her his can of lager, which she snatched gratefully and gulped from noisily. Tor finished wiping the sweat away and started kissing her breasts as he continued to rub her most private parts with the towel. Gradually, he turned her round and began to kiss her thighs and mound. She felt his probing tongue inching its way between her thighs. 'It's Pary next.'

Maggie saw that the brown-haired, green-eyed defender of Claire's fantasies was already stripping. It wasn't difficult to understand what Claire saw in him.

74

He had the most blatantly sensuous eyes Maggie had ever stared into.

'Bring her over here.' Pary lay back on the grass and took his cock in one hand. 'Stick her on this.' He ran his fingers up and down his erection.

Maggie put the can down and pushed herself free. Her earlier feeling of total recklessness returned and intensified. She had always sensed her potential to be good at domination. Very good. It was time to turn the tables on them. With an exaggerated roll of her hips, she strode across and stood astride him.

'You think you can satisfy me?' she questioned as she began to lower herself down on to his hard knob. 'Not quite right,' she complained. 'Move it back.' She warmed to her new role.

Pary did as requested and she felt his tip slide up between her sex lips. 'Good boy,' she encouraged him as she lowered herself down over him.

The others cheered approvingly. 'I reckon you've bitten off more than you can chew,' Troy goaded Pary. 'She's already beaten three of us, so far.'

Pary grinned confidently. 'No problem.' He gritted his teeth as she sank down to encompass him totally. 'I can take care of her,' he rasped hoarsely.

'Not before I fuck your brains out,' Maggie retorted in a voice similar to her own but using words she could hardly believe were coming from her mouth. She rolled her hips aggressively and squeezed her muscles. Pary groaned again.

Tor laughed. 'Now you're for it. We'll pick up the pieces after she's finished with you.'

'Yeah. We'll even give you a nice funeral,' Troy chuckled.

Maggie glanced down and realised that Pary wasn't listening to them anymore. His face was screwed up in total concentration and his breathing was already ragged. She grinned. She wasn't even moving up and down yet;

just massaging him with her inner muscles. She put her hands on his chest and increased her relentless pressure. She mouthed the ice hockey term for a ten-minute over-time session to determine the winner. 'Sudden death.'

'Ahh, Jesus!' Pary tightened his buttocks and tried to thrust up into her, but Maggie curled her fingers and dug her nails into his chest. 'Keep still,' she hissed, so softly none but he could hear.

Pary lowered himself back to the ground and gritted his teeth as she continued to squeeze him. He placed his hands on her buttocks and, with every movement of her muscles, he tightened his grip. One hand slid round to her mound and he started to finger her clit in time to the rhythm of her vaginal massage.

Maggie felt the perspiration starting to run down her again with the effort of maintaining her muscle contrac-tions. Pary's finger had found its way up beside his cock and his fingertip seemed to have discovered her G-spot. She wriggled with pleasure at his relentless caress.

'Get on with it, for Christ's sake.' The voice of one of the others broke their desperate concentration, reminding Maggie of her audience. Pary pulled his finger out and seized her left breast. Taking a deep breath, he forced his buttocks up under her and thrust hard and fast inside her.

'No!' he cried desperately as he lost the fight.

As soon as she had squeezed him dry, Maggie stood up stared down at him. 'Not bad, but I think you need a little more self-control, too,' she said.

She swung round to face the onlookers. Her eyes lighted on the squad's baby-faced, golden-haired net-minder known as Pele. He looked like a young Greek god in the moonlight. He would make a fortune if he did open a garage. Women would bring their cars from miles around for the chance to see him in action. 'Well? What are you waiting for?' she demanded. 'Strip.'

Pele jumped at her words. One hand started to pull at

his shirt while the other struggled to undo his zip. As he pulled his trousers down, hopping on one foot, he staggered and nearly fell. Maggie suppressed a giggle and wondered how on earth a professional ice skater could manage to look so ungainly. Finally, he was naked. She examined his cock critically.

'Lie down and wank yourself while I have another beer,' she instructed. Was that what was affecting her, she wondered, marvelling at her total lack of inhibition? Or was it just the pheromone-laden night air? Whatever it was, she was burning for more.

Tor handed her a can of ice-cold beer and she rubbed it over her breasts, smiling as she remembered Justin's coke can. Her nipples puckered and doubled in size. She pulled the ring and felt the cold spray of froth across her chest. She gasped with delight, then glared at him.

'You shook the can,' she accused him. She stepped closer. 'Lick it off.'

Tor grinned and moved eagerly to obey. As his tongue played across her breasts, Maggie poured some of the beer over her pubes. 'There as well.' She looked at the others. 'Give him some help,' she demanded. 'Not you,' she added as Pele began to get up. 'You just carry on with what you're doing.' She ran her eyes greedily over his swollen cock, which was clutched tightly in his fist. She reached behind her and poured more beer down her buttocks.

By the time the men had finished their task, Maggie had polished off the last of the beer and recovered her energy. She tossed the can aside and moved closer to Pele. She stood across his chest, facing his groin, and looked round at the other men. Her confidence was growing by the second. She was in charge now.

'I want to see you all wanking,' she told them calmly. 'Even you,' she added, glaring at Ean, whose penis hadn't even started to recover yet. For a moment, she thought they were going to refuse but then Bri, the last of the six, unzipped his flies and whipped his cock out. Maggie smiled, remembering how he had been trying to rearrange himself earlier. After all this time watching, she thought, he must be fit to bust!

Maggie moved around, guiding the men into a straight line near Pele. She encouraged each of them in turn and smiled at the sight of Pary trying to coax some life back into his little willy. She gave him a couple of taps on the rump and ran her hand under his balls to help him along, then moved back over Pele. She lowered herself on to his chest so that her engorged sex lips were just above his mouth and her face was resting just inches from his cock.

By just moving her eyes she found she could see the other men quite clearly illuminated by the light from the van door. She felt Pele push his tongue up into her. Glancing down, she noticed his hand already sliding more rapidly up and down his shaft.

Maggie pushed back with her hips, forcing his tongue in deeper. A glance at the others told her that Pary was getting into it again, while Bri looked as if he was almost ready to let go. His hand was literally flying up and down his cock and his face had that urgent look of deep concentration as he fought to prolong his gratification.

She was so engrossed in watching him struggle that she almost missed Pele. A sudden, urgent thrust of his tongue and a loud grunt as his muscles tensed, just warned her. As she rolled herself clear of his body his cock exploded and a jet of spunk sprayed up into the air before splattering across his chest.

Pele groaned again as the first jet was followed by another, then another, until his chest was covered with his come. Maggie's eyes widened. He looked like a volcano erupting. She lifted her head. The other five were still engrossed in their play. How Bri was still holding on was a mystery. His face was beetroot and his chest was heaving with the exertion. She moved over to him and stood in front of him with her hands on her hips and her legs apart.

'Do you like what you see?' she taunted as she slipped a finger down over her mound and on to her clit.

Bri opened his eyes and stared longingly at her crotch. His hand stopped moving and she saw he was squeezing his tip tightly to hold himself back. He licked his lips and nodded silently.

'Then show me.' She put her other hand over his and forced his fist to resume pumping. Without moving her finger from her clit, she crouched down so that she could see his balls drawn tightly up against his body. She took her hand off his speeding fist and cupped them in her palm. Her fingers caressed the soft flesh and Bri cried out. A thick stream of come burst from his tip and ran down his fingers.

His cry was enough to set off Tor and Troy, too, so that Maggie felt as if she was standing under a waterfall of spunk. She moved over to the almost-recovered Ean and lowered her lips over his growing enthusiasm. As she began to suck him, she felt his stiffness increase further and heard him starting to pant. She sucked harder.

As Ean finally lost it again, she felt a gentle slap on her bottom. She spun round to face Troy. He slipped his arm round her waist and kissed her cheek. 'You're quite something, baby,' he told her as he handed her a towel. 'That was fantastic.' He kissed her cheek. 'Maybe we could have a one-on-one rematch sometime?' he added softly. 'Sometime soon.'

Tor took her by the arm. 'If we hadn't stopped to argue over which turning to take, none of this would have happened. For once, Roland actually did us a real favour.' He stared at her. 'You never did say what you're doing out here all alone.'

'I, er ... I was just out for a walk,' Maggie told them.

'My friends and I are staying just up the road there and I needed some fresh air.' She pointed back down the lane.

Troy grinned. 'Lucky for us.' He put his arm round her waist again. 'Tell you what, sugar. Give us five minutes to put some clothes on and we'll give you a ride back.' He chuckled. 'A sweet thing like you shouldn't be out all on her own at this time of night. No telling what might happen to her.'

Chapter Four

On the short journey back to the B&B, Troy insisted that Maggie sit up in front with him. Maggie was surprised at just how easily she was able to sit and chat with him. It was almost as if her abandoned and wanton actions of the past hour had not taken place.

'So, how come you managed to get yourselves lost then?' she teased him.

'Roland drives like a maniac,' Troy explained ruefully. 'Besides, you can't really expect this old wreck to keep up with a brand new XK8,' he added.

Maggie was impressed. She had seen the car in the car park at the rink but hadn't realised who it belonged to. Thanks to Justin's obsession with fast cars, she had a pretty fair idea how much an XK8 was worth. She hadn't realised that the Trojans' manager did so well out of them. Still, it would take more than a fancy car to change her opinion of its owner. 'So, what will you do now?' she asked him.

Troy shrugged nonchalantly. 'Keep looking, I guess. If we don't find the hotel soon, we'll just curl up in the back of the van. Unless there's room for us in your bed?'

Maggie grinned at the idea of how her friends would

react if she sneaked back in with half a dozen of the Trojans in tow. Totally impractical, but very tempting.

Troy pulled up outside the B&B and turned to face her. 'There you go, Maggie. All safe and sound.' He kissed her cheek. 'Thanks again for an unreal time.'

Tor leant forward over the front seat and put his hand on her shoulder. 'We will be seeing you again real soon, won't we?'

Maggie twisted round and nodded. 'Probably.' She remembered that he was from Canada and had only been with the team a few weeks. 'I'm working the morning shift all next week.'

'Oh yeah, that's right. You work on reception, don't you?' He smiled warmly at her.

Maggie undid her seatbelt and opened the door. 'I might see you on Monday then?' She was flattered he had noticed her.

Tor grimaced. 'I've got to do a spot of house hunting first thing on Monday. Now I've signed on with the Trojans for next season I'm going to need somewhere better to live. The place I'm in at the moment is a real pigsty.'

Maggie stared at him thoughtfully. 'I've got a friend who's an estate agent,' she told him. 'You met her earlier this evening. Blonde hair and glasses?'

'Yeah. I remember her.' Tor said and nodded.

'She works for Hardy's in the High Street. I'll ask her if she can help you find something, shall I?' Just try to stop Jan from helping once she's heard about it, Maggie thought, remembering the way Jan had been eyeing Tor up earlier on.

'Great.' Tor smiled. 'Thank you.'

Boy oh boy, was Jan ever in for a big surprise, Maggie smiled to herself as she crept in the back door and tiptoed upstairs to the room.

* * *

Claire Patrick started her next shift at the rink at 7 a.m. the following Monday morning. She had had trouble getting off to sleep the night before and felt as if she had barely closed her eyes before the alarm clock jarred her back awake. When she had finally dozed off, her dreams had been haunted by muscular ice hockey players. It was hard to believe that she had really met them all in person.

In her exhausted daze, everything seemed to take twice as long as usual. Her eyes had dark shadows under them and her hair refused to obey the comb. She applied foundation and concealer to her face and rubbed a handful of mousse through her wayward locks. Still munching a piece of toast, she ran for the bus, catching it with only seconds to spare. By the time she slipped into the staff locker room to change out of her Gap jeans and into her crisp black and white uniform, she was already running very late.

There was a hastily scrawled note stuck on her locker door from the personnel manager informing her that she had been assigned to the players' changing rooms that morning. Claire read the note and then screwed it up angrily.

She hated it when she was reassigned from her normal work in the public locker rooms. It might be boring but at least she could get on in her own time and, usually, without anyone else interfering. The players' showers and changing area were always in such a mess after a match or a practice session. The women's junior ice hockey team had been playing a friendly match the previous afternoon and their changing rooms were bound to be in a right state. It was virtually guaranteed that she would end up wet and soggy before she was finished.

As she resentfully pushed her cleaning trolley along the corridor, Claire consoled herself with the thought that she might bump into Justin if he were on duty that morning. She had secretly lusted after him for ages but everyone knew that he and Maggie had a bit of a thing going, and she really liked Maggie.

Besides, if she was being completely honest with herself, Justin terrified her. He was so suave and sophisticated. If only she didn't always get tongue-tied at the wrong moment. If only she could be a bit more like Maggie or Jan. Even the quiet Sara seemed to find it easier to talk to men than she did.

'Good morning, Claire. You're late.' Justin had stepped out into the corridor in front of her. He glanced impatiently at his watch.

Claire jumped. Her pulse started to race as she realised who it was, and her face immediately reddened. 'I'm, I'm, er, sorry.'

'Well, you'd better get a move on,' Justin chided. 'I was promised you would be here by seven at the latest.'

'I'm sorry,' she said again, as her colour deepened. 'I overslept.' She wondered if he knew how good-looking he was in his dark suit and crisp white shirt, with his long blond hair tied back and his eyes sparkling against his tanned skin. Almost like one of the Trojans.

Justin put his hand on hers and flashed her one of his most dazzling smiles. 'Did you enjoy yourself on Saturday, by the way? We really slaughtered the 'Birds, didn't we?'

'Oh yes. It was wicked,' Claire replied nervously, thrilled that he was paying her so much attention. She remembered the way she had noticed him watching her once or twice while she was working and how some of his comments to her had seemed almost suggestive. After all, it wasn't as if he and Maggie were an item or anything. Maybe he really did fancy her? If only she could be sure.

Justin smiled again and his fingers tightened round hers. 'Perhaps I'll see you again when you've finished? You'd better start in the women's changing room first. I'll be in my office if you want anything.'

As he strolled off down the corridor, Claire watched his buttocks twitch up and down tantalisingly. Did he really mean for her to go and see him in his office later? Why else would he make a point of telling her where he would be? Maybe he was simply being a good manager or, then again, maybe he really did want her.

Shit. If only she could be certain. She would feel such a prat if he hadn't meant anything by his comments. Still, it wouldn't hurt to let him know she had finished, would it? Perhaps she could try to persuade him not to complain about her being late. It was not the first time she had overslept and she knew the personnel manager was unlikely to be sympathetic.

As she resumed pushing the trolley down the corridor, Claire pictured herself sitting on Justin's lap telling him how sorry she was for being late while he did wonderful things to her with his hands and lips. She sighed, already knowing that she would not dare to go and find him. If only she could learn to be a bit more assertive and confident, but she had always been too shy and reserved, even as a child. If only Justin had ordered her to his office so that she would have had no choice but to go. Maybe she could pretend that she thought he had.

Her mind still full of outrageous fantasies of herself and Justin making passionate love over his desk, Claire arrived at the women's home changing room and pushed her trolley through the door. She looked around and her heart sank. The place was an utter wreck. It looked as if it hadn't been cleaned properly for a week. It was going to take her ages to get this mess sorted out and she still had to do the men's room afterwards.

Claire scurried about frantically, picking up discarded paper towels and sweet wrappers. She even found a pair of knickers under one bench. Quite sexy but too big for her. She shoved them into the laundry bag with the damp towels. Let the laundry company worry about them.

She peered into the shower cubicles and grimaced when she saw the discarded shampoo bottles, the sticky globs of soap on the tiles and the strands of long hair blocking every drain. Talk about slobs. The women were far worse than the men. Angrily, she yanked at the cleaning hose, braced herself against the far wall and turned the tap full on. She had forgotten how much pressure it generated and before she could reach the tap to turn it down, she lost her footing. The nozzle slipped from her fingers and the hose began to writhe around on the floor like an angry python, spraying water in every direction.

'Bugger it!' Before she could regain her footing and scramble across the floor to the tap, she was soaked to the skin and the whole area was flooded. Justin would be livid if she didn't get this mopped up before anyone saw it. As she tried to brush the water off herself and wring out the hem of her sodden skirt she waded across the room to fetch the squeegee mop.

Maybe she could pretend that the drains had been blocked with paper towels. What if she lost her job? She wouldn't be able to afford her little bedsit if she was out of work. As she began frantically pushing the puddle of lying water towards the central drain, she pictured herself standing, dripping, in Justin's office and begging him not to report her.

'Please, Mr Edwards, I'm sorry. It was an accident. I'll do anything you want to make up for it.' Maybe she would undo her top button first so that he could see what she was offering. She could almost imagine his wolfish smile growing larger as he stared down her cleavage. She would have no choice but to do whatever he told her. Even her boyfriend would have to understand that she had had no choice. It was either that or move back home with her parents, and he would hate that even more, wouldn't he?

Having found an excuse to relieve the guilt of her

thoughts about Justin, she quickly warmed to her fantasies again. Her friend Sally said that if your boss took advantage of you, then it wasn't really a betrayal. Claire felt that if you deliberately flirted the way Sally did, it couldn't really be right, but she was coming round to her friend's way of thinking.

She must have been feeling like this because of Saturday. She was still excited from being with all the Trojans. She had been so turned on thinking about them all last night that, if her boyfriend had been there, she knew she would have let him. She hadn't been going out with Nick very long and, so far, she hadn't allowed more than heavy petting. Tonight, the two of them were going to try that new club in Guildford that she'd heard about. Claire adored clubbing. She could wear that brilliant new skirt she'd bought last week. Then again, maybe not. Nick only had a motorbike. She couldn't wear such a short, tight skirt on a bike.

Claire felt her cheeks start to glow as her thoughts drifted back to the Trojans and the way she had pleasured herself with her fingers under the bedclothes last night just thinking about them. Her mind had been so full of them that she couldn't get to sleep. Her fingers had been between her legs before she had even realised what she was doing. The Trojans were all so hot. They made Nick look like a skinny little boy. When she had come, her orgasm had been so intense she had cried out, then lay shivering in the darkness, hoping no one had heard her through the thin walls of her bedsit.

Claire pushed the last of the water into the drain, then wiped round the cubicles in record time. It wasn't a very good job, but it would have to do. She was running so late that she would never get finished otherwise. Hastily stuffing her cleaning things back on to her trolley, she hurried to the men's changing rooms.

In her rush, she forgot to hang the 'cleaning in progress' sign on the door. She didn't even stop to knock;

she just dashed inside and started gathering up the dirty towels and rubbish. Secretly, she often fantasised that she would walk in and catch a roomful of naked men prancing around, although, to be honest, if she ever had, she knew that she would probably die of embarrassment!

The room was empty and, thankfully, it was also fairly clean and tidy compared to the women's room. If she hurried she would be able to catch up on her work. As soon as she had mopped around, she unlocked the big walk-in storage cupboard and began sorting out a pile of freshly laundered towels.

She had just placed clean towels on the bench outside and returned to finish checking how many were left when she heard the outer door open and the sound of men's voices laughing and joking. In a blind panic, Claire reached out, pulled the cupboard door closed on her and switched off the light. So far as she could remember, the reserve team wasn't due to play again until Wednesday. Was there a practice session on this morning that no one had told her about? Holding her breath, she peered out awkwardly between the wooden slats in the door.

What if it was Justin coming to check up on her work? How would she explain what she was doing shut inside a dark cupboard with her clothes all wet? Why on earth had she panicked like that? She had every right to be in here. Then she remembered: the door! She had forgotten to put the cleaning sign on the door!

Four, no five men came into view, laughing and joking. Jesus! If she had only stayed where she was, she could have just said good morning and wheeled her trolley out. Now what was she going to do? Claire instinctively crouched down, making herself as small as possible, straining her ears to hear what was going on while she tried to remember whether she had left the key in the lock or not.

'That turned out to be quite a match on Saturday.'

'I thought we'd lost it when you nearly let that second one in.'

'Me let it in? It was your lousy checking that caused all the trouble.'

Claire heard the sounds of playful punches and raucous laughter, as if the men were scuffling with each other. She wiggled around and pushed her eye to the crack between two of the slats. As the room came back into focus, she put her hand over her mouth to stifle her gasp of shock. It couldn't be them! It just couldn't be. She was certain the Trojans weren't due to train again until tomorrow.

Pele, the golden-haired net-minder, was standing just in front of the door with his jeans unzipped so that she could clearly see the bulge of his penis under his pants. She swallowed her instinctive gasp and almost lost her balance.

Pele slipped his pants and trousers down his thighs and calves and stepped out of them. Claire could feel herself glowing from the tip of her toes to the roots of her hair as she stared at his nakedness. Her eyes began to sting and she realised that she had forgotten to blink. She rubbed them with one fingertip and twisted her head round to get a better view.

A second Trojan moved into range and Claire watched avidly as he, too, started to undo his trousers. She remembered that he was called Tor, and that he had just joined the team from Canada to play centre. She stifled another gasp. Jesus Christ! They were all stripping off!

Pele swung round so that his cock seemed to be pointing straight at her. He gave Tor a prod in the ribs.

'What about the lovely lady afterwards?' he chortled. We should have asked her who was the best. I bet she would have been more than happy to judge.'

'She was quite something wasn't she?' Tor responded. 'What a body.'

Claire wondered enviously who they were talking

about. She saw Troy turn round towards her so that his cock almost seemed to be dancing back and forth just for her benefit. She realised that she had involuntarily put her hand down between her clenched thighs and she quickly pulled it away. Supposing they heard her moving about? She could hardly bear the thought of being caught spying on them like this. She would die of shame. It didn't stop her moving her eyes from crack to crack trying to see all of them.

'This was all she really wanted,' Troy boasted, as he gave his genitals a loving caress. 'After me, she only took care of the rest of you to be polite.'

Pele snorted contemptuously.

'Truth is, if she hadn't been so polite, she would have been happier just to wait for me to recover,' Troy added softly.

'She would have grown old waiting for you,' Pele retorted.

'Look who's talking.' Pary slapped Pele on the back. 'If I remember correctly, you shot your wad without even getting your pencil-dick inside her.'

Claire swallowed hard. She had never heard men talking together like this. They were worse than women. She pushed her face even closer to the door and squinted her eyes so that she could examine the way Tor's cock was nestled up against his soft blond pubes. She could almost imagine herself gently coaxing him to respond to her body. The idea both shocked and excited her. She knew she was blushing but she didn't care.

Tor looked around the room and then began walking towards the cupboard. Claire watched, mesmerised at the way his balls bounced up and down in time with each step and how his cock flopped from side to side. As he drew closer, she shrank back away from the door, terrified that he was about to discover her. Her head twisted back and forth, seeking an escape route. What could she say? What possible excuse could she give for being in here like this?

Just a few steps short of the door, Tor stopped and leant over to pick up a towel from the bench. Claire released her breath again and peered out at him. His movements seemed so graceful yet so powerful as his muscles rippled under his tanned skin. Poised on one leg, with the other raised to provide a counter-balance, he looked just like one of those erotic sculptures Sara had once taken her to see. His penis was only inches from her face and she could see the individual hairs covering his balls.

She opened her lips. Her tongue slipped out towards him as if eager to taste his manhood. Tor turned his head towards the door and she froze, certain that he must have caught a glimpse of her movements. She sighed with a mixture of relief and regret as he suddenly turned round and leant his body against the door. His buttocks were pressed up into the wooden slats, and she had an almost irresistible urge to reach through and pinch him, just to prove this wasn't all a dream. She raised her hand up towards the door and ran her fingertips gently along the slats. Her heart was hammering so loudly in her chest that she was half-afraid he would hear it.

She leaned forward and peered up through the gaps until she could see the line of curly hairs under his legs, leading her eyes on up towards the curve of his scrotum. Overcome with guilt, she strained harder, twisting her head awkwardly, until she could make out the root of his penis. She longed to wrap her fingers around it and slide her hand slowly and teasingly up towards the smooth tip.

Tor stepped away and Claire remembered to breathe again. She could feel the cold dampness of her wet panties pressing against her sex and a trickle of perspiration ran down between her breasts. Her face was burning with a flush so deep that she felt almost faint with the heat.

As Pele moved back into view, Claire fastened her gaze on his groin. She could feel her bra cutting into her and she reached behind her to undo the catch. As her breasts flopped forward against her still-damp blouse, she put her hand under the bottom of the blouse and pushed the cups right up. She ran her fingers over her tiny breasts and was surprised at how hard her normally small nipples had become.

She pinched one of her super-hard nipples between her thumb and forefinger and felt a deep burning sensation between her legs. If only Nick were here with her now. She wouldn't mind him looking at her breasts like this. In fact, she was aching for him to fondle her. She couldn't remember ever feeling so hot. Was it because it was so unusual to see men like this? Or was it just the fear of being caught spying? Whatever the reason, she was burning all over with excitement and desire.

She pulled her skirt up her thighs as far as she could get it and ran her fingers over her mound and on to her sex lips. She was so aroused that it was all she could do to stop herself from pulling her knickers down and rubbing herself.

She couldn't do it. Not here. What if she cried out, like she had last night? Her clit burned and she closed her legs tightly together, squeezing her mound urgently as she continued to fondle her breasts with her fingers. She imagined the feel of Nick's hand probing urgently between her clamped thighs, forcing his way through her defences so that there was nothing she could do but surrender to him.

A bare leg banged against the door, making it rattle, and Claire jumped and almost toppled over backwards. She peered out again. Troy had snatched Pary's jock strap and was holding it up above his head teasingly. Pary was leaping naked about the changing room as he tried to retrieve it. His genitals bounced and flopped around in front of him, taunting her. His hip banged against the cupboard door again and Claire jumped, praying that it would not spring open and give her away. Quickly, she straightened her skirt. Her fingers were much too shaky to do her bra up again so she slipped her arms out of her sleeves and removed it completely. Before she could get her blouse back on there was another heavy crash and she had to cover her mouth to stifle her scream.

As she crouched back deeper into the cupboard, struggling with the sleeves of her blouse, she was practically sobbing with fear. She could feel her chest heaving in and out as she gulped lungfuls of stale air and fought to calm herself. Another pair of naked buttocks pressed against the slats and she shrank back until she was pushed up against the far wall. As her fingers fiddled desperately with the buttons she was certain that the door would spring open at any moment.

The shouting outside seemed to be growing fainter. What were they doing now? Claire leaned forward again and peered out. The men were heading for the showers. She could hear their laughter echoing down the tiled corridor as they continued to tease Pary.

What now? Should she creep out quickly before they returned? Supposing they came back in before she could gather up her cleaning things? Maybe she could just leave them where they were until later. Claire dithered, undecided, trying not to think about them all naked and covered in soap. She knew that she ought to get out, fast, but she was scared to move.

Before she had pulled herself together, it was too late. Claire heard damp footsteps approaching and realised that the men were returning to dress. She peeped out through the slats and watched in fascination as they finished drying themselves and donned their padded hockey gear. Thank God she had put enough fresh towels out or they might have opened the cupboard to fetch more!

After what seemed like forever, they were finally ready. Claire waited as they laced up their skates and picked up their hockey sticks before heading out to the rink. She hesitated another few minutes to make sure that she was quite alone, then stuffed her bra into her pocket and peered out at the wall clock. Just after eight: she had no time to lose. Quickly, she pushed the door open and stepped out.

As she moved towards her trolley, she realised that her panties were still rolled down round her thighs. She began pulling them up with one hand while she reached for her cleaning tools with the other. The broom slipped from her shaking fingers and crashed to the floor. She snatched it up again and quickly ran her eyes round the room to make quite sure she hadn't forgotten anything.

'Oh!' Her hands flew to cover her face and her eyes opened wide in shock.

Pele was standing on the far side of the changing room with an amused grin on his lips. She peered out at him between her fingers.

'You've tucked your skirt into your knickers,' he told her calmly. He started to walk towards her. The skimpy towel around his waist would have left little to the imagination, even if she hadn't already seen him without it. Claire stood as if made of stone, too shocked and horrified to speak or move. Where on earth had he come from? Hadn't he dressed and left with the rest of them? She couldn't remember.

Pele reached out and pulled her fingers from her face. She stared at him in silence, acutely aware of the way her breasts were heaving as she struggled to catch her breath. Pele took her arm and stepped backwards towards the bench, tugging her along with him. Claire moved her feet woodenly in his wake.

'You were in the cupboard just now watching us, weren't you?' he accused her softly. 'Naughty girl.'

As the back of his thighs made contact with the bench, Claire lowered her eyes and stared down at his crotch. The towel seemed to have pulled even tighter across him so that she could clearly see the outline of his cock. She glanced back up at his face and shuddered with shame at his words and at the knowing smile on his lips.

'It's lucky I like to take my time over my morning shower,' he continued with a wide grin. 'Or I might not have caught you.'

Her heart skipped a beat. God, he had a gorgeous smile. Despite her humiliation, she found herself smiling back. His grin was infectious, like when someone starts giggling helplessly and everyone else finds themselves joining in without really knowing why.

He sat down on the bench with his legs spread wide. He pulled her nearer to him and closed his thighs around hers. She flinched at the contact.

'Don't worry. I'm not gonna tell on you,' he reassured her. 'But, I couldn't let you go like this, could I?' He let go of her arm and moved his hand round to the back of her rucked-up skirt. Claire overbalanced and fell forward so that her breasts brushed across his face. She quickly put her hands up on the wall behind him and arched her back, pulling her body away from him. She could feel the warmth of his breath caressing the skin at her cleavage.

Pele slid his hands up her thighs and gently lowered her panties enough to free the hem of her skirt. Every touch of his skin against hers made Claire shudder with longing. Every shudder caused her breasts to brush against his face again. She twisted her head to try and see what he was doing and spotted their reflection in the mirrored tiles on the far wall. A small sigh dropped from her lips.

Pele had draped the hem of her skirt around her waist. As she watched, he slid his hands down over the curve of her hips and on to the top of her panties. Claire stared in silence as his fingers slid under the elastic. She felt and saw them lowering. Another shiver of fear and longing tore through her and her sweaty palms started to slip down the wall. He immediately let go of her panties and grabbed her round the waist to steady her.

Claire put her left hand on his shoulder and tried to push herself upright. He grinned and moved his head forward to suck one of her buttons into his mouth. If she kept struggling, the button would probably come open, revealing her naked breasts. She stood perfectly still and tried not to notice his fingers caressing her buttocks and thighs. She was almost afraid to look at their reflection again, yet at the same time she desperately wanted to watch.

Slowly and carefully, Pele pulled her knickers back up over her buttocks and ran his fingers over the material, smoothing it into place. His fingertips slipped round to the front and lightly caressed the swell of her mound. A sharp tingle of longing surged through her trembling body. With a soft whimper, Claire slumped forward and sank her teeth into his shoulder. Her head felt dizzy, and her whole being was shaking with a mixture of fear, shame and uncontrollable passion. She had never experienced anything quite like this.

As if oblivious to her reactions, Pele calmly released the hem of her skirt and tugged it back down over her knickers. Realising that she still had her teeth buried in his skin, Claire relaxed her jaws and raised her head again. She could see the reddened imprint of her teeth marks quite clearly. Her eyes travelled down his body and she stared in fascination at the shiny smooth tip of his engorged penis now peeping hungrily over the top of the towel.

Pele used his hands to guide her upright, although his legs were still holding her tightly in front of him. Uncontrollable shivers wracked her body and her mouth was so dry that she would not have been able to speak even if she could have thought of anything to say.

'Do you know what happens to naughty girls who hide in the men's changing rooms?' he questioned her teasingly.

Claire just shook her head helplessly. Her terror of public exposure flooded back.

'Yeah you do. They get their bottoms spanked,' he threatened her.

She shook her head again, already picturing one of his huge hands whacking her tiny buttocks red raw.

'Good and hard.'

She could see the lust on his face as he turned her sideways and flicked her hem back up before pulling her down so that she was sitting on his right knee. As her buttocks made contact with his bare flesh, Claire felt a jolt like an electric shock race through her body. There was a desperate, almost painful, ache deep inside her, growing stronger and stronger until she felt as if she were about to explode. What was wrong with her? She had never felt like this with anyone. Every touch of his body against hers seemed to burn her skin and she just couldn't stop herself from shaking. She had to get away.

Mustering all her strength and willpower, she leant forward and tried to pull herself back up on to her feet. Pele laughed and held her down as easily as if she were a small child. As soon as she stopped struggling, he pushed her face forward over his left thigh with her buttocks in the air. His crotch was hard up against her left hip so that she could feel his cock burning into her side as he thrust himself on to her. She could hear his breath coming in rapid, shallow gasps.

'Please stop,' she begged him. 'Please.'

Her words seemed to steady him. She heard his breathing quieten and he stopped thrusting himself against her. Claire turned her head sideways to look up at him and experienced another little shiver of lust when she saw his hungry smile.

'Oh no, missy,' he informed her loudly. 'You've got to be punished.' His voice sounded strange, as if he were having trouble speaking and Claire realised that he was no longer totally in control of himself. Instead of frightening her, this realisation caused another rush of desire that made her whole body feel weak. She felt her panties slipping down her thighs again and his fingers began stroking and squeezing her naked cheeks.

Claire bit her bottom lip and tried to stop herself from twitching. She wanted to beg him not to touch her between her legs. She knew what would happen if he did. She was so close to climaxing that his touch there would be all it would take. As inexperienced as she was, Claire hadn't realised that it was possible to get so close to coming without doing so.

Oh shit. Would he be able to tell? What would he think of her if she came that easily? Even the thought of her humiliation did not seem to help. She had never known such intense feelings of arousal as those she was now experiencing. It was all she could do to stop herself groaning aloud with the desperation of her passion.

'What a delightful little arse,' Pele growled softly as he tucked the hem of her skirt securely into its waistband. 'I don't know whether to smack it, kiss it or just eat it. It's gorgeous.' She felt his tongue caressing her left cheek, and another shudder of desire coursed through her.

'I bet your boyfriend can't stop fucking this, can he?' Pele's fingertip prodded the opening of her anus. Claire gasped and clenched her buttocks against his probing. No one had ever touched her there before. Her fear overcame her excitement.

'Please don't,' she mumbled. 'Please stop. I can't . . .'

'What's the matter? You're not afraid to let yourself go, are you? I've seen plenty of women climax.' Pele told her calmly. 'I love watching them wank. Watching them really letting themselves go.'

The lust in his voice made his words sound hard and Claire shivered with fear at how far he might be intending to go. She felt him deliberately pull her up against his cock again.

'Do you wank for your boyfriend?' he demanded hoarsely. 'I bet you do. Would you wank for me?'

Claire was unable to stifle a small squeal as he thrust his hand underneath her and she felt his fingers brushing insistently back and forth over her clit. 'Oh! No!' she clenched her teeth as she came. Wave after wave of pleasure rushed through her, leaving her breathless and trembling. Pele was seemingly unaware of what had happened; his finger continued to gently rub her, while his other hand caressed her buttocks and teased her anus.

As the last tremors of her orgasm died away, Claire struggled upright and sat shaking helplessly on his knee with her head resting on his chest. She could still feel his erection pushing against her thigh and knew that he wasn't finished with her yet. Was he planning to fuck her? She shuddered as she imagined him lowering her down on to his massive cock. What if someone walked in on them? Justin might come looking for her at any moment.

She trembled as Pele began to undo the buttons on the front of her blouse. She moved her thigh gently against his penis and savoured the feel of him twitching in response. She really should put a stop to this. She couldn't let him take her there in such a public place. She didn't want him to stop. He pulled the two sides of her blouse back and ran his tongue across her naked breasts. She flinched but he seemed not to notice. His tongue circled one nipple while his fingers began gently teasing the other.

'You have the loveliest tits I've ever seen,' he whispered. 'So tiny and firm.'

99

Claire flushed at the unexpected compliment and tried to decide if she should finish removing her blouse or wait for him. She wished she was sitting the other way round so that she could see herself reflected in the tiles. What must she look like? Christ, this was the men's changing room! Claire almost giggled. What did it matter? She wouldn't be any better off if it were the women's. Just, please God, don't let anyone come in and catch them.

Pele slid one hand back down between her legs and his finger started to fondle her clit again. Claire was amazed at the renewed rush of excitement pulsing through her. She felt his fingertips parting her engorged lips and tried to open her thighs wider for him but her panties stopped her.

Pele tugged her knickers down over her knees to her ankles. 'Lift up.'

Claire lifted one foot to kick them free and Pele immediately pushed her legs as wide as possible, clamping her with his thighs. She could see that he was staring hungrily at her exposure and the thought of his desire for her sent little shivers of delight up and down her spine. She found herself twitching helplessly as his hands explored her sex and his tongue devoured her nipples.

Pele finished undoing her blouse and began to slip the sleeves from her arms. 'Close your eyes,' he instructed her. She felt him placing something around her head and realised that he had bound her eyes with her rolled-up blouse. He lifted her into his arms and moved her along the bench.

'That's not fair,' she complained, amazed at her own daring. 'You can see everything and I can't.' She lifted her hands up towards her face, but he caught her wrists gently and moved them back into her lap. She felt herself being shifted around so that she was sitting on his lap with her back against his chest.

Claire could feel his cock pushed up into her crack and

realised that his towel must either have fallen off or he had removed it. The tip of his cock was pushed up against her arsehole. Maybe she would let him put just the tip of it up into her, she told herself. She whimpered as he pulled her legs wider apart and his finger slipped back between her sex lips. His other hand cupped her left breast and resumed teasing her nipple. She sensed her passion building up again and shuddered all over at the feel of his lips nuzzling the back of her neck.

The blindfold seemed to be heightening all her senses so that his every caress drove her wild. It was as if not being able to see somehow alleviated the guilt and fear of what was happening. All her inhibitions seemed to be melting away and she began to relax, giving herself up to the pleasure of his touch. She felt him take her hands and push the flattened palms down on her thighs, just inches from her mound.

'You do it.' His fingers guided hers towards her pussy while his tongue and teeth continued to lick and nibble her neck and ears.

Claire hesitated. Her clit was on fire from the touch of his knowing fingers, but she'd never played with herself in front of anyone else. She was scared to do it and scared not to. What if he got angry with her?

Timidly, Claire ran her fingertips over her tiny bud, trying not to squirm with the pleasure of it. Pele stopped kissing her neck and sat perfectly still. She knew that he was staring at her and she could feel his cock juddering excitedly under her. She stopped moving her finger and took a deep, shuddering breath.

'Don't stop,' he pleaded urgently. His words were faint and breathless and Claire licked her lips excitedly at the note of desperation she detected in his voice. She tried to assume a look of total submission as she lifted her hand slightly. She was automatically clenching her buttocks against his erection and she could feel him thrusting rhythmically back and forth in his excitement.

With a deep breath, Claire raised her finger to her lips and sucked it into her mouth. She heard the whoosh of his breath as she lowered her hand back between her thighs and ran the dampened fingertip over herself. A thrill of excitement raced up inside her and, for a second, she thought she was going to come again. Quickly, she pulled her finger back, breathing deeply to try to control her lust.

'Oh yeah! Don't stop, baby.' His voice was hoarse with need and the sound of it drove her crazy. She had always enjoyed teasing Nick and watching him getting all horny and breathless, but she had never experienced this sort of power over a man before. Careful not to actually touch her sensitive little bud, Claire returned her fingers to her pussy, rubbing the soft, damp flesh and savouring the feel of his bursting cock grinding relentlessly into her crack. She felt her orgasm rushing to overwhelm her again. What would he think of her lack of self-control if she came again so soon?

Quickly, Claire twisted away from him and lifted her leg over his. She heard him groan loudly as she pushed herself down between his thighs until she was kneeling, facing him. Blindly, she reached out, searching for his cock. She ran her hands up towards his groin. Pele groaned again.

'Sorry. Did I hurt you?' she questioned anxiously, pulling her fingers back.

'No. It's OK,' he assured her softly, as her questing fingers caressed his balls and started to inch their way back up his rigid shaft. She felt him raise his buttocks, thrusting his cock towards her. Her fingers tugged the towel away from his waist, exposing him totally.

'My turn,' she gloated as she felt her way down on to his thighs. Her fingers found their way back on to his cock and she ran them inquisitively all over it, trying to picture it in her mind from touch alone. It felt so huge and swollen that a momentary panic engulfed her at the idea of him pushing such a monster up inside her.

Remembering the sound of his voice and breathing when she had done it before, Claire put her fingers to her mouth and licked them again, before gently sliding her clenched palm down his length from tip to base. She could feel the thick bush of his hair at the base, but his cock seemed silky smooth to her touch. She wondered if he had deliberately shaved it.

Nervously, she raised her buttocks and leaned forward so that she could suck him into her mouth. She had only ever done this once before and had been excited by the reaction. When she had made him as desperate as she herself had been, she would stop and start to play with herself again. Maybe she could make him come too, so that he would know how it felt to lose it like that.

Pele groaned with pleasure and put his hands on her shoulders. She could already taste his spunk, warm and salty. She pushed one hand underneath him, fingering the skin behind his balls and trying to push her fingertip up into his crack the way he had done to her.

'Jesus!' She felt a rush of triumph at his desperate whisper, and smiled to herself at the way he was lifting his buttocks up so that she could push deeper and deeper into him. She could feel his cock jerking up and down in her mouth and knew that he was close.

Her own excitement was getting the better of her again, too. Claire ran her other hand down her body and between her legs, rubbing urgently to relieve the pressure. Suddenly, he seized her by the hair and pulled her lips off his cock.

'Not yet, baby,' he told her softly. 'I've got other plans for you first. After what you did, you won't get away with just sucking me off.' She felt his fingers pushing into her anus again.

Claire shivered all over at his words. She knew what he wanted. He wanted to fuck her. Fuck her in the arse.

Despite her fear, part of her wanted him to. Yet part of her wanted him inside her cunt too. She wanted to feel him come as she came.

'Jesus Christ! Will you look at that? Trust Pele. We leave him playing with his dick in the shower and he finds himself some juicy pussy!' The unknown male voice chuckled with delight.

Claire shot upright and ripped the blindfold from her eyes. She spun round and blinked in horror at the sight of three of the other Trojans lined up by the far door. How long had they been there? How much had they seen? She felt the colour flooding to her cheeks as she remembered what she had been doing. Pele must have known they were watching. She turned back to him.

'You bastard! You, you wanker!' she yelled furiously.

'Not guilty,' Pele grinned. 'I'm not so sure about them, though.'

Claire suddenly realised that the other Trojans were all openly fondling themselves through their clothing as they stared at her. She shook her head in disbelief, then squealed as she felt herself being lifted up from behind.

'What are you doing?' she cried as Pele stood her on the bench and raised her leg up over his shoulder. 'Stop it! Oh!' She sagged back against the wall as he leaned down and pushed his tongue into her pussy. His hands tightened around her buttocks, pulling her harder on to his mouth and she felt her passion growing again as his tongue probed deeper and deeper into her warm dampness.

She could hear herself making little mewing noises in the back of her throat as his relentless tongue rapidly carried her towards climax. A slight grunt caused her to lift her head, and her eyes widened as she saw that the other Trojans had unzipped themselves and were now caressing their swollen cocks while they watched Pele devour her. Claire gulped and closed her eyes. None of this could possibly be happening. Not here. Not to her.

Her hips writhed urgently as her inevitable orgasm burst inside her.

'There now. All nice and dry.' She opened her eyes again and saw that Pele had already used a paper towel to wipe her thighs. She allowed him to help her climb down from the bench. Glancing down, she saw his still-urgent erection thrust out in front of him like a sword. It was so gorgeous, she felt a desperate compulsion to take him back into her mouth and give him as much pleasure as he had given her.

Before she could move, however, one of the other Trojans stepped closer and knelt down behind her. She had almost forgotten about them. Panic engulfed her as his hands started to pull her thighs apart.

'No!' she screamed. She couldn't take anymore. She just couldn't. What if they all wanted her? She pulled the hem of her skirt back down and snatched her blouse up from the floor. Before anyone could react she fled out, across the corridor and into the women's changing room.

Claire perched breathlessly on the seat of one of the loos, breathing deeply as she struggled to regain her composure. Her mind was full of images of naked Trojans with enormous erections, and her whole body was still tingling from Pele's caresses. She stared out of the partially open door at the clock on the wall. Incredibly, it was still barely 8.30 a.m. Nick probably wasn't even awake yet.

Chapter Five

When Maggie awoke on Monday morning, for a moment she couldn't think where she was. She had been living in a kind of exhausted daze ever since the events of Saturday night and couldn't remember much of what had happened on Sunday. For reasons that she couldn't explain even to herself, she had said nothing to her friends about her adventure. Considering that any one of them would have given a week's pay for such an opportunity, her reluctance to even speak about it was peculiar. Was it because she felt she had gone too far, or because she was not sure they would believe her anyway? She was no longer certain that it had ever really happened.

She climbed out of her bed, emitting a small groan, and tottered into her bathroom. Five minutes under an almost cold shower cleared her head sufficiently to allow her to function as a human being again. She patted herself dry and slipped into an old pink robe before heading into the kitchen for several cups of strong black coffee.

As she sipped the steaming liquid, her mind filled with memories of Saturday. The whole episode seemed so incredible. Could it have been nothing more than a figment of her overstimulated imagination? It had seemed so real. What if it wasn't a dream? If it had really happened?

She thumped her coffee cup down on the work surface and moved across the room to pick up the phone. As she dialled the number her fingers trembled slightly. Her call was answered on the fifth ring.

'Jan. It's Maggie.'

'Maggie! Hi. Shit. Hang on a sec. Try the top drawer on the left.' Maggie heard her friend's muffled voice yelling. 'No. The left one.' There were a few bumping noises and Jan's voice returned. 'Men, honestly. Are they really all that helpless or is it just something about me? Do you have any idea what time it is, Mags?'

'Yes. Sorry. I figured you would be gone if I didn't catch you first.'

'I would be if everything wasn't going haywire this morning. When I got back yesterday I found Marcus had arrived back early from his trip. I had a hell of a job explaining where I had been. He was convinced that I'd been out with someone else behind his back.' Jan paused to take a breath and Maggie jumped in quickly.

'Talking about Saturday . . .' she began.

'Yes. If Marcus says anything to you, you will confirm I was in Bristol with you, won't you?' Jan pleaded.

'What's with you all of a sudden? I thought you and Marcus had an understanding?' Considering how Jan usually totally dominated Marcus, Maggie was feeling more than a little confused by this conversation. It was doing little to help clear her own muddled thoughts.

'We do,' Jan replied. 'It's just that I don't like him assuming I've been up to something when I haven't. Besides, the poor thing was in a real state about it. It took me ages to soothe him.'

I bet, Maggie thought to herself, picturing what Jan had probably done to soothe him. No wonder she sounded nearly as tired and ratty as Maggie felt. 'OK. No problem. I'll tell him you were with me. Now, shut up and listen for a minute, will you? I didn't get a chance to say anything to you yesterday, but there's something you need to know about.'

Jan practically dropped the phone back into its cradle. As she rushed into the bedroom to dress she was already planning her strategy. Christ Almighty. Her boss would be delirious if she managed to get one of the Trojans as a client. Just think of the publicity. Just think about the chance to see Tor again.

Maggie had sounded really strange on the phone, Jan mused to herself as she carefully applied her favourite lipstick. It was almost as if she were hiding something. Come to think of it, she had been acting funny all day yesterday. Sort of quiet and moody, as if her mind had been elsewhere. When had she had the chance to discuss house hunting with Tor? And, why hadn't she said anything about it sooner? She and Maggie obviously needed to have serious chat.

As soon as Jan was ready, she picked up her bag, grabbed her car keys and gave Marcus a cheery wave. 'Sorry, I've got to go. I've got a great chance of making a real coup if I hurry.'

'Who was that on the 'phone?' Marcus glared at her suspiciously.

'Only Maggie.' Sod it, she really didn't need another of his sulks right now. She had to get hold of Tor before one of their competitors got wind of him. Marcus would just have to get on and sulk. She could make it up to him later, once the deal was in the bag.

'How about dinner at Francesco's tonight? My treat.' she bribed him. It was their favourite restaurant.

'Well. OK.' His lips curled into a slight smile. 'How about giving me a proper goodbye?' He ran his eyes over her body suggestively.

'I can't now, Marcus.' Jan was certainly tempted. What-ever else you might say about Marcus, he was a great lover. She saw his mouth start to pout again. 'Look. I'll make it up to you tonight. Promise.' She blew him a kiss and hurried out the door before he could argue.

After grabbing himself some breakfast in the small hotel dining room, Tor returned to his room. If he left it up to Roland there was no telling how long he would be stuck in this sleazy hotel. Knowing from bitter experience what it was like to live out of a suitcase for weeks on end, he felt that it would be a good idea if he found himself somewhere to rent as soon as possible. He checked the 'phone book for local estate agents and then took a taxi to the address of the agents that Maggie had mentioned.

He wondered if she had remembered to speak to her friend about it, then shrugged. It didn't matter. One advantage of being a bit of a local celebrity was that people were always eager to drop everything once they realised who you were. He might not have been with the Trojans for very long, but long enough to know that they were pretty popular around there. He was quite sure that Jan would recognise him.

Tor leant back in the seat of the taxi and stared out the window. He liked being back in England. Most people assumed that he was Canadian and he was content to let them. It made him seem more interesting. There was nothing very glamorous about being born in the eastend of London. Besides, he had been living in Montreal since he was a child and had practically come to think of it as his home. The Trojans were a good career move for him, though. A few more years and, who knows, maybe he could return to Canada and sign with one of the top nationals.

'Here you go, mate.' The taxi driver's voice broke into his thoughts as the car pulled up outside the estate agents. 'That'll be £6.50 please.'

Tor climbed out of the car and handed the driver the money. 'Cheers.' The half-forgotten English expressions from his childhood had come back to him easily, although he was not sorry to have swapped his harsh London accent for the softer, gentler Canadian tones. As the car pulled off, he looked around him with interest. Fairwood was a nice little town. Small and friendly. The sort of place where everybody knew everybody else.

As Tor pushed the door open and stepped inside, a bell jangled insistently. He studied the interior carefully. The door led straight into the large front room of what had clearly once been an old house. The room was fitted out as an office, with three large desks. It seemed to be deserted and Tor wondered if they were even open for business yet.

'Hello. Anybody there?' he called out in his deep baritone voice. 'Am I too early?'

'Too early for what?' A tall, slim woman with blond hair and glasses walked through from a back corridor on the far side of the room. Tor recognised her immediately from the dinner on Saturday. He had forgotten just how attractive she was.

'Hi. Your friend, Maggie, said you might be able to help me find a place to rent.' He examined her critically. Very nice. Firm breasts, long shapely legs. Yeah. Very nice. He would enjoy her company this morning. Then, maybe lunch and . . .

'Finished?' Her voice sounded slightly harsh and Tor started guiltily. He lifted his eyes back to her face and laughed uneasily when he saw the way she was looking at him.

'I'm sorry, I . . .' his voice dried up. He hadn't realised that his stare had been quite so blatant. But, hell, she was an attractive woman. She must have been used to men looking at her.

'It's not a problem. Just so long as you know it's only

110

property we rent out. I'm Jan Nichols.' She held out a slim, well-manicured hand.

Although the tone of voice was still hard, there was a twinkle in her eye and a slight smile at the corners of her mouth as she spoke and Tor breathed a little more easily as he shook her hand. He had been afraid that he had put his foot in it. You could never be sure anymore. Some career women seemed to get totally pissed off at the slightest hint of anything that might be taken as sexist. 'Tor,' he responded softly.

He risked giving her another admiring look and grinned as she immediately twirled around for his benefit. Her skirt had a wide, flared hem so that it floated up away from her body as she moved, giving him a tantalising glimpse of her legs and the lacy tops of her stockings. God, she was sexy.

When she had finished her twirl Jan stared into his face and raised a sardonic eyebrow. 'Well?'

Tor swallowed hard. 'Perfect,' he murmured.

Jan's eyes seemed to focus on his crotch and he was certain that the bulge there was already expanding. He resisted the urge to cover himself and was relieved when she returned her gaze to his eyes. There was a slight flush on her cheeks that had not been there before, but he was not sure whether it was from excitement, embarrassment, or both.

'Well?' he mimicked her earlier question and Jan laughed and nodded.

'Just fine,' she agreed. 'So, now that we know we both come up to spec, perhaps we should get down to business,' she added suggestively. 'Considering who you are, I assume you are looking for something secluded and private? Something a bit out of town, perhaps?'

Tor nodded. Had she and Maggie been chatting about him? Would Maggie have told her friend what had happened on Saturday night? Guys would boast about that sort of thing, but he wasn't so sure about women.

111

'Did you come by car?' Jan questioned.

Tor shook his head. 'Taxi.'

'That's OK. We'll use mine. I've got three places that I think might be suitable for you.'

Jan walked over to one of the desks and bent over to open the bottom drawer. Tor watched the curve of her legs and buttocks through the soft material of the skirt and decided that she must be wearing a thong. He made a pretence of tucking the front of his shirt back in, and did his best to rearrange his ever-hardening cock.

Jan pulled out a folder and opened it on the desk. She picked up some advertising leaflets and spread them out side by side. Tor moved closer to look at them so that he was standing right beside her. He could just catch a subtle whiff of her perfume. He hated those strong body sprays some women wore so that you could smell them coming ten feet away. Jan's scent was just right. Sexy and suggestive – just like the lady who was wearing it.

Tor shifted closer so that he could study the information on one of the houses. His hip brushed against hers and he was pleased to notice that she did not move away. She didn't move any closer either. The warmth of her body aroused him even more. Did she realise the effect she was having on him? He glanced at her nipples. Yeah. They were definitely hard but then, they had been earlier too.

'This is probably the most suitable.' Jan tapped a long, varnished fingernail on one of the leaflets and turned her head to smile into his eyes. Her lips were only inches away from his.

'Well, OK.' His voice was a high-pitched squeak. He turned his head and coughed to clear his throat. 'Let's get started then.' He still sounded more like a soprano than a baritone. Unable to resist touching her, her put his arm loosely around her waist as if to guide her.

'Where's your car?' He felt suddenly foolish, steering

112

her across the office without knowing where they were headed.

'Out the back. I have to lock up first. I'm on my own this morning.' Jan slipped easily from his grasp and walked across to fasten the lock on the front door.

Tor watched her move, enjoying the way her skirt swirled round her legs and moulded itself to her thighs. The light seemed to shine straight through it and the view was definitely worth looking at. His pants were feeling extremely tight and uncomfortable. He shifted his hips and moved his hand round towards his waistband to try to adjust himself again. The bolt shot across and Jan started to turn round.

Tor whipped his hand away and thought quickly. 'I, um, I need to use the bathroom first if that's OK?'

'Sure. I'll show you the way.' He was almost certain that she deliberately brushed against him as she walked passed. His cock was showing its predictable lack of good timing. Instead of shrinking in response to his discomfort, the damned thing was actually so hard that it was difficult to walk.

Tor gritted his teeth and shuffled awkwardly in her wake. One day he was going to actually ask a woman like Jan if she realised what she could do to a man without seeming to even try, or if it was just accidental. Either way, it was a relief to get out of sight and slam the door behind him.

Tor unzipped himself and put his hand down inside his pants. His prick was as hard as a rock. He dropped his trousers to his ankles and bent awkwardly over the bowl. It was bloody difficult to piss straight when you had a hard-on. As he finished, his cock started to soften. He redressed himself carefully, adjusting his prick inside his pants so that if, or rather when, he expanded again, he would be more comfortable.

As he rejoined her, Jan glanced pointedly at his crotch

113

and Tor was certain that the look on her face was far less innocent than it seemed. Did she know?

'Better?'

He saw the way her lips were crinkling with suppressed laughter. Well, that answered his question. She obviously knew exactly why he needed to get out of sight. Thank God, he had resisted the temptation to jerk off.

'Yes thank you,' he answered and nodded awkwardly.

'Good. My car's through here.' Jan led the way along a dark narrow corridor leading to the rear entrance. Tor trouped after her like a lost sheep following the shepherd girl; his eyes were mesmerised by the way her buttocks swayed so seductively.

As soon as they were outside, Jan stopped to lock the back door and then slipped the key into her bag. Tor took her arm to help guide her down the narrow brick steps. Not that she needed any help, but it was an opportunity to get closer to her and she didn't seem to object. When they reached the bottom step, she pressed the remote button on her keyring and unlocked a white BMW.

'Nice wheels,' said Tor.

'Thank you.'

He steered her towards the car and opened the driver's door for her. As she slid gracefully in under the wheel, he caught a quick glimpse of her lacy white bra and bronzed skin through the buttons of her blouse. It was only a flash but it was more than enough to cause another surge of blood to his groin.

As he closed the door and walked round the front, Tor pondered over why he always seemed to turn into a tongue-tied, clumsy moron whenever he was alone with a beautiful woman. Considering what he and the other guys had got up to with Maggie the other night, it seemed unbelievable that he could be so unsure of himself now. Funny how he always knew what to do when opportunities like that presented themselves or when he was with the others, yet on his own, with a lady like Jan in a situation like this, he was reduced to a stammering idiot. It was almost as if he were two separate people: Tor the Trojan on the outside, yet still hapless old Andy Robbins underneath. Drink helped, but he could hardly walk around permanently drunk.

He climbed into the passenger seat and gave Jan another quick stare. How far was she prepared to let things go? He leaned forward and slipped his jacket off so that he could put it on his lap to cover himself. Now, at least, he could sit back and enjoy the view. He should have thought of it before.

'Safety beat, please.' Jan's voice snapped him out of his daydreams. Tor yanked at the belt, tugged it across his broad chest and plugged the end in with a sharp click. He twisted his body slightly so that he could just see the tops of her stockings and enjoyed the way the soft material of her skirt had moulded itself around her thighs again. She had wonderful legs. His fingers tingled with the urge to caress them but he resisted the temptation; instead he made do with imagining how soft and smooth her flesh would feel if he ran his hand up over the top of the nylon and on to her bare skin.

He pictured his fingers gliding up over her thigh and on to her hips and stomach. He was fairly certain that she was only wearing a tiny thong. Was it cotton or silk? His fingers would slip down over it and feel the outline of her mound. Would she have shaved? She had a good suntan, so she was bound to have at least shaved to the bikini line. His fingers would rub gently over her, exploring the slight sponginess of her remaining pubes. His cock twitched impatiently. Perhaps his other hand could slip in between the buttons and fondle those luscious breasts.

His thoughts were interrupted again as Jan suddenly slammed on the brakes. His jacket slipped off his lap on to the floor. Oh Jesus. Had she guessed what he was thinking? He reached down and grabbed the jacket quickly before she saw the evidence of his fantasy.

'Sorry about that.' Jan blasted the horn and glared out the windscreen. 'That stupid sod needs to take driving lessons.' She pulled round the car in front of them.

Tor slipped his hand under his jacket to try and make himself more comfortable. Zips might be convenient but they could certainly be a pain at times. He winced at his sudden memory of the first time he had ever been with a girl when he was fifteen.

He had just finished removing his clothes when her older sister had walked in on them. In his panic, he had jumped off – what was her name? Oh yeah, Charlotte. He had jumped up off Charlotte and whipped his jeans up without bothering about his pants. As he had tugged the zip up, he had caught himself. Shit, that had been painful. He never did know the name of Charlotte's sister, but he would never forget her cruel smile at the way he was doubled over in his agony.

'Forget something?' she had sniggered, holding his underpants out on the end of her finger. She had stood in front of the door and watched while he removed his jeans and dressed himself properly. He had never been so embarrassed, especially when she'd caught sight of his, by then, shrivelled cock. Her final words were permanently etched into his subconscious: 'Well, little sis, I don't think he could have done much damage with that!'

Tor frowned in disbelief. Normally, the memory of that incident was more than enough. Today, it wasn't working. His cock seemed to be as hard and desperate as ever. Carefully, so Jan wouldn't see, he pushed it sideways away from the zip. He tried staring out the window to distract himself but he could see the reflection of her face in the glass. It was a very lovely face, full of character as well as classic English beauty. Although he couldn't see the colour of her eyes, he was very aware of the way they kept flicking from the road ahead to glance at him. There was something almost regal about her features but he could detect no emotion, just concentration. It made her seem even more beautiful and desirable.

'You don't sound very Canadian,' Jan said, breaking into his thoughts. 'Where abouts do you come from?'

'Montreal. Although actually I was born in London.'

'Really? I guess that explains it.'

'It was a long time ago.' He wasn't entirely sure if he was talking about living in London or his humiliating first attempt to lose his virginity. He wanted to continue the conversation, but was becoming tongue-tied again.

Five minutes later she turned the car into a driveway and stopped at the closed gates. She released her seatbelt.

'No, I'll get them.' Tor opened the door.

'Thank you, but don't you think it would be easier if you undid your safety belt first?'

In his rush to be helpful, Tor had forgotten about the belt. Her words were spoken kindly, and he had a feeling that she was more than used to men making total arses of themselves around her. He unclipped the belt sheepishly, then had to laugh at the warmth of her smile. It was worth playing the fool just for that.

After he had opened one gate, he had to scrabble around looking for something to prop it open with while he held the other. As he moved an old brick into place and walked across to the other gate he could feel her eyes appraising his every move.

As soon as Jan had driven inside, Tor closed the gates and climbed back into the passenger seat. It didn't take him long to realise that one of her blouse buttons had come undone. He smiled to himself. If she thought that he wouldn't spot something like that, then she had seriously underestimated him. He might be having trouble remembering his own name, but there wasn't much about her he hadn't noticed. He knew exactly how many buttons she had on the front of her blouse and which side of her skirt the zip was on. He even knew that her bra did up at the back with two hooks.

The car reached the end of the drive and stopped. As Jan switched off the engine, Tor jumped out and practically ran round to hold the door for her. As she turned to climb out, he again took the opportunity to look down the top of her blouse. He thought he could just catch a glimpse of the pinkish outline of her nipples and the idea of them was enough to set the blood boiling in his veins. He took her arm and helped her out, doing his best to make it difficult for her to straighten her skirt.

'Well, this would be my choice.' Jan stood by the side of the car and let her eyes roam around the house and grounds. He could see now that her eyes were blue: a deep almost violet-blue, enhanced by the magnifying properties of her glasses so that they made the sky pale into insignificance.

'Rather large grounds, but there's a gardener who comes in once a week so you won't have to worry about that,' she told him.

She had turned slightly so that the sun was shining straight through the front of her blouse. The material seemed to have become almost transparent and Tor could not take his eyes off the clearly defined outline of her breasts. Was she posing like that deliberately, or was she totally unaware of the effect she had created? His cock certainly wasn't unaware. Somehow, his single-minded friend had managed to get itself into an even more uncomfortable position; his zip was really cutting into him.

Tor realised that Jan was staring at him again, waiting for some reaction to the house. He forced his eyes from her breasts and glanced round swiftly. 'Yeah. I like the idea of large grounds. What's the back like?' His eyes locked on to her cleavage again.

'Let's go and see, shall we? I think you'll find it even better.' She was glancing at the advertising blurb again.

'Very private and mostly south facing. Although I guess it's a little early in the year for that to matter much.'

As they started round the back Tor took her arm again. The pathway was narrow and winding so that they were forced to walk quite close together and Tor caught another heady whiff of her perfume. He slipped his arm round her waist and pulled her gently towards him.

'Careful –' he nodded down at the moss-covered paving slabs '– those look very slippery.'

'Oh yes. Thank you.' Jan made no attempt to escape his embrace. In fact, to his delight, she put her arm round him. 'Just in case I slip. You don't mind, do you?' She looked up at him and raised one eyebrow inquisitively.

Tor struggled to resist the urge to place his lips on hers. 'Just make sure that if you fall, you fall on me,' he muttered.

Jan laughed. 'It's a promise,' she responded huskily.

Thigh to thigh, they continued walking along the narrow path. Tor's hand slid down on to her hip so that he could feel her muscles tightening and loosening with each step she took. His cock jerked violently against his zip and he had to bite his bottom lip to stop himself from groaning at the exquisite pain of it. He looked around, trying to distract himself.

'What's that over there?' He pointed to a small building, partly hidden under the branches of a huge weeping willow tree, which was already beginning to bud.

'I'm not sure,' Jan admitted. 'I don't remember anything about it in the write-up. Let's take a look.' She took a step off the pathway and then pulled a face. 'Maybe not. The ground's so soft that my heels are sinking in to it.'

'No problem. I'll carry you.' Tor swept her up into his strong arms before she had time to protest.

Jan looked startled and then smiled. 'Well, if you don't mind?' She wrapped her arms around his neck and snuggled more comfortably against his muscular chest.

119

Tor could feel the softness of her breasts pushed against him and the scent of her perfume grew stronger, making his head feel light and fuzzy.

With one arm under her legs and the other wrapped around her back, Tor began to stride confidently across the lawn towards the small building. He could feel her skirt slipping against the nylon of her stockings and he shifted his hand higher up her thigh so that he could feel the lacy top. It was all he could do to keep the triumphant grin off his face. His fingers felt as if they had been charged with electricity where he was touching her and, impossibly, his cock seemed to be looking for room to expand further. He shifted his other arm further round her so that his fingers were just touching the curve of her left breast. Jan snuggled so close against him that he was sure she would hear his heart racing. Thank God she couldn't see his crotch. Nothing could hide his obvious arousal now.

As they drew closer he could see that the building was some kind of old summerhouse, clearly disused and badly neglected. He mounted the wooden steps warily, uncertain that they were strong enough to take their combined weights.

'You can put me down now.' Jan's words cleared his fuzzy brain.

'Of course.' Tor reluctantly lowered her legs to the ground, turning her body into him. As she slid down, her skirt slid up. He held her at the waist, pulling her stomach against his rock-hard erection. He couldn't really see much, but his imagination was running riot. Lust rippled through his body as he pulled her closer. If she would just give him a sign, do something. He caught the knowing smile on her face. Quite obviously, she was not only aware of the effect she was having, but was also revelling in his clumsy attempts to get closer to her. He gritted his teeth and felt the familiar rush of anger he always experienced when he sensed he was being teased.

He had always hated the idea of being toyed with. It drove him mad with desire. He wanted to see Jan squirming helplessly in his grasp, hear her sighing and moaning with her uncontrollable passion and desperate need. Shit! He released her so quickly that she stumbled slightly before regaining her balance.

'Thank you for the lift,' she said with an innocent smile that was so endearing that Tor felt his heart skip. She could melt an iceberg with that smile. He noticed the laughter dancing playfully in her eyes and felt his own mouth grin in response. She was so beautiful. He wanted her so much.

Jan stepped away, bending forward to brush down her skirt. Tor caught a quick glimpse of her panties – an image that would remain in his mind for a long time. God, he just wanted to drop to his knees and beg her to let him fuck her.

Walking across the outer veranda, he peered inside the filthy windows and took several deep breaths to calm himself down. The adrenalin was still rushing through his veins, making his hands shake. He made a fist with one hand and slammed it into the other one, then gripped it tightly, trying to physically stem the trembling. Dimly outlined in the dirty windowpane, he could see Jan standing just behind him. Even without looking up, he could feel her eyes boring into his back. He was determined not to turn around until he got himself back under control.

Tor twisted his head to the left and let his eyes roam over the gardens. He hoped to have a place like this of his own one day. Not that he was an avid gardener or anything, but he could learn. It would be a while before he could afford something quite so grand, unless his income improved dramatically. There always seemed to be so many expenses.

'The garden extends to those trees beyond the bushes,' Jan's voice broke his meditation. 'There's a vegetable plot behind the bushes, though I doubt there are any vegetables in it.'

Tor realised that she had moved closer to him. He could feel the warmth of her body and he sniffed the air to catch another hint of her alluring scent.

'Do you want to see?' she questioned. 'That is, if you don't mind carrying me again?'

It was tempting, very tempting. The feel of her lithe body in his arms, those pert little breasts pressed against his chest . . . 'No.' His voice sounded a bit harsh, even to his own ears. Jesus, she made him so randy! 'No, I'll take your word for it.' He made a show of tucking his shirt in and surreptitiously slipped a bit more material between his cock and the zip. Much better!

Jan moved closer still and took his arm. 'Would you like to see the house now then?'

Tor turned and looked at her. He nodded silently and Jan raised one arm up round his neck.

'Well?' she challenged him. He was trapped. House or vegetable garden. It made no difference. Either way, he would have her in his arms once more. His heart began to race as another surge of adrenalin coursed through his burning veins.

'OK.' This time, as her lifted her, he deliberately put his fingers under her skirt and allowed his other hand to slide even further round than before, so that he was cupping her breast. He was having trouble keeping his breathing steady and, as he began to move, his trousers tightened over his groin, rubbing his tormented cock. All his efforts to calm himself were completely wasted. He was shaking all over with passion. Although he could not see, he could vividly imagine the way her skirt was rucked up so that the tops of her thighs were visible.

'I'm not too heavy am I?' Even her voice drove him wild.

'No. You're perfect. I mean, perfect weight for me to carry.'

Jan twisted round to smile up at him and his hand moved even further on to her breast. He struggled to resist the urge to squeeze it between his fingers as he felt the outline of her lacy bra and the soft warmth of her flesh underneath. His fingertip made contact with the small rise of her nipple and a surge of lust caused him to stumble. His fingers instinctively tightened and her nipple became more distinct to his trembling fingers.

Jan turned slightly and pointed to a small rose garden. Her other breast pushed hard against him and his cock spasmed. Her skirt had ridden up over the top of her stockings so that his eyes were mesmerised by the soft whiteness of her bare thighs. He was almost overwhelmed by a surge of panic at the realisation of how close he was to losing it. He quickened his pace, feeling the sweat trickling down his body as he raced towards the path. As he lowered her to the ground again, he pulled his body back away from her. He didn't dare even so much as let her touch him until he had calmed down a little.

'This way.' Jan took his arm. 'The alarm can be switched off from the front or the back. It's linked to the local police station. If you set if off by mistake remember to call them or you'll have the local plod swarming all over you.' She stopped outside the back door.

Tor just nodded. He wasn't thinking about alarms. He was certain that she knew exactly what she was doing to him. The only question was how far she was willing to go. Shit, she had him shaking like a leaf. He'd never been so expertly teased in his life. He couldn't stop now. If she wouldn't go all the way, he was going to take his cock out and wank right in front of her. The idea excited him even more. It was a favourite fantasy. If she said no, he would do it. He would lie her on the floor, sit astride her and wank all over her breasts while he told her all the things he wanted to do to her.

'Are you all right? You look a bit pale.' Jan's question brought him back to earth.

'No, I'm fine.' Stop fantasising, he told himself sternly. She's running rings around you and you're making it worse. Don't let her get the better of you. He took a long, deep breath.

'Let's look inside, shall we?' he suggested in his deepest, strongest voice. 'After you.' He pushed the door open and stood back to let her go first. He followed after her, only just avoiding walking straight into her when she stopped to reset the alarm before it went off. He watched her breasts move tantalisingly under her blouse as she reached up to key in the numbers.

'Man of stone,' he muttered to himself.

'Sorry? Did you say something?'

'No, nothing.' He couldn't take his eyes off her. 'Just thinking aloud.'

'The number can be changed to whatever you choose if you decide to take the place,' Jan informed him as she began to move on down the corridor. 'Now, let's see. I think this must be the kitchen.' Jan pushed a door open and peered in. 'Freezer, microwave, gas oven and hob, plenty of cupboards and workspace.' She moved into the room while he stood by the door and watched as she pointed out the various utilities. 'It's fully fitted and complete with all the cutlery and crockery you'll need.'

Tor swallowed hard as she stood on tiptoe to peer in a wall cupboard, then bent over from the waist to pry under the sink. The sun poured through the large window so that he could clearly see the outline of her buttocks through her skirt.

'Washing machine and tumble dryer through here.' Jan moved towards another door. 'Whenever you need to wash something.'

'Any second now if you keep doing that,' Tor mumbled to himself.

'I'm sorry?' Jan looked confused.

'Nothing,' Tor grunted softly. Christ. He was going to have to be careful. He had never actually lost it in his pants before but he couldn't stop fantasising about her. He shifted his weight from one foot to the other, trying to relieve the almost unbearable pressure.

'Do you cook?'

'I'm sorry. What was that?' She had obviously asked him a question. His thoughts had been elsewhere.

'I was just wondering if you enjoy cooking. It's such a beautiful kitchen.'

'Why not come round one evening and find out?' His question took him by surprise. Better, much better, he congratulated himself. That had sounded very suave and sophisticated. He was tired of making such a fool of himself in front of her.

'Perhaps I will,' Jan replied. 'What's your speciality?'

'Um, well I can turn my hand to most things, though I don't get much chance during the season.' There was no way he was going to admit that he couldn't boil an egg to save his life. He always ate out or bought take-away.

Jan smiled again and headed back into the passage-way. Tor followed her around each room in turn, doing his best to look at what the house had to offer and not what her body was tempting him with. He kept his hands behind his back and leaned forward slightly as he walked to conceal the obvious outline of his groin. It had got to such a state that every move provoked him more, so that he was having one long fantasy about her. He had already imagined her begging for it at least three times. As they started up the stairs, Tor tried not to look at the back of her legs or the way her skirt was tightening across her buttocks.

'Oh.' Suddenly Jan stumbled and lost her footing. Tor's reactions were lightning fast: he leapt forward and wrapped an arm around her waist while reaching out with his other hand to grasp the banister.

'Thank you.' Her voice was genuinely shaky. 'I must

have caught my heel. If you hadn't caught me, I would have fallen.' Her lips were so close to his that he just couldn't resist. Her mouth tasted as sweet as honey. Although she wasn't kissing him back, she wasn't trying to pull away either.

He lifted her effortlessly into his arms and carried her to the top of the stairs. She said nothing. He stood with her like that, then gently kissed her again. This time, he felt the pressure of her own lips returning the kiss. She parted them slightly and he pushed his tongue eagerly on to hers.

Jan pulled her head back and smiled sweetly. 'It seems my knight in shining armour is claiming his reward.' She wriggled out of his arms and then stood on tiptoe to wrap her own arms around his neck. Pulling his head down towards her, she started to kiss him passionately.

Tor responded with equal ardour. He wrapped his arms around her slim body and pulled her tight on to him. He could feel her body warmth radiating from her and sending a blaze of heat all through him. His aching cock jerked and juddered against his clothing and he groaned helplessly as he savoured the feel of her soft, slippery tongue probing his.

As she pulled back from him and turned away, Tor grabbed her and pulled her back hard on to his body. Slowly, he slid his hands up her waist to cup both breasts, while his lips began to kiss her neck and ears. He could definitely feel her hardened nipples pushed against his eager fingers and he moaned softly as he began to undo the buttons of her blouse. Her skin was so soft and smooth. Gently, he slipped one hand up under her bra to caress the tender flesh of her breasts while his other hand tugged his zip open to relieve the pressure.

Jan whimpered softly and the sound drove him crazy. His pulse was racing and his cock felt as if it was about to split wide open with the pressure of his ever-increasing excitement. With shaking fingers, Tor tugged the sleeves of her blouse down her arms and over her wrists.

As the blouse fell from his fingertips, Tor bent forward and ran his tongue and lips down her back. His fingers fumbled with the catch on her bra. They both sighed as it came undone and Tor continued his journey down her back to her waist. He slid his hands round over her flat stomach and back up to caress her breasts. Moving more quickly now in his excitement, he peeled her bra straps off her arms and dropped it on the floor beside her blouse. He could feel her whole body trembling at his touch and see the goose bumps rising up on her soft white flesh.

Consumed with his burning passion, Tor ripped his own shirt off and pulled her back hard against his chest. His fingers started to toy with her engorged nipples as he savoured the thrill of her burning skin pressed against his own.

'You're so beautiful,' he whispered softly in her ear. 'So very desirable. I have to have you.' He felt her body tremble in response to his words and a fierce pang of longing coursed through him, setting his loins on fire. He felt as if he had never wanted any woman as much as he wanted Jan at that moment.

Tor's heart stopped as she pulled away from him, but then she took hold of his hand and started to lead him into one of the bedrooms. She guided him over to the large double bed, pushed him down on to the bare mattress and stepped back to undo the zip on her skirt. As it fell down her body, she stepped out of it and swung her leg over him so that she was straddling his thighs. With a tiny smile, she ran her fingers across his hard stomach and opened the catch at his waistband.

Tor shuddered with pleasure at her touch and held his breath as her sure fingers discovered that his zip was already open. He writhed from side to side, gritting his teeth in his effort to contain his excitement. He was too close again. Much too close. It was only sheer willpower holding himself back. Dear God, when she touched him there, he wouldn't be able to help himself.

Her burning fingers started to peel his pants down off him. His cock leapt out into the air as if loaded on springs with its swollen, purple head damp and ready. So ready. Just one touch was going to be all it would take. Tor closed his eyes and gave himself up to the inevitable.

He felt her pull his pants down as far as she could, then put her hands back on to his stomach and slide them round under his buttocks. He jumped at the pressure of her fingers pulling him up and realised that she wanted him to raise himself. Totally under her spell, he lifted himself off the bed, gritting his teeth and ready to feel his cock make contact with her breasts. As soon as he touched her, he would lose it. He knew he would. He needed to take control, to play with her until his overexcited body had a chance to calm down a bit.

Jan slipped his clothing down over his buttocks and thighs then bent forward and pushed him back on to the bed while she kissed his nipples. His cock rubbed against one of her breasts and Tor groaned in desperation and despair as he exploded. His penis juddered uncontrollably, spitting and spurting urgently as all the pent-up pressure and longing of the morning finally burst from him.

As the first hot spurt splattered her breast, Jan sat up and watched silently. Dimly, through the almost excruciatingly pleasurable sensation of his release, Tor could see the tiny smile of amusement on her lips as she witnessed his complete loss of control. He moaned incoherently, vaguely aware of just how humiliated he was going to feel, once the pleasure was over. As the final burst of his orgasm died away and his still-rigid cock ceased its jerking, Jan's smile seemed to widen.

'Hmm. A bit sensitive aren't we?' she mocked.

His eyes fell from her grinning lips to the sight of his dripping cock finally beginning to shrivel back to size, and he felt the first wave of utter shame sweep through him. He could actually feel the tears of humiliation burning in the back of his eyes. He closed them tightly so that he couldn't see her face, but the image of her amused expression was burnt on to his memory. He lay silently as she stood up and walked across the room. A door opened and he heard the sound of water running in the adjoining bathroom.

What was going through her mind? The smile on her face had seemed to indicate that she had enjoyed what she had done to him. Had she? Is that what she had intended all along? To push him so far so that he finally lost all self-control? If so, she must be very pleased with herself. The trouble was, he was still feeling incredibly randy. His explosion had done little to relieve his over-whelming passion, just taken away his immediate ability to do anything about it.

Tor stood up and finished stripping his clothing off. Naked, he walked through into the bathroom. Jan moved over to him and gently wiped the sweat from his broad chest.

'You know, in a way that was probably one of the most flattering things that has ever happened to me.' She smiled sympathetically.

Tor tried a weak smile in return. Well, it was a hell of a lot better than anger. After all, it had shown her just how much she turned him on, hadn't it? He stepped under the shower and started feeling a lot better.

When he had washed the sweat and semen from his body, he took a towel from the rail and wrapped it around his waist. Jan had already returned to the bedroom and replaced her skirt. She started towards the door, presumably to fetch her bra and blouse from the landing.

'Wait.' Tor grabbed her arm. 'Aren't you going to finish showing me around?'

Jan looked surprised and then stared around the room as if looking for something else to show him. 'Well, there are some built-in cupboards over there but I think you've seen the rest.'

Tor shook his head. 'No, I haven't seen everything, yet.' He was looking at her, not at the room. The sight of her naked breasts was already having a positive effect on his treacherous organ.

'Well, there are two other, smaller bedrooms and a separate bathroom.' Jan shrugged her shoulders. 'Don't you want to get dressed first?'

Tor shook his head. 'I'm still a bit damp. Come on.' He led her out the door and down the landing, not giving her time to stop for her clothing. As they walked, he watched the way her breasts bounced up and down.

'This is the second-largest bedroom,' she told him as they opened another door. 'If I remember correctly, this one has got a lovely view of the back garden.' She jumped at his touch. 'What are you doing?' she questioned as he quickly opened the zip on her skirt and tugged it back down her legs.

Tor turned her to face him. The towel dropped from his waist and fell to the floor. He saw her eyes glance down and then widen slightly. He leant forward and ran his tongue across her breasts while his hands glided over her waist and on to her tummy. He slipped his fingers under the elastic of her thong and started to pull it down, gradually revealing her mound.

Jan's lips parted slightly and he could hear the soft sigh of her breath as his lips wandered down her body. The feel of her trembling at the touch of his hands and tongue excited him further, so that his cock sprang back to full size and its shiny head joined his fingers, teasing her willing flesh.

'Oh yes,' Jan moaned and writhed in pleasure as his

130

tongue reached her partially shaved mound and its soft tip found her tiny pink clit. Her body spasmed and the air rushed from her lungs in a sudden whoosh as he sucked her swollen bud up into his lips. Tor felt her straining against the elastic of her thong as she tried to pull her legs wider apart. She grabbed his head, pushing him harder against her and he felt her fingers winding and tugging his hair as her passion mounted.

Tor felt the elation washing over him, adding to his own increasing excitement. This was much better. After his earlier loss of control, his total humiliation, now he was calling the shots. He was pushing her. Already, her little squeals of delight were becoming louder and more urgent. He could feel her clit swelling and hardening even more as he teased and licked her. The dampness on her sex lips and thighs was increasing by the second as her arousal intensified.

Soon, very soon now, he would push her just a little further. Then a little further still. He was going to give her the fuck of her life. Before he was finished, she would be begging him to stop. His cock jerked as his tongue slipped effortlessly into her and her whole body shuddered yet again. He wouldn't stop, no matter how hard she begged. He would drive her mad with passion as he explored every inch of her body. He was much calmer now; he had plenty of time.

'Oh my God,' Jan whimpered as Tor lost himself in his fantasies. 'Oh, yes . . .'

Chapter Six

Sara Williams was humming contentedly to herself as she bustled around the huge kitchen. She actually enjoyed her work, although the kind of fast food they served in the ice rink's café certainly didn't challenge her skills as a cook.

For the past few days, however, Sara had been somewhat preoccupied with her own thoughts to give more than passing attention to beefburgers and chips. Ever since the away match in Bristol, and the dinner afterwards, her mind had been filled with amorous thoughts about the dark-haired Trojan defender, Ean.

She had only spoken with him for a few minutes. In fact, she had spent more time talking with the big, blond centre player, Tor. Nevertheless, those few minutes, during which her body had brushed against his, had been enough to set more than her imagination on fire. As she had always suspected, Ean was the image of Mark twenty years ago. Well, almost, if you overlooked the muscles.

Sara finished stacking the dishwasher from the early morning breakfasts for the staff and looked around the kitchen critically. Everything was done except for restocking the freezer and preparing for the first coffee and snacks when the rink opened to the public at 10 a.m.

As she started buttering the rolls, Sara found herself worrying about why the Office Services Manager at the catering agency wanted to see her when she clocked off at noon. Ms Jamison's voice had given nothing away, but then it was always difficult to fathom out what was going through the woman's mind. She was super-efficient and friendly enough, but impossible to read. Neither her face nor her voice ever gave an inkling of what she was actually thinking. A week or so back, Sara had asked if she could work some extra shifts: with her son at college, money was always a bit tight. Hopefully that was all Ms Jamison wanted to see her about.

An hour and a half after their meeting, Sara was on the far side of town, standing outside the gates of a long winding driveway leading to a big old house. She double-checked the address written on the piece of paper in her hand and then stared apprehensively at the intercom system fitted on to one gatepost.

At least Ms Jamison had not kept her in suspense for long.

'Hello Sara. Sit down. I'll be with you in a minute.'

While the Office Services Manager had flicked through Sara's file, Sara had watched nervously, wondering if someone at the rink had complained about her work. She couldn't think of any reason why they should have done.

'Some of our clients are feeling the pinch of the rising interest rates and strong pound,' Ms Jamison had begun. 'They are tightening up on expenditure wherever they can and, as a result, our own business is suffering.'

Sara had felt her heart sink; suddenly she was afraid that she was about to be laid off. But that didn't make any sense. The rink was doing really well. She had heard Justin telling Maggie that the Trojans' successful season had made skating more popular than ever.

'Here, at Butterflies, we've decided that we need to make a few changes of our own in order to survive. So, we've decided to branch out and cater for a wider clientele.' Ms Jamison had looked up at Sara thoughtfully. 'I believe you said you would be interested in some additional work?'

Sara wrapped in the misery of imminent redundancy, was taken by surprise by the woman's words.

'Well, yes,' she had stammered. 'Things are a bit tight at the moment, what with my son . . .' Sara had stopped herself. Normally, she was a very private person, but she had always had a habit of talking too much when she was nervous and later regretting her hasty revelations.

'Well, I have a new client who is looking for a housekeeper for a few months. Someone who is both efficient and discrete. I see from our records that you have done this kind of work before.' She had looked up expectantly. 'Can I take it that you would be interested? It'll mean giving up the ice rink for a while, but it will be easier to replace you there than it is to find a good housekeeper. It will pay extremely well.'

When Ms Jamison had gone on to explain just what she meant by 'pays well', Sara had not hesitated. With Kevin away at college much of the time there was nothing to keep her at home anyway.

'Of course, you will have to attend an interview, but I'm sure that will only be a formality.'

As Sara smoothed her dress down and reached up to press the intercom button, her mind was already busy running over various recipes. Ms Jamison had said that she would probably have to contend with quite a lot of entertaining. It had been years since she had catered for dinner parties. What if she had forgotten how to cope on her own?

'Yes.' The voice sounded both cold and suspicious.

Sara reminded herself that this was a client who valued his privacy.

'Good afternoon. My name is Sara Williams. I was sent by Butterflies, the catering services group.'

The only reply she received was a short buzz, followed by a sharp click as the gates started to swing open.

Sara scowled. 'Please come in. I've been expecting you,' she muttered sourly to herself as she began walking down the long gravel driveway. Obviously, her prospective new boss was not a man given to wasting words.

'Sara Williams?' The man standing on the front step of the imposing redbrick house was middle-aged and overweight. There was something very familiar about him. Was he someone famous or had she seen or met him somewhere before? She racked her brains. If he was famous he might be offended if she didn't recognise him.

'Welcome, my dear. I've been so looking forward to your arrival.'

His words took her by surprise and she found herself swiftly re-evaluating her first impressions. Perhaps he wasn't unfriendly, just cautious with strangers? Where had she seen him before? She was certain that they had met quite recently.

The man hurried down the steps and shook her hand. 'Roland Donaldson. Call me Roland.' He took her arm. 'Please, come inside and let me show you around.' He glanced down in apparent surprise. 'You don't seem to have any suitcases with you? Are your things being sent on?'

'Well, um, no.' His hand felt damp and clammy on her skin and his body odour was not entirely masked by the heavy aftershave he appeared to have bathed in. Who was he? Suddenly she remembered. Roland Donaldson. Of course. He was the Trojans' manager! How could she have not recognised his name straight away?

'I was just told to come for an interview,' she added

135

quickly as she stared at him. She was certain that it was him.

'Interview? No need for that. You come highly recommended, Sara. I am delighted to take you on. Now, in you come. I can arrange for your things to be collected later.'

'Haven't we met?' she asked quickly.

'Met?' Roland looked puzzled.

'Yes. You're the Trojans' manager aren't you? I work, have been working, at the rink café. And, thanks to Justin, I was at their away match in Bristol last week.'

'Ah yes, of course. That's why you seem familiar. You were one of the lovely ladies who joined us for dinner after the game, weren't you?'

Sara nodded and felt her cheeks colour slightly. Her head was in a whirl of confusion.

'And a fan, too?' He raised his eyebrows in a questioning way. 'You are a fan?'

Sara nodded again.

'Splendid!' Roland started to guide her up the steps and through the wide oak doorway. 'How nice that we've all already met,' Roland continued. 'Some of the lads spend so much time here that it's practically their second home. I'm sure they'll all be delighted to see you again. Besides,' he gave her a sly wink and tightened his grip on her arm. 'None of them are what you might call domesticated. Prepare them a good home-cooked meal, Sara, and the boys will all become your instant and willing slaves. Ah, talk of the devil.'

Sara's eyes widened as several of the Trojans filed into the room. She was tempted to pinch herself to make sure that she wasn't dreaming. She almost laughed at the idea of Roland calling them 'boys'. Her stare found Ean, and her legs started to tremble.

'Lads, this is Sara. She has just agreed to move in and take care of me.'

Sara was too shocked to mention that she had agreed

to no such thing. She just stared at the ice hockey players and felt a flush of colour flow up her neck and on to her cheeks as they returned the compliment.

'In case you've forgotten, this is Tor, Troy, Ean, Pele, Pary and my little brother, Bri.' Roland pointed to each of the men in turn then put his arm across Bri's shoulders. 'Or, rather, ex-little brother,' he added.

Sara stared at him in bemusement.

'Roland used to be married to my sister,' Bri explained as he pulled away from Ronald's clasp and held out his right hand. 'Welcome aboard.'

Sara shook hands with each of them. When she took Ean's hand, she felt her blush deepen even more and a tingle like an electric shock run down her arm. His dark eyes twinkled at her cheerfully. He was the image of Mark.

'I know you from somewhere, don't I?' Tor questioned her as he shook her hand briefly. Sara nodded. 'I was at your game down in Bristol the other week,' she responded softly.

Tor grinned. 'How flattering,' he laughed. 'Everywhere I go, I seem to keep bumping into loyal female fans. I had no idea we were so popular.'

'Justin managed to get Maggie some complimentary tickets,' Sara explained. 'You know, Maggie. She works on reception at the rink. I work, used to work, as a cook in the café,' she added, wondering who else he had come across and where.

'Ah, um, yes. We know Maggie,' Tor agreed quickly and Sara could have sworn the men exchanged a highly meaningful glance at the mention of her friend's name. How curious. Had she missed something?

'A cook. Great.' Pele broke into her thoughts. 'What's for dinner?' he questioned. 'I'm famished.'

Roland laughed. 'Always thinking about your stomach. Don't scare her off.' He put his arm around

Sara's shoulders and gave her a friendly squeeze. 'She hasn't even seen her room yet.'

Sara pulled away from him and tried to think. Things were moving much too fast for her. 'I couldn't possibly start before tomorrow,' she told him firmly.

Ean pulled a face. 'Tomorrow? Take pity on us, Sara. I can't face another meal cooked by Roland and I'm sick to death of take-away.'

Pele took her hand. 'We'll waste away if we don't get some decent food soon. How can we possibly win matches if we don't eat a balanced diet?'

'Yeah. Please, Sara. There's only one thing worse than Roland's cooking,' Tor added pitifully as he dropped down on one knee in front of her.

Sara grinned. 'What's that?'

'Eating it,' Tor responded mournfully.

Sara shook her head and gave in. 'OK. I'll look around and see if I can rustle you up something.' She looked at Roland. 'If that's all right with you?'

Ean held her playfully by the waist. 'You angel of mercy.' He kissed her cheek and took her hand. 'You can feel me wasting away,' he complained as he placed her fingers on his hard stomach.

. Sara shivered and ran her fingers lightly up his chest. 'I think you're exaggerating just a little,' she chided him softly, although she certainly couldn't feel an ounce of fat on his gorgeous body.

'Well, that's settled then.' Roland sounded extremely happy. 'As for the menu, just cook whatever is easiest for you. Right. Come on lads. We have some work to do. Especially in defence.' He glared at Pary and Ean. 'Your checking in the second period was pathetic. Sara here could do a better job of taking control.'

'It's because we never eat properly,' Pary muttered.

Sara laughed and felt another little tremor of excitement at the fun to come. Who would ever have thought she would end up playing 'mum' to the Trojans and their manager? Although, to be honest, she wasn't feeling the least bit maternal. Far from it!

Later, as she bustled around the beautifully equipped kitchen, Sara could feel the beads of perspiration gathering between her breasts. Not surprisingly, from what the men had said, she had found Roland's kitchen cupboards virtually bare and had been forced to make a trip to the supermarket to purchase what she needed. Roland had thrust a generous fistful of notes into her hands, assuring her that there was no need to worry about expense and that they would sort the finances out properly later.

The room was hot and steamy with a roast sizzling in one of huge ovens and three kinds of green vegetables simmering gently on the gas hob. Sara could feel her pulse hammering at her temples and her hands were trembling slightly when she removed the meat tray from the oven to drain the succulent beef juices into the gravy boat. She kept trying to tell herself that there was nothing to worry about. She often prepared a roast at the weekend for herself and her son Kevin. This was no different; there was just more of it.

Sara prodded the huge baron of beef with a long fork. The juices ran slightly pink, just the way she liked it. With a small grunt of satisfaction, she wrapped the joint in foil and bent down to check on her Yorkshires. They were perfect: the raised edges golden brown and crispy and the shallow centres soft and spongy – just waiting for a lavish helping of her rich dark gravy. Her stomach rumbled at the delightful combination of savoury aromas filling the air.

'Something smells wonderful.' The masculine voice behind her almost made her drop the pan of roast potatoes. She quickly put it back on to the shelf and stood up, closing the oven door and spinning round nervously. Ean was standing just behind her and the room suddenly seemed to grow even hotter.

139

'It will be ready in about five minutes,' she stuttered as she hastily wiped the steam off her brow and pushed her silvery-blonde curls back behind her ears.

'Great. I'm so hungry I could eat a horse.'

She noticed that his eyes were appraising her with interest and she wished that she'd had time to remove her cooking apron.

She tried to lighten the atmosphere with a weak joke. 'Well, you'll have to make do with half a cow.' When he didn't respond, she turned her back on him and gave the gravy an extra stir.

'The smell reminds me of home.' Ean had moved closer to her. 'My mother always does a roast at the weekends.'

Sara stiffened. With the thoughts she had been having about him lately, this untimely reminder of their age difference was the last thing she wanted to hear. 'Let's hope I can come up to her standards,' she muttered.

Ean grinned. 'Tough challenge. She is pretty good,' he replied and Sara felt her heart sink. 'Mind you, she's had a lot more practice at it than you. She and dad have been married almost twenty-five years.'

Sara felt her burning face flush even deeper at the compliment. She was grateful for the steamy atmosphere to hide her blushes. 'I'm just about ready to start serving up.' Sara reached for the colander to begin straining the vegetables. 'Do you think you could round everyone up for me?'

'Sure.' Ean gave her another cheeky grin and casually brushed a strand of his soft dark hair out of his eyes. 'Believe me, they're not far away.' His stomach rumbled noisily. 'Whoops.' He patted it. 'Excuse me.'

His face was now glowing pink from the heat and steam, and she could see herself reflected in the depths of his huge, almond-coloured eyes. The skin on his cheeks looked as soft and smooth as buttermilk, contrasting starkly with the dark shadow of stubble over his lip and chin. Sara lowered her gaze and took in his wide shoulders, the swell of his biceps and the narrowing waist above his almost concave stomach. His casual grey trousers were thin and tight and the slight bulge of his manhood drew her eyes like a magnet.

'Then I'll come back and give you a hand, shall I?'

She pulled her thoughts away from her fantasises and nodded dumbly. As he left the room, her eyes followed every wiggle of his hips and buttocks and a lump began to form in her throat. If only he were not so much like Mark. She turned quickly and forced her attention to serving the food.

Five minutes later, as Sara and Ean loaded up the dining table with plates and dishes, Tor examined the place settings in surprise. 'Where's your plate?' he questioned her.

'I'm not really all that hungry,' Sara replied quickly. 'I'll just have a small plate in the kitchen.'

'What? A cook who won't eat her own food?' Roland grinned. 'What are you trying to tell me?'

'Another time, maybe. I've still got a lot to do.'

Pele and Troy childishly started to bang the table with their spoons. 'Join us. Join us,' they chanted in unison. Sara laughed.

'Behave yourselves, or you won't get any pudding,' she threatened.

'Pudding?' Tor's eyes lit up. 'What's for pudding?'

'Blackcurrant pie and cream,' she replied.

'You know, I think we should let Sara return to her work after all.'

'Seconded,' Ean agreed. 'But only this once,' he added, almost as an afterthought.

Back in the kitchen, Sara smiled to herself as she sipped a glass of red wine and pushed her portion of blackcurrant pie around her plate. She still couldn't believe how much fun the Trojans were to be with. She had barely stopped laughing at their antics all afternoon. Roland had made her feel so welcome too. More like an old friend come to stay than a hired help.

She raised her hand and massaged her aching neck and shoulders. It was much more tiring than she had anticipated though, cooking for such a large number all on her own. She looked around ruefully at the huge pile of dirty dishes. She would have to make a start on stacking the dishwasher or she'd never get finished.

'Let me do that.' Ean's voice took her by surprise. She had thought that they had all retired to Roland's big living room to watch a film and polish off a few beers.

Sara jumped as she felt his large hands push hers aside before his fingers started to massage her shoulders. She rolled her head, luxuriating in the feel of his strong fingers easing her knotted muscles.

'You're as tense as a coiled spring,' he chided her softly, as he moved his hands down her back. 'What you need is something to relax you completely.'

Yes please, Sara thought to herself dreamily. She imagined his hands running all over her body and her stomach suddenly felt as if it was full of butterflies. This couldn't be happening, could it?

'I think I should give you a proper massage,' he continued. 'After all, if you are going to cook regularly for us we don't want you off work with a bad back, do we?'

Before she could pinch herself to see if she was already asleep, Ean had pulled her chair out from under the table and twisted it round so that she was facing him. Crouching in front of her, he lifted her left leg and gently slipped one of her shoes off.

'From the bottom up,' he told her as his fingers started doing delightful things to the soles of her foot. Her thighs prickled at the implication of his words and her imagination was already running wild. She sighed softly and leant back against the chair with her eyes closed.

Ean lifted her foot on to his thigh and began to caress

142

each of her toes in turn. Through the softness of her stocking, his fingers felt incredibly smooth and their caress unexpectedly erotic. Sara felt her nipples hardening in response and the muscles at the top of her legs spasmed. His fingers slid under the sole of her foot and encircled her slim ankle. Sara shivered from head to toe and opened her eyes again to stare at him.

'We need to get you somewhere more comfortable,' he told her. He looked thoughtful for a moment, then nodded. 'I know. There's a big soft couch in Roland's library.'

Before she had a chance to protest, to insist that she still had work to do, Ean stood up and swung her up into his arms as easily as if he was lifting a small child. Cradling her against his broad chest, he carried her gently out the door, along the hall and into the large, deserted library. Sara snuggled guiltily against him, enjoying the feel of his muscles rippling under his shirt as he moved.

Ean placed her on a long, velvet-covered couch in front of the fireplace and stood in front of her. Sara looked around the room. A huge cabinet behind Roland's desk was filled with ice hockey trophies.

'Did you win all those?' she asked him nervously.

Ean nodded without taking his eyes off her. 'Well not all of them. At least, not personally. Some of them are from before I joined the squad. Now, slip off your dress and lie down on your stomach,' he commanded. 'I won't look, I promise,' he added when he saw her hesitation. 'It's OK, Sara. I know what I'm doing,' he assured her softly.

His words seemed full of double meaning. Or was it just that she wanted them to? Maybe he knew what he was doing, but did she? All the things Sara knew she should say fled from her mind. She forgot that she was a hired housekeeper with duties to attend to, forgot that he was a Trojan. It was as if she was a client at some exclusive clinic and he the concerned therapist.

Sara stood up slowly with her back to him. She lifted her dress up over her head and tried not to think about him standing there. She breathed a quick, silent prayer of thanks that she was wearing her most expensive undies and tried not to remember that she had been thinking of him that morning when she had put them on. As she turned back, she saw him watching her avidly.

'I thought you promised not to look,' she reprimanded him.

Ean grinned and put his head on one side. 'I had my fingers crossed,' he confessed and helped her down on to the couch.

Sara lay face down and rested her forehead on her arms. Almost immediately, she felt his firm fingers caressing her smooth calves. Another shiver of desire raced through her body and she felt the quick rush of moisture aound her pussy. She pushed her thighs as tightly together as his hands would allow, and raised her chest slightly so that her engorged nipples were not chaffing against the lace of her bra.

'Relax,' he chided her. 'I can't massage you properly while you keep tensing your muscles like that.'

'Sorry.' Sara tried hard to comply. It wasn't easy. His hands were slowly but gradually working their way up her leg, squeezing and kneading every inch of her. She stifled a gasp as his fingers reached the top of her stocking and slipped on to the bare skin of her upper thigh. His touch felt hot, even to her already burning flesh.

'Where did you learn to do that so well?' she asked him.

'I once did a course in remedial massage,' he replied. 'I was thinking about doing it for a living, before I got my break with the Trojans. Maybe I will still, later.'

'You'd never be short of clients,' Sara assured him with a gentle sigh.

'You know, you have a really sexy body,' he compli-
mented her in return. 'I bet you work out regularly.'

Sara failed to stop another tiny sigh of pleasure as his
knowing fingers slid over the curve of her left buttock
and began to knead the knotted muscles at the base of
her spine.

'Does that feel better?' he questioned in response to
her sigh.

'It feels wonderful,' she mumbled softly.

His hands moved on up her body and she felt his
fingers release the catch at the back of her bra. Her aching
breasts flopped forward on to the couch. Her nipples felt
as hard as marbles. He pulled her bra straps out of the
way and she felt his hands making large sweeping
motions all over her back.

'Why are you doing this?' she questioned sharply.

Ean's hands stopped in the centre of her back. 'Don't
you like it?'

'Yes. Of course. It feels incredible. I just wondered
why. I mean, wouldn't you rather be with the others?'
She wanted to ask why he, of all of them, should have
singled her out. Was it just a coincidence or had he
sensed her special attraction to him, even if he didn't
know the reason for it.

'We threw dice,' he admitted. 'And I won.'

It was the first time a man had ever gambled over her.
Sara wasn't sure how she felt.

'Look at it from my point of view,' he told her, as if
sensing her confusion. 'A few beers with the lads or get
my hands on your beautiful, sexy body. I don't believe
that's a serious question.'

Sara twisted her head slightly and peered up at him
curiously. Did he mean that? Did he really think of her
as a beautiful woman? She felt beautiful. Young, beautiful and desirable. He was beautiful too. And desirable.
So very, very desirable.

'You know, you've got incredible skin. It's like massaging

145

silk or ivory.' Ean patted her buttocks. 'You've also got a really sexy arse.' He pulled the sides of her panties up into her crack.

Sara had been about to protest but closed her mouth quickly. The tingling sensation in her buttocks was not entirely due to his slap. 'Flattery will get you every-where,' she whispered huskily.

Ean was crouched over the couch, level with her breasts. The zip of his trousers was unsettlingly close to her face. His penis was pushed across to the left and, from the way the material was stretched so tightly, there could be little doubt that he was at least partially aroused. Sara felt another trickle of lubrication dampen the crotch of her panties and her head began to spin as the faint but unmistakably masculine odour of his body teased her nostrils.

'I can't believe how stiff you are.' His hands started to squeeze her neck and shoulder muscles. He leaned even closer over her, so that his crotch and thighs were resting lightly against her upper torso and she felt the unmistak-able hardness of his erection expanding through his trousers.

'So are you,' she murmured softly. 'Perhaps you should massage yourself?' Christ! What a thing to say! What had come over her? She buried her blushing face in the cushion and gave herself up to the exquisite sensations of pleasure and arousal coursing through her whole body.

'Roll over,' he instructed her suddenly.

She responded without hesitation and heard the slight catch in his breathing as she turned herself on to her back. Ean slipped her bra straps down her arms and pulled the loose material off her breasts. Sara automati-cally crossed her arms to cover herself, but Ean gently lifted them back out of the way. His lips were opened slightly and his eyes seemed to grow even bigger as he stared down at the soft swell of her naked breasts and dark swollen nipples. Almost reverently, he placed his hands on the front of her shoulders and began massaging her upper chest muscles.

Sara tried to hold herself rigid. She could feel the way her breasts were wobbling gently up and down in time with his movements. Her panties were now so damp that he could be in no doubt as to the extent of her arousal. She shivered as his hands glided down either side of her body and his fingertips brushed the edges of her aching breasts. She felt his hands coming together over her navel and was powerless to stop the little tremors in her stomach and thigh muscles. His fingers met in the middle and began to move outwards again, retracing their path.

Sara moaned and clenched her thighs tightly together. Her clit was tingling with the rapidly building rhythm of her passion and it was all she could do to stop herself pushing her fingers between her legs to satisfy her desperate longing.

She turned her head and stared up at his groin again. His zip was now bulging so tightly that she could see the stitches straining. It seemed impossible that the material could continue to resist the pressure. She half-expected it to burst open so that his rampant manhood might spring out and ravish her. His fingers reached her neck again and started on a new journey down over her breasts. Sara cried out when he cupped them lightly in his hands. The deep tingle between her legs turned into an urgent ache and she arched her back, instinctively pushing her nipples hard on to his huge palms.

'Relax,' he murmured again, 'just let yourself go.'

Let herself go! Jesus. It was all she could do to stop herself from letting go. She couldn't remember when she had last been this excited. Yes she could. The first time Mark had made love to her. Every time Mark had made love to her. She felt one of Ean's hands wander down her stomach and trace the outline of her navel before moving on over the lace of her panties. She bit her bottom lip and tried to keep her hips still as his feather-light touch caressed her mound and ventured on down between her dripping thighs.

'Please,' she sobbed. She wasn't sure whether she meant please stop or please keep going. She was too confused to think straight. What if one of the other Trojans walked in on them like this? What if Roland found them? She would probably get the sack. She'd have one hell of a time explaining that to the super-efficient Ms Jamison!

Ean's right hand had begun to squeeze and knead the soft flesh of her inner thigh. His other hand was still playing with her right breast and she could feel his fingertips gently teasing the hardness of her nipple. Every inch of her flesh in between his two hands was glowing. Her clit was on fire and she was desperate to feel his lips kissing her there.

Before she had time to think about what she was going to do, Sara lifted her hands and took hold of the waistband of his trousers. She fumbled awkwardly with the button and then took hold of the zip with her forefinger and thumb. She could almost of sworn that she heard the material heave a sigh of relief as she tugged it open and released the tension.

She lifted her head to stare at him. His underpants were bulging out of the opening and she could just see the shiny tip of his engorged penis over the elastic waistband. She ran her fingertip over it and felt him shudder. She put her finger to her mouth and licked it, then moved it back to rub him again.

Ean sighed heavily and his fingers stopped all pretence of massaging her thighs. She felt him tugging urgently on her panties and she whimpered when his finger started exploring her hot damp sex.

'Take these off.' Sara tugged at his trousers. 'I want to see you.' She slid her hand down his shaft as she started to pull his pants down.

Ean stood up quickly and pulled his trousers and pants off in one smooth movement. His cock was as hard as granite and swollen dark purple-red with his lust. As she stared at it, a single drop of moisture bubbled out of the tip and trickled down his length. She reached out for him greedily, catching the liquid on her finger and smearing it over him. His cock bobbed excitedly and, suddenly, she just couldn't wait any longer.

'Please,' she whispered again. This time, neither of them could be in any doubt what she wanted.

Ean kicked his clothing free from his ankles and knelt over her on the couch. He took his cock in one hand and leant forward to guide himself into her. Sara spread her thighs and eagerly lifted her buttocks up to meet him.

Instead of penetrating her, Ean held the tip of his cock against her sex lips and used his hand to rub himself gently up and down over her hard little bud. She groaned loudly with a mixture of enjoyment and impatience. It felt so good. Her pussy was so damp and slippery with her juices that his cock seemed to glide over her effortlessly. She was only moments away from her climax. She had to have him inside her.

Sara reached out and seized his buttocks, pulling him down on to her. Her fingernails raked across his skin, gouging red deep welts in his flesh. Ean grunted with the shock and pain of her attack and thrust himself hard into her waiting dampness. The force of his penetration was so strong that she felt his balls slapping hard against her thighs.

'Oh Mark. I've missed you so much,' she cried helplessly. She ground her clit against his pelvis and a powerful orgasm rippled through her as she felt him draw back ready to thrust in to her again.

Outside, across the hall in the living room, the TV was blaring loudly. Somebody yelled something and others began to cheer and whistle enthusiastically. Totally oblivious, Ean continued to pump urgently in and out of her. Sara responded eagerly, her desire rapidly building up towards another climax as their lovemaking gradually massaged all her pent-up tensions and longings away.

Chapter Seven

'Good morning, Maggie.'

Maggie looked up from the reception desk in surprise. She had thought that she was the only one around. Her spirits sank when she saw who it was.

'Mr Donaldson. Good morning.' She forced herself to be polite. 'Is there something I can do for you?' She rather hoped that there wasn't. She didn't much like the idea of having anything to do with Roland Donaldson. He was such an unpleasant man.

'Several things spring to mind,' Roland responded suggestively, as he placed a hand on her arm. Maggie repressed a shudder. 'You can start by calling me Roland. Then, perhaps you would like to join me for a cup of coffee . . .'

'I can't. Sorry. I'm on duty until twelve o'clock,' Maggie interrupted him quickly.

'So late? I thought you finished sooner.' Roland looked at his watch. 'In that case, shall we make it lunch? What do you say to a quick drink and a bite to eat in the Royal Standard?'

'Well, that's very kind of you, but I already have plans for this afternoon.' This was actually true. After what she had said to the little girl with the sprained ankle, Maggie had been thinking seriously about her own lack of skills and qualifications. Or was it because of what she had learned about Troy? Either way, she had been wondering if there was something she could do about it. Jan had been attending business studies evening classes for some time now and Maggie had talked herself into a visit to the local library, just to see what courses were on offer.

'I won't take much of your time, I promise,' Roland persisted. 'But there is something I want to discuss with you. Something I'm sure will interest you.'

'Such as?' Despite herself, Maggie was intrigued. She might dislike Roland, but he was the Trojans' manager. Besides, she hated secrets. Roland grinned.

He repeated his invitation: 'Lunch?'

'I'll have to be away by two at the latest.' Maggie gave in to her curiosity.

'I'll see you at twelve, then.' Roland removed his sweaty palm from her arm and she breathed a sigh of relief. She was already half-regretting her haste. What could he possibly have to discuss with her that was worth spending at least an hour in his company for? Oh well, too late now. At least she'd get a free meal.

The Royal Standard was a popular local and it was already filling up when they arrived. Roland found a place by the window and held the back of Maggie's chair for her while she sat down. She had to admit that he had good – if somewhat old-fashioned – manners. She had enjoyed the ride in his flashy red XK8 too – even though, as Troy had said, he drove it like a maniac.

'What will you have to drink?'

'Vodka and tonic, please.'

'I'll order the food before it gets too busy, shall I?' he suggested. 'The Ploughman's here is excellent. Unless you'd prefer something from the menu?'

'Yes, I know. A Ploughman's will be fine, thank you.'

Maybe she had been a bit too hasty in her assessment of Roland? He wasn't that bad, after all. Quite distinguished-looking too, with his short, dark hair shot through with silver and his deep brown eyes. A bit plump maybe, and definitely too fond of himself, but he wasn't the only man she knew with that particular fault! She smiled as she thought immediately of Justin.

When Roland returned with their drinks he took the chair opposite and smiled across the table at her. 'Cheers.' He took a long swig of his beer. Maggie returned the smile and took a small sip of her vodka.

'You seem to be a number one fan of ours, Maggie. Do you reckon we're in with a chance for the Championship this season?'

Maggie was surprised. It seemed a strange question for the Trojans' manager to be asking her. 'You tell me,' she retorted brightly. 'I'd say it's looking good.'

'Providing the players keep their minds on their game and don't allow themselves to become distracted by anything,' Roland agreed. 'Or anyone.'

So, that was it. Don't say he had asked her out just to tell her to keep away from Troy and the others? Like some overprotective, Victorian father! Maggie was having trouble keeping a straight face.

'I'm sure the players all want to win as much as you do,' she told him.

'They'd better, if they all want to keep their places next season,' Roland replied. 'Ah, here's the food. Thank you.' He beamed at the pretty young waitress who had brought their meal over to the table. 'Do you think I could have some French mustard, please?'

They ate in silence for a few minutes before Roland spoke. 'Incidentally, are you planning to be at the match this weekend?'

Maggie frowned. Was he trying to tell her to stay away? Who the hell did he think he was? If she wasn't so broke she would buy a ticket just to spite him. 'I haven't decided yet,' she told him stiffly. 'Why?' Go on, say it, she thought. Just try to tell me not to go and see what happens.

'Oh, it's just that I need someone to act as the official hostess for the squad. The young lady who usually takes care of it has broken her leg skiing.' He looked almost put out, as if the girl had done it deliberately, just to spite him.

Maggie stared at him in astonishment. After his earlier comments this was the last thing she expected.

'I just thought that as you work for the rink anyway, and since you're obviously such a huge fan, you might be interested in filling in. Free accommodation and a top seat at the game, of course.' He stared at her. 'I realise that it's very short notice,' he added, when she remained silent. 'Perhaps you have other plans for the weekend?'

'No. Nothing important,' Maggie assured him, her mind racing. 'Thank you, Roland. I'd love to do it.' She had seriously misjudged him, she decided. He was really rather nice, once you got to know him. Not only would she get a free ticket to the match, but she was going to spend the whole weekend with the Trojans! She felt like jumping up and giving him a big hug.

'Good,' he said and beamed. 'That's settled then. I'll let you have all the details later in the week. I've hired a coach to take everyone this time. I don't want another farce like we had in Bristol, with half the lads getting lost after the match.' Fortunately, he didn't seem to notice her sudden, guilty flush. He reached out and patted her hand. His eyes locked on to her cleavage with a lecherous glint.

Maggie felt a tingle of apprehension. Had she just made a bad mistake? Did he think that she was now in his debt? He certainly wasn't that attractive! Oh well, what the hell! With a hotel full of Trojans, she wasn't going to have much time for anyone else. If Roland thought that he had just bought himself a cosy little

154

liaison with her in Nottingham, he was in for a big disappointment.

Maggie was outside the ice rink just after 2 p.m. on Friday, with her suitcase packed and ready. She hadn't been able to find anyone to take over her morning shift, but fortunately the rink had been fairly quiet and she had managed to get away on time at 12 p.m. to change and pack.

A small luxury coach was waiting in the main car park and a few of the squad were already milling around aimlessly, laughing and joking. Stephen Jackson, the squad coach, and their physiotherapist, Gemma Sullivan, were also there. Gemma looked calm and relaxed as she bantered with the players, while Stephen was rushing around like a headless chicken, clutching a large clipboard.

'Maggie. Good.' As soon as he saw her, Stephen rushed over. 'Here's a list of everyone who should be on the coach. Make very sure we don't leave any of the equipment behind. Check and double check. These lads can be worse than a bunch of naughty kids on a school outing.'

Maggie took the list and nodded gravely.

'When we arrive, the hotel will give you a room list. See everyone gets to the right place and make certain no one leaves anything on the coach. Somebody is always losing something.' Stephen grinned ruefully. 'I hope you know what you've let yourself in for, Maggie. Playing nursemaid to this bunch of *prima donnas* is hard work!'

She grinned confidently, far too excited to allow Stephen's warnings to daunt her. 'No problem. I'm great with naughty kids,' she informed him.

'Just as well. Excuse me, I need to have a quick word with the driver.' Stephen dashed off towards the coach and Maggie glanced down at the checklist.

Gemma ambled over to stand beside her. 'Hi Maggie. Welcome to the mad house,' she said.

Maggie looked up and smiled at the pretty young woman. Although she was still the tiniest bit jealous of Gemma's position with the squad, she realised that it might be good to have some female company. Besides, Gemma must have been on dozens of away matches and would know the score. 'Hello. How are you?' asked Maggie.

Gemma pulled a face. 'Bloody exhausted, to be perfectly honest. I was clubbing until the early hours and I've been at the rink since first thing this morning, packing everything the boys conceivably might need: from aspirin to spare jock straps!' She pushed a strand of long brown hair behind her ear and reached into her shoulder bag for some gum. She held out the packet. 'Want some?'

'No thanks.' Maggie wasn't all that fond of gum. It made her feel a bit like a cow chewing the cud.

Gemma rolled up a wad and popped it into her mouth. Maggie watched without comment, trying not to smile at the thought of the gum getting stuck around Gemma's tongue stud. She had often tried to imagine what it would be like trying to eat with a stud through your tongue, and was almost tempted to ask Gemma whether she had ever swallowed the stud by mistake. She had also wondered what it would be like to kiss someone with a stud. Gemma would have to be very careful giving head or the passion could easily turn sour! Maggie's smile broadened but, fortunately, Gemma didn't seem to notice.

'As soon as we get on board, I'm going to sprawl out and catch up on my beauty sleep,' she informed Maggie. 'Unless any of them get hurt or sick, they're all yours. Good luck.' She headed back towards the coach just as Stephen reappeared, looking, if anything, even more harassed than before.

'Start getting everyone on board will you, Maggie,' he

called. 'I'd like to get on the road as soon as possible. The driver says there are major roadworks on the motorway.'

She looked around again and noticed that most of the squad seemed to have arrived. She spotted Tor and Troy stowing their gear in the baggage compartment under the coach and her heart began to race. She was burning to know how Tor had got on with his house hunting with Jan. She had been meaning to call Jan and find out. She felt the colour rushing to her cheeks at the memory of what Tor had done to her. Jan should be so lucky!

Troy stood up and turned around. When he spotted Maggie a wide grin appeared on his sensual lips. He nudged Tor and then swaggered over towards her.

'Hi babes. I heard you were coming along to take care of us. Nice. Real nice.' He winked suggestively.

'Hi yourself,' Maggie muttered awkwardly. 'I hope you and the others aren't going to give me any trouble. I hear you can be a bit of a handful at times.'

Troy flashed her another lecherous grin. 'You'd better believe it, sugar,' he drawled teasingly.

'Right then, let's get everyone on the coach.' Maggie tried her best to look and sound businesslike and professional. 'Is everybody here?' She moved over to the door of the coach and began checking names on the list as the players piled in beside her.

'Come and sit at the back with us, Maggie,' Tor told her, as he swung himself up into the coach. 'We'll keep a seat warm for you.'

By the time the last member of the squad was safely inside and Maggie had assured Stephen that everyone was present and accounted for, she could already hear some sniggering coming from the back seats and wondered what they could possibly be up to already.

'OK. Listen up everyone.' Stephen leapt on board and held up his hand for silence. 'Keep the noise down and remember that any damage comes out of your pay packet. No obscene gestures or bare arses out of the windows and absolutely no alcohol. Try to remember that you've got a crucial match to play tomorrow.' He sank down wearily in the front seat and looked up at Maggie. 'Ready?'

She nodded.

'OK,' he told the driver, 'let's get going.'

'I'm just going to check everyone's all right,' Maggie told Stephen. The noise from the back was becoming more raucous and her curiosity was getting the better of her.

'Sure. Whatever,' Stephen responded. 'If you don't come back, I'll send a search party.'

Maggie made her way down the centre isle of the moving coach, smiling at the soft whistles and suggestive whispers as she passed. Stephen had been right. It was just like taking a bunch of kids on a school outing – extremely attractive and well-endowed kids, mind you.

Several of the men were leaning over their seats, facing the back. Everyone was laughing.

'Look out! Here comes trouble,' Pary yelled as she approached. Troy turned around and grinned up at her innocently. Maggie smiled back and moved past them to the back seat. Gemma was spread out on the seat, sleeping peacefully. Lying beside her with one arm across her pert breasts and the other under the hem of her skirt was a full-sized blow-up doll, stark naked and anatomically correct in every detail.

'Meet Anna,' Bri chuckled.

'She's sort of our unofficial mascot,' Troy told her. 'The perfect woman: mouth always open, but never says a word,' he added cheekily.

'Hey, watch it you,' Maggie scolded. 'We'll have no sexist comments while I'm in charge.'

'Yeah, shove it, black boy,' Bri chided.

'Hey, whitey! Watch who you're calling black or I'll set Maggie on to you.'

Before Maggie could think up a witty reply to this,

Gemma stirred and opened her eyes. 'What the fuck . . .' She sat up quickly and pushed the doll on to the floor. 'OK. Very funny.' She glared round at her laughing audience. 'Just wait till I get you on my massage table, that's all,' she threatened them.

'But, you and Anna make such a lovely couple,' Ean insisted. He ducked quickly as Gemma took an angry swipe at him.

'In your dreams,' she retorted.

'OK. Settle down everyone,' Maggie told them. 'If you don't cool it, Stephen will blow a fuse and I'll never get asked to play hostess again.'

Troy shifted over in his seat to make room for her. 'Come and sit by me,' he suggested. 'I'll show you what your duties are.'

Now, there's an offer no girl could refuse, Maggie thought to herself as she wriggled in next to Troy and snuggled herself up against him amidst the raucous catcalls. As she had anticipated, it was promising to be quite a weekend.

Roland caught Maggie just as she was coming out of her room later that afternoon.

'Ah, there you are, Maggie. I thought you might like to join me for dinner tonight. Not here. Somewhere where we can be alone.' He pulled a face. 'It's not that they're not a great bunch of lads, but, with an average age of around twenty-five, I do find some of their antics a bit childish at times, don't you?'

She smiled. Childish was not the word that immediately sprang to her mind. Demanding might be more apt. At least she now knew why Gemma always wore trousers when she was on duty. So far, she had been unable to come up with any threat of punishment that didn't encourage them all the more.

'I've already agreed to eat with them,' she told Roland. 'After all, I am working this weekend.'

'Your hostess duties don't require you to spend the evening with the squad. On the contrary, you should be helping the coach and me make sure that the lads restrain themselves. Remember that they have an important match tomorrow,' Roland told her stuffily.

'In that case, shouldn't you have dinner with them yourself?' Maggie suggested cheekily.

'I'm their manager, not their babysitter,' Roland retorted. He put his hand on her arm. 'I was rather hoping that you would want to show your appreciation. After all, if not for me you wouldn't be here.'

Maggie shook his hand off impatiently, annoyed but not totally surprised by his words; she had been half-expecting something like this. 'I'm here to do a job. I wasn't aware it involved any obligation to you. I appreciate your invitation, Roland, but I already have plans this evening.'

Roland's eyes narrowed. 'I see. My mistake. I shan't make it again. Excuse me.' He turned on his heels and briskly strode away.

Damn! Maggie watched his retreating back with dismay. Not the best of starts to the weekend. Oh well, it couldn't be helped. She had already known that Roland's interest in her went beyond her interest in him. The sooner he realised that he was wasting his time the better. Still, she might as well make the most of this opportunity. It seemed unlikely now that Roland would ask her to act as hostess for the squad again.

Later that night, Gemma stood in front of the mirror and turned her head from side to side as she admired the new silver-blonde highlights in her shoulder-length brown hair. Although she had been a bit taken aback by the cost, she was delighted with the results. Under the flashing lights of a nightclub they would look really wicked.

She twirled round slowly, critically examining her short lycra skirt and tight-fitting red top. Her breasts

160

were firm and round under the thin crop top and her nipples stood out clearly. She pushed a diamond stud into her nose and added two more sets of earrings in each of her multi-pierced ears, then pulled on some stay-ups, buckled her feet into her favourite ankle boots and picked up her suede jacket. Pausing only to apply another quick burst of body spray, she dashed out of her room and hurried down to the reception area. If Roland thought she was going to hang around here all night, he had another think coming. The squad might be in training, but she certainly wasn't.

The club she was heading for apparently had a bit of a reputation as a gay haven but, according to the cute young hotel waiter who had told her about it, it also had the best music and cheapest drinks. She hurried out of the hotel and hailed a passing cab.

After she bought herself a drink at the bar, Gemma headed upstairs to where dozens of hot, sweaty punters – men and women – were already dancing energetically under the strobe lights. She found herself a tiny table against the wall and sat down to watch the dancers; most of them were male, and some were obviously trying hard to attract attention to themselves. The hotel waiter had obviously been correct. She would be hard-pressed to find any talent here. By the look of it, most of the men only had other men on their minds.

Gemma's eyes brightened as she spotted a group of young women dancing together in a ragged line. Despite her protests about being partnered with Anna, she had nothing against gay sex, under the right circumstances. With her blood already boiling from the combination of the loud music and the strong alcohol, Gemma jumped up and made her way over to join the women. Soon, she was lost in the excitement and stimulation of gyrating her body to the compelling beat, while the overhead lights flashed hypnotically across their colourful outfits.

Gradually, a kind of sensual feeling of peace and

wellbeing flowed through her whole body, making her skin tingle as if it was electrified. There was almost nothing Gemma enjoyed more than a good night out. She smiled at the pretty blond dancing next to her and felt a small shiver of lust between her thighs as the blonde parted her lips and ran her tongue invitingly over her full, red lips. Almost nothing except a suitable partner to end the night with.

Gemma had been dancing for about ten minutes when her attention was captured by the arrival of two men who, even in the low rippling lights, quite obviously had bodies to die for. Given where they were, Gemma assumed that the two of them were probably together and could not help reflecting on what a waste that was.

The two men leaned up against one wall to sip their drinks, and Gemma grinned as she moved closer and saw who they were. She had assumed that Stephen and Roland would have the squad all safely tucked up in bed by this time, as they usually did. How in the world had these two managed to slip away?

'Pary! Bri! I see you managed to escape? I ought to report you both you know.' She had secretly lusted after Pary for ages but, until now, had never found the opportunity to do more than massage his aching body after a game. She kept her hips swaying seductively in time with the beat as she moved over to stand just in front of them.

'So, what are you doing here?' she questioned, wondering if they knew what kind of a reputation this place had. Maybe they were gay? Several of their fellow players were quite open about it. She hoped they weren't.

Pary shrugged. 'It was the first place we came across that looked worth trying. This town is really dead, you know.'

'Not as dead as that crummy hotel,' Bri added. 'We were bored stiff with sitting around listening to Stephen rabbiting on about tactics. The way he's acting, anyone would think we've never played an away match before.'

'We sort of sneaked out when he and Roland got into an argument about something,' Pary confessed. 'They probably think we're safely asleep by now and dreaming about winning the game. You won't tell on us, will you?'

'Depends,' Gemma giggled. 'I doubt if they would approve of me being here either, so I guess we'll just have to trust each other.'

'It's a good job you are here,' Pary told her. 'The local talent doesn't seem much to get excited about. Most of the women look a bit suss, if you get my drift.'

Gemma giggled again. 'Hardly surprising. You do realise that this is considered to be *the* spot for gays around here, don't you?'

'I thought the bartender was giving us a funny smile,' Pary joked. He stared at her thoughtfully. 'So, what brings you here?' he questioned. 'Don't ruin my evening and tell me I'm wasting my time.'

Gemma grinned. 'I heard it was a great place to dance and that the drinks are cheap,' she explained quickly. 'Besides, you never know who you might come across.'

'Maybe we'd better move on somewhere else,' Bri suggested somewhat nervously.

'I've only just got here,' Gemma protested. 'Don't you want to dance?' She began to sway her hips seductively.

'I don't suppose Maggie's with you, is she?' Pary questioned hopefully.

Gemma felt a surge of jealousy. What was his interest in Maggie? She must be heaps older than him. It had never even occurred to her to ask Maggie if she wanted to come. 'You're kidding!' she replied scornfully. 'Miss Goody-goody didn't think Roland would like it if we went out without asking him,' she lied. 'She's probably already asleep.' She was tempted to add that Maggie probably needed the rest, but she bit her tongue. She didn't want to sound bitchy.

Pary looked disappointed, then shrugged. 'Why don't

163

you go down and get us another round of drinks,' he suggested to Bri. 'What are you drinking, Gemma?'

'Oh, I'll have a Campari and soda, please.'

'Off you go, Bri. I'll have another Scotch.' He drained his glass and handed it over. Bri took it grudgingly and headed off towards the stairs. Gemma suspected that it was a deliberate ploy to get rid of him. She was still a bit miffed about Pary's interest in Maggie, but was willing to forgive him.

'You do realise we'll probably never see Bri again, don't you?' she chuckled as she reached up to put her arms around Pary's neck. 'Wandering around on his own like that, he's bound to attract attention.'

'I was sort of thinking that the bartender might keep him busy for a while,' Pary admitted as he put his arms around her waist and pulled her tightly against his body.

'If he gets that far,' Gemma replied. She had seen several men watching with more than a passing interest as Bri walked across the dance floor. Poor guy.

'Forget about Bri.' Pary pulled her even tighter against him so that she could feel his cock pressed into her navel. She wriggled her hips, deliberately rubbing herself against him until she felt his trousers growing tighter. It always turned her on to feel a cock stiffening against her body.

'One–nil to me,' Pary muttered softly.

'You what?'

'Nothing.' Pary lowered his head and put his lips over hers. She felt his tongue probing her mouth and she quickly swallowed her gum and opened her lips. His tongue slid in, hot and slippery, and wrapped itself around hers like a hungry snake. His mouth tasted of Scotch and his chin was prickly with the day's growth. His skin smelt warm and musky.

The music changed to something much faster and Gemma reluctantly released her arms from his neck and stepped back. Her lips were tingling from his kiss and

164

her tongue felt too big for her mouth. Her panties were dripping and her whole body was covered in a fine sheen of perspiration.

Pary began to dance alone in front of her. His every move was filled with the grace and beauty of an athlete; his limbs seemed to flow like liquid and his muscles rippled under his clothes as if they had a life of their own. She couldn't take her eyes off him.

Neither could anyone else. She gradually became aware that most of the people nearby had stopped dancing to watch him. She could see the admiration and lust burning in several pairs of eyes, male and female alike. She grabbed his arm and pulled him back into her embrace.

'That's probably not such a good idea,' she whispered in his left ear.

'Sorry?' He stared down at her with a puzzled look on his face.

'Your dancing. If you value your backside, you had better stop wiggling it like that,' she sniggered. 'Maybe Bri was right. Maybe we should go somewhere else before it's too late.'

'I was just getting going,' Pary protested.

'So are they.' She nodded towards a group of men nearby who were all openly fingering their crotches as they watched him. 'Come on, let's go and rescue Bri and get the hell out of here.'

As she led Pary by the hand across the dance floor, Gemma could feel every eye following them: willing him to stay, willing her to disappear. She held on to him possessively and ignored the stares.

At first, she could see no sign of Bri at the bar. They were probably already too late. Someone would have snapped him up by now, with or without his consent. Well, he was a big boy – no doubt about that – he would just have to take care of himself. She tugged Pary towards

165

the door, wondering where they could go to be alone. Somewhere close. She couldn't wait much longer.

They found Bri just inside the main doorway, talking with a couple of attractive women who were holding on to each other possessively. Boy, was he going to be in for a shock if he thought he was getting anywhere with them! Gemma grinned to herself.

Bri was in full flow, explaining something to them that had both women in fits of giggles. He said something else and they doubled over, clutching each other for support as their tears of mirth mingled with their mascara. Gemma could see that Bri appeared to be quite drunk. His babyface was flushed and his dark eyes were hooded and reddened. She hoped it was only drink. Trying anything else on sale in a place like this would be sheer madness. Either way, Stephen would kill him if he found out. He'd probably kill her too, for not taking better care of him.

Pary stepped forward and grasped Bri firmly by the elbow. 'Time to go,' he announced firmly as he steered his fellow Trojan away from the two near-hysterical women.

'What were those two dykes cracking up about?' Gemma asked him as they headed out the door.

'Dykes?' Bri's cheeks grew even pinker. 'You're kidding? I thought I was well-in there.' He glowered angrily as Gemma and Pary both started to snigger. 'Well? How was I to know?'

Pary shook his head. 'Only you . . .' he muttered. 'Come on, let's go.' He took Gemma's hand.

As they walked through the deserted town centre, Gemma flicked her eyes from one to the other trying to decide which of her two dark-haired escorts she fancied most. Truth was, she wanted them both. Where could they go? She didn't know Nottingham at all. Shame she was sharing with Maggie, or they could have tried to sneak back into the hotel without being seen. Did Pary and Bri have a room together, or were they sharing with any of the others?

Pary's hand slipped off her arm and slid down round her waist. She felt his fingers caressing the top of her buttocks. She wondered if he would try to send Bri packing again so he could have her to himself. Well, that was OK with her, but it still didn't solve the problem of where they could go.

Just then, as they drew level with the entrance to a dark alleyway between two shops, Pary stopped. He pulled her round so that she was facing him and put his lips over hers again. His tongue quickly resumed its urgent exploration of her mouth and she melted against him.

She felt her skirt being lifted from behind and then Bri's hand moved in to fondle her buttocks. Moving like one giant and ungainly six-legged monster, the two men guided her backwards into the concealing darkness. Her foot stepped on an empty beer can and it loudly rolled away into the hidden shadows.

Pary moved his hand round and pulled her top up over her breasts. His fingers started to squeeze her left nipple while his other hand pulled up the front of her skirt. Behind her, Bri gradually lowered her knickers, and she felt him thrust his fingers between her thighs.

'This is what you wanted, isn't it, Gemma?' Pary had moved his mouth away from hers and placed it over her right ear. His words sent a ripple of lust right through her. 'You've wanted us ever since you got the job as physio for the team, haven't you? Wanted to feel our cocks pushed up in you?'

'Yes. Oh yes.' She squirmed at his words. Dirty talk always did it for her. Her nipples formed into hard pebbles between his fingers.

Whimpering in her excitement, Gemma raised her own trembling hands and unzipped Pary's fly. She wanted to touch his cock. Her groping fingers slid inside the opening and quickly released his penis from the tiny pouch he was wearing. It was hard and thick, thicker than she would have believed possible. She traced one fingertip over his glans, marvelling at its well-formed ridge, and then on down the solid stem with its raised cords of engorged veins. His pubic hair was thick and fluffy, so unlike her own wiry curls. She ran her fingers gently through it and reached down further to caress the swell of his heavy balls.

Pary was nibbling her earlobe, sending sweet shivers right through her body. As she caressed him he shifted restlessly from one foot to the other and she felt his hot breath sighing inside her ear. Behind her, Bri opened his zip and she could feel him begin to pump his cock back and forth between her legs while his inquisitive fingers explored all her secret places.

Back in the main shopping precinct, footsteps approached and stopped. A beam of light shone blindingly down the alleyway and a deep, male voice called out: 'Anyone there?'

The six-legged beast froze, cowering motionless in the scant safety of a narrow doorway. Gemma could feel Bri's cock jerking impatiently between her thighs and Pary's stubby manhood seemed to twitch between her fingers.

The torch explored the far wall and then hovered curiously over a bulging black bin bag in the centre of the alleyway. A lump formed in Gemma's throat and her heart was pumping so rapidly that she was certain the policeman would hear it thudding. Bri's cock twitched again, so fiercely that she almost cried out. She felt him start to move back and forth again, his lust clearly overcoming his fear of discovery. Terrified that the policeman would hear his movements, Gemma clamped her thighs, trapping him. She almost squealed as Pary pushed his warm tongue into her ear.

The torch beam went out, leaving them blind in the

darkness. The heavy footsteps faded and Pary began to chuckle.

'Jesus!' Gemma could feel her whole body shaking with the after-effects of her fright. She could clearly imagine the headlines in the newspaper:

YOUNG PHYSIO CAUGHT IN PUBLIC PLACE WITH
RAMPANT HOCKEY PLAYERS
ICE HOCKEY HEROES SCORE HOME GOAL IN ALLEYWAY!

If Roland could see them now she'd be out of a job like a shot.

Pary started to tweak her nipples again and the tremors of pleasure soon overcame her panic. Both men seemed to be as hard as ever. Didn't anything put them off their stroke? Obviously not. She gasped aloud as Bri increased his urgent thrusting and Pary took his own cock and started to rub it round her sensitive clit.

She felt another urgent thrust from behind, so hard and deep that Bri's long, snakelike penis was rammed right through between her legs. Immediately, she lowered her hands and touched the tip protruding in front of her. An erotic thrill enveloped her. It was as if she had suddenly grown a penis of her own, poking out, swollen and ready. She squeezed it between her fingers, smoothing his dribbles of lubrication all over the soft round tip. Pary continued to caress her clit with his own cock and she felt the tingles of her arousal deep inside her. Her pussy spasmed as an unexpected orgasm overcame her and she felt her juices dribble down her legs.

Bri groaned desperately as her fingers slid frantically up and down his tip and Gemma felt the first spurt of his come shoot out between her fingers. She pumped harder as burst after burst poured from him and the stem of his cock writhed and jerked between her hot, wet thighs.

'Hey, watch where you're pointing that thing, will

you?' Pary stepped back to avoid the sudden shower of semen spurting up into the air in front of her. He laughed softly as he smoothed a condom down his rigid shaft. 'Now that you've shot your bolt, why don't you get out the way and watch a real artist in action?' he muttered.

Before Gemma knew what was happening, Pary stepped forward and swung her up into his arms. As she locked her fingers around his neck, he moved his hands down under her and lifted her legs. Following his lead, she wound them tightly round his waist and groaned as she felt his left hand pushed between them, guiding his huge cock into her. She was so wet that it slipped in easily, despite its unaccustomed circumference.

'Oh Christ,' she moaned with delight as he sank up into her, filling her completely. Despite having so recently climaxed, she could already feel another orgasm building as his cock pummelled her and his fingers continued to tease and caress her clit.

'Oh yeah, baby,' Pary grunted urgently, as she began raising and lowering her buttocks, sliding herself up and down his hard pole. 'Feel good?' he mumbled in her right ear. The words enflamed her further.

'Feels great,' she whispered. 'Just great.' Another pang of lust engulfed her. 'Harder,' she begged. 'Harder.' She felt him respond to her voice, thrusting his cock in and out like a piston.

Gemma turned her head and glanced down at Bri. He was standing so close to them that, even in the almost non-existent light of the alleyway, she could see the gleaming white flesh of his naked lower body. His eyes were fixed on her buttocks and she saw that his long, thin cock was rapidly swelling once more.

Bri looked up at her and grinned. Deliberately, he reached down and grasped his cock between his fingers. Without taking his eyes off hers, he began to knead and caress his tip and stem. His cock grew even longer and Gemma was reminded of how she had felt with it poking

170

out between her own thighs. She licked her lips, then gasped again as Pary increased the pace and depth of his own thrusting.

'Almost there baby,' Pary breathed. 'Almost there. You ready for it?'

'Ready for it!' What with the way he was ramming himself into her and the sight of Bri wanking away, Gemma was almost fit to bust. She bit her bottom lip to stifle the deep moan that was welling up inside her as her vagina went into spasm again. She sensed the first burst of his own release, hot and hard inside her, at the same time as she felt another shower of Bri's spunk splashing across her buttocks and thigh. Pary gave a final long thrust and she felt his cock twitch violently as he let go.

Finally, it was over and Pary lifted her gently off him and lowered her carefully to the ground. No one said a word as they wiped themselves off as best they could and tried to readjust their dishevelled clothing.

'All we have to do now,' Pary muttered as the three of them re-emerged from the alleyway into the deserted town centre, 'is to figure out how to get back into the hotel without getting sprung.'

Roland paced up and down furiously, his face contorted in anger. Stephen Jackson sat passively, as if mentally steeling himself for the outburst to come. Roland finally turned and glowered at the coach, his face black as thunder.

'What the hell went wrong, Stephen? 5–2, for Christ's sake! This match should have been a doddle. My fucking grandmother could have run rings around them. Another one like this and our chances for the Championship will be over.'

Stephen shook his head. 'I realise that. I don't understand it. The lads were in such good form during training last week. I don't know if it was nerves, or . . .'

'Or what?' Roland snapped.

Stephen shrugged. 'Oh, I don't know. Just a feeling that one or two of the lads were a bit sluggish out there today. Maybe they were too keyed-up to sleep properly last night or something? I mean, there's a lot riding on them at the moment. We've never been this close to getting into the finals. I think they're just a bit stressed-out. Don't worry. I'll sort it.'

'You'd damn well better. That's what you're paid for, after all. There's no point in having the best players going if they can't take the pressure of being at the top. You should have seen this coming and sorted it before the match.'

Stephen's eyes narrowed dangerously. 'If you want my opinion, you ought to keep a tighter rein on them. Maybe they'd play a damn sight better if there was a lot less fucking around going on. I know for a fact that several of the lads were out boozing and whoring last night when they should have been resting.'

'You're their coach,' Roland snapped.

'And you're their manager. Why don't you get off my back and start acting like one?' Stephen stood up and stamped furiously out of the room.

Roland stood, fuming. How dare Stephen talk to him like that? If he didn't need him so much right now he'd kick his arse right out of the squad. As for the players! He'd read them the riot act. They were under contract and they'd bloody well better remember it or else.

Maggie! She had turned him down the previous evening so that she could have dinner with some of the team. She and Troy were obviously far too interested in each other. His jealousy burned at the idea. The little slut. Troy might as well have been playing with his eyes closed out there today. He'd probably screwed the bitch silly all last night.

Maybe he would have a little chat with Justin about Maggie. He remembered that Justin and she had something going between them too. Shit! The bloody woman was nothing but trouble. Using him to get free tickets to the matches, manipulating the rink manager for her own benefit and now interfering with the players' training and costing them vital points. She would have to go. Somehow, he'd have to find a way of making Justin see what a liability she was. An idea began to take shape in his mind and, as it grew, he started to feel much better.

'Yeah. You'll rue the day you turned me down, you little whore,' he muttered softly.

Chapter Eight

'*I*'ve never known you to be so evasive. It's like getting blood out of stone.' Maggie glared impatiently at Jan. 'Don't forget it was because of me that he came to you in the first place.' It was the first time Maggie had seen Jan since they had got back from Bristol and she was still burning with curiosity to find out about Tor's house hunting.

Jan smiled. 'I know. I know. How many times do you want me to say thanks?' She sipped her drink. 'How's your coffee? I made it hot and black, just the way you like it.'

'Don't keep changing the subject,' Maggie complained, doing her best to ignore Jan's pointed comment. Did Jan fancy Troy as well, or was she just being deliberately provocative? Maggie wasn't in the mood for playing games. She was too worried about what Justin had said to her earlier.

Jan shrugged. 'I don't know what else you expect me to say. You're the one with all the hot news. You haven't said anything about Nottingham yet.'

Maggie shrugged. She wasn't sure that she was ready to talk about herself and Troy. Besides, she was determined to find out what had happened between Jan and Tor, and she was more than a little anxious to know if Tor had said anything about her to Jan. If anything serious was going on between them, she certainly didn't want her friend to find out how wantonly she had behaved with him in Bristol that night. It might have been a fantasy come true but fantasies were private!

'Was it just Tor you showed round, or did any of the others come with him?' Maggie questioned. In her mind, she could almost picture Jan pleasuring all of them, including Troy. Her jealousy burned.

'It was only Tor,' Jan replied with a dreamy look in her eyes.

So, she hadn't been with Troy. Maggie felt much better. Mind you, she was still consumed with curiosity as to exactly what had gone on between the two of them. Tor hadn't really mentioned Jan at all at the weekend, although he had said that his new house was just what he'd been looking for. Was Jan planning to see him again? If so, would she admit to it?

'Sod it.' Maggie swore as a drop of coffee splashed down the front of her dress. She brushed at the stain angrily. 'I've only just had this dress cleaned.'

Jan peered at her curiously. 'What's got you so ratty today, anyway? You've had a face like a thundercloud ever since you arrived. Have I done something?'

Maggie shook her head. 'Sorry. It's not you. It's work. Some money's gone missing from the ticket office till and Justin is in a real rage about it.'

'So? What's it got to do with you? It's his problem.' Jan took another sip of her coffee. 'Do you fancy a biscuit? I think I've got some somewhere, if Marcus hasn't scoffed them all.'

Maggie shook her head again. 'No thanks.' She frowned. 'The thing is, he was acting really weird when he told me about it. It was almost as if he suspected that I might have taken it.'

175

'Surely not? Justin knows you better than that. You must have imagined it.'

'Yes, I suppose so. It's just that I can't see who could or would have. I mean, a thief,' Maggie reiterated. 'It just doesn't bear thinking about, does it?' She pictured each of her colleagues in turn. There were only two or three who officially had access to his office but then nobody ever bothered to lock up, so it could have been anyone. 'It's horrible to think that one of your workmates can't be trusted.' Maggie tried to force a smile. 'Maybe I will have that biscuit, after all.'

Jan stood up and opened a cupboard to reach for the biscuit tin. 'How about another coffee?' she suggested. 'Then I want to hear all the lurid details about your weekend in Nottingham.'

Justin shrugged. 'I just don't know what else to say, Maggie. I'm sorry.'

It was two days after her conversation with Jan when a message had been delivered by one of the office juniors to tell Maggie that Justin wanted to see her in his office immediately. Annoyed at being summoned in such an offhand manner, Maggie had hurried to obey, wondering what was so urgent that it couldn't wait until her shift was over. He had not kept her wondering for long. As she had listened to what he had to say, she had felt herself growing cold all over. It was like some ghastly nightmare.

'You can't seriously believe that I would do something like that, Justin. You know I wouldn't.' Maggie protested feebly when he finally fell silent.

'If it was the first time but, well, there was the money from the till as well.' Justin replied awkwardly.

'I've already told you that I didn't have anything to do with that,' Maggie retorted angrily. 'It could have been anyone. Shit. This is ridiculous. Why on earth would I want to steal some petty cash for Christ's sake?'

'Hardly anyone else knew that the money was in my office,' Justin reminded her. 'Apart from myself, only you and Stephen. And he's not been around for several days.'

'If Stephen knew, then Roland probably knew as well, didn't he?' Maggie persisted.

'Of course. But it was his money! You're not suggesting that Roland would sneak into my office and steal his own money, are you?' Justin demanded incredulously.

'Why not? It's no more ridiculous than suggesting that I sneaked in and took it.' Maggie glared at him. 'So, what are you going to do now? Have me arrested?'

Justin looked pained. 'No, of course not. Look, the thing is, Roland agrees with me that we don't want any bad publicity. If we call the police in, it will be all over the local papers and might reflect badly on the squad. With the Championship going so well, we don't want that.'

'No, of course not,' Maggie interrupted him sarcastically. 'What the hell has all this got to do with Roland anyway?'

Justin frowned. 'Please don't make this any more difficult than it already is, Maggie.' He drummed his fingers nervously on the desk. 'Look. The staff have to see that I'm not prepared to tolerate this sort of thing. I'm sorry, but I'm going to have to let you go.'

Maggie gasped. 'You can't. If you sack me for alleged thieving, without any proof, I'll have you up for unfair dismissal,' she threatened. 'See what that does for Roland's precious publicity image!'

'I'm not letting you go for thieving,' Justin told her coldly. 'Your contract is up in a couple of months and I've decided not to renew it. Call it downsizing or staff rationalisation, if you like. Our recent internal review has revealed that we just don't need so many part-time staff.'

'You bastard!' Maggie spluttered, finally realising just how well she had been stitched up. Had Roland known that her contract was due for renewal too, or was that just a lucky coincidence? She felt a blaze of hatred. Just because she had turned him down! The slimy, stinking bastard had had her sacked because she wouldn't go to bed with him. Justin obviously didn't realise. Maggie tried to explain what had happened.

Justin listened in silence then looked wary. 'Did anyone see or hear any of this?' he asked her.

'No.'

'I'm sorry Maggie. You'd never prove a thing,' he told her.

'You know I didn't steal anything, Justin. You know I didn't!' Maggie could feel the tears welling up at the corners of her eyes.

'You can have your two months' pay, of course.' Justin ignored her appeal. 'I'll even throw in an extra month's bonus. No need for you to work out your contract.'

'I have no intention of working it out,' Maggie yelled. 'I wouldn't stay here another minute – whether you paid me or not.' She stood up and started to turn towards the door.

He gave her a feeble smile. 'I hope we can still be friends, Maggie?'

She tossed her head and stamped haughtily out of the room before he caught a glimpse of the tears that began openly trickling down her cheeks. She was damned if she would give him the satisfaction.

As soon as Sara had served Roland his breakfast and cleared up in the kitchen, she headed into town to meet her friends for coffee. She had a lot to tell them. They didn't know about her new job yet. Maggie was probably wondering why she hadn't been at the rink lately.

Her mind was in a whirl. Roland had invited some of the team around again that night to discuss their next match, and Sara was wracking her brain trying to think of something really special to cook for them. She was also wondering if Ean was to be one of the guests and, if so, whether he would slip away to see her again. She knew she ought to feel a bit guilty about her behaviour with Ean. After all, it wasn't exactly the way Ms Jamison would expect her to conduct herself. She smiled. Ms J. had said Roland wanted someone discreet. No one had said anything about her not having any fun.

Roland had brushed himself up against her in the kitchen again that morning. It had happened too often now to be put down to coincidence. She would have to draw the line there, she decided. After all, he was her employer, wasn't he? Besides, without being unkind, Roland wasn't exactly irresistible.

Not like Ean. Had they really thrown dice for her company? It was an incredibly exciting thought. She wondered if they would do it again. Sara pictured herself naked and helpless in front of them all while they competed for the pleasures of her body. Perhaps she should visit the beautician later and have a complete facial. She could afford the odd luxury now.

She was so caught up in her daydreams that she almost walked straight past the table where Maggie and Jan were seated. An impatient shout brought her back to her senses.

'Sara! Over here.'

'Whoops, sorry.' Sara hurried back to their table and plonked herself down beside Maggie. 'Sorry, I'm a bit late. Have you already ordered?'

'You looked as if you were in another world,' Jan teased her. 'I sense a man. Just what have you been up to?'

Sara felt the sudden rush of colour to her cheeks. What would Maggie and Jan say if she told them about Ean? No, she couldn't. Well, not in so many words, anyway. She could tell them about her job though and maybe drop a few hints. They could draw their own conclusions.

'You'll never believe this,' she began, 'but I've been reassigned by the agency. That's why I wasn't at the ice rink this week.' She drew a deep breath and tried to make her voice sound matter-of-fact. 'I've got a new job as Roland Donaldson's housekeeper. In fact, I'm cooking dinner for him and several of the Trojans tonight.'

'You poor bitch. I'd watch my back if I were you.' Maggie's voice was dripping with sarcasm and Sara stared at her in surprise, wondering what she was so mad about. It wasn't like her at all.

'Don't mind Maggie,' Jan told her. 'She's not feeling very happy at the moment. So, tell all. Are you staying with Roland? I mean, actually living in?'

Sara nodded. 'He insisted,' she told them. 'He said it was silly for me to travel back and forth every day when he had plenty of room. He's been very nice.'

Maggie raised an eyebrow. 'Nice?' she questioned icily. 'Nice is not the word I'd use to describe that stinking rat. Has he tried it on yet?'

Sara frowned again at the venom in Maggie's voice. Something was obviously very wrong. She thought about Roland's advances and felt a tingle of apprehension.

'I just meant that he's been very considerate and that he's paying me a more than generous salary,' Sara replied cautiously.

Maggie snorted rudely and took a sip of her coffee. Jan shrugged her shoulders apologetically. 'As you might have gathered, Maggie doesn't like Roland very much,' she said.

'Like! I could tell you what I'd like to do to him,' Maggie interjected. Her face was twisted with hatred.

'What's going on?' Sara demanded as she stared in confusion from one to the other.

'Maggie's been given the push. Some money went missing from the rink and, well, Justin suspects she might have been responsible,' Jan explained bluntly.

'What? But that's ridiculous! Justin would never ... I mean, why Maggie?' Sara was lost for words.

'Because your precious new boss wanted Justin to

think it was me, that's why,' Maggie retorted loudly. 'He probably took the money himself to make me look guilty. Just because I wouldn't fuck him,' she yelled.

The café suddenly fell silent and several heads turned to stare in curiousity.

'Shush! You don't know that, Maggie,' Jan replied softly. 'You've no proof.'

'Nor has Justin. That didn't stop him, did it? I know it was Roland. It had to be him. It's his way of getting back at me.' She snatched her bag and fled sobbing towards the loo.

Sara stared at Jan. 'Could you please tell me exactly what's been going on?' she demanded. She really didn't want to believe what Maggie had seemed to be implying.

Later that day, Maggie stood outside Tor's rented house and asked herself what on earth she was doing there. It was Troy she really wanted to see, but somehow they had never got around to swapping addresses. Was he in there with Tor now? They were often together. He had even told her that he was thinking of moving in with Tor and sharing the rent. What was she going to say to them? She hadn't seen them since Nottingham and she had no idea what they had heard or thought about what had happened at the rink. Surely they wouldn't believe that she was a petty thief, would they? But then again, why shouldn't they? Justin obviously did, and he knew her better than any of the Trojans.

Bugger it. Maggie put her hands on the gate and shook her arms angrily. It was all so humiliating and so bloody unfair. The gate began to swing open and Maggie hesitated. Her thoughts were so confused. She was angry and hurt and she wanted revenge but, most of all, she just wanted to be comforted. She desperately wanted, needed, to be believed.

Maggie slipped inside and pushed the gate shut behind her. As she walked down the driveway, she examined the house enviously. If only she could get a few of the right breaks maybe she could live in a place like this, instead of shacking up in a poxy flat barely big enough to swing a cat. Fat chance of that now. The way things were going, she would be lucky if she could even afford her flat for much longer. She had to find another job.

Funny, she had never before thought that her job at the rink was very important to her. She had often told Jan that one job was the same as another. Now, she was beginning to realise how much it had meant to her. She was good at it too. If she didn't organise everything for Justin the place would fall apart; now she hoped it would. Serve him right.

As she approached the house, Maggie could hear voices coming from the front room. She was certain that one of them was Troy. Deliberately avoiding the front door, Maggie followed the narrow pathway round to the back door and tried the handle. The door swung open on to a dark, narrow passageway. She called out but received no response. What were they up to? She waited to allow her eyes to adjust to the gloom, then took a few steps past the open kitchen door. An ear-splitting wail just behind her almost scared her witless. She froze as rapid footsteps approached the door in front of her.

'I bet it's Roland trying to sneak up on us.'

'Maybe it really is a burglar? Do you want me to go first?'

The male voices were coming closer by the second. It was too late to do anything except brazen it out. If only the goddamned alarm would shut up so that she could think. Maggie stood up straight, pulled her stomach in and thrust her breasts out.

'I don't suppose you know how to shut that bloody thing up?' she yelled as the door swung open and Tor and Troy appeared.

'Maggie? What are you doing here?' Tor pushed past her and reached up to punch a few numbers into the

alarm console. In the almost overpowering silence following the racket of the alarm Maggie could hear her heart
thumping.

'I'd better give the local cops a bell too,' Tor muttered.
'We don't want them bursting in on us as well.'

'Are you sure? I mean, you don't think she's dangerous
or anything, do you?' Troy was staring at her in open
amusement and Maggie could feel the blood flooding to
her cheeks.

'Oh, I think we can handle her, between us,' Tor
responded softly. Maggie turned her head to gaze up
into his sparkling grey eyes.

'Nice to see you,' Tor told her. 'Next time though, do
me a favour and just knock on the front door like
everyone else.'

'Sorry. I wanted to surprise you.' Maggie suddenly felt
stupid. What in the world had possessed her to sneak in
like that? Just like a thief. Her bottom lip started to
tremble. Troy immediately stepped forward and took her
hand in his. She could feel that she was trembling but
was powerless to stop herself.

'What's wrong Maggie?' he questioned. 'Shouldn't you
be at work this morning?'

Maggie flushed even deeper red. So, they hadn't heard.
'I don't work at the rink anymore,' she responded softly.

Troy stared at her a moment then turned to Tor and
nodded his head towards the door. Tor nodded in reply.
'I'll just go call the police,' he muttered, as he moved
through the door and closed it behind him.

Troy gave Maggie's hand a gentle squeeze. 'How come
you've deserted us? The rink will never run properly
without you there.'

'Maybe you should ask your boss,' Maggie snapped.

'Roland? What's he got to do with it?' A look of sudden
understanding came over his face. 'What's he been up
to? Look, how about a coffee or something? Then we'll

sit down and talk this over. I'm sure we can sort things out.'

Troy took her arm and steered her into the front room where Tor was waiting for them. Troy signalled for him to pour them some drinks. Maggie was surprised and deeply touched by the look of concern on both their faces. She perched herself on the arm of the couch and waited in silence while Tor poured them each a Scotch. As soon as he handed her a glass, Maggie took a quick sip, grimacing as the fiery liquid scalded her tongue. She had never been fond of neat spirits. At least she wasn't trembling quite so much any more.

'So, what exactly has Roland got to do with you leaving the rink?' Troy asked her. 'If he's been making a nuisance of himself you just shouldn't take any notice. He tries it on with everyone.'

Maggie was tempted to lie. It was horrible having to admit that she had been sacked and that Justin thought she was a thief. What if she lied and then they heard what had really happened? Wouldn't that just make her look even more guilty?

'Someone helped themselves to some money that I was responsible for and Justin fired me,' she hastily admitted.

'Shit. That's a bit off, isn't it?' Troy commented. 'Doesn't sound like Justin at all.' Maggie shrugged.

'I don't see what it's got to do with Roland, though,' Tor persisted.

'He set me up,' Maggie said, flaring up angrily. 'I know he did. He and I had a bit of a disagreement and this is his way of getting rid of me.'

'What kind of a disagreement?' Troy demanded.

'He wanted me to screw him, if you must know,' Maggie blurted out. She took another gulp of her Scotch. 'Look, can we just leave it? It's bad enough that everyone thinks I'm a thief without keeping talking about it.'

Troy moved over and put his arm around her. He gave her a hug. 'I don't think you're a thief,' he assured her.

184

Tor shook his head. 'I had begun to suspect that Roland could be a bit sharp, but I never thought he'd do something like this.'

'I don't have any trouble with the idea of him trying it on,' Troy replied, 'but I really don't think he's clever enough to come up with anything devious. There has to be some other explanation for the money.'

'Even so,' Tor continued, 'he shouldn't get away with it. Do you want us to have a chat with him?' He cracked his knuckles.

Maggie shook her head. 'No. Just forget it.'

Tor shrugged philosophically. 'OK. It's too bad, though. We'll really miss you. Where are you working now?'

'I'm not. There don't seem to be too many options for an ex-receptionist who doesn't have a reference.'

Troy gave her another squeeze. 'I'll give you a reference. You were the best hostess we ever had!'

Maggie giggled, already feeling much better. These two men were just the tonic she needed right now. She was suddenly very glad she had come. 'Thanks, but I don't see how that's going to be much help, unless I decide to look for a job at the local escort agency!'

'Now, there's a thought,' Tor smiled. 'You'd make a fortune.' He stared at her body thoughtfully. 'Hey! I don't suppose you can dance, can you?'

'Dance? What do you mean, dance?' Maggie glanced around the room and was grateful that she could see no sign of a CD-player. For one crazy moment she had thought that he was about to ask her to waltz with him or something!

'Dance. You know. I've got a friend who runs a night-club not too far from here. A fellow Canadian. I bet he'd be only too happy to take you on as a dancer if you were interested.'

She was just about to retort angrily that she was not planning on becoming a stripper, when she noticed the expressions on their faces. Although she had no intention of taking work as a dancer, she found that she just couldn't resist the opportunity to take advantage of them just a little.

'I've never really thought about it,' she lied. 'I mean, I suppose anyone can dance, can't they?' She thought about what she had done to Justin at the Cellar and a tingle of lust ran down her spine.

'Not the sort of dancing I had in mind,' Tor murmured softly.

'Why don't we all go out somewhere this evening and you can judge for yourselves whether or not I can dance?' she suggested brightly. A night out with these two was just what she needed to boost her spirits.

'What's wrong with dancing for us here?' Tor objected.

'What, now?' Maggie looked around the room again. 'For a start, you don't seem to have any music, unless you were planning to hum?'

Tor moved across the room and opened a heavy wooden cabinet to reveal an expensive-looking MiniDisc system. He flicked a couple of switches and the room was immediately filled with booming disco music. He sat himself down on the arm of a thick leather chair and an expectant grin spread over his face.

Maggie stood up and stared at each of them in turn. The men were watching her the way a cat watches a mouse, as though at any moment they might pounce on her. The loud music was insistent and compelling and she found herself beginning to sway her slender hips from side to side, thrusting her crotch forward suggestively as she moved. She heard Troy draw a sharp breath and was immediately overwhelmed by a desire to exert her power over them.

Gyrating faster, Maggie shuffled in front of Tor so that her crotch was almost touching him. She raised her arm and pushed firmly on his shoulder. Overbalanced, Tor slipped down into the leather chair and Maggie positioned herself in front of him, with her legs spread wide apart.

Bending forward from the waist, she thrust her breasts in front of his face and started to caress them through the thin material of her top. Her flattened palms made wide, circular movements across her chest and she felt her nipples harden in response. When she saw his eyes widen she knew that he had noticed, too.

Still rubbing her breasts with one hand, Maggie slid her other palm down over her mound. She could feel her clit swelling and sense the hot dampness of her own arousal. A quick glance downwards told her that she was not the only one. Tor's flies were already straining as his cock pushed hard and urgent against them. She leaned closer to him, so that her mound was hovering just inches above his groin, and smiled as she saw him involuntarily lift his buttocks off the chair, thrusting his crotch up towards hers. There was definitely more to lap dancing than she had thought!

Still smiling suggestively, Maggie wiggled back from him and swayed seductively across the room to stand in front of Troy. She put her hands behind her and ran them over her buttocks, then round her hips and up her stomach to her breasts. Troy watched her avidly, his white teeth gleaming and his black eyes burning.

'Don't you think you're a bit overdressed,' he muttered, reaching out to take hold of her waistband. His fingers began to tug clumsily at her button and Maggie shuffled out of his reach and moved back in front of Tor. As she repeated the suggestive caresses of her breasts and groin for his benefit, she experienced a rush of power that made her feel invincible. They were both already practically wetting themselves. She could see it in their eyes, their faces, and the way they were shifting their bodies awkwardly from side to side. She had them totally under her spell – yet again – and she intended to take full advantage.

Moving back into the middle of the room, Maggie started to undo the buttons on the front of her blouse. As soon as it was open, she slipped her arms out of the sleeves and let the garment drop slowly to the floor, leaving her in just her bra and skintight trousers.

Troy walked over to stand in front of her. He started to sway his hips in time with hers, his body not quite touching hers. His cock was a solid bulge behind the taut zip. Maggie put her hand on his waist and began to undo the buckle of his belt. As soon as it came loose, she tugged the leather strip out of his trousers and started to caress herself with it. As she pulled it tantalisingly back and forth between her legs, she heard his small sigh.

'Take your trousers off,' Troy whispered. 'Or let me take them off for you.' He stepped towards her again.

Maggie dropped the belt and opened her own trouser button. She kicked her feet free of her shoes and then began to peel the tight material over her buttocks and thighs. She took her time, posing carefully. Her skimpy silk panties were so damp with a mixture of sweat and lubrication that they clung to her body like a second skin, hiding nothing. She could smell the musky warmth of her own arousal wafting around her to mingle with another scent – the heady scent of fresh masculine sweat and sexual stimulation.

She stepped out of her trousers and kicked them up into the air with her left foot. They landed on Tor's knee but he didn't seem to notice. She slipped her feet back into her shoes and resumed dancing. Her fingers repeated their suggestive journey around her body, over her breasts and between her legs. The music seemed to grow louder and more insistent, throbbing and pulsing through her.

Maggie moaned softly and pushed her hand under the wet silk at the front of her crotch. Her fingertips encircled her engorged clit and she felt another rush of moisture on her already damp thighs. She pushed her hand down deeper, collecting the lubrication on her fingers, then pulled it out and raised it to her mouth. Slowly and deliberately, she inserted one finger between her pink lips, sucking on her own juices.

'Jesus Christ!' Troy had put his hand down the front of his trousers and wrapped his fingers around his rigid cock. As he moved it away from the zip, Maggie could see that he was gently squeezing himself. His face was flushed and his breathing ragged. She smiled provocatively and put her hand back down inside the front of her panties.

Her own need was like a searing burn deep inside her. She only just stopped herself from crying out as her fingertip remade contact with her hard little bud. Rubbing it rhythmically, she clamped her mouth closed to keep herself from panting and used her other hand to caress her aching nipples. She could feel the little ripples of excitement running up and down her body and raising goose bumps all over her tingling flesh. Troy stepped closer and wrapped his arms around her waist.

'Look, but don't touch,' she commanded as she twisted out of his gasp and pirouetted across the floor, closer to where Tor was still sitting in the big leather chair. Giving him a cheeky grin, she perched herself across his knees with her own legs spread wide. Fixing her eyes on his face, she reached behind her and undid the catch of her bra. She placed her other hand over the front and gradually slipped each strap in turn off her shoulders and down her arms.

Tor had had his eyes fixed on the dark, wet patch of silk between her open legs. Now, he raised his head and stared expectantly at the arm holding her bra in place. Maggie arched her back, thrust her chest forward and raised her arms above her head. The bra fluttered down on to his lap and her firm breasts bounced free, the nipples already dark and swollen.

Tor grinned appreciatively and stretched his neck out

189

towards her. She could see the tip of his pink tongue protruding between his lips: soft and wet. She could almost feel its satin caress on her hot, tingling skin. She longed to feel him suck her aching nipples into his mouth. Not yet, though. She wasn't finished teasing them yet.

Pushing her hands against his chest, Maggie leaped nimbly to her feet and twirled across the room with her naked breasts wobbling up and down in front of her. She came to a stop with her back against the door to the hallway and, her lips parted, looked around her. Slowly, she raised one leg and ran her hand teasingly down her bare thigh.

Tor was still sitting forward on the edge of his chair, while Troy was now standing in front of the settee. He still had his hand down the front of his trousers and was shifting restlessly from one foot to the other with his mouth partly open. She glanced down at his crotch and her own eyes widened at the size of the bulge. It looked as if he had stuffed a pair of socks down his front!

Troy's eyes followed her gaze and he gave her a knowing grin that was so suggestive she almost lost her balance.

'What have you stopped for, baby?' he challenged her. 'I was just getting into the beat.'

Maggie grinned. 'Not dressed like that, you weren't. Now it's you with too many clothes on.'

'We can soon fix that.' Troy pulled his hand out of his flies and started to tug his zip open.

'Not so fast. I want to enjoy this,' Maggie said.

Tor chuckled. 'You don't expect us to do the Full Monty for you, do you?'

'You got a problem with that?' Maggie retorted.

The two men exchanged glances and then Tor stood up. 'No problem at all,' he assured her.

Without taking her eyes off them, Maggie glided sensuously across the room and perched herself on the arm of a chair with her legs slightly apart and one hand absent-mindedly playing with her nipples. She put her hand over her mouth to stifle her little gasp as they stood side by side in front of her and then simultaneously spun around, lowered their trousers and raised their gyrating buttocks towards her.

Without breaking their stride, the two men whipped their shirts off and tossed them in the air. Turning in unison, they presented her with two pairs of over-tight briefs, each pair filled to bursting with a flatteringly enthusiastic hard-on. As the current track reached its final crescendo, Tor and Troy grinned and slowly lowered them. Two new dancers, one white, the other almost purple-black, took up the beat, swaying up and down in time with the men's gyrating hips.

It should have been funny. Maggie could feel a giggle building up inside her but, for some reason, her mouth was too dry to make a sound. She felt another tingle of lust between her legs and immediately crossed them, squeezing her tormented sex bud tightly between her thighs.

Without breaking his rhythm, Troy sidled closer and pushed his erection up towards her breasts. Without even thinking about it, Maggie leaned forward and sucked him up into her mouth. She slipped her left hand between his legs and cupped his massive balls in her palm. Slowly, teasingly, she slid him deeper and deeper into her mouth, using her tongue to caress the pronounced ridge of his shiny-smooth glans.

For the first time since they had begun to dance, she sensed Troy falter and lose his synchronisation with the rhythm of the music. With a soft sigh of pleasure, he tightened his buttocks and thrust himself into her, rocking gently back and forth on his heels and savouring the smooth wetness of her mouth and lips.

Out the corner of her eye, Maggie saw Tor edging in closer to her with his eyes riveted on what she was doing to Troy. She reached out and took hold of his cock. As she continued to run her tongue up and down Troy, she started to pump Tor with her eager fingers.

Troy crouched lower on his heels and stretched his arm out towards her until his fingers made contact with the crotch of her sopping wet panties. Unerringly, he homed in on her clit and started masturbating her.

'So, how did you like our dancing?' Tor murmured as he pushed his gigantic penis even harder into her willing fingers.

Even if she had not had her mouth full, Maggie would have been hard-pressed to think of a suitable reply. Her brain seemed to have abandoned her head and settled between her legs. She could think of nothing but the sensation of Troy's knowing fingers tormenting her clit. Her climax was already inevitable. She could feel the little tremors of pleasure running down her legs like electric shocks. The muscles inside her were contracting violently, creating further spasms of delight that seemed to travel all the way up to her nipples.

'Oh yes,' she breathed softly, as a surge of pure ecstasy swiftly engulfed her. She felt another rush of moisture pouring from her to coat Troy's fingers, but was too exhilarated by her climax to feel more than the tiniest twinge of embarrassment for her loss of control.

'Don't stop now,' Troy whispered.

With a start, Maggie realised that her fingers and tongue had both stopped moving. She had been so engrossed in her own gratification she had all but forgotten about them!

Troy pulled himself out of her slack lips and patted her on the top of the head. 'Maybe we should amuse ourselves for a bit and give Maggie time to recover.' His words made it quite clear that he was in no doubt about what they had done to her. Well, it was too late now to feel bashful!

She watched without comment as he took his still rigid

penis in his hand and started to fondle himself. If men only knew how exciting it was for a woman to watch them jerking off. She smiled to herself. Perhaps it was a good job they didn't?

Tor pulled himself back out of her half-hearted grip and begun to wank himself slowly and deliberately. Maggie stared silently from one to the other; she was mesmerised by the sight of them and not surprised to feel the first stirrings of renewed lust between her still-trembling thighs.

'Do you like to watch us wank, baby?' Troy questioned as he moved closer to her and began to fondle her nipples. 'You do, don't you? I can see it in your face.' He moved his hand up and down his shaft even faster. 'Maybe you'd like to watch us wanking each other?'

Her eyes widened as he reached out and grabbed Tor's cock, pushing Tor's own fingers away and then jerking him up and down at the same time as he continued to pump himself.

'That turn you on, eh, babe?'

Maggie nodded silently. She had never seen two men touching each other like that before. She was amazed at how stimulating it was. Her eyes grew even bigger as Tor slipped his hand underneath Troy's buttocks and started to fondle his huge black balls. He pushed his finger round until it was between Troy's solid buttocks and began rhythmically pushing his fingertip into Troy's arse crack. Maggie's eyes bulged.

'You like that, too?' Tor grinned. 'Want to watch me stick it in him? Or, maybe you want me to stick it in you again?' He pulled away from Troy and reached to grab her.

Maggie rose, unresisting, to her feet and allowed him to twist her round and push her stomach down over the arm of the chair. By twisting her head slightly, she could still see Troy pumping himself. Both men's balls seemed to have swollen to twice their previous sizes and the tips of their cocks were already wet and shiny.

She groaned again as she felt Tor forcing his cock between the backs of her thighs, using her own juices to slide back and forth against her skin. In the background, she could still hear the music thumping and pulsating urgently, feeding her passion. She felt a pricking, tingling sensation between her legs and knew that she was close to another climax.

Without warning, Tor pulled back from her and grabbed her firmly round the waist. Lifting her effortlessly, he swung her up high into the air and spun round on his heels, holding her out in front of him. As if this manoeuvre had already been rehearsed, Troy was standing up right in front of her, with his hips spread wide.

Grinning, he reached out and grasped her panties, tugging them down her thighs and over her knees and ankles in one, fluid motion. He tossed the skimpy damp silk over his shoulder and thrust his groin forward invitingly as he spread her thighs apart with his hands.

Tor lifted her even higher, took a couple of steps forward and lowered her gently on to Troy's awaiting cock.

'Oh my God,' she muttered softly, as Troy's manhood delved deeper and deeper inside her warm, welcoming embrace.

As Troy began to thrust firmly in and out, Tor continued to support her from behind. Every time he brought her down on to Troy's shaft, she felt his own hard cock prodding urgently against her buttocks. Maggie shut her eyes and gave herself up completely to the beat of the music and the multiple stimulation of her body.

Troy groaned urgently and pushed himself even deeper into her pliant cunt, and Maggie opened her eyes again just in time to see his face contort, then relax, as his pleasure consumed him. She felt her body slip effortlessly from his still twitching organ as Tor tumbled backwards and collapsed on to the chair. He pulled her sweat-drenched body tight against him and forced his rigid cock up between her slippery wet thighs. Maggie pushed her hand down between her legs, caressing his blood-engorged tip with her fingers while her thumb pushed hard on to her own tingling bud.

His grunt of release was masked by her own urgent cry as they climaxed together. She felt his come splatter powerfully on to her legs to mingle with her own flow of moisture. She whimpered again, a gentle sigh of complete and utter fulfilment, and relaxed her tense body against his hot damp chest. Almost as if on cue, the music came to an end and the sudden silence was only broken by the sound of heavy and irregular breathing, gradually dying away as they recovered.

'Well, I guess we've proved that she can dance,' Tor whispered hoarsely.

They were still laughing when they heard the sound of a car pulling up on the driveway.

'It's Roland,' Tor groaned. 'I recognise the sound of the engine.'

Troy jumped to his feet. 'Oh Lordy.' He rolled his eyes dramatically and flapped his hands around in mock terror. 'Massa Boss gonna whip my black ass if'n he catch me wid mah dick out. Oh Lordy!'

Tor and Maggie both howled with laughter, clutching on to each other helplessly as the tears of mirth trickled down their cheeks. Outside a car door slammed and Maggie began to pull herself together.

'Look, I'd better go. I'll leave the way I came,' she told them. 'I don't think Roland and I have anything to say to each other just now.' As she struggled into her sweaty and crumpled clothing, she couldn't help noticing that the two men were every bit as skilful at dressing quickly as they were at everything else she had seen them do.

* * *

To Sara's great disappointment, it was not Ean but Roland who came into the kitchen while she was stacking the dishwasher that evening. She kept her distance as he congratulated her on the meal and asked her if she was happy or whether there was anything else she needed. Her ears were strained for the slightest sound that would tell her what the others were up to, but the house seemed strangely still and quiet.

'Where is everyone?' she questioned finally.

'I believe they've all gone home,' he informed her. His voice sounded slightly huffy and she knew he was beginning to get the message that she was not interested in him. She started to imagine Ean tucked up alone in his bed, naked under the sheets. If only she were his housekeeper. She imagined herself popping up to his bedroom to see if he needed anything.

'Well, if you're sure you don't want anything, I guess I'll go and do some paperwork. It's a full-time job, just keeping up with the lads' expenses. I'll be in the library if you need me.'

After he had gone, Sara quickly finished her chores and then decided that she would have an early night. As she tiptoed softly past the open library door, she saw Roland huddled over his accounts, sipping a large Scotch. She remembered Maggie's bitchy comments about him and wondered if her friend's accusations could possibly be true. It didn't make sense. Why would Roland bother to have Maggie fired? Perhaps she would give the library a thorough clean tomorrow and tidy up Roland's messy desktop for him. Who knew what she might find?

Chapter Nine

*R*oland rubbed his weary eyes and ran his finger down the long column of figures. He nodded to himself in satisfaction. As always, he had done a neat job of hiding his tracks. Even someone who was good with figures would have trouble spotting any discrepancies. A bunch of brainless dickheads like the Trojans wouldn't stand a chance. Apart from Troy of course. Roland's eyes narrowed. That one was too clever for his own good. Roland still resented the fact that Maggie preferred Troy to him. Just look where that had got her though! If Troy ever gave him any trouble, he'd get rid of him just as quick. There were plenty of other good hockey players on the market and another transfer deal would help boost his own retirement fund.

Roland opened his personal account book and feasted his greedy eyes on the balance. Even with his heavy gambling losses, he was doing pretty well. If it kept up like this, he was going to be a very rich man before long. Those stupid prats had no idea how much they were raking in from sponsorship this season. He rubbed his hands together, polished off his Scotch and reached for his jacket. He had a little business to take care of at the bank. As he made his way down the hall, he could hear Sara singing to herself in the kitchen while she prepared his lunch.

Roland smiled. He had a little business to take care of there as well. With Maggie out of the way, he needed to turn his attentions elsewhere. It was ages since he'd had a woman. Stupid cow, Maggie. He could have shown her a much better time than Troy or any of the others. Still, one cunt was as good as another and Sara would probably do him just as well.

By the time her doorbell rang that evening, Jan was almost beside herself with nervous anticipation. Thank heavens Marcus was away on business again for a few days. Not that she should allow it to worry her. She was quite certain that he would not be sleeping alone while he was away. One day she would have to confront Marcus about his double standards where her sex life was concerned!

She checked her appearance one more time in the hall mirror, then opened the door.

'Hello Jan.' Tor was holding a huge bunch of flowers out in front of him. They must have cost a fortune. Jan could hardly believe her eyes. No one ever brought flowers on a date any more. It seemed almost ridiculously old-fashioned and totally unexpected.

'They're beautiful. Thank you.'

'Just my way of saying thanks for helping me out.'

Jan took the flowers from him and headed for the kitchen. 'I'll just put them in water.' She was very aware of Tor following along behind her. As she filled a large vase and fussed with the flowers, she could feel his eyes watching her, like a hungry lion ready to pounce.

She couldn't believe how awkward she was feeling. Like a teenager on a first serious date. It was quite ridiculous for someone of her age and experience.

Especially so, considering what had happened the last time they'd been together.

'So, what do you have in mind for us this evening then? I mean, where are we going?' she rephrased her words quickly.

'Well, I don't know this area very well yet but there's this nice little pub I came across, not too far out in the country. I think it's called the Blue Wren. I thought we might go there first, if that's all right with you?' Even his voice sent little shivers of desire coursing through her.

'Yes, I know it. I'll just get my coat.' Jan finally gave up fiddling with the flower arrangement and turned to walk past him into the hallway. Tor watched her silently and she had a feeling that he was tempted to touch her. She contemplated falling into his arms and making it easier for him. However, she knew that once they started neither of them would be able to stop. Well, so what? There was a big double bed in the other room, just waiting for them, and plenty of food and drink in the fridge if they were hungry later.

As she passed him, she looked up into his face and saw the lust smouldering in his eyes. She remembered his urgent desperation for her the last time and how he had lost it almost as soon as she had touched him. The memory caused a surge of fire in her loins. She wanted to do that to him again, wanted to see him squirming with his need for her. There was plenty of time. Why rush? They had the whole evening in front of them.

Jan picked up her coat. 'Ready?' she called.

Tor took the coat from her and held it open. As she shrugged her arms into the sleeves, he ran his hands teasingly over her shoulders. His touch made her feel quite weak at the knees and she was sorry when he let her go to open the front door. Once outside, she was pleased to see that he had borrowed Roland's flashy red sports car. She hadn't fancied the grubby old van she

199

had sometimes seen Tor and a few of the others driving round in.

'Nice of your manager to let you use his car,' she commented as he helped her in.

'Yes. I'm sure he will be only too happy, once he knows how generous he's been,' Tor responded with a cheeky, almost boyish grin.

Tor drove fast but carefully and Jan sank back into the deep leather upholstery and allowed herself to enjoy the speed and comfort. She was both surprised and disappointed that he kept his hands to himself but consoled herself with the fact that his eyes kept darting down on to her thighs in a very flattering way.

The pub was only half full and they soon found a small table for two in a secluded corner. Tor fetched them both a drink and picked up a menu. After a few awkward moments, they both began to relax and chat comfortably about nothing in particular. They sat side by side and the table was small enough for her to be able to feel the slight pressure of his thigh against her own. It was just enough to remind her of what was bound to happen sooner or later. The warm glow she was feeling right through her body had little to do with the alcohol.

They decided to order a cheese and pâté platter for two, washed down with a carafe of red wine. While they were waiting for the food to arrive, they continued to chat aimlessly. She found herself telling him all about her plans to open an estate agents of her own in the near future while in return, he described his life in Canada after his parents had inherited some money and decided to emigrate. Jan learnt that he had always been good at athletics and had originally planned to be a runner, until, that is, Canada introduced him to its favourite sport and he discovered he had a talent for skating.

'Of course, I did think about becoming a Mountie for a while too,' he told her with a twinkle in his eyes, 'but there was a slight problem with that.'

'Why, because you're British?' she questioned.

'No, because I can't ride,' he chuckled. As they both laughed, he casually slipped his arm around her shoulder and she snuggled up against him, enjoying his masculine scent.

'How do you fancy seeing a film after?' he suggested.

After what, Jan thought to herself as her excitement intensified. It had been a long time since any man had made her feel so damned horny as Tor did by simply being there. Her knickers already felt slightly damp and he hadn't so much as kissed her, yet.

'Yes, if you like. I've no idea what's on, though.'

'I do,' Tor assured her. 'Ah, great. Here's the food. I'm famished.'

During the meal, Tor moved his hand under the table and lightly on to her thigh. The action was so casual it almost seemed as if he was unaware that he was even touching her. Jan couldn't have felt more aroused if he had pushed his fingers down inside her knickers. The yearning was so intense, it was almost more than she could bear. She had never felt anything quite like this before.

When he finally removed his fingers in order to pay the bill, her sense of loss was like a physical blow. As she stood up to put her coat on, she found her limbs were trembling. It was as much as she could do just to walk across the room. She took his arm for support.

'Whoa! That wine must have been stronger than I thought,' she muttered as she swayed slightly, and Tor quickly steadied her with an arm around her waist.

The cold night air helped a bit but, as he helped her into the car, the touch of his hands on her skin sent another wave of desire washing over her, leaving her flushed and breathless – almost nauseous with the strength of her longing.

She didn't speak as he started the car and headed back into town. She didn't trust her voice not to betray her emotions. She could feel her heart thumping painfully in her chest and was intensely aware of the ache in the pit of her stomach. She closed her eyes and tried to make herself relax.

'Here we are then.' Tor had stopped the car and she heard the click of his door opening. She opened her eyes and looked out of the windscreen. They were parked in front of the gates of his rented house. Tor was already opening them.

When he climbed back in, she stared at him curiously. 'I thought you said a film?' Was he feeling as wound up as she was? Perhaps he had decided just to skip the film and take her back to his bed. Her desperate longing swept over her again, almost making her gasp.

'The TV and video are already set up and waiting,' he responded as he selected first gear and edged the car through the open gates. 'I thought it would be more fun, just the two of us. If that's OK with you?'

Jan nodded mutely, her mouth suddenly too dry for her to answer.

As soon as he had let them into the house and reset the alarm, Tor took her arm and guided her up the stairs and along the landing. His hand felt as if it were burning her skin through her clothes. Tor pushed a door open with his foot.

'The second largest bedroom with a lovely view of the back garden,' he mimicked her own words. 'Of course, it's a little too dark to appreciate the view now.' He grinned again.

Oh, I don't know about that, Jan thought, as she eyed him up and down. Would he think her too forward if she just started ripping his clothes off him now? Did she care what he thought, just so long as she got her hands on him?

'Make yourself comfortable,' he suggested. 'I'll just put the film on.'

She slipped out of her coat and looked around. The TV

and video were set up on a table at the end of the bed. There was nowhere else to sit. She sat down and swung her legs up on to the springy mattress. Tor was bent over the video and she admired the tightness of his trousers across his buttocks and thighs, longing to tug his trousers off him and sink her teeth into his solid flesh.

'Do you fancy a drink? I've got some champagne on ice in the bathroom.'

'Please,' she responded softly.

Now, that's what I call style, she thought, as he returned from the bathroom with two tall glasses of ice-cold bubbly. He sat down beside her and handed her a glass.

'I hope this is good,' he commented, pushing the video button. 'Troy had it sent to him from somewhere in Europe. He reckons it's terrific.'

Who cares about the film, Jan thought as she sipped her drink and placed the glass on the bedside table. There's only one thing I want to watch right now. She rolled closer to him and put her hand on his chest. As she began to fiddle with his top button, she glanced up at the TV and her fingers stopped moving.

The film had already started. Two muscle-bound men were knelt on the floor, wearing nothing but jock straps. Stretched out between them was a pretty young girl dressed in a skimpy, button-through white dress. Her hands and feet were bound with ropes and she had a blindfold over her eyes. The blond man on her left picked up a piece of velvet ribbon and trailed it softly up her bare legs. The girl writhed her hips and moaned softly.

Tor slipped his arm under her and pulled her closer. Jan rested her head on his chest and tried not to over-react as his fingers stretched round and found the swell of her right breast. She glanced down his body to the bulge of his groin and shivered at her memories of last time.

The girl in the film was moaning louder, her breath

sobbing from her. Jan looked back at the screen and saw that the man with the ribbon had unbuttoned her dress to reveal her tiny breasts. He was trailing the end of the ribbon round one of her nipples, which was already swelling and hardening. The girl arched her back, thrusting her breasts upwards. The man moved the ribbon on to her other nipple and teased it erect too.

Jan sighed gently. She could feel her own nipples rubbing against her bra and she rolled slightly so that Tor's fingers slipped further on to her breast. She felt his fingertip touch her own super-hard nipple and sighed again. A little tremor ran down her chest and stomach, like a small jolt of electricity. Her clit began to tingle expectantly.

The blond man pushed the hem of the girl's dress up, exposing a tiny triangle of white material, hardly big enough to cover her. The camera moved in closer so that they could see a few fluffy wisps of blonde pubic hair poking out each side. The second man had picked up a vibrator. He switched it on and placed it over the white triangle.

The girl's body jerked as if she had been stung by a scorpion. The camera panned back to show her face. She was rolling her head from side to side and groaning urgently. Her lips were slightly parted and the tip of her pink tongue repeatedly licked her ruby lips.

Jan turned her head and glanced up at Tor. He was staring avidly at the TV screen, totally engrossed. She lowered her eyes and examined his groin again. The bulge under his zip was much larger than before, and the sight of it caused another surge of desire to rush through her body. She forced her eyes back to the film.

The second man had slipped the vibrator under the girl's panties and was making small circular motions around her clit. The blond man was still tormenting her breasts with the velvet ribbon.

'Please. Stop. Oh please. I can't. I . . .' The girl was

rolling her whole body from side to side and drumming her heels against the floor. A close-up revealed a few droplets of perspiration trickling down between her breasts. She appeared to be about to climax.

Suddenly, both men stopped and sat up. The darker one switched the vibrator off and put it down. With the camera full on him, he pulled his briefs down and wrapped his hand round his already huge erection. Kneeling up over the girl, he began to pump himself up and down.

'Jesus!' Jan's gasp was out of her mouth before she could stop herself. She had watched plenty of porno films before, but never one with a fully erect cock.

Tor turned his head. 'What's wrong?' he asked.

'Eh. Nothing.' Jan could feel herself perspiring. 'Where did you say this film came from?'

The dark-haired man was still pumping himself enthusiastically while the blond man watched him and fondled his own groin. His other hand was gently caressing the bound and blindfolded girl, who was still trembling. Jan thought it was a good job the girl was blindfolded. If she'd been close to coming before, seeing what was happening now would certainly have set her off.

'Troy sent for it from somewhere. Holland, I think. Are you enjoying it?' His fingers moved gently over her breast again and Jan felt an expanding dampness inside the crotch of her panties. The camera had moved up even closer to the dark man. She could actually see the tip of his cock glistening with his lubrication. His penis looked purple and swollen and his balls were hard and tight with his need. It was difficult to see how he could be faking it. Without breaking his rhythm, he pushed his other hand down inside the girl's panties and started rubbing her.

The girl jumped again and pushed her hips up off the ground, grinding herself on to his palm. Without taking

205

her eyes from the screen, Jan reached down and put her hand over Tor's bulging flies. She heard his breath catch and felt his fingers pushing harder on to her breast. Her own fingers fumbled to open his zip and his trousers parted easily. She slipped her hand into the opening and closed her fingers around his cock.

Tor turned his head and pushed his tongue into her ear. Jan shuddered from head to foot as hot shivers of passion raced through her. On the TV, the dark-haired man ripped the girl's panties down her thighs and leaned forward to run his tongue over her sex lips. The girl cried out and her face and chest flushed red. The man smiled and resumed pumping himself. The other man whipped his own cock out and crouched over the girl's chest, using his hands to push her breasts up around his erection. Tor's cock was hard and urgent in Jan's trembling fingers. His tongue continued to probe her ear and his fingers had somehow found their way under her blouse and bra to torment her nipples.

Jan rolled round against him and pushed herself hard on to his thigh. Just the pressure of his body against her clit was enough to push her over the top. With a long, desperate moan, she climaxed violently, her whole body convulsing from the intensity of it. It was one of the most powerful orgasms she had ever had and it left her weak and trembling as she sucked in ragged breaths, waiting for her head to stop spinning.

'A bit sensitive, aren't we?' Tor whispered mockingly. 'I take it you are enjoying the film?'

Jan could think of no suitable reply. Her hand was still wrapped around his erection, although, lost in her own gratification, she had long ago stopped moving her fingers. Now, as she felt him twitching, she sensed her own strength returning.

She wriggled down his body slightly, undid his trouser button and eased him out. His cock was every bit as rigid and purple as the man's in the film, and twice as big. Jan

206

ran her tongue down his length and smiled at the enthusiastic response. On the TV, the blond man was now sucking and licking the girl's clit, while the dark man had pushed his cock between her lips and was pumping rapidly in and out of her mouth.

Jan licked her fingers and encircled Tor's glans. She started to pump him up and down, gradually building up speed until she felt his body stiffen. Immediately, she stopped pumping and squeezed him firmly. Tor groaned and pushed his hips up against her hand, trying to force her to continue. She moved her hand from top to base, centimetre at a time, then back up just as slowly.

The girl in the film cried out urgently, but neither Jan nor Tor looked up. Jan could feel Tor's whole body shuddering with his need for release. She increased her speed again, relentlessly bringing him back up to the brink.

'Oh Jesus!' Tor's words were faint, desperate. She slowed her hand again, waiting. Suddenly, he twisted out from under her. With all the agility of his profession, he rolled her on to her back and yanked her sodden undies down her thighs. Before she knew what was happening, he was on top of her and she felt the hot tip of his cock begin to enter her.

'Yes!' His cry was a mixture of desperation and triumph as he slid himself in effortlessly. The girl on the TV cried out again and Jan sank back on to the pillow and arched her back to meet Tor's relentless thrusting.

When he finally started to come, she felt herself responding yet again, so that their combined moans drowned the film out completely. Oblivious to the loss of their audience, the two men and the young girl continued to pleasure each other enthusiastically.

Sara's heart was thumping so hard in her chest that she could barely draw breath. She knew that it would be more sensible to wait until Roland was out of the house, but Maggie had been pushing her for days now to help her, and she didn't want her friend to think she didn't have any gumption. Though, just what good Maggie thought it would do, she had no idea. If Roland had been responsible for getting her fired, something Sara was not entirely convinced about, he was hardly likely to leave any evidence lying about the house. What did Maggie expect her to find anyway? A labelled envelope full of the missing ice rink money or a signed confession, perhaps?

Sara turned her head and strained her ears. Roland and a few of the squad were in the main living room with the coach, discussing tactics for their next game. Tor and Pary were both there and they were obviously annoyed about something because they were both shouting angrily. She could hear Roland's honeyed tones trying to soothe them, clearly unsuccessfully. It sounded as though they would be a while yet.

Sara looked around the library thoughtfully, wondering where to start. She eyed the safe door and smiled ruefully. If Roland had hidden the stolen money anywhere, which was extremely unlikely, then that was the most obvious place. Fingers shaking, she pulled the desk draw open and rummaged around for the keys. Her hand found the big black book she had seen him working on most days. On impulse, she pulled it out and opened it.

As Roland had suggested, it was an account book and Sara was flabbergasted by how much money was involved. No wonder Roland lived like a lord, with lavish roast dinners every night and a huge cooked breakfast most mornings. She felt slightly aggrieved when she saw just how much Butterflies were charging for her services. Why, she didn't even see a half of that in her wage packet! At least it helped to explain why Ms Jamison had been looking so pleased with herself lately.

With frequent nervous glances over her shoulder, Sara

continued to work her way down the neat columns of figures. She didn't really have the first idea what she was looking for, of course. Maggie had also hinted that she thought Roland was probably on the fiddle but, if he was, evidence of the fact would hardly be obvious to her inexperienced gaze.

Sara's eyes came to rest on a recent sponsorship entry and her brow crinkled thoughtfully. Although the figure entered was an awful lot of money, it was not anywhere near as much as she had overheard Roland discussing with a smart-looking businessman a couple of evenings previously. She stared at the figures again in bewilderment. She was certain that the man had been the one whose company was responsible for the donation. Why would he and Roland discuss one figure and then Roland enter a much smaller amount in the accounts? It didn't make sense. Perhaps she had misheard, or perhaps the company had had second thoughts about how generous a donation they were prepared to contribute?

The living room door slammed and Sara heard footsteps in the hallway. She shut the book quickly and shoved it back into the drawer. She had hardly closed it, when the library door was flung open and Roland stomped into view.

'Sara? What are you doing in here?' he demanded.

She shook her feather duster in the air in front of her. 'Just a spot of dusting.' She flicked the duster over the top of the telephone on the desk as if to prove her point. 'Actually, I'm just about finished, so if you've got some work you need to be getting on with, I'll leave you to it.' She took a few steps towards the hallway.

Roland put his hand out and caught hold of her arm as she passed him. 'No need to rush off. How about a little drink?'

'Oh, eh, no thank you. It's much too early for me. I really should be getting on with lunch.'

'Do you like working here, Sara? I mean, would you consider making it a more permanent relationship?'

'I, um. Why, yes.' Sara was flustered. As far as she knew, Roland had only hired her services until the end of the current season. It was a much better job than working in the café at the rink. 'If it's all right with the agency, of course.'

'Never mind the agency. It's me you have to please.' Roland's voice was as sweet as syrup, but his eyes looked dark and dangerous. His meaning was quite clear and Sara felt her heart sink. Obviously, she wouldn't be able to stay on if he was going to start adding extra, unwritten, clauses to her contract.

'Well then, I'd better make sure I get your food on the table on time, hadn't I?' she responded brightly, as she shook his hand from her arm and backed away. Head down, she scurried from the room.

'Hey! You look as if you just stepped on something nasty. What's up?' It was Tor's voice. Sara had only just stopped herself from walking headlong into him.

'Oh, excuse me. I was miles away.' She said and gazed up into his rugged face. She wondered how it was possible to find one man so repugnant and another so attractive that it made her weak at the knees.

'Roland's in a bad mood, is he? Sorry about that. It's probably my fault. We were just arguing about our next match. Don't worry. His bark's worse than his bite.'

Sara smiled at the image, thinking how apt it was. Roland reminded her exactly of a great slobbering Rottweiler.

'Lunch won't be long,' she told Tor breathlessly. 'I hope you and the others will be staying?' She felt a rush of excitement when she saw the ravenous look on his face. Of course, he was thinking about her cooking not her body – but a girl was allowed to dream, wasn't she?

* * *

As soon as she had cleared the lunch things away, Sara phoned Maggie and arranged to meet her at their usual coffee house. She slipped out without anyone noticing.

Maggie was already waiting impatiently outside when Sara arrived. As soon as they had found a table and fetched some drinks, Sara told her friend what she had discovered.

Maggie's eyes glittered triumphantly. 'Your see! I told you the bastard wasn't to be trusted, didn't I?' she exclaimed excitedly.

Sara looked dubious. 'I still don't see that it proves anything. It's more likely that I just misheard the sum involved or he made a mistake.' Sara took a quick sip of her coffee and glanced around the almost-deserted coffee house.

Maggie shook her head impatiently. 'More likely he pretends to receive one amount, the amount he puts in the accounts, and then just keeps the rest for himself,' she suggested.

'It's taking one hell of a risk. It would be so easy for someone to catch him out. If I heard the sum involved, you can be sure others would, too,' Sara argued.

Maggie grunted angrily. 'Well, hell, I don't know. Maybe he's got two sets of books. The one he shows the squad and the taxman and the one he lines his own pocket from.'

Sara continued to look unconvinced. The conversation was giving her a bit of a headache. She decided that she wouldn't make a good private eye. All this creeping around and speculating was far too confusing.

'What else did you notice?' Maggie demanded.

'Well, nothing really. I didn't have much time and, anyway, I don't really know what I'm looking for.' Sara tried to imagine just what Maggie hoped to get out of all this. Roland was a low-life, certainly. She was finding that out all too well for herself. But, even if he was dishonest in his dealings with the Trojans, why would he have had Maggie fired from the rink? It was all too much for her. She didn't really want anything to do with it, yet she could clearly see how much her friend was hurting and she desperately wanted to help.

'I'll have to get back,' she excused herself. 'I've still got a lot of work to do.'

After Sara had left, Maggie continued to sit on her own, lost in thought. If Sara could just find a second account book she might have the proof that she needed to nail Roland. Without it, she was certain that the Trojans would not believe her. Troy had already more or less laughed at her suggestion that Roland was responsible for the missing money, assuring her that their manager was too stupid to try and get one over on anyone.

She thumped the table angrily. It just wasn't fair. She knew that Roland had been responsible for having her sacked. He had more or less told her he would. So far, she had had no luck in finding herself another suitable job, and money was already becoming tight. Besides, if she didn't clear her name, everyone would always half-believe that she was a thief. She had to prove her innocence to Justin. Not that she would ever have anything to do with him again after he had treated her so badly, but she had to prove him wrong.

'Well, well. Hello Maggie. How are you? No, don't get up.' Roland's voice broke into her thoughts and caused her to jump visibly.

'What are you doing here?' Maggie could feel her temper rising. After what he had done to her, where did he get the gall to come over to her now, all crocodile smiles? She was sorely tempted to punch him on his smug nose. Had he seen her talking with Sara? Maybe his guilty conscience was getting the better of him. Not about her, of course, but perhaps he was worried about what Sara might know – or find out.

'I was just passing when I saw you sitting here, all

212

alone,' he replied cheerfully. 'I wondered how you were getting on. I was sorry to hear you had lost your job. Complete nonsense, of course. I'm sure you would never do anything dishonest. I told Justin as much.'

Maggie swallowed. His concern was so blatantly insincere as to be sickening. She knew he had to be responsible for getting her fired, no matter what he said now. She was about to get up and walk off, when it occurred to her that this might be the opportunity she was looking for. If she lulled him into a sense of false security, maybe she could trap him into inadvertently saying something incriminating.

'Would you like some coffee?' she asked him politely.

'No thanks.' Roland shook his head and perched his ample backside on the chair opposite her. 'I've just had some.' He bared his large teeth at her and Maggie immediately understood how Little Red Riding Hood must have felt. She tried to suppress a shudder of revulsion.

'I really wish that there was something I could do to help you,' he told her. 'If I had any jobs going, but well, money is a bit tight at the moment.'

Maggie snorted. 'With all the sponsorship money you've been raking in? I find that hard to believe.'

Roland suddenly looked wary. 'I don't know where you got that idea from. Sponsorship money is extremely difficult to acquire and, with so many expenses, it really doesn't go very far,' he told her.

'No. I would imagine your XK8 put quite a dent in the coffers,' Maggie retorted sharply, before she could stop herself.

Roland frowned. 'I don't know what you're implying. My personal expenditure has got nothing to do with the squad's sponsorship money.' He pulled a grubby handkerchief out of his top pocket and mopped his brow.

'If you say so.' Maggie's tone made it quite clear that she did not believe him.

Roland's eyes narrowed and his mouth became a hard line. He stood up abruptly. 'Considering your own situation, young woman, I wouldn't have thought that you were in any position to start making insinuations about other people. You're lucky Justin didn't hand you over to the police.'

'Yes. I'm surprised you didn't arrange that, too,' Maggie replied. 'Or, perhaps you were reluctant to have them poking around the rink, in case they uncovered more than was to your own best interests.' As soon as the words were out of her mouth, Maggie wanted to bite her tongue off. The last thing she wanted to do was to warn Roland what she suspected. Why the hell had she allowed him to provoke her so easily?

'I think this conversation's gone quite far enough,' he snapped. His eyes flashed dangerously. 'I would advise you not to interfere with things that have nothing to do with you, my dear, or . . .' He stopped.

'Or what?' She hoped that he couldn't hear the tremble in her voice.

'I don't let anything come between me and business, Ms Lomax. Or anyone. You would do well to remember that if you know what's good for you.'

'Is that a threat?'

'I never make threats my dear. At least, not idle ones.'

Maggie stood up shakily.

'Nice to have talked with you.' He held out his hand. She ignored it and he grinned. 'I'm sure we understand each other better now.' He turned on his heel and strode away without looking back.

At least she knew that she was right now, anyway. Her rash comments had certainly found their mark. Had he really been threatening her? Surely not? What more could he possibly do? He'd already had her fired. He'd just been hoping to scare her off. Well, it took more than a fat pig like him to stop her, once she had made her mind up about something. She would have to get in touch with Sara again and push her a bit harder. One way or another, she was going to fix Roland Rat for good.

Chapter Ten

Maggie uttered profanities under her breath as she tried to ease her car out from in between two others that had thoughtlessly been parked much too close to hers. She and Jan had spent all evening talking over her job situation without getting anywhere, and Maggie was tired and grumpy. All she wanted to do was to get home to bed. As she pulled away, she was dazzled by a set of high beams from behind, reflected in her mirror.

'Sodding idiot!' Maggie flicked the rear-view mirror up to protect her eyes. The road was empty and she pulled out quickly, turning left towards home. Glancing in her wing mirror, Maggie saw the other car pull out behind her, driving much too close. Its headlights were still blazing, making it impossible to tell what make or colour it was. She increased the pressure on the accelerator, attempting to pull away. Reaching the end of the road, she slowed down and indicated right.

The other car was so close behind her that she could almost sense its presence, like when someone stands too close behind you, breathing down your neck and encroaching on your personal space. Thankfully, there was nothing coming and she pulled out too quickly, feeling the rear wheels slide as she fought to keep the turn under control. Her unwelcome shadow followed, riding her boot.

'That's it!' Maggie's temper snapped. She could feel herself shaking with a mixture of anger and fear and her heart was thumping erratically inside her ribcage. Flicking the left indicator on, she slammed her feet down on the brake and clutch and spun the steeringwheel towards the kerb. As she came to a stop, she heard a squeal of brakes and then the roar of an engine as the driver behind her shifted down.

The car shot past her so close that she half-expected her wing mirror to be ripped off. Staring wide-eyed through the side window, she caught a brief glimpse of the silhouettes of two large, well-built figures in the front of the big black car. With its boot level with her bonnet, the car slowed and stopped. She could see the two figures in the front twisted around to stare back at her. They seemed to be arguing and gesturing towards her.

Really frightened now, Maggie shoved her foot on the clutch and rammed the gearstick into reverse. Before she could move, the other car's engine revved loudly and it shot off into the night with its tyres screaming. Taking the next left, it disappeared from sight.

Trembling so much that she could barely control her limbs, Maggie put the car into first and moved off warily. As she passed the left-hand turn, her heart was in her mouth and her foot was poised over the accelerator, ready to make a sudden dash if the other car should be lying in wait. The road was completely deserted. She laughed shakily.

By the time she reached her flat, Maggie had almost got herself under control. After all, it had probably only been a couple of joyriders messing about. She parked her car and hurried inside. After throwing her jacket over the back of the settee, she kicked her shoes off and curled up wearily in her favourite chair with a book. Although she had been so tired earlier, suddenly, she didn't feel like sleeping at all.

Two days later, Maggie was on her way round to Jan's again. It was late afternoon and she had had a very bad day. All three interviews she'd attended that day had been a complete waste of time and she was beginning to think that she was never going to get another job.

If only she could bring herself to ask Justin for a reference. She was fairly certain that he would give her one, no matter what he suspected her of, but she just couldn't swallow her pride. She had been surprised at just how much his lack of trust in her had hurt, no matter how much Roland had twisted his arm. She hadn't realised that she cared that much.

As she pulled out, she glanced in her mirror and saw what looked like the strange black car behind her again. She felt her stomach churn. If it was the same car, then it couldn't possibly be just be joyriders, could it? Roland's threatening words popped unbidden into her mind: 'Don't interfere with things that have nothing to do with you or . . .'

Maggie tried to grin. It certainly wasn't Roland following her. She would recognise his portly build and flashy red car anywhere. But who was it who had been trying to call her yesterday evening? Twice, when she had answered the phone, no one had been on the other end. Honestly! Talk about an overactive imagination. There must be dozens of big black cars like this one, and wrong numbers were not that uncommon.

Maggie turned left towards Jan's house. She tried not to notice that the car was still behind her. If it was someone pissing about, she refused to play any more of their silly games. As she took another left turn, the car suddenly sped up and overtook her. She saw that it was a Ford Cosworth. As before, two shadowy figures lurked inside but they could have been anyone.

Her foot lifted slightly from the accelerator and she realised that she was still half-expecting the car to skid in front of her and block the road, like on TV police chases. The Cosworth continued to accelerate away from her at high speed and she smiled with a mixture of relief and disappointment as it disappeared from view. In a strange kind of way there had been something exciting, almost stimulating, about imagining she was being chased.

Maggie slowed and turned right into Peacock Lane. A man was crouching at the side of the road and she instinctively pulled out to avoid him. As she drew closer to him, she could see that he was fiddling with what looked like a reel of wire fence. Seemingly oblivious to her approach, the man stood up and threw something across the road. Maggie had no chance of stopping.

'Stupid bloody idiot,' she exclaimed angrily as she heard a peculiar rattle under the wheels. She slowed to turn left and glanced back at the man. He was already picking up whatever he had thrown. What kind of nut was he?

As she began to turn the steering wheel, Maggie felt the back of the car drift from under her. She fought the wheel, struggling to correct the skid. The vehicle was behaving like a bucking bronco. She had practically no control of it at all. Damn it to hell, she must have picked up a puncture. Cursing loudly, she managed to guide the car into the grass verge and come to a stop. Fortunately, it was less than a mile to Jan's place if she were forced to walk.

'Of all the stupid, idiotic morons!' She was trembling with both rage and fright as she got out and stared at the now very flat tyres. She might have been killed. She moved round to the near side. All four tyres were ruined.

As she turned her head, she saw the man hurrying towards her with whatever he had thrown tucked under his arm. So he should come over to apologise. Bloody fool. For the first time, it dawned on her that it might not have been an accident. The man had deliberately thrown that wire fence thing out in front of her. Didn't the police use some sort of spiked tyre-mat to stop joyriders? Her heart did a complete somersault. Were the police after her? Christ Almighty, perhaps the rink were going to bring charges against her after all!

'Get a grip on yourself, girl,' she muttered under her breath. Her alleged crime wouldn't warrant this kind of response, would it? The man was rapidly drawing closer and suddenly she was quite certain that he was not a policeman. She grabbed her bag and started to run down the road towards Jan's house. A quick glance over her shoulder confirmed her fears. The man was running in pursuit. She ran faster. If she could just get round the next corner there was a footpath that cut straight through some waste ground to Jan's road.

Running flat out, she reached the corner and glanced back. He was being left behind. If that was the best he could manage, she could easily outrun him. She rounded the corner and raced for the safety of the footpath. Soon, she would be out of sight altogether.

As she scrambled over the style, her skirt caught on a rusty nail and she heard the sound of it tearing. Yanking herself free, she lost her balance and tumbled awkwardly, winding herself. Before she could move, two hands grasped her round the waist and helped her to her feet. Maggie screamed.

'Are you all right?'

She peered up anxiously at the man. He was dressed in jogging pants, jacket and trainers. His hood was pulled up so that she could not see his face properly. 'Sorry,' she blurted. 'You made me jump.'

Out the corner of her eye, she saw her pursuer round the corner and start down the pathway. She grabbed the jogger by the arm. 'Please help me.' She pointed back down the path. 'That man is following me.' She gripped his arm tightly and tried to move round behind him.

As her pursuer reached the style and started to climb over it, Maggie felt the jogger flex his biceps. He was very well built. Very attractive in a rugged kind of way. She felt a wave of relief wash over her at the realisation that she was going to be all right.

The jogger smiled. 'It's OK,' he assured her. 'I'll take care of you. We wouldn't want anything to happen to you would we, Maggie?' He shook off her hand and took hold of her arm.

The blood in her veins turned to ice. She stared back at the original pursuer and saw that he had pulled a balaclava on over his head. He continued to advance slowly but surely. His eyes were two dark holes filled with menace.

Stupid bitch! She had run straight into their trap. A small whimper of fear and despair burst from her lips as she swivelled her head round, desperately seeking a way out. Back on the road, someone might have driven past; here, there was no one to help her.

Maggie shrank away from the jogger, tugging her arm to free herself. He gripped her harder and twisted her round so that her arm was pinned behind her back. Another sob welled up inside her.

'You've been sticking your nose in where it isn't wanted, Maggie.' She heard the man wearing the balaclava speak for the first time. His voice was as cold and menacing as his eyes.

'I don't know what you mean. Let me go.' Maggie had deliberately relaxed her body, hoping to catch the jogger off-guard. Now she used all her strength to try to break free. She almost succeeded. Blindly, she kicked out at his knee but he sidestepped her easily and increased the pressure on her arm. Her eyes began to water with the pain.

'Ow! Stop it. You're hurting me.' She was forced to lean over to find some relief. Drawing her stomach in, she pushed back as hard as she could. Her buttocks

221

smashed into the jogger's crotch but he barely seemed to notice.

'Now, behave yourself Maggie. We're just here to give you a message. A warning.' He stressed the word. 'It's nothing personal. Just a job.' He relaxed his grip enough for her to stand up straight once more.

'Normally, we'd just break a leg or an arm. Nothing too serious.' He looked around at the woods and fields thoughtfully. 'If anything like that happened to you here, it might be some time before anyone found you. That would be a pity.'

'A great pity,' the man in the balaclava agreed softly. His words seemed more gentle and Maggie felt a glimmer of hope. She was determined not to let them see how scared she was.

'OK. So you're not going to break my legs,' she responded stiffly. 'You've done your job. You've ruined my tyres and I've got your message. From now on, I'll mind my own business.'

They had to have been sent by Roland. Although she could hardly believe he would dare pull a stunt like this, at least it proved she was right about him.

'There. I knew you would be sensible about this. I could tell as soon as I saw you.' The jogger squeezed her wrist.

'Oh yes. Very sensible,' she agreed. 'Feet always firmly on the ground.' Her attempt at bravado sounded rather lame, even to her.

'Well that's good,' he replied. 'But, the thing is, we have to make sure that you understand. I mean, it's all very well saying it now, but what about later? What about once you've had a chance to think it over and get all sure of yourself again?' The jogger tugged on her arm and she stumbled. Immediately she lashed out at him again with her left foot. Again, she missed.

'See what I mean, Maggie? No, you are going to have

to be taught a lesson.' He twisted her arm savagely and Maggie cried out in pain as again she doubled over.

'If that kick had found its mark, I would do more than hurt you. I'd break your fucking legs.'

She knew that he meant it. As he eased the pressure and let her straighten, she could feel her eyes brimming with tears.

'It would be a pity to break such lovely legs.' The man in the balaclava stepped closer and reached down to run his hand up under her skirt and on to the tops of her stockings. Why the hell hadn't she worn her old jeans? Maggie gritted her teeth as his other hand began to explore the curve of her buttocks.

'We have ourselves one very sexy lady here,' the man informed his colleague. Maggie flinched as his fingers ran across the tops of her thighs. She tried to wriggle out of his reach but that just seemed to encourage him. She stood perfectly still and feigned disinterest.

They wouldn't dare do anything bad to her. Not really bad. Roland might be a creep but it wasn't as if he were a real hardened criminal. No, they were just going to scare her a bit, then let her go. Of course, there would be no way to tie any of this to him.

'Why don't you let us have a look at your tits? Have you got nice tits, Maggie?'

Maggie hated the way they both kept using her name. Like they owned her or something. She felt the jogger release her arm and wrap himself around her. His hands cupped her breasts.

'They feel good to me.' He flipped open one of her buttons and pushed his fingers inside her bra. His hand felt icy cold against her skin. She heard a rip as his other hand tore the next two buttons free. His fingers pinched her left nipple and she squealed.

'Bastard!' She felt him pinch harder in response and she bit her lip to stop herself saying anything else. Goose bumps sprang up all over her body and she could feel her legs trembling with conflicting emotions.

'Very nice.' His words galvanised her into action. She was tired of being treated like a piece of meat and angry with herself for responding to their caresses. She twisted out of his grasp, raised her hand and slapped his face with all the force she could muster. Her hand started to throb.

Caught off-balance, the jogger stumbled backwards. Not waiting to see what the other man was doing, Maggie started to run. Before she had gone three paces, she felt a sharp tug on her skirt and she stumbled on to her knees. There was another tug at her skirt and it ripped up one side to the belt. She felt herself being lifted up and pushed and pulled back and forth between the two of them as they toyed with her, like a couple of cats playing with a captive mouse. Her head began to spin.

'Stop it. Please stop it,' she begged. Her blouse was gaping open and her skirt was hanging in tatters. They were laughing at her and she hated it. She had to get away before it was too late.

The jogger grabbed her by the neck, pressing her head down, then dragged her across the grassy path. She twisted and turned, scratching and kicking. Her feet flailed out in all directions, seeking a target. The man with the balaclava crouched down in front of her, just out of reach, and spoke in a calm but threatening voice.

'The more you fight us, the more fun we're having,' he said. Maggie saw him reach into his pocket and pull something out. The click the blade made as it opened sent a cold chill right through her. She held her breath and stood completely still as he put his hand on her stomach and pushed her down to the ground.

'Lie still or I'll cut you.'

His words terrified her. All her remaining courage evaporated. She stared helplessly up at the shiny blade, too scared even to blink.

'Please. Just let me go,' Maggie whimpered.

He ignored her and continued waving the knife around, making jabbing gestures at her but stopping short of actually touching her.

Maggie couldn't take her eyes off the blade as its owner smiled at her fear.

'Now keep very still. I don't want to slip and have an accident.' He rubbed the blunt edge of the knife across her throat.

Maggie shook her head wordlessly. She was shivering with fear and her mouth was too dry to speak. She tried to plead with her eyes.

The pressure of the knife disappeared and Maggie heard the blade snap shut. The relief was so great she almost wet herself. The breath whooshed out of her tortured lungs and she began to gasp. Tears pooled in the corners of her eyes and dribbled down her cheeks as she lay there, horrified at what might happen next.

The jogger reached down and patted her shoulder. 'Do you think she's got the message now?' he questioned his companion.

'I'm not sure.' The other man took her hands and tugged her to her feet. 'Look me in the eyes, Maggie.'

Maggie didn't move. She stood in front of him with her head lowered.

'Now!'

Her head jerked up as if it were on strings. She watched his eyes devouring her naked body.

'You've got a very nice body, Maggie. Haven't you?'

She said nothing.

'Haven't you!'

She flinched. 'Yes,' she mumbled.

'You wouldn't want it to be scarred now, would you? You wouldn't want us to leave you so no man would ever want you again?'

She shook her head.

'Good. Then get up. Now.'

'I'll get the car,' the man in the balaclava muttered. He headed back towards the road.

'Come on, Maggie.' The jogger took her arm and Maggie found herself being dragged along beside him. 'Please let me go.' Whatever happened, she knew she mustn't dare get in the car with them. As they reached the style, she saw the car pull up and the other man begin to reverse it towards them.

'Look. You've got what you wanted. I'm scared. I'll forget everything that happened. I won't tell anyone. Just let me go,' she wailed.

'Shut up.' The jogger reached the car and opened the boot. He picked up a strand of rope and quickly tied her hands together. He reached back into the boot and picked up a black hood. Before she could react, he shoved it down over her head. She screamed.

'I told you to shut up.'

She felt herself being lifted into the air then dumped down on her back. There was a loud thud as the boot closed, trapping her inside.

Maggie tugged frantically at the ropes on her hands. She was sobbing uncontrollably. Jesus Christ. What were they going to do with her? 'Please God, don't let them kill me,' she whispered. She screamed again as she felt the car moving off. Where were they taking her?

A few minutes later, the car stopped again. She heard the doors slamming and then felt the cold evening breeze on her naked flesh as the boot opened. Hands lifted her up and she started kicking with her feet. She opened her mouth to scream but her throat was so dry with terror that she couldn't utter a sound.

'Remember, Maggie. Keep your nose out of things that don't concern you in future. We won't be so nice next time.' The disembodied words petrified her. She felt herself falling and something sharp grazed across her leg. The car doors slammed and the engine revved up. They pulled away with a squeal of tyres and a handful of gravel flew up and stung her bare skin. Everything grew silent.

Mustering all her remaining strength, Maggie struggled with the rope. The knot was not very tight and, after a few minutes, she managed to work her wrists free. She pulled the hood off her face and blinked as she stared around. She was lying in a ditch at the side of another lane and it didn't take her long to recognise where she was. She was only a couple of miles from where she had been attacked. If she remembered correctly, there was a telephone box at the far end of the lane. No more than half a mile.

Maggie glanced down at herself. She was dressed only in the remaining tatters of her skirt and her stockings. The stockings had not even laddered. A bubble of hysterical laughter escaped from her lips at this thought. She had to do something. She couldn't just lie semi-naked in a ditch forever.

It was a quiet lane with few houses and very little traffic. Maggie scrambled up the grassy bank and hurried along the lane as fast as her stockinged feet could carry her. After twenty yards or so, she broke into a kind of desperate jog. She felt terribly vulnerable and very scared. When she heard the sound of a car coming, she leaped into the ditch and huddled behind a small bush. What if it was the two men coming back for her? She held her breath, willing the car not to stop. She couldn't face anyone. Another small sob welled up inside her. Her whole body was shaking with the reaction to her ordeal, and the cold evening breeze chilled her right through.

The car passed without slowing and Maggie slipped out of the ditch and resumed her desperate dash for safety. The phone box was already in sight when she heard another car approaching. Maggie dived back into the ditch and ducked her head. She was panting hard and tears of fear and humiliation trickled down her pale cheeks. She just couldn't bear the idea of anyone seeing her like this.

Oh God! If only she had never got involved with the Trojans, or their sleazy manager. She didn't want anything more to do with any of them. From now on, she would forget all about ice hockey and just get on with her own life. Roland could do what he liked.

As soon as the car engine faded away, Maggie stood up and stared nervously at the phone box. It was so exposed, especially now that the daylight was fading and a light had come on inside. Still, what other choice did she have? Glancing all around her, she dashed for the phone box, picked up the receiver and dialled the operator.

While she waited for the operator to call Jan's number, Maggie huddled herself up as small as possible, tugging the tatters of her skirt around her and putting her arm protectively over her breasts. She continually scanned as far as she could see, and her ears strained for the slightest sound. She would just die if anyone found her in this state. As soon as she heard the operator ask if Jan would accept the charges, she started sobbing down the phone, begging Jan to take it.

'Yes. I'll take the call.' Jan's calm, sensible voice was like a lifeline. 'Maggie? Is that you? What's wrong? Are you all right?'

'Jan, please help me.' Her voice was no more than a feeble squeak.

'Where are you? Are you OK?'

'I'm in the phone box by the fields on Market Road. I need you to come and get me. Please hurry.' Maggie's nerve broke. She slammed the receiver down and scurried out to the comparative safety of the ditch. She crouched down behind a bush and rubbed her arms with her hands to try and keep warm. She would be all right soon.

228

Jan arrived about ten minutes later. She parked her car by the phone box and opened the door to climb out. 'Maggie? It's me. Jan. Where are you?'

Maggie started to sob with relief when she saw her friend. She stood up and scrambled up out of the ditch.

'Oh my God, Maggie. What's happened?' Jan took her coat off and wrapped it around Maggie's quivering shoulders. She helped Maggie over and into the car, then ran round to the driver's side. She started the engine and turned the heater up full.

'It won't take long to warm up,' she promised reassuringly, as she put the car into gear and headed for home.

Maggie huddled down in the seat. Now that she was safe, her last resolve disappeared and she could only sob helplessly as she tugged the coat around her nakedness. Thankfully, Jan didn't push her to tell her what had happened. She couldn't find the words to explain anything just yet.

By the time they arrived at Jan's house, Maggie had almost managed to stop crying. Jan helped her inside and steered her in front of the gas fire in the living room. Tiny sobs still wracked her body as she crouched in front of the welcoming warmth. Jan's coat slipped from her shoulders and fell to the floor.

'Here. Drink this.' Jan thrust a large glass of brandy in to her hands. Shakily, Maggie raised it to her lips and gulped the fiery liquid down. She gasped and started to cough, then drained the remaining drops. For the first time, she noticed that Jan was dressed only in a skimpy slip.

Jan followed her gaze. 'I was about to take a bath when you called,' she explained. 'I just grabbed my coat and keys and came running.' Her eyes anxiously scanned Maggie's semi-naked body.

'Are you hurt, Maggie? You have to tell me what's happened. Have you been raped? Do you want me to call the police or send for a doctor?'

Maggie shook her head, feeling stronger as the heat of the fire and the warmth of the brandy took effect. She was safe now. She sank down on to a nearby chair.

Jan knelt beside her and slipped her arm around Maggie's shoulders. 'Do you feel like telling me what happened?'

Maggie shuddered as she remembered lying in the boot of the car, wondering if they were going to kill her. Another small sob fell from her lips.

'OK. Never mind. Let's at least get you cleaned up.' Jan took Maggie's hand and led her unresisting upstairs to the bathroom. Passively, Maggie allowed Jan to peel her stockings and the remaining threads of her skirt from her trembling body. Jan topped up the now cooling bath water and motioned for Maggie to climb in. Gently, she soaped and rinsed her friend all over, before helping her out and drying her with a large fluffy towel. The remaining chill gradually left Maggie's body, and she was able to raise a feeble smile as Jan helped her into a warm dressing gown. The two women went back downstairs in front of the fire and Jan poured them both another brandy. She gave Maggie another small hug.

'Now can you tell me what happened?'

Maggie stared at her in silence for a few seconds, then looked round the room. 'Where's Marcus?' she whispered.

'Don't worry. He's not here. He won't be back until tomorrow at the earliest. It's just us two girls.' Jan pulled Maggie's head down on to her breasts and gently stroked her tousled hair. 'It's OK. You're safe now.'

At last, Maggie started to speak. As the words gradually tumbled out of her, the tears began to trickle down her cheeks.

Jan listened in silence until Maggie had finished speaking.

'You're certain it was Roland who arranged it?'

Maggie shrugged. 'Yes. I'm quite sure. But I can't prove it.'

Jan frowned. 'You're not going to let him get away with it are you?'

Maggie stared at her in surprise. 'Well, what do you expect me to do?'

Jan shook her head. 'I don't know yet, but if that bastard thinks he can do this to my best friend and get away with it, he's in for a nasty shock.'

Maggie had never heard Jan sound so angry or so determined. It made her feel strong and safe. 'I guess you're right. I don't see what I can do, though.' Another little tremor shook her body.

Jan stared at her. 'This can wait for now. You look completely done in. You'd better stay here tonight. I know it's a bit early, but you've had a bad scare and you could do with some sleep.'

'I don't want to be alone, Jan.'

'You'll be fine. I'll set the alarm and double check all the locks. Besides, I could do with an early night myself.'

Upstairs, Maggie quickly donned one of Jan's nighties and then snuggled down gratefully in Jan's big double bed. Jan stripped off and climbed in beside her. She pulled her close and Maggie snuggled up against the warmth and comfort of her friend's body. She could feel Jan's arm around her waist and her hand resting just under her breasts.

Maggie closed her eyes and tried not to think about what had happened, but it was impossible. At least she had not been the complete victim. Nevertheless, the whole ordeal was unforgivable. How dare Roland arrange to have her treated like that! Christ Almighty! She had been abducted, manhandled, threatened at knifepoint and dumped in a ditch. She might have been seriously hurt, even killed. How could she even think about letting him get away with it? Jan was right. Roland

231

had to be taught a lesson. What was it that he was so scared of her finding out, anyway?

Of course, it was easy to think like this now that she was lying safe and warm in Jan's arms. Maggie relaxed her body, pulling Jan's arm tighter around her. As she drifted towards sleep, she realised that Jan's hand was now covering her breast. She remembered the feel of Jan's hands soaping her body. She could feel her fingers gently teasing her nipple. Her touch felt very good. Warm and comforting.

Chapter Eleven

M aggie opened her eyes and gazed around in confusion, trying to remember where she was. As the events of the previous evening flooded back, she felt another rush of fear for what might have happened. A small whimper fell from her lips.

'Maggie? What is it? Are you all right?'

She turned her head and found herself staring into Jan's concerned eyes. She forced a feeble smile. 'Hello. Yes, I'm all right.'

Jan sat up and wiped the sleep from the corners of her eyes. She yawned widely and glanced around her. 'What time is it? Did you sleep OK?'

Maggie nodded. 'Yes, thanks. I must have gone out like a light. Brandy always has that effect on me.' She hesitated, uncertain what else to say. Her thoughts were so jumbled and confused. Her last memory was of her own hand on Jan's breast and of feeling safe and protected. She remembered thinking that touching Jan that way seemed right and natural, something she had wanted to do for a long time. Had Jan noticed or realised what she was thinking? She felt a faint flush of colour to her cheeks.

'It's only seven-thirty.' Jan had finally found her glasses and was peering through them at the bedside clock. 'There's no need for us to get up just yet. Do you fancy a cuppa?'

Maggie nodded. 'Yes please. I'd love one.' She watched without further comment as Jan climbed out of the bed and walked across the room to pick up her dressing gown. Her short nightie had ridden up over her thighs, exposing the swell of her buttocks, and Maggie found herself wondering what it would be like to run her fingers over all that soft, smooth flesh. She felt a tingle of excitement in her loins that both embarrassed and excited her.

Jan slipped her gown round her shoulders and padded silently out of the room to make the tea. Maggie pulled the duvet back and scurried across the room towards the bathroom. She rinsed her face and used her finger to brush round her teeth before gargling with mouthwash to freshen her breath. Her hair was still tangled and she ran a comb through it, surprised and pleased at how well she looked and felt, considering what she had been through. She must have slept like a top. She took a quick pee and was surprised to find that relieving the pressure on her bladder did little to ease the insistent tingling between her thighs. Hearing Jan's footsteps returning up the stairs, she dashed back into the bedroom and propped herself up in bed with a pillow.

Jan came back into the room, carrying a tray. 'Tea and toast in bed,' she announced with a smile. Maggie grinned.

'I feel like royalty,' she laughed. 'I can't remember the last time I had breakfast in bed. Probably not since I left home.'

Jan placed the tray over Maggie's knees, then pulled her dressing gown off and moved round to slip under the duvet beside her.

'No more than you deserve after what you've been though,' she commented.

Maggie grimaced, then forced another smile. 'Oh, it wasn't all that bad,' she protested, trying not to remember how terrified she had felt when she had been trussed up in the boot of the car. 'You should see the other guys,' she laughed flippantly.

Jan gave her a hard stare, then reached for the tray. She lifted it up on to the bedside table, then turned back and slipped her arm round her friend's shoulders. 'Poor love. You've had a pretty bad time of it lately, one way and the other, haven't you,' she murmured softly, as she pulled Maggie into her comforting embrace.

Maggie gulped back the ready tears and snuggled gratefully against her friend, so that her head was resting on Jan's soft breasts. She closed her eyes and tried to relax. Jan's hair brushed against her face; it felt soft and gentle and smelt fresh and clean, like a summer's day. Maggie felt a little tremor of excitement run down her spine. Tentatively, she lifted her hand and brushed her fingertips lightly over Jan's breast.

Jan flinched but didn't pull away. Maggie peered anxiously up into her friend's face. 'You, you don't mind, do you?' she whispered huskily.

Jan shook her head. 'No, I don't mind at all,' she responded softly.

Maggie smiled. 'You've got lovely breasts,' she murmured as her hand resumed its slow exploration of Jan's body. 'I want to . . .'

'Yes? Want to what?' Jan asked.

'I want to run my tongue over them,' Maggie admitted.

Jan wriggled out from under her and drew back the duvet. Slowly, she raised her arms and tugged her nightie off over her head. Her naked breasts fell free in front of her, bouncing delightfully. Maggie sighed with pleasure and bent her head forward. Slowly, she ran the tip of her tongue down Jan's shoulder and on to her left breast. As her lips gently caressed the nipple, she felt it harden in response and heard Jan's quiet sigh. Her stomach flipped and her own nipples began to stiffen.

'Oh yes,' Jan breathed. 'That feels so good.' She arched her back, pushing her breast up harder on to Maggie's lips. Maggie sucked the rigid nipple into her mouth and circled it with her tongue. Jan sighed again and Maggie felt another powerful surge of lust between her thighs. Impatiently, she sat up and pulled her own nightie over her head. Her own breasts were already aching with her passion and her nipples were hard, dark buds. She gasped with delight as she felt Jan's silky smooth tongue exploring them. Her thighs dampened and her clit started to tingle.

'Pinch me, somebody. I must be dreaming. Unless I've died and gone to heaven?' Marcus was standing beside the door, watching them. Maggie gasped with shock and horror. Quickly, she pulled back from Jan's caress and tugged the duvet up over her nakedness.

'Marcus?' Jan looked distinctly surprised and uncomfortable. 'I wasn't expecting you back until later.'

'So I see.' Marcus took a step into the room and Maggie could see the lust blazing in his eyes. She tried to imagine what it must be like for him to creep up into his bedroom, expecting to find Jan asleep, and catching her and her girlfriend. Despite her embarrassment, Maggie couldn't help but see the funny side of it. She could also imagine the affect it would be having on him. She was now well aware of how men fantasised about this sort of thing. This thought made her feel even more horny. Marcus or no Marcus, she wanted Jan more than ever.

Marcus took a few more steps, so that he was standing at the foot of the bed and Maggie no longer had to imagine his reaction. She could see the outline of his cock, already hard and rigid beneath his trousers. Another ripple of longing raced through her.

236

'Maggie's had a bit of a shock,' Jan explained. 'I was just comforting her . . .'

'I could see what you were doing,' Marcus interrupted her. His voice sounded strange. Hard and tight. A bit like his trousers, Maggie giggled to herself.

'Don't stop on my account,' he continued. 'Just pretend that I'm not here.' As he spoke, he pushed his hand down the waistband of his trousers to adjust himself and Maggie shivered again, both at the sight of his obvious arousal and at the implication of his words.

She was already nervous enough about what she and Jan had been doing. How could she possibly carry on now, with him watching? On the other hand, how could she possibly stop? She was feeling more and more aroused by the second. Her body was burning to feel Jan caress her again and, if she was perfectly honest, the sight of him so obviously turned on by watching them was only adding to her passion. It was just what she had been secretly fantasising about for some time. Maybe not with Marcus, but the result was the same.

Jan sat up and pulled the duvet around her. 'Do you want some breakfast?' she questioned him brightly, just as if there was nothing unusual about the situation.

Marcus shook his head. 'I'm not hungry.' He licked his lips. 'At least, not for food.' He moved round beside Jan and pulled the cover back down, exposing her. As she went to get up, he pushed her back on to the bed and pulled the cover off Maggie as well. Both girls watched his face silently.

Marcus placed his hand over Jan's left breast and pinched her rigid nipple between his fingers. Jan groaned and her body writhed with pleasure. Marcus pushed her towards Maggie. 'Suck her nipples,' he ordered hoarsely.

Jan shook her head but did as she was told, and Maggie felt another rush of dampness between her tightly clenched thighs. She stared up at Marcus, watching him watching them. He leaned over her, his face flushed with desire.

'Now you, Maggie. Suck her tits,' he commanded.

Quite unable to stop herself, Maggie lifted her head and sucked Jan's right nipple into her mouth. Jan moaned, arching her back so that the duvet slipped right down off her, revealing the damp, blonde curls of her pubes. She reached out and gently caressed one of Maggie's tingling nipples.

'Oh yes!' Maggie shuddered from head to toe and sucked harder on Jan's breast, using her tongue to make small, circular movements around the puckered nipple. She heard Marcus groan and, out the corner of her eye, saw him struggling with the zip of his straining trousers. Was he going to climb in bed with them? Maggie had never really thought about sex with him. He was certainly attractive enough, but she had secretly always thought him a bit of a wimp. Besides, he was Jan's lover and nothing but trouble ever came of playing around with your best friend's man.

Jan pushed them both away and sat back up. Her face was flushed and her eyes were sparkling with desire. 'One thing at a time, I think,' she whispered. She turned towards Maggie and winked mischievously. 'Since Marcus wasn't actually invited, I think he should sit back and wait his turn, don't you?'

Maggie stared at her friend in surprise. She had always thought that she was the more adventurous of the two where sex was concerned. Look at what she had got up to with the Trojans! Mind you, she didn't know for sure what Jan had done with them, did she? She was bloody certain something had happened between her and Tor, at least.

'What do you mean?' she muttered, doing her best to ignore the way Marcus was devouring her body with his eyes. Didn't Jan mind? Did she mind?

'I'll show you.' Jan climbed off the bed and took hold

238

of Marcus' arm. She led him unresisting across the room to a wooden chair and pushed him down on to it. 'I think you should be able to see everything from here,' she told him as she tugged the cord out of her dressing gown and calmly tied his hands to the back supports.

Maggie stared at them both in silence, realising for the first time the hidden advantages of Marcus' passive nature. Had Jan done this sort of thing with him before? She felt a slight twinge of jealousy at the idea of her not being the first.

Jan stood naked in front of the bound-up Marcus, with her hands on her hips. 'Hmm. Not quite right. You must be uncomfortable with so many clothes on.' She bent down and finished undoing his trousers. 'Lift up.' As she whipped both trousers and pants down his legs, his swollen cock sprang out in front of him, hard and desperate. Jan took no notice of it at all, while Maggie stared at it in astonishment.

After tugging his clothing free from his ankles, Jan moved across the room and removed the cord from his dressing gown, which was hanging behind the door. Without another word, she secured his ankles and then climbed back on to the bed beside Maggie.

Maggie stared at her shyly, her mouth gaping. Jan grinned. 'I often tie Marcus up like that while I pleasure myself for him,' she confessed softly. 'I like the idea of knowing that he can look but not touch. Not just me, but himself too. Don't worry. He likes it too.'

Another ripple of lust crawled down Maggie's spine at the implication of Jan's words. No matter how excited Marcus became, there was nothing he could do about it, until Jan allowed it. The concept appealed to Maggie enormously. She would have to try it with Justin. Her good mood evaporated as she remembered that it was all over between her and Justin.

'Now, where were we?' Jan edged closer to her and put her hand back on Maggie's breast.

Maggie shook her head. 'I don't know, Jan. I'm not sure . . .' Despite her change of mood, Maggie could still feel the little shivers of desire rushing through her body. Jan's fingers were so soft and so knowing. She moaned softly as she felt Jan's other hand creeping down her stomach towards her mound.

'You don't really want me to stop now, do you?' Jan whispered. Her hand reached between Maggie's legs and her fingertip unerringly sought for and found her hardened clit. She caressed it softly and Maggie moaned again, closing her eyes as she gave herself up to the exquisite little tremors of arousal coursing through her. Dumbly, she shook her head again.

Jan increased the pressure of her caress, rubbing Maggie's bud in a way no one had ever rubbed it before, except Maggie herself. However, she couldn't believe how much better it felt than when she pleasured herself. It was incredible. Already, she could feel the tingle of her mounting orgasm building deep inside her. She writhed her hips from side to side, moaning with delight.

Marcus groaned. 'Jesus!' he spluttered. His voice was a high-pitched squeak. 'Jan. Please untie me. I can't take this.'

Maggie opened her eyes and turned her head towards him. Marcus was leaning as far forward on the chair as his bindings would allow. His face was bright red and contorted with his lust. She lowered her gaze and feasted her eyes on the sight of his rampant cock, engorged with his need and twitching hungrily as he gazed pleadingly at the two women.

Jan peered round at him and smiled teasingly. 'Of course you can,' she contradicted him, clearly revelling in her position of power over both of them. 'If it gets too much, just close your eyes and think about something else.'

'I can't. Shit. I mean it, Jan.' Marcus strained harder against his bindings, causing the chair to rock forward on to its front legs, so that Maggie was afraid that he was about to tumble on his face. He had clamped his thighs together as tightly as possible and was wriggling his hips erratically in a desperate effort to rub his tortured cock. 'I have to . . . I want to . . . Oh God!'

Jan smiled and turned back to Maggie. Slowly and deliberately, she ran her tongue down Maggie's stomach and over her shaved mound. Maggie sank back on to the mattress and gritted her teeth. Jesus Christ! It felt so good. Jan's tongue was as soft and light as a feather and she seemed to know exactly where and how to touch for maximum effect. Maggie's clit was on fire and her orgasm inevitable. She could feel it welling up inside her dripping cunt, building like a thunderstorm. Any second now, it was going to burst and engulf her whole body; she could already feel the scream of ecstasy in the back of her throat as her chest heaved with her pent-up emotion and longing.

Jan lifted her head away from Maggie's cunt and put her hand between her own legs. Maggie groaned with frustration as her climax was halted right on the brink of engulfing her. It didn't seem possible to be so close to release and yet not to come. Every nerve in her body seemed to be on edge. One more caress was all it would take; just one more touch and she would be there. Her longing overwhelmed her and she rolled her hips from side to side again, savouring the exquisite torture of her desperate need.

'Please, Jan,' she sobbed. 'Please don't stop.' Already, she could feel the immediate urgency receding, although the need burned stronger than ever, so that her passion was consuming her.

Jan reached out and took Maggie's hand. Firmly, she placed it over her own mound, lifting her buttocks so that she could rub herself against Maggie's pliant fingers. Maggie could feel the warm dampness of Jan's juices trickling out on to her skin, and another surge of lust

241

shook her body. Slowly, she moved her hand down between Jan's silky lips and pushed her middle finger up deep inside her friend's welcoming dampness.

Jan clenched her buttocks and thrust herself down hard on Maggie's hand; rolling her whole body from side to side as she savoured her pleasure.

'Oh God, Jan. You have to untie me,' Marcus begged again.

Maggie looked at him once more and almost gasped aloud at the look of sheer desperation on his face. His cock was jerking up and down as if on strings and his balls were so hard and swollen that they looked like they were going to burst. She could see the dampness of his lubrication glistening on the hot, purple tip of his shiny cock and, still burning with her own desperation, could imagine only too well how he was suffering.

'Don't stop,' Jan begged her, pushing herself even harder on to Maggie's fingers.

Maggie looked back down at her friend and smiled. Just one look at Jan's face was enough to tell her that she was almost there. Teasingly, Maggie withdrew her finger, trembling all over with her own passion as she watched Jan writhe and shudder with the intensity of her need.

Jan sat up and grinned shakily. She climbed off the bed, moved over to Marcus and knelt down in front of him. Raising her arms, she cupped one hand round the base of his trembling penis and began to slide it up and over the swollen head. As she began to glide it back down the other side, she used her other hand to follow her first, so that she was effectively stimulating him with one long continuous stroke; over and over, without ceasing.

Marcus moaned, his whole body shaking. Maggie stared at them both in fascination, shivering with her own desire. Marcus seemed to be deliberately clenching himself, as if he could physically stem his approaching eruption with his pelvic muscles. Jan grinned at him and started to slap his engorged cock lightly back and forth with the palm of one hand. Maggie could have sworn that it was growing even harder and darker with every tap. Marcus groaned again.

'Naughty boy,' Jan chided. 'I should give you a really good spanking for watching us like this.'

'Please, Jan. Untie me.' Marcus pleaded again.

Jan gave his cock another light tap and sat back on her heels. She shook her head. 'Not yet, my lover,' she murmured. 'Not yet.' She stood up, walked back across the room and climbed onto the bed, positioning herself so that she could place her tongue back between Maggie's still trembling thighs, while Maggie could now do the same for her. As the two women lowered their heads eagerly over each other's sex lips, Maggie heard Marcus groan again, and the sound of the chair bouncing along the floor as he edged himself ever closer to the bed.

Maggie flinched as she felt Jan's tongue run over her aching bud and then slip up inside her welcoming cunt. Tingles of ecstasy ran up and down the backs of her legs, and her overdue climax rapidly began to build again. Whimpering with delight, she pushed her own tongue deep inside Jan's hot dampness and began to thrust it firmly in and out. There was a hard thump as Marcus' chair collided with the edge of the bed.

When she finally came, Maggie's orgasm was so intense that she could not even cry out. The spasms of pleasure enveloping her were so strong and so powerful that the top of her head felt as if it was coming off. Her whole body shook, and she was so overwhelmed with her own gratification that she only just registered the fact that Jan was crying out as she also came.

As the last little tremors of her climax died away, she lifted her head to look at Marcus. His face was swollen with his passion and she could see the sweat literally pouring off him. His cock was stuck up in the air in front of him like a mast.

'I think he enjoyed himself too, don't you?' Jan chuckled.

Maggie couldn't resist. She licked her finger and, leaning over, ran it down his erection towards his balls. Marcus groaned urgently and she pulled back with a surprised yelp as his seed began spurting helplessly from him to shower his chest and thighs.

Maggie could feel the satisfied grin on her face as she snuggled back down on the bed and savoured the warmth of Jan's body and the unmistakable scent of their combined enjoyment. It was a pity about the tea and toast though, she thought sleepily, they must be stone-cold by now!

In the end, Maggie stayed with Jan and Marcus until the end of the week. She used the time to work through her confused and conflicting emotions about what had happened to her. By the time she was ready to go home, the fear, anger and humiliation had been almost completely consumed by her appetite for revenge. Before, she had only been partly serious about catching Roland out, now she was deadly earnest.

It was an interesting time in many ways. By the end of it Maggie no longer had any lingering questions about what it would be like to make love with another woman. No questions, only lots of happy memories and a much closer relationship with Jan than ever before.

Her opinions about Marcus had changed too. He really was a very sweet and delightful man. Jan was lucky to have him. Maggie felt slightly guilty at how she had treated him during her stay. Not that he appeared to mind. On the contrary, he seemed to enjoy her abuse almost as much as she had enjoyed abusing him. Still, she had never used anyone for her own gratification like that before. She had teased him unmercifully and it was almost as if every act of humiliation she had made him suffer had served to make her stronger and more determined to seek her revenge on Roland.

As she had hoped, Jan was not lacking in ideas for exposing Roland. Three days after Maggie had been attacked, the two of them had just about completed their overall strategy. All that remained now was to take care of a few details. It was time for them to have a little chat with Sara and Claire. If the plan were going to have any real chance of success then Sara's co-operation would be vital.

Chapter Twelve

'Maggie?' Sara's whisper was barely audible. 'Are you there?'

'Finally!' Maggie stepped out from behind some bushes and brushed a couple of twigs from her dress. The mild spring weather had taken a recent turn for the worse and her teeth were almost chattering. 'About time too. I thought you had forgotten all about me. It's freezing out here.'

'Shush!' Sara put her fingers to her lips. 'Sorry. I had to wait until everyone had arrived and been served with drinks.'

The thought of all her friends supping drinks in the warm with the Trojans, while she shivered outside in the undergrowth like an outcast, did little to improve Maggie's temper. 'I'm surprised you didn't wait until you'd all had something to eat and watched a movie as well,' she snapped sarcastically. She stepped up to the French windows and peered in at Sara, who was wringing her hands together and shooting nervous glances over her shoulder. Don't say she was going to lose her nerve now.

'Where's the Rat?'

Sara's lips twitched. 'Jan's just about to take him off somewhere for a little chat.'

Maggie grinned. Good old Jan! Knowing her friend, Roland should be well out of the way for the time being. 'OK, then.' She stepped into the room. 'Lead the way. Let's have a good look at those accounts of his, and find out what dirty little secrets he keeps in his safe.'

Jan moved across the room and touched Roland's shoulder. She stood on tiptoe so that she could whisper in his ear. 'Have you got a few minutes? I've got something I'd like to discuss with you.'

Roland grinned lecherously at her and gave her bum a familiar pat that made her clench her teeth to hide the anger. 'Of course, my dear,' he answered. 'I can always find time for a pretty lady. Why don't we adjoin to the library? We can be quite alone there.'

'Um, no. Not the library,' Jan replied. She thought quickly. 'I hear you've got a tank of tropical fish somewhere. Do you think I could see them? I love fish.'

'Why not?' He tucked her arm in his and led her down the passageway towards the far end of his luxurious house and into his immaculate drawing room. He turned the wall lights down low and guided her over to the wide, comfy couch, which rested in front of a blazing fire.

'Would you like a drink?' He indicated a well-appointed bar in one corner of the room.

'Please. A gin and tonic if you have one. Ice and lemon.' Jan ignored the couch and moved over to stand in front of the large fish tank set into the far wall. She peered curiously into its murky depths. 'They're lovely. Somehow, I didn't really picture you as an animal-lover.'

'I'd hardly call fish animals,' Roland laughed. 'Actually, I find them very soothing. The fish, I mean.' He walked across and stood beside her. 'Here's your drink.'

247

He nodded at the tank as he handed her a glass. 'It's a wonderful way to unwind, just watching them.'

Jan took the glass from his outstretched hand. 'Thank you.' She deliberately allowed her fingers to brush lightly over his knuckles and pretended not to notice the way his eyes lit up. 'You really do have a beautiful home, Roland.' She let her eyes wander around the room. 'I had no idea ice hockey managers were paid so well.'

He took her hand and led her back over to the couch. He sat down beside her so that his thigh was touching hers. Jan smiled coyly over the top of her glass, then licked her lips seductively. 'Cheers.' She sank back on to the soft cushions and smiled contentedly.

'You said that you had something you wanted to discuss with me?' he remarked, and took a long gulp of his own drink before leaning back on the couch with his arm behind her. Jan grinned to herself as she felt the pressure of his thigh against hers increasing. She knew he wanted her, but suspected there might be something he wanted even more.

'Yes.' She smiled encouragingly. 'I've recently come into some money,' she told him. 'An inheritance from a maiden aunt. I'm looking for the best way to invest it.' It sounded a little corny but he didn't seem to notice. Besides, there was nothing like a bit of flattery to get to his ego. 'The lads all said you were the one to talk you.'

Roland dropped his arm so that it was resting lightly across her shoulders. His fingers started toying with her hair. 'I see. Just how much money are we talking about here?'

'A lot.' She forced herself to let her body relax against his.

He took another swig of his Scotch and stared down at his almost-empty glass. His face was slightly flushed and Jan could smell his perspiration. She glanced at the carriage clock on the mantelpiece and estimated that she needed to keep him occupied for at least another fifteen minutes.

He dropped his hand over her shoulder so that his fingers were resting on the top of her breast. Jan glanced down at his groin and saw that his flies were already straining. Two over-excited pricks together, she thought to herself. How delicious. She rested her hand casually on his thigh and suppressed a grin at the way his muscles immediately twitched.

'What type of investment did you have in mind?' he questioned. 'Long-term secure or short-term high risk, high return?'

'No risk. Just a sure, steady return.' She paused, then played her ace. 'Actually, I think I could be interested in investing in the Trojans,' she told him coyly. 'If the incentives were right.'

Roland's eyes sparkled greedily. 'Incentives?' he questioned carefully.

She nodded. 'I'd have to have a vested interest, wouldn't I? Something too irresistible to ignore.'

Roland grinned hungrily and leaned forward to place his lips over hers. Jan returned his kiss with as much pretence of passion as she could muster. She wondered how Maggie and Sara were doing. Maybe just another ten minutes would be enough.

'I think I can provide that,' Roland muttered as he increased the pressure of his fingers on her breast.

'Why don't you unzip yourself and show me just what you have to offer?' Jan whispered huskily. She had a feeling that it would not take much to satisfy him. Most probably just a few words and suggestions would do it. She set herself the challenge. Could she make him come without so much as touching him, before Maggie and Sara got through? It was an interesting concept. She could feel her thighs and buttocks tingling with anticipation.

* * *

When Maggie and Sara finally walked into the living room, Maggie couldn't hide the smug satisfaction on her face. The evidence against Roland was overwhelming and spoke for itself. Once the Trojans saw it and heard what she had to say, they could be in no possible doubt that their manager was fleecing them. She had even found two entries for payments she was certain he had made to have her taken care of. One was shortly before her ordeal, the other the day afterwards. She would never be able to prove that part of it, of course.

Claire rushed over to them excitedly. 'What took you so long?' she hissed. 'I was getting frantic.'

'Where's Roland?' Maggie questioned breathlessly.

'Over there. He and Jan reappeared a couple of minutes ago. He doesn't look very happy,' Claire giggled. 'I don't think Jan's proposition agreed with him.' She glanced anxiously at Maggie. 'Well? Did you find anything?'

'You could say that,' Maggie nodded. She turned her head as she saw Justin moving towards her with a questioning look on his face. Her temper flared at the memory of how he had treated her. After what she had been through, she was definitely going to enjoy the rest of this evening.

'Maggie! What on earth are you doing here?'

Ignoring Justin completely, Maggie stepped into the middle of the room and cleared her throat. She turned to face Roland and held up his personal account book that she had been concealing behind her back. Roland was staring at her in astonishment. When he saw what she was holding, his eyes bulged and his face drained of colour.

'Where the hell did you get that?' Roland made a lunge for the book, but Maggie side-stepped him easily. 'Give it here. I should have thought that you would have learned your lesson . . .'

'What? From your thugs?' Maggie smiled sweetly.

'Didn't they tell you? They had a bit of a change of heart when they realised that they were on the wrong side. In fact, you could say that we became quite friendly . . .'

'Would somebody mind telling us what the hell is going on here?' Tor was staring in bewilderment from Maggie to the enraged Roland.

'I'm sure Roland will be only too happy to explain,' Maggie replied. 'You do have an explanation for why you keep a second set of accounts, don't you, Roland? And, I'm sure there's a perfectly good reason why a large percentage of the squad's sponsorship money never gets any further than your own pocket. On the other hand, I know that you were prepared to go to great lengths to keep it quiet. Your pet gorillas proved that.'

'I don't have the faintest idea what you're talking about,' Roland mouthed through gritted teeth. 'You're not making any sense, whatsoever.' He glared angrily at Sara. 'What's this silly bitch doing in my house?' he demanded.

Maggie threw the account book to Tor. 'Go on. See for yourself.'

Tor flicked the book open and stared at the figures in silence. His face hardened as he quickly checked a few entries against dates and the implications of what Maggie was saying began to sink in. He swung round and stared questioningly at their manager. 'Well?'

Roland shrugged.

'There do seem to be rather a lot of deposits,' Tor continued softly.

'I don't think this is the time, or the place,' Roland muttered. 'I don't know what she's talking about, but I promise you that there's a perfectly logical explanation for everything. There are no irregularities. You know I do a lot of investment.'

'Yeah, but all I can see are deposits,' Tor persisted. 'All one way. Your way.'

'Never mind that. What's all this talk about thugs?' Troy demanded as he stared curiously at Maggie.

'When Roland realised that Maggie was growing suspicious, he sent a couple of bruisers round to teach her a lesson,' Jan responded angrily. 'They stripped her, knocked her about, threatened to rape her and damnnear half-killed her.'

Troy swung round on Roland. 'Is that true?' His voice was as cold as an icicle and the side of his mouth twitched dangerously. His hands closed into tight fists as he struggled to control his fury. He took a few menacing steps towards the now frightened-looking manager.

Roland shook his head frantically. 'No. The woman is clearly deranged,' he stuttered. 'I have no idea what she's on about.'

Tor moved himself deliberately between Roland and Troy. 'I think you're right, Roland. This isn't the place to discuss it. I suggest we arrange a meeting with the chairman as soon as possible. The sooner the better. You can explain everything to him.' He turned to Maggie.

'If even part of what you've suggested is true, I expect we all owe you an apology. I suppose Roland was responsible for having you sacked from the rink, too. I never did believe you were a thief.'

'I never believed that Maggie was guilty either,' Justin interrupted quickly. 'I told you that, didn't I, Maggie? I just didn't have any choice in the matter.'

'Just a minute. You can't be seriously intending to take this crazy woman's word over mine,' Roland blustered. 'Not after everything I've done for you. I made you. You owe me.' He made another grab for the account book.

Tor held it easily out of his reach. 'From the look of it, you've been collecting for months. You could say that you owe us. Do you want us to collect?' He raised an eyebrow. One or two of the other Trojans took a couple of steps towards him.

'You'll be sorry. You won't get away with this. You'll never play again. Any of you. I've, I've got friends.'

'Not here you haven't,' Tor assured him.

Roland glared furiously at Maggie. 'It's a pity they didn't really take care of you, you interfering little bitch,' he hissed under his breath.

'Why, you sodding bastard!' Troy side-stepped Tor before anyone could react. With an angry snarl, he hit Roland full in the gut. Roland squealed pitifully and doubled over, gasping for breath.

Tor quickly grabbed Troy, pulling him away. 'Let it go, Troy. Half killing him won't help.'

Troy struggled furiously. 'I'll tear his fucking head off,' he yelled.

Maggie reached for his arm. 'Troy. It's OK. I've got my revenge. I just wanted to clear my name. There's no need for any more violence.'

An uncomfortable silence fell over them all. Jan looked at Maggie and winked, and Maggie smiled weakly. Her whole body was trembling so much that she could practically feel her knees knocking together, and her stomach was churning queasily. She looked up at Troy's angry face. 'Come on, let's go out and get some fresh air,' she suggested gently.

Maggie led Troy along the hallway, through the kitchen, and out of the back door on to a wide patio. It was a cloudy night with a distinct chill in the air and Troy pulled her closer as he felt her shivering.

'Looks like some kind of seat over there.' He guided her down some wide steps on to a velvet-smooth lawn. As they sat down side by side on a comfy garden hammock, Troy took her icy hands in his.

'I can't believe that bastard,' he muttered. 'Look. I'm really sorry I didn't believe you before. I just thought you were upset. I should have listened to you. I'm sorry.'

Maggie was surprised at the genuine anguish in his

voice. She shuddered as she remembered the terror she had endured in the boot of the car. 'It's OK,' she told him, 'there was no real harm done and it's all over now. I've got my name back.'

'You should have let me shove his teeth down his throat,' Troy ranted.

Maggie smiled. She leaned across and kissed his cheek. 'What, and risk hurting yourself before the big game? Besides, it doesn't matter now. The important thing is that he's been caught out.'

'What made you suspect he was conning us, anyway? And, how did he realise that you were on to him?' Troy shook his head. 'I can't believe all this was going on and we never noticed a thing. If only I had listened to you before. How did you know?'

Maggie laughed. 'I don't know. I just knew. Let's just call it women's intuition, shall we?'

Troy pulled her into his arms and put his lips on hers. A surge of lust raced down her spine as she felt his soft tongue slipping into her mouth. She put her hands behind his head and buried them in his short wiry hair.

Without breaking the kiss, Troy reached up and started to lower the zip on the front of her dress. He pushed his hands inside and cupped her left breast. Maggie moaned with pleasure as her nipples started to pucker. Her thighs began to prickle with anticipation.

Troy groaned and started to tug his own zip open. He took one of her hands and pushed her willing fingers inside his fly. He wasn't wearing any underpants and his cock was already hot and hard. Maggie wrapped her fingers round it and squeezed gently. Her clit burned as she felt him trembling to her touch.

'Jesus. I have to have you. Now,' he mumbled desperately.

'Aren't you supposed to be in training, or something?' Maggie teased.

'I don't need any training for what I'm going to do to

254

you,' Troy assured her softly, and Maggie shivered as she felt him lift her up and swing her round so that she was standing in front of him. Urgently, he tugged her dress down her arms. Before it had even dropped to the ground, he was already stripping her panties down over her thighs. Maggie whimpered as she felt his tongue probing her damp pussy. Automatically, she spread her legs, falling forward over him so that her breasts were pressed flat against the top of his head.

Troy moaned again and raised his buttocks off the seat so that she could peel his trousers down his hips. His dark skin glistened and his already damp-tipped cock seemed to be steaming in the cold night air. He grasped her hips and lifted her up into his arms. In one smooth, fluid motion, he lowered her down over him so that she was perched astride his lap and Maggie felt his rigid shaft beginning to penetrate her. She put her hands on his shoulders and ground her pelvis on to him, pushing his cock up even harder and deeper into her.

Still holding her around the waist, Troy started to thrust his buttocks up and down, raising and lowering her body as his cock pumped in and out of her. His tongue caressed her nipples and his fingers dug into her skin.

Maggie threw her head back and thrust her breasts harder on to his lips as she used her inner muscles to tease and caress his hard wet cock. She could already feel her climax building and sending little ripples of fire right through her.

'I'm going to fuck you until you can't stand up,' Troy threatened her hoarsely. Maggie shuddered at the note of longing in his voice, and increased the pressure of her muscles around him. Troy laughed and his hot breath steamed in the icy chill. 'You'll have to do a lot better than that, baby,' he told her breathlessly. 'Not that it will do you any good. You can't possibly win. I'm going to make you come at least three times before you get the better of me.'

Just the threat was enough. With a sharp cry, Maggie felt her clit spasm as her first orgasm enveloped her. She cried out again, shuddering all over as the little tremors of her pleasure shook her whole body. Troy laughed again.

'One,' he taunted her, as his cock thrust even harder and deeper into her pliant dampness. 'Two more to go. I hope you're feeling strong.' He sucked her right nipple back into his mouth and nibbled it softly.

Maggie drew a deep breath and tightened her grip around his muscular thighs. She rolled her hips, grinding herself on to his shaft and willing him to lose control. Troy chuckled knowingly and pumped himself even harder into her.

'Oh Christ. That feels so good,' she simpered. 'I love to feel your hard hot cock shoved right up inside my cunt like that.'

'Nice try, Maggie. Talk as dirty as you like. It won't work.' Troy lifted her up into the air so that his cock sprang free. He twisted her round and pushed her down face forward over the seat. 'Let's see how it feels from this side,' he suggested as he stood up behind her and started to guide his cock between her thighs.

Maggie grunted and sprawled forward over the seat with her buttocks thrust up in the air. She whimpered as she felt his hardness gliding back up into her. Gradually, she felt him building up speed again until he was pumping rhythmically in and out. She reached round behind her and grabbed his buttocks, pulling him harder on to her so that she could feel his groin slapping against her thighs. She pushed one hand down underneath them and cradled his massive balls in her palm.

Troy groaned with delight and took her breasts between his fingers. As he started to tweak her aching nipples in time with his thrusting, his other hand homed in on her clit and she instantly knew that he was about to win again.

'Oh Christ!' she cried out as she felt another powerful climax engulf her. She tensed all her muscles and her whole body spasmed in response to her pleasure. She felt the sudden rush of moisture trickle down her thighs and she slumped forward on to the seat and took a long, shuddering breath. Troy's cock slipped out from her dripping cunt and rubbed itself teasingly all over her tingling buttocks.

'Two,' he counted triumphantly. 'Do you concede yet?'

Maggie shook her head wearily and pushed herself upright. She tugged him down on to the seat and pushed his legs apart. Crouching between his thighs, she took his cock in her fingers and ran her tongue softly down his length.

Troy groaned softly and closed his eyes. She saw him lift his buttocks up off the seat to push himself up towards her lips, and she smiled with satisfaction. Even he would not be able to withstand this. Maggie closed her lips around him and sucked him deeper into her mouth. With her eyes fixed on his face, she started to pump him in and out.

Troy's mouth tightened and she saw the beads of sweat breaking out on his brow as he struggled to keep control. His cock twitched urgently between her lips and she tasted the saltiness of his lubrication. Immediately, she pushed her hand under him, cupping his balls in her palm again. They were tight and swollen. It wouldn't be long now.

'Put your hand between your legs and play with yourself. I want to see you wanking.' His voice was nearly as tight as his balls. The words enflamed her. Without breaking the rhythm of her mouth, Maggie slipped her hand down her stomach and over her mound. Her clit was still swollen like a grape and so sensitive that she whimpered as her fingers caressed it.

257

Her sex lips were still engorged and damp from her previous orgasms. Slowly, she pushed her middle finger up inside her smooth, wet cunt and started to pump it back and forth.

Troy leaned forward so that he could watch what she was doing. His cock jerked inside her mouth and she felt his body stiffen, fighting her. She pumped harder, revelling in the double sensation of his cock twitching in her mouth and her own finger tormenting her cunt and bud. He was about to come. She knew that he just couldn't hold out any longer. She moaned urgently, then moaned again as yet another orgasm of her own took her by surprise.

'Three,' Troy muttered hoarsely. 'I warned you. Oh shit!' He thrust himself so deeply into her mouth that she could feel the tip of his cock in the back of her throat. 'Oh yeah.'

Maggie tasted the first powerful spurt of his climax. She swallowed hard and sucked him again as she felt another jet of spunk burst from him, then another. She kept sucking, pumping him in and out of her lips until he had nothing left to give.

'I win,' Troy told her softly as soon as he had recovered his breath. Maggie laughed.

'It's the final tomorrow night,' she reminded him. 'Will you win that, too?'

Troy gave her a fierce hug. 'Of course. With you back as our mascot, how could we possibly lose?'

'I don't think I shall go back to work at the rink, though,' Maggie told him, surprised to discover that her mind was made up. She thought about the little girl with the sprained ankle and remembered her words of encouragement to the youngster. 'I've got a chance to start over and I'm not going to waste it. It's too late for me to become a doctor now, but I think I might train as a nurse, or perhaps a physiotherapist.'

Troy kissed her on the nose. 'Any time you want to

play at doctors and nurses is fine with me, baby,' he teased.

Maggie noticed that it had started to snow. She smiled contentedly as she snuggled up against his smooth, broad chest and watched the soft flakes melting on his hot skin – ebony and ivory, fire and ice. Definitely a winning combination.

BLACK LACE NEW BOOKS

Published in September

DEVIL'S FIRE
Melissa MacNeal
£5.99

Destitute but beautiful Mary visits handsome but lecherous mortician Hyde Fortune, in the hope he can help her out of her impoverished predicament. It isn't long before they're consummating their lust for each other and involving Fortune's exotic housekeeper and his young assistant Sebastian. When Mary gets a live-in position at the local abbey, she becomes an active participant in the curious erotic rites practised by the not-so-very pious monks. This marvellously entertaining story is set in 19th century America.

ISBN 0 352 33527 0

THE NAKED FLAME
Crystalle Valentino
£5.99

Venetia Halliday's a go-getting girl who is determined her Camden Town restaurant is going to win the prestigious Blue Ribbon award. Her new chef is the cheeky over-confident East End wide boy Mickey Quinn, who knows just what it takes to break down her cool exterior. He's hot, he's horny, and he's got his eyes on the prize – in her bed and her restaurant. Will Venetia pull herself together, or will her 'bit of rough' ride roughshod over everything?

ISBN 0 352 33528 9

CRASH COURSE
Juliet Hastings
£5.99

Kate is a successful management consultant. When she's asked to run a training course at an exclusive hotel at short notice, she thinks the stress will be too much. But three of the participants are young, attractive, powerful men, and Kate cannot resist the temptation to get to know them sexually as well as professionally. Her problem is that one of the women on the course is feeling left out. Jealousy and passion simmer beneath the surface as Kate tries to get the best performance out of all her clients. *Crash Course* is a Black Lace special reprint.

ISBN 0 352 33018 X

Published in October

LURED BY LUST
Tania Picarda
£5.99

Clara Fox works at an exclusive art gallery. One day she gets an email from someone calling himself Mr X, and very soon she's exploring the dark side of her sexuality with this enigmatic stranger. The attraction of bondage, fetish clothes and SM is becoming stronger with each communication, and Clara is encouraged to act out adventurous sex games. But can she juggle her secret involvement with Mr X along with her other, increasingly intense, relationships?

ISBN 0 352 33533 5

ON THE EDGE
Laura Hamilton
£5.99

Julie Gibson lands a job as a crime reporter for a newspaper. The English seaside town to which she's been assigned has seen better days, but she finds plenty of action hanging out with the macho cops at the local police station. She starts dating a detective inspector, but cannot resist the rough charms of biker Johnny Drew when she's asked to investigate the murder of his friend. Trying to juggle hot sex action with two very different but dominant men means things get wild and dangerous.

ISBN 0 352 33534 3

To be published in November

LEARNING TO LOVE IT
Alison Tyler
£5.99

Art historian Lissa and doctor Colin meet at the Frankfurt Book Fair, where they are both promoting their latest books. At the fair, and then through Europe, the two lovers embark on an exploration of their sexual fantasies, playing dirty games of bondage and dressing up. Lissa loves humiliation, and Colin is just the man to provide her with the pleasure she craves. Unbeknown to Lissa, their meeting was not accidental, but planned ahead by a mysterious patron of the erotic arts.

ISBN 0 352 33535 1

THE HOTTEST PLACE
Tabitha Flyte
£5.99

Abigail is having a great time relaxing on a hot and steamy tropical island in Thailand. She tries to stay faithful to her boyfriend back in England, but it isn't easy when a variety of attractive, fun-loving young people want to get into her pants. When Abby's boyfriend, Roger, finds out what's going on, he's on the first plane over there, determined to dish out some punishment.

And that's when the fun really starts hotting up.

ISBN 0 352 33536 X

If you would like a complete list of plot summaries of Black Lace titles, or would like to receive information on other publications available, please send a stamped addressed envelope to:

Black Lace, Thames Wharf Studios,
Rainville Road, London W6 9HA

BLACK
lace

BLACK LACE BOOKLIST

Information is correct at time of printing. To check availability go to www.blacklace-books.co.uk

All books are priced £5.99 unless another price is given.

Black Lace books with a contemporary setting

THE NAME OF AN ANGEL £6.99	Laura Thornton ISBN 0 352 33205 0	☐
FEMININE WILES £7.99	Karina Moore ISBN 0 352 33235 2	☐
DARK OBSESSION £7.99	Fredrica Alleyn ISBN 0 352 33281 6	☐
THE TOP OF HER GAME	Emma Holly ISBN 0 352 33337 5	☐
LIKE MOTHER, LIKE DAUGHTER	Georgina Brown ISBN 0 352 33422 3	☐
THE TIES THAT BIND	Tesni Morgan ISBN 0 352 33438 X	☐
VELVET GLOVE	Emma Holly ISBN 0 352 33448 7	☐
DOCTOR'S ORDERS	Deanna Ashford ISBN 0 352 33453 3	☐
SHAMELESS	Stella Black ISBN 0 352 33485 1	☐
TONGUE IN CHEEK	Tabitha Flyte ISBN 0 352 33484 3	☐
FIRE AND ICE	Laura Hamilton ISBN 0 352 33486 X	☐
SAUCE FOR THE GOOSE	Mary Rose Maxwell ISBN 0 352 33492 4	☐
HARD CORPS	Claire Thompson ISBN 0 352 33491 6	☐
INTENSE BLUE	Lyn Wood ISBN 0 352 33496 7	☐
THE NAKED TRUTH	Natasha Rostova ISBN 0 352 33497 5	☐
A SPORTING CHANCE	Susie Raymond ISBN 0 352 33501 7	☐

---------✂-------------------

Please send me the books I have ticked above.

Name ....

Address ....

....

....

.... Post Code ....

Send to: **Cash Sales, Black Lace Books, Thames Wharf Studios, Rainville Road, London W6 9HA.**

US customers: for prices and details of how to order books for delivery by mail, call 1-800-805-1083.

Please enclose a cheque or postal order, made payable to **Virgin Publishing Ltd**, to the value of the books you have ordered plus postage and packing costs as follows:
  UK and BFPO – £1.00 for the first book, 50p for each subsequent book.
  Overseas (including Republic of Ireland) – £2.00 for the first book, £1.00 for each subsequent book.

If you would prefer to pay by VISA, ACCESS/MASTER-CARD, DINERS CLUB, AMEX or SWITCH, please write your card number and expiry date here:

....

Please allow up to 28 days for delivery.

Signature ....

---------✂-------------------